THE SN

NIGHT OF ERROR

Desmond Bagley was born in 1923 in Kendal, Westmorland, and brought up in Blackpool. He began his working life, aged 14, in the printing industry and then did a variety of jobs until going into an aircraft factory at the start of the Second World War.

When the war ended, he decided to travel to southern Africa, going overland through Europe and the Sahara. He worked en route, reaching South Africa in 1951.

Bagley became a freelance journalist in Johannesburg and wrote his first published novel, *The Golden Keel*, in 1962. In 1964 he returned to England and lived in Totnes, Devon, for twelve years. He and his wife Joan then moved to Guernsey in the Channel Islands. Here he found the ideal place for combining his writing and his other interests, which included computers, mathematics, military history, and entertaining friends from all over the world.

Desmond Bagley died in April 1983, having become one of the world's top-selling authors, with his 16 books – two of them published after his death – translated into more than 30 languages.

'I've read all Bagley's books and he's marvellous, the best.'   ALISTAIR MACLEAN

By the same author

DESMOND BAGLEY

The Snow Tiger

AND

Night of Error

HARPER

HARPER
an imprint of HarperCollins*Publishers*
77-85 Fulham Palace Road
Hammersmith, London W6 8JB
www.harpercollins.co.uk

This omnibus edition 2009
1

The Snow Tiger first published in Great Britain by Collins 1975
Night of Error first published in Great Britain by Collins 1984
Interview with Desmond Bagley first published by the
Evening Standard 1978

Desmond Bagley asserts the moral right to
be identified as the author of these works

Copyright © Brockhurst Publications 1975, 1984
Interview with Desmond Bagley © *Evening Standard* 1978

ISBN 978 0 00 730481 3

Printed and bound in Great Britain by
Clays Ltd, St Ives plc

 Mixed Sources
Product group from well-managed
forests and other controlled sources
www.fsc.org Cert no. SW-COC-1806
© 1996 Forest Stewardship Council
FSC

FSC is a non-profit international organisation established
to promote the responsible management of the world's forests.
Products carrying the FSC label are independently certified
to assure consumers that they come from forests that are managed
to meet the social, economic and ecological needs
of present and future generations.

Find out more about HarperCollins and the environment at
www.harpercollins.co.uk/green

CONTENTS

THE SNOW TIGER

This book is a work of fiction with its roots deeply embedded in fact. Many of the organizations mentioned exist, but it is not my intention to denigrate them in any way, and if I am thought to do so, I apologize.

The book would have been impossible to write without the help of many men and their expertise. My thanks go to Ken Parnell, one-time mountain guide in the Mount Cook National Park; Bob Waterhouse and Philip Brewer, both of the Cold Regions Research and Engineering Laboratory of the US Army Terrestrial Sciences Centre; Dr Barrie Murphy, MD; Lt-Comdr F. A. Prehn and Lt-Comdr Thomas Orr, both of Antarctic Development Squadron Six (VXE-6), Operation Deep Freeze.

My thanks also go to the staff of William Collins (New Zealand) Ltd, and the Librarian and staff of New Zealand House, London, for incredible patience in the face of a barrage of questions. I asked many stupid questions but never once got a stupid answer.

To JOAN, on her birthday.
I said I would and I did.

Snow is not a wolf in sheep's clothing
– it is a tiger in lamb's clothing.

Matthias Zdarsky

Absence of body is preferable to
presence of mind.

Anon.

PROLOGUE

It was not a big avalanche, but then, it did not need to be very big to kill a man, and it was only because of Mike McGill's insistence on the Oertel cord that Ballard survived. Just as a man may survive in an ocean with the proper equipment and yet drown in a foot of water, so Ballard may have perished in a minor slippage that would have gone unrecorded even in avalanche-conscious Switzerland.

McGill was a good skier, as might be expected considering his profession, and he had taken the novice under his wing.

They had met in the ski lodge during an après-ski session and had taken an immediate liking to each other. Although they were the same age McGill appeared to be the older man, possibly because of his more varied life, but he became interested because Ballard had much to teach of areas other than snow and ice. They complemented each other, which is not an uncommon basis for friendship among men.

One morning McGill proposed something new. 'We've got to get you off the piste,' he said. 'And on to soft snow. There's nothing like cutting a first track.'

'Isn't it more difficult than on the piste?' queried Ballard.

McGill shook his head decisively. 'A beginner's myth. Turning is not quite as easy, but traversing is a cinch. You'll like it. Let's look at the map.'

They went up by the chair-lift, but instead of going down by the piste they struck off to the south, crossing a level plateau. After half an hour they arrived at the top of the clear slope which McGill had chosen, following local advice. He stopped, resting on his sticks, while he surveyed the slope. 'It looks all right, but we won't take chances. Here's where we put our tails on.'

He unzipped a pocket of his anorak and produced a bundle of red cord which he separated into two coils, one of which he handed to Ballard. 'Tie one end round your waist.'

'What for?'

'It's an Oertel cord – a simple device which has saved a hell of a lot of lives. If there's an avalanche and you get buried there'll be a bit of that red cord showing on the surface to show where you are so you can be dug out fast.'

Ballard looked down the slope. 'Is there likely to be an avalanche?'

'Not that I know of,' said McGill cheerfully, knotting the cord around his waist.

'I've never seen anyone else wearing these.'

'You've only been on the piste.' McGill noted Ballard's hesitancy. 'A lot of guys don't wear cords because they think it makes them look damn fools. Who wants to go down a slope wearing a red tail? they say. To my mind they're damn fools for not wearing them.'

'But avalanches!' said Ballard.

'Look,' said McGill patiently, and pointed down the slope. 'If I thought there was a serious avalanche risk down there we wouldn't be going down at all. I checked on the snow reports before we left and it's probably as safe as the nursery slopes. But *any* snow on *any* slope can be dangerous – and it doesn't have to be in Switzerland; people have been caught in avalanches on the South Downs in England. The cord is just a precaution, that's all.'

Ballard shrugged and began to tie the cord. McGill said, 'We'd better continue your education. Do you know what to do if the snow does slide?'

'Start praying?'

McGill grinned. 'You can do better than that. If it goes at all it will go under your skis or just behind you. It doesn't go in a rush so you have time to think about what to do – not much time, mind you. If it goes underfoot you might have time to jump higher up the slope, in which case you'll be out of it. If it starts sliding behind you and into you remember just one thing – you can't ski out of it. I might be able to, but not you.'

'So what do I do?'

'The first thing is to get your wrists out of the loops of the sticks. Throw the sticks away, then snap off the quick release fastenings on your skis. They're supposed to release automatically in a fall but don't trust them. When the snow hits you start swimming upstream and try to head up to the surface. Hold your breath and don't get bunged up with snow. When you feel yourself slowing bring one arm in front of your face, but not too close – that will give you an air space to breathe, and maybe you can shout so that someone can hear you.' He laughed at the expression on Ballard's face, and said lightly, 'Don't worry, it may never happen. Let's go. I'll go first, not too fast, and you follow and do what I do.'

He launched himself down the slope and Ballard followed and had the most exhilarating ride of his life. As McGill had said, turning was not as easy in the soft snow and his ankles began to ache, but schussing was a joy. The cold wind stung his cheeks and whistled past his ears with a keening sound but, apart from that, the only sound was the hiss of his skis as they bit into the virgin snow.

Ahead of him, at the bottom of the slope, he saw McGill execute a stop christiania and come to a halt. As he drew alongside he said enthusiastically, 'That was great! Let's do it again.'

McGill laughed and pointed. 'We have a way to go to get back to the chair-lift; it's around the spur of the mountain. Maybe we'll have another crack at it this afternoon.'

At about three in the afternoon they arrived at the top of the chosen slope and McGill pointed to the two sets of tracks. 'There's been no one here but us chickens. That's what I like about this – it's not as crowded as the piste.' He handed an Oertel cord to Ballard. 'You go first this time; I want to watch your technique on the way down.'

As he knotted the cord he studied the slope. The late afternoon winter's sun was already sending long shadows creeping across the snow. McGill said, 'Keep to the centre of the slope in the sunlight; don't go into the shadowed areas.'

As he spoke Ballard took off, and McGill followed leisurely, keeping an eye on the less experienced skier and noting any faults for future instruction. All went well until he noted that Ballard was swinging to the left and towards slightly steeper ground where shadows lay. He increased speed, calling out as he did so, 'Keep to the right, Ian. Keep to the main slope.'

Even as he shouted he saw Ballard apparently trip, a slight hesitation in the smooth downward movement. Then the whole slope started to slide taking Ballard with it. McGill skidded to a halt, his face pale, and kept his eyes on Ballard who was now plunging out of control. He saw him throw away his right stick and then Ballard was hidden in a swirl of powder snow. A rumble filled the air with the noise of soft thunder.

Ballard had got rid of his sticks but found himself in a world of mad instability. He managed to release his right ski but then found himself upside down and rotating violently. He struck out vigorously with his arms, sternly repressing the rising tide of panic within him, and tried to remember

McGill's instructions. Suddenly he felt an excruciating pain in his left thigh; his foot was being twisted outwards inexorably until it felt as though his leg was being unscrewed from the hip.

He nearly passed out from the pain but, after a sharp intensification, the pain eased a little. The tumbling motion ceased and he remembered what McGill had said about making an air space about his mouth, so he brought up his left hand across his face. Then all motion stopped and Ballard was unconscious.

All that had taken a little over ten seconds and Ballard had been carried not much over a hundred feet.

McGill waited until there was no further snow movement and then skied to the edge of the disturbed scar of tumbled snow. He scanned it quickly then, jabbing his sticks into the snow, he removed his skis. Carrying one stick and one ski he walked carefully into the avalanche area and began to quarter it. He knew from experience that now time was of the utmost importance; in his mind he could see the graph he had been shown a few days earlier at the local Parsenndienst Station – the length of time buried plotted against the chance of survival.

It took him half an hour to explore the area and he found nothing but snow. If he did not find Ballard he would have to begin probing with little chance of success. One man could not probe that area in the time available and the best bet was to go to find expert help – including an avalanche dog.

He reached the lower edge of the slide and looked up indecisively, then he squared his shoulders and began to climb upwards again through the centre of the slide. He would make one quick five-minute pass and if he did not find anything by the time he reached the top he would head back to the ski lodge.

He went upwards slowly, his eyes flickering from side to side, and then he saw it – a tiny fleck of blood red in the

shadow of a clod of snow. It was less than the size of his little fingernail but it was enough. He dropped on one knee
and scrabbled at the snow and came up with a length of red
cord in his hand. He hauled on one end which came free, so
he tackled the other.

The cord, tearing free from the snow, led him twenty feet
down the slope until, when he pulled, he came up against
resistance and the cord was vertical. He started to dig with
his hands. The snow was soft and powdery and was easy to
clear, and he came across Ballard at a little more than three
feet deep.

Carefully he cleared the snow from around Ballard's
head, making sure first that he was breathing and second
that he could continue to breathe. He was pleased to see
that Ballard had followed instructions and had his arm
across his face. When he cleared the lower half of Ballard's
body he knew that the leg, from its impossible position, was
broken – and he knew why. Ballard had not been able to
release his left ski and, by the churning action of the snow,
the leverage of the ski had *twisted* Ballard's leg broken.

He decided against trying to move Ballard, judging that he
might do more harm than good, so he took off his anorak
and tucked it closely around Ballard's body to keep him
warm. Then he retrieved his skis and set off down to the
road below where he was lucky enough to stop a passing car.

Less than two hours later Ballard was in hospital.

Six weeks later Ballard was still bed-ridden and bored. His
broken leg was a long time in healing, not so much because
of the broken bone but because the muscles had been torn
and needed time to knit together. He had been flown to
London on a stretcher, whereupon his mother had swooped
on him and carried him to her home. Normally, when in
London, he lived in his own small mews flat, but even
he saw the force of her arguments and succumbed to her

ministrations. So he was bedridden and bored in his mother's house and hating every minute of it.

One morning, after a gloom-laden visit from his doctor who prophesied further weeks of bed-rest, he heard voices raised in argument coming from the floor below. The lighter tones were those of his mother but he could not identify the deeper voice. The distant voices rose and fell in cadences of antagonism, continuing for a quarter of an hour, and then became louder as the running fight ascended the stairs.

The door opened and his mother came into the room, lips pursed and stormy in the brow. 'Your grandfather insists on seeing you,' she said curtly. 'I told him you're not well but he still insists – he's as unreasonable as ever. My advice is not to listen to him, Ian. But, of course, it's up to you – you've always done as you pleased.'

'There's nothing wrong with me besides a bad leg.' He regarded his mother and wished, not for the first time, that she would show more sign of dress sense and not be so dowdy. 'Does he give me any option?'

'He says if you don't want to see him he'll go away.'

'Does he, by God? He must have been touched by an angel's wing. I'm almost inclined to test this improbability.' Sending Ben Ballard from a closed door was fit for inclusion in the *Guinness Book of Records*. Ian sighed. 'You'd better show him in.'

'I wish you wouldn't.'

'Bring him in, Mother; there's nothing wrong with me.'

'You're as pig-headed as he is,' she grumbled, but went to the door.

Ian had not seen old Ben for a year and a half and he was shocked at the transformation in the man. His grandfather had always been dynamic and bristling with energy but now he looked every day of his eighty-seven years. He came into the room slowly, leaning heavily upon a blackthorn stick; his cheeks were hollow and his eyes sunk deep into his head so that his normally saturnine expression was rendered skull-like. But there was still a faint crackle of authority as he turned his head and said snappily, 'Get me a chair, Harriet.'

A small snort escaped her but she placed a chair next to the bed and stood by it. Ben lowered himself into it creakily, planted the stick between his knees and leaned on it with both hands. He surveyed Ian, his eyes sweeping the length of the bed from head to foot and then back to the head. A sardonic grin appeared. 'A playboy, hey! One of the jet-set! I suppose you were at Gstaad.'

Ian refused to be drawn: he knew the old man's methods. 'Nothing so grand.'

Ben grinned widely like a shark. 'Don't tell me you went on a package tour.' One of his fingers lifted to point to the leg. It trembled slightly. 'Is it bad, boy?'

'It could have been worse – it could have been taken off.'

'Must you say such things?' Harriet's voice was pained.

Ben chuckled softly, and then his voice hardened. 'So you went skiing and you couldn't even do that right. Was it on company time?'

'No,' said Ian equably. 'And you know it. It was my first holiday for nearly three years.'

'Humph! But you're lying in that bed on company time.'

Ian's mother was outraged. 'You're heartless!'

'Shut up, Harriet,' said the old man without turning his head. 'And go away. Don't forget to close the door behind you.'

'I'll not be bullied in my own home.'

'You'll do as I say, woman. I have to talk business with this man.'

Ian Ballard caught his mother's eye and nodded slightly. She made a spitting sound and stormed out of the room. The door slammed behind her. 'Your manners haven't improved,' Ian said flatly.

Ben's shoulders shook as he wheezed with laughter. 'That's why I like you, boy; no one else would have said that to my face.'

'It's been said often enough behind your back.'

'What do I care about what's said? It's what a man does that matters.' Ben's hands tightened momentarily upon his stick. 'I didn't mean what I said about you lying in bed on company time – because you're not. We couldn't wait until you're up and about. You've been replaced.'

'Fired!'

'In a manner of speaking. There'll be a job for you when you're fit enough. I think it's a better job, but I doubt if you will.'

'That depends on what it is,' said Ian cautiously.

'Nearly four years ago we opened a mine in New Zealand – gold. Now that the price of gold has gone up it's beginning to pay its way and the prospects are good. The managing director is an old idiot called Fisher who was brought in for local reasons, but he's retiring next month.' The stick thumped on the floor. 'The man is senile at sixty-five – can you imagine that?'

Ian Ballard was cautious when the Greeks came bearing gifts. 'So?'

'So do you want the job?'

There had to be a catch. 'I might. When do I have to be out there?'

'As soon as possible. I suggest you go by sea. You can rest your leg as well on board a ship as here.'

'Would I have sole responsibility?'

'The managing director is responsible to the Board – you know that.'

'Yes, and I know the Ballard set-up. The Board dances on strings pulled from London. I have no wish to be office boy to my revered uncles. I don't know why you let them get away with what they're doing.'

The old man's hands whitened as he clutched the knob on top of the blackthorn. 'You know I have no say in Ballard Holdings any more. When I set up the Trust I relinquished control. What your uncles do is their business now.'

'And yet you have a managing directorship in your gift?'

Ben offered his sharklike grin. 'Your uncles are not the only ones who can pull strings from time to time. Mind you, I can't do it too often.'

Ian thought about it. 'Where is the mine?'

'South Island.' Ben's voice was studiedly casual. 'Place called Hukahoronui.'

'*No!*' It was torn from Ian involuntarily.

'What's the matter? Scared to go back?' Ben's upper lip drew back showing his teeth. 'If you are then you're no good blood of mine.'

Ian took a deep breath. 'Do you know what it means? To go back? You know how I loathe the place.'

'So you were unhappy there – that was a long time ago.' Ben leaned forward, bearing down heavily on the stick. 'If you turn down this offer you'll never be happy again – I can guarantee it. And it won't be because of anything I'll do, for there'll be no recriminations on my part. It's what you'll have to live with inside yourself that'll do the trick. For the rest of your life you'll wonder about it.'

Ian stared at him. 'You're an old devil.'

The old man chuckled deep in his throat. 'That's as may be. Young Ian, now listen you to me. I had four sons and three of them aren't worth the powder to blow 'em to hell. They're conniving, they're unscrupulous and they're crooked, and they're making Ballard Holdings into a stink in the City of London.' Ben drew himself up. 'God knows I was no angel in my time. I was rough and tough, I drove a hard bargain and maybe I cut a corner when it was needed, but that was in the nature of the times. But nobody ever accused Ben Ballard of being dishonest and nobody ever knew me to go back on my word. With me it was a word and a handshake, and that was recognized in the City as an iron-clad contract. But nobody will take your uncles' words – not any more. Anyone dealing with them must hire a regiment of lawyers to scrutinize the fine print.'

He shrugged. 'But there it is. They run Ballard Holdings now. I'm an old man and they've taken over. It's in the nature of things, Ian.' His voice became milder. 'But I had a fourth son and I hoped for a lot from him, but he was ruined by a woman, just as she damned near ruined you before I had the wit to jerk you out of that valley in New Zealand.'

Ian's voice was tight. 'Let's leave my mother out of this.'

Ben held up his hand placatingly. 'I like your loyalty, Ian, even though I think it's misplaced. You're not a bad son of your father just as he wasn't a bad son of mine – not really. The trouble was I handled the matter badly at the time.' He looked blindly into the past, then shook his head irritably. 'But that's gone by. It's enough that I got you out of Hukahoronui. Did I do right there?'

Ian's voice was low. 'I've never thanked you for that. I've never thanked you for that or for anything else.'

'Oh, you got your degree and you went to the Johannesburg School of Mines and from there to Colorado; and after that the Harvard Business School. You have a good brain and I didn't like to see it wasted.' He chuckled. 'Bread cast on the waters, boy; bread cast on the waters.' He leaned forward. 'You see, lad; I've come for repayment.'

Ian felt his throat constrict. 'What do you mean?'

'You'll please an old man by taking this job in Hukahoronui. Mind, you don't have to take it – you're a free agent. But I'd be pleased if you did.'

'Do I have to make up my mind now?'

Ben's voice was sardonic. 'Do you want to talk it over with your mother?'

'You've never liked her, have you?'

'She was a whining, puling schoolmarm, afraid of the world, who dragged a good man down to her crawling level. Now she's a whining, puling woman, old before her time because she's always been afraid of the world and of living, and she's trying to do the same to another man.' Ben was harsh. 'Why do you think I call you "boy" and "lad" when you're a grown man of thirty-five? Because that's all you are yet. For Christ's sake, make a decision of your own for once in your life.'

Ian was silent. At last he said, 'All right, I'll go to Huka-horonui.'

'Alone – without her?'

'Alone.'

Ben did not appear to be elated; he merely nodded his head gravely. He said, 'There's quite a town there now. I doubt if you'd recognize it, it's grown so much. I was there a couple of years ago before my damned doctor said I shouldn't travel any more. The place even has a mayor. The first mayor's name was John Peterson. Quite a power in the community the Petersons are.'

'Oh Jesus!' said Ian. 'Are they still there?'

'What would you expect? Of course they're still there. John, Eric and Charles – they're still there.'

'But not Alec.' Ian appeared to be addressing the back of his hands.

'No – not Alec,' Ben agreed.

Ian looked up. 'You're really asking for something, aren't you? What the hell do you expect of me? You know damned well that putting a Ballard into Huka is like putting a detonator into a stick of dynamite.'

Ben's eyebrows rose. 'The Petersons being the dynamite, I presume.' He leaned forward. 'I'll tell you what I want. I want you to run that bloody mine better than it's been run up to now. It's a tough job I've handed you. That old fool,

Fisher, couldn't keep control – that's one thing. For another, Dobbs, the mine manager, is a chronic fence-sitter – and, for number three – Cameron, the engineer, is a worn-out American has-been who is holding on with his fingertips because he knows it's the last job he'll ever have and he's scared witless that he'll lose it. You have to put some back-bone into that lot.'

Ben leaned back in his chair. 'Of course,' he said musingly, 'the Petersons won't welcome you with open arms. It's not likely, is it, when it's a family tradition of theirs that they were robbed of the mine? A lot of poppycock, of course, but that's what they believe – and, Ian, always remember that men are not governed by facts but by what they believe.' He nodded. 'Yes, I can see you might have trouble with the Petersons.'

'You can stop needling,' said Ian Ballard. 'I said I'd go.'

The old man made as if to rise, then paused. 'There is one thing. If anything serious should happen – to Ballard Holdings or to me – get in touch with Bill Stenning.' He thought awhile. 'On second thoughts, don't bother. Bill will get in touch with you fast enough.'

'What's this about?'

Don't worry; it may never happen.' Ben got slowly to his feet and made his way to the door. He stopped halfway across the room and held up his blackthorn. 'I doubt if I'll want this any more. I'll send it to you tomorrow. You'll need it. When you've finished with it don't send it back – throw it away.'

He paused outside the door and raised his voice. 'You can come in now, Harriet. No need to listen at the keyhole.'

GOVERNMENT OF NEW ZEALAND

The Hearing
of the
Commission of Inquiry
into the
Disaster at Hukahoronui

CHAIRMAN: Dr H. A. Harrison

ASSESSORS: Prof. J. W. Rolandson

Mr F. G. French

SECRETARY: Mr J. Reed

in the Canterbury Provincial Chamber
CHRISTCHURCH, SOUTH ISLAND

THE HEARING

First Day

ONE

The great hall was unexpectedly and floridly magnificent. Built in the mid-nineteenth century at the height of the Gothic Revival and designed by an architect who was, equally unexpectedly, a direct descendant of Simon de Montfort, it brought medieval England to the Southern Hemisphere and to that more-than-English city, Christchurch. Lofty, with an arched ceiling, painted and carved, it abounded in corbels, pillars, lancets and wood panelling, and every surface that could possibly be carved was carved to a fare-thee-well. There was also a lot of stained glass.

Dan Edwards, doyen of the Press of Christchurch, was blind to the incongruity of the scene; he had seen it too often before. He was more concerned about the floor which creaked abominably as the ushers walked beneath the Press gallery setting out note-pads and pencils. 'The acoustics are lousy,' he said. 'And that bloody kauri floor doesn't make things better.'

'Can't they oil it or something?' asked Dalwood, who was from Auckland.

'They've tried everything but nothing seems to work. I'll tell you what – let's do a pool. If I miss anything I'll take it from you – and vice versa.'

Dalwood shrugged. 'Okay.' He looked over the edge of the Press gallery to the dais immediately beneath. Three high-backed chairs were set behind the rostrum, and before each chair was a new foolscap note-pad with two ball-point pens to the left and three newly sharpened pencils to the right. Together with the water carafes and the glasses, the whole looked remarkably like place settings at a dining table.

Edwards followed his glance and then nodded towards the public gallery, already full, at the north end of the hall. 'They're going to make a meal of this.'

Dalwood nudged him and indicated the door beneath the public gallery. 'There's young Ballard. He's brought a legal army with him.'

Edwards studied the young man who walked at the head of a phalanx of older, soberly dressed men. He pursed his lips. 'The question is whether they're representing him or the company. If I were Ballard I'd be keeping a tight sphincter.'

'A sacrificial lamb?'

'A lamb to the slaughter,' agreed Edwards. He looked down at the rostrum. 'Things are happening.'

The hum of conversation died as three men took their places at the chairs behind the rostrum. One of the two stenographers looked up and held his hands poised expectantly over the keys of his machine. There was a rustle as everyone arose.

The three men sat down and a fourth came forward and sat at the desk in front of the rostrum. He laid a sheaf of papers before him and consulted the uppermost document. The man above him, in the centre of the rostrum, was elderly with a shock of white hair and deeply lined face. He looked down at the virgin pad in front of him and pushed it away. When he spoke he spoke quietly and in an even voice.

'In the winter of the year, on the eighteenth of July, a disaster occurred in the township of Hukahoronui on the South Island of New Zealand in which fifty-four people lost their lives. The New Zealand Government has appointed a Commission of Inquiry, of which I am Chairman. My name is Arthur Harrison and I am Rector of Canterbury University.'

He moved his hands apart. 'With me are two assessors, both well qualified by their knowledge and experience to sit on this Commission. On my left we have Professor J. W. Rolandson of the Department of Scientific and Industrial Research.' Harrison paused. 'In the interests of brevity his department will, in future, be referred to as the DSIR.'

Rolandson smiled and nodded.

'On my right sits Mr F. G. French of the New Zealand Mines Department. The gentleman immediately below me is Mr John Reed, barrister-at-law; he is Secretary to the Commission.' Harrison surveyed the tables in the hall. 'There are several interested parties present. Perhaps they would identify themselves, beginning from the right.'

The well-fed, middle-aged man seated next to Ballard rose to his feet. 'John Rickman, barrister, representing the Hukahoronui Mining Company, Proprietary, Limited.'

There was a long pause before the man at the next table got to his feet, and Edwards whispered, 'Ballard has no personal representation.'

'Michael Gunn, barrister, representing the General Miners' Union of New Zealand and the relatives of its members who lost their lives in the disaster.'

'Alfred Smithers, barrister, representing the Ministry of Civil Defence.'

'Peter Lyall, barrister, representing Charles Stewart Peterson and Eric Parnell Peterson.'

There was a sound of surprise in the room, a compound of sudden involuntary movement and indrawn breath. Edwards looked up from his notes. 'Why should they think they need legal help? This sounds promising.'

Harrison waited until the stir died away. 'I see we are greatly endowed with legal aid. I must therefore warn the legal gentlemen present that this is not a Court of Law. It is a Commission of Inquiry which is empowered to make its own rules of procedure. Evidence will be heard here which would not necessarily be admissible before a Court of Law. The object of this Commission is to find the truth of what happened during the events which led up to the avalanche at Hukahoronui, during the avalanche itself, and what happened afterwards.'

He leaned back in his chair. 'Adversary tactics, such as are common in law courts, will be frowned upon here. We wish to find the truth unimpeded by legal technicalities, and the reason we wish to find the truth is to make certain that such a disaster does not happen again. The force of this consideration is so great that the Commission hereby rules that any evidence given here may not be used in any future legal action other than criminal which may eventuate as a result of the avalanche at Hukahoronui. The protection of lives in the future is of more importance than the punishment of those who may be felt to be guilty of acts of omission or commission arising out of the disaster. The Commission is legally empowered to make such a ruling and I hereby do so.'

Gunn hastily rose to his feet. 'Mr Chairman; do you not think that is an arbitrary decision? There will be matters of compensation arising. If interested parties are denied the use of evidence in a future legal action, surely an injustice will be done.'

'Mr Gunn, I have no doubt that the government will appoint an arbitrator who will study the findings of this Commission and make the necessary dispositions. Does that satisfy you?'

Gunn bobbed his head, a pleased expression on his face. 'Indeed it does, Mr Chairman.'

Dalwood murmured to Edwards, 'No wonder he's pleased. It's all going to happen here – a bloody drumhead courtmartial with no holds barred.'

Edwards grunted. 'He'll not get much past old Harrison.'

'And now we come to the question of witnesses. Some citizens have come forward voluntarily to give evidence here, others have been subpoena'd by one or more of the interested parties.' Harrison frowned. 'I, and my fellow members on the Commission, have been much exercised as to how the evidence should be taken, and we have decided that it shall be taken in chronological order, insofar as that is possible. Because of this, any person giving evidence may be asked to step down before his evidence is wholly completed if we find it necessary to do some filling in. It follows, then, that all witnesses should hold themselves in readiness at all times during the sitting of the Commission.'

'Mr Chairman!'

Rickman was on his feet. Harrison said, 'Yes, Mr Rickman?'

'Such a condition is likely to be onerous on certain of the witnesses. Some of them are busy men with duties which lie outside this room. This is likely to be a long inquiry and I do not feel that such a condition is entirely fair.'

'When you refer to certain of the witnesses can I take it that you refer to Mr Ballard?' asked Harrison drily.

'Mr Ballard is one such witness,' conceded Rickman. 'Out of consideration for him it would be better if he could give his evidence and retire.'

'Is Mr Ballard a citizen of New Zealand?'

'No, Mr Chairman; he is a United Kingdom subject.'

'And would his retirement from this hall be as far away as England?'

Rickman bent down and spoke quietly to Ballard who replied in equally low tones. Rickman straightened. 'It is true that there are certain matters in the United Kingdom which urgently require Mr Ballard's attention.'

Harrison's voice was cold. 'If I thought it was Mr Ballard's intention to leave New Zealand during the sitting of this Commission I would ask the relevant authority to relieve him of his passport. This inquiry is a serious matter, Mr Rickman.'

'I am sure it is not Mr Ballard's intention to flout the authority of the Commissioners,' said Rickman hastily. He bent down again and spoke to Ballard, then he rose and said, 'Mr Ballard has no intention of leaving New Zealand at the present time.'

'I would prefer to hear that from Mr Ballard.' Harrison leaned forward. 'Is that correct, Mr Ballard?'

Ballard stood, and said in a low voice. 'That is correct, sir. My time is at the disposal of the Commissioners.'

'In that case you will have no objection to attending this inquiry with the rest of the witnesses. Thank you.'

In the Press gallery Edwards said, 'My God! Whoever Rickman is representing, he's not representing Ballard. He set him up just to knock him down.'

Harrison said, 'This inquiry will not have the formality of a law court, but neither will it be a free-for-all. Representatives of the interested parties may address the witnesses at the discretion of the Chairman. It will not be necessary to disturb the sacro-iliac by standing each time – a mere raising of the hand will suffice. The assessors may question the witnesses in their respective fields of expertise.'

He put his hands together. 'Since we are gathering information in chronological order it becomes necessary to decide at which point of time to begin. From depositions laid before the Commission I gather that it was the appearance of Mr Ballard in Hukahoronui which led to a series of events which may – or may not – have relevance to the disaster which took place some weeks later. That is for this inquiry to decide. Be that as it may, I think the first witness should be Mr Ballard.'

Reed, the secretary, said, 'Will you come forward, Mr Ballard, and sit down there?' He indicated an ornately carved chair a little to the right of the rostrum. He waited until Ballard was seated, then said, 'Your name is Ian Dacre Ballard?'

'Yes, sir.'

'And you are managing director of the Hukahoronui Mining Company, Proprietary, Limited?'

'No, sir.'

A hum as of a disturbed hive of bees filled the air. Harrison waited until it had died away, then said quietly, 'All present will be silent during the questioning of witnesses.' He leaned forward. 'Thank you, Mr Reed; I'll take it from here. Mr Ballard, at the time of the avalanche were you managing director of the company?'

'Yes, sir.'

'Can you give me a reason why you are no longer in that position?'

Ballard's voice was colourless. 'I was suspended from my duties a fortnight after the disaster.'

'I see.' Harrison's eyes flicked sideways as he saw a hand raised. 'Yes, Mr Gunn?'

'Can the witness tell us who owns the Hukahoronui Mining Company?'

Harrison nodded to Ballard, who said, 'It's a wholly-owned subsidiary of New Zealand Mineral Holdings, Limited.'

'And that company is just a shell instituted for legal and financial reasons, is it not? Who owns it?'

'It is owned substantially by the International Mining Investment Corporation.'

'And who has the controlling interest in the International Mining Investment Corporation?'

'Mr Chairman!' Rickman said sharply. 'Is there provision in your procedure for objections?'

'Of course, Mr Rickman. What is your objection?'

'I cannot see what this line of questioning has to do with an avalanche on a hillside.'

'Neither can I,' said Harrison. 'But no doubt Mr Gunn can make it clear.'

'I think the answer to my last question will make it quite clear,' said Gunn. 'I asked who owns the controlling interest in the International Mining Investment Corporation.'

Ballard raised his head and said clearly, 'Ballard Holdings, Limited, registered in the City of London.'

Gunn smiled. 'Thank you.'

'Well, well!' said Edwards, scribbling rapidly. 'So he's one of those Ballards.'

Dalwood chuckled. 'And Gunn is gunning for Rickman. Up the workers and down with international capital. He smells money.'

Harrison tapped lightly with his gavel and the hall became quiet again. 'Mr Ballard, do you own shares – or any interest whatever – in Ballard Holdings? Or in any of the companies mentioned?'

'No, sir.'

'Does any of your family own any such interest?'

'Yes; my three uncles and some of my cousins.'

'Not your father?'

'He is dead.'

'How did you come to be appointed managing director of the Hukahoronui Mining Company?'

Ballard shrugged. 'The company is an old family concern and I suppose that. . .'

'Can the witness describe his qualifications for the position?'

Harrison jerked his head around to identify the source of the interruption. 'You will oblige me by not calling out in this hall, Mr Lyall. Further, you must not interrupt a witness.' In a milder voice he said, 'However, the question is relevant and the witness will answer.'

'I have a degree in mining engineering from Birmingham University. I have done post-graduate studies in South Africa and the United States.'

Lyall had his arm firmly in the air by this time. 'But no *practical* experience as a mining engineer?'

Pink spots glowed in Ballard's cheeks but he appeared to be in control as he said to Harrison, 'May I finish answering Mr Lyall's *first* question?'

'Of course.' Harrison looked at Lyall. 'Mr Lyall: you will *not* interrupt the witness, and you *will* address your questions through me unless I indicate otherwise. Go on, Mr Ballard.'

'I was about to say that, apart from the engineering studies, I attended the Harvard Business School for two years. As for practical experience as a mining engineer, that would be called for if I professed to be a mining engineer, but as managing director my field was rather that of business administrator.'

'A valid point,' said Harrison. 'A managing director need not have the technical expertise of the men he directs. If it were so a large number of our managing directors would be immediately unemployed – and possibly unemployable.'

He waited until the laughter died away, then said, 'I do not see the point in further questioning along those lines, Mr Lyall.' As Lyall's hand remained obstinately raised, he said, 'Do you have a further – and different – question?'

'Yes, Mr Chairman. I am reliably informed that when Mr Ballard appeared in Hukahoronui he was unable to walk except with the aid of a stick. Is this correct?'

'Is this relevant, Mr Lyall?'

'I believe so, sir.'

'Witness will answer the question.'

'It is correct.'

Lyall, his hand up, remained punctiliously silent until Harrison nodded at him curtly. 'Can you tell us why?'

'I broke my leg in a skiing accident in Switzerland.'

'Thank you, Mr Ballard.'

'I can't say that I see the relevance,' observed Harrison. 'But no doubt it will appear in time.'

'It was in an avalanche,' said Ballard.

There was dead silence in the hall.

TWO

Harrison looked across at Lyall. 'The significance still escapes me,' he said. 'And since Mr Lyall does not see fit to pursue the subject I think we should carry on. Mr Ballard, when did you arrive in Hukahoronui?'

'On the sixth of June – six weeks before the avalanche.'

'So you had not been there very long. Was Hukahoronui what you expected?'

Ballard frowned in thought. 'The thing that struck me most was how much it had changed.'

Harrison's eyebrows rose. 'Changed! Then you had been here before?'

'I lived there for fifteen years – from infancy until just after my sixteenth birthday.'

Harrison made a note. 'Go on, Mr Ballard. How had Hukahoronui changed?'

'It was bigger. The mine was new, of course, but there were more houses – a lot more houses.' He paused. 'There was a lot more snow than I seem to remember from my childhood.'

Professor Rolandson of the DSIR said, 'It is a matter of record that the snow precipitation in the Southern Alps was exceptionally high this past winter.'

Ballard had been depressed as he drove west from Christchurch in a company Land-Rover. He was going back

33

to his origins, to Hukahoronui which lies in an outrider of
the Two Thumbs Range, and which he had never expected
to see again.

Hukahoronui.

A deep valley in the mountains entered by a narrow
rock-split gap and graced with stands of tall trees on the
valley slopes. A river runs through, cold from the ice water
of the high peaks, and there is a scattering of houses up the
valley, loosely centred about a church, a general store and a
village school. His mother had once been the schoolteacher.

He hated the place.

It was a bad place to get to in thick snow. There had been
heavy snowfalls and even with snow tyres and four-wheel
drive Ballard found the going tricky. As far as he could remember there had not been a snow like that in those parts since
1943, but of that his memory was understandably hazy – he
had been four years old at the time. But he had particular
reasons for remembering the heavy snow of that year.

After a lot of low gear work he eventually reached the Gap
and he pulled off the road on to a piece of level ground overlooking the river gorge where he contemplated Hukahoronui.

It had certainly changed, just as old Ben said it had. In
the distance was a little township where no township had
been. On one side, under the western slope of the valley,
was a cluster of industrial buildings, presumably the milling
works and refinery belonging to the mine. A streamer of
black smoke coming from a tall chimney was like a stain
against the white hillside beyond.

The township spread along the valley floor with most of
the houses to the west of the river which had been bridged.
The valley people had talked inconclusively for years about
putting a bridge across the river, and now it had been done
at last under the prodding thrust of an affluent economy.
That was probably to be chalked up on the credit side; you
had to pay the price of the mine to get the bridge.

Beyond the township there did not seem to be much change. In the far distance Ballard saw Turi's house beneath the great rock called Kamakamaru. He wondered if the old man was still alive or whether the smoke coming from that distant chimney rose from the fireside of another. Turi had been an old man even when Ballard left the valley, although age in a Maori is difficult to estimate, especially for a youth of sixteen. At sixteen anyone over forty is verging on decrepitude.

But there was something else about the valley that was strange and Ballard was puzzled to determine what it was. A change had occurred which had nothing to do with the mine or the new town and he tried to match up sixteen-year-old memories with the actuality before him. It was nothing to do with the river; that still ran the same course, or seemed to.

And then he found the change. The hill slope on the western side was now almost completely treeless. Gone were the stands of tall white pine and cedar, of kahikatea and kohekohe – the hillside had been stripped almost completely bare. Ballard looked up at the higher slopes of the mountain to where the snows stretched right up to the base of the crags in one smooth and beautiful sweep. It looked good for skiing.

He switched on the engine and went on down into the new town. As he approached he was impressed by the way it had been laid out. Although much detail was blanketed by snow he could see the areas which, in summer, would be pleasant open gardens and there was a children's playground, the swings and slides, the seesaws and the jungle gym, now white-mantled and stalactited with icicles and out of use.

Although the house roofs were heavily laden with snow the road was quite clear and had apparently been swept recently. Coming into the town centre he came across a bulldozer clearing the road with dropped blade. There was a name on its side: HUKAHORONUI MINING CO. (PTY) LTD. It seemed as though the mine management took an interest in municipal affairs. He approved.

There were houses built along the bluff that projected into the river; when Ballard was a child that was called the Big Bend and that was where they had their swimming hole. Peterson's store used to be at the base of the bluff, and so it still was, although it took him a long time to recognize it. In his day it had been single-storey with a corrugated iron roof, a low building with spreading eaves which protected against the summer sun. There used to be chairs on the veranda and it was a favourite place for gossip. Now it was two-storey with a false façade to make it look even larger, and there were big plate-glass windows brightly lit. The veranda had gone.

He pulled the Land-Rover into a designated parking place and sourly wondered when parking meters would be installed. The sun was setting behind the western slopes of the valley and already the long shadows were creeping across the town. That was one of the drawbacks of Hukahoronui; in a narrow valley set north and south night-fall comes early.

Across the street was a still-raw building of unmellowed concrete calling itself the Hotel D'Archiac – a name stolen from a mountain. The street was reasonably busy; private cars and industrial trucks passed by regularly, and women with shopping bags hurried before the shops closed. At one time Peterson's had been the only store, but from where he sat in the car Ballard could see three more shops, and there was a service station on the corner. Lights glowed in the windows of the old school which had sprouted two new wings.

Ballard reached for the blackthorn stick which was on the back seat and then got out of the car. He crossed the road towards the hotel leaning heavily on the stick because he still could not bear to put too much weight on his left leg. He supposed that Dobbs, the mine manager, would have accommodated him, but it was late in the day and he did not want to cause undue disturbance so he was quite prepared to spend a night in the hotel and introduce himself to the mine staff the following morning.

As he approached the hotel entrance a man came out walking quickly and bumped his shoulder. The man made a mutter of annoyance – not an apology – and strode across the pavement to a parked car. Ballard recognized him – Eric Peterson, the second of the three Peterson brothers. The last time he had seen Eric he had been nineteen years old, tall and gangling; now he had filled out into a broad-shouldered brawny man. Apparently the years had not improved his manners much.

Ballard turned to go into the hotel only to encounter an elderly woman who looked at him with recognition slowly dawning in her eyes. 'Why, it's Ian Ballard,' she said, adding uncertainly, 'It *is* Ian, isn't it?'

He hunted through his memories to find a face to match hers. And a name to put to the face. Simpson? No – it wasn't that. 'Hello, Mrs Samson,' he said.

'Ian Ballard,' she said in wonder. 'Well, now; what are you doing here – and how's your mother?'

'My mother's fine,' he said, and lied bravely. 'She asked to be remembered to you.' He believed white lies to be the social oil that allows the machinery of society to work smoothly.

'That's good of her,' said Mrs Samson warmly. She waved her arm. 'And what do you think of Huka now? It's changed a lot since you were here.'

'I never thought I'd see civilization come to the Two Thumbs.'

'It's the mine, of course,' said Mrs Samson. 'The mine brought the prosperity. Do you know, we even have a town council now.'

'Indeed,' he said politely. He looked out of the corner of his eye and saw Eric Peterson frozen in the act of unlocking his car and staring at him.

'Yes, indeed,' said Mrs Samson. 'And I'm a councillor, imagine that! Whoever would have thought it. But whatever are you doing here, Ian?'

'Right now I'm going into the hotel to book a room.' He was sharply aware that Eric Peterson was walking towards him.

'Ian Ballard.' Peterson's voice was flat and expressionless.

Ballard turned, and Mrs Samson said, 'Do you two know each other? This is Eric Peters . . .' Her voice tailed away and a wary look came into her eyes, the look of one who has almost committed a social gaffe. 'But of course you know each other,' she said slowly.

'Hello, Eric.'

There was little humour in Peterson's thin smile. 'And what are you doing here?'

There was no point in avoiding the issue. Ballard said, 'I'm the new managing director of the mining company.'

Something sparked in Peterson's eyes. 'Well, well!' he said in tones of synthetic wonder. 'So the Ballards are coming out of hiding. What's the matter, Ian? Have you run out of phoney company names?'

'Not really,' said Ballard. 'We've got a computer that makes them up for us. How are you doing, Eric?'

Peterson looked down at the stick on which Ballard was leaning. 'A lot better than you, apparently. Hurt your leg? Nothing trivial, I hope.'

Mrs Samson suddenly discovered reasons for not being there, reasons which she explained volubly and at length. 'But if you're staying I'll certainly see you again,' she said.

Peterson watched her go. 'Silly old bat! She's a hell of a nuisance on the council.'

'You a member, too?'

Peterson nodded abstractly – his thought processes were almost visible. 'Did I hear you say you are booking a room in the hotel?'

'That's right.'

Peterson took Ballard's arm. 'Then let me introduce you to the manager.' As they went into the lobby he said, 'Johnnie and I own half of this place, so we can certainly find room for an old friend like you.'

'You're doing well for yourself.'

Peterson grinned crookedly. 'We're getting something out of the mine, even if it isn't raw gold.' He stopped at the reception desk. 'Jeff, this is Ian Ballard, an old friend. You would say we were friends, wouldn't you, Ian?' He drove over any reply that Ballard might have made. 'Jeff Weston is manager here and owns the other half of the hotel. We have long arguments over which half he owns; he claims the half with the bar and that's a matter for dispute.'

'Glad to meet you, Mr Ballard,' said Weston.

'I'm sure you can find a good room for Mr Ballard.'

Weston shrugged. 'No difficulty.'

'Good,' said Peterson jovially. 'Give Mr Ballard a room – the best we have.' His eyes suddenly went flinty and his voice hardened. 'For twenty-four hours. After that we're full. I wouldn't want you to get the wrong idea of your welcome here, Ballard. Don't be fooled by Mrs Samson.'

He turned on his heel and strode away, leaving Weston open-mouthed. Ballard said lightly, 'Eric always was a joker. Do I sign the register, Mr Weston?'

That night Ballard wrote a letter to Mike McGill. In it, among other things, was the following passage:

I remember you telling me that you'd be in New Zealand this year. Why don't you come out earlier as my guest? I'm in a place called Hukahoronui in South Island; there's a hell of a lot of snow and the skiing looks great. The place has changed a bit since I was here last; civilization has struck and there are great developments. But it's not too bad really and the mountains are still untouched. Let me know what you think of the idea – I'd like to meet your plane in Auckland.

THREE

Harrison sipped water from a glass and set it down. 'Mr Ballard, at what point did you become aware of danger by avalanche?'

'Only a few days before the disaster. My attention was drawn to the danger by a friend, Mike McGill, who came to visit me.'

Harrison consulted a document. 'I see that Dr McGill has voluntarily consented to appear as a witness. I think it would be better if we heard his evidence from his own lips. You may step down, Mr Ballard, on the understanding that you may be called again.'

'Yes, sir.' Ballard returned to his seat.

Reed said, 'Will Dr McGill please come forward?'

McGill walked towards the rostrum carrying a slim leather satchel under his arm. He sat down, and Reed said, 'Your name is Michael Howard McGill?'

'Yes, sir; it is.'

Harrison caught the transatlantic twang in McGill's voice. 'Are you an American, Dr McGill?'

'No, sir; I'm a Canadian citizen.'

'I see. It is very public-spirited of you to volunteer to stay and give evidence.'

McGill smiled. 'No trouble at all, sir. I have to be here in Christchurch in any case. I leave for the Antarctic next

month. As you may know, the Operation Deep Freeze
flights leave from here.'

Professor Rolandson stirred. 'You're going to the
Antarctic and your name is McGill! Would you be the Dr
McGill who wrote a paper on stress and deformation in
snow slopes which appeared in the last issue of the *Antarctic
Journal?*'

'Yes, sir.'

Rolandson turned to Harrison. 'I think we are fortunate in having Dr McGill with us. I have read many of his
papers and his qualifications as an expert witness are
unimpeachable.'

'Yes, indeed.' Harrison waggled an eyebrow. 'But I think
his qualifications should be read into the record. Will you
tell us something about yourself, Dr McGill?'

'I'd be glad to.' McGill paused, marshalling his thoughts.
'I took a B.Sc. in physics at the University of Vancouver and
then spent two years with the Canadian DSIR in British
Columbia. From there I went to the United States – M.Sc.
in meteorology at Columbia University and D.Sc. in glaci-
ology at the California Institute of Technology. As to practical experience, I have spent two seasons in the Antarctic,
a year in Greenland at Camp Century, two years in Alaska
and I have just completed a year's sabbatical in Switzerland
doing theoretical studies. At present I work as a civilian
scientist in the Cold Regions Research and Engineering
Laboratory of the United States Army Terrestrial Sciences
Centre.'

There was a silence which was broken by Harrison. He
gave a nervous cough. 'Yes, indeed. For simplicity's sake,
how would you describe your employment at present?'

McGill grinned. 'I have been described as a snowman.' A
ripple of laughter swept across the hall, and Rolandson's lips
twitched. 'I should say that I am engaged on practical and
theoretical studies of snow and ice which will give a better

understanding of the movement of those materials, particularly in relation to avalanches.'

'I agree with Professor Rolandson,' said Harrison. 'We are very fortunate to have such a qualified witness who can give an account of the events before, during and after the disaster. What took you to Hukahoronui, Dr McGill?'

'I met Ian Ballard in Switzerland and we got on very well together. When he came to New Zealand he invited me to visit him. He knew that I was coming to New Zealand on my way to the Antarctic and suggested that I arrive a little earlier than I had originally intended. He met me at the airport in Auckland and then we both went down to Hukahoronui.'

Lyall held up his hand, and Harrison nodded to him. 'How long did the witness know Mr Ballard in Switzerland?'

'Two weeks.'

'Two weeks!' repeated Lyall. 'Did it not seem strange to you on such a casual acquaintanceship that Mr Ballard should undertake such a long journey involving an air flight from South Island to North Island to meet you at the airport?'

Harrison opened his mouth as though to object, but McGill, his face hardened, beat him to it. 'I don't understand the import of the question, but I'll answer it. Mr Ballard had to attend a board meeting of his company in Auckland with which my arrival coincided.'

'I didn't understand the tenor of that question, either, Mr Lyall,' said Harrison grimly. 'Does the answer satisfy you?'

'Yes, sir.'

'It will speed this inquiry if irrelevant questions are kept to a minimum,' said Harrison coldly. 'Go on, Dr McGill.'

In the Press gallery Dan Edwards said, 'There was some sort of malice behind that. I wonder what instructions the Petersons have given Lyall.'

McGill said, 'There was a lot of snow on the way to Hukahoronui . . .'

Fifteen miles from Hukahoronui they came across a Volkswagen stuck in a drift, the skis strapped on the top proclaiming its purpose. It contained two Americans help-lessly beleaguered by the snow. Ballard and McGill helped to haul the car free and received effusive thanks from the two men who were called Miller and Newman. McGill looked at the Volkswagen, and commented, 'Not the best car for the conditions.'

'You can say that again,' said Newman. 'There's more snow here than in Montana. I didn't expect it to be like this.'

'It's an exceptional season,' said McGill, who had studied the reports.

Miller said, 'How far is it to Huka . . ., He stumbled over the word but finally got it out by spacing the syllables. 'Huka-horo-nui?'

'About fifteen miles,' said Ballard. He smiled. 'You can't miss it – this road goes nowhere else.'

'We're going for the skiing,' said Newman. He grinned as he saw Ballard's eye wander to the skis strapped on top of the car. 'But I guess that's evident.'

'You're going to get stuck again,' said Ballard. 'That's inevitable. You'd better go on ahead and I'll follow, ready to pull you out.'

'Say, that's good of you,' said Miller. 'We'll take you up on that offer. You've got more beef than we have.'

They hauled the Volkswagen out of trouble five times before they reached Hukahoronui. On the fifth occasion Newman said, 'It's real good of you guys to go to all this trouble.'

Ballard smiled. 'You'd do the same, I'm sure, if the position were reversed.' He pointed. 'That's the Gap – the entrance to the valley. Once you're through there you're home and dry.'

They followed the Volkswagen as far as the Gap and watched it descend into the valley, then Ballard pulled off the road. 'Well, there it is.'

McGill surveyed the scene with a professional eye. Instinctively he looked first at the white sweep of the western slope and frowned slightly, then he said, 'Is that your mine down at the bottom there?'

'That's it.'

'You know something? I haven't asked what you get out of there.'

'Gold,' said Ballard. 'Gold in small quantities.' He took a packet of cigarettes and offered one to McGill. 'We've known the gold was there for a long time – my father was the first to pick up the traces – but there wasn't enough to take a chance on investment, not while the gold price was fixed at thirty-five dollars an ounce. But when the price was freed the company risked a couple of million pounds sterling in establishing the plant you see down there. At present we're just breaking even; the gold we're getting out is just servicing the capital investment. But the pickings are getting richer as we follow the reef and we have hopes.'

McGill nodded abstractedly. He was peering through the side window at the rock walls on either side of the Gap. 'Do you have much trouble in keeping the road clear just here?'

'We didn't seem to have trouble years ago when I used to live here. But we're having a fair amount now. The town has got some of the company's earth-moving machinery on more-or-less permanent loan.'

'It'll get worse,' said McGill. 'Maybe a lot worse. I did a check on meteorological conditions; there's a lot of precipitation this year and the forecast is for more.'

'Good for skiers,' said Ballard. 'Bad for mining. We're having trouble getting equipment in.' He put the car in gear. 'Let's get down there.'

He drove through the town and then to the mine office. 'Come in and meet the senior staff,' he said, then hesitated. 'Look, I'm going to be a bit busy for maybe an hour.' He grinned. 'Finding out if they've made a fortune while I've been away. I'll get someone to take you to the house.'

'That'll be fine,' said McGill.

They went into the office building and Ballard opened a door. 'Hello, Betty. Is Mr Dobbs in?'

Betty jerked her thumb. 'Inside with Mr Cameron.'

'Fine. Come on, Mike.' He led the way to an inner office where two men were discussing a plan laid on a desk. 'Hello, Mr Dobbs; hello, Joe. I'd like you to meet a friend who'll be staying in Huka for a while – Mike McGill. This is Harry Dobbs, the mine manager, and Joe Cameron, the mine engineer.'

Dobbs was a thin-faced New Zealander with a dyspeptic expression who looked as though his wife's cooking did not agree with him. Cameron was a broad-shouldered American pushing sixty but not admitting it. They shook hands, and Ballard said, 'Everything okay?'

Cameron looked at Dobbs and Dobbs looked at Cameron. Dobbs said in a thin voice, 'The situation is deteriorating at the same rate.'

Cameron chuckled. 'What he means is that we're still having trouble with this goddam snow. We had a truck stuck in the Gap yesterday; took two 'dozers to get it out.'

'If we can't keep up essential supplies then output is going to be restricted,' said Dobbs.

'I don't think we'll make a profit this half year,' said Ballard.

'Mike, here, says things will get worse, and he ought to know – he's a snow expert.'

'Don't take that as gospel,' protested McGill. 'I've been known to be wrong.' He looked through the window. 'Is that the mine entrance?'

Cameron followed his gaze. 'Yes, that's the portal. Most people think of a mine as having a vertical shaft, but we just drove an adit into the mountainside. It slopes down inside, of course, as we follow the reef.'

'It reminds me of a place in British Columbia called Granduc.' McGill slanted his eyes at Cameron. 'Know it?'

Cameron shook his head. 'Never heard of it.'

McGill looked oddly disappointed.

Dobbs was saying, '. . . and Arthur's Pass was closed for twelve hours yesterday, and the Haast has been closed since Tuesday. I haven't heard about Lewis Pass.'

'What have those passes to do with us?' asked Ballard. 'Our supplies come from Christchurch and don't cross the mountains at all.'

'They're the main passes across the Southern Alps,' said Dobbs. 'If the government can't keep them open, then what chance do we have? They'll be using every machine they've got, and no one is going to send a snow plough to clear a way to Hukahoronui – it's a dead end.'

'We'll just have to do the best we can, Mr Dobbs.' Ballard jerked his head at McGill. 'Let's get you settled in, Mike.'

McGill nodded and said to the room at large, 'Nice to have met you.'

'We'll have to get together,' said Cameron. 'Come over to my place and have dinner some time. My daughter's a great cook.'

Dobbs said nothing.

They went into the outer office. 'Betty will show you where the house is. The bedroom on the left at the back is yours. I won't be more than an hour.'

'Take your time,' said McGill.

It was nearly three hours later when Ballard turned up and by that time McGill had unpacked, taken a walk around

town which did not take long, and returned to the house to
make an urgent telephone call.

When Ballard came into the house he looked tired and
depressed. When he saw McGill he winced as recollection
came back. 'Oh hell! I forgot to tell Mrs Evans we were
coming back. There's no grub ready.'

'Relax,' said McGill. 'There's something in the oven –
McGill's Antarctic Burgoo, as served in all the best restau-
rants south of latitude sixty. We'll eat well.'

Ballard sighed in relief. 'I thought we'd have to eat in the
hotel. I'm not too popular there.'

McGill let that pass. 'There's just one thing I can't find –
your booze.'

Ballard grinned. 'Come on.'

They went into the living-room, and McGill said, 'I used
your phone. I hope you don't mind.'

'Be my guest.' Ballard opened a cupboard and took out a
bottle and two glasses.

'You get your supplies from Christchurch. I know you're
tight for space but is there a chance of getting a parcel in for
me?'

'How big?' McGill made sketching motions with his
hands, and Ballard said, 'Is that all? We can do that.' He
checked his watch. 'That truck Cameron had trouble with is
leaving Christchurch with a load. I might be able to catch it
before it leaves.'

He crossed the room and picked up the telephone. 'Hello,
Maureen. Ian Ballard here. Can you get me the Christchurch
office?'

'I had a look round town,' said McGill. 'It looks mostly
new.'

'It is. When I lived here it was a tenth of the size.'

'Nicely laid out, too. Is most of it mine property?'

'A lot of it. Houses for the married couples and single
quarters and a club house for the bachelors. This is a mine

house. My predecessor lived in one of the old houses but I prefer this one. I like to be on the spot.'

'How many mine employees?'

'At the last count it was a hundred and four – including office staff.'

'And the total population?'

'A bit over eight hundred, I'd say. The mine brought a fair amount of prosperity.'

'That's about what I figured,' said McGill.

An electronic voice crackled in Ballard's ear, and he said, 'This is Ballard at the mine. Has Sam Jeffries left yet? Put him on will you?' There was a pause. 'Sam, Dr McGill wants to talk to you – hold on.'

McGill took the telephone. 'McGill here. Do you know where Advanced Headquarters for Operation Deep Freeze is? Yes . . . near Harewood Airport. Go to the Headquarters Building and find Chief Petty Officer Finney . . . yes, finney as in fish . . . ask him to give you the parcel for me . . . McGill. Right.'

'What was all that about?' asked Ballard.

McGill took the drink which Ballard offered. 'I just thought I'd keep myself occupied while I'm here.' He changed the subject. 'What's with your Mr Dobbs? He looks as though he's swallowed a lemon.'

Ballard smiled wearily and sat down. 'He has a chip on his shoulder. He reckons he should have been put on the board of directors and have my job, instead of which he got me. To make it worse, my name is Ballard.'

'What's that got to do with anything?'

'Don't you know? If you trace things back far enough the whole mine is owned by the Ballard family.'

McGill spluttered into his drink. 'Well, I'll be god-damned! I've been hobnobbing with the plutocratic capitalists and never knew it. There's a name for that kind of thing – nepotism. No wonder Dobbs is acid.'

'If it's nepotism it isn't doing me any good,' said Ballard. There was a touch of savagery in his voice. 'I don't have a penny except my director's fees.'

'No shares in the company?'

'No shares in this or any other Ballard company – but tell that to Dobbs and he wouldn't believe you. I haven't even tried.'

McGill's voice was soft. 'What's the matter, Ian? Come from the wrong side of the family?'

'Not really.' Ballard got up to pour himself another drink. 'I have a grandfather who's an egotistical old monster and I had a father who wouldn't co-operate. Dad told the old boy to go to hell and he's never forgotten it.'

'The sins of the fathers are visited on the children,' said McGill thoughtfully. 'And yet you're employed by a Ballard company. There must be something there some-where.'

'They don't pay me any more than I'm worth – they get value for money.' Ballard sighed. 'But God, I could run the company better than it's run now.' He waved his glass. 'I don't mean this mine, this is a piddling little affair.'

'You call a two million pound company a piddling affair!' said McGill in wonder.

'I once worked it out. The Ballards control companies with a capital value of two hundred and twenty million pounds. The Ballards' own shareholdings are about forty-two million pounds. That was a few years ago, though.'

'Jesus!' said McGill involuntarily.

'I have three rapacious old vultures who call themselves my uncles and half a dozen cousins who follow the breed. They're only interested in loot and between them they're running the show into the ground. They're great ones for merging and asset-stripping, and they squeeze every penny until it hurts. Take this mine. Up in Auckland I have a Comptroller of Accounts who reports to London, and I can't sign a cheque for more than a thousand dollars without his say-so. And I'm supposed to be in charge.'

He breathed heavily. 'When I came here I went underground and that night I prayed we wouldn't have a visit from the Inspector of Mines before I had time to straighten things out.'

'Had someone been cutting corners?'

Ballard shrugged. 'Fisher, the last managing director, was an old fool and not up to the job. I doubt any criminal intent, but negligence combined with parsimony has led to a situation in which the company could find itself in serious trouble. I have a mine manager who can't make decisions and wants his hand held all the time, and I have a mine engineer who is past it. Oh, Cameron's all right, I suppose, but he's old and he's running scared.'

'You've got yourself a packet of trouble,' said McGill.

Ballard snorted. 'You don't know the half of it. I haven't said anything about the unions yet, not to mention the attitude of some of the town people.'

'You sound as though you earn your pay. But why the hell stick to a Ballard company if you feel like this?'

'Oh, I don't know – some remnants of family loyalty, I suppose,' said Ballard tiredly. 'After all, my grandfather did pay for my education, and quite extensive it was. I suppose I owe him something for that.'

McGill noted Ballard's evident depression and tiredness and decided to change the subject. 'Let's eat, and I'll tell you about the ice worms in Alaska.' He plunged into an improbable story.

FOUR

The next morning was bright and sunny and the snow, which had been falling all night, had stopped, leaving the world freshly minted. When Ballard got up, heavy-eyed and unrested, he found Mrs Evans in the kitchen cooking breakfast. She scolded him. 'You should have let me know when you were coming back. I only learned by chance from Betty Hargreaves last night.'

'I'm sorry,' he said. 'I forgot. Are you cooking for three?' Mrs Evans usually ate breakfast with him; it was a democratic society.

'I am. Your friend has gone out already, but he'll be back for a late breakfast.'

Ballard consulted his watch to discover that he had overslept by more than an hour. 'Give me ten minutes.'

When he had showered and dressed he felt better and found McGill in the living-room unwrapping a large parcel. 'It came,' said McGill. 'Your truck got through.'

Ballard looked at what was revealed; it was a backpack which appeared to contain nothing but sections of aluminium tubing each nestling in an individual canvas pocket. 'What's that?'

'The tools of my trade,' said McGill. Mrs Evans called, and he added, 'Let's eat; I'm hungry.'

Ballard toyed with his breakfast while McGill wolfed down a plateful of bacon and eggs, and pleased Mrs Evans by asking for more. While she was out of the room he said, 'You asked me here for the skiing, and there's no time like the present. How's your leg?'

Ballard shook his head. 'The leg is all right, but sorry, Mike – not today. I'm a working man.'

'You'd better come.' Something in McGill's tone made Ballard look at him sharply. McGill's face was serious. 'You'd better come and see what I'm doing. I want an independent witness.'

'A witness to what?'

'To whatever it is I find.'

'And what will that be?'

'How do I know until I find it?' He stared at Ballard. 'I'm serious, Ian. You know what my job is. I'm going to make a professional investigation. You're the boss man of the mine and you couldn't make a better witness. You've got authority.'

'For God's sake!' said Ballard. 'Authority to do what?'

'To close down the mine if need be, but that depends on what I find, and I won't know that until I look, will I?' As Ballard's jaw dropped McGill said, 'I couldn't believe my eyes at what I saw yesterday. It looked like a recipe for instant disaster, and I spent a damned uneasy night. I won't be happy until I take a look.'

'Where?'

McGill got to his feet and walked to the window. 'Come here.' He pointed at the steep slope above the mine. 'Up there.'

Ballard looked at the long curve, blinding white in the sunlight. 'You think . . .' His voice tailed away.

'I think nothing until I get evidence one way or the other,' said McGill sharply. 'I'm a scientist, not a soothsayer.' He shook his head warningly as Mrs Evans came in with a fresh plate of bacon and eggs. 'Finish your breakfast.'

As they sat down he said, 'I suppose you can find me a pair of skis.'

Ballard nodded, his mind busy with the implications of what McGill had said – or had not said. McGill dug into his second plateful of breakfast. 'Then we go skiing,' he said lightly.

Two hours later they were nearly three thousand feet above the mine and half way up the slope. They had not talked much and when Ballard had tried McGill advised him to save his breath for climbing. But now they stopped and McGill unslung the backpack, dropping one of the straps over a ski-stick rammed firmly into the snow.

He took off his skis and stuck them vertically into the snow up-slope of where he was standing. 'Another safety measure,' he said conversationally. 'If there's a slide then the skis will tell someone that we've been swept away. And that's why you don't take off your Oertel cord.'

Ballard leaned on his sticks. 'The last time you talked about avalanches I was in one.'

McGill grinned. 'Don't fool yourself. You were in a little trickle – a mere hundred feet.' He pointed down the mountainside. 'If this lot goes it'll be quite different.'

Ballard felt uneasy. 'You're not really expecting an avalanche?'

McGill shook his head. 'Not right now.' He bent down to the backpack. 'I'm going to do a little gentle thumping and you can help me to do it. Take off your skis.'

He began to take aluminium tubing from the pack and to assemble it into some kind of a gadget. 'This is a penetrometer – an updating of the Haefeli design. It's a sort of pocket pile-driver – it measures the resistance of the snow. It also gives us a core, and temperature readings at ten-centimetre intervals. All the data for a snow profile.'

Ballard helped him set it up although he suspected that McGill could have done the job just as handily without him. There was a sliding weight which dropped down a narrow rod a known distance before hitting the top of the aluminium tube and thus driving it into the snow. Each time the weight dropped McGill noted the distance of penetration and recorded it in a notebook.

They thumped with the weight, adding lengths of tubing as necessary, and hit bottom at 158 centimetres – about five feet.

'There's a bit of a hard layer somewhere in the middle,' said McGill, taking an electric plug from the pack. He made a connection in the top of the tubing and plugged the other end into a box with a dial on it. 'Make a note of these temperatures; there'll be fifteen readings.'

As Ballard took the last reading he said, 'How do we get it out?'

'We have a tripod and a miniature block and tackle.' McGill grinned. 'I think they pinched this bit from an oil rig.'

He erected the tripod and started to haul out the tube. As the first section came free he disconnected it carefully and then took a knife and sliced through the ice in the tube. The sections were two feet long and the three of them were soon out. McGill put the tubes back into the pack, complete with the snow cores they contained. 'We'll have a look at those back at the house.'

Ballard squatted on his heels and looked across the valley. 'What now?'

'Now we do another, and another, and another, and another in a line diagonally down the slope. I'd like to do more but that's all the core tubing I have.'

They had just finished the fourth trial boring when McGill looked up the slope. 'We have company.'

Ballard turned his head to see three skiers traversing down towards them. The leader was moving fast and came around in a flashy stem christiania which sent the snow spraying before he stopped. When he lifted blue-tinted goggles Ballard recognized Charlie Peterson.

Peterson looked at Ballard with some astonishment. 'Oh, it's you! Eric told me you were back but I haven't seen you around.'

'Hello, Charlie.'

The two other skiers came up and stopped more sedately – they were the two Americans, Miller and Newman. Charlie said, 'How did you get here?'

Ballard and McGill looked at each other, and Ballard wordlessly pointed to the skis. Charlie snorted. 'You used to be afraid of falling off anything steeper than a billiard table.' He looked curiously at the dismantled penetrometer. 'What are you doing?'

McGill answered. 'Looking at snow.'

Charlie pointed a stick. 'What's that thing?'

'A gadget for testing snow strength.'

Charlie grinned at Ballard. 'Since when did you become interested in snow? Your Ma wouldn't let you out in it for fear you'd catch cold.'

Ballard said evenly, 'I've become interested in a lot of things since then, Charlie.'

He laughed loudly. 'Yes? I'll bet you're a hot one with the girls.'

Newman said abruptly, 'Let's go.'

'No, wait a minute,' said Charlie. 'I'm interested. What are you doing with that watchamacallit?'

McGill straightened. 'I'm testing the stresses on this snow slope.'

'This slope's all right.'

'When did you have this much snow before?'

'There's always snow in the winter.'

'Not this much.'

Charlie looked at Miller and Newman and grinned at them. 'All the better – it makes for good skiing.' He rubbed the side of his jaw. 'Why come here to look at snow?'

McGill bent down to buckle a strap. 'The usual reason.'

The grin left Charlie's face. 'What reason?' he asked blankly.

'Because it's here,' said McGill patiently.

'Funny!' said Charlie. 'Very funny! How long are you going to be here?'

'For as long as it takes.'

'That's no kind of answer.'

Ballard stepped forward. 'That's all the answer you're going to get, Charlie.'

Charlie grinned genially. 'Staying away for so long has made you bloody prickly. I don't remember you giving back-chat before.'

Ballard smiled. 'Maybe I've changed, Charlie.'

'I don't think so,' he said deliberately. 'People like you never change.'

'You're welcome to find out any time you like.'

Newman said, 'Cut it out, Charlie. I don't know what you have against this guy and I don't much care. All I know is he helped us yesterday. Anyway, this is no place to pick a fight.'

'I agree,' said Ballard.

Charlie turned to Newman. 'Hear that? He hasn't changed.' He swung around and pointed down the slope. 'All right. We go down in traverses – that way first. This is a good slope for practising stem turns.'

Miller said, 'It looks good.'

'Wait a minute,' said McGill sharply. 'I wouldn't do that.'

Charlie turned his head. 'And why not, for Christ's sake?'

'It could be dangerous.'

'Crossing the road can be dangerous,' he said contemptuously. He jerked his head at Miller. 'Let's go.'

Miller pulled down his goggles. 'Sure.'

'Hold on,' said Newman. He looked down at the penetrometer. 'Maybe the guy's got something there.'

'The hell with him,' said Charlie, and pushed off. Miller followed without another word. Newman looked at Ballard for a moment, then shrugged expressively before he followed them.

McGill and Ballard watched them go down. Charlie, in the lead, skied showily with a lot of unnecessary flair; Miller was sloppy and Newman neat and economical in his movements. They watched them all the way to the bottom.

Nothing happened.

'Who's the jerk?' McGill asked.

'Charlie Peterson. He's set up as a ski instructor.'

'He seems to know you.' McGill glanced sideways. 'And your family.'

'Yes,' said Ballard expressionlessly.

'I keep forgetting you were brought up here.' McGill scratched his cheek reflectively. 'You know, you could be useful. I want to find someone in the valley who has lived here a long time, whose family has lived here a long time. I need information.'

Ballard thought for a moment and then smiled and pointed with his ski-stick. 'See that rock down there? That's Kamakamaru, and a man called Turi Buck lives in a house just on the other side. I should have seen him before now but I've been too bloody busy.'

McGill hung his backpack on a convenient post outside Turi Buck's house. 'Better not take that inside. The ice would melt.'

Ballard knocked on the door which was opened by a girl of about fourteen, a Maori girl with a cheerful smile. 'I'm looking for Turi Buck.'

'Wait a minute,' she said and disappeared, and he heard her voice raised. 'Grandpa, there's someone to see you.'

Presently Turi appeared. Ballard was a little shocked at what he saw; Turi's hair was a frizzled grey and his face was seamed and lined like a water-eroded hillside. There was no recognition in his brown eyes as he said, 'Anything I can do for you?'

'Not a great deal, Turi,' said Ballard. 'Don't you remember me?'

Turi stepped forward, coming out of the doorway and into the light. He frowned and said uncertainly, 'I don't . . . , my eyesight's not as good as . . . Ian?'

'Your eyesight is not so bad,' said Ballard.

'Ian!' said Turi in delight. 'I heard you were back – you should have come to see me sooner. I thought you had forgotten.'

'Work, Turi; the work comes first – you taught me that. This is my friend, Mike McGill.'

Turi beamed at them. 'Well, come in; come in.'

He led them into the house and into a room familiar to Ballard. Over the great fieldstone fireplace was the wapiti head with its great spread of antlers, and a wood fire burned beneath it. On the walls were the wood carvings inlaid with paua shell shimmering iridescently. The greenstone *mere* – the Maori war axe – was still there and, in pride of place, Turi's *whakapapa* stick, his most prized possession, very intricately carved and which gave his ancestry.

Ballard looked around. 'Nothing has changed.'

'Not here,' said Turi.

Ballard nodded towards the window. 'A lot of change out there, though, I didn't recognize the valley.'

Turi sighed. 'Too much change – too quickly. But where have you *been*, Ian?'

'A lot of places. All over the world.'

'Sit down,' said Turi. 'Tell me about it.'

'Tell me about yourself first. Did that beautiful young lady call you "Grandpa"?'

'I am a grandfather five times now.' Turi's shoulders shook. 'My sons are men and all married. Both my daughters are mothers.'

'Tawhaki,' said Ballard. 'How is Tawhaki?' He had been Ballard's playmate as a child and a constant companion as he grew older.

'He does well,' said Turi. 'He went to the University of Otago and took a good degree.'

'In what?'

Turi laughed. 'In economics. Imagine a Maori knowing about economics. He has a post in the Department of Finance in Auckland. I don't see him often.'

'You must give me his address. I'll look him up when next I'm in Auckland.' Ballard saw Turi regarding McGill with interest. 'Mike, here, is very interested in snow. He's so interested he's going to Antarctica later in the year.'

Turi's seamed face broke into a grim smile. 'Then there's something for you here, Mike. We have a lot of snow; more than I can remember since 1943.'

'So I've seen.'

Ballard went to the window. On the other side of the valley the cedar branches drooped heavily under the weight of snow. He turned, and said, 'What happened to the trees on the west slope, Turi?'

'Above the mine?'

'Yes,' said Ballard. 'That slope has been stripped.'

McGill became alert. 'The slope used to be timbered?'

Turi nodded and then shrugged. 'When they put in the mine they wanted props. *Kahikatea* make good mine props.' He looked up. 'The Petersons own that land; they made a good profit.'

'I bet they did,' said Ballard.

'Your mother shouldn't have sold it to them.' Turi clasped his hands. 'Then they blasted out the stumps and put the land down to grass for hay. They run cattle on the river flats; Herefords for beef and a few dairy cows. That's also become profitable now the town has grown.'

Ballard said, 'Didn't anybody think of what would happen when the snow came?'

'Oh yes,' said Turi. 'I did.'

'Didn't you say anything? Didn't you object when they put up the mine building? When they built the township?'

'I objected. I objected very loudly. But the Petersons were louder. Who would listen to an old man?' His lips twisted. 'Especially one with a brown skin.'

Ballard snorted and looked at McGill who said slowly, 'The stupid bastards! The stupid, greedy bastards!' He looked about the room and then at Turi. 'When did you come to the valley, Mr Buck?'

'My name is Turi, and I was born here.' He smiled. 'New Year's Day, 1900. I'm as old as the century.'

'Who built the house?'

'My father built it in about 1880, I think. It was built on the site of my grandfather's house.'

'And when was that built?'

Turi shrugged. 'I don't know. My people have lived here a long time.'

McGill nodded. 'Did your father give any reason for building on the same site? Under this big rock?'

Turi answered obliquely. 'He said that anyone building in Hukahoronui must take precautions.'

'He knew what he was talking about.' McGill turned to Ballard. 'I'd like to test those samples pretty quickly. And I'd like to come back to talk to you, Turi, if I may?'

'You must both come back. Come to supper and meet a couple of my grandchildren.'

As Turi accompanied them to the door Ballard said, 'You don't think much of the mine, do you, Turi?'

'Too many changes,' he said, and shook his head wryly. 'We now have a supermarket.'

'You know I'm in charge of the mine now – and I don't like it much, either. But I think my reasons are different.

You're going to see more changes, Turi, but these I think you'll like.'

Turi thumped him gently on the arm. '*He tamariki koe?* You're a man now, Ian; a real man.'

'Yes,' said Ballard. 'I've grown up. Thanks, Turi.'

Turi watched them put on their skis and, as they traversed the slope which led away from the house, he waved and called, '*Haere ra!*'

Ballard looked back over his shoulder. '*Haere ra!*' They headed back to the mine.

FIVE

The late afternoon sun poured through the windows of the hall, rendered multi-coloured by the stained glass. Patches of colour lay across the tables; the carafe of water in front of Ballard looked as though it was filled with blood.

Dan Edwards loosened his tie and wished he could have a cold beer. 'They'll be adjourning pretty soon,' he said to Dalwood. 'I wish old Harrison would get a bloody move on. All this talk of snow doesn't make me feel any cooler.'

Harrison poured himself a glass of water and sipped. He set down the glass, and said, 'So you took samples of the snow cover on the western slope in the presence of Mr Ballard. What were your findings?'

McGill unzipped the leather satchel and took out a sheaf of papers. 'I have written an entire report on the events that occurred at Hukahoronui – from the technical side, of course. I submit the report to the Commission.' He gave the report to Reed who passed it up to Harrison. 'Part One consists of my findings on the first series of snow profiles which was submitted to the mine management and, later, to the municipal authorities of Hukahoronui.'

Harrison flipped through the pages and frowned, then he passed the papers to Professor Rolandson. They conferred for a moment in low voices, then Harrison said, 'This is all very well, Dr McGill; but your report appears to be highly technical and contains more mathematical formulae than the majority of us are accustomed to. After all, this is a *public* hearing. Could you not describe your findings in a language that can be understood by others apart from yourself and Professor Rolandson?'

'Of course,' said McGill. 'Indeed, I did so to the people in Hukahoronui.'

'You may proceed; and you may expect to be questioned – in the interests of clarity – by Professor Rolandson.'

McGill clasped his hands in front of him. 'Snow is not so much a substance as a process; it changes in time. It begins with a snowflake falling to earth and becoming part of the general snow cover. It is a six-sided crystal and not very stable, and sublimation begins – a sort of evaporation. Eventually the crystal becomes a small, rounded granule. This is called destructive metamorphism and results in a higher density because the air is squeezed out. At the same time, because of the evaporative process, there is water vapour in the snow mass and, due to the low temperature, the separate granules tend to bond together by freezing.'

'This bond is not particularly strong, is it?' asked Rolandson.

'The bond is not strong, when compared with other materials.' Rolandson nodded and McGill went on. 'The next thing to take into account is the temperature through the snow cover. It's not constant – it's warmer at the bottom than the top, thus forming a temperature gradient. If you look at Graph One you will find the temperature gradient of those first five samples.'

Rolandson flipped pages. 'Not a very steep gradient – not more than two degrees.'

'It's enough for the next stage in the process. There is still a lot of air in the snow cover and the relatively warm air at the bottom begins to rise carrying water vapour with it. The vapour precipitates on the colder granules above. There is now a building process at work which is called constructive metamorphism, and a new kind of crystal begins to form – a cup crystal.'

'Could you describe a cup crystal, Dr McGill?'

'It's a conical shape with a hollow in the blunt end – the cup.'

'And how large is a cup crystal?'

'A well-developed crystal may run to half an inch long, but you can take a quarter-inch as average.' McGill paused, and when Rolandson remained silent, he said, 'Graph Two shows the penetrometer readings – that is the resistance of the snow to stress.'

Rolandson studied it. 'This is the resistance in kilograms plotted against depth?'

'Yes, sir.'

'There's a discontinuity half way down on all five samples.'

'Yes, sir; that's a layer of surface hoar.'

Harrison interrupted. 'If it is not on the surface how can it be described as surface hoar?'

'It *was* on the surface. When the surface of the snow is colder than the air above it then there is more sublimation of water vapour – something like the condensation on the outside of a glass of cold beer.' (In the Press gallery Dan Edwards sighed in anguish and licked his lips.) 'In this case I should imagine it happened on a clear and cloudless night when there would be a lot of outgoing radiation. Then the hoar, or frost, would form on the surface producing flat plates of thin ice.'

Again Harrison brought up the objection. 'But this discontinuity, as Professor Rolandson calls it, is not on the surface.'

'No,' agreed McGill. 'Normally, when the sun hits it in the morning it disappears. In this case, I imagine that clouds came over before sunrise and it began to snow again quite heavily. The layer of hoar was covered and preserved.'

'With what significance?' queried Rolandson.

'Several things could happen. The layer is quite hard, as you can see from the penetrometer readings. It is also quite smooth and could form a sliding surface for the snow above it.' McGill extended two fingers. 'Secondly, a layer of hoar is formed of flat plates of ice fused together – that is, it is relatively impermeable to air. This means that the most likely place for cup crystals to form would be just under the hoar layer.'

'You emphasize cup crystals. In what way are they dangerous?'

'They are dangerous because of their rounded shape and because there is very little bonding between one crystal and another.' McGill tugged at his ear. 'As a very rough analogy I would suggest that it would be very difficult for a man to walk on a floor loosely packed with billiard balls. It's that kind of instability.'

'Was there any evidence of cup crystals forming at this time?'

'They had begun to form in sample one, the highest up the slope. I had reason to believe that the process would continue which would result in a marked decline in stability.'

'Go on, Dr McGill.'

McGill put up a third finger. 'Three, the weather forecast at the time indicated more snow – more weight – on that slope.' He dropped his hand. 'All things considered I came to the conclusion that the snow cover on the western slope of the valley of Hukahoronui was relatively unstable and thus formed a potential avalanche hazard. I so informed the mine management.'

'You mean Mr Ballard?' asked Harrison.

'Present at the meeting were Mr Ballard; Mr Dobbs, the mine manager; Mr Cameron, the mine engineer; Mr Quentin, the union representative.'

'And you were present during the whole of that meeting?'

'Yes, sir.'

'Then I think we can take your evidence as best evidence of what occurred at the meeting, subject to later appraisal. However, the time has come to adjourn for today. We will gather here at ten in the morning when you, Dr McGill, will again be a witness. The hearing is adjourned.'

SIX

The participants of the hearing flooded on to the pavement of Armagh Street and began to disperse. Dan Edwards, heading rapidly beerwards, stopped when Dalwood said, 'Who is the tall redhead talking to Ballard? The girl with the dog.'

Edwards craned his neck. 'Good God! Now what the hell goes on there?'

'Who is she?'

'Liz Peterson, the sister of Charlie and Eric.'

Dalwood watched Ballard pat the Alsatian and smile at the girl warmly. 'They seem on good terms.'

'Yes – bloody funny, isn't it? Charlie has got his knife so deep into Ballard that he's in blood up to his armpit. I wonder if he knows Liz is fraternizing with the enemy?'

'We'll soon know,' said Dalwood. 'Here come Charlie and Eric now.'

The two men came out of the building, unsmiling and exchanging monosyllables. Charlie looked up and his face became thunderous. He snapped something at his brother and quickened his pace, elbowing his way through the crowd on the pavement. At that moment a car drew up and Ballard got into it and when Charlie reached his sister Ballard had gone. Charlie spoke to his sister and an argument seemed to develop.

Edwards watched the by-play, and said, 'If he didn't know he does now. What's more, he doesn't like it.'

'And the dog doesn't like Charlie. Look at it.'

The Alsatian's upper lip was curled back in a snarl and Liz Peterson shortened her grip on the lead and spoke sharply to it.

Edwards sighed. 'Let's get that beer. The first one will hiss going down.'

Mike McGill was driving the car. He slanted an eye at Ballard and then returned his attention to the road. 'Well, what do you think?'

'Your evidence was good. Very concise.'

'Rolandson helped; he fed me some good lines. He makes a good straight man to my comedian. You didn't do too well, though.'

'I'm doing all right.'

'Wake up, Ian! That son of a bitch, Rickman, is going to deliver you bound and gagged if you don't stop him.'

'Save it, Mike,' said Ballard shortly. 'I'm too bloody tired.'

McGill bit his lip and lapsed into silence. After ten minutes he swung off the road and parked in the forecourt of their hotel. 'You'll feel better after a cold beer,' he said. 'It was goddam hot in that courthouse. Okay?'

'All right,' said Ballard listlessly.

They went into the hotel bar and McGill ordered two beers and took them to a discreet table. 'Here's mud in your eye.' He drank and gasped with pleasure. 'God, how I needed that!' He replenished his glass. 'That courthouse is sure some place. Who designed it – Edward the Confessor?'

'It's not a courthouse – it's a sort of provincial House of Parliament. Or it was.'

McGill grinned. 'The bit I like about it are those pious texts set in the stained glass windows. I wonder who thought those up?' In the same even tone he said, 'What did Liz Peterson want?'

'Just to wish me well.'

'Did she?' said McGill sardonically. 'If she really meant it she'd operate on that brother of hers with a sharp knife.' He watched the condensation form on the outside of his glass. 'Come to think of it, a blunt knife might be better. The Peterson lawyer was really sniping at you this morning.'

'I know.' Ballard took another draught. It seemed to do him good. 'It doesn't matter, Mike. You and I know the evidence is on our side.'

'You're wrong,' said McGill flatly. 'Evidence is how a lawyer puts it – and talking about lawyers, what about Rickman? You know what he did to you this morning, don't you? He made it look as though you were trying to renege. Hell, everyone in that hall thought you were trying to slip the country.'

Ballard rubbed his eyes. 'I said something to Rickman just before the hearing opened, and he got it wrong, that's all.'

'That's all? That's not all – not by a thousand miles. A smart guy like that doesn't get things wrong in a courtroom. If he got it wrong then he meant to get it wrong. What did you say to him, anyway?'

Ballard took out his wallet and extracted a piece of paper. 'I was leaving the hotel this morning when I got this.' He passed it to McGill. 'My grandfather's dead!'

McGill unfolded the cablegram and read it. 'Ian, I'm sorry; I really am.' He was silent for a moment. 'This Harriet – is she your mother?'

'Yes.'

'She wants you to go home.'

'She would,' said Ballard bitterly.

'And you showed this to Rickman?'

'Yes.'

'And he got up on his hind legs and, by inference, demonstrated that you are a coward. Hell, Ian; he's not representing you! He's representing the company.'

'Six of one and half a dozen of the other.'

McGill regarded Ballard and slowly shook his head. 'You really believe what the Chairman of the Commission said, don't you? That all they want is to get at the truth. Well, that may be what Harrison thinks but it's not what the public want. Fifty-four people died, Ian, and the public want a scapegoat. The President of your company knows . . .'

'Chairman.'

McGill waggled his hand. 'To hell with semantics. The Chairman of your company knows that, too, and he's making goddam sure the company isn't the goat. That's why he's employed a sharp cookie like Rickman, and if you think Rickman is acting for you then you're out of your mind. If the company can get out from under by sacrificing you then that's what they'll do.'

He thumped the table. 'I can write the scenario right now. "Mr Ballard is new to the company. Mr Ballard is young and inexperienced. It is only to be expected that so young a man should make unfortunate mistakes. Surely such errors of judgment may be excused in one so inexperienced."' McGill leaned back in his chair. 'By the time Rickman is finished with you he'll have everyone believing you *arranged* the goddam avalanche – and the Petersons and that snide lawyer of theirs will fall over themselves to help him.'

Ballard smiled slightly. 'You have great powers of imagination, Mike.'

'Oh, what the hell!' said McGill disgustedly. 'Let's have another beer.'

'My round.' Ballard got up and went to the bar. When he came back he said, 'So the old boy's dead.' He shook his head. 'You know, Mike, it hit me harder than I thought it would.'

McGill poured more beer. 'Judging by the way you talked about him, I'm surprised you feel anything at all.'

'Oh, he was a cantankerous old devil – stubborn and self-opinionated – but there was something about him . . .' Ballard shook his head. 'I don't know.'

'What happens to the parent corporation . . . what's it called?'

'Ballard Holdings.'

'What happens to Ballard Holdings now he's dead? Is it up for grabs?'

'I shouldn't think so. The old man established a trust or something like that. I never really got the hang of it because I knew I wouldn't figure in it. I imagine that things will remain pretty stable, with Uncle Bert and Uncle Steve and Uncle Ed running things pretty much as they are now. Which is to say badly.'

'I don't see why the shareholders put up with it.'

'The shareholders don't have a bloody thing to do with it. Let me tell you a fact of financial life, Mike. You don't really need fifty-one per cent of the shares of a company to control it. Thirty per cent is enough if the other shares are fragmented into small parcels and if your lawyers and accountants are smart enough.' Ballard shrugged. 'In any case, the shareholders aren't too unhappy; all the Ballard companies make profits, and the kind of people who are buying into Ballard companies these days aren't the type to inquire too closely into how the profits are made.'

'Yeah,' said McGill abstractedly. This was not really of interest to him. He leaned forward and said, 'Let's do some strategy planning.'

'What do you mean?'

'I've been figuring how Harrison's mind works. He's a very logical guy and that works in our favour. I'm going to give evidence tomorrow about the meeting with the mine management. Why me?'

'Harrison asked if you'd been present during the entire meeting – and you had. He picked you because you were already on the stand and it was quicker than calling another witness. That's what I think, anyway.'

McGill looked pleased. 'That's what I think, too. Harrison said he'd take evidence in chronological order, and he's doing just that. Now what happened after the mine meeting?'

'We had the meeting with the town council.'

'And what will Harrison ask me?'

'He'll ask if you were present during the whole of that meeting – and you'll have to say no, because you left half way through. So?'

'So I want to pick the next witness, and knowing how Harrison's mind works, I think I can swing it.'

'Who do you want for the next witness?'

'Turi Buck,' said McGill. 'I want to get on record the history of Hukahoronui just to ram things home. I want to get on record the sheer stupidity of that goddam town council.'

Ballard looked broodingly into his glass. 'I don't like doing that to Turi. It might hurt.'

'He wants to do it. He's already put himself forward as a voluntary witness. He's staying with his sister here in Christchurch; we'll pick him up tomorrow morning.'

'All right.'

'Now, look, Ian. Turi is an old man and may be likely to become confused under hostile cross-examination. We've got to make sure that the right questions are asked in the right order. We've got to cover the ground so thoroughly that no one – not Lyall nor Rickman – can find a loophole.'

'I'll make out a list of questions for Rickman,' said Ballard.

McGill rolled his eyes skyward. 'Can't you get it into your thick skull that if Rickman questions Turi it will be in a hostile manner.'

Ballard said sharply, 'Rickman is representing me and he'll follow my instructions.'

'And if he doesn't?'

'If he doesn't then I'll know you're right – and that will free me completely. We'll see.' He drained his glass. 'I feel sticky; I'm going to have a shower.'

As they left the bar McGill said, 'About that cablegram. You're not going back, are you?'

'You mean running home to Mamma?' Ballard grinned. 'Not while Harrison is Chairman of the Commission. I doubt if even my mother could win against Harrison.'

'Your mother isn't Jewish, is she?' asked McGill curiously.

'No. Why do you ask?'

'Oh, it's just that Jewish mothers are popularly supposed to be strong-willed. But I think that your mother could give a Jewish mother points and still win.'

'It's not a matter of a strong will,' said Ballard soberly. 'It's just straightforward moral blackmail.'

THE HEARING

Second Day

SEVEN

McGill and Ballard found Turi Buck waiting outside his sister's home at nine-thirty next morning. Although it was still early the weather showed signs of becoming oppressively hot. Ballard leaned over to open the back door of the car, and said, 'Jump in, Turi.'

'I'm past jumping anywhere, Ian,' said Turi wryly, 'But I'll endeavour to accommodate myself in this seat.'

Sometimes Turi's phrases had an oddly old-fashioned ring about them. Ballard knew he had never been formally educated but had read a lot, and he suspected that Sir Walter Scott was responsible for some of the more courtly expressions.

'It's good of you to come, Turi.'

'I had to come, Ian.'

In the Provincial Chamber, at precisely ten o'clock, Harrison tapped the top of the rostrum gently with his gavel, and said, 'We are now prepared to resume the inquiry into the avalanche disaster at Hukahoronui. Dr McGill was giving evidence. Will you please resume your seat?'

McGill walked to the witness chair and sat down. Harrison said, 'Yesterday you referred to a meeting of the mine management at which you presented a report. What happened at that meeting?'

McGill tugged at his ear thoughtfully. 'The problem was to explain the evidence and to get them to accept it. Mr Ballard had already accepted it. Mr Cameron wanted to go through the figures in detail, but he came around in the end. The others weren't as convinced. It went like this . . .'

It was Cameron, the engineer, who saw the true significance of the cup crystals. 'Could you draw a picture of one of those, Mike?'

'Sure.' McGill took a pencil from his pocket and made a drawing. 'As I said, it's conical in shape – like this – and it has this hollow in the blunt end. That's why it's called a cup crystal.'

'I'm not worried about the hollow.' Cameron stared at the drawing. 'What you've sketched here is a pretty good picture of a tapered roller bearing. You say these are likely to form under that layer of hard hoar frost?'

'Correct.'

'That's not good,' said Cameron. 'That's not good at all. If you get a lot of weight on top pushing downwards vertically by gravity then there'll be a resultant force sideways on the slope. The whole hillside could come down on ready-made bearings.'

Cameron passed the drawing to Dobbs who looked at it with Quentin, the union man, peering over his shoulder. 'Any of those cup things there now?'

'There are indications of them forming in one of the samples I took. I'd say the process is well under way.'

'Let's have a look at your stress figures.' Cameron grimaced as he began to go through the equations. 'I'm used to working with stronger stuff than snow.'

'The principle is the same,' said McGill.

Dobbs handed the drawing to Ballard. 'Are you seriously telling us that there'll be an avalanche which will fall on this mine?'

'Not exactly,' said McGill carefully. 'What I'm saying, at this moment, is that there is a potential hazard that must be watched. I don't think there is a present danger – it's not going to come down in the next hour or even today. A lot depends on future events.'

'Such as?' asked Ballard.

'The way the temperature goes. Future snow precipitation. An appreciable rise in wind speed wouldn't help much, either.'

'And the forecast is for more snow,' said Ballard.

McGill said, 'When you have a potential hazard like this you have to take precautions. Protecting the mine portal, for instance. There's a steel construction called Wonder Arch which comes in useful. It was developed at Camp Century in Greenland specifically for this type of application. It's used a lot in the Antarctic.'

'Is it expensive?' asked Dobbs. His voice was clouded with doubt.

McGill shrugged. 'It depends on how much money you put against lives on the balance sheet.' He turned to Cameron. 'Joe, remember me asking if you'd heard of Granduc in British Columbia?'

Cameron looked up from the figures. 'Yeah. I hadn't.'

'Granduc is remarkably like your mine here. They installed Wonder Arch – put in a covered way to the mine portal.' He rubbed the side of his jaw. 'It was like closing a stable door after the horse has gone; they put in the arch in 1966 after the avalanche of 1965 when twenty-six men died.'

There was a silence broken after a while by Cameron. 'You make your point very clearly.'

Ballard said, 'I'll put it to the Board of Directors.'

'That's not all,' said McGill. 'You got to look at the situation in the long term. That slope is dangerous mostly because it's been stripped of timber. It will have to be stabilized again, and that means building snow rakes. Good snow rakes cost sixty dollars a foot run – I doubt if you'd get away with under a million dollars.'

The sound of Dobbs's suddenly indrawn breath was harsh.

'Then there's the snow deflection walls at the bottom,' went on McGill inexorably. 'That's more – maybe even half a million. It's going to cost a packet.'

'The Board won't stand for it,' said Dobbs. He stared at Ballard. 'You know we're just paying our way now. They're not going to put in all that extra capital for no increase in production. It just isn't on.'

Quentin stirred. 'Would you want to close down the mine?'

'It's a possibility,' said Ballard. 'But it's not my decision.'

'My people would have something to say about that. There's a lot of jobs at stake.' Quentin looked at McGill hostilely and threw out his hand. 'And who's to say he's right? He comes busting in here with his tale of doom, but who the hell is he, anyway?'

Ballard straightened. 'Let's get one thing clear,' he said. 'As of yesterday Dr McGill became a professional consultant employed by this company to give us advice on certain problems. His qualifications satisfy me completely.'

'You didn't talk to me about this,' said Dobbs.

Ballard gave him a level stare. 'I wasn't aware I had to, Mr Dobbs. You are so informed now.'

'Does the Chairman know about this?'

'He'll know when I tell him, which will be very soon.'

Quentin was earnest. 'Look, Mr Ballard; I've been listening carefully. There's not been an avalanche, and your friend hasn't said there's going to be one. All he's been talking about are potentials. I think the Board is going to need a lot more than that before they spend a million and a half dollars. I don't think this mine is going to close – not on this kind of talk.'

'What do you want?' asked McGill. 'Avalanche first – and protection later?'

'I'm protecting the men's jobs,' said Quentin. 'That's what they put me in here for.'

'Dead men don't have jobs,' said McGill brutally. 'And while we're at it, let's get another thing quite clear. Mr Ballard has said that he has engaged me as a professional consultant, and that is quite true. But fundamentally I don't give one good goddamn about the mine.'

'The Chairman will be delighted to hear it,' said Dobbs acidly. He looked at Ballard. 'I don't think we need carry on with this any more.'

'Carry on, Mike,' said Ballard quietly. 'Tell them the rest. Tell them what's really worrying you.'

McGill said, 'I'm worried about the town.'

There was a silence for the space of ten heartbeats and then Cameron cleared his throat. 'It's snowing again,' he said, not altogether inconsequentially.

'That just about finished the meeting,' said McGill. 'It was decided that the mine management should consult with the town council that afternoon, if possible. Then Mr Ballard was to communicate by telephone with the Presi . . . Chairman of his company.'

Gunn had his hand up, and Harrison said, 'Yes, Mr Gunn?'

'May I question the witness, Mr Chairman?' Harrison inclined his head, and Gunn proceeded. 'Dr McGill, the meeting you have just described took place a long time ago, did it not?'

'The meeting took place on the sixteenth of July. On the Friday morning.'

'It is now December – nearly five months later. Would you say that you have a good memory, Dr McGill?'

'About average.'

'About average! I put it to you that you have a much better than average memory.'

'If you say so.'

'Indeed, I do say so. When I listened to your evidence – when you related the conversations of others *ad verbatim* – I was put in mind of a stage performance I saw quite recently in which a so-called memory man amazed an audience.'

'Mr Gunn,' interjected Harrison. 'Irony and sarcasm may, or may not, have their place in a law court; they have certainly no place here. Please refrain.'

'Yes, Mr Chairman.' Gunn did not seem put out; he was aware that he had made his point. 'Dr McGill, you have given evidence that Mr Quentin, the elected union leader at Hukahoronui mine, *seemed* – and I use the word advisedly – seemed to be more intent on filling the pockets of his comrades than in preserving their lives. Now, Mr Quentin is not here to defend himself – he was killed in the disaster at Hukahoronui – and since I represent the union I must defend Mr Quentin. I put it to you that your recollection of this meeting so long ago may be incorrect.'

'No, sir; it is not incorrect.'

'Come, Dr McGill; note that I said that your evidence *may* be incorrect. Surely there is no loss of face in admitting that you may be wrong?'

'My evidence was correct, sir.'

'To traduce a dead man when it is not necessary is not thought to be good manners, sir. No doubt you have heard the tag, *"De mortuis nil nisi bonum."* ' Gunn waved his arm largely. 'The good and wise men who caused this hall to be built saw fit to include cogent aphorisms in these windows to guide them in their deliberations. I draw your attention to the text in the windows just above your head, Dr McGill. It reads: "Be not a hypocrite in the sight of men, and talk good when thou speakest."'

McGill was silent, and Gunn said, 'Well, Dr McGill?'

'I was not aware that I had been asked a question,' said McGill quietly.

Harrison shifted uneasily on his seat and seemed about to interrupt, but Gunn waved his arm again. 'If it is your claim to have a memory so much better than other men then I must accept it, I suppose.'

'I have an average memory, sir. And I keep a diary.'

'Oh!' Gunn was wary. 'Regularly?'

'As regularly as need be. I am a scientist who investigates snow, which is an evanescent and ever-changing substance, so I am accustomed to taking notes on the spot.'

'Are you saying that while that very meeting was in progress you were actually taking written notes of what was said?'

'No, sir.'

'Ha! Then a period of time must have elapsed between the meeting and when you wrote down your impressions. Is that not so?'

'Yes, sir. Half an hour. I wrote up my diary in my bedroom half an hour after the meeting ended. I consulted my diary this morning before I came to this hearing to refresh my memory.'

'And you still insist on your evidence as it relates to Mr Quentin?'

'I do.'

'Do you know how Mr Quentin died?'

'I know very well how Mr Quentin died.'

'No more questions,' said Gunn with an air of disgust. 'I am quite finished with this witness.'

McGill glanced at Harrison. 'May I add something?'

'If it has a bearing on what we are trying to investigate.'

'I think it has.' McGill looked up at the roof of the hall, and then his gaze swept down towards Gunn. 'I also have been studying the texts in the windows, Mr Gunn, and one, in particular, I have taken to heart. It is in a window quite close to you, and it reads: "Weigh thy words in a balance lest thou fall before him that lieth in wait."'

A roar of laughter broke the tension in the hall and even Harrison smiled, while Rolandson guffawed outright. Harrison thumped with his gavel and achieved a modicum of quiet.

McGill said, 'As for your Latin tag, Mr Gunn, I have never believed that latinity confers virtue on stupidity, and therefore I do not believe that one should never speak ill of the dead. I believe in the truth, and the truth is that the death toll in the Hukahoronui disaster was much higher than need be. The reason lies in the actions, reactions and inactions of many men who were confronted with an unprecedented situation beyond their understanding. Mr Quentin was one such man. I know that he died in the disaster, and I know that he died heroically. Nevertheless, the truth must be told so that other men, in the future, when faced with a similar situation will *know* the right things to do.'

'*Mr Chairman!*' Gunn was waving his arm, but Rickman had beaten him to it. He was on his feet, finger upraised. 'This is monstrous! Must a witness make speeches and lecture us to tell us our duty? Must . . . '

Harrison's gavel cracked down sharply, cutting off Rickman in mid-spate. 'Mr Rickman, may I again remind you that this is *not* a court of law and that procedure is at my sole discretion. Dr McGill has just restated the nature and intention of this Commission of Inquiry in words more well chosen and acute than I myself used yesterday during the opening proceedings. I have noted in counsel a regrettable tendency to adversary tactics, a practice against which I warned you. I will have no more of it.'

There was a dead silence.

Dan Edwards was busily scribbling. 'Boy, oh boy, oh boy! Good copy at last.' He tore off a sheet and handed it to a youth behind him. 'Get that back to the office as fast as you can.'

Harrison laid down his gavel. 'Dr McGill: you say that the mine management had a meeting with the Hukahoronui Town Council on the afternoon of Friday, the fifth of July.'

'No, sir. I said that was the arrangement at the meeting in the morning. In the event it proved to be impossible.'

'Why?'

'Three of the councillors were absent from town that day and it was impossible to find a quorum. The meeting was held next morning – the Saturday morning.'

'A delay of half a day.'

'Yes, sir.' McGill hesitated. 'Mr Ballard and I debated whether or not to approach the two councillors who remained in town and we decided against it. Our view was that such an important matter should be communicated to the council as a whole; we did not want to tell a complicated story twice.'

'So you met on the Saturday?'

'Yes, sir. There was one other person present at my request.'

'Oh, who was that?'

'Mr Turi Buck. I have to tell you that I was not present during the entire meeting. I left half way through.'

Harrison bent forward and said to Reed, 'Is Mr Buck present?'

'Yes, Mr Chairman.' Reed turned in his seat. 'Will you step forward, Mr Buck?'

Turi Buck came forward and stood before the rostrum. 'Were you present during the entire meeting under discussion, Mr Buck?' Harrison asked.

'Yes, sir; I was.' Turi's voice was strong.

'Then you will replace Dr McGill in the witness chair.'

McGill stepped down and went back to his place, winking at Ballard as he passed.

EIGHT

Harrison said, 'Mr Buck, would you be related to that illustrious member of your race, Sir Peter Buck?'

A ghost of a smile hovered on Turi's seamed face. 'No, sir.'

'I see.' Harrison drew his note-pad towards him. 'Can you tell us who was present at this meeting?'

'There was Ia . . . Mr Ballard and Mr Cameron from the mine. Dr McGill was there. And there was Mr Houghton, the mayor, and Mr Peterson – that's to say John Peterson – and Eric Peterson, Mr Warrick and Mrs Samson.'

'The last five were members of the council?'

'Yes, sir.'

Harrison consulted a list. 'Wasn't Mr Quentin present?'

'Oh yes; he was there. I forgot about him.'

'Well, Mr Buck, perhaps you can tell us what went on at the meeting.'

Turi frowned. 'It started off by Dr McGill telling of what he'd found. From what I've been hearing while I've been here I'd say it was just what he'd said at the meeting at the mine on the Friday. He told them there was a danger of avalanche and he told them why.'

'What was the general reaction?'

'They didn't believe him.'

Lyall put up his hand. 'Mr Chairman.'

'Yes, Mr Lyall?'

'It is incumbent on me to point out that of the ten people present at that meeting only four are able to be here at this inquiry. I ought to add that of the five council members only Mr Eric Peterson is able to be here.'

Harrison stared at him. 'Now that you have given me that information – of which, I might add, I was well aware – what am I supposed to do with it?'

'With respect, sir, one might think that Mr Eric Peterson is best qualified to give the reaction of the council.'

'Does Mr Peterson wish to be a witness?'

'He does.'

'Then he will have his chance later. At present we are hearing the evidence of Mr Buck.'

'Again with respect, Mr Chairman; may I point out that of the original mine management only Mr Ballard is here. Mr Dobbs and Mr Quentin are dead, and Mr Cameron is in hospital. It is well known in Hukahoronui that Mr Ballard and Mr Buck are friends of many years standing, and there has been evidence given here of the friendship between Mr Ballard and Dr McGill. It may be thought that the evidence given here is, shall we say, too one-sided.'

Harrison leaned back in his chair. 'It is evident, Mr Lyall, that you are doing at least one of two things. You are impugning the integrity of this Commission, or you are questioning the honesty of Mr Buck. Possibly you are doing both. Do I understand you correctly?'

'I do not question the integrity of the Commission, sir.'

Turi's face was stricken as he half rose from his chair. Ian Ballard wriggled in his seat. He dug his elbow into Rickman's ribs, and said, 'The bastard! the utter bastard! Intervene and get on with that line of questioning I gave you.'

Rickman shook his head. 'It would be most unwise. It wouldn't be in the interests of the company.' He twisted his head and looked at Lyall. 'See how he's stirring things up.'

'But, God damn it, he's making us into some sort of conspiracy.'

Rickman stared at him unwinkingly. 'But not involving the company,' he snapped.

Turi Buck lifted his hands helplessly. They were trembling as he said to Harrison, 'May I be excused from the witness chair, sir?'

'No, you may not, Mr Buck.' Harrison turned his head. 'Yes, Mr Ballard?'

Ballard lowered his hand. 'I would like to question Mr Buck.'

Harrison frowned. 'I thought you had representation, Mr Ballard. I gave warning at the beginning of this hearing that I would not allow it to be turned into a free-for-all.'

Ballard said, 'As of thirty seconds ago Mr Rickman ceased to represent me personally. He will, of course, continue to represent the company.'

A wave of noise washed across the hall. Amid the uproar Rickman said, 'You bloody young fool! What the devil do you think you're doing?'

'You're fired,' said Ballard briefly.

Harrison wielded his gavel lustily and at last achieved relative quietness. 'If there is any more uproar I will have the public gallery cleared,' he announced. 'These proceedings will be conducted in an orderly manner.' He waited until there was utter silence, broken only by the creaking of the old wooden floor, before he addressed Ballard. 'Are you asking for an adjournment so that you may obtain a new legal adviser?'

'No, sir. For today, at least, I am content to represent myself. I do not wish to waste the time of the Commission.'

Harrison allowed himself a wintry smile. 'Very laudable. I wish the legal fraternity would follow your example. And you wish to interrogate Mr Buck?'

'Yes, sir.'

'I object,' said Rickman. 'Apart from the personal insult to me in being dismissed so cavalierly and in public, I consider this to be most irregular.'

Harrison sighed. 'Mr Rickman, you have been told many times that the procedure of this Commission is a matter for my discretion. Even in a law court it has not been unknown for a person to represent himself, choosing not to enlist the aid – or otherwise – of a lawyer. Therefore I will allow it.' He held up his hand. 'And I will entertain no argument about it. Proceed, Mr Ballard.'

Ballard smiled at Turi. 'I will not comment on any remarks that have been made here, but will go on from your last relevant statement. Mr Buck, you said that the councillors did not believe Dr McGill when he informed them of avalanche hazard. What were their reasons for disbelief?'

'They said there had never been avalanches in the valley.'

'Did they? Mr Chairman, is it possible to have a map of the valley on view?'

'Provision has been made. Mr Reed, will you see to it.'

Presently a large-scale map was set up on an easel behind the witness chair. Harrison said, 'Since this map is evidence of a sort we must be sure that it is the best evidence. Mr Reed, call your technical witness, please.'

'Call Mr Wheeler.'

Wheeler was new to Ballard, who regarded him with interest. He returned his gaze to the map, and his eyes narrowed suddenly. Reed said, 'What is your full name?'

'Harold Herbert Wheeler.'

Harrison said, 'There is no need for you to take the witness chair, Mr Wheeler. Your evidence is technical and will not take long. What is your occupation?'

'I am a cartographer employed by the Lands and Survey Department of the New Zealand Government.'

'And you have prepared this map especially for this Inquiry?'

'That is correct, sir.'

'What does the map represent?'

'It depicts the Hukahoronui Valley, including the township of Hukahoronui. The scale is one in two thousand, five hundred; that is twenty-five inches to the mile approximately.'

'Does it represent the valley before or after the disaster?'

'Before, sir. It is drawn according to the latest information available to the Topographical Office.'

'Thank you, Mr Wheeler. That will be all.'

Ballard said, 'Could Mr Wheeler hold himself available for possible further questions?'

Harrison wrinkled his brow. 'I suppose so, Mr Ballard. You will stay available, Mr Wheeler.'

Ballard studied the map. 'Mr Buck, I would like you, if you will, to point out on this map your own house.' Turi stood up and indicated a point on the map with his finger. 'And the Peterson store.' Turi's hand came up around in an arc and stopped. 'Now my house.' Again Turi pointed. 'And the mine portal.'

'I fail to see the point of this,' said Rickman.

'The point is to prove that Mr Buck can read a map as well as the next man,' said Ballard pleasantly. 'Mr Buck, at the meeting with the council was a map produced?'

'Yes, but not as big as this one.'

'And were you asked to point out various places on that map?'

'Yes, sir.'

'Now I want you to think very carefully. I don't want you to say anything here, because of my questioning, that was not said at the meeting with the council. Do you understand?'

'Yes.'

'Why did you attend the meeting?'

'Because Dr McGill asked me to go.'

'Do you know why he asked you to go?'

'He said I knew more about the history of Hukahoronui than anyone else he'd met.'

'You say the reaction of the council was that there had, hitherto, never been avalanches in the valley. Was that the reaction of *all* the councillors?'

'It was – at first.'

'So their views changed, then. Let us find out why. Mr Buck, you are of the Maori race. Do you understand the language?'

'Yes, sir.'

'Can you give us a translation – a free translation, if you like – of the name, Hukahoronui?'

'Yes, sir; it means "The Great Snow Slide".'

There was a subdued murmur from behind Ballard. 'Would you point out your own house again, Mr Buck. There is a great rock between your house and the mountainside, is there not? What is the name of that rock?'

'Kamakamaru.'

'Kamakamaru,' repeated Ballard. 'Can you translate that into English?'

'It means "The Rock of Shelter".'

Again came that quickly suppressed sound in the hall. 'When was your house built, Mr Buck?'

'It was built by my father about 1880, but there was a house there before built by my grandfather.'

'Let us get one thing straight. Your family did not live in Hukahoronui before the incursion of the white settlers into New Zealand?'

'Before the Pakeha! No, sir, my family came from North Island.' Turi smiled. 'It was said that we came to South Island to escape the Pakeha.'

'Did your family name the valley and the rock?'

'No, they were already named. There were some of my people living close by. Not in the valley, but close by.'

'Did your father replace your grandfather's house because, let us say, it had been damaged by an avalanche?'

'No, sir. He replaced it because the house was in bad condition and because the family was growing larger.'

Ballard was silent for a moment as he consulted a paper. At last he raised his head and asked quietly, 'Mr Buck, do you, of your own knowledge, know of any avalanches in the valley of Hukahoronui?'

'Yes, there was an avalanche in 1912 when I was a boy. A family called Bailey had built a house quite close to ours but not protected by Kamakamaru. My father warned the Baileys but they took no notice of him. There was an avalanche in the winter of 1912 and the Bailey house was swept away. The whole family died – all seven of them.' He looked at Ballard and said definitely, 'I was there – I helped dig out the bodies.'

'So the rock – Kamakamaru – acted as a splitting wedge. Is that it?'

'The snow flowed around Kamakamaru, and our house was safe.'

'But the Bailey house was destroyed. Any more avalanches?'

'There was one in 1918.' Turi hesitated. 'I was not there; I had joined the army. I had a letter from my father saying there had been an avalanche.'

'Again on the western slope?'

'Yes. There were no lives lost nor damage to property, but the snow blocked the flow of the river and there was flooding. The farmers lost a lot of stock by drowning.'

'A six-year gap. Any more?'

'There was the avalanche of 1943.'

'Did you see that avalanche actually fall?'

'No – but I remember it broke a lot of trees on the west slope. I used to collect firewood there afterwards.'

'Yes,' said Ballard. 'There was a lot of good firewood around there for two or three years. Were there any fatalities in the avalanche of 1943?'

Turi's eyes opened wide. 'Why, yes, Ian. Your father was killed.'

The hall had been quiet as Ballard led Turi through his evidence but now there was a gust of pent-up emotion let loose in a wave of sound. Harrison let it die away before he rapped gently with his gavel.

Ballard said, 'Could you point out on the map the place where my father was killed?'

Turi stretched out his hand. 'There,' he said. 'Just where the mine office is now.'

'How do you know it was there?'

'Because you showed me three days after it happened. You had seen it happen.'

'And how old was I then, Mr Buck?'

Turi considered. 'Maybe four years.'

'Mr Buck, you have given us a lot of information. Was the same information given to the councillors at the meeting?'

'Yes, it was.'

'Thank you, Mr Buck.'

Ballard leaned back and glanced sideways at Lyall who already had his hand up. 'I would like to ask Mr Buck one or two questions.'

Harrison nodded. 'Very well.'

'Was the avalanche of 1943 a very large one?'

Turi thought about it, then nodded his head vigorously. "Very large – bigger than the one in 1912.'

Lyall looked pleased. 'I see. Could you say, perhaps by indicating on the map, just how far down the slope it came?'

'Just to the bottom. Mr Ballard's father was killed here. It didn't go much farther than that'

'It didn't go as far as the Peterson Supermarket?'

'It didn't go anywhere near the Peterson store.'

'Remarkable. Now tell me, Mr Buck: if the Peterson Supermarket was not destroyed by a very big avalanche in 1943, why then was it destroyed this year?'

Turi looked blank, then said, 'The trees, of course.'

Ballard let out a long sigh and let Lyall dig his own pit. Lyall said, 'The trees! Oh, you mean that timbered area marked on the west slope?'

Turi turned to look at the map. He examined it for a moment, then said, 'But this is all wrong.'

Ballard put up his hand. 'Mr Chairman – on a point of evidence. I would like to have Mr Wheeler recalled briefly. It would seem that his map is not the best evidence.'

Harrison looked startled, then raised his eyebrows. 'Mr Lyall?'

Lyall frowned, but said, 'No objection.'

Wheeler was brought back and Ballard said, 'Look at the map, Mr Wheeler. Do you see that forested area on the western slope of the valley?'

'Yes, sir.'

'I can bring five hundred witnesses to swear that that area was not forested before the avalanche struck. What do you say to that?'

Wheeler did not know what to say to it. He twitched nervously for a while, then said, 'The information I put into that map comes from the latest sources available.'

'But not late enough, it would seem. In respect of a vital piece of evidence – the lack of timber on the western slope – this map is untrue. Is that correct?'

Wheeler shrugged. 'If you say so. I have never been to Hukahoronui myself.'

'It is not for me to say,' said Ballard. 'But let us ask Mr Buck. When were the trees cut?'

'They started cutting when the mine opened. The timber went into the mine and for building houses.'

'That was four years ago?'

'Yes. The cutting went on for two years. By that time the slope was just about stripped.'

Rolandson stirred, and said, 'Mr Ballard, are we to understand that you regard the cutting of that timber as a contributory factor which led to the avalanche?'

Ballard hesitated. 'I am not an expert on avalanches, sir. I would prefer you to direct that question to Dr McGill.'

'I will,' growled Rolandson, and conferred for a few moments with Harrison. They both looked at Wheeler who shuffled his feet nervously. 'You have not been to Hukahoronui and yet you present this map as evidence,' said Harrison unbelievingly. 'That is what you said, isn't it?'

'Yes,' said Wheeler unhappily.

He was even more unhappy when Harrison had finished with him and sent him off. When Lyall was asked if he had further questions he warily said that he had none. Ballard raised his hand. 'I would like to ask Mr Buck one more question.'

'Very well.'

'Mr Buck, what was the immediate reaction of the councillors towards your revelations about the incidence of avalanches in Hukahoronui?'

Turi Buck froze. In a low voice he said, 'I would rather not say.'

'Mr Buck – I must ask you the question.'

Turi shook his head. 'I will not say.'

'You must answer the question, Mr Buck,' said Harrison, but Turi shook his head dumbly.

Harrison looked at Ballard blankly for a moment and Ballard shrugged. The hall was very quiet when someone said, 'I can answer that question.'

Harrison's head jerked. 'Dr McGill, this is most unseemly.'

McGill stepped forward. 'Mr Chairman, there are only four people who can answer the question. Mr Buck refuses for reasons I can understand. Mr Eric Peterson will not answer, again for reasons I can understand. In all propriety Mr Ballard cannot, because he is interrogating Mr Buck – he cannot be questioner and witness simultaneously. I am the only one left who was present at the meeting.'

Harrison sighed. 'Very well, you will answer the question. What was it, Mr Ballard?'

'What was the immediate reaction of the councillors to Mr Buck's evidence?'

McGill unzipped his satchel and drew forth a flat notebook. 'As is my habit, I took notes immediately after the meeting. I can read here exactly what was said.' He selected a page and stared at Eric Peterson where he sat next to Lyall. 'Mr Eric Peterson's exact words were, "Turi Buck is an ignorant old black man. He knows nothing – he never has and he never will".'

There was pandemonium in the Press gallery.

The hall errupted in a babble of noise and Harrison hammered in vain on the rostrum but the crash of his gavel was lost in the uproar. When, at last, he could make himself heard, he said in anger, 'This hearing is adjourned until further notice and until those present can control themselves.'

NINE

'Turi Buck is an ignorant old black man. He knows nothing – he never has and he never will.'

The words hung heavily in an embarrassed silence in the residents' lounge of the Hotel D'Archiac which did duty as a council chamber. At last Matthew Houghton coughed nervously, and said, 'There's no call for that sort of talk, Eric'

Ballard was angry. 'I should bloody well think not.'

John Peterson, who was standing, put his hand on his brother's shoulder. 'Eric, if you can't talk sense you'd better keep your big mouth shut. You're starting to behave like Charlie.' He looked at Turi. 'My apologies.'

'Maybe you'd better let Eric make his own apologies,' said Ballard tightly.

Eric went red in the face but said nothing. John Peterson ignored Ballard and addressed himself to McGill. 'So you've come up with past avalanches, and now you say there's going to be another.'

'I have *not* said that.'

'Then what *are* you saying?' demanded Houghton.

McGill spread his hands. 'Who cares if a few thousand tons of snow falls off a mountain? It's happening all the time in the Southern Alps. But if someone is standing underneath at the time then it's downright dangerous.

That's the position you're in. You have a potential hazard here.'

'Not an actual hazard?' queried John Peterson.

'I can tell you more after another series of tests. But I'll tell you this – the hazard isn't getting any less.'

Peterson said, 'It seems pretty flimsy to me. From the line you're shooting it seems to me that you want us to spend a lot of money because of something that may never happen.'

'There's something I don't understand,' said Houghton. 'If there have been avalanches in the past, why weren't the houses knocked down? My house was the second one built in the valley; my grandfather built it in 1850, two years after the Otago Settlement.'

Ballard said, 'Let's have a look at the map.' He pushed the map across the table to Houghton. 'Matt, I want you to cast your mind back, say, twenty years – before all the houses were built when the mine started. I want you to mark all the houses you can remember.' He handed Houghton a pen.

'Well, there's my house there, and Turi Buck's house – but we know why that's still there. And there's the Cunningham house, and the Pearman house . . . '

'. . . and the Jackson place and the old Fisher house,' said Mrs Samson.

Slowly Houghton marked them all and then leaned back. Ballard said, 'Don't forget the church and the school – and Peterson's store.'

Houghton scratched more crosses on the map, and Ballard said, 'Just look at it. All those buildings are well scattered and if you look at the terrain you'll see that every one of them is protected against falls from the western slope to a greater or lesser degree.' He picked up the pen. 'But we do know there was another building – the Bailey house.' He marked its position on the map. 'That's gone now.'

Mrs Samson said, 'What are you getting at?'

'When the settlers first came here, back in the middle of last century, they didn't bother overmuch about keeping records, so we don't know a lot about houses destroyed. We only know about the Bailey house because of Turi. My bet is that the houses Matt has just marked are the survivors.'

Phil Warrick said, 'That makes sense. If a man had a house knocked down he wouldn't rebuild in the same place. Not if he had any brains.'

'Or if he survived,' said McGill. 'The Baileys didn't.' He put his hand flat on the map. 'Those houses survived because the builders were lucky or knew what they were about. But now you've got a whole township here – not just a few scattered houses. That's where the hazard comes in.'

'So what are you asking us to do?' asked John Peterson.

'I want you to accept the fact that avalanche hazard exists – that's the first step and all follows from that. So you'll have to take the necessary precautions, first in the short term and, later, in the long term. You must notify the appropriate authority outside the valley that a hazard exists. Then you must be ready for it if it comes. You must have rescue gear stored in safe places where it can be got at in case of disaster. And you'll have to have men trained to use that equipment. And you'll have to have contingency planning in case it becomes necessary to evacuate the town. I can help in advising on a lot of that.'

Eric Peterson said, 'My brother is right. It seems to me that you're asking us to spend a lot of money guarding against something which might never happen. If we have to train men we have to pay them; if we have to have equipment we have to pay for it. Where do we get the money?'

Quentin laughed bitterly. 'You haven't heard anything yet. Wait until you hear about the long-term precautions.' His finger stabbed out. 'If this man has his way the mine will shut down.'

'What the hell!' John Peterson stared at Ballard. 'What foolish talk is this?'

'Ask McGill how much it will cost to protect the mine,' said Quentin. 'At the last meeting we had they were talking in millions of dollars – and we all know the company won't stand for that.'

'Not to protect the mine,' snapped Ballard. 'To protect the town. In a case like this you'll get a government grant.'

Eric Peterson laughed shortly. 'Everyone knows that government grants don't cover everything – not by a long chalk. We learned that when we were extending the school. And you are talking in millions of dollars, not in thousands.' He looked up at his brother. 'Guess how much the town rates will be next year if this damn silly caper carries on.'

Ballard said, 'How much is your life worth, Eric?'

'That's a hell of a question! But I'll give you a short answer. My life is worth that of one of my brothers – that much and no more.'

'There's no call for that,' said Houghton quickly.

'Well, he brought it up,' said Eric. 'In any case, according to him, I'm safe.' He tapped the map. 'My place is one of the survivors.'

'Not any more,' said Ballard. 'Not since the trees were cut down on the west slope. Did you do that, Eric?'

'What the hell has that got to do with anything?'

'The only reason the store survived in 1943 was because of the trees. Now they're gone there's nothing between you and the snow. You made a bad bargain there.'

Eric stood up. 'Too right I made a bad bargain, or rather, my old man did. You know damned well that when your mother sold him the property she cheated him of the mineral rights. Oh, she was bloody clever, wasn't she? She even kept hold of that bit of land at the bottom where the mine is now -just enough land to put up the crushing mill to work the ore she gets out of *our* land.'

Ballard rubbed his eyes. 'That's not the way it was, Eric. It was my father who separated the mineral rights from the property. He did it in his will. Your father didn't buy the land for five years after that. 1948, wasn't it?'

'The hell with it!' said Eric. 'She still gets the gold.'

'No, she doesn't,' said Ballard. 'She doesn't hold the mineral rights.'

'Pull the other one,' scoffed Eric. 'You're all Ballards.'

Matt Houghton drummed his fingers on the table. 'We seem to have left the subject.' He glanced nervously at Eric.

'Yes,' said McGill. 'I don't know what this is all about but I don't think it has anything to do with snow on a hillside. But those missing trees do; there's nothing left to bind the snow.'

Eric shrugged and sat down again. 'It's a lousy piece of land, anyway. Too bloody steep for cattle, and I couldn't even get in the hay crop this year.'

McGill's head jerked up. 'What hay crop?' he said sharply.

'What do you care?'

'You'd better tell me. What happened to your hay crop?'

John Peterson rolled his eyes towards the ceiling. 'For God's sake, Eric! Indulge his curiosity. Then perhaps we can get this meeting over. I've got things to do.'

Eric shrugged. 'First it was the rain – the crop was sodden, so we couldn't take it in. I thought we'd have a dry spell, but we didn't – it rained right in to the winter, so I gave it up. It was rotting in the fields, anyway.'

'And you just left it,' said McGill. 'And it's still there uncut. Is that it?'

'That's right,' said Eric, and added touchily, 'But what's it got to do with you I'm damned if I know.'

McGill speared him with a long stare. 'So you cut down the trees, which is bad enough. Then you leave uncut grass, which is worse. Long, wet grass on a hillside is just about the slipperiest stuff there is. The chances of an avalanche have just gone up considerably.'

Warrick said, 'It was slippery, I know. I tried to get up there during the rain myself. After the third try I gave up.'

'What am I? Some kind of public enemy?' demanded Eric. 'Who the hell is this joker to come with his accusations?'

'I'm not accusing anyone of anything except maybe short-sightedness,' said McGill. 'The first sign of potentially dangerous terrain is a mountain with snow on it; and you have one right on your doorstep but none of you seems to have seen it.'

'Dr McGill is right,' said Ballard.

Eric Peterson lunged to his feet. 'Anyone called Ballard is the last person to accuse me of anything at all,' he said with a jagged edge to his voice. 'Anyone with a yellow . . .'

'That's enough,' cut in Mrs Samson sharply. 'What's past is gone.'

'What's this about?' asked Warrick, looking from Ballard to Eric Peterson. He wore a baffled look, as of a man who feels he is missing the obvious.

Matt Houghton looked bleak. 'It's old history and nothing to do with the subject here.'

McGill stood up. 'Gentlemen, you have my report. It's there on the table before you written up in technical language, and I've explained what it means in words of one syllable. I can do nothing more. I shall leave you to your deliberations.'

'Where are you going?' asked Houghton.

'To do some work.'

'Where can we get hold of you if we need further information?'

'At Mr Ballard's house,' said McGill. 'Or up on the west slope – it needs further investigation. But don't send anyone up there to find me. In fact, no one should be allowed on that slope from now on. It's damned dangerous.'

He left the meeting.

TEN

Ian Ballard swam another length of the pool and then climbed out. He walked to the canvas chair where he had left his towel and began to rub himself down. It was good to relax after spending all day at the Inquiry. He poured himself a beer and checked his watch before slipping it on to his wrist.

Mike McGill came sauntering across the lawn and held out an envelope. 'Business as usual. Old Harrison must have got over his tantrum. This will be your notification to attend; I've had mine.'

Ballard opened the envelope. McGill was right; the letter was from Reed, the Secretary to the Commission. He dropped it on the grass next to his chair, and said, 'So we go on. What comes next in the evidence?'

'The first avalanche, I suppose.' McGill grinned and spread a newspaper before Ballard. 'Eric has got his name in print.'

Ballard looked at the black headline bannered across the front page:

'IGNORANT BLACK MAN' JIBE

He shook his head. 'He's not going to like that.'

McGill chuckled. 'Think he'll come after me with a gun?'

'Eric won't – but Charlie might,' said Ballard soberly. 'He's crazy enough to do it.'

McGill laughed and sat down on the grass. 'Got yourself a lawyer yet?'

'No.'

'You'd better start looking.'

'I've discovered I have an unsuspected talent,' said Ballard. 'I can defend myself very well.'

'You did all right with Turi, and you got Lyall to walk out on a limb before you sawed it off. Not bad going for a novice.'

'Mr Ballard?' Ballard looked up and saw the young man from the hotel office. 'A telegram just came. I thought it might be important so I brought it right out.'

'Thanks.' Ballard ripped open the envelope. 'It's a cable-gram from England.' He scanned it rapidly and frowned. 'Now why should . . .?'

'Trouble?'

'Not really.' Ballard handed the cable to McGill. 'Why should a man suddenly fly half way across the world to see me?'

'Who is Stenning?'

'A friend of my grandfather.' Ballard looked at the pool abstractedly.

McGill began calculating. 'He says he's leaving on the night flight. It doesn't really matter whether he comes east or west, it's still about forty hours to Auckland. Then he'll have to catch an internal flight down to here. Say two full days – that means Saturday afternoon.'

'The Commission won't sit on Saturday. I'll meet Stenning at the airport.'

'You'd better have a message awaiting him at Auckland so you can arrange to meet him here.'

Ballard nodded. 'Old Ben said something about Stenning the last time I saw him. He said that if anything were to happen to him or the company then I should get in touch with Stenning. Then he said to forget it because Stenning would get in touch with me fast enough. It seems as though he really meant it.'

'Who is Stenning, apart from being your grandfather's friend?'

'He's a lawyer.'

'Then he's arriving just in time,' said McGill. 'Just the man you need.'

Ballard shook his head. 'He's not the right sort of lawyer. He specializes in taxes.'

'Oh, one of those boys.' McGill chuckled. 'He's probably come to confess all – that he slipped up on sorting out the death duties bit, and instead of three million from the old man you're just going to get three thousand.'

Ballard grinned. 'I'm not going to get three cents. Ben warned me about that. He said that he'd educated me and I'd have to stand on my own two feet as he'd done at my age. I told you that all his money is tied up in some trust or other.' He stretched. 'I'm beginning to feel chilly. Let's go inside.'

'It's warmer in the bar,' agreed McGill.

THE HEARING

Third Day

ELEVEN

The Press gallery was jammed as Harrison led Eric Peterson through his evidence. Dan Edwards had shamelessly bought space for himself by bringing in two cub reporters and then sending them away when the proceedings began. But it was to no avail; protests from other reporters soon led to the seats being occupied, and Edwards was compelled to scrawl his shorthand in as cramped conditions as anyone else.

Harrison made a note on his pad, and raised his eyes. 'So we arrive at the point when Dr McGill left, having delivered his bad news. What happened then, Mr Peterson?'

Eric Peterson shrugged. 'Well, the meeting went on for a long time. In all honesty I have to say that some of us were not convinced of the gravity of the situation. You must remember that this whole thing had been jumped on us suddenly – had taken us by surprise, if you like. After all, if someone steps up to you and says, "The end of the world is at hand!" you're going to need a lot of proof before you believe him.'

'I appreciate your position,' said Harrison. 'Can you give some specific examples of the views of members of the council?'

'Well, my brother argued that, even if McGill was any-where near right, we didn't want to start a panic. I agreed with that and so did Matt Houghton, the mayor. Phil

Warrick didn't seem to have any views at all. He just blew along with the wind and agreed with everybody. Mrs Samson wanted to go all out with preparations for evacuation right there and then.'

'What position did the mine management take?'

'Mr Ballard agreed with Mrs Samson. Mr Quentin said he didn't think there was any danger – he said it was all a lot of hot air. Mr Cameron tended to go along with Mr Ballard.' Peterson clasped his hands before him. 'You must realize that any decision concerning the town had to be made by the council. It wasn't up to the mine management to tell the town what to do. Dr McGill had told us there was no immediate hazard from the west slope, and to some of us there seemed to be no reason for going off half-cocked on a project that might cost the town a lot of money and wasted time.'

'And lose votes if nothing happened,' remarked Edwards cynically.

'Well, as I said, there was a lot of talk and we went round in circles for some time. Eventually Matt Houghton came up with an idea. He said that maybe there was something in what McGill had said, but he'd like a second opinion. He said he'd telephone Christchurch and get some advice.'

'To whom was he going to speak?'

'That was the rub. He didn't know and neither did anyone else. Mr Cameron suggested he talk to someone in the Forestry Department – he said they'd probably know about avalanche conditions. Someone else, I forget who, suggested the Department of Civil Defence. It was decided he'd try both. Mrs Samson said the police should be notified and that was agreed to.'

'Did the mine management make any concrete suggestions?'

'We had the offer of transport – trucks and suchlike. Also bulldozers.'

'Who made that offer?'

Peterson glanced sideways at Ballard. He hesitated, then said, 'I don't remember. It may have been Mr Cameron.'

Ballard smiled thinly.

'And what happened then?'

'The meeting broke up and it was decided we'd meet at eleven the next morning, even though it was Sunday.'

'I see.' Harrison looked around. 'Has anyone any further questions to ask Mr Peterson?'

Smithers raised his hand. 'I represent the Ministry of Civil Defence. Was a telephone call in fact made to the Civil Defence authorities?'

'Not to my knowledge.'

'Why not?'

'I talked with Matt Houghton after the meeting. He was a bit wavery about things. He said he'd do what he always did before making a decision. He said he'd sleep on it.'

'And the police – were they notified?'

'That was a bit difficult. Arthur Pye was away; he was up at the head of the valley investigating a case of sheep worrying.'

'Who is Arthur Pye?'

'Our policeman. Hukahoronui is only a small place – we just had the one policeman.'

'Do you mean to tell me that when you discussed notifying the police it was your intention to tell Constable Pye?' said Smithers incredulously.

'Well, he'd know what to do about telling his superiors,' said Peterson defensively.

'So *nobody* outside Hukahoronui knew of the situation?'

'I suppose that is correct.'

'And in Hukahoronui the knowledge was confined to a handful of people.'

'Yes, sir.'

Smithers consulted his note-pad. 'You say that when it was decided to get a second opinion on Dr McGill's diagnosis of the situation nobody knew whom to consult.' He lifted his head and looked at Peterson with an air of disbelief. 'Did no one on the council read the directives which were sent out by my Ministry?'

'We get a lot of stuff from the Government.' Peterson shrugged. 'I didn't read it all myself.'

'Apparently no one on the council read it.' Smithers took a deep breath. 'Mr Peterson, you were a councillor and a responsible official. Would you not agree that preparations for a crisis in your community were conspicuous by their absence? I am not speaking of avalanches only – we do live in an earthquake prone country, a major reason for the existence of the Ministry of Civil Defence.'

'May I object?' said Lyall quickly.

Harrison looked up from his notes. 'What is your objection?'

'I would like to point out that the township of Hukahoronui was relatively new and the population was largely composed of recent immigrants to the valley. In such a situation the degree of community spirit would naturally be less than in a longer established community.'

'Mr Lyall, is that your objection? You seem to be answering for the witness.'

'It is not my objection, Mr Chairman. My objection is that it is improper for Mr Smithers to ask such a loaded question of Mr Peterson. He is usurping the function of this Commission, which is to decide whether the state of affairs implicit in his question was actually the case.'

'A thin point, but valid nevertheless,' conceded Harrison. 'But it would have come better with the accompanying speech of extenuation. Mr Smithers, your last question was out of order. Have you any further questions?'

'None that I would care to ask this witness,' said Smithers curtly.

'Then you may step down, Mr Peterson, on the understanding that you may be recalled.'

Peterson left the witness chair with an air of relief, and Harrison bent forward to have a word with Reed. He then sat back in his chair, and said, 'Mr Cameron, the engineer of the Hukahoronui Mining Company, has been hospitalized for many months due to the injuries he received in the disaster. However, he has notified the Commission that he feels well enough to give evidence at this time and he is now present. Will you come forward, Mr Cameron?'

There was a low murmur as Cameron limped across the hall leaning heavily on the arm of a male nurse. He had lost a lot of weight and was now almost emaciated; his cheeks were sunken and his hair, pepper and salt at the time of the avalanche, was now quite white. He looked an old man.

He sat in the witness chair and the male nurse drew up another chair behind him. Reed said, 'What is your full name?'

'Joseph McNeil Cameron.'

'And your occupation, Mr Cameron?'

'I was a mining engineer,' said Cameron flatly. 'Specifically for the Hukahoronui Mining Company at the material times under investigation by this Commission.' His voice was strong if slow.

'Mr Cameron,' said Harrison, 'if at any time you feel unable to continue, please do not hesitate to say so.'

'Thank you, Mr Chairman.'

'I understand that you have evidence to give about the events of the evening of the day you had the meeting with the council. That would be the Saturday evening, would it not?'

'Yes, sir,' said Cameron. 'There was a dinner-dance at the Hotel D'Archiac that night. I had invited Mr Ballard and Dr McGill to be my guests. My daughter, Stacey, was also present – she was on vacation from the States at that

time and was due to go back the following week. There
was a certain amount of table-hopping during the dinner
and it was then I learned that the mayor had not made the
telephone calls. That, combined with a new and most disturbing report from Dr McGill, worried all of us very
much.'

'Could you go into that in more detail?' said Harrison.

'Why, yes. We were just starting dinner . . .'

McGill inspected the menu. 'Colonial goose,' he said. 'That
sounds good.'

Ballard chuckled. 'Don't expect poultry.'

'I was going to order that,' said Stacey Cameron. She was
a tall, dark girl with typical American svelte good looks.
McGill had measured her with a knowledgeable eye and
classed her as a long-stemmed American beauty, Californian
variety. She said, 'What is it if it isn't a bird?'

'A Texas nightingale isn't a bird, either, honey,' said
Cameron. 'It's a donkey. This is a similar New Zealand
joke.'

Stacey was horrified. 'You mean it's horse meat?'

'No,' said Ballard. 'It's hogget and stuffing.'

'Now you've lost me,' complained McGill. 'What's hogget?'

'Midway between lamb and mutton. There are millions
of sheep in New Zealand and just about as many ways of
cooking the animal. Colonial goose is a colonial joke, but it's
not bad.'

'A trap for the unwary tourist,' commented McGill.
'Talking of that, when are you going back to the States,
Stacey?'

'Just ten days left,' she said with a sigh.

'I've been trying to talk her into staying,' said Cameron.

'Why don't you?' Ballard asked her.

'I'd like to,' she said regretfully. 'If only to look after this
crazy man.' She leaned over and patted her father's hand.

'But I have a boss back in San Francisco who's depending on me – I wouldn't want to let him down.'

Cameron said, 'No one is indispensable. How long would it take you to cut free?'

She thought about it. 'Maybe six months.'

'Then what about it?'

'I'll consider it,' she said. 'Really I will.'

Over dinner Cameron yarned about some of the practical difficulties they had run into when getting the mine going. 'The trouble was mainly with the people. The folks around here weren't very enthusiastic at first. They'd got pretty set in their ways and didn't like change. All except old man Peterson, of course, who saw the possibilities.'

'That reminds me,' said McGill. 'What's with the Petersons? And how many of them are there, for God's sake?'

'Three brothers,' said Ballard. 'John, Eric and Charlie. The old man died last year.'

Cameron said, 'John has the brains, Eric has the drive, and Charlie has the muscle and precious little else. If Charlie-boy had twice the brains he has now he'd be a half-wit. The Petersons own the Supermarket and the filling station, they have a half share in this hotel, run a couple of farms – things like that. Charlie wants to develop Huka as a ski resort but he's finding it tough sledding; his brothers don't think the time is ripe for it. Old Peterson saw the possibilities and his boys are carrying on where he left off.'

'You forgot Liz,' said Stacey. 'She's over there – fourth table along.'

Ballard turned his head. He had not seen Liz Peterson since his return to the valley and his image was still of a freckled, gawky girl with pigtails and skinned knees. What he saw was something quite different and he drew in his breath.

Liz Peterson was a rarity – a really beautiful girl whose loveliness did not depend on the adventitious aid of cosmetics. Her beauty lay deeper than the surface of her skin – in the bone structure of her skull, in the sheen of good health and youth, in the smooth and controlled movements of her body. She was beautiful in the way a healthy young animal is beautiful and she had the unconscious arrogance that can be seen in a thoroughbred racehorse or a fine hunting dog.

'By God!' he said. 'She's grown up.'

Cameron chuckled. 'It tends to happen.'

'Why haven't I seen her around?'

'She's been visiting in North Island; just got back this week,' said Cameron. 'She had dinner with us on Monday. Stacey was quite impressed, and it really takes something to impress my girl.'

'I like Liz,' said Stacey. 'She has a mind of her own.'

Ballard looked studiously at his plate. 'Any of the Petersons married yet?'

'John is – and Eric's engaged.'

'Charlie?'

'No – he hasn't had to – not yet; but it's been a close call once or twice from what I hear. As for Liz, she should have been married long ago but Charlie has a way of scaring the young men. He looks after his sister like a hen with one chick.'

McGill said, 'The Petersons don't like you, Ian. What was all that about this morning?'

'An old quarrel,' said Ballard shortly. He glanced at Cameron. 'Know about it, Joe?'

'I've heard,' said Cameron. 'Something about the Ballards cheating the Petersons out of the mine.'

'That's the way the Petersons tell it,' agreed Ballard. 'Not John – he's too sensible; but Eric tends to drive it into the ground a bit. What happened was that my father had a row with my grandfather and emigrated to New Zealand. Although he'd left the family, he was still enough of a Ballard to be interested in gold when he found it on his land. He knew there wasn't enough sign to start a serious operation, the price of gold being what it was, but when he made his will before he joined the army he left the land to my mother, but the mineral rights he left to my grandfather.'

'In spite of the fact that they'd quarrelled?' asked McGill.

'He was a Ballard. What would my mother do with mineral rights? Anyway, after he died my mother had to sell the land – she couldn't farm it herself. She sold most of it – that's the west slope – to old Peterson, who neglected to check if he had the mineral rights. I don't know if he cared about that one way or the other, but when my grandfather bought the rest of the land from my mother – the bit at the bottom of the slope – and started to exploit the mineral rights under Peterson land then all hell broke loose. Accusations of bad faith were tossed around like confetti. The Petersons have always been convinced it was a deep-laid plot on the part of the Ballards. Actually, of course, it was nothing of the kind, but because my name is Ballard I'm stuck with it.'

'When you put it that way it doesn't sound too bad,' said Cameron. 'All the same, I'm not surprised that the Petersons are riled.'

'I don't see why they should be,' said Ballard. 'The only people making a profit out of the mine are the Petersons; the mine brought prosperity to this valley and the Petersons are creaming it off. The Ballards certainly aren't making a profit. You've seen the operating figures, Joe, and you know the company is just breaking even.' He shook his head. 'I don't know what's going to happen if we have to put in extensive avalanche protection. I've been trying to get hold of Crowell all day but he's not available.'

'Who is he?' asked McGill.

'Chairman of the company. He lives in Auckland.'

'I've been thinking of avalanche protection,' said McGill meditatively. 'I've got some figures for you, Joe. When you design the avalanche gallery over the mine portal allow for an impact pressure of ten tons a square foot.'

Cameron flinched. *'That much?'* he asked incredulously.

'I've been talking to people who witnessed the 1943 slide. From all accounts it was an airborne powder avalanche, and so was the 1912 slide, according to Turi Buck. The next may not be any different.'

'Airborne powder! What's that?'

'This is no time for a lecture on avalanche dynamics. All you need to know is that it's fast and it packs a hell of a wallop.'

Ballard said, 'The 1943 avalanche turned a hundred acres of big trees into firewood.'

Cameron put down his fork. 'Now I *know* why you're worried about the town.'

'I wish to hell the council was as worried as I am,' said McGill bleakly.

Cameron looked up. 'Here comes Matt Houghton. If you tell him what you've just told me maybe he'll become as scared as I am.' As Houghton came up, his bald head gleaming, Cameron pulled out a chair. 'Sit down, Matt. What did the Civil Defence people have to say?'

Houghton sat down heavily. 'I haven't had time to talk to them yet. We'll be posting signs on the slope; Bobby Fawcett's scouts are making them and they'll be putting them up tomorrow. Got any stakes we can use, Joe?'

'Sure,' said Cameron, but his voice was abstracted. He was looking at McGill.

Ballard leaned forward. 'What do you mean, Matt – you didn't have time? I thought it was agreed . . .'

Houghton flapped his hands. 'It's *Saturday,* Ian,' he said plaintively, and shrugged. 'And tomorrow is Sunday. We probably won't be able to get through to them until Monday.'

Ballard looked baffled. 'Matt, do you really think that Civil Defence Headquarters closes down at weekends? All you have to do is to lift the bloody telephone.'

'Take it easy, Ian. I have enough trouble with the Petersons. Charlie takes the line that no one can prevent him from walking – or skiing – on his own land.'

'For Christ's sake! Is he out of his mind?'

Houghton sighed. 'You know Charlie. It's that old feud getting in the way.'

'What the hell did I have to do with buying and selling mineral rights? I was only a kid at the time.'

'It's not that; it's the other thing. Charlie *was* Alec's twin, you know.'

'But that was nearly twenty-five years ago.'

'Long memories, Ian; long memories.' Houghton rubbed his jaw. 'That stuff you told us about your training – you know, Johannesburg and Harvard. Eric was inclined to disbelieve you.'

'So he thinks I'm a liar as well as a coward,' said Ballard sourly. 'What does he think it takes to be in charge of a company like this?'

'He did mention a rich grandfather,' said Houghton wryly.

He dropped his eyes under Ballard's steady stare. Ballard said, 'I'm expecting a call from old Crowell. You can talk to him if you like. He'll tell you my qualifications.' His voice was chilly.

'Take it easy – I believe you. You've made a success of your life, and that's all that matters.'

'No, it isn't, Matt. What matters is that bloody snow on the slope above this town, and I don't want any ancient history getting in the way. I'm going to make sure the right thing is done, and if the Petersons get in my way I won't go around them – I'll go through them. I'll smash them.'

Houghton gave him a startled look. 'My God, but you've changed!'

'Turi Buck said it first – I've grown up,' said Ballard tiredly.

There was an embarrassed silence at the table. McGill, who had been quietly watchful, said, 'I don't know what that was all about, Mr Houghton, but I can tell you this. The situation is now more serious than that I outlined at our meeting this morning. I've taken more samples from the slope and the stability is deteriorating. I've also been talking to people about previous avalanches, with the result that I've just notified Mr Cameron to prepare for something hitting the mine very hard indeed. I have to tell you that also applies to the town.'

Houghton was affronted. 'Why the hell didn't you talk like that this morning instead of pussyfooting around with scientific quibbles? This morning you said the hazard was potential.'

McGill was exasperated. 'I sometimes wonder if we talk the same language,' he snapped. 'The hazard still is potential and it will be until something happens and then it'll be actual hazard and too goddam late to do anything about it. What do you want me to do? Go up on the slope and trigger it just to prove to you that it can happen?'

Ballard said, 'Go back to your council and tell them to stop playing politics. And tell the Petersons from me that no one votes for dead men.' His voice was like iron. 'You can also tell them that if they don't do something constructive by midday tomorrow I'll go over their heads – I'll call a public meeting and put it to the people direct.'

'And telephone Civil Defence as soon as you can,' added McGill.

Houghton took a deep breath and stood up. His face was red and shiny with sweat. 'I'll do the best I can,' he said, and walked away.

Ballard stared after him. 'I wonder if this is a good time to get drunk?'

TWELVE

'Did Mr Ballard drink heavily that night?' asked Lyall.

Cameron's lips compressed and then he relaxed. 'Not more than most,' he said easily. 'It was a party, you must remember. For instance, he didn't drink as much as me.' As an apparent afterthought he added, 'Or as much as your clients there.'

Lyall said sharply, 'I must protest. The witness cannot be allowed to make gratuitous innuendoes of that nature.'

Harrison was trying unsuccessfully to hide a smile. 'It appears to me that Mr Cameron was merely trying to put Mr Ballard's drinking in the scale of things. Is that not so, Mr Cameron?'

'It was a party in a small town,' said Cameron. 'Sure, there was drinking. Some of the boys from the mine got pretty smashed. Some of the town folk, too. I was a bit rosy myself towards the end. But Mr Ballard was nowhere near drunk. I don't think he's really a drinking man. But he had a few.'

'I think that answers Mr Lyall's question. Go on, Mr Cameron.'

'Well, at about eleven-thirty that night Mr Ballard again tackled the mayor about whether he'd telephoned anybody – Civil Defence or whatever – and Houghton said he hadn't. He said he didn't see that a few hours would make any difference and he wasn't going to make a fool of himself in the middle of the night by ringing up some caretaker and asking him damn silly questions.'

Harrison looked across at Ballard. 'Mr Cameron, it would be improper to ask you why Mr Ballard, at this point, did not make the call himself. Mr Ballard is here to answer for himself, as I am sure he will. But, if there was this urgency, why did *you* not make the call?'

Cameron looked embarrassed. 'We'd been told, quite bluntly, to keep our noses out of town business. And up to that time we thought the call *had* been made. When we found it hadn't we thought the likelihood of getting anyone at Civil Defence who could tell us what we wanted to know was slight. Another thing was that Mr Ballard still hoped to co-operate with the council, and if he made the call they'd think he'd gone over their heads on what they would consider to be town business. Relations between mine and town might be permanently damaged.'

'What did Dr McGill think of this?'

'He wasn't around at the time; he'd gone out to check the weather. But afterwards he said that Mr Ballard was a damned fool.' Cameron scratched his cheek. 'He said I was a damned fool, too.'

'It seems that Dr McGill is the only person to come out of this with any credit,' observed Harrison. 'There appears to have been a lot of buck-passing for reasons which pale into insignificance when one considers the magnitude of the disaster.'

'I agree,' said Cameron frankly. 'But Dr McGill was the only person who had any conception of the magnitude of the trouble which faced us. When he told me to prepare for an impact pressure of ten tons a square foot I thought he was coming it a bit strong. I accepted his reasoning but at the back of my mind I didn't really believe it. I think that Mr Ballard was in the same case, and he and I are technical men.'

'And because the members of the council were not technical men do you think that excuses their dilatory conduct?'

'No,' said Cameron heavily. 'We were all guilty to a
greater or lesser degree. It does not excuse our conduct, but
it goes a long way towards explaining it.'

Harrison was silent for a long time, then he said gently,
'I'll accept that, Mr Cameron. What happened next?'

'Mr Ballard and I stayed at our table talking and doing a
little drinking. If Mr Ballard did any drinking that night it
was then that he did it. He hadn't had more than two drinks
up to then.'

Cameron talked with Ballard for some time, maybe twenty
minutes, and then they were joined by Stacey Cameron.
Ballard cocked an ear towards the dance floor; it was late
enough for the jigging rock rhythms to have been replaced
by the night-club shuffle. 'Dance?' he suggested.

Stacey grimaced. 'Thanks all the same, but no thanks.
I've been danced off my feet tonight.' She sat down and
flexed her toes, then looked up at him. 'Liz Peterson wants
to know if you think she has smallpox.'

He blinked. 'What!'

'She seems to think that you're ignoring her. She could
be right, at that.'

Ballard smiled slightly. 'I'd forgotten she existed until
tonight.'

'Well, you know she exists now. Why don't you ask her
for a dance? She's sitting this one out.'

Ballard's jaw dropped, and then he smiled. 'Well, for
God's sake, why not?' He drained his glass and felt the lump
of whisky hit bottom with a thud. 'I'll give it a whirl.' He
left, heading for the dance floor.

'Are you crazy?' demanded Cameron. 'Don't you know
that Ballard and the Petersons get on like the Hatfields and
McCoys? What are you trying to do – start a war?'

'They've got to start talking to each other reasonably sometime,' said Stacey. 'Huka isn't big enough for them to ignore each other forever.'

Cameron looked unconvinced. 'I hope you know what you're doing.'

'Dad, what's all this about an avalanche?'

'What avalanche?'

'Don't talk to me as though I were a half-wit,' said Stacey. 'The avalanche you were discussing over dinner.'

'Oh, that one!' said Cameron with an ill-assumed air of surprise. 'Nothing to it. Just some precautions McGill wants us to take.'

'Precautions,' she said thoughtfully. 'That's not what I understood by the way Ian was reaming out Houghton.' She looked past her father. 'Here's Mike now. How's the weather, Mike?'

'Heavy snow setting in.' McGill checked his watch. 'Nearly midnight. How long do these shindigs go on?'

'The dancing will stop dead on midnight,' said Cameron. 'Very religious guys, these New Zealanders. No dancing on Sunday.'

McGill nodded. 'I won't be sorry to get to bed.' He stretched. 'What did the Civil Defence crowd have to say?'

'Houghton didn't call.'

'He *didn't*!' McGill grabbed Cameron by the arm. 'What have you done about it? Did Ian try?' Cameron shook his head. 'Then he's a goddamned fool – and so are you. Where's the telephone?'

'There's one in the lobby,' said Cameron. 'Look, Mike, there'll be no one there at this time of night qualified to tell you anything.'

'Tell me – hell!' said McGill. 'I'm going to tell them. I'm going to raise the alarm.'

He walked away rapidly with Cameron on his heels. As they skirted the dance floor there was a shout and a sudden disturbance. McGill jerked his head sideways and saw Charlie Peterson with his hand on Ballard's shoulder. 'Just what we need,' he said disgustedly. 'Come on, Joe,' and crossed the floor to where the two men bristled at each other.

Ballard had been dancing with Liz Peterson when he felt the heavy thud of Charlie's meaty hand on his shoulder and felt himself spun round. Charlie's face was sweaty and his eyes were red-rimmed. Alcohol fumes came from him as he whispered hoarsely, 'Stay away from my sister, Ballard.'

Liz's face flamed. 'Charlie, I told you . . .'

'Shut up!' His hand bore heavily on Ballard's shoulder. 'If I catch you with her again I'll break your back.'

'Take your hand off me,' said Ballard.

Some of the ferocity left Charlie and he grinned genially. 'Take it off yourself – if you can.' His thumb ground viciously into the muscle at the top of Ballard's arm.

'Stop this nonsense,' said Liz. 'You get crazier every day.'

Charlie ignored his sister and increased the pressure on Ballard. 'What about it? You won't get into trouble with your momma – she's not here.'

Ballard seemed to droop. His arms hung down in front of him, crossed at the wrists, and suddenly he brought them up sharply, hitting Charlie's arm at the elbow with considerable force and thus breaking free.

Charlie lunged forward but Cameron grabbed one arm and twisted it behind Charlie's back. It was done with expertise and it was evident that Cameron was no stranger to a rough house.

'Break it up,' said McGill. 'This is a dance floor, not a boxing ring.'

Charlie pressed forward again but McGill put his hand flat on Charlie's chest and pushed. 'All right,' said Charlie. 'I'll see you outside when you don't have your friends to help you.'

'Christ, you sound like a schoolboy,' said McGill.

'Let the bastard speak for himself,' said Charlie.

In the distance a voice was raised. 'Is Mr Ballard around? He's wanted on the telephone.'

McGill jerked his head at Ballard. 'Take your call.'

Ballard shrugged his shoulders into his rumpled jacket and nodded briefly. He walked past Charlie without so much as looking at him. Charlie twisted in Cameron's grip and yelled, 'You've not changed, you bastard. You still run scared.'

'What's going on here?' someone demanded.

McGill turned to find Eric Peterson at his elbow. He took his hand off Charlie's chest, and said, 'Your kid brother has gone off his rocker.'

Eric looked at Liz. 'What happened?'

'The same thing that happens every time I get too close to a man,' she said wearily. 'But worse than usual this time.'

Eric said to Charlie coldly, 'I've told you about this before.'

Charlie jerked his arm free of Cameron. 'But it was Ballard!' he pleaded. 'It was Ballard.'

Eric frowned. 'Oh!' But then he said, 'I don't care who it was. You don't make these scenes again.' He paused. 'Not in public.'

McGill caught Cameron's eye and they both moved off in the direction of the lobby and found Ballard at the reception desk. The desk clerk was pointing. 'There's the phone.'

'Who'd be ringing you?' asked McGill.

'Crowell, if I'm lucky.'

'After you with the phone – I want to ring Christchurch.' McGill turned to the desk clerk. 'Have you a Christchurch telephone book?'

Ballard picked up the telephone as McGill flipped through the pages. 'Ballard here.'

A testy voice said, 'I have half a dozen message slips here asking me to ring you. I've just got in so it had better be important.'

'It is,' said Ballard grimly. 'We're in a bad situation here. We have reason to suppose that the mine – and the town – is in danger of destruction by avalanche.'

There was a blank silence broken only by a surge of music from the dance floor. Crowell said, 'What!'

'An avalanche,' said Ballard. 'We're going to be in dead trouble.'

'Are you serious?'

Ballard put his finger to his other ear to block out the noise of the music. 'Of course I'm serious. I don't joke about things like this. I want you to get on to the Ministry of Civil Defence to let them know about it. We may need help fast.'

'But I don't understand,' said Crowell faintly.

'You don't have to understand,' snapped Ballard. 'Just tell them that the township of Hukahoronui is in danger of being blotted out.'

McGill's finger marked a line in the telephone book. He looked up as someone ran past and saw Charlie Peterson heading for Ballard at a dead run. He dropped the book and jumped after him.

Charlie grabbed Ballard by the shoulder, and Ballard shouted, 'What the hell . . .?'

'I'm going to break you in half,' said Charlie.

Lost in the uproar was a soft rumble of distant thunder. Ballard punched at Charlie, hampered by the telephone he held. From the wildly waving earpiece came the quacking sound of Crowell in Auckland. McGill laid hands on Charlie and hauled him away bodily.

Ballard, breathing heavily, put the telephone to his ear. Crowell said, '. . . going on there? Are you there, Ballard? What's . . .?'

The line went dead.

McGill spun Charlie around and laid him cold with a right cross to the jaw just as all the lights went out.

THIRTEEN

'After the lights went out things got pretty confused,' said Cameron. He half turned in his chair and spoke to the nurse in a low voice. The nurse got up and poured him a glass of water, and when Cameron took it, his hand was shaking.

Harrison watched him carefully. 'You've been giving evidence for quite a long time, Mr Cameron, and I think you should stand down for the moment. Since we are taking evidence chronologically the next witness should naturally be Mr Crowell. Thank you, Mr Cameron.'

'Thank you, sir.' Cameron got to his feet painfully, assisted by the male nurse, and hobbled slowly across the hall.

Reed said, 'Will Mr Crowell come forward?'

A short, stout man got to his feet and walked up to the rostrum with some reluctance. As he sat down he turned his head sideways to look at Rickman, who nodded reassuringly. Reed said, 'What is your full name?'

Crowell licked his lips nervously, and coughed, 'Henry James Crowell.'

'And your occupation, Mr Crowell?'

'I'm the chairman of several companies, including the Hukahoronui Mining Company.'

Harrison said, 'Do you own shares in that company?'

'I have a minority holding, yes.'

'Mr Ballard was the managing director of that company, was he not?'

'Yes.'

'What were his responsibilities?'

Crowell frowned. 'I don't understand the question.'

'Come, Mr Crowell. Surely Mr Ballard had duties which were defined.'

'Of course, sir. He had the normal duties of a managing director – to see to the total interests of the company under the guidance of the board of directors.'

'Which was headed by yourself.'

'That is correct.'

'You have been listening to evidence relating to a telephone call which you made to Mr Ballard. Did you, in fact, make that call?'

'Yes.'

'Why?'

'I had been away from home and arrived back late on the Saturday night. My secretary had left a list of messages from Mr Ballard to the effect that I should contact him. From the number and tenor of these messages I judged the matter to be urgent, so I telephoned him immediately.'

'And what did he say?'

'He said something about an avalanche. I didn't quite understand – he was very indistinct.'

'Didn't you ask him to explain further?'

'Yes.' Crowell's hands twitched. 'There was a lot of noise going on at his end – music and so forth. He wasn't very coherent.'

Harrison regarded him thoughtfully, and then moved his eyes sideways. 'Yes, Mr Smithers?'

'Can the witness state whether or not Mr Ballard asked him to contact the Ministry of Civil Defence to warn them of impending danger at Hukahoronui?'

Harrison's eyes returned to Crowell who wriggled in his seat. 'He did say something along those lines, but there was a lot of noise on the line. A lot of shouting and screaming.' He paused. 'Then I was cut off.'

'What did you do then?' asked Harrison.

'I talked it over with my wife.'

A ripple of amusement passed over the hall. Harrison knocked sharply with his gavel. 'Did you contact the Ministry of Civil Defence?'

Crowell hesitated. 'No, sir.'

'Why not?'

'I thought it was some sort of practical joke. With that music and uproar on the line . . . well, I thought . . .' His voice tailed away.

'You thought Mr Ballard was joking?' queried Harrison.

Both Lyall and Rickman had their hands up. Harrison picked Rickman and nodded. 'Did you think Mr Ballard was drunk?' asked Rickman. Lyall grinned and hauled down his hand.

'I did.'

'When you said that Mr Ballard was incoherent that was what you meant, wasn't it?'

'Yes,' said Crowell. He smiled gratefully at Rickman.

'You must not lead the witness,' said Harrison mildly.

'I'm sorry, Mr Chairman.' Rickman smiled encouragingly at Crowell. 'Who appointed Mr Ballard as managing director?'

'The instruction came from London – from a majority shareholder.'

'You had nothing to do with his appointment, then. Could we say that Mr Ballard was foisted upon you?'

'As a minority shareholder I didn't have much say in the matter.'

'If you had had a say in the matter whom would you have picked as managing director?'

'Mr Dobbs, who was mine manager.'

'And who is now dead.'

Crowell bowed his head and said nothing.

'That is all,' said Rickman.

'What did you think of Mr Ballard when you first met him?' asked Harrison.

Crowell shrugged. 'I thought he was a personable enough young man – perhaps a little too young for the job.'

'Did you suspect him of any proclivities towards drunkenness or practical joking?'

'They did not present themselves – then.'

'But they did eventually? When?'

'On that evening, Mr Chairman.'

Harrison sighed, exasperated at Crowell's woolly-mindedness. 'But we have heard evidence that Mr Ballard was neither drunk nor playing a practical joke. Why should you not believe what he said on that occasion?'

Crowell shook his head unhappily and looked towards Rickman, whose head was down as he busily scanned a sheet of paper. 'I don't know – it was just that it sounded that way.'

'It has been suggested that Mr Ballard was "foisted" upon you.' Harrison uttered the word as though it had a nasty taste. 'Upon his appointment, did you make any complaint of any kind – to anyone?'

'No.'

Harrison shook his head slowly as he regarded this most unsatisfactory witness. 'Very well. I have no further questions He looked down from the rostrum. 'Yes, Mr Ballard?'

'I would like to ask some questions.'

'I see that you still have no legal representation. Do you think that wise? You must have heard the saying that the man who argues his own case has a fool for a lawyer.'

Ballard smiled. 'That may hold good in a law court, but, Mr Chairman, you have repeatedly said that this is not a court of law. I think I am quite capable of asking my own questions.'

Harrison nodded. 'Very well, Mr Ballard.'

Ballard looked at Crowell. 'Mr Crowell, two weeks after the disaster the board suspended me from my duties. Why?'

Rickman's hand shot up. 'Objection! What happened two weeks after the incident does not come within the scope of this inquiry.'

'Mr Rickman has a point,' said Harrison. 'I cannot really see that this is helpful.'

Ballard stood up. 'May I argue the point?'

'Certainly.'

Ballard picked up a note-pad. 'I took notes of your remarks when this inquiry began. You ruled that evidence given here may not be used in a future civil action. It seems to me that this inquiry may be the only public hearing possible.'

He turned a page. 'On the second day Dr McGill said that the death-roll in the disaster was higher than need be. You overruled an objection to that on the grounds that this is not a court of law and the procedure is at your sole discretion.'

He looked up. 'Mr Chairman, this inquiry is being widely reported in the Press, not only in New Zealand but also in the United Kingdom. Regardless of your findings, the public is going to blame someone for those unnecessary deaths. Now, certain imputations have been made about my character, my drinking habits and a supposed propensity for practical joking which, in my own interests, I cannot allow to pass unchallenged. I ask to be allowed to question Mr Crowell about these matters, and the fact that I was suspended from my duties a fortnight after the disaster certainly seems to me to be a legitimate reason for inquiry.'

Harrison conferred briefly with his two assessors, then said, 'It is not the wish of this Commission that a man's reputation be put lightly at stake. You may sit down, Mr Ballard, and continue your questioning of Mr Crowell.'

Rickman said warningly, 'There may be grounds for appeal here, Mr Chairman.'

'There may, indeed,' agreed Harrison tranquilly. 'You will find the procedure set out in the Commissions of Inquiry Act. Continue, Mr Ballard.'

Ballard sat down. 'Why was I suspended from my duties, Mr Crowell?'

'It was a unanimous decision of the board.'

'That is not exactly answering my question, but we'll let it pass for the moment. You said in evidence that you had nothing to do with my appointment, that you would rather have chosen another man, and that the instructions came from London. Do you usually take your instructions from London, Mr Crowell?'

'Of course not.'

'Then where do you take your instructions from?'

'Why, from . . .' Crowell stopped short. 'I do not take instructions, as you put it, I am chairman of the company.'

'I see. Do you regard yourself as a sort of dictator?'

'That is an insulting question.'

'Maybe you might think so. All the same, I'd like you to answer it.'

'Of course I'm not a dictator.'

'You can't have it both ways,' said Ballard. 'Either you take instructions or you do not. Which is it, Mr Crowell?'

'As chairman I assist the board in making decisions. All decisions are made jointly.'

'A most democratic process,' commented Ballard. 'But the decision to appoint me as managing director was not made jointly by the board, was it, Mr Crowell?'

'The decision need not be unanimous,' said Crowell. 'As you have pointed out, this is a democratic process where the majority rules.'

'But not so democratic as to be a one man, one vote system. Is it not a fact that he who controls most votes controls the company?'

'That is the usual system.'

'And you said in evidence that the instruction to appoint me came from a majority shareholder in London. Is that shareholder a member of the board?'

Crowell twitched nervously. In a low voice he said, 'No, he is not.'

'Then is it not a fact that your board of directors has no real power and is thus a democratic sham? Is it not a fact that the power to control the company lies elsewhere? In the City of London?'

'That is a misreading of the situation,' said Crowell sullenly.

'Let us turn from my appointment to my suspension,' said Ballard. 'Did the instruction to suspend me also come from London?'

'It may have done.'

'Surely you know. You are the chairman of the board.'

'But not concerned with the day to day running of the company.'

'No,' agreed Ballard. 'That was the function of the managing director. You said so yourself in your evidence. Surely you are not suggesting that I suspended myself?'

Dan Edwards could not contain himself. There was a loud snigger from the Press gallery and Harrison looked up, frowning.

'You are being ridiculous,' said Crowell.

Ballard said drily, 'Any ridiculousness inherent in this situation certainly does not emanate from me. There remains one alternative. Are you suggesting that the suspension of the managing director was a minor bit of day to day business that was beneath your notice as chairman?'

'Of course not.'

'Then you will know where the idea of my suspension originated, won't you?'

'Now I come to think of it, the instruction for your suspension did come from London.'

'I see. But that again is not an exact answer to the question. Is it not a fact that you communicated with London because the board is a puppet dancing to strings held in the City of London? Is it not a fact that a suggestion was made – by you – that the company was in danger of being in bad odour because of evidence to be given at this inquiry? And is it not a fact that you intimated that I, as a Johnny-come-lately, was an ideal person to shuffle the responsibility on to, and that it was then that the instruction was given – from London – that I be suspended?'

'Objection!' cried Rickman. 'Mr Ballard cannot lead the witness in this way.'

'I tend to agree,' said Harrison. 'Such a compendium cannot be permitted, Mr Ballard.'

'I withdraw the question.' Ballard knew, from the rustle in the Press gallery, that he had made his point where it mattered. 'I shall return to the telephone conversation between Mr Crowell and myself. When you were cut off, what did you do? Oh yes; you talked it over with your wife, didn't you? What was the substance of that conversation?'

'I don't remember.' Crowell added irritably, 'It was late at night and we were both very tired.'

'When you were cut off, did you attempt to replace the call?'

'No.'

'No? Why not?'

'You heard my evidence. I thought you were drunk.'

'How long did you think I'd been drunk, Mr Crowell?'
asked Ballard softly.

Crowell looked startled and uncomprehending. 'I don't
understand the question.'

'It's quite a simple question. Please answer it.'

'I didn't give it a thought.'

Ballard picked up a sheet of paper. 'You said in evidence
that your secretary had left a number of messages from me.
You also said that you judged, from the number and tenor
of those messages, that the matter was urgent. Did you
think I'd been drunk all day? The first call I had was at
eleven-thirty that morning.'

'I told you. I didn't give it a thought.'

'Evidently not. So you did not try to call me back?'

'No.'

'And you did not try to communicate with the Ministry
of Civil Defence?'

'No.'

'As a matter of interest, Mr Crowell, what *did* you do?
After you had discussed it with your wife, I mean.'

'I went to bed.'

'You went to bed,' repeated Ballard slowly. 'Thank you,
Mr Crowell. That will be all.' He waited until Crowell was
rising from the chair and was in a half crouch. 'Oh, there is
just one further thing. Did you come forward voluntarily to
give evidence here, or were you subpoena'd?'

'I object,' said Rickman. 'That has nothing to do with anything.'

'I agree, Mr Rickman,' said Harrison smoothly. 'This
Commission need not be instructed that Mr Crowell was
subpoena'd – it already knows.' He ignored the indescribable sound that came from Rickman, and continued blandly,
'And now I think we shall adjourn for lunch.'

FOURTEEN

Over lunch in the restaurant near the Provincial Buildings, McGill said, 'You're doing all right, Ian. You got in some good stuff this morning.'

Ballard poured a glass of water. 'I didn't think Harrison would let me get away with it.'

'Get away with it! God, he compounded with you. He ticked you off when he had to, but he didn't stop you. I thought I'd split a gusset when he brought out the bit that Crowell had been subpoena'd. He agreed with Rickman and harpooned him in the same breath.' McGill paused. 'I don't think Harrison likes Crowell.'

'I don't like him much myself.'

'You're not doing yourself much good with your family. That histrionic speech about the company dancing to strings pulled in the City of London won't go down well with your uncles back home. Where did you learn to pull a trick like that?'

Ballard grinned. 'Watching the Perry Mason Show.' He shrugged. 'It won't make much difference. I've already decided to leave the Ballard Group.'

'After a speech like that you'll have to. I can't see any Ballard company hiring you now. What will you do?'

'Haven't made up my mind yet. Something will turn up.' He frowned. 'I keep wondering what Stenning wants.'

'Do you know him at all?'

'Not well. The old man relied on him a lot, and I know why. He's a tough old bird, about as ruthless as old Ben was himself. Ben told him what he wanted to do, and Stenning figured out a legal way of doing it. He's as sharp as a tack.'

'You say he's old – how old?'

Ballard reflected. 'He'll be pushing seventy now, I suppose. He was much younger than Ben. One of the bright young men that Ben surrounded himself with in the early years.'

'An old guy of seventy flying half way across the world,' mused McGill. 'Could be important, Ian.'

'I can't see how.'

McGill looked up. 'Here comes someone else who is not doing herself much good with her family.' He stood up. 'Hi, Liz.'

Liz Peterson put her hand on Ballard's shoulder. 'Don't get up, Ian. Hi, Mike.'

McGill drew up a chair for her and then sat down. He put out his hand and rubbed Liz's dog behind the ears. 'Hi, Victor; how's the boy?' The Alsatian lolled his tongue and his tail wagged vigorously.

'I didn't see you at the hearing this morning,' said Ballard.

'I was there. Wouldn't miss it for anything. It's just that I wasn't sitting with the boys. I don't like Lyall – he gives me the cold grues. Where's Joe?'

'Gone back to the hospital. Giving evidence this morning took it out of him.'

Liz tapped on the table. 'My charming brother, Charlie, manufactures the bullets and Lyall fires them.' She burlesqued Lyall's accent. ' "Did Mr Ballard drink heavily that night?" I damn near cheered when Joe fired that right back. It wounded Charlie to the heart.'

'You're not doing yourself much good with them,' warned Ballard.

'To hell with both of them,' she said pleasantly. 'I only stuck around because of Johnnie, and now he's dead I'll be leaving Huka. Maybe I'll be leaving New Zealand.'

'A fine pair you are,' said McGill. 'Don't either of you believe in family ties at all?'

'Not with that pair,' said Liz. 'I nearly gave Charlie a heart attack just now. I said that if anyone implied that Ian was drunk just once more I'd offer my services as your witness. I said that I can tell well enough when the man I'm dancing with is drunk, and that Ian wasn't but that Charlie certainly was.' She laughed. 'I've never seen a man go red and white at the same time.'

'I'd be careful, Liz,' said Ballard soberly. 'Charlie can be violent.'

'Don't I know it! I once had to crown him with a bottle. But I can handle him.'

McGill smiled satirically. 'So unlike the home life of our own dear Queen,' he observed.

Ballard said, 'Thanks for the support, Liz. Ever since the avalanche I've been depressed, but now the depression is lifting. I've made a couple of decisions and now the way ahead seems a lot clearer. You've had a lot to do with it.'

'I bring more than support, sir – I bring information. Rickman and Lyall are cooking up something together. I was driving past the company office just now when they both came out together, laughing fit to bust.'

'Watch it, Ian,' warned McGill. 'It'll be a pincer movement.'

'Thanks, Liz,' said Ballard.

She looked at her watch. 'I think I'll sit with the boys this afternoon. I might learn something more. See you at the hearing.' She stood up. 'Come on, Victor.'

As she walked away McGill said, 'The prettiest spy I ever did see.' He finished his coffee and looked around for the waitress. 'We'd better be going, too. By the way, what are these couple of decisions you've made?'

'You've heard one – I'm leaving the Ballard Group.'

'And the other?'

'I'm getting married,' said Ballard placidly.

McGill paused, his wallet half way from his breast pocket. 'Well, congratulations. Who's the lucky girl?'

Ballard dabbed at his mouth with a napkin. 'Liz Peterson – if she'll have me.'

'You must be insane,' said McGill. 'Who'd want Charlie as a brother-in-law?'

FIFTEEN

MacAllister was an electrical engineer, stolid and given to precise answers. When Harrison asked him when the power lines were cut, he answered, 'Two minutes and seven seconds to midnight.'

'How do you know?' asked Professor Rolandson.

'There is a recording device on the circuit breakers. When they kicked out the time was recorded.'

Harrison said, 'What did you do?'

'Established where the break was.'

From Rolandson: 'How?'

'I put a current on the line and measured the resistivity. That gave a rough idea of the distance to the break. I put it as a little short of Hukahoronui.'

'And then?'

'I rang my opposite number in Post Office Telephones and asked if he had the same trouble. He had, and he confirmed my findings. I then sent out an inspection crew.'

'With what result?'

'They rang me nearly two hours later to say that they had found the trouble. They said it was due to a fall of snow. A Post Office crew was also there and my men had used their portable telephone.'

'They just said it was due to a fall of snow?'

'Yes, sir. It didn't seem reasonable to me that a fall of snow could cut the cables so I asked for further information. The entrance to the valley of Hukahoronui is by a cleft or gap, and my men said the gap was filled with snow to a height farther than they could see in the darkness. I know the place, sir, and I asked if the river which runs out of the valley was still flowing. My man said there was a little flow but not very much. I assumed there would be flooding on the other side of the snowfall so I immediately notified the police.'

'Very quick-witted of you,' remarked Harrison. 'But why the police?'

'Standard instructions, sir,' said MacAllister stolidly.

'Did you take further steps?'

'Yes, sir. I went to the scene of the break in the cable. It was snowing quite heavily as I set out and conditions became worse as I proceeded. When I arrived at the break it was snowing very heavily – something like a blizzard. On my truck I had a spotlight but there was too much back reflection from the falling snow to show how high the blockage in the Gap was. I also investigated the flow of the river and found it to be minimal. I judged the situation serious enough to telephone the police again.'

'And what was the reaction from the police?'

'They noted the facts as I gave them, sir.'

'Nothing more?'

'They told me nothing more.'

'You say you could not tell the height of the blockage. Obviously you could not tell the depth – how far back it extended into the Gap?'

'No, sir.'

'Did you take steps to find out?'

'Not at that time. It was snowing heavily and it was dark. To investigate in those conditions would have been most dangerous. I would not climb up there myself, nor would I send anyone else. I judged it better to wait until daylight when we could see what we were doing.'

Harrison looked at Smithers. 'It appears from the evidence of Mr MacAllister that this was the first occasion that anyone outside Hukahoronui had any inkling of trouble.' He switched his gaze to Crowell who was sitting next to Rickman and amended his statement. 'Or anyone who did something constructive about it, that is. Have you any questions, Mr Smithers?'

'No, Mr Chairman. But I think the witness ought to be congratulated on the sensible steps he took – especially his quickness in passing on news of a potentially hazardous situation.'

'I concur.' Harrison turned to MacAllister. 'To what time does your evidence take us?'

'I made the second call to the police at three-thirty on the Sunday morning.'

'Thank you. You may step down, Mr MacAllister, with the knowledge that you have done your duty well.'

MacAllister left the witness chair, and Harrison said, 'I think it is time to get back to what happened in Hukahoronui after the lights were extinguished. We have just heard of a fall of snow which blocked the Hukahoronui Gap. I would like to hear Dr McGill's professional views on that.'

McGill rose, walked to the witness chair, and set his briefcase on the floor. Harrison said, 'You were present in the lobby of the Hotel D'Archiac when the lights went out?'

'Yes, sir. As Mr Cameron said, there was a lot of confusion at that time. Mr Ballard was trying to talk to Mr Crowell and had difficulty in doing so because of the actions of Mr Charles Peterson. I went to his aid and it was about then that the lights went out. Mr Ballard said that the telephone had also gone dead.'

'Did you *hear* the snow falling into the Gap?'

'No. There was too much noise in the hotel.'

'So what happened?'

'The management of the hotel got busy and provided light. There were candles and kerosene lanterns ready for use. I was told that a breakdown of electricity supply was not uncommon, and there had been a similar occurrence only the previous month. Everybody took it as a matter of course. I asked about the dead telephone but no one seemed worried about that, either. The dance was over, anyway, so everybody went home.'

'Including you?'

'Yes. I went home with Mr Ballard and went to bed.'

McGill was woken from a sound sleep by Ballard. He awoke to darkness and automatically flicked at the switch of the bed-side lamp, but nothing happened. It was then he remembered about the power failure. Ballard was a deeper shadow in the darkness. McGill said, 'What time is it?'

'Five-thirty. Cameron just rang up with a funny story. It seems that one of his men, Jack Stevens, left early this morning to go to Christchurch to see his mother. He says he can't get out of the valley.'

'Why not?'

'He says the Gap is closed off with snow. He says he can't get through.'

'What sort of car does he have?'

'A Volkswagen.'

'Well, it's not surprising, is it? Look at what happened to those two Americans the other day. Is it still snowing?'

'Very heavily.'

'Well, there you are. It's probably been snowing all night. I couldn't guarantee to get through myself with a Land-Rover.'

'According to Cameron, Jack says it's not like that. He's talking of a wall of snow so high he can't see the top. I told Cameron to bring him here.'

McGill grunted. 'Light that candle on the dressing-table, will you?'

Ten minutes later he was saying, 'You're sure, now. This is not just a deep drift across the road?'

'I've told you it's not,' said Stevens. 'It's a bloody great wall of snow.'

'I think I'd better go and look at it,' said McGill.

Ballard said, 'I'll come with you.' He looked at the telephone and then at Cameron. 'If there's no power how did you manage to ring me?'

Stevens said, 'The exchange has a bank of batteries and an emergency diesel generator to top them up. We're all right for local calls.'

McGill nodded. 'Whatever happened at the Gap must have taken out the electricity cables and the telephone lines both.' He picked up a heavy anorak. 'Let's get going.'

'I'll come, too,' said Cameron.

'No,' said McGill. 'I've just been handed an idea. Do you have diesel generators at the mine?'

'Sure.'

'Then you see that they're in working order. I have a notion that we're going to need power before long.'

'That means me,' said Stevens. 'I'm the mine electrician.' He winked at Cameron. 'Do I get double time for Sunday work?'

Ballard left to put on ski pants and an anorak and then he joined McGill in the garage. He got behind the wheel of the Land-Rover and pushed the self-starter; it whined but the engine did not fire. 'She's cold,' he said as he pushed again. He tried several times but still the engine did not take. 'Confound the bloody thing.'

'Take it easy,' said McGill. 'You've flooded her. Wait a couple of minutes.' He pulled the anorak about him and then put on gloves. 'What's between you and Charlie Peterson? Last night he acted like a bull moose in rutting season.'

'It's an old story,' said Ballard. 'Not worth repeating.'

'I think I'd better know. Look, Ian: the Petersons are forty per cent of the town council and that fool of a mayor, Houghton, will do whatever John Peterson tells him to do.'

'John's all right,' said Ballard.

'Maybe. But Eric is steamed up about the mine and he hates your guts. As for Charlie – I don't know. There seems to be something else sticking in *his* craw. What did you do? Take away his girl or something like that?'

'Of course not.'

'If an old quarrel is getting in the way of co-operation with the council I'd better know about it. Charlie did enough damage last night.'

'It goes back a long way.'

'So tell,' said McGill. 'The snow in the Gap won't go away if what Stevens says is true. We have the time.'

'I never knew my father,' said Ballard. 'I was born in the January of 1939 in England, and I was brought here as a babe in arms. Something else also happened in '39.'

'The war?'

'That's it. My father had split with old Ben and he decided to leave England and farm here. He bought the land and then the war came and he joined the army. He was in the Western Desert with the New Zealand Division and I didn't see him to recognize until he came back in 1943 when I was four years old. My mother wanted him to stay – a lot of the men who came back in '43 refused to return to active service – and there was a bit of a quarrel between him and my mother. In the end it was academic because he was killed in the avalanche here. I saw it happen – and that's all I got to know of my father.'

'Not a lot.'

'No. It hit my mother hard and she turned a bit peculiar. Not that she went round the bend or anything like that. Just peculiar.'

'Neurotic?'

'I suppose you could call it that.'

'What form did it take?'

Ballard stared past the whirling snowflakes eddying in the wind beyond the open garage doors. 'I think you could say she became over-protective as far as I was concerned.'

'Was that what Charlie meant when he said she wouldn't let you out in the snow for fear you'd catch cold?'

'Something like that.'

'He made another crack about you wouldn't go on a slope steeper than a billiard table.'

Ballard sighed. 'That was it. It was made worse because my mother was the schoolteacher here. She tried to run the farm herself but she couldn't, so she sold off most of the land to old Peterson, just keeping the bit the house was on. To earn a living she took the job of schoolmistress. She was qualified for it. But there I was – in the middle. Over-protected and regarded as a teacher's pet into the bargain.'

'"Don't go near the water until you learn how to swim,"' quoted McGill.

'You don't know how true that was, Mike.' There was an edge of bitterness in Ballard's voice. 'Like all kids everywhere we had our swimming hole over by the bluff behind the Petersons' store. All the kids could swim well except me – all I could do was dog-paddle in the shallows and if my mother had known about that she'd have given me hell.'

He took out a packet of cigarettes and offered one to McGill who produced a lighter. Inhaling smoke, he said, 'I was twelve when it happened. It was in the spring and Alec Peterson and I were down by the river. Alec was the fourth of the Peterson brothers. There was a lot of melt water coming down from the mountains – the river was full and flowing fast and the water was bloody cold, but you know what kids are. I dipped in and out of the shallows – more out than in – but Alec went farther out. He was tough for a ten-year-old, and a strong swimmer.'

'Don't tell me,' said McGill. 'He got into trouble.'

'I think he got cramp,' said Ballard. 'Anyway, he let out a yell as he was swept out into the main stream. I knew I wouldn't have a hope in hell of getting him out, but I knew that river. It swirled around the bluff and on the other side there was an eddy where anything floating usually came ashore. It was common knowledge among the kids that it was a good place to collect firewood. So I belted across the bluff, past the Peterson store as fast as I could run.'

He drew on the cigarette in a long inhalation. 'I was right. Alec came inshore and I was able to wade in and grab him. But on his way around the bluff he'd bashed his head on a rock. His skull was cracked and his brains were leaking out and he was stone dead.'

McGill blew out his breath. 'Nasty! But I don't see how you could be blamed for anything.'

'Don't you? Well, I'll tell you. Two other people heard Alec when he yelled but they were too far away to do anything. And they saw me running like hell. Afterwards they said they'd seen me running away and leaving Alec. The two witnesses were Alec's brothers – Charlie and Eric.'

McGill whistled. 'Now I'm beginning to see.'

'They made my life a misery for the next four years. I went through hell, Mike. It wasn't just the Petersons – they set all the other kids against me. Those were the loneliest years I've ever spent. I think I'd have gone nuts if it hadn't been for Turi's son Tawhaki.'

'It must have been tough.'

Ballard nodded. 'Anyway, when I was sixteen years old Ben appeared in the valley as though he'd dropped from the sky. That was when the preliminary exploration was made for the mine. He listened to the local gossip, took one look at me and another at my mother, and then they had a flaming row. He beat her down, of course; very few people could withstand Ben. The upshot of it was that I went back to England with him.'

'And your mother?'

'She stayed on for a few years – until the mine started – then she went back to England, too.'

'And latched on to you again?'

'More or less – but I'd learned the score by then. I'd cut the apron strings.' Ballard flicked his cigarette butt out into the snow.

There was a brief silence before McGill said, 'I still don't get it. Grown men don't behave like Charlie's behaving because of something that happened when they were kids.'

'You don't know Charlie,' said Ballard. 'John's all right and, apart from what he believes about the mine, so is Eric. But for one thing, Charlie and Alec were very close – Alec was Charlie's twin. And for another, while you can't call Charlie retarded, he's never really grown up – he's never matured. Only last night you said he sounded like a schoolboy.'

'Yeah.' McGill stroked the side of his cheek. He had not shaved and it made a scratching sound. 'Anyway, I'm glad you told me. It makes things a lot clearer.'

'But there's nothing much any of us can do about it.' Ballard prodded at the starter again and the engine caught with a steady throb. 'Let's go up to the Gap.'

He drove into town, and as they were passing the Supermarket, McGill pointed to a car just pulling out. 'Looks as though he's leaving, too.'

'That's John Peterson.' Ballard accelerated to get ahead and then waved Peterson down.

As Peterson drew alongside McGill wound down the side window. 'Going far, Mr Peterson?'

John said, 'I've an early business appointment in Christchurch tomorrow, so I thought I'd leave early and get in a couple of rounds of golf there today.' He laughed as he waved at the snow. 'Not much chance of golf here, is there?'

'You may be disappointed,' said McGill. 'Our information is that the Gap is blocked.'

'Blocked? Impossible!'

'We're just going to have a look. Maybe you'd like to tag along behind.'

'All right. But I think you'll find yourself mistaken.'

McGill closed the window. 'As the White Queen said – I can think of six impossible things before breakfast. Carry on, Ian.'

They drove up the road that rose towards the Gap and which paralleled the river. As the headlights' beam swept across the ravine which the river had cut McGill said, 'Jack Stevens could be right. Have you ever seen the river as full as that?'

'I'll tell you when we come to the next bend.' At the next corner Ballard stopped the car. The beam from the headlights played in calm waters which swirled in smooth eddies. 'I've never seen it so high. The ravine is more than thirty feet deep here.'

'Let's get on.' McGill turned in his seat. 'Peterson is still with us.'

Ballard drove as far as he could until he was stopped by a cliff which suddenly appeared from out the darkness – a cliff which had no right to be there. 'My God!' he said. 'Just look at it!'

McGill opened the door of the car and got out. He walked towards the wall of snow and was silhouetted in the headlights. He prodded at the snow and then looked upwards, shaking his head. With a wave of his hand he gestured for Ballard to join him.

Ballard got out of the car just as John Peterson drew alongside. Together they walked to where McGill was standing and beating his gloved hands together. Peterson looked at the piled snow. 'What caused it?'

McGill said blandly, 'What you are seeing, Mr Peterson, is the end result of an avalanche. Not a big one, but not a small one, either. Nobody will be leaving Hukahoronui for quite some time – at least, not in a car.'

Peterson stared upwards, holding his hand above his head to stop snow driving into his eyes. 'There's a lot of snow there.'

'Avalanches tend to have a lot of snow in them,' said McGill drily. 'If the slope above the town gives way there'll be a hell of a lot more snow than you see here.'

Ballard walked over to one side and looked at the river. 'There'll be floods in the valley if the water keeps backing up.'

'I don't think so,' said McGill. 'The water is deep here and there'll be considerable pressure at the bottom. It will soon drill a hole through this lot – I'd say before the day is over. That will leave a snow bridge over the river, but it won't help any to clear the road.'

He went back to the snow wall and took out a handful of snow and examined it. 'Not too dry but dry enough.'

'What do you mean?' asked Peterson.

'Nothing. Just being technical.' He thrust his hand under Peterson's nose, palm upwards. With the forefinger of his left hand he stirred the snow around. 'Soft, harmless stuff, isn't it? Just like lamb's wool.' His fingers closed on the snow, making a fist. 'There was a man in my line of business called Zdarsky,' he said conversationally. 'He was a pioneer working before the First World War. Zdarsky said, "Snow is not a wolf in sheep's clothing – it is a tiger in lamb's clothing."'

He opened his fist. 'Look at that, Mr Peterson. What is it?'

In the palm of his gloved hand lay a lump of hard ice.

'So that was the first avalanche,' said Harrison.

'Yes, sir.'

'And it meant that no vehicles could leave or enter the valley?'

'That is correct.'

'So what happened next?'

McGill said, 'It had been my intention to persuade the town council that the best course of action was to evacuate the population of the valley until the danger had receded. This was now impossible.'

'You say impossible. Surely the obstacle could be climbed.'

'It could be climbed by the fit and active, of course; but what of the elderly, the handicapped and the children? But at least one member of the town council was now convinced that avalanches were something to be reckoned with in Hukahoronui. He was now ready to go back to town and throw his full weight into implementing any action I recommended. Mr John Peterson had been the first mayor and his words and actions would count for a lot. We went back to the town to get some action going.'

Harrison nodded and made a note. 'What was the name of the man you quoted to Mr Peterson? How do you spell it?'

'Z-D-A-R-S-K-Y, Matthias Zdarsky. He was an Austrian and an early pioneer in snow studies.' McGill hesitated. 'I have an anecdote which may have some bearing on what I quoted to Mr Peterson.'

'Proceed,' said Harrison. 'As long at it does not take us too far from our purpose here.'

'I don't think it does. A couple of years ago I was in Western Canada as a technical adviser on avalanche protection. There was a cartographic draughtsman who had been given the job of drawing a map of the area showing all the sites of avalanche hazard. It was a long job but he had nearly finished when, one day when he got back from lunch he found that some joker had written in medieval lettering on each avalanche site the words "Here be Tygers", just as on an old map.'

He smiled slightly. 'The draughtsman didn't think much of it as a joke, but the boss of his department took the map, had it framed, and hung it on the wall of his office as a reminder to everyone about avalanche hazard. You see, everyone in the game knows about Matthias Zdarsky and what happened to him.'

'An interesting anecdote,' said Harrison. 'And perfectly relevant. At the risk of wasting more time I would like to know what did happen to Zdarsky.'

'He was in the Austrian army during the First World War. At that time both sides – Austrians and Italians – were using avalanches as weapons in the Dolomites and the Tyrol. It's said that eighty thousand men died in avalanches during the war. In 1916 Zdarsky was going to the rescue of twenty-five Austrian soldiers who had been caught in an avalanche when he himself was caught in one. He was lucky enough to be rescued alive but that's about all you can say. He had eighty broken bones and dislocations, and it was eleven years before he could ski again.'

The hall was hushed. Presently Harrison said, 'Thank you, Dr McGill.' He looked up at the clock. 'I think we will now adjourn for the weekend. This hearing will recommence at ten in the morning on Monday.' He tapped lightly with the gavel 'The hearing is now adjourned.'

SIXTEEN

Next morning Ballard went to the hospital to visit Cameron. He tried to do this as often as possible to keep the old man company and cheer him up. It was a fact that Cameron now *was* an old man; his experience in the avalanche had almost killed both spirit and body. McGill said, 'I'll go to see him to-morrow. I have things to do at Deep Freeze Headquarters.'

'I'll be out that way this afternoon,' said Ballard. 'I'm picking up Stenning at Harewood. Want a lift back?'

'Thanks,' said McGill. 'Ask for me in the office.'

Ballard found Cameron out of bed but in a wheelchair with a blanket tucked around him in spite of the fact that it was a hot day. He was talking to Liz Peterson when Ballard walked into the room. 'Hi!' said Liz. 'I've just been telling Joe how Mike tried to freeze our blood when he gave evidence yesterday.'

'Yes, I think he made Harrison shiver a bit.' Privately he thought it tactless to describe the sufferings of an avalanche victim such as Zdarsky to one who had himself been caught in an avalanche, and he wondered how much Liz had said. 'How are you feeling, Joe?'

'A bit better this morning. I could have stayed yesterday afternoon in spite of my damn fool doctor.'

'You do as he says,' Ballard advised. 'What do you think, Liz?'

'I think Joe should do as he likes. Doctor doesn't always know best.'

Cameron laughed. 'Oh, it's good to have a pretty girl here – especially when she's on my side. But you really shouldn't be here, Liz.' He nodded towards the window. 'You should be out there, enjoying the sunshine. On a tennis court, maybe.'

'I've got plenty of time for tennis, Joe,' she said. 'The rest of my life. Are they looking after you well here?'

'Okay, I guess – but it's just like any other hospital. The food is terrible – they have too many dieticians and too few cooks.'

'We'll have something sent in,' said Ballard. 'Won't we Liz?'

She smiled. 'I'm not bad at home cooking.'

They stayed until Cameron sent them off, saying that young people must have something better to do than to sit around in hospitals. Outside, in the sunshine, Ballard said, 'Doing anything in particular, Liz?'

'Not really.'

'What about having lunch with me?'

She hesitated fractionally, but said, 'I'd like that.'

'We'll go in my car. I'll bring you back on my way to the airport this afternoon. I'm meeting someone.'

'It'll cost you lunch for two. I'll have to bring Victor. I can't leave him in my car.'

'Sure.'

She laughed. 'Love me – love my dog.'

As Ballard started the engine of his car, he said, 'Did you mean what you said yesterday – about leaving New Zealand?'

'I've been thinking about it.'

'Where would you go?'

'England, I suppose – at first anyway. Then perhaps America. You've travelled around a bit, haven't you? I've always wanted to travel – to see things.'

He drove out of the hospital grounds. 'Yes, I've been places, but they've always been working trips. I'll tell you one thing – I certainly never expected to come back to New Zealand.'

'Then why did you?'

Ballard sighed. 'My grandfather wanted me to. He was a forceful old bird.'

'He *was*! I didn't know he was dead.'

'He died a few days ago.'

'Oh, Ian! I am sorry.'

'So am I, in a way. We didn't always see eye to eye, but I'll miss him. Now that he's gone I won't be staying with the Ballard group. In fact, I've just about made that impossible.'

'It's like Mike says – neither of us get on with our relatives.' Liz laughed. 'I had a row with Charlie last night. Someone saw us in the restaurant yesterday and split to Charlie.'

'Don't get into trouble because of me, Liz.'

'I'm tired of Charlie's tantrums. I'm a grown woman and I'll meet whoever I like. I told him so last night.' She rubbed the side of her face reflectively.

Ballard glanced sideways and caught the action. 'He *hit* you?'

'Not for the first time, but it's going to be the last.' She saw the expression on Ballard's face. 'Not to worry, Ian. I can defend myself. I'm reckoned to be a pretty aggressive tennis player and those smash services develop the muscles.'

'So you hit him back. I doubt if that would make much of an impression on Charlie.'

She grinned impishly. 'I happened to be holding a plate-ful of spaghetti at the time.' When Ballard burst out laughing she added, 'Eric socked him, too. We're quite a happy family, we Petersons.'

He turned the car into the hotel car park. As they walked into the foyer he said, 'The grub's not bad here; they serve quite a good lunch. But what about a drink first?'

'Something long and cold,' she agreed.

'We'll have it by the pool,' he said. 'This way.' Suddenly he stiffened and halted in his stride.

'What's the matter?'

'The forces are rallying. It's Cousin Francis. Now where the devil did he spring from?'

A youngish man in a business suit stepped in front of them. 'Morning, Ian,' he said, abruptly and unsmilingly.

'Good morning, Frank,' said Ballard. 'Miss Peterson, this is my cousin, Frank Ballard.'

Frank Ballard gave her a curt nod. 'I want to talk to you, Ian.'

'Sure. We're just going to have drinks by the pool. Join us.'

Frank shook his head. 'In private.'

'All right. After lunch, then.'

'No, I haven't the time. I'm catching a plane back to Sydney almost immediately. It'll have to be now.'

'Don't mind me,' said Liz. 'I'll wait for you by the pool. Come on, Victor.' She walked away without waiting for an answer.

Frank said, 'What about your room?'

'All right.' Ballard led the way. They walked in silence until they reached the room. As he closed the door Ballard said, 'What brings you from Australia, Frank?'

Frank swung around. 'You bloody well know what brings me. Why the hell did you put old Crowell through the hoops the way you did yesterday? He was on the phone to me, crying on my shoulder long distance.'

Ian smiled. 'Just trying to elicit a bit of truth.'

There was no answering smile from Frank. 'Now look here, Ian. You're getting the company into a right mess. A fine bloody managing director you are.'

'Aren't you forgetting that Crowell suspended me from duty? Or is what you've just said an offer of the job back?'

'You flaming idiot! The suspension was only until the Inquiry was over. If you'd have used your brains and kept quiet everything would have been all right, and you'd be back in the saddle next week. As it is, I'm not so sure. You've been throwing so much mud at the company that I'm not sure you're fit for the position.'

Ian sat on the bed. 'If I'd kept quiet I'd be a dead duck, and you know it. Between the company and the Petersons I wouldn't stand a chance. Did you really think I'd stand still and let you make a patsy out of me?'

'This is a *Ballard* company,' said Frank furiously. 'We take care of our own. Have you no family feeling?'

'You'd take care of me like a fox takes care of a rabbit,' snapped Ian.

'If that's what you think, I'm sorry.' Frank's finger shot out. 'When the inquiry starts again on Monday you'd better keep quiet. No more appeals to the grandstand like those you've been making. If you promise to do that then maybe there'll still be a job for you in the Group. I doubt if I'll be able to swing the managing directorship of Hukahoronui – my old man's hopping mad – but I still think I can guarantee some kind of job.'

'Thanks,' said Ian ironically. 'But I'm underwhelmed by your generosity. You know what I think of the Group – I've never made a secret of it.'

'For Christ's sake!' burst out Frank. 'You know how big we are. We just have to pass the word around and you'll never get a job in mining again. Look, you don't even have to *do* anything – just stop asking damn fool questions in public.'

Ian stood up. 'Don't push me, Frank,' he warned.

'I haven't even started yet. For God's sake, be reasonable, Ian. Do you know how much the share price of the company has dropped since yesterday? All this adverse publicity is having an effect even in London. We're dropping money fast.'

'I bleed for you.'

'You know we're going to float a new issue of Hukahoronui shares. What chance do you think we'll have if you continue to hold up the chairman of the board as a bloody fool?'

'The foolishness of Crowell is none of my doing – he's a self-made idiot. That's why you have him there – because he'll jump when he's told. You ought to be getting rid of Crowell, not me.'

'You're impossible,' said Frank disgustedly. 'We're *not* getting rid of you.'

'No,' agreed Ian. 'I'm leaving under my own power, and in my own way. I don't take easily to blackmail, Frank, and the way you're going you're likely to cook your own goose.'

Frank looked up and said sharply, 'What do you mean?'

'Have you considered the composition of the Commission of Inquiry? There's Harrison, the chairman, and his two assessors, both experts in their fields. Rolandson knows about snow, and French is from the Department of Mines. He hasn't said much yet.'

'So?'

'So any more pressure from you and I'll start asking questions about conditions in that mine, and by the time I'm through French will write a report that'll curl your hair – a report that the shareholders won't like at all. Then you'll see something really happen to the share price.'

'You're being really hard-nosed about this, aren't you? Why, Ian?'

'Do you have to ask after what you've been doing? I don't like being manipulated, Frank. I don't like being pushed around. I'm no Crowell. And another thing: the day before I was fired – and let's give it the right name, Frank; none of this bull about suspension – I saw the result of the latest assay. Rich pickings, Frank, my boy; *very* rich pickings.

But can you tell me why those results haven't been given to the shareholders?'

'That's none of your bloody business.'

'It might be if I buy some shares. Not that I will, of course. That mine is going to make someone a fortune, but the way you'll set it up I don't think the ordinary shareholders will see much of it.'

'Nobody will make anything if you get on your hind legs and start asking damn fool questions about avalanche defences,' said Frank sourly. 'Good God, do you know how much it will cost us if this bloody Commission goes the wrong way?'

Ian stared at him. 'What do you mean – the wrong way? Were you thinking of *not* putting in avalanche defences?'

'Hell, there's only an avalanche every thirty years or so. By the time the next one comes the mine will be worked out.'

Ian took a deep breath. 'You damned fool! That was when the trees were still on the west slope. Now they're gone there's likely to be a fall in any period of heavy snow.'

'All right.' Frank flapped his hand impatiently. 'We'll re-afforest the slope. That'll cost less than the snow rakes your friend McGill wants to have.'

'Frank, do you know how long it takes for a tree to grow? I thought you lot were bad enough but now I know the depth of your greed.' Ballard's voice was hard. 'And I suggest we bring this conversation to a sudden halt.' He crossed to the door and threw it open.

Frank hesitated. 'Think again, Ian.'

Ian jerked his head. 'Out!'

Frank walked forward. 'You'll regret it.'

'How's Uncle Steve?'

'He's not going to like the answer I take back to Sydney.'

'He should have come himself and not sent a half-wit to do his dirty work. He's too intelligent to think threats would have any effect – he'd have tried a bribe, if I know him. Tell him from me that that wouldn't have worked, either. Maybe you'll be able to keep a whole skin that way.'

Frank paused outside the door, and turned. 'You're finished, Ian. I hope you know that.'

Ian closed the door in his face.

As he drove Liz back to the hospital to pick up her car he said, 'Sorry about the gloomy lunch, Liz. I have a few things on my mind.'

'It was a bit glum,' she agreed. 'What's the matter? Trouble with the family? You were all right until you saw your cousin.'

He did not answer immediately but pulled the car off the road and parked by the kerb. He turned to face her, and said, 'We both seem to have trouble that way. When were you thinking of going to England, Liz?'

'I haven't thought that far ahead.'

'I'll be going as soon as the inquiry is over. Why don't you come with me?'

'My God!' she said. 'Charlie would have kittens. Is this by way of being a proposal, Ian?' She smiled. 'Or do I come as your mistress?'

'That's up to you. You can take it either way.'

Liz laughed. 'Shakespeare didn't write this script. I know we're like the Montagues and Capulets, but Romeo never made an offer like that.' She put her hand on his. 'I like you, Ian, but I'm not sure I love you.'

'That's the problem,' he said. 'We haven't known each other long enough. Just two or three days at Huka, rudely interrupted by a disaster, and a week here. Love doesn't flourish under those conditions, especially when overlooked by brother Charlie.'

'Don't you believe in love at first sight?'

'I do,' said Ballard. 'Evidently you don't. It happened to me at the dance on the night everything started. Look, Liz: when I get on that plane I won't be coming back to New Zealand. I'd hate it like hell if I never saw you again. Maybe you don't love me, but it would be nice if you gave it a fighting chance.'

'Propinquity!' she said. 'A lovely word. Do you think it works?'

'What have you got to lose?'

She looked pensively through the windscreen, staring at nothing. Presently she said, 'If I do go to England with you – and I'm not saying right now that I will – but if I do there'll be no strings. I'm my own woman, Ian; a very private person. That's something Charlie can never understand. So if I come it will be my choice, and if after a while I leave you, it will be my choice again. Do you understand?'

He nodded. 'I understand.'

'And let me tell you something else, just to clear up something which may have been on your mind. Eric is against the Ballards on principle – it's not just you. But with Charlie it definitely is you. Now, I was only two when Alec died; I never knew him – not to remember. And you were twelve then, and now you're thirty-five. A person at twelve and a person at thirty-five are two different people, not to be confused with each other as Charlie does. I don't know the rights and wrongs of Alec's death – and I don't care. I'll be going to England with a man, not a boy.'

'Thanks,' said Ballard. 'Thanks, Liz.'

'Not that I've said I'm going with you yet,' she warned. 'I'll have to think about it. As to the question you asked – what have I got to lose?' She patted his knee. 'The answer, my dear Ian, is my virginity!'

SEVENTEEN

Ballard dropped Liz at the hospital and went on to Deep Freeze Headquarters. He did not find McGill at the office but finally ran him down at the Officers' Club where he was talking shop. Ballard said, 'I thought I'd pick you up first. Old Stenning will have travelled a long way and he'll be tired, so I thought I wouldn't keep him waiting around.'

'Sure,' said McGill. 'I'll come right along. When is he due in?'

'In fifteen minutes, if the plane's on time.'

They drove to Harewood Airport, two minutes away, and stood chatting on the concourse while they waited. McGill said, 'I've never met a millionaire's lawyer. Will you recognize Stenning when you see him?'

Ballard nodded. 'He's a tall, thin chap with white hair. Looks a bit like Bertrand Russell.'

The aircraft was on time and, as the passengers streamed through the terminal, Ballard said, 'There he is,' and McGill saw a tall, old man with the face of an ascetic. Ballard stepped forward. 'Good afternoon, Mr Stenning.' They shook hands. 'This is Mike McGill, a friend. He's come to carry the suitcases. I don't think they'll be long in coming.'

Stenning smiled. 'Are you the Dr McGill who has been giving evidence at the Inquiry?'

'Yes, sir.'

'If you're carrying suitcases you've come down in the world.'

'The luggage is coming now,' said Ballard. Stenning pointed out his cases, and Ballard said, 'Let's get this stuff out to the car, Mike.' As they left the terminal he said to Stenning, 'I've booked you a room at the hotel where I'm staying. It's quite comfortable.'

'Just point me towards a bed,' said Stenning. 'I find it difficult to sleep on aircraft. How is the Inquiry going?'

'I've kept the newspapers for you. It's getting good coverage in Christchurch.'

Stenning grunted. 'Good! I've been in aircraft for two days so I've fallen behind with the news. I'm looking forward to discussing the disaster with you, Dr McGill.'

'Any time I'm not in court, Mr Stenning.'

At the hotel McGill tactfully made himself scarce while Ballard showed Stenning his room. Stenning said, 'I'm not as resilient as I used to be, Ian. I'm going to bed. Your grandfather would have said a thing or two about that, were he here. At my age he was an assiduous globe-trotter.' He shook his head. 'I'm sorry he's gone.'

'Yes,' said Ballard. 'So am I.'

Stenning regarded him curiously. 'Are you?' he asked in a sceptical tone. 'If you'd have said the other thing I wouldn't have been surprised – or shocked. Your grandfather was a hard man to get on with. In my opinion he didn't treat you very well.'

Ballard shrugged. 'I'll miss him all the same.'

'So will I, Ian. So will I. Now, if you'll excuse a tired old man . . .'

'Have you eaten? I can get something sent in.'

'No – I just want my bed.'

Ballard indicated a cupboard. 'I laid in some drinks. There's whisky, gin and brandy – with the trimmings.'

'A kindly thought. A whisky before bed will go down very well. I'll see you tomorrow, Ian.'

Ballard left him and found McGill having a beer by the pool. McGill raised an eyebrow. 'Well?'

'Nothing,' said Ballard. 'He didn't say a damned thing.'

McGill frowned. 'I'll tell you something,' he said. 'He sure as hell didn't fly thirteen thousand miles to discuss a disaster with Mike McGill.'

Stenning was absent from breakfast next morning. McGill buttered a slice of toast. 'He doesn't seem to be in much of a hurry. Just like a lawyer; they work to a different sort of time from the rest of us.'

'I had a visit from one of my relatives yesterday,' said Ballard. 'My cousin Frank.' He told McGill what had happened.

McGill whistled. 'You Ballards play rough. Can he do what he threatened to do? Have you blackballed in the industry?'

'I doubt it. He might like to think he can. He could certainly make life bloody difficult.'

'How come Frank was in Sydney? Very convenient, wasn't it?'

'The Ballard Group has interests in many countries, including Australia. It's not unusual to find a member of the family popping up almost anywhere. I think my Uncle Steve, Frank's father, is also in Sydney. That's what Frank implied.'

McGill helped himself to marmalade. 'Goddamn convenient, all the same. Crowell knew they were in Australia because he blew the whistle on you. Frank came running fast enough.'

They talked desultorily until McGill had finished his coffee. 'I'm going to the hospital to see Joe. If Stenning has anything important to say he won't want me around.' He went away leaving Ballard to finish his breakfast alone.

Ballard read the Sunday papers by the pool, concentrating first on the account of the Inquiry. That did not take long, and he went on to the rest of the news which did not take long, either. He felt restless and thought of going to see Liz, but he did not want to leave the hotel without having seen Stenning. He went to his room and put on swimming trunks and worked out his frustration in several lengths of the pool.

It was eleven-thirty before Stenning appeared, carrying several newspaper clippings. 'Good morning, Ian,' he said briskly.

'Did you sleep well?'

'Like a babe. Only to be expected, of course. I had breakfast in my room. Where's Dr McGill?'

'He's gone to see Joe Cameron, the mine engineer. He's still in hospital.'

The clippings fluttered in Stenning's hand. 'So I gathered.' He looked around. 'We could do worse than have a chat here. Very nice place.'

Ballard unfolded another garden chair. 'The town is all right, too. Christchurch prides itself on being more English than England.'

Stenning sat down. 'I'm looking forward to seeing it.' He regarded the clippings, then folded them and put them into his pocket. 'You're having quite a time at this Inquiry. I don't think your family is going to like the things you've been saying.'

'I know they don't like it,' said Ballard. 'I had a visit from Frank yesterday. He wants me to shut up.'

'What did you do?' asked Stenning interestedly.

'I showed him the door.'

Stenning did not comment but he looked pleased in an indefinable way which Ballard could not place. 'You know, I was more than your grandfather's lawyer. I was also his friend.'

'I know he placed a lot of trust in you.'

'Trust,' said Stenning, and smiled. 'Trust – that's what I want to talk about. What do you know about the way your grandfather organized his affairs – I mean his financial affairs?'

'Practically nothing,' said Ballard. 'I knew that he put all, or most, of his money into some kind of trust a few years ago. He made it quite clear that I was not going to inherit, so I didn't take much interest. It was nothing to do with me.'

Stenning nodded. 'Yes, it was a little over seven years ago. Do you know anything about estate duties in the United Kingdom?'

'Death duties? Nothing much.'

'Then I shall enlighten you. A man may give his money away – to his family usually – to a charitable foundation, as Ben did. However, if he dies within seven years of the trans-action having taken place then his gift is assessed for estate duty just as if he hadn't made it at all. If he dies after seven years have elapsed then the gift escapes the tax.'

'I had heard about that,' Ballard smiled. 'I didn't worry too much about it, myself. I don't have much to leave, and I've no one to leave it to.'

Stenning shook his head. 'Every man must make provi-sion for the unknown future,' he said in a lawyerly way. 'Ben died after the seven-year period.'

'Therefore the foundation doesn't have to pay the tax.'

'Precisely. But it was a near-run thing. For one thing, the government changed the law and Ben squeezed in just under the deadline. For another he died just two weeks after the seven years were up. In fact, he nearly didn't make it at all. Do you remember him coming to see you just before you came to New Zealand?'

'Yes. It was when he offered me the job in Hukahoronui.'

'The effort nearly killed him,' said Stenning. 'The next day he took to his bed and never left it again.'

'He sent me his stick,' said Ballard. 'I had a bad leg at the time. He said he wouldn't need the stick again.'

'He didn't.' Stenning looked at the sky contemplatively. 'It was very important to Ben that he should see you at that time. The breaking of your leg was a minor disaster – you couldn't go to see him, so the mountain had to go to Mahomet. It was so important to him that he put at risk a very large sum of money – and more beside.'

Ballard frowned. 'I don't see how it could have been important. All he did was to twist my arm into taking the job at Hukahoronui – and look how that's turned out.' His voice was bitter.

'An avalanche wasn't part of Ben's plans – but it came in useful.' Stenning laughed as he saw the bafflement on Ballard's face. 'You think I'm talking in riddles? Never mind; all will be made clear. Let us look at the charitable foundation. Ben gave it all his personal fortune except what he needed to live on until his death, which wasn't much. Ben was not a man to flaunt prestige symbols; he had no Rolls Royce, for example. His needs were few and his life austere. But the foundation got a lot of money.'

'I could see how it might.'

'It does good work. The money or, rather, the interest on the money, supports several laboratories working mostly in the fields of mining safety and health. Very good and necessary work, indeed.'

'My God!' said Ballard in astonishment. 'Do the trustees know how the Ballard Group works? Every safety regulation is normally bent, or broken if they think they can get away with it. That's like giving with one hand and taking with the other.'

Stenning nodded. 'That perturbed Ben, but there was nothing he could do about it at the time for reasons you shall see. Now let us take a look at the trustees. There are five.' He ticked them off on his fingers. 'There's your uncle

Edward, your cousin Frank, Lord Brockhurst, Sir William Bendell and myself. I am the Chairman of the Board of Trustees of the Ballard Foundation.'

'I'm surprised that two of the family are trustees. From what Ben said the last time I saw him he had no great regard for them.'

'Ben made them trustees for tactical reasons. You'll see what I mean when I come to the nub. You're right, of course, in your assessment of Ben's attitude to the family. He had four sons, one of whom died here in New Zealand, and the other three turned out in a way he couldn't stomach. He had no great regard for any of his grandchildren, either, except one.' Stenning jabbed forward a thin forefinger. 'You.'

'He had funny ways of showing it,' said Ballard wryly.

'He'd seen how his sons had turned out and he knew that whatever else he was good at he was not a good father. So he saw to your education and left you strictly alone. He watched you, of course, and he liked what he saw. Now consider – what could Ben do a few years ago when he contemplated what was likely to happen to his personal fortune? He wouldn't give it to his family whom he didn't like, would he?'

'Not on the face of it.'

'No,' said Stenning. 'Anyway, as Ben saw it they already had enough. In all honesty, could he give it to you? How old were you then?'

'Seven years ago? Twenty-eight.'

Stenning leaned back. 'I rather think that when Ben and I first talked about setting this thing up you were twenty-six. Just a fledgling, Ian. Ben couldn't see himself putting so much money and power – and money is power – into the hands of one so young. Besides, he wasn't too sure of you. He thought you were immature for your years. He also thought your mother had something to do with that.'

'I know. He was scathing about her at our last meeting.'

'So he set up the Ballard Foundation. And he had to do two things: he had to make sure that he retained essential control – and he had to live for seven years. He did both. And he watched you like a hawk because he wanted to see how you turned out.'

Ballard grimaced. 'Did I come up to expectations?'

'He never found out,' said Stenning. 'He died before the Hukahoronui experiment was completed.'

Ballard stared at him. 'Experiment! What experiment?'

'You were being tested,' said Stenning. 'And this is how it went. You were now thirty-five; you were more than competent at any job you'd been given, and you knew how to handle men. But Ben had a feeling that you have a soft centre and he discovered a way to find out if this was indeed so.' He paused. 'I gather that you and the Peterson family have never got on too well together.'

'An understatement,' said Ballard.

Stenning's face was firm. 'Ben told me that the Petersons had walked all over you when you were a boy. He sent you to Hukahoronui to see if the same thing would happen.'

'Well, I'll be damned!' Ballard was suddenly angry. 'I knew he had a power complex, but who the hell did he think he was? God? And what the devil was it all for?'

'You can't be as naive as that,' said Stenning. 'Look at the composition of the Board of Trustees.'

'All right; I'm looking. Two Ballards, yourself and two others. What about it?'

'This about it. Old Brockhurst, Billy Bendell and I are all old friends of Ben. We had to have two of the family on the board so they wouldn't smell a rat. If they had suspected what Ben was up to they'd have found a way to shove their oar in and wreck Ben's plan. Any half-way criminal lawyer could have found a way of torpedoing the Foundation before Ben died. But for seven years the three of us have been playing the Ballards on a length of line so the boat wouldn't be rocked. We've been playing along with the two Ballards on the board, only forcing our hand in things which didn't matter too much to them. They think it's going to continue in this way – but it's not.'

'I don't see what this has got to do with me.'

Stenning said evenly, 'Ben wanted you on the Board of Trustees.'

Ballard gaped at him. 'So?'

'So it's arranged like this. The board is self-perpetuating. If a member retires there is a vote to elect his replacement and – this is important – the retiring member has a vote. Brockhurst is nearly eighty and has only held on to please Ben. When he retires you'll have his vote, you'll have Billy Bendell's vote, and you'll have my vote – and that's a majority and there's nothing the Ballards can do about it.'

Ballard was silent for a long time. Presently he said, 'This is all very well, but I'm not an administrator, at least, not of the trustee kind. I suppose there'd be an honorarium, but I have a living to earn. You're offering me a job for a retired business man. I don't want to run a charitable fund, no matter how big.'

Stenning shook his head sadly. 'You still don't get the point. Ben set up the foundation for one reason and one reason only – to prevent his fortune from being dissipated and to keep the Ballard Group intact but out of the hands of his sons.' He took an envelope from his pocket. 'I have here the share quotations of the companies in the Ballard Group as at the middle of last week.'

He extracted a sheet of paper from the envelope. 'It's astonishing what can be put on to a small sheet of paper like this.' He bent his head. 'The total value of the shares is two hundred and thirty-two million pounds. The holdings of the Ballard family – that is your uncles and all your cousins – is about fourteen million pounds. The holding of the Ballard

Foundation is forty-one million pounds, and the Foundation is by far the largest shareholder.'

He slipped the paper back into the envelope. 'Ian, whoever can swing most votes on the Board of Trustees controls the Ballard Foundation, and whoever controls the Foundation controls the Ballard Group of companies. For seven years we've been waiting for you to come into your inheritance.'

Ballard felt as though the wind had been knocked from him. He stared blindly into the shimmering pool and knew that the dazzle in his eyes did not come only from the sunlight reflected from water. That wonderful, egotistical, crazy old man! He rubbed his eyes and was aware of wetness. Stenning had been saying something. 'What was that?'

'I said there's a snag,' said Stenning.

'I suppose it's inevitable.'

'Yes.' A fugitive smile chased across Stenning's face. 'Ben knew he was dying. Two days before he died he extracted a promise from me to come out here and see the results of the Hukahoronui experiment – to see if the Petersons were still walking over you. As Ben's friend – and his lawyer – I feel bound to honour his last wish and to do what he would want to do himself were he alive.'

'So it's not settled.'

'I've been reading the newspaper accounts of the Inquiry with great interest. You've been putting up a good fight, Ian, but it seems to me that the Petersons are still walking over you. Ben considered that the man who cannot defend himself is not the man to control the Ballard Group – and I must say I tend to agree with him. The exercise of so much power demands steel in a man.'

'That's the second shock you've handed me today,' said Ballard softly.

'Not that I'm going on newspaper reports,' said Stenning. I'm too much of a lawyer to believe all I read. You'll get a fair judgment, Ian; but out of respect for Ben it must be an honest one.'

'And you are my judge. My sole judge?'

Stenning inclined his head. 'Ben relied on me a lot, but the last task he set me is the hardest burden I have had to bear. Still, I can't run away from it.'

'No,' said Ballard pensively. 'I don't suppose you can.' He thought of his own eagerness to escape from Hukahoronui when he was a boy of sixteen. The urge to run away from the oppressions of the Petersons had been overwhelming. 'I'd like to go away and think about this for a while.'

'Very understandable,' said Stenning. 'Will I see you at lunch?'

'I don't know.' Ballard stood up and picked up his towel. 'Mike McGill will be around. You can ask him about the avalanche.'

He walked across the lawn to his room.

THE HEARING

Fourth Day

EIGHTEEN

When, at breakfast the following morning, Stenning announced his intention of attending the Inquiry, Ballard said, 'That might not be easy. There's a great deal of interest and there are queues for the public seats. You can sit with me, if you like.'

'I doubt if that would be advisable,' said Stenning. 'The news of that would get back to your uncles very quickly. But it's all right, Ian. I telephoned Dr Harrison on Saturday before I went to sleep and he has found me a place.' He smiled. 'A courtesy to a visiting lawyer.'

Sharp! thought Ballard. *Very sharp!* He said, 'If you are there at all the news might get back to the family.'

Stenning cut a slice of grilled bacon in two. 'I doubt it. I'm not known in New Zealand and you tell me none of the family is here.'

At ten minutes to ten Ballard was in his seat and running through his notes. He saw Stenning come in preceded by an usher who showed him to a seat in the distinguished visitors' section. Stenning sat down and viewed the hall with interest, and his eyes passed Ballard without a flicker. He produced a notebook and a pen from his briefcase and laid them on the table before him.

As Ballard returned to his notes a shadow fell athwart the table and he looked up to see Rickman. 'May I have a word with you, Mr Ballard?'

Ballard nodded towards the rostrum. 'It will have to be a quick word. We'll be starting soon.'

'This won't take long.' Rickman leaned on the edge of the table and bent down. 'Mr Crowell was most annoyed on Friday at your treatment of him on the witness stand, but he's had the weekend to think it over and now he's in a more considerate frame of mind.'

'I'm glad to hear it,' said Ballard, keeping his face straight.

'You may not know it but Mr Crowell is about to be . . . er . . . translated to a higher station. He is taking the chairmanship of New Zealand Mineral Holdings, the parent company of the Hukahoronui Mining Company. It's been in the wind for quite some time.'

'That will be nice for him.'

'He feels that to do the double job – chairmanship of both companies – would be too much for him. Consequently the chairmanship of the mining company will fall vacant.'

'Interesting,' said Ballard neutrally. He said no more. He wanted Rickman to do the running.

'You know that assays at the mine before the avalanche showed a highly enhanced gold enrichment, and the board decided to float a share issue to capitalize extensive development work. Whoever is appointed chairman will be in a most favourable position. A considerable number of stock options will go with the job – that is, an option to buy so many shares at par.'

'I know what an option is.'

Rickman spread his hands. 'Well, then. When the news of the increased gold values is released the share price will inevitably go up. Anyone with options will be in a position to make a lot of money.'

'Isn't that illegal? Inside deals are frowned on.'

'I assure you that the way it will be done will be perfectly legal,' said Rickman smoothly.

'I'll take your word for that, Mr Rickman. You're the lawyer and I'm not. But I don't see what this has to do with me.'

'As chairman of the parent company, Mr Crowell will have a great deal to say in the appointment of the chairman of the mining company. He feels that you have qualities that make you suitable for the position should you wish to be considered as a candidate.'

'For what consideration?' Ballard asked bluntly.

'Come, now, Mr Ballard. We're both men of the world and we both know what we're talking about.'

'I detect the hand of Uncle Steve,' said Ballard. 'He jerks a string in Sydney and Crowell jumps.' He pointed to the empty witness chair. 'Crowell sat there on Friday and I roasted him to a turn. Now he offers me the chairmanship of the company from which he's just fired me as managing director. What sort of a man does that make Crowell, Mr Rickman?' He shook his head. 'I don't think you can count me in your list of candidates.'

Rickman frowned. 'It's a position few young men would turn down – especially in view of the evidence which may be forthcoming presently at this Inquiry – evidence particularly damaging to yourself. The effect of that evidence *could* be minimized.' He paused. 'Or vice versa.'

'I wouldn't want to be a man of your world, Mr Rickman, or that of Crowell. I'm a plain-speaking man and I'll tell you what I think. First you attempt to bribe me, and now you threaten me. I told Frank Ballard that neither would work. Now I'm telling you the same. Get lost, Mr Rickman.'

Rickman's face darkened. 'If I had a witness to that little speech I'd have you in court for slander.'

'You're making damned sure you don't have a witness,' retorted Ballard. 'Why have you been whispering?'

Rickman made an ejaculation of disgust, turned his back and walked to his seat where he held a rapid conversation with Crowell. Ballard looked at them for a moment and then turned his attention to the seats reserved for witnesses. Mike McGill raised his eyebrows in silent interrogation, and Ballard winked at him.

He had told Mike in confidence why Stenning had flown to New Zealand in such a hurry, and McGill had choked over his beer. 'Two hundred and thirty-two million pounds . . .!' He set down his glass and gazed into space, his lips moving silently. 'That's over six hundred million bucks – even by American standards that's not puny.'

'It's not mine,' said Ballard drily. 'It belongs to the shareholders.'

'That may be, but you'll control it. You'll be able to steer it wherever you like. That's a hell of a lot of power.'

'I'm not a trustee yet. It's Stenning's decision.'

'No, it isn't,' said McGill sharply. 'It's your decision. All you have to do is to steamroller the Petersons. Stenning told you as much. My God, but that grandfather of yours must have been a hellion in his time. He could think up the nicest tricks.'

'Steamroller the Petersons,' repeated Ballard. 'Liz might not think a hell of a lot of that.'

'The world well lost for a woman – is that what you think?' McGill snorted. 'Well, Stenning has made the issue quite clear. If he'd spelled it out in words of one syllable and had them tattooed on your chest he couldn't have been clearer. You've got to nail the Petersons' hides to the barn door, and you have to do it publicly at the Inquiry. That's your last chance.'

Ballard was acid. 'And just how am I going to do that?'

McGill shrugged. 'I don't know. Up to the time of the first avalanche they were pussyfooting around with local politics

and they might come in for a bit of censure on that score.
But after that they didn't put a foot wrong. They did all the
right things at the right time and they'll get the credit for it.
Charlie even volunteered to go on the slope with me after
the avalanche when I thought there might be a second fall.
That took guts. There's no faulting the Petersons from here
on in.'

'So there's no steamroller.'

McGill laughed – a humourless bark. 'Oh, sure there is.
There are going to be questions asked about your decision
about the mine. Eric made the right suggestion and you
turned it down. Over fifty people died, Ian. There's a steamroller, all right; but the Petersons are driving it, and they're
going to trundle it right over you.'

NINETEEN

Eric Peterson was giving evidence.

'It must have been somewhere between half past six and seven o'clock on the Sunday morning when my brother, John, came and woke me. With him were Mr Ballard and Dr McGill. They said there'd been an avalanche. At first I didn't believe them. I'd heard nothing, and according to the scare story the town would be blotted out if they were right. But John said the Gap was blocked and that no one could get in or out.'

He shrugged. 'I still didn't really believe it, but John was very convincing. Then he said that if the Gap could be blocked like that then perhaps Dr McGill was right about the danger to the town from the west slope. My brother got busy on the telephone and called an emergency council meeting. It was getting on towards eight o'clock by then and beginning to get light. We held the meeting in the Supermarket.'

There was no cold glare from the overhead fluorescent tubes that Sunday morning. Two oil lamps gave a warmer glow which paled as the sky grew brighter. There was no sunlight yet; the sun had to rise high to clear the eastern slope of the valley and to burn off the mist which hung heavily.

Eric Peterson stoked up the old-fashioned pot-bellied stove with billets of wood, and commented, 'I'm glad we didn't get rid of this relic.' He jerked his thumb towards the back of the store. 'Back there I have two thousand gallons of fuel oil that's good for damn all. The central heating system needs two electric motors to drive it.'

'What's keeping Matt?' asked Mrs Samson fretfully.

'He'll be along,' said John Peterson. 'You know Matt – slow but reliable.'

Eric put the lid back on to the stove. Then there are the fridges and the cold room, all with no power. A good thing this didn't happen in summer.'

'For Christ's sake!' said John irritably. 'Use your bloody brains for once. How in hell could it happen in summer?'

Eric paused in surprise. 'I was forgetting. What I meant was . . .'

'To the devil with what you meant. If you can't talk sense, shut up!'

Tempers were becoming uncertain. McGill said calmly, 'I think we ought to begin without waiting for Mr Houghton. We can fill him in later.'

'No need,' said Phil Warrick. 'He's here now.'

Houghton walked up the aisle towards the group around the stove. 'I know we agreed to meet this morning, but this is beyond a joke. Do you know the time?'

John Peterson raised his hand. 'There's been an avalanche in the Gap, Matt. It's blocked completely. There's so much snow in there you can't see the top.'

'You mean we can't get out?'

'Not in cars,' said McGill.

Houghton looked about uncertainly, and John Peterson said, 'Sit down, Matt. When there's been one avalanche there can be another. I suggest we apologize to Dr McGill and listen to his suggestions.'

'No apology needed – and here's my first suggestion.' McGill surveyed the small group. 'There aren't enough of us here. I want more men brought in; strong men who don't scare easy. And women, too; but no shrinking violets – I want the bossy kind.' Three people started to speak at once and he held up his hand. 'Mrs Samson, will you act as secretary. Take down the names of those who are suggested.'

Eric said, 'There's paper and pencil at the cash desk. I'll get it.'

Ten minutes later McGill said, 'That ought to be enough. Mrs Samson, will you go out immediately, round up all those people and see they get here as soon as possible.'

She got up. 'They'll be here.'

Ballard gave her a note. 'Give that to Joe Cameron. I think you'll find him at the mine, not at his house.'

Mrs Samson left. McGill looked outside at the thin light. 'The first thing that should be done is to let outside know what's happening here. As soon as it gets light enough I want men to climb out; two teams of two men each, for insurance. I'll write letters for them – we don't want the information garbled.'

Ballard said, 'You'll need a secretary for that stuff. You can have Betty from the mine.'

McGill nodded shortly. 'If what comes down the hill is a powder avalanche – which it might be – then this store is going to go.'

'You think it might?' asked Eric.

'I'm certain, now the trees are gone.'

'For God's sake!' snapped Eric. 'Every time I ask a question he blames me for cutting trees.'

McGill hit the side of a display stand with the flat of his hand. It made a noise like a pistol shot and Warrick jumped visibly. 'Now listen to me,' said McGill in a harsh voice. 'We'll all get on better if there are no recriminations. I wasn't blaming anybody; I was just stating the obvious.'

Ballard chipped in, and pointed to the door. 'There'll be a lot of people coming in just now, and we're going to tell them they're facing disaster. They'd better not find out that the town council has had the information for nearly twenty-four hours and has been sitting on it. Got the picture, Eric?'

John's voice was cold. 'I told you once, Eric: if you can't talk sense then shut up.' He nodded to McGill. 'Go on.'

'All right. Accept that this place is likely to go. I want all these shelves stripped and the food taken to a safe place.' His eyes shifted and settled on Phil Warrick. 'Could you organize that, Mr Warrick?'

'Sure,' said Warrick. 'But where's a safe place?'

'Turi Buck's house for a starter – I'll let you know of others later. Begin with staples – leave the chocolate biscuits until last. And if you can find some empty drums you can drain off fuel oil from the tank that Eric mentioned. If we're hit we'll need heat as well as food.'

'Right,' said Warrick with decision. Ballard thought that Warrick was a good man as long as he had to take orders and not give them.

'Don't forget the stock-rooms at the back,' said John Peterson.

Houghton said, 'That's all right for the food, but what about the people? We can't put the whole population in Turi Buck's house. I think we all ought to go up the east slope.'

'That's out for a start,' said McGill. He leaned forward. 'I hope it doesn't happen, Mr Houghton, but if a powder avalanche comes down the west slope it will cross the valley bottom and go clean across the river. I don't know how far it will go up the east slope.' Houghton looked sceptical, and McGill tapped him on the knee. 'It will be moving very fast, Mr Houghton. Not only faster than you can run, but faster than you can drive a car.'

'Is that your guess, McGill?' asked Eric.

'That's my estimate. The snow in the avalanche at the Gap was a bit too dry for my liking. The drier it is the more likely it is to form a powder avalanche, and the drier it is the faster it moves. What's more, the more the temperature drops the drier it will get.' McGill nodded to the window. 'The temperature is dropping very quickly.'

Warrick said, 'If the temperature is dropping what about the mist out there? You'd think it would freeze out of the air.'

McGill frowned, then said, 'Take it from me the temperature is falling. It's dropped a degree and a half since I got up this morning.'

'So where do the people go?' reiterated Houghton.

'We'll know better when I look at the map we had yesterday.' There was a movement at the entrance to the Super market, and McGill said to Warrick, 'Go up there and keep those folk corralled for a while. We've got to talk to them all at once. Let me know when they're all here.'

'All right,' said Warrick.

'And don't tell them a damn thing,' said McGill. 'We don't want panic. Just say they'll know everything in – ' He cocked his head and looked past Houghton at John Peterson – 'fifteen minutes.' John nodded.

Warrick went away, and Eric said, 'Of course, there's a perfect place to put the people. What about the mine? It's like a bloody big air raid shelter. It's right inside the mountain.'

'Hey, that's a thought!' said Houghton.

'I'm not sure it's a good one.' McGill dropped his chin into his hand. 'The portal is right at the bottom of the slope and any avalanche is going to go right over it.'

'That's all right,' said John Peterson. 'That's why they build snow galleries over roads. I've seen them in Switzerland. The snow goes straight over the top.'

'And if, as you said, most of the snow will go right across the valley, then there'll be no trouble in getting out when it's over,' said Houghton.

'That's when I was talking about a powder avalanche,' said McGill. 'But supposing the temperature starts to rise, then it won't be a powder avalanche. It will be slower and wetter and a hell of a lot of snow will pile up at the bottom of the slope. And that blocks the mine portal. Wet snow sets like concrete after an avalanche.'

'The mine has the equipment,' said John Peterson. 'If they can mine rock, they can mine snow – or ice. They could be out an hour after it's over.'

McGill stared at him. 'I don't think we're on the same wave-length. Do you know how much snow there is on the west slope?'

'I don't suppose I do – not really.'

'Well, I've done some figuring, and my estimate is a million tons – plus.'

Eric burst out laughing, and Houghton said flatly, 'Impossible!'

'What's so goddamn impossible about it? You've got nearly two thousand acres up there covered with over six feet of snow. Ten inches of new-fallen snow equals an inch of rain – but the rain runs off while the snow stays. But that snow up there has been compressed so I reckon you have the equivalent of about eight inches of water lying up there – maybe more. You don't need a goddamn slide rule to work out the weight of that lot. And it's been snowing like crazy for the last thirty-six hours, so I'm likely to be underestimating.'

There was silence. McGill rubbed the side of his jaw with a rasping sound. 'What do you think, Ian?'

'As far as the mine goes, I'm more worried about the powder avalanche. From what I've seen of your mathematical description of a powder avalanche I'd say you are using fluid dynamics.'

McGill nodded. 'That's right.'

'I thought so. Well, if you have a fluid flowing past the portal at the speeds you've been describing you'll get some weird effects inside the mine. It'll be like blowing across the top of a beer bottle, but more so.'

'Suction,' said McGill. 'Goddamn it – it might pull all the air right out. I hadn't thought of that one.'

'I'll talk to Cameron,' said Ballard. 'Perhaps we can build a baffle or gate of some kind.'

'Let's leave it at that,' said McGill. 'It's something to think of if we run out of other places to go. Let's move on to the next step. Suppose there is an avalanche and someone gets caught. What do we do about it?'

'There won't be much anyone can do,' said Houghton. 'Not from the way you've been talking. They'll be dead.'

'Not necessarily, and it's a defeatist assumption no one must make. Freakish things happen during avalanches. Now, what we've got to get over to these people here is the necessity for speed in rescue once we've been hit. We have to tell them what to do.'

'You have to tell them what to do,' said John Peterson.

'I accept that,' said McGill grimly.

Someone walked along the aisle from the entrance. Ballard turned his head and saw a uniformed policeman walking towards them. A sudden inspiration hit him and he smote McGill on the back. 'Radio!' he said. 'Pye has a transmitter – he must have.'

Arthur Pye stopped. 'Morning, John. What's the trouble? Ma Samson said you wanted to see me on the double.'

Ballard cut in. 'Arthur, you have a radio transmitter, don't you?'

Pye turned. 'Yes, Mr Ballard, normally I do. But not right now. It's been acting up a bit, so it went in for servicing on Friday. I'll have it back tomorrow.'

McGill groaned. 'It's a flaming conspiracy!'

'What's going on?' demanded Pye.

Matt Houghton opened his mouth to speak, but John Peterson put up his hand and explained the problem concisely. Pye regarded McGill with interest. 'This true?'

McGill nodded. 'That's how the power and phone lines were cut. Has anyone else got a transmitter? No radio hams?'

'Not that I know of,' said Pye. 'Maybe one of the scouts. I'll ask Bobby Fawcett.' He turned to John Peterson. 'What's being done about this?'

John indicated the growing crowd at the entrance. 'We're getting together some of the steadier people. I'll tell them the score, and McGill will advise on what to do about it.' He shrugged. 'He's the only one who knows.'

'You'd better do it quickly,' advised Pye. 'They're getting a bit restive.'

John Peterson looked at McGill who nodded. 'Right. Let's get to it.'

McGill said to Ballard, 'Ring up Turi Buck and tell him to prepare to play host to a crowd of kids.' He stood and joined Peterson and Pye. 'We'll be forming an avalanche committee but it's not going to be a talking shop – not if I can help it.'

'It won't be,' promised Pye.

McGill nodded in appreciation. 'You're on it, Mr Pye; and we'd better have a doctor. Now let's go and break the bad news.'

Eric Peterson said, 'So my brother told those people that Mrs Samson had brought in. They didn't believe it at first – not until someone came in from the street and said he couldn't get through the Gap. Even then they took a lot of convincing that the town was in danger.' He shrugged. 'It was just like that first council meeting, but on a bigger scale. Everybody wanted to argue the toss.'

'What time was it then?' asked Harrison.

'Half past eight, going on nine.'

'Then it would be light?'

'Yes and no. In Huka there are mountains on both sides so we don't get direct sunlight until fairly late in the morning. The sky was light enough but there was a thick mist.'

Professor Rolandson held up a finger and Harrison nodded. 'You have said that Dr McGill told you the temperature was falling. And that Mr Warrick queried that because of the mist. I must say I don't understand it myself. I would have thought that, in those conditions, the mist would have frozen out as hoar frost. Was any explanation given for this?'

'None that I heard.'

'And was it still snowing at this time?'

'No, sir, it had stopped. It didn't snow for the rest of that day.'

Rolandson leaned back, and Harrison said, 'How was this situation finally resolved? I mean the convincing of the chosen group.'

'It was Arthur Pye who did it. He listened to the arguments for a while, then jumped in and said it was time to cut the cackle. He was very forceful about it.'

Harrison raised his head and addressed the hall. 'It is a great pity that Constable Pye cannot be here to give evidence. As you may know, he was killed after the avalanche in a most valiant rescue attempt. Yesterday I was informed that Constable Pye and Mr William Quentin, the union representative at the mine, have been posthumously awarded the George Cross by Her Majesty.'

There was a murmur of voices and sporadic clapping which grew quickly into a storm of applause. The Press gallery bubbled and boiled. Harrison let the applause run its course and then tapped on the rostrum. 'Let us get on with the evidence.'

The hall quietened, and Harrison said to Eric Peterson, 'Can you tell us what Mr Ballard was doing at this time?'

'He used the telephone, and then talked to Mr Cameron for a while.'

'He did not participate in any of the arguments?'

'Not then. He took Mr Cameron on one side and they talked together.'

'You did not hear what they said?'

'No, sir.'

Harrison looked at Ballard. 'In view of a certain decision that was made about this time, I would like to hear what was said in that conversation. You are excused, Mr Peterson. Will you step forward, Mr Ballard?'

TWENTY

Ballard was tense. In Hukahoronui he had made a decision, and now he was called upon to justify it. Because of that decision fifty-four people had died who might now be alive and the knowledge lay heavily upon him. He clasped his hands tightly to prevent his fingers trembling.

Harrison said, 'Can you give us the gist of the conversation you had with Mr Cameron at that time?'

Ballard's voice was steady. 'We talked about Mr Eric Peterson's proposal that the mine be used as a shelter. I had already talked with Dr McGill about what to expect of avalanches, and he said that powder avalanches were very fast – anything up to a maximum of two hundred and eighty miles an hour.' He paused. 'That's the translational speed, of course.'

'You mean the general speed of the advancing snow mass?' asked Rolandson.

'Yes. But inside the mass there would be a considerable turbulence, according to Dr McGill. There would be a swirling action resulting in momentary gusts of up to twice the translational speed.'

Rolandson raised his eyebrows. 'You mean there could be gusting at speeds in excess of five hundred miles an hour?'

'So I was informed by Dr McGill.'

'I see your problem. You were afraid of an organ pipe effect as the avalanche swept past the portal of the mine.'

'Yes, sir. The suction would be tremendous.'

'And what of the second type of avalanche?'

'The wet snow avalanche would come down much more slowly – possibly at a speed of thirty to forty miles an hour. As a result of this relatively slow speed it would tend to pile up before the portal, and Dr McGill told me that snow of that nature sets hard into ice immediately. I was faced with the possibility of having several hundred thousand tons of ice of an unknown thickness between hundreds of people in the mine and the outside world. These were the problems discussed by myself and Mr Cameron.'

'And what were Mr Cameron's views?' asked Harrison.

Cameron was pungent. 'Jesus!' he said incredulously. 'You want to put the whole population into a hole in a mountain?'

'It's a shelter.'

'Okay, it's a shelter – I know that – but there are problems. So many problems. I don't know where to start. For instance, when is this disaster supposed to happen?'

'It may never happen.'

'Exactly. So how long are they going to sit in there just waiting? They might stand it a day, but when nothing happens they'll want out. Do you think you can stop them?'

'The town council might.'

Cameron made a hawking sound at the back of his throat which indicated his opinion of the council. 'To tell the truth, I'm not too happy about *anyone* being in the mine if there's going to be a fall. A million tons of snow falling an average vertical height of three thousand feet must set up *some* vibrations.'

Ballard narrowed his eyes. 'What are you getting at, Joe?'

'Well, you know we've been cutting a few corners.'

'I've seen some of the corners that have been cut. In fact, I've written a report for the board. I've not been here long, Joe; not long enough to put things right. I'm telling you now that it's got to stop. Why, in the name of God, did you let them get away with it?'

'I wasn't high man on the totem pole,' snapped Cameron. 'My immediate boss is that spineless lump of jelly, Dobbs – and above him was Fisher with one leg in the grave and incompetent in the first place. And the men were just as bad. That production bonus you've been handing out is goddamn near criminal. The guys are only human and if a shot-firer, say, can earn a fast buck by ignoring a regulation he'll go for the dough every time. And Dobbs looked the other way because he got a piece of the cake, too.'

'And you?'

Cameron looked at the floor. 'And maybe me, too.' He looked up at Ballard challengingly. 'I'm not justifying it. I'm just giving you the facts. I'm not like Dobbs – I didn't do it for the money. I did it for the job, Ian. I had to hold on to the job. This is the last job I'll hold as chief engineer. If I lose it I'll be on the way down – I'll be assistant to some smart young guy who is on his way up – and when you get to my age you can't afford to take chances like that. If I hadn't played along I'd have been fired.'

He laughed humourlessly and tapped Ballard on the chest. 'But don't tell me you haven't had your worries already. I did my best, I tell you I really did, but those business sharks in Auckland are a tight-fisted lot of bastards – all take and no give. I pleaded with Dobbs – I pleaded with Fisher – for more money to go into safety, to go into supporting structures. All I got was the one answer – "Make do."'

Ballard rubbed his eyes. 'All that's water under the bridge. What's worrying you?'

'I'll tell you. If that lot falls off the mountain – wet snow or dry, it doesn't matter – it's going to make a hell of a big thump. Now, maybe we've been interpreting the rules a mite too freely but I wouldn't want to be in there when it happens. I don't think the supporting structures will take it.'

Ballard drew in his breath. 'That's a hot one, Joe. Anyone in the mine now?'

'Sunday maintenance crew. Half a dozen guys. Engineers and electricians.'

Ballard's voice was as cutting as a knife-edge. 'Get them out. Get them out now. And bloody well jump, Joe.'

He turned on his heel and went to the noisy argumentative crowd near the door. Arthur Pye raised his voice in a bull bellow. 'Quiet! Let's hear what McGill has to say about that.'

McGill turned as Ballard arrived at his elbow. 'We've been discussing Eric Peterson's idea of using the mine as a shelter. I think it's not such a bad idea. I think we can discount the suction effect if Joe Cameron can put a stopper at the entrance. And it will easily hold everyone.'

'No,' said Ballard. 'Nobody is going in. I've just ordered the men who are already in the mine to come out.'

There was a babble of voices, cut short again by a blast from Pye. He said, 'Why not, Mr Ballard?'

'Because I don't think it's safe. Mr Cameron has just pointed out that a million tons of snow hitting the valley bottom will make quite an impact. I don't think the mine is safe.'

Pye frowned. 'Not safe?'

'It's my decision, and I've made it,' said Ballard. 'As soon as the men are out I'm having the entrance sealed.'

'Well, that's it,' said McGill. 'No need to argue any more about it.' He looked curiously at Ballard before he turned to Pye. 'I want four men, experienced in the mountains if possible. They'll need ropes and ice-axes, if you have them.'

'Some of the scouts are good climbers.'

'They'll do,' said McGill briefly. 'Where's the secretary you promised me, Ian?'

'And that's how it was,' said Ballard.

Harrison opened his mouth and then closed it. He leaned back and said to the assessor on his left, 'Do you have any questions, Mr French?'

'Indeed I have.' French drew his chair around so that he could get a good view of Ballard. 'You know that I am from the Department of Mines, Mr Ballard?'

'Yes.'

'I have followed your evidence with great care. Are we to believe that you ordered the mine sealed because you thought there would be a danger of tunnel collapse in the event of an avalanche?'

'That is correct.'

'Are you aware that because of the particular nature of this country the mining regulations are framed in such a way as to take account of earthquakes?'

'I am.'

'And so, even if a large quantity of snow did come down the west slope above the mine, there would be little or no damage providing the regulations had been followed. Do you believe that?'

'Yes.'

'And so, by pursuing the course of action which you did, you evidently believed that the regulations, as laid down in law by my department, had not been followed?'

'I believe, with Mr Cameron, that the regulations had been rather too freely interpreted, largely in the interests of economy. It was not a thing I would have relished arguing with an Inspector of Mines, had there been one there.'

'That, Mr Ballard, is a very damaging admission,' said French coldly.

'I admit that, sir.'

'And so, believing this, you had the mine sealed. In the ensuing disaster fifty-four people were killed. After the disaster the mine was unsealed and the supporting structures had, in the event, proved to be equal to the shock. Nothing had collapsed in any part of the mine. If the whole population of Hukahoronui had sheltered in the mine, as was proposed by Mr Eric Peterson, they would have been all safe. What do you say to that, Mr Ballard?'

Ballard looked troubled. 'It has weighed heavily on my mind ever since the avalanche. It is evident that I made the wrong decision, but it is only evident in hindsight. I was there and the decision was up to me, so I made it on the basis of available evidence.' He paused. 'I must add that were I placed in the same position again I would not vary my decision.'

There was an uneasy rustle from the public gallery and the floor creaked. Harrison said gently, 'But the mine *should* have been safe, Mr Ballard.'

'Yes, sir.'

'And it was not?'

'It was not.'

Rolandson leaned forward, his elbows spread wide on the rostrum, and looked across at French. 'Was the mine unsealed by a member of the Inspectorate of Mines, Mr French?'

'Yes, it was.'

'What were his views on the supporting structures that he found?'

'His report was unfavourable,' said French. 'I might add that he made a verbal report to me immediately after his inspection, and his remarks were unprintable.'

Ballard said, 'I made a similar report to the board of the company. I request that it be introduced as evidence.'

Harrison leaned forward. 'Mr Rickman, can that report be produced?'

Rickman conferred in whispers with Crowell for a few minutes, then he looked up. 'I am instructed to inform the Commission that no such report has been received from Mr Ballard.'

Ballard was pale. In a controlled voice he said, 'I can provide the Commission with a copy of that report.'

'With respect, Mr Chairman,' said Rickman. 'The fact that Mr Ballard can provide a copy of a report does not necessarily mean that a report was sent to the board of the company. In point of fact, any report that Mr Ballard may present to the Commission may have been written *post facto*.'

Harrison looked interested. 'Are you seriously suggesting that the report Mr Ballard has offered to me has been fraudulently written after the event?'

'With respect, I am merely pointing out the possibility that it could have been written yesterday.'

'An interesting suggestion, Mr Rickman. What do you think of it, Mr Ballard?'

Ballard looked at Rickman who looked back at him blandly. 'Mr Rickman is imputing that I am a liar.'

'Oh no!' said Rickman with an ingenuous air. 'Only that you very well could be.'

'Mr Rickman is also not improving my present frame of mind,' said Ballard. 'I would delight in answering any questions concerning the safety of the mine from Mr French, from Mr Gunn, who represents the General Mining Union, or from any other interested person.'

The smile disappeared from Rickman's face as Gunn seized upon the offer. 'Mr Ballard, you have said the mine was not safe. Apart from this disputed report, did you mention the matter to anyone else at that time?'

'I did. I talked about it in conversations with Mr Dobbs, Mr Cameron, and Dr McGill, both before and after the avalanche.'

'Had you taken steps to right matters?'

'I wrote the report and was preparing to follow it up.'

'How long was it before the disaster that you took up your position with the company?'

'Six weeks.'

'Only six weeks!' echoed Gunn in well-simulated surprise. 'Then Mr Rickman, or even Mr Lyall, can hardly suggest that you were responsible for the state of affairs in the mine.'

'I had no intention of suggesting it,' said Lyall drily.

Rickman remained silent.

'But someone must have been responsible,' pursued Gunn. 'What, in your opinion, was the reason for this scandalous state of affairs?'

'The mine was teetering on the verge of profitability. If it was not to make an actual loss all margins had to be shaved. Any money that went into the mine went towards productivity – towards profit. Anything that did not conduce towards productivity went to the wall – and that included safety margins.' Ballard moved in his chair and looked towards Rickman. 'Now that a rich vein of conglomerate ore has been struck one hopes that more money will go to safety.'

Rickman leaped to his feet. 'Mr Chairman, I must protest. The witness is giving away the very secrets of the company – secrets he acquired in the course of his duties. Is this the conduct of a responsible managing director?'

Pandemonium broke out in the Press gallery. Lost in the uproar was Ballard's retort, 'Don't you mean ex-managing director?'

TWENTY-ONE

When the Commission of Inquiry reconvened in the afternoon Harrison said acidly, 'I hope we do not have a recurrence of the behaviour which led to the adjournment of this morning's session. Whether Mr Ballard was wise to say what he did is not for me to judge. However, I believe he was goaded into it by the adversary tactics I warned against at the opening of this Inquiry. Mr Rickman, I give you a final warning: you must not be over-zealous in the protection of your client's interest. One more instance like that of this morning and I shall have to ask your client to find someone else to represent him.'

Rickman stood up. 'I apologize to the Commission if I have offended in any way.'

'Your apology is accepted.' Harrison consulted his notes. 'I would like to ask one further question of Mr Ballard. It will not take long and you may keep your seat. Mr Ballard, you say that you consulted with Mr Cameron. I have looked through your evidence most carefully and I find that Mr Dobbs, the mine manager and Mr Cameron's superior, has figured little. Where was Mr Dobbs all this time?'

Ballard hesitated. 'I don't really know. Something seemed to have happened to him.'

'Such as?'

'Something psychological, I'd say. He seemed to retreat into himself. He relinquished all his duties into my hands. Naturally I was perturbed about this, so I sent Dr Scott to talk with Mr Dobbs to see if he could discover what was the matter. I think his evidence would be best. I am not a medical authority.'

'Yes, that would be best. I will call him later, if it proves necessary.' Harrison consulted his notes again. 'Dr McGill seems to have effectively taken charge at this time. He was, as it were, the organizing force because only he had any idea of what was to come. I think we had better hear his testimony.'

McGill took his seat, and said immediately, 'I think I can clear up a point that was worrying Professor Rolandson. The mist.'

Rolandson looked up. 'Yes, I'd like to know about that.'

'It worried me, too,' said McGill. 'Although I tried not to show it. I couldn't see how there could be so much mist in a rapidly falling temperature. It was quite thick – almost to be classified as a fog – and was very troublesome to us. It was only after the avalanche that I got it figured out.'

He knew he would be giving evidence all afternoon so he made himself comfortable in his seat. 'You may remember that the first avalanche blocked the river as well as the road. The river had been frozen, but of course the water flowed freely under the ice. When the river was blocked the water rose and broke the ice. That water was relatively warm and on contact with the cold air produced the mist. It was actually freezing out into frost all the time, but as the water spread over low ground there was a great deal of surface area presented to the air, and mist was being generated faster than it was frozen out.'

'An ingenious theory,' said Rolandson. 'And no doubt correct.'

'As I say, it gave us a great deal of trouble that day. It hampered our operations considerably.'

'What was the prime consideration in your mind?' asked Harrison.

'The safety of the people,' said McGill promptly. 'And I had a great deal of co-operation once the gravity of the situation was made clear. I would like to say now that those who had already realized that gravity gave of their utmost. I would like especially at this time to commend John Peterson.'

Harrison nodded and made a note. 'What steps were taken?'

'It was important to communicate with outside. Two teams were sent to climb out of the valley as soon as light permitted. One team was to climb the avalanche debris blocking the Gap, while the other took a more circuitous route. Once that was set going, I had all the children rounded up and sent to Turi Buck's house which was on the record as being safe. At this time I became worried about the vulnerability of the central, and I – '

'The central?' queried Harrison.

'I'm sorry,' said McGill. 'A transatlantic – or transpacific – confusion. You'd call it the exchange – the telephone exchange. It was right in the open and sure to be hit – and yet we had to have communications. A failure of the telephone system during the organizing period would have made things most difficult. I discussed this with Mr Ballard and Mr Peterson, and one of the mine electricians volunteered to man the board. However, Mrs Maureen Scanlon, the operator, would not give up the board. She said she would be derelict in duty and refused to leave, She also said that it was her board and that no one else was going to touch it.'

McGill lowered his voice. 'The telephone system worked perfectly all during the organizing period and right up to the time of the avalanche, when the exchange was destroyed and Mrs Scanlon was killed. Mr John Peterson was also killed at that time in an effort to save Mrs Scanlon.'

The silence in the hall was total, and then there came a long, shuddering sigh.

Harrison said quietly, 'You seem to have had your hands very full.'

'Well, Mr Ballard and John Peterson were very able joint chiefs of staff, as you may say. Mr Ballard provided all the resources of the mine and did the organizing from that end, while Mr John Peterson did the same for the town, aided by the other members of the council. The main problem at first was to convince the town people that we were serious, and this is why the telephone system was so important. The council members spoke personally by telephone to every head of household in the valley. For myself, I merely provided overall direction in order to prevent mistakes being made and, after a while, I was able to think of what to do after the avalanche hit.'

Professor Rolandson said, 'How certain were you, at this time, that there would be another avalanche?'

'I was not dealing in certainties but in probabilities. As a scientist I am accustomed to doing this, but it does tend to preclude exactness. Avalanches are notoriously unpredictable. I know of a case in Switzerland where a five-hundred-year-old-building was swept away, thus proving that no avalanche had followed that path for five hundred years. No one could have predicted that. But based upon my investigation of the slope and upon what little theory we have and my own past experience I put the chance of an avalanche at about seventy per cent – and rising as the temperature fell.'

'Would you say rising to eighty per cent?'

'Yes, I'd say that, or even higher.'

'Let me put that in lay terms,' said Rolandson. 'What Dr McGill is saying is that the chance of *not* having an

avalanche was the same as throwing a die and showing a six
on the first throw. The chances of an avalanche occurring,
in his opinion, was about four or five to one.'

'Odds that only an inveterate gambler would accept,'
commented Harrison. 'I take it that the people were advised
to go to safe places. Who determined those places?'

'I did, sir.' McGill hesitated. 'Safety is relative. To tell the
truth, I wasn't even too sure of the safety of Turi Buck's
house with all the trees gone from the slope. But it was the
best we had and that's why we put most of the children
there. As for the rest, I looked at the map and as much of
the actual ground as I could – the mist made that difficult –
and tried to take advantage of topographical features; anything to put something between the people and the snow.'
He paused. 'In one case I have to say I made a bad error of
judgment.'

'No one can blame you for that,' said Harrison.

'Thank you, sir. The main difficulty was to get the people
to move. No one wanted to leave a warm house to stay in
the open in the snow, and the thick mist didn't make the
prospect more inviting. Constable Pye, a very forceful man,
did a lot there.'

'You say there came a time when you were able to think
of what to do after the avalanche. What did you mean by
that?'

'Speed in rescue after an avalanche is the first essential,
but the rescuers must know what they're doing. To find a
person buried in snow is exceptionally difficult. Swiss experience shows that it takes a trained team of twenty men
twenty hours to thoroughly probe an area of one hectare.'

'A hectare being two-and-a-half acres,' interjected
Rolandson.

'Well, we had no trained men and we had no equipment.
We couldn't be sure of outside help so we had to improvise
with what we had. We stripped TV antennae from the

houses; these provided aluminium tubing to make probes for the rescue teams. Mr Cameron, at the mine workshop, made them up into lengths of ten feet. I organized three teams, a total of sixty men, and tried to give a crash course in avalanche rescue.'

'At what time was this?'

McGill shook his head. 'I couldn't say, sir. I was too busy to keep my eye on the time.'

The mist was clammy against the skin. It wreathed in coils as the slight breeze shifted and the range of vision changed sharply. A large group of men, bulky in cold weather clothing, milled about somewhat aimlessly, some stamping their feet to keep warm, others blowing on their fingers and beating their arms across their chests.

'All right, you guys,' yelled McGill. 'Those who have probes step forward and line up.' He inspected them with a critical eye. 'Line up as though you're in the army and on parade – shoulder to shoulder and standing at ease. Feet about ten inches apart.'

The men shuffled about. There was embarrassed laughter as they realized the spectacle they must make. 'There's nothing funny about this,' snapped McGill. 'You other guys gather around and watch.'

He walked forward, holding a ball of string and gave the end to the man on the extreme left of the line. 'Hold that.' He walked along the line, unreeling string, until he was at the extreme right, then he cut the string, and gave it to the man on the end. 'Now, you two guys are the markers. Bend down and stretch that string tight on the snow. Everyone else put the toes of their boots against the string.'

He watched them get into position. 'Right. Now, in front of you is an area in which you think someone is buried, but you don't know exactly where. You put the probe just in front of the toe of your left boot, and push down. You'll hit

bottom hereabouts at less than three feet. If there's an avalanche there'll be a hell of a lot more snow than that.'

All the men probed. 'Okay, now you do the same at the
toe of your right boot.'

Someone called out. 'How do we know when we've
found a body?'

'You'll know,' said McGill. 'It's unmistakable. If you hit a
body go easy on the pressure – don't use that probe as a
spear. Call your team leader who will mark the spot for the
digging team. Right, now you markers take a step forward –
not more than a foot – and stretch that string again. All you
others put your toes against it and probe again the same
way as before.'

He turned to the crowd of watchers. 'You see what
they're doing? They're probing every square foot; we call
this a fine search, and there's a ninety-five per cent chance
of finding a body if there's one there. For a really fine search
you probe in front of each boot and then again in the middle. That gives a hundred per cent chance, providing the
body isn't deeper than your probe.'

Someone said, 'It's bloody slow, though.'

'Right,' said McGill. 'It's slow. When the next lot of
probes comes I'm going to teach you guys coarse probing.
There's a thirty per cent chance of missing a body, but it's
faster and sometimes speed is more efficient than thor-
oughness.'

'Here comes Cameron with more probes now,' someone
called.

McGill swung around to see the truck coming towards
them. As it pulled to a halt he said, 'Okay, get them out of
there.'

He pulled out a packet of cigarettes. Cameron got out of
the cab and crunched across the snow to take a cigarette
from the outheld packet. 'Thanks, Mike. How are you
doing?'

McGill looked about to make sure he was out of earshot of the men. 'Not good. You know how long it takes to train the men of the Parsenndienst in Switzerland? And *they* have the equipment.'

'What's that . . . what you said? Some sort of snow rescue service?'

McGill nodded. 'These guys are enthusiastic enough, but when it comes to the crunch they'll not be much use. Some of them might be under the snow, instead of on top where I want them. The rest will be good for nothing.'

'How do you mean?'

'A million tons of snow – or anything else, for that matter – dropping close by takes the pith out of a man.' McGill blew a long plume of smoke. 'It's known as disaster shock. We'll need outside help and we'll need it fast, and I hope to hell they have dogs. A trained dog can find a body in a tenth of the time it takes a twenty-man team. Half the victims of avalanches in Switzerland are found by dogs.'

Cameron turned and watched the line of men probing into the snow. 'Then what are you doing all this for?'

'Just to keep up morale. It helps if they have something to do. How many probes did you bring?'

'Twenty. There'll be another twenty in under an hour.' He looked back at the truck. 'They've unloaded. I'll be on my way.'

'Okay, Joe.' As Cameron drove away McGill stepped forward. 'You guys with the new probes come over here. I'll show you coarse probing.' He paused as a Land-Rover swept up and stopped close by. Two men got out, one of them Ballard. McGill had not seen the other man before.

Ballard hurried over. 'Mike, this is Jack MacAllister. He came over the Gap.'

'We met a couple of your people on top,' said MacAllister. 'They've gone on to get to a telephone. They told us what was happening so I came on down to see for myself.'

'Thank God!' said McGill. It was a cry from the heart. He sized up MacAllister. 'What are the chances of evacuating the valley – all the people?'

MacAllister shook his head. 'Not a chance. It took me all my time getting over. That snow has set solid – it's more like ice now. In places it's a vertical climb. But the telephone boys are trying to get a line over now.'

'That'll be a help.' McGill dropped his cigarette and put his foot on it. 'At least we've got through to outside. Better late than never.'

'They knew last night,' said MacAllister unexpectedly. I telephoned the police. There's a whole gang of them on the other side of the Gap right now. They pitched up just as I started to climb.'

'Better and better.' McGill turned to Ballard. 'You know what's been worrying me?'

'What?'

McGill pointed upwards. 'Not being able to see that god-damn slope because of the mist. It's been giving me a real prickly feeling.'

'Hush!' said MacAllister. 'What's that?'

'What's what?'

'Listen!'

There was a faint drone from overhead, growing louder. 'An airplane,' said McGill, straining his eyes against the mist.

'He can't land in this,' said Ballard.

They listened while the aircraft circled overhead but they did not see it. It droned for about ten minutes and then went away, only to return five minutes later.

'And that's it,' said McGill. He put his hands flat on the arms of the witness chair and looked at Harrison. 'That's when the avalanche hit us.'

TWENTY-TWO

Harrison drew in a long breath. 'And so we come to the avalanche itself. It has been suggested in the Press that the sound of that aeroplane, which had been sent to investigate by Civil Defence, was the trigger which set the avalanche in motion. What are your views on that, Dr McGill?'

'That's utter nonsense, sir,' said McGill baldly. 'The idea that sound can trigger an avalanche is a myth, an old wives' tale. In the United States supersonic aircraft studies have been made. Even the high overpressure of two pounds a square foot caused by a military aircraft like the Hustler has had no detectable effect.' He paused. 'But that's in normal use. In Montana experiments were made by F–106 aircraft making aimed dives and pulling out at supersonic speeds. Those did cause avalanche release. But the plane I heard flying over Hukahoronui could not in any way have triggered that avalanche.'

Harrison smiled. 'The pilot of that aircraft will be very glad to hear that. I believe it has been on his conscience.'

'It needn't be,' said McGill. 'That snow was ready to come down, and it came down without his assistance.'

'Thank you, Dr McGill. It appears that the pilot and observer of that aircraft were the only people to see the avalanche as it began to fall. From the depositions I have read

211

it appears that the observer has more to offer in evidence. You are excused, Dr McGill. Please call Flying Officer Hatry.'

Hatry took his seat. He was a fresh-faced young man of about twenty, wearing the uniform of the RNZAF. Reed asked, 'Your name?'

'Charles Howard Hatry.'

'Your occupation?'

'Flying Officer, Royal New Zealand Air Force.'

Harrison said, 'How was it that you came to be flying over Hukahoronui at that time?'

'Orders, sir.'

'And what were your exact orders?'

'To fly to Hukahoronui, and to land if possible. To find out the situation and radio back. I believe the orders originated with Civil Defence. That's what I was told, anyway.'

'Just so. Carry on.'

'Flight-Lieutenant Storey was the pilot and I was the observer. We flew to Hukahoronui from Harewood Airport, here in Christchurch. When we got there we found that landing was out of the question. There was a thick layer of cloud or mist on the valley floor. It would have been pretty dangerous going into that. We radioed this information back to Christchurch and were told to fly around for a while in case the mist lifted.'

'What were weather conditions like – other than the low mist?'

'Very good, sir. The sky was clear and the sun very strong. The clarity of the air was exceptional. Very good for photography. I remember saying to Lieutenant Storey that I thought it would be cold outside. It was that sort of day – crisp and cold.'

'You mentioned photography. Were you instructed to take photographs?'

'Yes, sir. I took two complete spools of the area around the valley – seventy-two exposures in all. These included

photographs of the misted area just in case it meant anything. I couldn't understand the mist, sir, because everything else was so clear.'

Harrison shook out some glossy black-and-whites from
an envelope. 'And these are the photographs you took?' He
began to hold them up one at a time.

Hatry leaned forward. 'Yes, sir, those are the official photographs.'

'I see you took a picture of the snow which blocked the
Gap.'

'Yes – we flew low to take that one.'

'You say these are the official photographs. Are we to
understand that there are some *unofficial* photographs?'

Hatry shifted in his seat. 'I'm keen on cine-photography
and I just happened to have my camera along. It isn't up to
much – just eight millimetre. Conditions were so good and
the mountains looked so beautiful that I decided to shoot off
a reel.'

'And while you were shooting this film the avalanche
began and you managed to film it?'

'Some of it, sir.' Hatry paused. 'It's not a very good film,
I'm afraid.'

'But when you had it developed you realized its importance and you offered it to this Commission as evidence. Is
that it?'

'Yes, sir.'

'Well, then, I think the film will be the best evidence
available. Please have the screen set up, Mr Reed.'

The hall buzzed with voices as the ushers set up the
screen and projector. Curtains were drawn over the windows. In the semi-darkness Harrison said, 'You may begin at
any time.'

There was a click and a whirr, and the screen lit up with a
series of rapidly flashing letters against a blurred white background. Suddenly a recognizable scene appeared – white

mountains and a blue sky. It disappeared to be replaced by a shot of the ground. 'That's the valley,' said Hatry. 'You can see the mist.' He stopped as though conscious of committing *lèse-majesté*. 'I'm sorry, sir.'

'That's all right, Mr Hatry. Make whatever comments you please.'

'There's not much during the first half,' said Hatry. 'Just mountains. Some good views towards Mount Cook.'

The film ran on. It could have been any amateur travelogue – hand held and unsteady. But the tension in the hall grew as the seconds went by and scene followed scene.

Presently Hatry said, 'I think it's coming along about now. I asked Lieutenant Storey to fly north along the Hukahoronui valley.'

'How high were you flying?' asked Rolandson.

'A little over two thousand feet above the valley floor.'

'So that the west slope of the valley actually stretched above you.'

'Yes, sir. Afterwards I found the slope was six thousand feet from crest to valley. Here it is now.'

It was an upward shot showing a little blue sky at the top of the screen, then there were a few scattered rocks jutting up, and then the snow so white as to make the eyes ache which filled the rest of the screen. As an artistic composition it was terrible, but that did not matter.

The scene suddenly jogged and blurred, and then steadied again. 'That's it,' said Hatry. 'That's when it started.'

A faint plume of grey had appeared, a shadow cast by rising snow, which grew larger as it moved down the slope. It disappeared sideways as though the camera had panned away. The next shot was of distant mountains and sky, very wobbly. 'We had trouble in positioning the aircraft,' said Harry apologetically. 'I suppose we were excited.'

There came another shot of a boiling cloud of whiteness shadowed by grey which plunged down the mountainside, growing in extent continually. Ballard licked dry lips. He had once seen a big oil fire, and watching this growing cloud advancing down the slope reminded him of the billowing clouds of black smoke from that fire, but seen, as it were, on negative film.

Again the scene jerked off the screen and there came a dizzying view of the ground whirling in a spiral. 'I asked Lieutenant Storey to bank,' said Hatry, 'so I could get a good view into the valley. He did it a bit too quickly.'

The camera steadied and it could be seen that the whole of the upper slope was in motion and the line of advance was incredibly fast, even when seen from a distance. Blurred and unsteady though the film was, the sight was impressive.

Suddenly there was a complete change of scene. The moving front of the avalanche was now much farther down the mountain, almost near the bottom, and approaching the bank of mist which covered the valley floor. Hatry said, 'We were flying out of distance. We had to make a quick circuit and come back.'

Something surprising was happening to the mist. Long before the approaching front of snow was near it, the mist was driven back as though an invisible jet was playing on it. It cleared magically and buildings could be seen briefly. Then the snow swept over everything.

The screen flashed blindingly white and there was a flapping sound as the tail of the film was slapped around by the reel of the projector. 'That's when the film ran out,' said Hatry.

'Will someone draw the curtains?' said Harrison. The curtains were drawn open and he waited until the hum of conversation ceased. 'So you took the film. What did you do next?'

'We radioed back, telling what we'd seen.'

'And what was the result of that?'

'They asked us if we could land. I checked with Lieutenant Storey and he said not. There was still some mist about, but that wasn't it. You see, he didn't know *where* to land after the snow had gone over everything. We were then ordered to return to Christchurch.'

'Thank you, Mr Hatry. You may step down.' Harrison looked towards McGill. 'Have you any comments on what you have just seen, Dr McGill? You may answer from where you are sitting.'

'It was most interesting from a professional point of view. If we know the number of frames per second of that film we can measure the speed of the avalanche very accurately and in detail. One of the most interesting features is that it showed something which we have always suspected and, in a sense, knew, but could not prove. Because of the mist we could see that there was an air blast in advance of the moving mass of snow. At a very rough estimate I would put that air blast as moving at something over two hundred miles an hour. Apart from the actual snow impact, such a blast could cause considerable damage. I think the film should be preserved and, indeed, duplicated. I wouldn't mind having a copy of it myself for study.'

'Thank you.' Harrison looked at the clock. 'The time has come for our adjournment. We meet here again at ten o'clock tomorrow morning.'

His gavel tapped on the rostrum.

TWENTY-THREE

McGill joined the throng leaving the hall. Ahead he saw the tall figure of Stenning walking next to Ballard. They were not talking to each other and, once through the doorway, they made off in different directions. He smiled and thought that neither of them was giving the Ballard family any grounds for suspicion.

'Dr McGill!' Someone caught his elbow and he turned to find the Peterson brothers just behind him, first Eric, and then the bulkier figure of Charlie behind. Eric said, 'I'm glad you said what you did about Johnnie. I'd like to thank you for that.'

'No need,' said McGill. 'Credit should be given where it's due.'

'All the same,' said Eric a little awkwardly, 'it was good of you to say so in public – especially when you're on the other side, so to speak.'

'Now hold on a minute,' said McGill sharply. 'I'm a neutral around here – I'm on no one's side. Come to that, I didn't know there were sides. This is an inquiry, not a court battle. Isn't that what Harrison insists?'

Charlie looked unimpressed. 'You're a neutral like I'm the fairy queen. Everybody knows that Ballard and you are in each other's pockets.'

'Shut up, Charlie!' said Eric.

'Why the hell should I? Harrison said he wants the truth to come out – but is it? Look at the evidence this morning. Not nearly enough was made of the fact that Ballard made a bad mistake. Why didn't you prod Lyall into going for him?'

'Oh, Charlie, enough is enough.' Eric looked at McGill and shrugged expressively.

'Not for me it isn't,' said Charlie. 'All I know is that I used to have three brothers and now I've got one – and that bastard killed two of them. What do you want me to do? Stand still while he murders the whole Peterson family?'

'Give it a rest, for Christ's sake!' said Eric exasperatedly.

'Fat chance,' said Charlie, and tapped McGill on the shoulder. 'Now, Dr Neutral McGill – don't tell me you won't be seeing Ballard tonight.'

'I'll be seeing him,' said McGill evenly.

'Well, you tell him what I think. Eric made the suggestion of using the mine as a shelter but Ballard turned him down because the mine wasn't safe. The safety of the mine was Ballard's responsibility – he was in charge, wasn't he? And the mine wasn't safe. In my book that's criminal irresponsibility and I'm going to see he gets nailed for it. You're his friend – you tell him that.' Charlie's voice rose. 'You tell him, if I can't get him for murder I'll get him for manslaughter.'

Eric held his arm. 'Keep your voice down. Don't make one of your bloody scenes in here.'

Charlie shook his arm free. 'Don't tell me what to do.' He stared at McGill with hot eyes. 'And tell that bloody murdering friend of yours to keep out of my way, because if I ever come across him I'll tear him apart piece by piece.'

McGill looked about him. Apart from the three of them the hall was now empty. He said, 'Threats like that are very unwise. Threatening a witness in this Inquiry could get you into trouble.'

'He's right,' said Eric. 'For God's sake, keep your mouth shut. You talk too much – you always have.'

'I'll do more than talk before I'm through.' Charlie's forefinger bored into McGill's chest. 'Tell Ballard that if he so much as looks at Liz again I'll kill the bastard.'

'Take your goddamn hand off me,' said McGill softly.

Eric pulled Charlie away. 'Don't start a fight here, you damned fool.' He shook his head wearily. 'Sorry about that, McGill.'

'Don't apologize for me,' shouted Charlie. 'Christ, Eric, you're as chicken as everybody else. You go arse-creeping to McGill – the high and mighty Dr Know-it-all-McGill – and thank him kindly for putting in a nice word for the Petersons. What the hell is this? Damn it, you know that he and Ballard are running a cover-up operation that makes Watergate sound like a fairy story. What the hell's got into you?'

Eric took a deep breath. 'Charlie, sometimes I think you're going out of your mind. Now will you, for God's sake, shut up? Let's go and have a beer and cool down.' He took Charlie by the arm and steered him towards the door.

Charlie allowed himself to be led away, but twisted his head and shouted to McGill, 'Don't forget to tell Ballard. Tell that son of a bitch I'll have him in jail for ten years.'

At the hotel Stenning went to his room to clean up. The climate was hotter than he was used to and he felt uncomfortably sticky. His suit was too heavy for the New Zealand summer and he made a mental note to buy a lightweight suit since it seemed that the Inquiry would continue for some time to come.

He felt better after he had bathed and he sat for a while in his dressing-gown while he made notes of the events of the day, amplifying the hasty scrawls he had made during the Inquiry. He shook his head over the evidence and thought that young Ballard was not in a favourable position; the business of the safety of the mine might go heavily against him should someone try to push the point. He thought about it and decided that Rickman would let it lie; he wouldn't want to bring up anything that would reflect on the company. Gunn, the union lawyer had gone out of his way to be kind to Ballard while still sticking his knife into the company. Stenning was surprised that the Petersons' lawyer, Lyall, had not made an issue of it. Perhaps that was to come.

After a while he dressed and went outside to find Ballard sitting at a table near the pool with an extraordinarily beautiful young woman. As he approached, Ballard caught sight of him and stood up. 'Miss Peterson, this is Mr Stenning, a visitor from England.'

Stenning's white eyebrows lifted as he heard the name, but he merely said, 'Good evening, Miss Peterson.'

'Have something cooling,' suggested Ballard.

Stenning sat down. 'That would be most welcome. A gin and tonic, please.'

'I'll get it.' Ballard strode away.

'Didn't I see you at the Huka Inquiry this afternoon?' asked Liz.

'I was there. I'm a lawyer, Miss Peterson. I'm very interested in your ideas of administrative justice here in New Zealand. Dr Harrison was kind enough to provide me with a place.'

She fondled the ears of her dog which sat by her chair. 'What's your impression so far?'

He smiled, and said with a lawyer's caution, 'It's too early to say. I must read a transcript of the early part of the Inquiry. Tell me, are you related in any way to the Peterson family that is involved?'

'Why, yes. Eric and Charlie are my brothers.'

'Ah!' Stenning tried to add things up and failed to find an answer, so he repeated his observation. 'Ah!'

Liz picked up her Cuba Libre and sipped it while regarding him over the rim of the glass. She said, 'Have you known Ian Ballard long?'

'We're fellow guests in the hotel,' he said, blandly avoiding the question. 'Have *you* known him long?'

'All my life – on and off,' she said. 'More off than on. There was a big gap in the middle.' She had noted Stenning's evasiveness and began to wonder just who he was. 'That was when he left for England.'

'Then you must have known him when he was a boy in Hukahoronui.'

'I don't think you need to read a transcript of the Inquiry,' she said, a little tartly. 'That wasn't in evidence today.'

'No,' he agreed. 'I think I read it in a newspaper report.'

Ballard came back and put a frosted glass in front of Stenning. Liz said, 'Mr Stenning is being mysterious.'

'Oh! What about?'

'That's what's mysterious. I don't know.'

Ballard looked at Stenning and raised his eyebrows. Stenning said easily, 'Miss Peterson is a remarkably sharp young lady, but perhaps she sees mysteries where none exist.'

Liz smiled, and said, 'How long have you known Mr Stenning, Ian?'

'Twenty years – or a little under.'

'And you're just good friends,' she suggested. 'And fellow hotel guests, of course.'

'Perhaps I prevaricated, Miss Peterson,' said Stenning. 'But I had my reasons. Perhaps you would be good enough not to mention my name in connection with Mr Ballard.'

'Why should I mention you?'

Stenning picked up his drink. 'It happens. Casual conversations cover a lot of ground.'

Liz turned to Ballard. 'What is all this?'

'It's just that Mr Stenning and I have business which we'd prefer not to parade before other people at this time.'

'Something to do with the Inquiry?'

'Nothing to do with the Inquiry,' he said flatly. He turned to Stenning. 'Talking of the Inquiry, Rickman tried to pull a couple of fast ones this morning before the opening. He came over to me and . . .'

He stopped as Stenning raised his hand and said, 'Am I to take it that you don't mind if Miss Peterson hears about this matter?'

'Why shouldn't she hear it?' asked Ballard in surprise.

Stenning frowned. 'I'm sure I don't know,' he said perplexedly.

'All right, then. First Rickman tried to bribe me, then to blackmail me.' He retailed what Rickman had said.

Stenning grimaced. 'Was there a witness to this interesting conversation?'

'No.'

'A pity. I'd take delight in having the man disbarred.'

Liz laughed. 'You have wonderful friends, Ian. Such nice people.'

'Not nearly as wonderful as the Petersons.' Ballard looked up. 'Here's Mike. What kept you?'

McGill put a glass and a bottle of 'DB' beer on the table. 'A run-in with Liz's charming brothers. Hi, Liz. I won't ask "How's the family?" because I know. Did you enjoy the show, Mr Stenning? It was a nice movie.'

'It had its moments of drama.' Stenning sat back in his chair and watched Ballard and Liz Peterson with curious eyes.

'What about my brothers?' Liz asked.

McGill filled his glass. 'Eric's all right,' he said, intent on not letting the beer foam over. 'But have you ever wondered about Charlie? If I were a psychiatrist I'd tend to diagnose paranoia.'

'Did he make another of his big scenes?'

'And how!' McGill jerked his head at Ballard. 'He threatened to dismember Ian from limb to limb if he ever meets him.'

'Talk!' said Liz scornfully. 'That's all he ever does.'

'Maybe,' said McGill. 'Ian, if you and this wench are going to consort you'd better wear a blindfold. He said that if you so much as look at Liz he'll kill you.'

Stenning broke in. 'And was there a witness to *this* conversation?'

'Just me and Eric.'

'And he used the word "kill"?'

'The very word.'

Stenning shook his head. Liz said, 'I'll have a talk with Master Charlie. He's got to get it into his thick skull that my life is my own. This time it won't be a plate of spaghetti that I'll crown him with.'

'Liz, be careful,' warned McGill. 'I'm getting the idea that he's genuinely unbalanced. Even Eric thinks he's losing his marbles. It took Eric all his time to hold him in.'

'He's just a big blow-hard,' she said. 'I'll sort him out. But let's not talk about the Petersons – let's not talk at all. How's your tennis, Ian?'

'Not bad,' said Ballard.

She held up her glass. 'Bet you another of these you can't beat me.'

'Done,' he said promptly.

'Let's go,' she said, and stood up.

McGill turned his head and watched them as they walked towards the tennis courts with Victor trotting behind, then he turned back and grinned at Stenning. 'Do you find our conversation stimulating, Mr Stenning?'

'Interesting, to say the least. Miss Peterson is also interesting.'

'An understatement typical of a lawyer.' McGill topped up his glass. 'Tell me – If Ian marries a Peterson, does that count in your Peterson Bashing Contest?'

Stenning moved nothing except his eyes which he slanted at McGill. 'So he told you about that. Your question is hard to answer. I doubt if it is what Ben had in mind.'

'But circumstances alter cases.'

Stenning said austerely, 'That truism has no legal validity.'

Avalanche

TWENTY-FOUR

High on the western slope and deep in the snow layer the processes of disaster were well advanced. Destructive metamorphism had long since ceased and constructive metamorphism was well under way. Air, slightly warmed from the ground, rose upwards through the snow laden with water vapour until it reached the impenetrable layer of hoar frost half way through the snow mass. Here it cooled giving up the vapour to create the tapered cup crystals.

By now the cup crystals were large and well formed, some of them being over half an inch in length.

The heavy snow-fall of the past two days had added an increased weight which, operating vertically through gravity against the cup crystals on the slope, had led to a delicately unstable position. A man may take an orange pip, hold it gently between forefinger and thumb, and squeeze ever so gently – and the orange pip will be propelled with considerable velocity. So it was on the western slope. A heavy-footed hawk alighting on the snow could provide that little extra pressure and set the cup crystals in motion.

Something like that did occur and a small slippage started. It was not very much and could have been spanned by a man with outstretched arms. The new-fallen surface snow, very cold, dry and powdery, was lifted a little by the sudden movement and a small white plume arose like a puff of smoke. But underneath chaos had begun. The fragile ice plate of the hoar layer cracked, jostling the cup crystals beneath which began to roll. The delicate bonds which held the snow together sheared, and cracks spread wide, zig-zagging at high speed from the point of original breakage. It was a chain reaction; one event followed another in lightning succession and suddenly a whole section of the snow fifty feet across slumped forward and downward, adding its weight to the untouched snow farther down the slope.

Again the inevitable action and reaction. Event followed on event even faster and presently the whole of the higher slope across a front of a hundred yards was in movement and plunging downwards.

As yet it was not moving very quickly. Five seconds after the first slippage an agile man caught in the open two hundred yards down the slope could have avoided death by running aside not very quickly. The speed of the young avalanche at this time was not much more than ten miles an hour. But the motion and the air resistance caused the light, feathery surface snow to rise and, as the speed increased, more and more of the snow powder became airborne.

The powder mixed turbulently with the air to form essentially a new substance – a gas with a density ten times that of air. This gas, tugged down the slope by the force of gravity, was not checked very much by friction against the ground, unlike the snow in the main avalanche. The gas cloud picked up speed and moved ahead of the main slide. Twenty seconds after the first slippage it was moving at fifty miles an hour, hammering gustily at the snow slope and smashing the delicate balance of forces that held the snow in place.

This was a self-energizing process. More snow was whirled aloft to increase the gas cloud and the avalanche, no longer an infant but lustily growing, fed hungrily on the snow lower down the slope. Already the whole of the upper slope was boiling and seething across a front of four hundred yards, and clouds of snow rose like the thunderheads of a hot summer's day, but incredibly faster.

The avalanche cloud poured down the mountainside even more quickly. At seventy miles an hour it began to pull into itself the surrounding air, thus increasing its volume. Growing thus, it again increased its speed. At a hundred miles an hour the turbulence in its entrails was causing momentary blasts of two hundred miles an hour. At a hundred and thirty miles an hour miniature tornadoes began to form along its edges where it entrained the ambient air; these whirlwinds had internal velocities of more than three hundred miles an hour.

By this time the mature avalanche was encountering air resistance problems. It was moving so fast that the air in front did not have time to get out of the way. The air was compressed and this caused its temperature to rise sharply. Pushed by the heavy avalanche cloud, an air blast began to develop in front of the rapidly moving snow, a travelling shock wave which could destroy a building as effectively as a bomb.

Now fully grown, the avalanche rumbled in its guts like a flatulent giant. A million tons of snow and a hundred thousand tons of air were on the move, plunging down towards the mists at the bottom of the valley. By the time the mist was reached the avalanche was moving at over two hundred miles an hour with much greater internal gusting. The air blast hit the mist and squirted it aside violently to reveal, only momentarily, a few buildings. A fraction of a second later the main body of the avalanche hit the valley bottom.

The white death had come to Hukahoronui.

I

Dr Robert Scott regarded Harold Dobbs with a professionally clinical eye. Dobbs looked a mess. Apparently he had not shaved for a couple of days and the stubble was dirtily grey on his cheeks and chin. His eyes were bloodshot and red-rimmed and he sullenly refused to meet Scott's gaze. His fingers twitched jerkily in his lap as he sat in the armchair, his face averted.

Scott noted the nearly empty gin bottle and the half full glass on the occasional table by the chair, and said, 'That's the only reason I'm here. Mr Ballard asked me to call in. He's worried that you might be ill.'

'There's nothing wrong with me,' said Dobbs. His voice was so low that Scott had to bend forward and strain his ears to catch the words.

'Are you sure you're the best judge of that? I'm the doctor, you know. What about me opening the little black bag and giving you a check over?'

'Leave me alone!' flared Dobbs in a momentary access of energy. The effort seemed to exhaust him and he relapsed into inanition. 'Go away,' he whispered.

Scott did not go away. Instead he said, 'There must be something wrong, Harry. Why haven't you been working for the past couple of days?'

'My business,' mumbled Dobbs. He picked up the glass and drank.

'Not entirely. The company is entitled to some sort of explanation. After all, you *are* the mine manager. You can't just abdicate without saying anything.'

Dobbs eyed him sullenly. 'What do you want me to say?'

Scott used shock tactics. 'I want you to tell me why you're swinging the bloody lead, and why you're trying to climb into that gin bottle. How many of those have you gone through, anyway?' Dobbs was obstinately silent, and

Scott persisted, 'You know what's going on out there, don't you?'

'Let Ian Bloody Ballard handle it,' snarled Dobbs. 'It's what he's paid for.'

'I think that's unreasonable. He's paid to do his own job, not yours as well.' Scott nodded towards the window. 'You should be out there helping Ballard and Joe Cameron. They've got their hands full right now.'

Venom jetted from Dobbs. 'He took my job, didn't he?'

Scott was puzzled. 'I don't know what you mean. He took nothing. What happened was that you stayed at home and cuddled up to a bottle.'

Dobbs flapped his hand; it wobbled loosely at the wrist as though he had no proper control over it. 'I don't mean that – I don't mean manager. The chairman promised me the job. Crowell said I'd go on the board and be managing director when Fisher went. But oh no! Along comes this young Pommy sprout and gets the job because he's called Ballard. As though the Ballards don't have enough money – they've got to take mine.'

Scott opened his mouth and then closed it again as Dobbs continued to speak. He looked pityingly at the older man as he ranted on. The floodgates of resentment had burst open and Dobbs was in full spate. Spittle drooled from the corner of his mouth. 'I'm getting no younger, you know. I've not saved as much as I hoped – those thieves on the stock exchange took a lot of my money. Rogues, the lot of them. I was going to be managing director – Crowell said so. I liked that because I'd have enough to retire on in a few years. Then the Ballard family decided otherwise. They not only took my job but they expect me to serve under a Ballard. Well, they can damn well think again.'

Scott said gently, 'Even so, that's no excuse for pulling out now without a word. Not when there's trouble. You won't be thanked for that.'

'Trouble!' Dobbs ground out the word. 'What does that whippersnapper know about trouble? I was running a mine when he was having his nappies changed!'

'It's not the mine,' said Scott. 'It's the town.'

'A lot of bloody nonsense. The man's an idiot. He's talking of spending millions to stop a few flakes of snow falling off a hillside. Where's the money to come from – I ask you that? And now he's got everyone running in circles like chickens with their heads cut off. And they tell me he's closed down the mine. Wait until they hear about that in Auckland – to say nothing of London.'

'You seem well informed for one who hasn't been out of the house for a couple of days.'

Dobbs grunted. 'I have my friends. Quentin came in to see what we could do to stop this fool.' He picked up the glass and drank again, then shook his head. 'Quentin knows the score all right but there's nothing he can do. There's nothing any of us can do. It's all cut and dried, I tell you.'

Scott's eyes narrowed. It had not taken him long to come to the conclusion that Dobbs was definitely unbalanced. Resentment had been festering within him and something had happened to cause it to burst out, and he had a good idea of what it was. Deliberately he said, 'Do you think you could have handled the job of managing director?'

Rage burst from Dobbs. 'Of course I could,' he yelled. 'Of course I could have done it.'

Scott stood up. 'Well, it doesn't matter now. I think we'd better get you to a safer place than this. If anything happens out there this house will be one of the first hit.'

'Poppycock!' jeered Dobbs. 'A lot of flaming poppycock! I'm not moving and no one can make me.' He grinned, his lips drawn back ferally over his teeth. 'I might move if young Ballard comes here and apologizes for taking my job,' he said sarcastically.

Scott shrugged and picked up his bag. 'Suit yourself.'

'And close the door when you leave,' Dobbs shouted at Scott's back. He wrapped his arms about his thin body. 'I *could* have done the job,' he said aloud. 'I *could* have.'

When he heard Scott's car start up he picked up his drink and went to the window. His eyes followed the car until it went out of sight and then he shifted his gaze to the mine buildings. It was difficult to see very far because of the mist, but he could just make out the outline of the office block. He shook his head sorrowfully. 'Closed down!' he whispered. 'All closed down!'

Suddenly the mist cleared as though by magic and he felt a strange vibration through the soles of his feet. The office block, now clearly to be seen, lifted off its foundations and floated through the air towards him. He looked at it, mouth gaping, as it soared right over his house. He actually saw his own desk tumbling out of it before it went out of sight overhead.

Then the window smashed before his eyes and a sliver of glass drove through his throat. He was hurled across the room before the house exploded around him, but of course he did not know that the house was destroyed.

Harry Dobbs was the first man to be killed in Hukahoronui.

As Dr Scott left Dobbs's house he reflected on the strengths and weaknesses of the mind, particularly the weaknesses. Fundamentally a weak man, Dobbs had wanted the managing directorship and had deliberately suppressed the knowledge that he could not really handle it, and that knowledge was a canker inside him like a worm at the core of an apple.

The poor devil, thought Scott as he started his car. *A retreat from reality.*

He drove to the corner and turned, heading into town.
He had gone about three hundred yards when he found
there seemed to be something wrong with the steering – the
car would not answer to the wheel and he had an eerie sensation of floating.

Then he saw, to his astonishment, that the car really was
floating and that the wheels were a good three feet from
the ground. He had not time even to blink before the car
was flipped over on its back and he struck his head against
the window plinth and was knocked unconscious.

When he came round he found he was still behind the
wheel of the car, and the car was upright and on its four
wheels. He lifted his hand and winced as his fingers
explored the bump on his head. He looked about him and
saw nothing; there was a heavy coating of snow on all the
windows and they were opaque.

He got out of the car and stared blankly at what he saw.
At first he could not recognize where he was, and when he
did recognize his position his mind refused to believe it. A
sudden spasm took him and he leaned against the car and
vomited.

When he had recovered he looked again at the impossible. The mist was nearly gone and he could see as far as the
Gap on the other side of the river. The *other* side. He moistened his lips. 'Right across!' he whispered. 'I've been carried right across the bloody river!'

He looked across the river to where the township of
Hukahoronui should have been. There was nothing but a
jumble of snow.

Afterwards, quite understandably, he measured the distance
he had been taken by the avalanche. His car had been carried nearly three-quarters of a mile horizontally, across the
river, and lifted nearly three hundred feet vertically to be
deposited on its four wheels a fair distance up the east slope.

The engine had stopped but when he turned on the ignition it purred away as sweetly as ever.

Dr Robert Scott was caught in the avalanche and freakishly survived. He was lucky.

II

Ralph W. Newman was an American tourist. The 'W' in his name stood for Wilberforce, a fact he did not advertise. He had come to Hukahoronui for the skiing, having been led to believe by a man he had met in Christchurch that the slopes were exceptionally good. They may well have been but it takes more than snow on slopes to make a ski resort, and the essentials in Hukahoronui were lacking. There was no chair-lift, no organization and precious little après-ski conviviality. The two-bit dance they held Saturday nights at the hotel was not much of a substitute.

The man he had met in Christchurch who had told him of the charms of Hukahoronui was Charlie Peterson. Newman judged him to be a con man.

He had come to Hukahoronui for the skiing. He had certainly never expected to find himself in the middle of a line of twenty men, holding a long aluminium pole botched up out of a television antenna, and methodically driving it into the snow at the toe of each boot to the rasped commands of a Canadian scientist. It was all very improbable.

The man next to him nudged him and nodded at McGill. 'That joker would make a bloody good sergeant-major.'

'You're right about that,' said Newman. He felt the probe hit bottom and hauled it out.

'Think he's right about this avalanche?'

'He seems to know what he's doing. I ran across him up on the slope and he had some scientific gear with him. Said it was for testing snow.'

The other man leaned on his probe. 'He seems to know what he's doing down here, too. I'd never have thought of this way of searching. Come to think of it, the subject never entered my mind until half an hour ago.'

The line of men advanced one foot and Newman set his toes against the tautened string. The string slackened and he drove the probe into the snow again. 'My name's Jack Haslam,' said the man. 'I work at the mine. I'm a stoper.'

Newman didn't know what a stoper was. He said, 'I'm Newman.'

'Where's your friend?'

'Miller? I don't know. He went out early this morning.

'What's a stoper?'

Haslam grinned. 'The chap at the sharp end of a mine. One of the elite. I get the gold out.'

In went the probes again. Newman grunted. 'If we have to do this for long it's going to be tiring.'

'Listen!' said Haslam. 'I think I hear a plane.'

They stopped and listened to the drone overhead. Soon the whole line of men had stopped and were staring at the greyness above. 'Come on!' called the team leader. 'Haven't you heard a plane before?'

The line moved ahead one foot and twenty probes were raised for driving downwards.

Newman worked methodically. Drive down left . . . haul out . . . drive down right . . . haul out . . . advance one foot . . . drive down left . . . haul out . . . drive down . . .

A sudden yell from McGill stopped him. There was something in the quality of McGill's shout that made the hair prickle at the nape of his neck and caused a sudden hollowness in his belly.

'Take cover!' shouted McGill. 'Take cover right now! You've got less than thirty seconds.'

Newman ran towards the place that had been allotted to him in case of emergency. His boots crunched crisply on the snow as he ran to the cluster of rocks, and he was aware of Haslam at his elbow. McGill was still shouting hoarsely as they reached the rocks.

Haslam grabbed Newman by the arm. 'This way.' He led Newman to a cranny not more than two feet wide and three feet high. 'In here.'

Newman crawled inside and found himself in a small cave. Haslam was breathing heavily when he hauled himself in. Between gasps he said, 'Used to play in here when I was a kid.'

Newman grunted. 'Thought you miners all came from outside.' He felt apprehensive. This was a silly time and place for inconsequential conversation.

More men came through the narrow hole until seven of them were jammed in the small cave. It was a tight fit. One of them was Brewer, the team leader, who said, 'Quiet, everyone!'

They heard a distant shouting which suddenly cut off, and then a faint faraway thread of noise difficult to interpret because it was like nothing any of them had heard before. Newman checked his watch. It was dark in the cave but he peered at the luminous second hand as it marched steadily around the dial. 'Must be more than thirty seconds.'

The air quivered imperceptibly and the noise grew a little louder. Suddenly there was a violent howl and air was sucked out of the cave. Newman choked and fought for breath and was thankful that the suction ceased as suddenly as it had begun.

The live rock underneath him quivered and there was a thunderous drumming noise overhead, deafening in its intensity. The air in the cave filled with fine particles of snow which settled everywhere. More and more snow came in and began to build up thickly about the tangle of huddled bodies.

The noise grew louder and Newman thought his eardrums would split.

Someone was shouting. He could not make out the words but, as the sound eased, he knew it was Brewer. 'Keep it out! Keep the bloody snow out!'

The men nearest the entrance scrabbled with their hands but the snow came swirling in faster and faster, much more quickly than they could cope with. 'Cover your mouths,' shouted Brewer, and Newman brought his arm across his face with difficulty because of the restricted space.

He felt the snow build up about him, cold but dry. Finally, what space in the cave not occupied by bodies was filled completely with snow.

The noise stopped.

Newman kept still, breathing deeply and evenly. He wondered how long he could go on breathing like that – he did not know if air could penetrate the snow mass. Presently he sensed someone stirring and he made a tentative movement himself.

He was able to push with his arm and found that by pushing he could compress the snow into a smaller volume and thus make a bigger air space. From what seemed a hundred miles away he heard a faint voice and he stopped moving so that he could listen. 'Can anyone hear me?'

'Yes,' he shouted. 'Who are you?'

'Brewer.'

It seemed pretty silly that you had to shout at the top of your voice to a man not many feet away. 'Newman here,' he yelled. He remembered that Brewer had been nearest to the cave entrance. 'Can you get out?'

There was a pause and presently he heard another voice. 'Anderson here.'

Brewer called, 'Not a chance. There's a lot of snow outside.'

Newman was busy clearing a space. He pushed the powdery snow away, plastering it on the rock wall of the cave. He shouted to tell Brewer what he was doing, and Brewer told everybody else to get busy and do the same. He also asked them to call out their names.

Newman was aware of the dead weight of Haslam next to him. Haslam had not moved or made a sound. He put his hand out and groped for Haslam's face and found his cheek. Still Haslam did not move, so Newman pinched the flesh between thumb and forefinger very sharply. Haslam remained inert.

'There's a guy called Haslam here,' he said. 'He's unconscious.'

Now that there was increased air space there was no need to shout. Brewer said, 'Wait a minute. I'm trying to get my torch from my pocket.' There were gasping sounds in the darkness and the wriggling of contorted bodies, then suddenly a beam of light shot out.

Newman blinked, then turned to Haslam. He moved his hand and pointed. 'Shine that light here.' He bent over Haslam, and Brewer crawled forward with the light. Newman felt for Haslam's wrist pulse but could detect no movement so he leaned down and pressed his ear against Haslam's chest. When he lifted his head he turned towards the light. 'I think the guy's dead.'

'How can he be dead?' demanded Brewer.

'Give me the light.' Newman shone it on Haslam's face which was leaden grey. 'He didn't die of asphyxiation, that's for sure. I've seen that and he's the wrong colour. He'd be purple.'

'There's snow in his mouth,' said Brewer.

'Yeah.' Newman passed back the light and put his finger in Haslam's mouth. 'But not much. Not enough to stop him breathing. Can you guys give me some room? I'm going to try the kiss of life.'

Room was made with difficulty. 'Maybe he died of shock,' someone suggested.

Newman breathed air into Haslam's lungs and then pumped his chest. He kept it up for a long time but Haslam did not react. All that happened was that his body became colder. After fifteen minutes Newman stopped. 'No good. He's gone.' He turned his head to Brewer. 'Better switch off that light. It won't last forever.'

Brewer snapped off the light and there was darkness and silence, each man occupied with his own thoughts. At last Newman said, 'Brewer.'

'Yes?'

'Nobody is going to find us with probes – not in this cave. How much snow do you reckon is out there?'

'Hard to tell.'

'We'd better find out. It looks as though we'll have to save ourselves.' Newman groped about and found Haslam's hat which he placed over the dead man's face. It was a futile but human gesture there in the darkness. He remembered Haslam's last words – *Used to play in here when I was a kid*. It was too goddamn ironic to be true.

There were six men jammed in that narrow cleft in the rock: Newman, Brewer, Anderson, Jenkins, Fowler and Castle.

And the dead man – Haslam.

III

Turi Buck was coping remarkably well with the influx of children. The house under the great rock of Kamakamaru was large – too large now that his family had grown up and gone out into the world – and he welcomed the bustle and clamour. He relished less the glacial eye of Miss

Frobisher, the schoolteacher who accompanied the children. There is something about schoolteaching in isolated communities which tends to acidulate the feminine temperament and Miss Frobisher had a high acid content. Turi listened to her comments which tended to a criticism of the civil authorities, the stupidity of men, and other cognate matters. He took her measure and thereafter ignored her.

His daughter-in-law, who was his housekeeper, and his granddaughter were occupied in laying out bedding and allocating quarters for the horde of noisy small fry. This was woman's work and they would brook no interference, so Turi went to the back of the house to see how the emergency generator was to be installed.

Jock McLean, the mechanical engineer from the mine, was a Scot from the Clyde. He tapped the toe of his boot on the level area of concrete where the lines for hanging laundry were suspended from steel poles. 'And how thick is this, Mr Buck?'

'My name is Turi, and the concrete is six inches thick. I laid it myself.'

'Good. We drill four holes for the foundation bolts an' anchor 'em wi' masonry plugs. We don't want this thing shiftin'.'

'How are you going to drill the holes?' queried Turi. 'We have no power.'

McLean jerked his thumb over his shoulder. 'Air compressor wi' an air drill.'

Turi looked down at the concrete and shook his head. 'Not there. Can your drill make holes in rock?'

'Wi' a diamond drill I can go through armour plate.'

Turi pointed. 'Then put the machine over there. Fasten it to the rock.'

McLean stared at the old man, and smiled. 'I think six inches o' concrete should hold her,' he said tolerantly.

'Have you been in an avalanche, Mr McLean?' asked Turi softly.

'People call me Jock.' McLean shook his head. 'We didna' have them in the Gorbals – not when I was a laddie there forty years gone by. Maybe at Aviemore.'

'I have been in an avalanche. I have dug dead bodies from the snow.' Turi nodded his head towards the north. 'Just over there – about two hundred yards away. Put your machine on the rock.'

McLean scratched his head. 'Are they as bad as that?'

'When the avalanche comes it will be worse than anything you have ever known in your life.'

'I doubt it,' said McLean. 'I went ashore at Anzio.'

'I also have been in a war,' said Turi. 'Possibly a worse war than yours. I was in Flanders in 1918. When the avalanche comes it will be worse than that.'

'Aye, well.' McLean looked about. 'We'll have to find a flat bit o' rock an' that willna' be easy.' He strode away, his eyes roving. At last he thumped with his heel. 'It's flat enough here. This'll do.'

Turi walked over and stood on the place which McLean marked. He looked up at Kamakamaru and shook his head. 'This is not the place.'

'An' why not?' demanded McLean.

'In 1912 my father had a workshop here. It was built very strongly because my father believed in building strongly. When the snow came down that winter the workshop vanished. We never found so much as a brick.' He pointed. 'I believe that when the wind comes, followed by the powder, there is an eddy here. This place is not safe.'

'You're a cheery soul,' said McLean. 'What about over there, right under the rock?'

'That would do,' said Turi gravely. 'In 1912 I had some rabbits in a hutch there. The hutch wasn't strongly made because my father didn't make it – I did. But the rabbits were unharmed.'

'Well I'll be damned!' said McLean. 'Let's go an' see what the footin' is like.'

It proved to be satisfactory. Turi said, 'It will be all right here.' He went away, leaving McLean staring after him.

A truckload of canned goods had arrived and there were some drums of fuel oil. Turi showed Len Baxter and Dave Scanlon where to put the oil and then supervised the unloading of the food by some of the older children. After he had done this he went to the back of the house where he found Baxter and Scanlon helping McLean with the generator.

McLean had drilled four holes in the rock and had inserted bolts in the holes, secured by expanding fasteners. Turi marvelled at the speed with which McLean had drilled the holes; evidently McLean had been right to trust his diamond-tipped drill. Now he had erected a tripod and was lowering the generator by means of a block and tackle, while Scanlon and Baxter guided it so that the bolts would enter the holes in the base plate.

At last it was done and McLean grunted with satisfaction. 'Right, boys,' he said, and took four steel nuts from his pocket. 'I can carry on from here.'

Dave Scanlon nodded. 'I'd like to get back. I want a word with Maureen.' The two men went away and presently Turi heard the truck start up and drive away.

Turi's daughter-in-law came out with a laden tray. 'Will you have some tea, Mr McLean? And there are home-made cakes.'

McLean dropped the nuts back into his pocket. 'I'll be glad o' that. Thanks, Mrs . . . Miss . . . er . . .'

'This is Ruihi, my daughter-in-law,' said Turi.

McLean's eyes lit up as he bit into a cake. 'Good,' he said rather indistinctly. 'An old widower like me doesn't often get the chance o' real home cookin'.'

Ruihi smiled at him and went away, leaving the tray, and Turi and McLean spent a few minutes chatting over the tea and cakes. Presently McLean helped himself to a second cup of tea, then waved his arm towards the valley. 'Those dead bodies you were speakin' of a while back – how many were there?'

'Seven,' said Turi. 'A whole family – the Baileys. There was a house there. It was completely destroyed.' He told McLean of how he had helped his father dig.

McLean shook his head. 'Now that's a terrible thing. Not somethin' for a laddie of twelve to be doin'.' He finished the tea and looked at his watch. 'Well, this isna' tyin' down yon generator.' He took the nuts from his pocket and picked up a spanner. 'I'll secure it.'

Turi cocked his head on one side. He had heard a noise and, for a moment, thought it was the aeroplane that had been flying overhead. Then he heard and recognized the eerie bass hum and a higher whistling sound, something he had not heard since 1912.

He grabbed McLean's arm. 'Too late. Into the house – quick.'

McLean resisted. 'What the hell! I've got to – '

Turi hauled at him. 'The snow is coming,' he yelled.

McLean looked at the old man's contorted face and believed him instantly. They both ran to the back door, which Turi immediately slammed closed and locked as soon as they were inside. He took a step forward. 'The children . . .'

McLean saw Turi's mouth opening and closing but he did not hear the end of that sentence because the noise reached a deafening pitch.

Then the avalanche hit.

McLean had heard the barrage which opened the battle of El Alamein and that, in his opinion, had been the ultimate in noise, even exceeding that of the boiler shop where he had been apprenticed on the Clyde. He now knew with a depressing certainty that he had a new measure of the ultimate.

The fundamental note was low cycle, deep in the bass – a sound which grabbed his stomach as though he was being squeezed by a giant hand. He opened his mouth and air was expelled forcibly from his lungs as his diaphragm kicked sickeningly. Superimposed on the bass was a whole series of high-pitched whistles of ear-piercing intensity, tones which collided with each other to produce strange and eerie harmonics. He had the impression that the sound entering his ears was compressing his brain.

The old house quivered on its foundations. The light had suddenly gone as though by an eclipse of the sun, and all he saw through the window in front of him was a dirty grey blur. The house lurched as it received two swift buffets and the windows smashed inwards. He heard no sound of breaking glass.

Fine snow dust jetted into the room through the broken panes as though squirted from a great hose pipe. The dust hit the wall to one side of McLean and sprayed outwards, and then it stopped coming in as suddenly as it had begun. Instead there was an opposite reaction, although not as strong. Air was sucked from the room, taking some of the snow with it.

It seemed to McLean that he had been standing there for an eternity. He was wrong, of course, because, from first to last, the avalanche swept by the rock of Kamakamaru in under twenty seconds. When it was over he stood as still as a statue. He was covered from head to foot with fine snow powder which gave him the appearance of a ghost. There was a ringing sound in his ears and he heard distant cries which seemed to be coming from as far away as the town.

Turi Buck stirred. Slowly he lifted his hands and put them to his ears, and he shook his head as though to assure himself that it would not fall off his trunk. He said, 'It is over.' His voice crashed out unnaturally loudly as it reverberated in the cavities of his skull. He turned his head and looked to McLean, saying again, 'It is over.'

McLean did not move so Turi put out his hand and touched him gently on the arm. A shudder went through McLean and he looked at Turi. His eyes were glazed and staring. Turi said, 'It's finished, Jock.'

McLean saw Turi's lips moving and heard his voice coming as though from a long way off, almost drowned out by the persistent buzzing in his ears. He frowned stiffly and deep cracks appeared in the powdering of snow that covered his lean face, accentuating the grooves that ran from the base of his nose to the corners of his mouth. He swallowed convulsively and his hearing improved. The distant cries he had heard before became louder, shrilling in his ears almost like the noise of the avalanche.

Every child in the house was screaming.

'The children,' said Turi. 'We must see to the children.'

'Yes,' said McLean. His voice came out creakily. He looked down at his hands and saw that he was still holding four steel nuts in his left hand and a spanner in his right hand. He took a deep breath and looked at Turi again. 'You're bleeding,' he said.

The cut on Turi Buck's face, caused by a fragment of flying glass, was the only physical wound suffered by anyone in the house. Psychic wounds were something else again.

Other houses in the valley were not as lucky.

IV

Matt Houghton was confident he had nothing to fear from any snow falling down the west slope. His house was built on the other side of the river and a considerable way up the east slope so that it had a commanding view of the valley.

The view from his front porch was a source of considerable satisfaction to Matt Houghton and it was his habit, on fine summer days, to sit there and drink beer in the evenings. He had a streak of vanity and, since his election as mayor of Hukahoronui, he liked to think he was overlooking his kingdom. To his mind, the view from the house added two thousand dollars to the value of the property.

Not that he was sitting on his front porch this Sunday morning. For one thing, it was too cold, and for another, the porch was cluttered with hastily packed suitcases brought by his unexpected visitors. His wife, Mamie, was in the kitchen making gallons of tea and cutting piles of sandwiches, and he was playing the genial host.

'It's so very good of you to have us here,' said Mrs Jarvis tremulously. Mrs Jarvis was the oldest person in Hukahoronui. She was eighty-two.

'No need to thank me.' Houghton laughed jovially. 'I'm only doing it to get your vote in the next election.'

She looked at him uncertainly, then said, 'Do you think we're safe here?'

'Of course we're safe,' he assured her. 'This house has been here a long time – second oldest in the valley. It's not been knocked down by an avalanche yet, so I can't see it happening now.'

Sam Critchell, sitting in a big over-stuffed armchair, said, 'You never know. Avalanches can do funny things.'

'What do you know about avalanches, Sam?' Houghton's voice was scornful.

Critchell placidly continued to fill his pipe with liver-spotted hands. 'I've seen a few.'

'Where?'

'At the end of the war I was in the mountains back of Trieste. There were a lot of avalanches that winter. They used the army for rescue work.' He struck a match. 'I saw enough to know that avalanches can be damned unexpected.'

'Well, if I thought this house wasn't safe I wouldn't be here, would I?' demanded Houghton rhetorically.

A long plume of smoke jetted from Critchell's lips. 'Neither would I. All I said is that avalanches can do funny things.'

A tall, stringy woman walked over to Houghton and he took the opportunity to escape this pointless conversation. 'Well, how are things, Mrs Fawcett?' he asked heartily.

Mrs Fawcett carried a clipboard. She was one of the live-wires of the community. She ran the dramatic society with a rod of iron and was the mainspring of the debating society. Her son, Bobby, ran the scout troop. She was bossy and a born organizer and Houghton always had the uneasy feeling that she regarded him with contempt. She consulted the list on the clipboard, and said, 'All here except for Jack Baxter.'

'How many in all?'

'Jack will make twenty-five. With your family there will be twenty-nine of us here.'

Houghton grunted. 'Let's hope the food holds out.'

She gave him the peculiar look she reserved for fools. 'Old people have small appetites,' she said tartly. 'I wonder what's keeping Jack?'

'Who is bringing him?'

'Jim Hatherley.' She held her head on one side and looked up at the ceiling. 'That aeroplane is here again.'

'Doesn't that fool of a pilot know that any sound can start an avalanche?' said Houghton irritably. He left the room, went through the hall and out on to the porch where he stared at the sky. There was nothing to be seen.

He was about to go back inside when Jim Hatherley ran up, somewhat out of breath. 'I've got trouble, Mr Houghton. Jack Baxter slipped on the snow when he was getting out of the car. I'm pretty sure he's bust his leg.'

'Oh, hell!' said Houghton. 'Where is he?'

'Lying by the car just around the corner.'

'Better telephone the doctor; the phone's in the hall. I'll go down and see to Jack.' Houghton paused, biting his lip. He did not like Mrs Fawcett, but she'd know what to do about a broken leg. 'And ask Mrs Fawcett to come out.'

'Okay.' Hatherley went into the house and looked about for Mrs Fawcett. He did not see her but he did see the telephone so he decided to make the call first. He picked up the handset and got Maureen Scanlon at the exchange.

'What number do you want?'

Hatherley said, 'Maureen, this is Jim Hatherley at Matt Houghton's house. Old Jack Baxter took a bad fall and we think he's broken his leg. Do you think you can find Dr Scott?'

There was a pause before she said, 'I'll try.' The line clicked as she broke the connection.

Hatherley tapped on the telephone table as he waited to be put through. He looked about him and saw Mrs Fawcett just entering the hall. He waved her over and rapidly explained what had happened to Baxter. 'Oh, the poor man,' she said. 'I'll go at once.'

She turned, took two steps in the direction of the front door, and died.

When the avalanche hit the valley bottom the dense cloud of snow powder and air ceased to pick up speed but it did not come to a halt at once. The energy it contained had to be dissipated by friction against the ground and the surrounding air and it continued to cross the valley quite rapidly.

It was only when it got to the other side that it really began to slow down. Now it was climbing the east slope gravity was working against it and eventually it came to a halt a hundred yards from the Houghton house and perhaps a hundred feet of vertical distance below it. There was no danger of Matt Houghton's house being overwhelmed with snow.

But the air blast did not stop. It came up the hill from underneath the house moving at about one hundred and fifty miles an hour. It caught under the eaves and ripped off the roof. Because of this the walls were no longer tied together so when the blast slammed at them the house exploded as though hit by a bomb. All who were in the house at that time – twenty-eight people – died. Some were struck by masonry, some were trapped in the wreckage and died of exposure. Two died of heart attacks. Some died immediately while others died in hospital a few days later.

But all in the house died.

Matt Houghton was not in the house, and neither was Jack Baxter. When the house was hit Houghton was bending over Baxter and asking, in what he conceived to be the cool, professional tones of a doctor, where the pain was. He was protected by the car, and the car was protected more by a small hillock hardly more than three feet high which stood between it and the descending hillside. When the air blast roared up the hill and hit the house the car did nothing more than rock heavily on its springs.

Houghton looked up, mystified, but not alarmed. He looked under the car and, finding nothing, he stood up and walked around it. Wind beat at him, the aftermath of the air blast, but it was not so abnormal as to tickle his curiosity. Standing on the other side of the car, he could see into the valley. The curtain of mist had been torn aside and his gaze shifted as he tried to fit what he saw with what he expected.

He shook his head bemusedly and climbed up on to the hillock to get a better view. At first he thought he could not be looking in the right direction so he changed his stance, but that made no difference. His problem was that he could not find the town of which he was mayor.

He rubbed the back of his neck perplexedly and then solved the problem to his own satisfaction. Of course, that was it! There had been a heavy fall of snow during the night and the town was covered in snow. It must have been a heavy snowfall, indeed, to cover the buildings so they could not be seen, but what with that and the mist it was not entirely unexpected.

Baxter moaned behind the car, and Houghton thought it was time to get Mrs Fawcett. He turned, still standing on the hillock, to go up to the house, and then stopped dead. *There was no house!* There was no front porch, no tall stone chimney – nothing! If he had been a little farther up the hill he would have seen the wrecked foundations and the scattered bodies, but from where he stood it was as though the house with the two-thousand dollar view had never existed.

A strangled noise came from him and froth came from his lips. Stiffly he toppled forward and never knew when he hit the ground.

Presently a querulous voice said, 'Matt! Matt? Where is everybody?'

Jack Baxter, his leg broken but untouched by the avalanche, was still very much alive. He did not understand then, or ever after, how lucky he was to have broken his leg at the exact moment he did.

V

Stacey Cameron took her father's car and drove it to Dr Scott's house which was where he held his surgery. Because she had first-aid training she had volunteered to help on the medical side should such help be necessary, and Scott, being the only doctor, was the hub around which all medical problems revolved. She drew up behind a station wagon which was parked outside Scott's house.

Liz Peterson was there. 'Hi, there,' said Stacey. 'You a volunteer nurse, too?'

'More of an almoner,' said Liz. 'Dr Scott wants us to round up medical supplies. He's had to go because Ballard wants him to look in on Harry Dobbs.'

'Harry?' Stacey shook her head. 'Isn't he at the mine office?'

'No,' said Liz. 'That seems to be the trouble.'

Stacey offered Liz a cigarette. 'Talking about Ian – what exactly happened last night?'

'My idiot brother happened,' said Liz. 'Charlie's a great big pain in the neck.' She accepted a light. 'Tell me, how are things in California?'

Stacey was puzzled. 'What do you mean – how are things?'

'Conditions of living – and working. I'm thinking of leaving here.'

'That's a laugh,' said Stacey. 'I'm thinking of moving in here.'

Liz smiled. 'Perhaps we can do an even swap: jobs, houses – everything.'

'I don't live in a house. I rent an apartment.'

'Any particular reason for burying yourself in a hole like Huka?'

'My father.' Stacey hesitated. 'And other reasons.'

'What's the other reason's name?' asked Liz drily.

'You were dancing with him last night.'

Liz raised her eyebrows. 'And at your invitation, too. I'm not blind or stupid, you, know. You were talking to me, and then you went to talk to him. Ian wasn't drunk but he'd had just enough to say, "I'll dance with Liz Peterson and to hell with her quarrelsome brothers." And you gave him the idea. That's a funny way for a girl to act towards her reason.'

'I don't want to appear possessive. At least, not at this delicate stage in our relationship.'

'And what stage is that?'

Stacey smiled. 'The stage at which he hasn't noticed I exist.' She sighed. 'And I only have a few days more.'

'Well, he has a lot on his mind right now. Maybe your chance will come during the avalanche. All you have to do is to be gallantly rescued by Ian Ballard. Then he'll have to marry you – it's as good as making you pregnant, according to all the films I've seen.'

'What do you think of him?'

'A very nice man,' said Liz coolly. 'But I go more for his friend, Mike McGill.' She shook her head. 'There's no joy there.'

'Why not?'

'He says he's been bitten before. His wife divorced him three years ago; she said she couldn't live with a snowman who's never at home. Mike said he couldn't blame her. Who'd want a husband who alternates between the North Pole and the South Pole like a yo-yo?'

Stacey nodded commiseratingly. 'Tell me – what's this quarrel between your brothers and Ian?'

'Too old to bear repeating,' said Liz briefly. She stubbed out her cigarette. 'This isn't stocking up the medical supplies. Let's get busy.'

They drove to the chemist's shop in the main street and Liz got out of the car and tried the door, which proved to be locked. She knocked repeatedly but there was no answer and finally she gave up. 'That bloody fool, Rawson, was told to be here,' she said angrily. 'Why the devil isn't he?'

'Perhaps he's been held up.'

'I'll hold him up when I find him,' said Liz grimly. She looked past Stacey at a truck coming down the street, then stepped forward and waved it down. As it stopped she called, 'Len, have you seen Rawson anywhere?'

Len Baxter shook his head and turned to consult Scanlon. 'Dave says he saw him going into the hotel about half an hour ago.'

'Thanks.' Liz turned to Stacey. 'Let's part him from his beer. Come on.'

In any community there is a sizeable proportion of fools, and a large number of these were congregated together in the Hotel D'Archiac. The philosophy of the management appeared to be 'Business as usual', and perhaps business was better than usual. A rumble of male voices came from the crowded bar and the dining-room was being prepared for lunch as though it was any other Sunday of the year.

Liz saw Eric standing at the entrance to the bar and brought him across the lobby with a jerk of her head. 'What's going on here? Don't these people know what's happening?'

'I've told them and I've told them,' said Eric. 'It doesn't make a blind bit of difference. There are a lot of miners in there being stirred up by Bill Quentin. They seem to be holding a protest meeting about the mine being closed down.'

'It's the first I've heard of it,' said Stacey. 'Dad said nothing about it.'

'Bill Quentin says it's a certainty.'

Liz looked at a waitress carrying a loaded tray of drinks into the dining-room. 'This place should be closed down. Close it, Eric. We do own half the business.'

Eric shrugged. 'You know as well as I do that Johnnie and me are just sleeping partners. We agreed with Weston that we shouldn't interfere with the day-to-day running. I've talked to him, but he says he's staying open.'

'Then he's a damned fool.'

'He's a fool who's coining money.' Eric waved his hand towards the bar. 'Look at it.'

'To the devil with them!' snapped Liz. 'Is Rawson in there?'

'Yes, I saw him talking to – '

'Get him out. I want him to open his shop. We need medical supplies.'

'Okay.' Eric went into the bar and was away a long time. Presently he came back with Rawson, a tall, gaunt man who wore thick-lensed spectacles.

Liz took a step forward and said crisply, 'Mr Rawson, you promised to be at your shop half an hour ago.'

Rawson smiled. 'Do you think this situation is so serious, Miss Peterson?' His tone was of amused tolerance.

Liz took a deep breath and said with iron control, 'Whether it's serious or not, the fact remains that you weren't at your shop as you promised.'

Rawson cast a longing look at the bar. 'Oh, very well,' he said ungraciously. 'I suppose I'd better come.'

'Are you staying here?' Liz asked Eric.

He shook his head. 'I'm going to join Johnnie. This crowd won't be shifted.'

'Do it now,' she advised. 'Come on, Mr Rawson.' As they left the hotel Stacey looked over her shoulder and saw Quentin come out of the bar to join Eric. They seemed to be starting an argument.

When Rawson unlocked his shop he said fussily, 'I don't know that I'm not breaking the law by doing this.'

'Pharmacists are allowed to open on Sunday in emergencies,' said Liz. 'I seem to know more about the law than you do.'

Rawson went inside and snapped a light switch. When nothing happened he said, 'Oh, I forgot. Never mind, I have a few candles at the back.'

Liz said, 'It's light enough without candles. Let's get on with it.'

Rawson went behind the counter and adopted a professional stance. 'Well, ladies,' he said brightly. 'What can I do for you?' Stacey suppressed a smile. She had half-expected him to put on a white coat.

'I have a list,' said Liz, and gave it to him.

Rawson scanned the papers slowly, going with maddening deliberation from one paper to the next. 'My!' he said at last. 'This *is* a lot'

'Yes,' agreed Liz patiently.

Rawson looked up. 'Who is going to pay for all this?'

Liz looked at him expressionlessly and then glanced at Stacey who stood with open mouth. She leaned over the counter, and said sweetly, 'Would you like payment before or after delivery, Mr Rawson?'

Obtusely, he did not catch the danger underlying her tone.

'Well, this lot will take quite a time to add up.' He chuckled. 'It's a good thing I bought one of those new electronic calculators. It makes things like this so easy, you know.'

Liz slammed her hand on the counter. 'Start producing, Rawson. If you're worried about the money put it on Johnnie's account – or don't you think his credit is good?'

'Oh no, that will be quite all right,' said Rawson hastily. He peered at the list again. 'Right, let's begin. Bandages – ten dozen boxes of two-inch, ten dozen boxes of three-inch, the same of six . . .' He broke off. 'We'll have to go into the stock room for those.'

'Right, let's get into the stock room. Where is it?'

'Wait a minute,' he said. 'There's something not quite right here, Miss Peterson. All this morphine – here on the third page.' He held it out to her. 'I can't really issue that without a prescription. And the quantity!' He shook his head. 'I could lose my licence.'

'If you turn to the last page you'll find Dr Scott's signature.'

'That's not good enough, Miss Peterson. For one thing, page three isn't signed, and for another, it should be done on the prescribed form. The Dangerous Drugs Act is very precise about this kind of thing. This is most irregular and I'm surprised that Dr Scott should have countenanced it.'

'For Christ's sake!' exploded Liz. Rawson was shocked and startled. 'You could be killed at any time and you're worried about names on bloody bits of paper. Now look here: if you don't get moving and produce everything on that list I'll have Arthur Pye confiscate your whole damned stock. He'd do it, too.'

Rawson was affronted. 'You can't threaten me with the police!'

'What do you mean – I can't? I've just done it, haven't I? Stacey, use that telephone and find Arthur Pye.'

Rawson threw up his hands. 'Oh, very well – but I insist on delivering any drugs on the dangerous list to Dr Scott personally.'

'Good!' said Liz briskly. 'That means you'll be helping at last. Where's the stock room?'

Rawson waved. 'That door back there.' As Liz strode towards it he said, 'But it's locked. Can't be too careful about things like that.' He joined her and took a chain from his pocket on the end of which dangled a bunch of keys. He unlocked the door. 'All the bandages are on those shelves to the right. I'll be in the dispensary getting the drugs together.'

The two girls marched past him and he turned, shaking his head at the impetuosity of modern youth. Who would have thought that a nicely brought up girl like Elizabeth Peterson was capable of using language which hitherto he had only associated with bar-rooms?

He went into the dispensary and unlocked the cupboard in which he kept the registered drugs. He took a box and began filling it with ampoules, keeping careful count and making a note every so often in the Poisons Register. This naturally took up time. He was a most meticulous man.

He was not to know it but the combination of his broken promise and his scrupulosity meant that he was a dead man.

If he had been on time at the shop he would have been there when the girls arrived and there would have been no waste of time in extracting him from the hotel bar. His meticulousness in putting everything in the Poisons Register meant that he was still in the dispensary when the avalanche hit.

When the front of the shop caved in, the shock transmitted through the foundations caused a half-gallon bottle to leap off a shelf and fall and smash on the table before him. It was full of hydrochloric acid which splashed all over his face and the front of his body.

Liz Peterson was saved by something which had begun five years earlier. In the winter of that year, which had also been cold, a drop of water had frozen in a minute crack in the concrete which formed the footing of the rear wall of the stock room. The water drop, turning into ice, had expanded and widened the crack. The following year the same thing happened, but with a little more water, and year by year the crack had widened until at this time it constituted a serious danger to the stability of the wall.

Had Rawson known of this he would have had it repaired immediately, being the sort of man he was. But he did not know of it because it was underground. Consequently, when the shock of the avalanche struck, the rear wall constituted a weakness and it gave way easily and without resistance.

Liz was hurled forward against stacked boxes of bandages which cushioned the shock, although the edge of a shelf broke two of her ribs. The whole mass, shelving, boxes and the bodies of Liz and Stacey, was forced against the rear wall which gave immediately, and Liz was precipitated through the air in a tangle of streaming and unwinding bandages.

She fell on to snow, and more snow covered her, holding her body and clamping her arms and legs. She was quite conscious and rational and she wondered if she were about to die. She did not know that Stacey Cameron was in much the same position not more than ten feet away. Both girls lost consciousness at about the same time, roughly one-and-a-half minutes after being buried.

Rawson was also buried about twenty yards away and was dying slowly and quite painfully as the acid ate at his flesh. Fortunately, when he opened his mouth to scream it filled with soft snow and he died mercifully and quickly of asphyxia.

The Hotel D'Archiac, that abode of fools, was speedily demolished. Jeff Weston, the king of fools who had been coining it, was parted from more than his money. Business was so brisk that he had gone behind the bar to help the overworked bartender and when the building was hit he was struck on the head by a bottle of scotch whisky which left the shelf behind him like a projectile.

Most of the men who were drinking in the bar were killed by flying bottles. Behind the bottles came the whole wall and, after that, came the snow which covered every-thing. They died because they were fools, although a cynic might have said they died of acute alcoholism. But there were no cynics left in Hukahoronui after that Sunday morning.

Those in the dining-room died when the roof fell in. Alice Harper, the waitress who had served McGill with colonial goose on the previous evening, was killed by a heavy suitcase which fell from the bedrooms above. The suitcase belonged to the American, Newman, who had his own troubles at the time.

Newman's room no longer existed as a room and the same applied to the room next door which had been taken by his friend, Miller. Miller was most fortunate to be absent.

Bill Quentin was exceptionally lucky because he had left the hotel with Eric Peterson only moments before the hotel was destroyed. He had gone into the lobby from the bar and found Eric. 'Look here,' he said. 'Does the council know what's going on?'

'About what?'

'About closing the mine.'

'The mine has been closed. Ballard closed it this morning.'

'I don't mean that. I mean closing it permanently.'

Eric shook his head a little wearily. 'No one has said anything to us – yet.'

'Well, aren't you going to do anything about it?'

'What the hell do you expect us to do when we haven't been notified officially? I don't believe it will close.'

Quentin snorted. 'Ballard said it would. He said it at a meeting yesterday. He said the company couldn't afford to spend money on avalanche protection. I think this avalanche scare is a lot of balls. I think the company is trying to weasel out.'

'Weasel out of what? I don't know what you're talking about.' Eric moved towards the door.

'You know what these big companies are like.' Quentin took a couple of steps to keep up with him. 'I hear that Ballard is related to the big boss back in London. Know anything about that?'

'I've heard it.' Eric quickened his pace. 'It's true.'

'I'll bet he's been sent to do the hatchet job. Hey – where are you going?'

'To join Johnnie in the old Fisher house.'

'I think I'll come with you,' said Quentin. 'I think the council ought to know about this. Where's Matt Houghton?'

'At home.'

They stepped off the pavement, and Quentin said, 'That means he's the only sensible man around here. Everybody else is shutting themselves up in holes.'

Eric glanced at him. 'Like me?'

'Don't tell me you believe in Doomsday?'

Eric stopped on the opposite pavement. His back was to the Fisher house and so he did not see his brother run across the road towards the telephone exchange. 'Johnnie's no fool and he believes it,' he said deliberately. 'And I'm beginning to.'

He resumed his stride at a quicker pace and Quentin, a much smaller man, was forced to trot to keep up with him. They entered the house and Eric glanced into the empty room off the hall. 'He'll be in the cellar.'

The two men were just going down the steps into the basement when the house was hit. Eric tumbled the rest of the way and fell on top of young Mary Rees, breaking her leg. Bill Quentin fell on top of Eric and broke Eric's arm. He himself was quite unhurt; he was untouched and inviolate and was not even scratched by the falling rubble of the collapsing house.

VI

After shouting his warning, McGill dropped into his own selected shelter, jostled by Ballard. He grabbed the telephone which had been installed by a mine electrician and rang the exchange which was busy. 'For Christ's sake, come on!' he muttered.

He waited for ten seconds which were more like ten minutes before the operator, Maureen Scanlon, came on the line. He said quickly, 'Plug me into John Peterson, Mrs Scanlon, and then get the hell out of there – fast.'

'I understand,' she said, and the ringing tone came into his ear.

'John Peterson here.'

'McGill. Get your people under cover. She's coming down.'

'What about Maureen Scanlon?'

'I've told her to get out. You can see the exchange from where you are. Keep an eye open for her.'

'Okay,' Peterson slammed down the telephone and snapped at Bobby Fawcett, 'Everyone downstairs. Move it, Bobby.'

Fawcett left the room on the run and Peterson looked out of the window at the telephone exchange up the street. The street was deserted with not a sign of movement. He thumped the table nervously and wondered what to do.

As soon as Mrs Scanlon had put the call through to Peterson she took off the headset, stood up, and lifted her coat from a hook. She knew exactly what to do because Peterson had told her. She was to join him in the old Fisher building, one of the few houses in town which had a basement. She did not bother to put on the coat but had taken only one step to the door when the switchboard buzzed at her. She turned back, plugged in and lifted the headset. 'What number do you want?'

'Maureen, this is Jim Hatherley at Matt Houghton's house. Old Jack Baxter took a bad fall and we think he's broken his leg. Do you think you can find Dr Scott?'

She bit her lip. 'I'll try.' She plugged in a jack and rang Scott's house.

In the Fisher house Peterson made up his mind. He ran from the room and into the hall. A freckled-faced fourteen-year-old girl was standing in the doorway, and he said, 'Into the basement, Mary. On the double.'

The crackle of authority in his voice moved her body without her consciously willing it. But she said, 'Where are you going?'

'To fetch Mrs Scanlon.' He ran out into the street, and Mary Rees went down into the basement to join the others.

Peterson ran up the empty street towards the telephone exchange. He reached the corner where a road ran off to the left towards the mine, cast a hurried glance along it, and skidded to a frantic halt. What he saw was incredible. The mist was gone and he could see as far as the mine, but that was not what held his attention. A building was flying through the air directly at him, disintegrating at it came, and in that split second he recognized the mine office block.

He jumped back and dived behind a concrete wall, landing heavily, and then he twisted over so that he could see. There was a fierce blast of wind in his face and then he saw the office block fall squarely on to the telephone exchange, obliterating it.

The wind gusted at him again and he felt a tremendous pain in his chest. *Heart attack!* he thought dimly, *I'm having a heart attack.* Even while fighting the pain he lost consciousness and died very soon thereafter.

In the basement of the Fisher house Mary Rees added her screams to those of the others as the structure collapsed overhead and something or someone fell on top of her. No one died in the basement but there were several serious injuries, including Mary's broken leg.

VII

In the Supermarket Phil Warrick looked about him and said with satisfaction, 'We've just about got it cleared.' He lifted the lid of the stove and dropped in some chunks of wood.

The Reverend Howard Davis, vicar of St Michael's Anglican Church, agreed. 'Just about,' he said. 'This will be the last load. He wheeled a pushcart before the biscuit counter and began to fill it with packets.

Warrick watched him and grinned. 'McGill said no chocolate biscuits.'

'I don't know what Dr McGill knows about nutrition, but he certainly knows nothing about children,' said Davis with a smile. 'Chocolate biscuits are better than baked beans for keeping up morale.'

Warrick nodded. 'I hope he knows what he's doing about this avalanche. I swear my arms have lengthened two inches because of lugging around all these cases of canned food.' He replaced the lid of the stove.

Davis regarded him with amusement. 'Do you mean you'll feel sorry if there is no avalanche?'

'Oh, you know I don't want an avalanche, but it would be a shame to see all this hard work go for nothing.'

'I don't want an avalanche, either, but there's no harm in being prepared. If John Peterson is willing to have his store looted like this then he must believe McGill, and John is a level-headed man.'

A truck pulled up outside, and two men got out and came into the Supermarket. Warrick said, 'Hi, Len . . . Dave.'

Len Baxter said, 'That plane has come back. It's still float-ing around up there. Wonder what he wants?'

'He's not going to land,' said Warrick. 'This fog's too thick.'

Davis picked up a coffee-pot and put it on the stove top. 'You'll need something to warm you up.'

Dave Scanlon held out his hands to the stove. He wore a worried look. 'That'll go down well. I'll swear it's getting colder.' He glanced at Davis. 'I'm getting worried about Maureen. Someone said the exchange is too exposed.'

'John Peterson told me he'd look after her,' said Davis. 'I'm sure she'll be all right.' He laid the back of his finger on the coffee-pot to test the heat. 'Won't be long.'

'Got any more oil?' asked Len.

'Two more forty-five-gallon drums,' said Warrick. 'The last I could find. But we must have taken nearly six hundred gallons out of that tank.'

'I was talking to one of the mine engineers up at Turi Buck's place,' said Len. 'He's fixing up a generator there. He said the diesel engine could use fuel oil at a pinch. I never knew that.'

Dave said, 'I think I'll go and check on Maureen after I've had some coffee.'

As Davis picked up a cup, Len Baxter said, 'That reminds me. Does anyone know where my old man is? I've been so busy this morning I've lost track of things.'

'He's gone up to Matt Houghton's house. McGill thought it was one of the safest places in the valley.'

Warrick nodded. 'We discussed that in the council meeting. That and Turi Buck's place are the two oldest houses. The kids have gone to Turi Buck and the old people to Matt's place.'

'Not all the kids,' said Dave. He took a cup of coffee from Davis. 'I saw Mary Rees just now.'

Warrick frowned. 'Where?'

'Here in town. She was standing in the doorway of the old Fisher house.'

'That's all right,' said Davis. 'It has a basement. That's where Maureen will go. John Peterson organized all that.'

'Where will you hide out?' asked Len.

'I will be in the church,' said Davis firmly. His tone rejected any suggestion that he would be hiding anywhere.

Len considered it. 'Not bad,' he commented. 'The church must be the strongest building here. The only one built of stone, anyway.'

Dave Scanlon finished his coffee. 'I'll just pop along and see Maureen, then I'll be back to help you load.' He waved his hand. 'I've never seen the town so deserted, not even on Sunday.'

He turned to go, and froze in mid-stride. 'The mist's go . . .'

The three-ton truck parked outside was picked up bodily and thrown through the plate glass windows of the Supermarket like a monstrous projectile. Even as it came the building was collapsing around them. It had not been built too strongly in the first place and, hit by the giant fist of the avalanche, the showy false front sheared off and fell through the roof.

Suddenly the Reverend Davis found himself floundering in snow. He was dazed, and when he put his hand to his head it came away bloody. He was up to his waist in snow and, to his surprise, in his right hand he still held the coffee-pot. He opened it and looked inside and found it half full of steaming liquid. His head was spinning and hurt when he moved it suddenly. Darkness spiralled before his eyes and everything became dim just before he fell unconscious. The coffee-pot dropped from his hand and fell over on its side, and coffee stained the snow.

Dave Scanlon died instantly. He was hit by the truck and mashed to a bloody pulp. Len Baxter was hit on the head by a falling brick which was driven through the roof from the false front. His body was quickly covered by rubble which, in turn was covered by a rush of snow. He was still alive at that time but he died within a few minutes.

The cast-iron stove was ripped from the concrete plinth to which it was secured by four half-inch bolts. It was driven through the rear wall of the store and hit the fuel oil tank, which ruptured. Phil Warrick went flying after the stove and fell on top of it. He had been stoking it up liberally all morning and it was nearly red hot. The lid came off and a stream of hot embers shot out, igniting the fuel oil which streamed from the tank. Flames ran about and a cloud of black smoke went up, to be shredded immediately by the roaring wind.

The fire could not last long because of the snow which drove over the area, but it lasted long enough to kill Phil

Warrick. Embracing the hot stove, he was burned alive under six feet of snow.

VIII

Joe Cameron, driving the truck back to the mine after delivering the load of snow probes, was caught right in the open. Not for him the eerie sensation of driving a floating car as experienced by Dr Scott. The air blast slammed at the truck broadside on and it rocked violently. The left wheels rose from the ground and the truck went careering along for a few yards on two wheels and it was within a breath of toppling over. Then the wheels came down again with a crunch and Cameron fought to keep control.

After the air blast came the snow cloud of a much denser material. It pounded the side of the truck much more forcibly and this time toppled it over on to its side. The truck did not lie there. Pushed by the snow it began to roll over faster and faster.

In the cab Cameron was getting a mauling. His right foot was trapped between the accelerator and brake pedals; every time the truck rolled the gear lever ground into his stomach as his body flopped helplessly from side to side, and once, when his arm went through the spokes of the driving wheel, a blow on the front axles made the wheel spin and his arm broke with a dry crack which he did not hear.

When the truck finally came to rest it was upside down under fifteen feet of snow. Cameron was also upside down, his head resting against the top of the cab and his foot still trapped. The windscreen was smashed and there was much snow in the cab but enough of an air space left to provide the breath of life for a fairly long time. He was bleeding profusely from a gash on his cheek and the blood stained the snow a bright red.

He was unconscious, but presently he stirred and groaned. As he came round he felt as though he had been through a grinding machine and then stretched on a rack; every part of him ached and there were bits that were very painful. He tried to move his arm and felt the edges of bone grind together at the same time as a hot knife was stuck into his shoulder-blade. He did not try to move his arm again.

The danger of death in the snow was very real, but what Cameron did not know was that he was in much more danger of dying by drowning.

First came the air blast and then the heavy hammer fist of the snow cloud. Following these came the sliding surface snow. Not as fast as its predecessors, it moved in a flowing tide inexorably across Hukahoronui. It washed around the church and the spire shuddered; it obliterated the wreckage of the Hotel D'Archiac and swept over the remnants of Mr Rawson's shop; it reached the Supermarket and covered the burned body of Phil Warrick, then it went on across the bluff to the river where it spilled over the edge and filled the river bed with snow.

Across the river its energy was spent and it slowed until it was moving at no more than the speed of a man running fast. A little later, when it encountered the rising ground of the east slope, it stopped entirely having clothed destruction in immaculate whiteness.

The avalanche had finished.

The disaster had not.

IX

McGill climbed to the top of a small mound of snow in order to get a good view. He looked down the valley, and said softly, 'Oh my God!'

Most of the town had gone. The only building he could see was the church, which looked as though it had been given a coat of whitewash. Finely powdered snow had been driven into the stonework so that it looked like the ghost of a church. For the rest, there was just a hummocky expanse of snow.

He went back to Ballard and bent over him. 'Come on, Ian. It's over now and we have work to do.'

Ballard raised his head slowly and looked up at McGill. His eyes were dark smudges in a white face and showed no comprehension at all. His lips worked a little before he said, 'What?'

McGill felt compassion because he had a good idea of what had happened to Ballard. His senses had been so assaulted in an unexpected manner that the wits had been driven from him as a soldier might be shell-shocked in an artillery barrage. McGill was not feeling too good himself, but because of his knowledge and experience he had known what would happen and thus armoured had been able to ward off the worst effects.

Ballard was suffering from disaster shock.

McGill shook his head slowly. Compassion was not enough. A lot of people must have died and, if the rest of the survivors were like Ballard, then a lot more would die from want of help. He drew back his arm and slapped Ballard across the face very hard. 'Get up, Ian,' he said harshly. 'Jump to it!'

Slowly Ballard lifted his hand and fingered the red marks on his cheek. He blinked rapidly, weak tears coming to his eyes, and mumbled, 'What did you do that for?'

'You'll get worse than that if you don't get up.' McGill put a crackle in his voice. 'On your feet, man!'

Ballard heaved himself up and McGill led him to the viewpoint. 'Take a look.'

Ballard looked down the valley and his face crumpled. 'Christ!' he breathed. 'There's nothing left.'

'There's plenty left,' contradicted McGill. 'But we have to find it.'

'But what can we do?' said Ballard in despair.

'You can wake up for a start,' said McGill brutally. 'Then we look for the rest of the guys who were around here, and we wake them up. We have to get some sort of organization going.'

Ballard looked once more at the desolation and then stepped down from the mound. He rubbed his stinging cheek, and said, 'Thanks, Mike.'

'Okay,' said McGill. 'You look over there and see who you can find.' He turned his back on Ballard and walked away. Ballard trudged slowly in the direction McGill had indicated. His brain still felt pummelled.

Fifteen minutes later they had grown from two to twenty. One by one the stunned survivors were ruthlessly extracted from the holes where they were hiding, and McGill showed no mercy in the way he handled them. They were all shocked in varying degrees and all showed a marked aversion to looking up at the slope, now visible, from which disaster had come. They stood around apathetically with their backs to the west.

McGill selected the brightest of them and set them searching in their turn and more survivors came to light. In half an hour he was beginning to believe they might stand a chance. He gave one man his notebook and a ball pen and instructed him to take the name of each survivor. 'And ask him who he was standing next to just before he ran for cover. We want to find out who's missing.'

To Ballard he said, 'Take three men and go to Turi Buck's house. Find out how they're shaping.' Others he sent to Matt Houghton's house and he himself set off for the town.

His last command was: 'If anyone finds Dr Scott, he's to report to me.'

As it happened, Dr Scott was also on his way to town. He had to cross the river and the bridge had been swept away, but there was no need for a bridge because the river bed was full of snow and he was able to walk across, but with difficulty because the snow was soft. He crossed the river opposite the bluff about where the Supermarket had been and he was still unable to take in the enormity of the disaster. It did not seem either reasonable or possible that the Supermarket should have disappeared.

He trudged through the hampering snow holding his bag, the contents of which were precious. In the distance he saw something black outlined against the prevailing whiteness which, when he came nearer, proved to be a man buried to his waist. Next to him was an overturned coffee-pot.

Scott bent down, turned the man's head and recognized the Reverend Davis. He was alive but his pulse was weak and fluttery. Scott scrabbled at the snow, digging with his gloved hands. The snow was not very compacted and the digging was comparatively easy; within ten minutes Davis was freed and lying on the surface.

As Scott was opening his bag he heard voices in the distance, so he stood up and saw a group of men picking their way over the snow where the town had been. He shouted and waved, and presently they came up to him. The man in the lead was the Canadian, McGill.

'I'm glad you survived, Doctor,' said McGill. 'You're going to be needed. How is he?'

'He'll live,' said Scott. 'He needs to be kept warm. Hot soup would help.'

'He'll have it if Turi Buck's house held up. The church is still standing so we'll use that as a base. Better take him there.' McGill looked down at Davis and noted the clerical collar. 'Seems appropriate. As for heat, he'll have that if we have to burn all the pews.'

Scott looked around. 'What a hell of a mess.'

McGill turned to MacAllister, the man from the power station. 'Mac, you take a couple of guys and go to the Gap. If anyone is coming over tell them we need help real bad. But we need trained help – men who know about snow rescue. We don't want a lot of amateurs lousing the place up.'

MacAllister nodded and turned away. McGill said, 'And, Mac, if there are trained snow dogs in New Zealand we need those, too.'

'Right,' said MacAllister, and selected his men.

Others helped pick up Davis, and McGill led the way to the church.

Turi Buck had left McLean when the engineer was still in a shocked stupor. He went to the source of the screaming, taking with him a jar of barley sugar which he found in the kitchen. It took him a long time to subdue the terrified children, but presently he was helped by Ruihi.

'The barley sugar is good,' she said. 'But hot, sweet cocoa would be better.' She went into the kitchen and had to remake the fire which had been extinguished, and when she lit the fire the kitchen filled with smoke because the flue was choked with snow.

Miss Frobisher was of no use at all. She was curled into a foetal ball and whimpered from time to time. Turi ignored her and directed his attention to the children.

McLean looked down at the spanner in his hand and frowned. Slowly his mind began to work. *Why am I holding this spanner?* he asked himself, and the answer came creaking into his mind. *The generator!*

He moved stiffly towards the door and opened it. A light breeze came into the room, whirling up the powdered snow on the floor. He stepped outside and looked towards the rock of Kamakamaru and crinkled his eyes in disbelief. The generator stood where he had left it, even though it had not been bolted down. *Thank God!* he thought. *What's good for rabbits is good for generators.*

But the portable air compressor he had used to drive the drill had vanished, and he remembered it had stood on the place on the rock where he had first proposed to put the generator. He walked forward past a tree which had been sheared at a height of ten feet. He stopped and grunted in his throat as he saw the drill. The air hose which had connected it to the compressor had snapped and now swayed in the breeze; the drill itself was driven deep into the trunk of the tree as though it had been flung like a giant dart.

When Ballard and his team arrived at the house he was thankful to hear the voices and even laughter. Children are resilient, and, once the shock had worn off, they became excited, even over-excited. He went inside and saw Turi sitting in a big armchair surrounded by a flock of children and looking somewhat like a biblical patriarch. 'Thank God!' he said. 'Are you all right, Turi?'

'We're all fine.' Turi nodded across the room to where Ruihi was supporting Miss Frobisher and administering tea. 'She was shaken up a bit.'

From behind the house came a whine which settled into a steady throb. Startled, Ballard said, 'What's that?'

'I think Jock McLean will be testing the generator.' Turi stood up. 'Would you like some tea?' he asked, as politely as though they were ordinary guests visiting his home.

Ballard nodded dumbly. Turi sent one of the older children into the kitchen with instructions to bring back tea and sandwiches. Then he said, 'What happened to the town?'

'Turi, there is no town.'

'Gone?'

'I saw nothing standing except the church.'

'And the people?'

Ballard shook his head. 'I don't know. Mike is there now.'

'I will come to help search,' said Turi. 'After you have refreshed yourselves.'

Presently the tea and sandwiches arrived and Ballard ate as hungrily as though he had not eaten for a week. The hot tea was welcome, too, especially as Turi had laced it liberally with brandy.

When he had finished he idly picked up the telephone and held it to his ear. All he got was silence. As he cradled it he said, 'Communications – that's what we're going to need. There was some food supposed to come here, Turi.'

'It came. We have plenty of food.'

'We'll take some back to town. It will be a load to carry but we'll have to manage.'

Ruihi said, 'The car's in the garage, isn't it?'

Ballard sat upright. 'You have a *car*?'

'It's not much of a car,' said Turi. 'But it goes.'

Ballard thought of the soft snow which covered Hukahoronui and thought that perhaps the car was not such a good idea after all; but he went out to have a look at it. It proved to be an elderly Australian Holden stationwagon and he ignored it because the Massey-Ferguson tractor standing next to it looked to be worth its weight in diamond-studded platinum. Fifteen minutes later it was loaded with canned goods and on its way to town, towing an improvised sledge.

*   *   *

When Ballard arrived at the church he found more people than he had expected, with McGill at an improvised desk by the altar, the centre of a growing organization. In one corner Scott was very busy, aided by three women. Most of his patients had broken bones and two men were breaking up a pew to make splints. Ballard saw that Eric Peterson was in line for attention, so he strode over to him. 'Is Liz all right?'

Eric's face was white and drawn. 'I don't know. She and that American girl were at Rawson's shop, I think, when we were hit.' His eyes were bleak. 'The shop's gone – not there at all.' There was hysteria in his voice.

'You have your arm fixed,' said Ballard. 'I'll check.'

He went over to McGill. 'Turi's place is okay,' he said. 'Everyone is fine there. They've got a generator working and I have a load of food outside – with a tractor. You'd better take charge of that.'

McGill gave a long sigh. 'Thank God the kids are safe.' He nodded. 'Good work, Ian. That tractor will be useful.' Ballard turned away and McGill said, 'Where are you going?'

'To look for Liz and Stacey. They were in the chemist's shop.'

'You'll do nothing of the kind,' snapped McGill. 'I don't want any half-assed rescue attempts.'

'But – '

'But nothing. If you go tramping out there you'll ruin the scent for a dog, and a dog can do better work than a hundred men. That's why everybody is being kept in this church – for a time, at least. If you have information about where people were when we were hit, take it to Arthur Pye over there. He's our Bureau of Missing Persons.'

Ballard was about to reply hotly but someone pushed past him and he recognized Dickinson who worked at the mine. Dickinson said quickly, 'I've just come from Houghton's house and it's like a bloody butcher's shop up there. I think some of the people are still alive, though. I reckon we need Dr Scott.'

McGill raised his voice. 'Dr Scott, will you come here?

Scott finished knotting an improvised bandage and walked across. McGill said to Dickinson, 'Carry on.'

'The house looks as though it blew apart,' said Dickinson. 'I found Jack Baxter and Matt Houghton outside the house. Jack's as chirpy as a cricket, but his leg's broken. There's something funny about Matt; he can hardly speak and he's paralysed all down one side.'

'Could be a stroke,' said Scott.

'I put them both in a car and brought them down as far as I could. I didn't dare cross the river on that soft snow so I left them on the other side.'

'And the house?'

'Oh, it's bloody awful in there. I didn't stop to count the bodies but there seemed to be hundreds. Some of them are still alive, I do know that.'

'What sort of injuries?' asked Scott. 'I'll need to know what to take.'

McGill grinned mirthlessly. 'You've not got much. Better take the lot.'

'Turi brought a first-aid kit from the house,' said Ballard.

Scott said, 'That I can use.'

They had not been conscious of the distant vibration in the air but now it burst upon them with a bellow. Ballard jerked and ducked his head, thinking it was another avalanche about to hit them but McGill looked up at the roof. 'A plane – and a goddamn big one!'

He got to his feet and ran to the church door, followed by the others. The aircraft had gone down the valley and was now banking and turning to come back. As it came closer they saw it was a big transport marked with United States Navy insignia.

A ragged cheer broke out and there was a beatific smile on McGill's face. 'A Navy Hercules from Harewood,' he said. 'The Marines have arrived in the nick of time.'

The Hercules finished its turn and steadied at a lower altitude, flying straight down the valley. From its stern black specks dropped and then the parachutes opened and blossomed like multi-coloured flowers. McGill counted: '. . . seven . . . eight . . . nine . . . ten. And those are just the experts we need.'

THE HEARING

Eighth Day

TWENTY-FIVE

John Reed, Secretary to the Commission, poised his pen expectantly. 'Your full name, please?'

'Jesse Willard Rusch.' The tall, squarely-built man with the decidedly unfashionable crewcut had a strong American accent.

'And your occupation, Mr Rusch?'

'By rank I am a Lieutenant-Commander in the United States Navy. By occupation I am, at present, Supply Officer to Antarctic Development Squadron Six. It's the outfit that does all the flying in the Antarctic in support of our Operation Deep Freeze.'

'Thank you,' said Reed.

Harrison regarded the American with interest. 'I understand that you were the first man trained in snow rescue to arrive in Hukahoronui after the avalanche.'

'I understand that, too, sir. But there were five of us. My feet happened to hit the ground first.'

'But you were the leader.'

'Yes, sir.'

'Can you tell us the chain of circumstances which took you there?'

'Yes, sir. I understand that your Civil Defence people put in a request to Commander Lindsey, the officer commanding our Advanced Base here in Christchurch. Because the request concerned snow rescue and because I am Supply Officer to VXE-6 – that's the squadron – he dumped the job in my lap.'

Harrison stared at the ceiling and the notion crossed his mind that Americans were strange people. 'I don't quite see the connection,' he said. 'What has snow rescue to do with you being Supply Officer? I take it that a Supply Officer is of the nature of a quartermaster.'

'Sort of,' said Rusch. 'I'll have to explain. There's always a lot to do in the Antarctic; there are usually more jobs than bodies, so it becomes normal for a man to wear two hats, as it were. It has become a tradition, a much prized tradition, that the Supply Officer of VXE-6 doubles up on rescue and is automatically in command of any rescue operations in the field, particularly those involving air transport.'

'I see. That explains it, then.'

'I ought to say that we are all trained parachutists. We do our parachute training at Lakehurst, New Jersey, and our field rescue training in the region of Mount Erebus in the Antarctic. Our training there is done with experienced instructors drawn from the Federated Mountain Clubs of New Zealand.' Rusch paused. 'So when a New Zealander makes a request we jump to it fast.'

'You have made yourself very clear.'

'Thank you, sir. At the time of the request, which was in mid-winter, the staff of our Advanced Headquarters here was run down. Flights to the ice – to the Antarctic – are not routine at that time of the year and any flights are for emergencies, or perhaps experimental reasons. We normally have twelve men tapped for rescue – all volunteers, I might add – but at that time only myself and four others were available.'

Harrison made a note. 'Have you ever run short of volunteers?'

Rusch shook his head. 'Not to my knowledge, sir.'

'Interesting. Please proceed.'

'We were briefed, together with the aircrew, and the aircraft was loaded with our equipment which is prepacked ready for instant use. The standard operating procedure is that a team of four men jump with one packed sled. However, in view of the briefing and the possible conditions at our destination I loaded extra sleds. We jumped with five men and five sleds and landed in Hukahoronui at 12.56 hours. To the best of my knowledge that was fifty-five minutes after the disaster.' Rusch smiled. 'Imagine my feelings when the first man to greet me turned out to be someone I already knew from the Antarctic – Dr McGill.'

Rusch smothered his parachute and snapped the quick release button. He pushed back his face mask and checked the others as they came down, then turned to meet the group of men who were stumbling towards him across the snow. Arms akimbo, he stared incredulously at the man in the lead. 'Well, I'll be a son of a bitch!' he said. As McGill approached Rusch stepped forward. 'Dr McGill, I presume.'

'Good morning, Lieutenant-Commander.' McGill rubbed his eyes tiredly. 'Or is it afternoon?'

'It's afternoon, and it doesn't look too good to me. Where's the town?'

'You're looking at it.'

Rusch looked about him and whistled softly. 'You've cut yourself a slice of trouble, Mike. Are you in charge here?'

'I guess I am.'

'No!' Ballard came forward, his hand gripping Eric Peterson's good arm. 'This is Eric Peterson, a town councillor – the only one around. He represents the civil authority.'

Rusch gave McGill a quizzical glance, then shook Peterson's left hand a little awkwardly. 'We could have met in better circumstances, Mr Peterson.'

Peterson was taken wrong-footed. 'Me!' he said to Ballard. 'What about Matt Houghton?'

'He seems to have had a stroke.'

Peterson's face worked. 'Well, now,' he said indistinctly, and indicated his right arm. 'I can't fly fast on a broken wing. You'd better be co-opted, Ian. You and McGill.'

'Right!' Ballard turned to Rusch. 'We need medical supplies.'

'Those we've got.' Rusch swung around and yelled, 'Hey, Chief, I want the medical sled – on the double.'

Ballard said, 'Dr Scott, you take charge of that, and make all necessary arrangements. What about communications, Lieutenant . . . er . . .?'

'Rusch. Lieutenant-Commander Rusch. We have five walkie-talkies, so we can set up a network. There's a bigger transmitter in one of the sleds for outside communication. We ought to be able to raise Chi-Chi . . . Christchurch, that is.'

'That had better go to the church,' Ballard decided. 'That's our headquarters. I'd like to talk to somebody at Civil Defence as soon as possible.' He paused. 'By the way, I'm Ian Ballard. Let's get busy.'

On the way back to the church McGill fell in step with Ballard. 'What did Turi feed you on at the house? Raw meat?'

'Someone must take charge of administration and it's not going to be you. You know about snow rescue, so get to it. But before you go let me have a list of what you need so I can make sense when I talk to Christchurch.'

'Okay.' They walked a few more paces, and McGill said, 'What was the idea of pushing Peterson forward like that? He's as much use as a fifth wheel.'

'Strategy. He abdicated – didn't you hear him? I knew it would happen. Look, Mike: I'm a trained administrator and I'd be wasted doing anything else. You're a snowman and you'd be wasted doing anything else. Let's get our priorities right.'

'Makes sense.' McGill grinned. 'And legal, too. We're now town councillors, you and me both.'

They went into the church, Rusch stopped just inside and frowned as he surveyed the scene. 'Worse than a war.'

The pews were full of white-faced, lethargic men and women with lustreless eyes. They sat or lay in abandoned attitudes, still and silent, gazing back in horror at the closeness of death. Only a few of them moved and, of those, only a scant half-dozen were attempting to help the others.

McGill said, 'You're not going to get much help from this lot. They've been hit badly by disaster shock.'

'Blankets,' said Ballard. 'We'll need blankets. Come up to the office.' He led the way to the desk that McGill had set up, and sat behind it. 'Right, Mike. What else do we need?'

'Trained rescue men – in quantity. They can come in by helicopter and light planes equipped with skis. And they can get these people out on the return trip.'

'We've got some helos at Harewood,' said Rusch. 'We've been stripping down for winter maintenance but I know that four are serviceable.'

'We need rescue dogs, too,' said McGill.

'I don't think so,' said Rusch. 'There are none in the country as far as I know. I could be wrong, though. Try Mount Cook and Coronet Peak.'

Ballard nodded. Those were popular skiing and climbing areas. 'There should be trained men there, too.'

Rusch said, 'Your doctor has gone to a house the other side of the valley. One of my guys has gone with him. I'll leave another here to help with the radio, and then he can help with the injured here. We're not exactly medicos but we can set bones. The rest of us will take a general look at the situation and set out a plan.'

Ballard raised his voice. 'Arthur, come here for a minute.'

Arthur Pye, who was trying to question one of the survivors and not getting very far, straightened up and

walked to the desk. His face was haggard and his movements stiff, but there was that spark of intelligence and
comprehension in his eyes which was missing from most
of the others.

Ballard said, 'What's the score, Arthur? How many
missing?'

'God, I don't know.' Pye wiped his face with a big hand.
'How could anyone know?'

'Then make a guess. I have to tell Christchurch something.'

'It's bloody hard getting anything out of anybody.' Pye
hesitated. 'All right – say three hundred and fifty.'

Rusch stiffened. *That many!*

Pye waved his hand. 'You've seen the town – or what's
left of it. They're still drifting in, one or two at a time. I reckon the final tally will be very much less.'

McGill said, 'The ones who are coming in now are the
lucky ones. There'll be others who are buried.'

'Come on, Mike,' said Rusch. 'Let's start looking. Our
radio man is fixing up the transmitter, Mr Ballard. If you
want to contact me use his walkie-talkie.'

Rusch and McGill left the church and Ballard looked up
at Pye. 'Are you sure about the number?'

'Of course I'm not sure,' said Pye wearily. 'But it's about
that. I think John Peterson bought it. Mary Rees says she saw
him run out into the street just before the avalanche hit.'

One of the Americans walked up the central aisle unreeling wire from a drum. He stopped in front of the desk and
said, 'CPO Laird, sir. I've got the radio set up outside; it's
better there because of the antenna. But I have a portable
handset you can use here. It's two-way – you use it like an
ordinary telephone.' He put the handset on the desk and
plugged it in.

Ballard looked down at the telephone. 'Who will I be
talking to?'

'Communications centre, Operation Deep Freeze. I've just been talking to them.'

Ballard took a deep breath and stretched out his hand. 'Hello, this is Ballard in Hukahoronui. Can you put me through to Civil Defence Headquarters? It's in the Reserve Bank Building, Hereford Str – '

A calm voice cut in. 'No need for that, Mr Ballard. They're on the line now.'

TWENTY-SIX

Rusch, McGill and two of the American servicemen crunched across the snow over the desolation that was Hukahoronui. McGill took off his glove and bent to feel the texture of the snow. 'It's hardening,' he said, and straightened up. 'I was training some guys in snow rescue before we got hit. I said then they'd be no good, and I was right. You know what's worrying me right now?'

'What?' asked Rusch.

'We're going to get a lot of people flying in here if Ballard does his stuff – maybe several hundreds.' McGill nodded to the west slope. 'I'm worried that she'll come down again. That would really compound this disaster.'

'Is it likely?'

'There's still a lot of snow up there, so I think only half of it came down, sliding on a hoar frost surface. I'd like to take a look.'

The man behind Rusch touched his arm. 'Sir.'

'What is it, Cotton?'

'Look at that dog, sir. It's sniffing at something in the snow.'

They looked to where Cotton pointed and saw an Alsatian pawing at the snow and whining. 'Maybe it's not trained,' said McGill. 'But it's the best we've got.'

As they approached, the dog looked up at them and wagged its tail – and then scraped at the snow with its forepaw. 'Good dog,' said Rusch. 'Cotton, use that shovel.'

Cotton found the body beneath three feet of snow and Rusch checked the pulse. 'This one is gone. Let's get him out.'

They pulled the body from the snow and Rusch's breath hissed from his lips. 'What in the name of God happened to his face? Do you know him, Mike?'

'His wife wouldn't know him,' said McGill bleakly. His face was pale.

The dog wagged its tail happily and trotted off across the snow, where it stopped and began to sniff and scratch again. 'Cotton, you're now the dog handler,' said Rusch. 'Harris, round up some able-bodied men and dig wherever that German shepherd scratches.'

McGill heard the familiar sound of skis hissing on snow and turned to see two men approaching. They stopped and the one in the lead pushed up his goggles. 'What can I do to help?' said Charlie Peterson.

McGill looked down at Charlie's feet. 'You can lend me your skis for a start. I'm going up the mountain.'

Miller pushed forward from behind Charlie and stared down at the body. 'Christ!' he said. 'What happened to him?' A retching sound came from him and he turned and vomited helplessly.

The body did not seem to worry Charlie. He looked down, and said, 'It's Rawson. What happened to him?'

'How do you know who it is?' asked Rusch. 'The guy's got no face.'

Charlie pointed. 'He lost the first joint of the little finger of his left hand.' He looked up at McGill. 'Take Miller's skis. I'll come with you.'

'That slope's not the safest place in the world, Charlie.'

Charlie grinned crookedly. 'You can get killed crossing the road. I said that before, didn't I?'

McGill gave Charlie a level stare, then made up his mind.

'Okay. Help me get them off him. He's in no condition to do it himself.'

Five minutes later Rusch watched them go. He looked up at the slope and frowned. It wasn't a job he would fancy doing. 'Sir!' called Cotton urgently. 'We've got another one – alive and female.'

Rusch strode over. 'Be careful with that shovel, Harris. Cotton, bring up that empty sled.'

The limp body of Liz Peterson was lifted on to the sled and covered warmly with a blanket. Rusch looked down at her. 'Lovely girl,' he commented. 'Take her to the church. We've just started to earn our pay.'

The Canterbury Provincial Chamber was very quiet as Lieutenant-Commander Rusch gave his evidence, although there had been a shocked whisper as he described the finding of Rawson's body.

'The dog was a big help in that first hour, sir,' said Rusch. 'He found three victims, two of whom were alive. But then he lost interest. I think he was tired – the snow was very deep and hard to get through, and maybe his scent was failing. He wasn't a trained animal, anyway.'

'Did you find out whom the dog belonged to?' asked Harrison.

'His name was Victor and he belonged to the Scanlon family. There were no survivors from the Scanlon family.'

'I hope Victor has found a good home.'

'I believe he has, sir. Miss Peterson is looking after him.'

Harrison looked across the room towards the Petersons' table. He smiled at Liz Peterson and nodded. 'Most appropriate,' he commented. He consulted his watch. 'Our next evidence deals with the activities of the Civil Defence authorities. As it is getting late in the afternoon this hearing will adjourn until ten o'clock tomorrow morning.'

He turned to Rusch. 'Thank you, Lieutenant-Commander. It only remains for me to thank you and your comrades for a job well done.'

The hard-bitten Rusch actually blushed.

TWENTY-SEVEN

'Listening to that evidence gave me a cold grue all over again,' said McGill. 'I was too busy at the time to think about it much, but when you get it all laid out then it really hits you.'

'A terrible experience,' said Stenning.

They were standing at the desk in the hotel waiting for the receptionist to finish telephoning. 'Where is Ian?' asked Stenning.

'Gone off somewhere with Liz,' McGill smiled. 'Have you come up with an answer to the question I asked? What happens if Ian marries her?'

Stenning shook his head. 'That will take a great deal of thought.'

The receptionist came off the telephone and took keys from a board. 'Mr Stenning. Dr McGill. There's a letter for you, Dr McGill.'

'Thank you.' McGill tossed the letter lightly in his hand. 'Care to join me in a drink?'

'I think not,' said Stenning. 'I think I'll take a short nap.'

Stenning went to his room and McGill went into the bar. He ordered a drink and then opened the letter. As he unfolded the sheets a cheque slipped out and fluttered to the bar counter. He picked it up, glanced at it, and his eyes

292

widened as he saw the amount it was made out for. He laid
down the cheque and his brows drew together as he read
the first page of the letter. He flipped over the sheet and
read absorbedly, the drink untasted at his elbow. He arrived
at the final page then, turning back to the beginning, he
read it all through again. Then he sat on the bar stool
and looked ahead of him broodingly, which unnerved the
bar-tender who happened to be at the focus of his blank
stare.

'Anything wrong with your drink, sir?'

'What?' McGill roused himself. 'No, give me another –
and make it a double.' He picked up the glass and swallowed
the neat scotch in one gulp.

When Ballard arrived McGill was waiting for him
and steered him into the bar. McGill crooked his finger
at the bar-tender. 'Two more doubles. We're celebrating,
Ian.'

'What's there to celebrate?'

'Guess what I've got in my pocket?'

'How could I possibly guess?' Ballard looked at McGill
closely. 'Mike, are you drunk? You look like a boiled owl.'

'In my pocket,' said McGill seriously. 'In my pocket I
have a steamroller. It arrived air mail from Los Angeles.'
He took the letter from his breast pocket and waved it
under Ballard's nose. 'Read it, my friend. Read it and
weep. I don't feel like cheering even though it's the saving
of you.'

'I think you *are* drunk.' Ballard took the envelope and
opened it. He glanced at the cheque and said, 'What the hell
is this? A bribe?'

'Read,' urged McGill.

Ballard started to read the first page and then, frowning,
glanced at the bottom of the last page to find that the letter was from the American, Miller. Its contents were
appalling.

'Dear Dr McGill,

'I have been wanting to write this letter for a long time but I have been putting it off because I guess I was scared. What happened has been on my conscience ever since the avalanche which caused so many deaths, including that of my good friend, Ralph Newman. A friend sent me newspaper clips about the inquiry into the Hukahoronui disaster. On reading the clips I relived that terrible experience and I know I have to speak up. I am having this letter notarized so that it may be used in evidence if you think it necessary, but I send it to you in the hope that you will not think it necessary. I leave it to your good judgment.

'Early on the morning of that dreadful Sunday I went skiing with Charlie Peterson. There was a mist in the valley but he said there would be sun on the higher slopes. I was a bit nervous because I had heard talk of avalanches at the hotel, but Charlie laughed at me and said that someone was pulling my leg. We went up into the hills at the head of the valley and did some skiing but the slopes were not very good there, and Charlie suggested that we go to the slopes nearer Hukahoronui. This we did.

'We finally arrived at the top of the west slope above the town and we saw a sign there saying that no skiing was allowed. I wanted to turn around and go another way, but Charlie said the land was Peterson land and that no one could stop him from doing what he wanted on his own land. He said all this talk of avalanches was nonsense and there had never been one in Hukahoronui. He laughed when he said the sign had been put up by boy scouts and it was just about their mark.

'We had quite an argument up there on the mountain. I said the scouts must have been told to put the sign there and I guessed it was you who had told them. I said that maybe you were right about the danger of an avalanche. Charlie just stood there laughing and there was something funny about him right at that time. He said that an avalanche might be a good thing and anything that could get rid of Mr Ballard couldn't be all bad.

'He went on about Ballard for quite a while, a lot of real wild talk. He said that Ballard had killed his brother and stolen the mine from his father and that it was about time someone stopped him from stealing the whole of Hukahoronui. He ranted on like this for maybe five minutes, then he said the mine wouldn't do Ballard much good if it wasn't there.

'I told him he was talking crazy and asked him how he could make a whole gold mine disappear. Suddenly he shouted, "I'll show you!" and took off down the hill. He wasn't going very fast and he kept jumping up and down very heavily. I went after him to try to stop him, but suddenly there was a crackling noise like French fries in the pan and Charlie gave a shout. I stopped and saw him jumping sideways up the hill.

'Nothing seemed to happen at first and then I saw the snow cracking where Charlie had been. A lot of cracks zigzagged very fast and a bit of snow went up into the air. Then the slide started. Charlie and I were safe because we were above the fall. We just stood there and watched it happen and I've never seen a more awful sight.

We watched it go down into the mist over the town and I started to cry. I'm not ashamed of that.

Charlie shook me and said I was a crybaby. He said
to keep my mouth shut. He said if I told anybody
about it he would kill me. I believed him when he
said that – he was crazy enough for anything.

'I asked him what we were going to do and he said
we were going into town to see what had happened.
He said it was just a lot of feathery stuff that had
gone and it had probably just given the people a good
scare, though he hoped it had done for the mine. He
laughed as he said that. So we went into the town
and saw the dreadful thing that had happened.

'Then Charlie threatened me again. He said that if
I as much as blinked an eyelid in his direction the
world would not be big enough; he would search me
out and find me wherever I was.

'As God is my witness this is the truth of what
happened that Sunday morning. I am deeply ashamed
of my silence and I hope this letter will go towards
making amends. I suppose there will be a public fund
for the families of the victims because there usually is.
I enclose a check for $10,000. This is nearly all my
savings and I cannot afford more.'

Ballard looked up. 'For God's sake!'

'It's like holding an unexploded bomb, isn't it?'

'But we can't use *this*.'

'Why not? Stenning would just love you.'

'To hell with Stenning. I wouldn't do that to anybody.
Besides . . .'

His voice tailed away, and McGill said, 'Lover's Lane must
run straight and narrow? Ian, you have the Ballard Trust
right in the palm of your hand.'

Ballard stared at the drink in front of him. He put his
hand out, but only to push it away in a rejecting gesture.
He turned to McGill. 'Mike, tell me something and tell me

honestly. Before the avalanche we were making every preparation possible. We *expected* an avalanche, didn't we? Does this really make any difference?' He tapped for emphasis on the bar counter and, as the bar-tender came running, he shook his head violently in negation. 'You exonerated the pilot of that plane – you said the snow was ready to come down. Do you still believe that?'

McGill sighed. 'Yes, I still believe it.'

'Then we don't use this.'

'You're too gentlemanly for your own good, Ian. This is a tough world we live in.'

'I wouldn't want to live in the kind of world where I'd use this letter.'

'It won't wash,' said McGill flatly. 'I know what you're thinking. If this letter is produced you can say goodbye to Liz. But it's not good enough. That son of a bitch killed fifty-four people. If Miller had claimed it was accidental I might have gone along, but he says Charlie did it deliberately. You can't suppress it.'

'What do I do, Mike?'

'There's nothing for you to do. It's my responsibility. The letter is addressed to me.' He took it from Ballard's fingers, replaced it in the envelope, and put it back in his pocket.

'Liz will never believe I didn't go along with you,' said Ballard gloomily.

McGill shrugged. 'Probably not.' He picked up his glass. 'Come to think of it, I don't think I'd like you as much if you'd grabbed the chance of hammering the Petersons with eager cries. You're a silly bastard, but I still love you.' He raised the glass in a toast. 'Here's to chivalry – still alive and living in Christchurch.'

'I still think you're drunk.'

'That I am, and I'm going to get a hell of a lot drunker – if only to forget how many shits there are in this world.' He drained his glass and set it down with a thump.

'When are you going to give the letter to Harrison?'

'Tomorrow, of course.'

'Hold off for a bit,' said Ballard urgently. 'I'd like to get straightened out with Liz first. I wouldn't want her to get this slammed at her cold at the Inquiry.'

McGill pondered. 'Okay, I'll save it for twenty-four hours.'

'Thanks.' Ballard pushed his untasted drink before McGill. 'If you're insistent on getting drunk there's my contribution.'

McGill twisted on his stool and watched Ballard walk out of the bar, then he turned back to the hovering bar-tender. 'Two more doubles.'

'Then the gentleman is coming back?'

'No, he's not coming back,' said McGill absently. 'But you're right about one thing. He *is* a gentleman – and there are damned few of them around these days.'

Ballard and Stenning dined together that night. Ballard was abstracted and in no mood for small talk. Stenning noted this and was quiet, but over coffee he asked, 'Ian, what is your relationship with Miss Peterson?'

Ballard jerked his head, a little startled by the intrusive question. 'I don't see that's any of your business.'

'Don't you?' Stenning stirred his coffee. 'You forget the matter of the Ballard Trust. It is still very much on *my* mind.'

'I don't see what Liz has to do with it.' His lip curled. 'Don't tell me you want me to walk over her, too.'

'I don't want you to do anything you don't wish to.'

'You'd better not try,' said Ballard.

'Yet I have to interpret Ben's wishes, and it's much more difficult than I anticipated. Ben didn't tell me about Liz Peterson.'

'The old man didn't think much of women,' remarked Ballard. 'He lived for business, and for him women had no place in business so consequently they didn't exist. He didn't tell you about Liz because, to him, she was a nonentity.'

'You understand Ben better than I thought.' Stenning paused with his coffee cup in mid-air, then set it down gently. 'Yes, that is certainly something to be taken into consideration.'

'I don't know what you're talking about.'

'It depends on your relationship with Miss Peterson. It was something McGill asked me – he wanted to know, if you married her, whether it would have any effect in the "Peterson Bashing Contest", as he called it.'

'And what answer did you give him?'

'A dusty one,' said Stenning. 'I had to think about it.'

Ballard leaned forward. 'Let me tell you something,' he said in a low, but intense, voice. 'Ben thought he was God. He manipulated me, and he's been manipulating the family through the Trust. Now that's all right if it's just in the course of business, but if the old bastard is going to control my private life from beyond the grave, then that's another thing.'

Stenning nodded. 'Your analysis of Ben's attitude towards women has proved quite illuminating. I think you are quite right when you say that Ben didn't mention Miss Peterson because he discounted her completely. This, therefore, has a strong bearing on how I intend to interpret his wishes. The conclusion I have come to is this: you may marry or you may not – you may even marry Miss Peterson or you may not. Whatever you do will have no bearing on my decision regarding your suitability as a trustee. If Ben discounted Miss Peterson, then so shall I.'

'Thanks,' said Ballard hollowly.

'Of course, the problem still remains with the Peterson brothers.'

'Thanks again,' said Ballard. 'For nothing. Do you really believe that if I walk over the Petersons, as you so delicately put it, I would stand a chance with Liz? God knows she doesn't get on with her brothers, but she wouldn't be the woman I think she is, the woman I want to marry, if she didn't have some family loyalty.'

'Yes, you would appear to have quite a problem.'

Ballard stood up. 'Then to hell with you, Mr Stenning.' He threw down his napkin. 'And to hell with the Ballard Trust.'

Stenning watched him walk away, his face expressionless. He lifted the cup to his lips and found the coffee cold, so he called for another cup.

THE HEARING

Twelfth Day

TWENTY-EIGHT

Witness after witness passed before Harrison and his assessors, their actions minutely scrutinized, their utterances
tested; a long parade of townsfolk, policemen, mountain
rangers, doctors, engineers, scientists, soldiers and civil
defence workers. Dan Edwards, wearied in the Press gallery,
said to Dalwood, 'I think the old bastard is hoping for a new
job when he dies – he's understudying the Recording
Angel.'

There was a movement in the valley. At first there was just
a handful of rescuers but the number swelled hour by hour,
brought in by helicopter and ski plane. The mountain
rangers came from Mount Cook, from Coronet Peak, from
Mount Egmont, from Tongariro – men knowledgeable and
skilled in their trade of snow rescue. Doctors came in Air
Force and US Navy helicopters, which took out the children
and the badly injured.

The mass of snow which blocked the Gap was attacked
fiercely. Steps were cut and guide ropes laid so that within
hours it was possible for any moderately active person to
enter or leave the valley. This was done by volunteers from
the mountain clubs who had come in dozens at a time to
the place of disaster, many of them flying from as far as
North Island.

These men knew what to do and, once in the valley, they formed teams to probe the snow, at first working under the general direction of Jesse Rusch. They were aided by a force of police and an even larger detachment of troops. Even so, they were not too many; the area to be patiently probed, foot by foot, was over four hundred acres.

At first Ballard acted as co-ordinator, but he was glad to be relieved by a professional civil defence man flown in from Christchurch. He stayed on to help Arthur Pye. The identification of the survivors and the dead and the listing of those still missing was work in which local knowledge was vital. There was pain in his eyes as he saw the name of Stacey Cameron on the list of the dead.

He said, 'Any news of Joe Cameron?'

Pye shook his head. 'Not a sign of him. He must be buried out there somewhere. They've found Dobbs dead. Funny thing about that: the chap who dug him out said that Dobbs had cut his throat. The body was drained of blood.' He rubbed his eyes. 'God, but I'm tired.'

'Take a break, Arthur,' said Ballard. 'Get something to eat and have a nap. I can carry on.'

'If I went to sleep now I feel as though I'd never wake up again.' Pye rose from his chair and stretched. 'I'll take a walk outside. The fresh air might do me some good.'

Ballard checked to find if he was needed and then walked over to a pew where Liz Peterson was lying swathed in blankets. Her face was deathly pale and she still appeared to be dazed. He knelt beside her, and said, 'How are you feeling, Liz?'

'A bit better now.'

'Have you had some soup?'

She nodded and moistened her lips. 'Have you found Johnnie yet?'

He hesitated, wondering whether to tell her or not. She had to know sooner or later, so he said gently, 'He's dead, Liz.' She closed her eyes and sighed. 'He died well. Young Mary Rees says he was trying to get Mrs Scanlon out of the exchange when it happened.'

Liz opened her eyes. 'And Stacey?'

Ballard shook his head.

'But she was with me – she was standing right next to me. How can she be dead when I'm not?'

'You were lucky. You were one of the first to be found. Stacey was only a few feet from you but nobody knew that. When there were enough men to make a proper search it was too late for Stacey. And Joe is still missing.'

'Poor Stacey. She was on holiday, you know.'

'I know.'

'She thought a lot of you, Ian.'

'Did she?'

'More than you know.' Liz leaned up on one elbow. 'I've seen Eric, but where's Charlie?'

'He's all right. Take it easy, Liz. He volunteered to go up the mountain with Mike. Mike is afraid there'll be another fall so he's gone to check.'

'Oh my God!' said Liz. 'It would be terrible if it happened again.' She began to shiver uncontrollably.

'Don't worry. Mike wouldn't be on the mountain if he thought it was that dangerous. It's just a normal precaution, that's all.' He put his hands on her shoulders and pressed her back, then tucked the blankets closer about her. 'I think you'll be going out on the next flight.' He looked towards his work table. 'I must leave now, but I'll see you before you go.'

He went back to the table where Bill Quentin was standing. 'I hope it's good news, Bill.'

Quentin nodded. 'Mrs Haslam – they've just got her out. She's still alive but in pretty bad shape. The doctor said she'll be all right, though.'

Ballard crossed her name off one list and added it to another. 'Any news of her husband yet?'

'Not a thing.' Quentin hesitated. 'I made a damn fool of myself before the avalanche, Mr Ballard. I'm sorry about that.'

Ballard looked up. 'Not to worry, Bill. I've made some monumental bloody mistakes in my time, too. And while we're about it, my name is Ian. Those who have gone through this lot together are entitled to be on first name terms.'

Quentin swallowed. 'Thanks. I'll be getting back.'

'Bring good news.'

Miller wandered up. His face was pasty white and his eyes looked like two burnt holes in a blanket. 'Any news of Ralph Newman yet?'

'I'm sorry, Mr Miller. Nothing yet.'

Miller moved away again, mumbling to himself as he went. He had been asking that same question at ten minute intervals.

Ballard looked down at his lists. The papers were dog-eared and the lists confused, with many scribbles and rough erasures. He took fresh paper and began to transcribe them anew in alphabetical order, a tedious and mundane but necessary task.

Brewer, Anderson, Jenkins, Newman, Castle, Fowler – and Haslam; seven men – one dead – locked in a cave by snow and ice. They had no key.

'It's cold enough to freeze the balls off a brass monkey,' said Anderson.

Newman did not reply. It was the eighth time Anderson had uttered that conversational gem and it did not improve on rehearing. He pulled his anorak closer about his body and tried to control his fits of shivering.

'How long has it been?' asked Brewer.

Newman peered at his watch. 'Nearly six hours.'

There was a spasm of coughing from Jenkins. He spluttered a while before he brought it under control, then he gasped, 'Where are they? Where the devil are they?'

Newman said into the darkness, 'Brewer?'

'Yes?'

'What about another try?'

'It's bloody useless. You dig into the snow and it falls in from the top. You could get trapped that way.'

'Is that light still working?' For answer Brewer switched it on and there was a feeble glimmer. 'What if I tried?'

'It's too bloody dangerous.'

Newman shivered violently. 'I'd still like to try.'

'You're safer here in the cave. They'll be coming for us pretty soon.'

'If there's anyone left up there. Like to bet on it, Brewer?'

'I'm not a rich Yank,' said Brewer. 'I don't have the money to bet with.'

'Just your life,' said Newman. 'If we stay here we'll die anyway.'

'Shut up!' shouted Jenkins. 'You flaming well shut up!'

'Yes,' said Brewer. 'That kind of talk's no good.' He paused. 'Let's have another sing-song.'

'Singing won't get us out, either,' said Newman. 'We've got to work at it. We can't rely on anyone digging down to us. Who would know where to look?'

'Jenkins is right,' said Brewer sharply. 'If you can't be more cheerful you'd better keep quiet.'

Newman sighed. *What's the use?* he thought. Something occurred to him, and he said urgently, 'Sound off!'

'What's that?'

'Call out your names. I haven't heard Fowler or Castle for a long time.'

Castle said, 'Fowler's asleep.'

'Then you'd better wake him up before he dies.' Newman was boiling with frustration. 'Brewer, how much snow above us, do you think?'

'Too bloody much.'

'It might be only ten feet – it could be six feet. That's nothing.'

'For the last time,' said Brewer. 'Shut your big mouth.' Newman stirred and inadvertently put his hand on Haslam's face, knocking the hat aside. It was icy cold.

Newman was wrong.

The cave was in a jumble of big rocks, the debris of long-gone glaciation. The rock immediately above the cave was a big one, more than sixty feet high, which was why the place had been chosen as offering good shelter from the avalanche. It was reckoned that, when the snow came, it would pour over the top of the rock and anything at the bottom would be relatively sheltered.

And so it was – but the hollow in front of the rock had filled with snow as a housewife fills a cup with flour. The snow was level with the top of the rock. Newman was entirely wrong. The depth of snow above the cave entrance was not ten feet, or an optimistic six feet.

It was sixty feet.

Cameron shouted.

He had been shouting for a long time and all he had achieved was a sore throat and a hoarse voice. The truck rested upside down and he was still trapped with his foot jammed in the pedals. He had tried to release it but the pain caused by his movements soon made him stop. Consequently he, like the truck, was still upside down and he had the eerie impression that his head was bulging with the pressure of blood.

He also had a headache of such intensity that it nauseated him.

He shouted again. Even to him it sounded weak and when he stared at the snow through the shattered windscreen, which was feebly illuminated by the last glimmer of the roof light, he knew that the sound was being absorbed by that cotton-wool whiteness. For the tenth time he decided to stop shouting in order to conserve his strength. He knew he would break that promise to himself; the idea that someone might be quite close and not know he was there was too frightening. But he did stop shouting for a while.

He wondered how much snow there was above him. Three feet? Six feet? Ten feet? There was no way of knowing. He thought he detected a little stuffiness in the air of the cab, and that made him afraid. It would be hell to die slowly of lack of oxygen. With his technician's mind he began to make calculations of the probable permeability of snow with regard to air, but his mind was confused in any case, he did not know enough about the variables. *McGill would know,* he thought dimly.

There was something else Cameron did not know, and it was better for him that he should not. The truck was upside down in the river bed, and the snow which had dammed the flow of water was being eaten into upstream of him. Slowly but inexorably the river was coming to him.

II

High on the west slope McGill paused for breath and leaned on his ski-poles. 'This'll do,' he said. 'We'll test it here.'

Charlie Peterson stared down the slope. 'Lots of activity down there.'

McGill watched another helicopter land. 'Yes, they're coming in faster.' He glanced at Charlie. 'We want no bouncing about. Try to imagine you're walking on custard and don't want to break the skin.'

'I'll be light-footed,' said Charlie, and laughed. 'I never thought I'd ever try to imitate a bloody ballet dancer.'

McGill grunted and looked along the line of the slope. 'Your brother told me he grew a hay crop here. Did you have cattle grazing?'

'Hell, no! It's too steep. You'd have to breed your cows with short legs on one side and long legs on the other.'

'That figures,' said McGill. 'Professor Roget was right about his cow test.'

'What sort of test is that?'

'It was in the early days of skiing in Switzerland. Someone asked Roget how to tell if a slope was safe for skiing. He said you had to think like a cow, and if you reckoned you'd be uncomfortable grazing then the slope wasn't safe.'

'I reckon we'll lose a lot of stock.' Charlie pointed up the valley. 'There's bad flooding up there on the farm.'

'The river is blocked, but it'll soon clear.' McGill turned his ski-pole over. 'This is eyeball science,' he said wryly. 'I lost my kit.' He pushed the stick into the snow, keeping up a steady pressure. When it hit bottom he marked the depth with his thumb and withdrew the stick. 'Under three feet – that's not too bad.' He looked down at the hole he had made. 'I wish to hell I knew what was down there.'

'Why don't we dig and find out?'

'That's just what I'm going to do. Charlie, you stand upslope from me about ten yards away. Keep your eyes on me. If anything gives then mark the place where you last saw me.'

'Hey, you don't think . . .?'

'Just a precaution,' said McGill reassuringly. He jerked his thumb towards the valley. 'If I thought what I'm doing would cause any more damage down there I wouldn't be doing it.'

Charlie climbed up the slope and turned to watch McGill, who started to excavate a hole. His movements were gentle but he worked quickly, piling the snow up-slope of the hole. Finally he thrust his arm down as far as it would go and came up clutching some brown strands. 'Long grass. That's not too good.'

He straightened. 'We'll go across diagonally and upwards, making a hole every hundred yards.' He shaded his eyes from the sun and pointed. 'I have a good idea that the avalanche broke up there by those exposed rocks. I'd like to have a look at the place.'

Charlie's eyes followed the direction of McGill's pointing arm. 'Is that necessary?'

'Not strictly necessary but I'd still like to see it.' He grinned. 'It's about six holes away. Come on, Charlie.'

They went on, making their way across and up the slope. When they had gone a hundred yards McGill stopped and dug another hole, then they went on again. For the first time Charlie showed signs of nervousness. 'You really think this is safe?'

'As safe as crossing the road,' said McGill sardonically.

'A pal of mine was killed in Auckland crossing a road.'

McGill dug another hole. Charlie said, 'What's the verdict?'

'Same diagnosis. Not too much snow but slippery underneath. If it went now it wouldn't do too much damage, but I hope to hell we don't get more snow before we're finished down there.'

They toiled higher. Charlie watched McGill digging and then looked upwards over his shoulder towards the rocks where McGill thought the avalanche had begun. They were about two hundred yards away. His gaze returned to McGill and he called out, 'What makes it slippery?'

'The grass.'

'I think we should get off the slope.'

'That's what we're doing,' said McGill equably. 'Not far to go now. Just as far as those rocks.' He straightened his bent body. 'I don't think we'll do any more digging. We'll head straight up.'

'I don't think that's a good idea,' said Charlie. His voice was edgy.

'What's the matter with you?' asked McGill. 'Why the sudden jitters?'

'I don't like standing out here. I saw what happened before.'

An aircraft went overhead very low and McGill looked up and saw the white blur of a face behind a window. Whoever it was seemed to be taking photographs. He shook his head and looked again at Charlie. 'It's quite safe,' he said. 'Take my word for it.'

There was a splintering noise from the valley behind him and he turned around. 'What was that?'

Charlie stared. 'I don't know. It's too far away to see.'

On the white floor of the valley the black specks which were men began to converge on one point like ants intent on dismembering a dead beetle. McGill could not see what was at the focal point. He said, 'Something odd seems to have happened. Are your eyes any better than mine, Charlie? Where are they all heading?'

Charlie shaded his eyes. 'Can't tell.'

They watched for a while but could not distinguish the cause of the sudden activity. At last McGill said, 'Well, let's get on.' Charlie did not move. He was standing very still, looking down into the valley. 'Snap out of it, Charlie.'

'Oh, Christ!' said Charlie. 'Look!'

McGill turned. In the valley there was a blossom of red fire which expanded as they watched, and a coil of oily black smoke grew upwards like a giant tree making an ugly stain in the air.

Breath whistled from McGill. 'What the hell was that?' he said as the sound of the explosion reached them. 'Let's get down there.'

'Sure thing,' said Charlie.

TWENTY-NINE

Jesse Rusch was going towards the church but turned aside sharply as someone yelled, 'I've found someone.' He ran towards the group of men who had broken their line, put aside the probes, and taken up spades. He stood on one side and watched them dig carefully, and had to smile as someone else said disgustedly, 'It's a flaming cow.'

Flaming it certainly was not. One of the men pushed at a hoof and the leg was seen to be as stiff as a rod. Rusch stepped forward. 'Dig it out, anyway.'

A man turned around. 'Why? It's a waste of time.'

'Because there might be someone under the cow,' said Rusch patiently. 'That's why.' It was a possibility but privately he thought it unlikely, so he said, 'Three men to the cow – the rest can carry on probing.'

The men dropped their spades and picked up the probes with alacrity, leaving the man who had queried the utility of digging out the cow alone with his spade. He stared at his mates in disgust, and said, 'Hey, the man said three.'

He turned and saw a group of men standing twenty yards away, their hands in their pockets. 'You lot,' he called. 'Come and give me a hand.'

They stared at him with blank eyes, then turned their backs on him and shuffled away slowly. The man flung down his shovel. 'God Almighty!' he said passionately. 'I've flown four hundred miles to help these bastards, and the bloody lead-swingers won't even help themselves.'

'Leave them be,' said Rusch quietly. 'They're not themselves. Regard them as dead men, if that's any help. Pick up your spade and get on with it. If you want help, ask your team leader.'

The man blew out his cheeks expressively, the picked up his spade and dug it viciously into the snow. Rusch watched him for ten seconds, then turned aside and went on his way.

Just outside the church he encountered a helicopter pilot from VXE-6 called Harry Baker, and he saw at once that Baker was angry, so steamed up that he should have melted the snow for yards around. He cut in before Baker opened his mouth and said quietly, 'When you tell me what's bugging you keep it soft.'

Baker jerked his thumb at the sky. 'Some goddamn maniac buzzed me up there as I was coming in. He was taking photographs.' His voice was choked with rage.

Rucsh shrugged philosophically. 'I guess those are the Press boys. They'll be chartering planes and coming in like locusts from here on in.'

'Jesse, up there it's already becoming more crowded than Times Square,' said Baker earnestly. 'If it gets any worse there'll be trouble.'

Rucsh nodded. 'All right, Harry. I'll see the Civil Defence people here and see what we can do about tightening up air control. If necessary, I'll insist on grounding all unauthorized flights. In the meantime keep your cool.'

He went into the church, where he nodded to Ballard who was talking to a woman lying on a bench, and went up to the altar to speak to the Civil Defence Local Co-ordinator.

Ballard said, 'I'm sorry, Liz. I know I promised you an early flight out but there are people in worse shape than you.

Mrs Haslam, for instance, needs hospital attention badly –
and there are some kids, too.'

'That's all right. I'm feeling much better now. Is Charlie
still up there with Mike?'

'Yes.'

She looked worried. 'I hope they're safe. I don't like
them being up there.'

'Mike knows what he's doing,' said Ballard.

The stretcher bearing Mrs Haslam was being loaded into the
helicopter by Arthur Pye and Bill Quentin. She moaned,
and said feebly, 'Where's Jack? I want my Jack.'

Pye said, 'You'll be seeing him soon, Mrs Haslam,' not
knowing whether he was a liar or not.

Harry Baker adjusted his helmet and said to the ground
controller, 'When I take off I want this crowd to stand back.
They were pushing a bit too close last time.' He jerked his
thumb at the sky. 'It's bad enough being crowded up there.'

The ground controller nodded. 'I'll shoo them away.'
He looked towards the helicopter and saw Pye and
Quentin walking away and, beyond them, the loadmaster
closing the sliding door. The loadmaster waved, and he
said, 'That's the last one. You can take off now.' Baker
climbed up into the cockpit, and the ground controller
shouted, 'All right, stand back, everybody. Get well away.
Come on, now.'

Baker said to his co-pilot. 'Let's get this thing off the
ground. We have time for three more trips before nightfall.'

Pye and Quentin walked with the rest, shepherded by
the ground controller. The engine of the helicopter fired
and the rotors began to move. It looked ungainly as it rose
from the ground, gathering vertical speed. Quentin was not
watching when the crash happened, but Pye saw it. The
helicopter rose directly into the path of a low flying light
plane which appeared from nowhere and struck it in the

rear. There was a splintering crash and, locked together, the two machines dropped straight into the snow.

Everyone began to run and Pye and Quentin were in the lead. Pye heaved on the sliding door of the helicopter but it had warped and would not budge. 'Give me a hand, Bill,' he panted, and Quentin also heaved at the door which slid half open creakingly and then jammed.

Immediately inside was the loadmaster whose helmet had saved him from being knocked totally unconscious. He was shaking his head groggily as Pye grabbed him by the arm and hauled him out bodily. Pye then climbed inside with Quentin just behind him.

Two children were strapped into a seat, their bodies lolling forward and supported only by the straps. Pye did not know whether they were living or dead as he fumbled at the straps, and he had no time to find out. He freed the first and passed her back to Quentin, and then tackled the second, a boy. From far away he heard a bellow from the ground controller – 'You guys in there had better be quick. She might go up.'

He freed the boy who was passed out to fall into waiting hands, then he said to Quentin, 'I'll have to go back there to get behind the stretcher. You take this end.'

There were two stretchers and when Pye looked at one of them he saw there was no use in doing anything about that one. The man lying in it had his head at a totally impossible angle and Pye judged, in that hasty glance, that his neck was broken. He turned to the other stretcher and heard Mrs Haslam say, 'Is that you, Jack?' Her eyes stared at him unwinkingly.

'Yes, that's right. I've come to take you home.' His finger nails tore and his fingers bled as he worked frantically at the straps which secured the stretcher. He got one loose and turned to find that Quentin had released the other. 'Right. Take it gently.' He bent forward and said to

Mrs Haslam reassuringly, 'We'll soon have you out of here.'

It was at that moment the petrol ignited. He saw a white flash and felt searing heat, and when he inhaled his next breath he drew flaming petrol vapour into his lungs. He felt no pain and was dead before he knew it, and so was Bill Quentin, Mrs Haslam, Harry Baker and his co-pilot, whom nobody had seen on the ground in Hukahoronui.

There was no sound in the inquiry room other than the creaking of the old kauri floor. Harrison said into the silence, 'A public inquiry has already been held into the reasons for this air crash. It was held by the inspector of Air Accidents as was his statutory duty. Its findings will be incorporated into the findings of this inquiry. However I propose to say a few words on the subject now.'

His voice was even and his demeanour grave. 'Lieutenant-Commander Rusch has already given evidence that the dead helicopter pilot had complained of the hazardous nature of the flying conditions and the reasons for the hazards. Even at the moment of the crash Lieutenant-Commander Rusch was talking to the authorities at Harewood Airport and you have heard, from his evidence and that of others, that he was most forthright, and indeed, aggressive in reinforcing the strictures of his fellow officer.

'At the time of the crash it was assumed that the aircraft which was the cause of this accident bad been chartered by a newspaper. In actual fact, it turned out to be an official flight made by a junior minister of the Government who was intent on finding the extent of the disaster area at Hukahoronui. Regardless of whether the flight was official or unofficial, it is evident that there was a grave breakdown of communication between the Ministry of Civil Defence and the civil and military air authorities, leading to what might be construed as criminal negligence.'

He looked up at the Press gallery with cold eyes, and Dan Edwards twitched in his seat. 'I might add that the Press acted most irresponsibly in their flights over the disaster area. While a reporter may think he has a duty to get at the facts, he has a higher duty to the community than to the newspaper which employs him. While I understand that certain civil air pilots have been reprimanded and suitably punished by the withdrawal of their flying licences, I regret that a similar punishment cannot legally be meted out to those who so irresponsibly chartered the aircraft and gave the orders.'

He switched his attention to Smithers. 'And I hope the Ministry of Civil Defence is reviewing its procedures immediately and not waiting for the findings of this Commission to be published. There could be a similar disaster tomorrow, Mr Smithers.'

He did not wait to hear anything Smithers might have to say, but tapped with his gavel. 'We stand adjourned until ten a.m. tomorrow.'

THIRTY

As Ballard left the hall he saw McGill talking to a bespec-tacled, middle-aged man whom he had previously noticed in the front rank of the Press gallery. When he approached he heard McGill say, 'I'd be much obliged if you could get them for me.'

Dan Edwards scratched the side of his jaw. 'Tit for tat,' he said. 'If there's a story in it I want an exclusive.' He smiled. 'It's all right for old Harrison to act pontifical, but I'm still a newspaperman.'

'If there's a story you'll have it first,' promised McGill. 'Even Harrison would agree that this is in the public interest.'

'When do you want them?'

'Yesterday – but today will have to do. Can I meet you in your office in half an hour?'

Edwards grimaced. 'I was looking forward to a beer, but I suppose that can wait.'

'If I find what I'm looking for I'll buy you a case of beer.'

Edwards said, 'I'll hold you to that,' and went away.

Ballard said, 'What's all that about, Mike?'

'Just checking on something – professional stuff. Seen Liz yet?'

'No. I'm meeting her later.'

'Don't waste time,' advised McGill. 'The balloon goes up tomorrow. If Harrison knew I was sitting on this he'd ream

me out for sure.' He looked past Ballard. 'Ah, there's the
guy I want to see.' He walked away with Flying Officer
Hatry, talking fast and making gestures with his hands.
Ballard looked after him curiously, then shrugged and went
to get his car.

He had missed Liz at lunch-time – she had left quickly
with Eric and Charlie – and she had not appeared for the
afternoon session. During the mid-afternoon recess he had
telephoned her at her hotel and asked to see her. 'You'd better not come here,' she had said. 'Charlie wouldn't like it.
I'll come to your hotel after dinner. What about nine
o'clock?'

At the hotel he avoided Stenning by the simple expedi-
ent of staying in his room. In view of what had happened
the previous night he had no wish for further conversation with Stenning. He whiled away the time by reading a
novel which bored him, and his thoughts went skittering
away from the narrative which should have held his
attention.

He wondered where McGill was and what he was doing.
He thought of how he was going to break the news to Liz –
that was going to be damned difficult. How do you tell the
woman you love that her brother is – to all intents and
purposes – a multiple murderer?

He had dinner in his room. At nine-fifteen he was pacing
the floor and, at nine-thirty, when Liz still had not shown
up, he contemplated telephoning her again. At nine-forty
the telephone rang and he grabbed it.

'Ballard.'

'A guest for you, Mr Ballard.'

'I'll be right there.'

He went to the reception desk where the clerk said, 'In
the lounge, Mr Ballard.'

Ballard walked into the hotel lounge and looked about.
In a corner he saw Stenning reading a newspaper but there

was no sign of Liz. From behind him a voice said, 'I'll bet you didn't expect *me*, Ballard.'

He turned and saw Charlie Peterson. 'Where's Liz?' he demanded.

Charlie swayed slightly on his feet. His face was reddened and covered with a film of sweat, and a tic worked convulsively under his left eye. 'She won't be here,' he said. 'I've made sure of that. I've told you before – stay away from my sister, you bastard.'

'What have you done with her?'

'She's got nothing to do with you – now or at any other time. You must be either stupid or deaf. Didn't McGill pass on my message?'

'He did.' Ballard contemplated Charlie for a long moment, then said, 'I asked Liz to come here because I had something important to tell her. Since she isn't here I'll tell you.'

'I have no interest in anything you have to say.' Charlie looked about the lounge. 'If we were anywhere else I'd break your bloody back. You're always careful never to be alone, aren't you?'

'You'd better listen, Charlie; it's for your own good. And you'd better sit down while you hear it, before you fall down.'

Something in Ballard's tone of voice caught Charlie's attention. He narrowed his eyes, and said, 'All right, say your piece.' He flopped down heavily on to a settee.

As Ballard sat down he saw Stenning looking across at them wearing a puzzled expression. He ignored Stenning and turned to Charlie. 'You're in trouble – bad trouble.'

Charlie grinned humourlessly. '*I'm* in trouble! Wait until you hear what's in store for you.'

'We know what went on on top of the west slope before the avalanche. We know what you did, Charlie.'

The grin disappeared from Charlie's face. 'I wasn't on the west slope and no one can say I was. Who says I was?'

'Miller says so,' said Charlie quietly. 'We have a letter.'

Ian

'He's a liar,' said Charlie tautly.

Ballard shrugged. 'What reason has he for lying? What reason has he for sending ten thousand dollars to the Disaster Fund? You tell me.'

'Where is this letter? I want to see it.'

'You'll see it. It will be given to Harrison tomorrow morning.'

Charlie swallowed. 'And what the hell am I supposed to have done? Tell me because I don't know.'

Ballard looked at him steadily. 'He says you deliberately started the avalanche.'

The tic on Charlie's face twitched. 'Lies!' he shouted. 'He's a bloody liar!'

'Keep your voice down,' said Ballard.

'Keep my voice down!' said Charlie in suppressed fury. 'I'm accused of murder and you tell me to keep my voice down!' All the same he spoke more softly and looked quickly about the lounge.

'Now listen to me. I asked Liz here so I could break it to her gently so she wouldn't hear it for the first time in open court tomorrow. I don't know how you've prevented her from coming here, but since you're here I decided to tell you. I'm giving you a chance, Charlie.'

'What chance?' he asked in a grating voice.

'Miller may be a liar or he may not. But whichever he is I'm giving you the chance to get on your hind legs tomorrow as soon as the session starts and get in your version to Harrison before the letter is produced. And don't think I'm doing it for you. I'm doing this for Liz.'

'Some chance,' sneered Charlie. 'You cooked up this, Ballard; you and McGill between you.'

'I know the truth of that,' said Ballard quietly. 'And so, I think, do you. And another thing – I don't know how you stopped Liz coming here but if you've hurt her you'll be responsible to me.'

Charlie stood up suddenly. 'You bloody bastard, no one is responsible for Liz *except* me, and no pommy son of a bitch is going to get near her least of all anyone called Ballard.' He looked around the crowded lounge and then jabbed out his finger. 'I tell you, if I catch you anywhere I can get at you, you'll wish you'd never heard of the Peterson family.' He turned on his heel abruptly and walked from the lounge.

'I almost wish that now,' said Ballard softly, and turned his head to look across at Stenning who looked back at him with an expressionless face.

McGill worked late that night, mostly in a photographic darkroom at Deep Freeze Advanced Headquarters. It was finicky and exacting work, involving fine measurement, but he was greatly helped by a US Navy photographer. Even so, it was long after midnight before he finished and all he had to show was an envelope containing some eight by ten glossies and a few transparencies.

He drove back to the hotel and parked his car in its slot next to Ballard's car and got out, taking the envelope with him.

He turned to go into the hotel, and then hesitated before walking around to look at Ballard's car. It was empty and the door was locked. He shrugged and was about to turn away again when he heard a thread of a sound so weak it would have been obscured had he moved his feet on the gravel. He stood very still and listened, straining his ears, but heard no more.

He walked to the other side of Ballard's car and stepped on something soft and yielding in the darkness. He stepped back and flicked on his cigarette lighter and peered downwards, then he drew in his breath sharply and, turning on his heel, he ran to the hotel entrance as fast as he could.

The night porter looked up in alarm as McGill burst into the foyer and skidded to a halt. 'Phone for a doctor and an ambulance,' said McGill breathlessly. 'There's a seriously injured man in the car park.' The porter was immobile with early morning stupidity, and McGill yelled, 'Move, man!'

The porter jerked and reached for the telephone and a minute later McGill was hammering on Stenning's door. 'Who is it?' Stenning's voice was muffled and sleepy.

'McGill. Open up.'

Presently Stenning opened the door. His white hair was tousled and his eyes still sleep-filled, and he was knotting the cord of a dressing-gown about his waist. 'What is it?'

McGill was curt. 'You'd better come with me and see the result of your goddamn meddling.'

'And what do you mean by that?' Stenning was coming awake quickly.

'You'll see. Come on. It's not far so you needn't dress.'

'Slippers,' said Stenning. 'I'll need slippers.' He went back into the room and reappeared seconds later.

As they went through the foyer McGill called out, 'What about that doctor?'

'On his way with the ambulance,' said the porter.

'Can you turn on the lights in the car park?'

'Yes, sir.' He turned and opened a door behind him and snapped switches. 'A car accident?'

McGill didn't answer that one. 'You'd better rouse the manager. Come on, Stenning.'

They hastened across the car park which was now brightly lit. Stenning said, 'Someone hurt?'

'Ian – and he's hurt bad. Over here.'

A startled exclamation was torn from Stenning as he looked down at the bloody body of Ballard. 'Oh my God! What happened?'

'It was no car accident, that's for sure.' McGill took Ballard's wrist, ignoring the blood. 'I think he's still alive – I'm not sure. Where's that goddamn doctor?'

'What do you mean – it isn't a car accident? It looks bad enough to be one.'

'How in hell could he be hit by a car here?' McGill waved. 'The space between these cars is only three feet.'

'He could have crawled in here.'

'Then where's the trail of blood he left?' McGill stood up. 'What you're looking at, Stenning, is a man who has almost been beaten to death – and I'm not sure about almost. It's what happens when a man gets *walked over*, Stenning.' His voice was harsh and accusing.

Stenning's face was white. McGill said in a shaky voice, 'You sit in your plush offices in the City of London and you manipulate men, and you set up what you call *experiments*, for God's sake, and you talk of people being walked over.' His finger stabbed down at Ballard's body. 'This is the reality, Stenning. Look at it, damn you!'

Stenning swallowed and his Adam's apple bobbed up and down in his skinny throat. 'There was no intention of . . .'

'No intention of murder?' McGill laughed and it was an ugly sound in the quiet night. 'What the hell else do you expect to happen when you interfere with a maniac like Charlie Peterson?'

Stenning was a lawyer and his mind worked on tracks as precise as a railway engine. 'I saw Charlie Peterson and Ballard in the hotel tonight. They had a long conversation and it wasn't amiable – but that's not proof of anything.' He turned his head and looked at McGill. 'Do you *know* it was Peterson?'

'Yes,' said McGill bluntly.

'How do you know?'

McGill paused. He suddenly realized he was still holding the envelope of photographs. He looked at it for a moment and his mind worked fast. 'I know,' he said, lying deliberately. 'I know because Ian told me before he passed out.'

In the distance a siren wailed as the ambulance approached.

THE HEARING

Last Day

THIRTY-ONE

At ten o'clock Harrison walked into the hall and sat on the rostrum flanked by Rolandson and French. He waited until the rustling had stopped, then said, 'I have to report that Mr Ian Ballard was seriously injured in a car accident in the early hours of this morning and is at present in Princess Margaret Hospital. He is in a coma and Dr McGill is, quite understandably, with him.'

There was a surge of noise. In the Press gallery Dan Edwards frowned, and said, 'Damn! I wonder if that affects the story?'

'What story?' asked Dalwood.

'Oh, nothing. Just something I was getting a line on.' He nudged Dalwood. 'Look at Charlie Peterson. He's laughing fit to bust a gut.'

Harrison tapped with his gavel to restore order. 'We are now at a stage of the Inquiry when the evidence of Mr Ballard and Dr McGill is not absolutely essential, so there is no need to adjourn. Call the first witness, Mr Reed.'

Twenty-four hours after the avalanche the number of those still missing had been cut down to twenty-one. All the others had been accounted for – dead and alive. Ballard said glumly, 'There's still no sign of Joe Cameron.'

Jesse Rusch said, 'A friend of yours?'

'I suppose so. I hadn't known him long. I don't suppose there's much hope for him now, but perhaps it's better that way. His daughter was killed.'

'There've been too many people killed here,' said Rusch, thinking of Baker. 'And some of those deaths were un-necessary.'

'All of them were,' said Ballard bleakly.

Turi Buck came up and silently held out a piece of paper. Ballard took it, then looked up. 'The Marshall family, all four of them?'

'We've just dug out the house – or what's left of it.'

'Dead! All of them?'

'Yes.' Turi went away, his back bent.

Ballard made four violent slash marks on the list before him. 'Seventeen.'

'We'll be able to get bulldozers in this afternoon,' said Rusch. 'That should speed things up.'

'And it could be dangerous,' said Ballard. 'A bulldozer blade could chop a man in half.'

'We'll be careful,' said Rusch. 'We'll be real careful. But speed is important now. If anyone buried is still alive now they can't last much longer.' By the tone of his voice he doubted if anyone could possibly be still alive.

Cameron was almost totally exhausted. He had been asleep or perhaps unconscious – it did not matter which – but now he was awake again. His whole body was racked with pain and the fierce headache was still with him. He had been sick during the night and had been afraid of choking on his own vomit, but he had managed to twist his head to one side and so had not suffered that particularly ugly death. Also during the night he had uncontrollably voided both urine and fae-ces and now the stench of himself sickened him.

He became aware of a sound and, at first, thought it was human and his hopes rose. It sounded as though someone was chuckling quietly. Cameron called weakly and then listened as the distant laughter went on. He thought he was going mad – who would be laughing in the middle of a snowdrift?

His senses swam and he passed out for a few minutes. When he awoke again he heard the sound but it had subtly changed. It was now more of a gurgle than a laugh or a chuckle, a sound such as might be made by a contented baby in its cot. After listening for a long time he knew what it was and again became afraid. He was listening to the sound of water.

Presently he was aware that his head was becoming wet. A trickle of water had entered the cab and swirled about his scalp as he hung there suspended upside down, and now he knew that he would drown. Not much water need come in to cover his mouth and nose – no more than six inches.

On the surface two young men were piloting a bulldozer through the hummocky snow alongside the river. The driver was John Skinner, a construction worker from Auckland; he was also a member of the Alpine Sports Club. His companion was a university lecturer and a member of the Canterbury University Ski Club called Roger Halliwell. Skinner stopped the bulldozer by the river, and said, 'The flooding upstream will stop as soon as the river clears that snow away.'

'I hear a lot of cattle were drowned,' said Halliwell.

'No people, though. That bloody avalanche must have been bad enough without the risk of drowning.' Skinner looked around. 'Now where was it that the Yank wanted us to dig?'

A section of snow in the river bed slumped as it was undercut by water and Halliwell looked at it idly. Then he said, 'I think I saw something down there.'

'What?'

'I don't know. Something dark. It was round.'

'A boulder, maybe.'

'Perhaps.' Halliwell frowned. 'I'm going to have a look.'

He dropped from the bulldozer and walked to the edge of the river and then put his foot delicately on to the snow. It was soft but bore his weight without him sinking too much. He walked on slowly, lifting each leg high. As he progressed the snow became more slushy because it had been penetrated by the river water, and suddenly he sank up to his waist. He had a nightmare vision of going right down, but he found himself standing on something.

He put his hand down into the snow and encountered a shape which he explored. It was a wheel with a tyre on it. 'There's a car in here,' he yelled.

Skinner jumped down and unclipped a wire rope from the rear of the bulldozer. There was a big snap-shackle on each end, one of which he clipped to a stout bar on the bulldozer. 'Can you catch this?' He whirled the other end of the rope around his head.

He missed on his first cast, but Halliwell caught it the second time. There was some difficulty in finding somewhere to attach the shackle. Halliwell knew it had to be an integral part of the chassis of the buried vehicle and he groped around in the snow for some time quite unsuccessfully.

In the cab Cameron was close to drowning. The water covered his nose even though he withdrew his head into his shoulders like a tortoise trying to retreat into its shell. There was only a matter of an inch to go before it covered his mouth. While he could do so he took a deep breath.

The truck lurched and water washed over his head. When the movement had finished Cameron's head was completely under water and he battled to keep his breath. The truck moved again, this time upwards, and Cameron screamed at the pain and thought his back was being broken. The bulldozer hauled the truck bodily from the river bed and on to the bank where it lay on its side.

Halliwell ran up to it. 'There's someone in here,' he said in wonder. 'And he's alive, by God!'

Within the hour Cameron was in a helicopter on his way to Christchurch. But he was a badly broken man.

Newman was unlucky.

All night he had been digging upwards in total darkness. He had to dig a hole at least two feet in diameter to accommodate the shoulders of a broad man. There had also to be steps cut in the side where he could stand. For digging he used whatever came to hand. His most useful tool was a ballpoint pen which he jabbed repeatedly into the snow above him, breaking it out, chunk by chunk. Often the snow dropped into his eyes, but that did not matter because it was dark anyway. Twice he dropped the pen and that did matter because he had to go down and grope with gloved hands until he found it. He lost time there.

In one sense he was lucky. He did not know how far he had to dig and had he known it was as much as sixty feet it is doubtful if he would have ever begun. But during the time he was under the snow it had begun to settle and compact as the air was squeezed out of it. While this made it a harder material to penetrate it also meant that it lessened the distance he had to dig to a little over fifty feet.

He dug alone because the others in the cave had lapsed into total apathy.

Fifty-two hours after the avalanche the sky was darkening and Sam Foster, a Ranger from Tongariro, debated with himself whether or not it was worth while having his team continue the search. There were still a few men missing but it was inconceivable that any would be alive even if found. Perhaps it would be better to call off the search until the morrow.

He strode into a gently sloping cup-shaped hollow and was somewhere in the middle of it when the snow gave under his feet. Newman had dug to within a foot of the surface, and when Foster's weight broke through one of Foster's boots slammed into his head. He fell down the hole he had made. It was not a long fall because the bottom of the hole was packed with the debris of his digging. But it was enough to break his neck.

The others, of course, were rescued, excepting Haslam who was dead already. Newman was the last person to die in the valley. The last person to die as a result of the disaster at Hukahoronui was Mrs Jarvis, the oldest inhabitant, who lingered tenaciously in hospital for a week before she succumbed.

There was a second avalanche on the west slope of Hukahoronui that year but it happened in the spring thaw. There was nobody there to kill.

THIRTY-TWO

At three-thirty in the afternoon McGill parked his car and hurried across Durham Street towards the Provincial Government Buildings. Instead of going into the chamber where the hearing was being held, he went upstairs to the entrance to the Press gallery and had a word with the usher. Presently Dan Edwards came out to see him.

'I keep my promises,' said McGill. 'You've got your story.' He gave Edwards an envelope. 'A photostat of a letter which is self-explanatory and some photographs which I'll explain to the Chairman. What's going on down there now?'

'Harrison is winding things up. A pathologist is giving medical evidence.' Edwards paused, his thumb beneath the flap of the envelope. 'Talking of that – how's Ballard?'

'In a bad way.'

'These bloody hit-and-run drivers.' He saw McGill's look of surprise, and said, 'One of the boys checked at the hotel. It was obviously hit and run, wasn't it?' He regarded McGill closely. 'Or am I missing something?'

McGill poked his finger at the envelope. 'You're missing your story.'

Edwards pulled out the copy of the letter and scanned it. His jaw dropped. 'Jesus! Is this straight up?'

'I'll be giving the original to Harrison in less than five minutes.'

'Thanks, McGill. Maybe I'll give *you* a case of beer.' He went back into the Press gallery and found a young reporter. 'Take this back to the office. Give it to the editor – in no one else's hands, understand. Off with you.'

He regained his seat and Dalwood said curiously, 'Anything doing?'

Edwards grinned broadly and nodded down into the hall. 'The fireworks are due to start any minute.'

McGill walked across the vestibule, past the two policemen standing outside the chamber, and went inside. Harrison turned his head, and said to the witness, 'Excuse me, Dr Cross. Good afternoon, Dr McGill. How is Mr Ballard?'

'He's still unconscious, Mr Chairman.'

'I'm sorry to hear it. It's good of you to return, but not really necessary under the circumstances.'

'I think my return was very necessary, Mr Chairman. I am in possession of fresh evidence.'

'Indeed? Step forward, Dr McGill. You are excused for the moment, Dr Cross.'

The pathologist stepped down and McGill stood before the rostrum. He took an envelope from his pocket. 'I received this letter and discussed the contents with Mr Ballard. We both agreed that it was too important to conceal even though it could destroy a man's reputation.'

He handed the letter to Harrison who opened it and began to read. It took him a long time and the lines of his face deepened as he read. At last he raised his head, and said, 'I see. Yes, it would have been wrong to withhold this.' He looked at the letter again. 'I see that each page is signed and countersigned, and has the seal of a notary public. Would that be the American equivalent of our own Commissioner for Oaths?'

'It is almost the exact equivalent, Mr Chairman.'

Harrison's eyes roved about the room. 'Mr Lyall, would you mind stepping over here?'

Lyall looked surprised, but said, 'Not at all, Mr Chairman.' He got up and walked over to stand next to McGill.

Harrison said in a low voice, 'This concerns one of your clients. I think you'd better read it.' He held out the letter.

A few minutes later Lyall said nervously, 'I don't really know what to say, Mr Chairman.' His face was pale. 'I feel inclined to withdraw from this case.'

'Do you?' Harrison's voice was grim. 'This is not a *case*, Mr Lyall; it is a Commission of Inquiry. Apart from that, I doubt if anyone would respect a lawyer who deserted his client when things became hard.'

Red spots burned in Lyall's cheeks. 'Very well,' he said abruptly. 'But is it admissible evidence?'

'That is something which I and the assessors will have to decide,' said Harrison heavily. He took the letter from Lyall and passed it to Rolandson.

McGill said, 'I have other supporting evidence.'

'No evidence can be brought to support this letter if the letter itself is not admissible,' said Lyall. 'And if you admit the letter there will certainly be grounds for appeal.'

'There'll be no appeal,' said McGill. 'And you know it.'

'You are not here to argue a lawyer's case, Dr McGill,' said Harrison in tones of freezing rebuke. He turned to Rolandson. 'What do you think?'

'I think it's appalling,' snapped Rolandson.

'I mean, is it admissible?'

'Let me read it all.' Presently Rolandson said, 'It has been witnessed under oath. It is admissible.'

Harrison gave the letter to French, who read it and soon looked as though there was a bad smell under his nose. He tossed the letter down. 'Certainly admissible.'

'I think so, too. I'm sorry, Mr Lyall.' Harrison passed the letter to the Secretary to the Commission. 'Read that aloud, Mr Reed.' He paused as though confused by the discord of what he had uttered.

Reed scanned the letter and then began, 'This is a letter from a Mr George Albert Miller of Riverside, California, and is addressed to Dr Michael McGill.'

He read the letter slowly and in an even tone which contrasted oddly with the events Miller described. When he had finished he said flatly, 'Each page is signed by Mr Miller and countersigned by Carl Risinger. Each page is impressed with the seal of a notary public.'

The silence in the hall was total and seemed to last forever. It was as though time had stopped. There was a strange movement as people twisted in their seats to look in one direction. It was as though Charlie Peterson had developed a new form of attractive force – all eyes turned towards him like compass needles towards a magnet.

He was sitting slumped in his chair, his face white and his eyes staring. Next to him Eric had withdrawn and was looking at Charlie with a baffled expression. Liz was sitting upright, her hands in her lap, and staring rigidly ahead. Her brow was contracted and her lips compressed. She was very angry.

Charlie's eyes flickered from side to side and he became aware that everyone was watching him in silence. He jumped to his feet. 'It's a lie!' he shouted. 'Miller is a liar. He started the avalanche, not me.'

The silence broke and a wave of sound washed around Charlie. Harrison hammered with his gavel furiously. With difficulty he achieved order and said icily, 'Any more disturbance and I will adjourn this session.' He looked at Charlie with cold eyes. 'You will sit down, Mr Peterson.'

Charlie's right hand stabbed out, pointing at Harrison and McGill's eyes narrowed as he observed the strip of sticking-plaster which decorated his knuckles. 'Aren't you going to hear me?' Charlie yelled. 'You were ready enough to hear Ballard when his reputation was at stake.'

Harrison turned to Lyall. 'You must control your client, Mr Lyall. Either he sits down or he leaves – by force, if necessary.'

Lyall called out, 'Sit down, Charlie. You're paying me to handle this.'

'And you're not doing too well,' grumbled Charlie. But he sat down and Eric whispered to him furiously.

Lyall said, 'I must formally protest against the admission of this unsubstantiated letter as evidence. It attacks my client's reputation seriously and, in my opinion, unjustifiably. Mr Miller is not available for my cross-examination and I must protest. Further, I give formal warning that a motion of appeal will be entered immediately.'

Harrison said calmly, 'As I remarked to Mr Rickman earlier in these proceedings, you will find the necessary procedure set out in the Act of Parliament which governs the holding of Commissions of Inquiry. Dr McGill, you mentioned that you have other evidence. Is this evidence in support of Mr Miller's allegations?'

'Yes, sir.'

'Then we will hear it.'

'Objection!'

'Overruled, Mr Lyall.'

'It is photographic evidence, Mr Chairman,' said McGill. 'I have taken the liberty of having the equipment made available. I would like to operate it myself.'

Harrison nodded abruptly. 'See to it, Mr Reed.'

In the few minutes it took for the apparatus to be set up, noise again swelled in the hall. Dalwood said to Edwards, 'You knew what was coming, you old fox.' He was still scribbling furiously.

Edwards offered him a self-satisfied grin. 'My boss will be remaking the front page right now. We've got a photocopy of Miller's letter.'

'How the hell did you get that?'

'McGill wanted something from us.' He nodded down at the hall. 'You'll see.'

Harrison called for silence and the hall quietened quickly. 'Proceed, Dr McGill.'

McGill stood next to a cine projector. 'I have here the original film taken of the avalanche by Flying Officer Hatry. The film he submitted to the Commission was a copy; the original is a better print. I don't think that Flying Officer Hatry should be censured for this, either by this Commission or by his superiors in the Air Force. For a keen photographer to part with an original would be a highly unnatural act.'

He switched on the projector. 'I will show only that portion of the film which is relevant.'

An unsteady picture appeared on the screen, the whiteness of snow and a few scattered rocks with blue sky beyond. A plume, as of smoke, arose and McGill switched off the projector to freeze the action. He stepped forward with a pointer in his hand.

'As you can see, the avalanche started here, just by these rocks. It was daytime and the sun was shining in a clear sky. Under those conditions rock and snow take up heat in a different way; the rock warms more quickly, and this difference may set up stresses in the snow just enough to upset an already critical balance of forces. That was my assumption when I first saw this film.'

He switched off the cine projector. 'I have here a greatly enlarged portion of that scene which I am going to put in this special projector. It is called a comparator.' He switched it on. 'The degree of enlargement is such that the image is very grainy, but it will suffice for our purposes.'

Again McGill went to the screen with the pointer. 'Here are the rocks and there is the plume of snow powder which is the start of the avalanche. This photograph is from a frame of the film which we will call frame one. The next slide you will see is a similar shot but taken thirty-six frames later. That is, there is a two-second difference between the taking of the two photographs.' He went back to the comparator and inserted the second slide.

'There is not much difference, as you can see. The plume of snow powder is marginally greater.' He paused. 'But if we alternate the slides rapidly, as this machine is designed to do, you will see something curious.'

The image on the screen began to flicker rapidly and the snow plume oscillated. McGill used his pointer. Two of what I thought to be rocks – those two specks there – are obviously moving. This one at the top does not move very much in the two-second interval, but the one beneath moves a fair distance upwards. I submit that the speck at the top is Mr Miller, and the one beneath is Peterson climbing up to him after the avalanche was triggered.'

The increased sound in the hall was almost like the growl of a wild beast, and Harrison's gavel slammed down. 'I must protest again,' said Lyall. 'Two grainy images on a film which cannot even be seen to be men! What sort of evidence is this? They could very well be flaws in the film.'

'I have not yet finished,' said McGill quietly.

'Neither have I,' retorted Lyall. 'I would like to talk to you in private, Mr Chairman.'

Harrison listened to the roil of noise in the hall. 'I think if you keep your voice down you'll be private enough here.'

'I must object,' said Lyall intensely. 'Dr McGill has been giving evidence about something he could not possibly know – evidence that reflects upon my client. He has stated flatly in this room that one of those specks on the film is Charlie Peterson. Further, he has also stated that the lower

of those specks *is* Mr Peterson and that he started the avalanche. Can he prove this?'

'Well, Dr McGill?' said Harrison.

McGill was silent for a moment. 'No,' he admitted.

'Assuming, for the sake of theoretical argument, that
those specks are men,' said Lyall. 'They could be anyone,
and nothing to do with my client.'

'Now wait a minute,' said McGill. 'Charlie just said
that Miller started the avalanche. If he knows that, then
it means he was there. And we have Miller's sworn
evidence.'

'I'm quite capable of drawing my own conclusions,' said
Harrison. 'I suggest you confine your evidence to that
which you know, Dr McGill.'

Lyall said, 'As I see it, it's Miller's word against that of my
client. And Miller isn't here to cross-examine.'

'What would he gain by accusing Charlie!' asked McGill.
'He'd have done better for himself by keeping his mouth
shut. As it is, he's out ten thousand dollars.'

'That's enough,' said Harrison sharply. 'As I said before,
you're not here to argue a lawyer's case, Dr McGill. Now
you say you have more evidence?'

'Yes, sir.'

'Photographic?'

'That and my own testimony.'

'Then I suggest we proceed.' Harrison again hammered
with his gavel until he succeeded in achieving silence. He
waited until the silence was absolute, then said quietly, 'Dr
McGill, you may continue.'

McGill returned to the projector. 'After the avalanche
I went up on the west slope to see if there was further hazard. As it turned out, the hazard was minimal in the immediate future. Charlie Peterson volunteered to accompany
me. We made an examination of the slope and Mr Peterson
was very cool and showed no sign of nerves. It was only

after I had indicated my intention to examine the site where the avalanche had begun that he showed signs of nervousness. At the time I put this down to a natural fear of being in a potentially hazardous situation.

'As we went up the mountain his nervousness increased rapidly and he suggested we go down. We were not far from the site which I wished to examine so I ignored his suggestion. In the event we never reached the site. There was the air accident in the valley and we went down the slope immediately.'

'Interesting,' said Harrison. 'But I don't see the point.'

'This is the point,' said McGill. 'While we were on the slope an aircraft flew over us at very low altitude and I saw someone taking photographs. I discovered afterwards that the plane had been chartered by a newspaper here in Christchurch. I went to the newspaper office last night and went through all the photographs that had been taken. Here are some of them.'

The projector clicked and flashed again, and a black-and-white photograph appeared on the screen. McGill said, 'In the bottom right-hand corner you can see Peterson and me. In the top left corner you see exposed rocks. By the rocks there are ski tracks here – and here. I think that Peterson didn't want me to see those tracks; that's why he was nervous.'

'An unwarranted suggestion,' snapped Lyall.

McGill ignored him, and put another picture on the screen. 'Here is an enlargement of the breakaway point of the avalanche. There is a ski track going into it, and this ragged line, and another here, is where a man jumped up the slope. It had been snowing heavily that night, and all these tracks could only have been made on the morning of the avalanche.'

He switched off the projector. 'I further state on oath that the first time I saw Miller and Peterson on that Sunday they were both on skis.'

The dark room exploded. 'Lights!' shouted Harrison. 'Turn on the lights!'

An electrolier sparked into brilliance, and then sunlight flooded the room as an usher pulled aside a curtain. Charlie was on his feet. 'Damn you!' he yelled, pointing at McGill.

'Shut up, Charlie!' called Lyall sharply, but he was too late.

'Damn you all!' cried Charlie. 'It was Ballard who killed my brother – everyone knows that. Nobody would have died if they'd gone into the mine as Eric wanted. And Alec wouldn't have drowned if it hadn't been for Ballard. He's a bloody murderer, I tell you!' Froth flecked his lips. 'He started the avalanche – him and Miller between them.'

Lyall sagged and McGill heard him say, 'He's crazy!'

Charlie's throat worked convulsively. 'Ballard didn't like Huka or anyone in it.' He threw his arms wide. 'He wanted to *destroy* it – and he *did*. Most of all, he didn't like us Petersons. He killed two of us – and he made a whore out of my sister.' His arm swung around and pointed to Liz.

Harrison's gavel cracked sharply, and he said, 'Dr Cross, is there anything you can do?'

Eric grabbed Charlie's arm, but Charlie tossed him aside effortlessly. 'And McGill was in on the whole thing and I'm going to kill the bastard!' He plunged across the hall towards McGill but before he could reach him Eric had recovered and was on his back.

'Let me go,' he screamed. 'Let me get at him!' Again he broke Eric's grip and started again for McGill, but this time several men had moved in to subdue him. There was a brief flurry and then Charlie broke loose and ran sideways and made for the door. It opened before he got there and he ran into the arms of two policemen. They both put an armlock on him and he was marched out of sight.

Harrison thumped his gavel in vain. Into the uproar he said quietly, 'This hearing is adjourned.'

THIRTY-THREE

Half an hour later McGill, still in the hall, was beseiged by reporters. 'No comment,' he kept repeating. 'I said all I had to say when I gave my evidence. There's nothing more.'

He broke free, went into the first room he saw and slammed the door behind him. He turned and saw Harrison and Stenning. 'Sorry, but do you mind if I take refuge for a few minutes. Those reporters are driving me crazy.'

'Not at all,' said Harrison. 'You've caused quite a stir, Dr McGill.'

McGill grimaced. 'Not as much as Charlie. How is he?'

'Dr Cross put him under sedation.' He paused. 'I think there's a case for a court order for psychiatric treatment.' Harrison recollected his manners. 'Oh, this is Mr Stenning, a visitor from England. He's here to see how we conduct our administrative justice. I've been telling him that not all our Inquiries are so rowdy. I don't think he believes me.'

'I'm acquainted with Mr Stenning,' said McGill. 'We stay at the same hotel.'

Harrison picked up his briefcase. 'I think it will be safe to leave by the back way, gentlemen.'

Stenning said, 'Could I have a word with you, Dr McGill?'

'Of course.'

'Feel free to use this office,' said Harrison. 'Will you attend the Inquiry tomorrow, Mr Stenning?'

345

'I think not. I have urgent business in England. I assure you it has been most interesting.'

'Well, then, we'll say goodbye now.' They shook hands.

When Stenning and McGill were alone Stenning remarked, 'Harrison was wrong – that letter was not admissible because Miller was not there to be cross-examined. I think the Inquiry will be adjourned while Harrison takes legal advice. It shows the inadvisability of setting a layman to do a lawyer's job.'

McGill shrugged. 'Does it matter now? We've seen that Charlie is as crazy as a loon.'

Stenning regarded him speculatively. 'You said in your evidence that Ian had agreed that the letter should be produced.'

'That's right.'

'Strange. At the end of our last conversation Ian told me to go to hell. He also consigned the Ballard Trust to the same destination. He must have changed his mind. It would be interesting to know exactly when he changed it.'

'I think he changed it when Charlie Peterson started beating the hell out of him.'

'You think it *was* Peterson?'

'For God's sake! Don't you? You've just seen Charlie in action. He tossed Eric around as though he was a rag doll, and Eric's no midget. And I got a good look at his hands this afternoon. His knuckles were pretty raw.'

'Is that the only reason you think it was Peterson? I have to be sure, Dr McGill.'

'Of course not,' said McGill, lying bravely with a frank open face. 'Ian told me himself when I found him in the car park. He said, and I remember his exact words, "It was Charlie, use the letter and smash him." Then he passed out.'

'I see.' Stenning smiled, and said obliquely, 'I think Ian is lucky to have you for a friend.'

'I'd do the same for anyone who was getting the raw end of a deal, Mr Stenning. He was getting it from both sides, you know. Your hands are not entirely clean in this matter.'

Abruptly he turned his back on Stenning and left the room. He crossed the Provincial Chamber, now deserted, and went into the vestibule where he ran straight into Liz Peterson. She lifted her hand and slapped his face with all the force she could muster, which was considerable.

His head rocked sideways and he grabbed her wrist. 'Steady, Liz.'

'How could you?' she said passionately. 'How could you do that to Charlie?'

'Someone had to stop him.'

'But not like that. You needn't have crucified him in public.'

'How would you suggest? He was mad, Liz; he was going insane. Even Eric thought so. Eric told him outright he was losing his mind. He was eaten up by guilt and he wanted to pour it all out on Ian.'

'Ian!' Liz said contemptuously. 'That man wanted to marry me. I never want to see him again. He could have suppressed that letter.'

'He wanted to,' said McGill. 'But I talked him out of it. It would have been a fool thing to do. He was supposed to see you last night. Did he?'

She shook her head. 'Charlie played one of his tricks. He got me into his car on some excuse and then drove me out of town going like a maniac.' She stopped as she realized what she had just said and then swallowed. 'Anyway, he dumped me on a country road and just drove away. It was nearly midnight when I got back into town. I phoned Ian but he wasn't in. I thought I'd see him this morning but he had the accident.'

'Did Charlie know you were going to see Ian?'

'Not unless Eric told him.'

'So you told Eric, and Eric mentioned it to Charlie. That was a fool thing to do.' He took her arm. 'You need talking to, my girl, and you'd better have a drink while you listen.'

Five minutes later at a discreet table in a hotel lounge McGill said, 'It's a bit of a convoluted story. When Miller's letter came, Ian read it and asked me just one question. He wanted to know if the avalanche would have happened anyway, regardless of what Charlie had done. I had to say that it would have come down. It was only a matter of time, Liz.'

He picked up his drink and stared at it. 'Once Ian heard that he wanted me to suppress the letter. I talked him out of that, but then he said he wanted to clear things with you.'

'And I didn't turn up,' Liz said dully.

'The next time I saw him he was a hospital case, and I was lying like a flat fish to a man called Stenning – you've met him.'

'What's he got to do with it?'

McGill told her about old Ben Ballard, the Ballard Trust and the task that had been laid upon Stenning. It took quite a while. He wound up by saying, 'Even when Ian knew about Miller's letter he told Stenning to go to hell. Stenning just told me that.'

'He was prepared to give all that up?' said Liz slowly.

'Not because he didn't want to hurt Charlie, but because he didn't want to hurt you. Don't blame Ian for anything. Anyway, it doesn't matter any more. Stenning has evidence that Ian did walk over the Petersons in the end. He might suspect a fiddle but he can't prove it, and because he's a lawyer he'll accept it.' McGill smiled. 'From something he said just now I rather think he likes it this way.'

'Aren't you cheating Stenning?' asked Liz with a half smile.

'Not really. I think old Ben was wrong. He said a man must have steel in him to run the Ballard Group but I think there are enough men of steel around – too many, perhaps. They're going out of fashion. What the Group needs now is a man-manager, an administrator, a diplomat – and Ian is all of those. And if he needs any steel he'll have it if he has a Peterson next to him.'

'Oh, Mike, do you think . . .?' Liz put her hand on McGill's and her eyes were bright with unshed tears. 'I'm torn, Mike. The police have taken Charlie away because of the avalanche and . . .'

'No!' said McGill sharply. 'Not because of the avalanche. That hasn't been proved – and may never be.'

'Then why?'

'Ian intended to meet you last night but, instead, he got Charlie. Stenning saw them at the hotel. And Charlie beat Ian half to death in the car park, probably when he was on his way to look for you. There was no car accident. The police were waiting to arrest Charlie for assault as soon as he came out of the hall.'

Liz was as pale as she had been when McGill had first seen her in the church after the avalanche. He said gently, 'He had to be stopped, Liz. I've often wondered what would have happened if he and I had gone that extra two hundred feet up the west slope after the avalanche and I'd seen those ski tracks. I think, maybe, there'd have been another avalanche victim. He's strong enough to have torn me in half. He had to be stopped and I took the quickest way I knew.'

Liz sighed shudderingly. 'I knew he was violent and had his strange ways, and I knew they were becoming worse. But not as bad as this. What will become of him, Mike?'

'He'll be all right. There'll be people to look after him. I don't think he'll stand trial for anything. He's beyond that, Liz – way beyond. You saw him this afternoon – you know what I mean. Harrison said as much, too.'

She nodded. 'So it's all over.'

'It's over,' he agreed. 'My masters want me to go south to the the ice. They've put up a geodesic dome at the South Pole – Buckminster Fuller strikes again – and they want a snowman to check the foundations.'

McGill leaned back in his chair and picked up his glass. He said casually, 'Ian is in the Princess Margaret Hospital – third floor. The Ward Sister is a tough old bird called Quayle but if you say you are Ian's fiancee she might let you . . .'

He became aware he was talking to thin air. 'Hey, you haven't finished your drink!'

But Liz was halfway across the room on her way, and beside her Victor trotted, his tail waving in a proud plume.

NIGHT OF ERROR

For STAN HURST, at last,
with affection

And when with grief you see your brother stray,
Or in a night of error lose his way,
Direct his wandering and restore the day.
To guide his steps afford your kindest aid,
And gently pity whom you can't persuade:
Leave to avenging Heaven his stubborn will,
For, O, remember, he's your brother still.

JONATHAN SWIFT

PREFACE

The Pacific Islands Pilot, Vol. II, published by the Hydrographer of the Navy, has this to say about the island of Fonua Fo'ou, almost at the end of a long and detailed history:

> In 1963, HMNZFA *Tui* reported a hard grey rock, with a depth of 6 feet over it, on which the sea breaks, and general depths of 36 feet extending for 2 miles northwards and 1 1/2 miles westward of the rock, in the position of the bank. The eastern side is steep-to. In the vicinity of the rock, there was much discoloured water caused by sulphurous gas bubbles rising to the surface. On the bank, the bottom was clearly visible, and consisted of fine black cellar lava, like volcanic cinder, with patches of white sand and rock. Numerous sperm whales were seen in the vicinity.

But that edition was not published until 1969.

This story began in 1962.

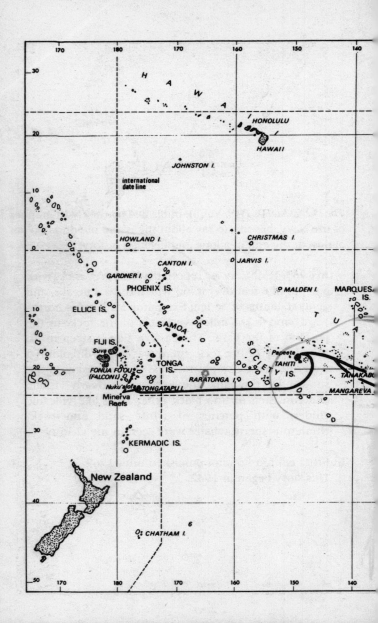

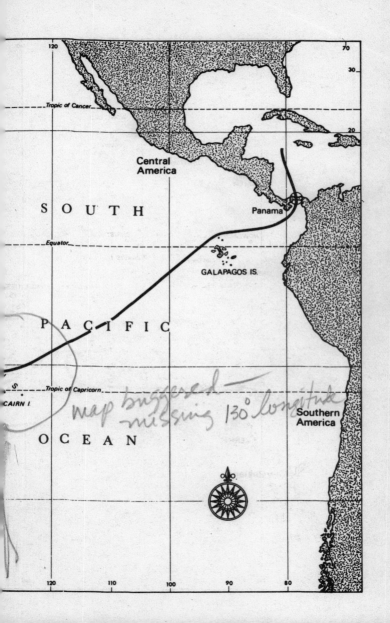

120   70

30

Tropic of Cancer

20

**Central
America**

S   O   U   T   H

Panama

Equator

GALAPAGOS IS.

P   A   C   I   F   I   C

S

Tropic of Capricorn

CAIRN I.

map buggered —
missing 130° longitude

Southern
America

O   C   E   A   N

120   110   100   90   80

ONE

I heard of the way my brother died on a wet and gloomy afternoon in London. The sky was overcast and weeping and it became dark early that day, much earlier than usual. I couldn't see the figures I was checking, so I turned on the desk light and got up to close the curtains.

I stood for a moment watching the rain leak from the plane trees on the Embankment, then looked over the mist-shrouded Thames. I shivered slightly, wishing I could get out of this grey city and back to sea under tropic skies. I drew the curtain decisively, closing out the gloom.

The telephone rang.

It was Helen, my brother's widow, and she sounded hysterical. 'Mike, there's a man here – Mr Kane – who was with Mark when he died. I think you'd better see him.' Her voice broke. 'I can't take it, Mike.'

'All right, Helen; shoot him over. I'll be here until five-thirty – can he make it before then?'

There was a pause and an indistinct murmur, then Helen said, 'Yes, he'll be at the Institute before then. Thanks, Mike. Oh, and there's a slip from British Airways – something has come from Tahiti; I think it must be Mark's things. I posted it to you this morning – will you look after it for me? I don't think I could bear to.'

'I'll do that,' I said. 'I'll look after everything.'

She rang off and I put down the receiver slowly and leaned back in my chair. Helen seemed distraught about Mark and I wondered what this man Kane had told her. All I knew was that Mark had died somewhere in the Islands near Tahiti; the British Consul there had wrapped it all up and the Foreign Office had got in touch with Helen as next of kin. She never said so but it must have been a relief – her marriage had caused her nothing but misery.

She should never have married him in the first place. I had tried to warn her, but it's a bit difficult telling one's prospective sister-in-law about the iniquities of one's own brother, and I'd never got it across. Still, she must have loved him despite everything, judging by the way she was behaving; but then, Mark had a way with his women.

One thing was certain – Mark's death wouldn't affect me a scrap. I had long ago taken his measure and had steered clear of him and all his doings, all the devious and calculating cold-blooded plans which had only one end in view – the glorification of Mark Trevelyan.

I put him out of my mind, adjusted the desk lamp and got down to my figures again. People think of scientists – especially oceanographers – as being constantly in the field making esoteric discoveries. They never think of the office work entailed – and if I didn't get clear of this routine work I'd never get back to sea. I thought that if I really buckled down to it another day would see it through, and then I would have a month's leave, if I could consider writing a paper for the journals as constituting leave. But even that would not take up the whole month.

At a quarter to six I packed it in for the day and Kane had still not shown up. I was just putting on my overcoat when there was a knock on the door and when I opened it a man said, 'Mr Trevelyan?'

Kane was a tall, haggard man of about forty, dressed in rough seaman's clothing and wearing a battered peaked cap.

He seemed subdued and a little in awe of his surroundings. As we shook hands I could feel the callouses and thought that perhaps he was a sailing man – steam seamen don't have much occasion to do that kind of hand work.

I said, 'I'm sorry to have dragged you across London on a day like this, Mr Kane.'

'That's all right,' he said in a raw Australian accent. 'I was coming up this way.'

I sized him up. 'I was just going out. What about a drink?'

He smiled. 'That 'ud be fine. I like your English beer.'

We went to a nearby pub and I took him into the public bar and ordered a couple of beers. He sank half a pint and gasped luxuriously. 'This is good beer,' he said. 'Not as good as Swan, but good all the same. You know Swan beer?'

'I've heard of it,' I said. 'I've never had any. Australian, isn't it?'

'Yair; the best beer in the world.'

To an Australian all things Australian are the best. 'Would I be correct if I said you'd done your time in sail?' I said.

He laughed. 'Too right you would. How do you know?'

'I've sailed myself; I suppose it shows somehow.'

'Then I won't have to explain too much detail when I tell you about your brother. I suppose you want to know the whole story? I didn't tell Mrs Trevelyan all of it, you know – some of it's pretty grim.'

'I'd better know everything.'

Kane finished his beer and cocked an eye at me. 'Another?'

'Not for me just yet. You go ahead.'

He ordered another beer and said, 'Well, we were sailing in the Society Islands – my partner and me – we've got a schooner and we do a bit of trading and pick up copra and maybe a few pearls. We were in the Tuamotus – the locals call them the Paumotus, but they're the Tuamotus on the charts. They're east of . . .'

'I know where they are,' I interrupted.

'Okay. Well, we thought there was a chance of picking up a few pearls so we were just cruising round calling on the inhabited islands. Most of 'em aren't and most of 'em don't have names – not names that we can pronounce. Anyway we were passing this one when a canoe came out and hailed us. There was a boy in this canoe – a Polynesian, you know – and Jim talked to him. Jim Hadley's my partner; he speaks the lingo – I don't savvy it too good myself.

'What he said was that there was a white man on the island who was very sick, and so we went ashore to have a look at him.'

'That was my brother?'

'Too right, and he was sick; my word yes.'

'What was wrong with him?'

Kane shrugged. 'We didn't know at first but it turned out to be appendicitis. That's what we found out after we got a doctor to him.'

'Then there was a doctor?'

'If you could call him a doctor. He was a drunken old no-hoper who'd been living in the Islands for years. But he said he was a doctor. He wasn't there though; Jim had to go fifty miles to get him while I stayed with your brother.'

Kane took another pull at his beer. 'Your brother was alone on this island except for the black boy. There wasn't no boat, either. He said he was some sort of scientist – something to do with the sea.'

'An oceanographer.' Yes, like me an oceanographer. Mark had always felt compelled, driven, to try and beat me whatever the game. And his rules were always his own.

'Too right. He said he'd been dropped there to do some research and he was due to be picked up any time.'

'Why didn't you take him to the doctor instead of bringing the doctor to him?' I asked.

'We didn't think he'd make it,' said Kane simply. 'A little
ship like ours bounces about a lot, and he was pretty sick.'

'I see,' I said. He was painting a rough picture.

'I did what I could for him,' said Kane. 'There wasn't
much I could do though, beyond cleaning him up. We talked
a lot about this and that – that was when he asked me to tell
his wife.'

'Surely he didn't expect you to make a special trip to
England?' I demanded, thinking that even in death it
sounded like Mark's touch.

'Oh, it was nothing like that,' said Kane. 'You see, I was
coming to England anyway. I won a bit of money in a
sweep and I always wanted to see the old country. Jim, my
cobber, said he could carry on alone for a bit, and he
dropped me at Panama. I bummed a job on a ship coming
to England.'

He smiled ruefully. 'I won't be staying here as long as I
thought – I dropped a packet in a poker game coming
across. I'll stay until my cash runs out and then I'll go back
to Jim and the schooner.'

I said, 'What happened when the doctor came?'

'Oh sure, you want to know about your brother; sorry if
I got off track. Well, Jim brought this old no-good back and
he operated. He said he had to, it was your brother's only
chance. Pretty rough it was too; the doc's instruments
weren't any too good. I helped him – Jim hadn't the stomach for it.' He fell silent, looking back into the past.

I ordered another couple of beers, but Kane said, 'I'd like
something stronger, if you don't mind,' so I changed the
order to whisky.

I thought of some drunken oaf of a doctor cutting my
brother open with blunt knives on a benighted tropical
island. It wasn't a pretty thought and I think Kane saw the

horror of it too, the way he gulped his whisky. It was worse for him – he had been there.

'So he died,' I said.

'Not right away. He seemed okay after the operation, then he got worse. The doc said it was per . . . peri . . .'

'Peritonitis?'

'That's it. I remember it sounded like peri-peri sauce – like having something hot in your guts. He got a fever and went delirious; then he went unconscious and died two days after the operation.'

He looked into his glass. 'We buried him at sea. It was stinking hot and we couldn't carry the body anywhere – we hadn't any ice. We sewed him up in canvas and put him over the side. The doctor said he'd see to all the details – I mean, it wasn't any use for Jim and me to go all the way to Papeete – the doc knew all we knew.'

'You told the doctor about Mark's wife – her address and so on?'

Kane nodded. 'Mrs Trevelyan said she'd only just heard about it – that's the Islands postal service for you. You know, he never gave us nothing for her, no personal stuff I mean. We wondered about that. But she said some gear of his is on the way – that right?'

'It might be that,' I said. 'There's something at Heathrow now. I'll probably pick it up tomorrow. When did Mark die, by the way?'

He reflected. 'Must have been about four months ago. You don't go much for dates and calendars when you're cruising the Islands, not unless you're navigating and looking up the almanack all the time, and Jim's the expert on that. I reckon it was about the beginning of May. Jim dropped me at Panama in July and I had to wait a bit to get a ship across here.'

'Do you remember the doctor's name? Or where he came from?'

Kane frowned. 'I know he was a Dutchman; his name was Scoot-something. As near as I can remember it might have been Scooter. He runs a hospital on one of the Islands – my word, I can't remember that either.'

'It's of no consequence; if it becomes important I can get it from the death certificate.' I finished my whisky. 'The last I heard of Mark he was working with a Swede called Norgaard. You didn't come across him?'

Kane shook his head. 'There was only your brother. We didn't stay around, you know. Not when old Scooter said he'd take care of everything. You think this Norgaard was supposed to pick your brother up when he'd finished his job?'

'Something like that,' I said. 'It's been very good of you to take the trouble to tell us about Mark's death.'

He waved my thanks aside. 'No trouble at all; anyone would have done the same. I didn't tell Mrs Trevelyan too much, you understand.'

'I'll edit it when I tell her,' I said. 'Anyway, thanks for looking after him. I wouldn't like to think he died alone.'

'Aw, look,' said Kane, embarrassed. 'We couldn't do any-thing else now, could we?'

I gave him my card. 'I'd like you to keep in touch,' I said. 'Perhaps when you're ready to go back I can help you with a passage. I have plenty of contacts with the shipping people.'

'Too right,' he said. 'I'll keep in touch, Mr Trevelyan.'

I said goodbye and left the bar, ducking into the private bar in the same pub. I didn't think Kane would go in there and I wanted a few quiet thoughts over another drink.

I thought of Mark dying a rather gruesome death on that lonely Pacific atoll. God knows that Mark and I didn't see eye to eye but I wouldn't have wished that fate on my worst enemy. And yet there was something odd about the whole story; I wasn't surprised at him being in the Tuamotus – it was his job to go poking about odd corners of the seven seas as it was mine – but something struck a sour note.

For instance, what had happened to Norgaard? It certainly wasn't standard operating procedure for a man to be left entirely alone on a job. I wondered what Mark and Norgaard had been doing in the Tuamotus; they had published no papers so perhaps their investigation hadn't been completed. I made a mental note to ask old Jarvis about it; my boss kept his ear close to the grapevine and knew everything that went on in the profession.

But it wasn't that which worried me; it was something else, something niggling at the back of my mind that I couldn't resolve. I chased it around for a bit but nothing happened, so I finished my drink and went home to my flat for a late night session with some figures.

II

The next day I was at the office bright and early and managed to get my work finished just before lunch. I was attacking my neglected correspondence when one of the girls brought in a visitor, and a most welcome one. Geordie Wilkins had been my father's sergeant in the Commandos during the war and after my father had been killed he took an interest in the sons of the man he had so greatly respected. Mark, typically, had been a little contemptuous of him but I liked Geordie and we got on well together.

He had done well for himself after the war. He foresaw the yachting boom and bought himself a 25-ton cutter which he chartered and in which he gave sailing lessons. Later he gave up tuition and had worked up to a 200-ton brigantine which he chartered to rich Americans mostly, taking them anywhere they wanted to go at an exorbitant price. Whenever he put into England he looked me up, but it had been a while since last I'd seen him.

He came into the office bringing with him a breath of sea air. 'My God, Mike, but you're pallid,' he said. 'I'll have to take you back to sea.'

'Geordie! Where have you sprung from this time?'

'The Caribbean,' he said. 'I brought the old girl over for a refit. I'm in between charters, thank God.'

'Where are you staying?'

'With you – if you'll have me. *Esmerelda*'s here.'

'Don't be an idiot,' I said happily. 'You know you're welcome. We seem to have struck it lucky this time; I have to do a bit of writing which will take a week, and then I've got three weeks spare.'

He rubbed his chin. 'I'm tied up for a week too, but I'm free after that. We'll push off somewhere.'

'That's a great idea,' I said. 'I've been dying to get away. Wait while I check this post, would you?'

The letter I had just opened was from Helen; it contained a brief letter and the advisory note from British Airways. There was something to be collected from Heathrow which had to clear customs. I looked up at Geordie. 'Did you know that Mark is dead?'

He looked startled. 'Dead! When did that happen?'

I told him all about it and he said, 'A damned sticky end – even for Mark.' Then he immediately apologized. 'Sorry – I shouldn't have said that.'

'Quit it, Geordie,' I said irritably. 'You know how I felt about Mark; there's no need to be mealy-mouthed with me.'

'Aye. He was a bit of a bastard, wasn't he? How's that wife of his taking it?'

'About average under the circumstances. She was pretty broken up but I seem to detect an underlying note of relief.'

'She's best to remarry and forget him,' said Geordie bluntly. He shook his head slowly. 'It beats me what the women saw in Mark. He treated 'em like dirt and they sat up and begged for more.'

'Some people have it, some don't,' I said.

'If it means being like Mark I'd rather not have it. Sad to think one can't find a good word to say for the man.' He took the paper out of my hand. 'Got a car I can use? I haven't been in one for months and I'd like the drive. I'll get my gear from *Esmerelda* and go out and pick this stuff up for you.'

I tossed him my car keys. 'Thanks. It's the same old wreck – you'll find it in the car park.'

When he had gone I finished up my paperwork and then went to see the Prof. to pay my respects. Old Jarvis was quite cordial. 'You've done a good job, Mike,' he said. 'I've looked at your stuff briefly and if your correlations are correct I think we're on to something.'

'Thank you.'

He leaned back in his chair and started to fill his pipe. 'You'll be writing a paper, of course.'

'I'll do that while I'm on leave,' I said. 'It won't be a long one; just a preliminary. There's still a lot of sea time to put in.'

'Looking forward to getting back to it, are you?'

'I'll be glad to get away.'

He grunted suddenly. 'For every day you spend at sea you'll have three in the office digesting the data. And don't get into a job like mine; it's *all* office-work. Steer clear of administration, my boy; don't get chair-bound.'

'I won't,' I promised and then changed tack. 'Can you tell me anything about a fellow called Norgaard? I think he's a Swede working on ocean currents.'

Jarvis looked at me from under bushy eyebrows. 'Wasn't he the chap working with your brother when he died?'

'That's the man.'

He pondered, then shook his head. 'I haven't heard anything of him lately; he certainly hasn't published. But I'll make a few enquiries and put you in touch.'

And that was that. I didn't know why I had taken the trouble to ask the Prof. about Norgaard unless it was still that uneasy itch at the back of my skull, the feeling that something was wrong somewhere. It probably didn't mean anything anyway, and I put it out of my mind as I walked back to my office.

It was getting late and I was about ready to leave when Geordie returned and heaved a battered, ancient suitcase onto my desk. 'There it is,' he said. 'They made me open it – it was a wee bit difficult without a key, though.'

'What did you do?'

'Busted the lock,' he said cheerfully.

I looked at the case warily. 'What's in it?'

'Not much. Some clothes, a few books and a lot of pebbles. And there's a letter addressed to Mark's wife.' He untied the string holding the case together, skimmed the letter across the desk, and started to haul out the contents – a couple of tropical suits, not very clean; two shirts; three pairs of socks; three textbooks on oceanography – very up-to-date; a couple of notebooks in Mark's handwriting, and a miscellany of pens, toiletries and small odds and ends.

I looked at the letter, addressed to Helen in a neat cursive hand. 'I'd better open this,' I said. 'We don't know what's in it and I don't want Helen to get too much of a shock.'

Geordie nodded and I slit the envelope. The letter was short and rather abrupt:

Dear Mrs Trevelyan,

I am sorry to tell you that your husband, Mark, is dead, although you may know this already by the time you get this. Mark was a good friend to me and left some of his things in my care. I am sending them all to you as I know you would like to have them.

Sincerely,

P. Nelson

I said, 'I thought this would be official but it's not.'

Geordie scanned the short note. 'Do you know this chap, Nelson?'

'Never heard of him.'

Geordie put the letter on the desk and tipped up the suitcase. 'Then there are these.' A dozen or so potato-like objects rolled onto the desk. Some of them rolled further and thumped onto the carpet, and Geordie stooped and picked them up. 'You'll probably make more sense of these than I can.'

I turned one in my fingers. 'Manganese nodules,' I said. 'Very common in the Pacific.'

'Are they valuable?'

I laughed. 'If you could get at them easily they might be – but you can't, so they aren't. They lie on the seabed at an average depth of about fourteen thousand feet.'

He looked closely at one of the nodules. 'I wonder where he got these, then? It's a bit deep for skin-diving.'

'They're probably souvenirs of the IGY – the International Geophysical Year. Mark was a physical chemist on one of the ships in the Pacific.' I took one of the notebooks and flipped the pages at random. Most of it seemed to be mathematical, the equations close-packed in Mark's finicky hand.

I tossed it into the open suitcase. 'Let's get this stuff packed away, then we'll go home.'

So we put everything back, higgledy-piggledy, and carted the case down to the car. On the way home Geordie said, 'What about a show tonight?' On his rare visits to a city he had a soft spot for big gaudy musicals.

'If you can get tickets,' I said. 'I don't feel like queueing.'

'I'll get them,' he said confidently. 'I know someone who owes me a few favours. Look, drop me right here and I'll see you at the flat in half an hour, or maybe a bit longer.'

I dropped him and when I got to where I lived I took Mark's suitcase first because it came handiest, then I went back to the car for Geordie's gear. For some time I pottered about estimating what I'd need for a trip away with him, but I had most of what I needed and the list of things I had to get was very short and didn't take long to figure out.

After a while I found myself looking at the suitcase. I picked it up, put it on the bed and opened it and looked at the few remnants of Mark's life. I hoped that when I went I'd leave more than a few books, a few clothes and a doubtful reputation. The clothing was of no particular interest but, as I lifted up a jacket, a small leather-bound notebook fell out of the breast pocket.

I picked it up and examined it. It had obviously been used as a diary but most of the entries were in shorthand, once Pitman's, but adapted in an idiosyncratic way so that they were incomprehensible to anyone but the writer – Mark.

Occasionally there were lines of chemical and mathematical notation and every now and then there was a doodled drawing. I remembered that Mark had been a doodler even at school and had been ticked off often because of the state of his exercise books. There wasn't much sense to be made of any of it.

I put the diary on my dressing table and turned to the larger notebooks. They were much more interesting although scarcely more comprehensible. Apparently, Mark was working on a theory of nodule formation that, to say the least of it, was hare-brained – certainly from the point of view of orthodox physical chemistry. The time scale he was using was fantastic, and even at a casual glance his qualitative analysis seemed out of line.

Presently I heard Geordie come in. He popped his head round the door of the bedroom and said triumphantly, 'I've got the tickets. Let's have a slap-up dinner first and then go on to the theatre.'

'That's a damned good idea,' I said. I threw the notebooks and the clothing back into the case and retied the lid down.

Geordie nodded at it. 'Find anything interesting?'

I grinned. 'Nothing, except that Mark was going round the bend. He'd got hold of some damn fool idea about nodules and was going overboard about it.'

I shoved the case under the bed and began to get dressed for dinner.

III

It was a good dinner and a better show and we drove home replete with fine food and excellent entertainment. Geordie was in high spirits and sang in a cracked and tuneless voice one of the numbers from the show. We were both in a cheerful mood.

I parked the car outside the block of flats and got out. There was still a thin drizzle of rain but I thought that by morning it would have cleared. That was good; I wanted fine weather for my leave. As I looked up at the sky I stiffened.

'Geordie, there's someone in my flat.'

He looked up at the third floor and saw what I had seen – a furtive, hunting light moving at one of the windows.

'That's a torch.' His teeth flashed as he grinned in the darkness. 'It's a long time since I've had a proper scrap.'

I said, 'Come on,' and ran up into the foyer.

Geordie caught my arm as I pressed for the lift. 'Hold on, let's do this properly,' he said. 'Wait one minute and then go up in the lift. I'll take the stairs – we should arrive on your floor at the same time. Covers both exits.'

I grinned and saluted. 'Yes, sergeant.' You can't keep an old soldier down; Geordie was making a military operation out of catching a sneak thief – but I followed orders.

I went up in the lift and stepped out into the lighted corridor. Geordie had made good time up the stairs and was breathing as easily as though he'd been strolling on the level. He motioned me to keep the lift door open and reached inside to press the button for the top floor. I closed the door and the lift went up.

He grinned in his turn. 'Anyone leaving in a hurry must use the stairs now. Got your key?'

I passed it to him and we walked to the door of my flat, treading softly. Through the uncurtained kitchen window I could see the flash of a torch. Geordie cautiously inserted the key into the lock. 'We'll go in sharpish,' he whispered, gave the key a twist, threw open the door and plunged into the flat like an angry bull.

As I followed on his heel I heard a shout – *'Ojo!'* – and the next thing I knew was a blinding flash in my eyes and I was grappling with someone at the kitchen door. Whoever it was hit me on the side of the head, it must have been with the torch because the light went out. I felt dizzy for a moment but held on, thrusting forward and bringing my knee up sharply.

I heard a gasp of pain and above it the roar of Geordie's voice from further in the flat – possibly the bedroom.

I let go my grip and struck out with my fist, and yelled in pain as my knuckles hit the kitchen door. My opponent squirmed out from where I had him pinned and was gone through the open door of the flat. Things were happening too fast for me. I could hear Geordie swearing at the top of his voice and the crash of furniture. A light tenor voice called, *'Huid! Huid! No disparéis! Emplead cuchillos!'* Then suddenly someone else banged into me in the darkness and I struck out again.

I knew now that this assailant would certainly have a knife and possibly a gun and I think I went berserk – it's wonderful what the adrenal glands will do for a man in an emergency. In the light from the corridor I caught a glimpse of an upraised knife and I chopped viciously at the wrist.

There was a howl of pain and the knife clattered to the floor. I aimed a punch at where I thought a stomach was – and missed.

Something was swung at the side of my head again and I went down as a black figure jumped over me. If he hadn't stopped to kick at my head he would have got clean away, but I squirmed to avoid his boot and caught his leg, and he went sprawling into the corridor.

I dived after him and got between him and the stairs, and he stood in a crouch looking at me, his eyes darting about, looking for escape. Then I saw what he must have swung at my head in the flat – it was Mark's suitcase.

Suddenly he turned and ran, towards the blank end of the corridor. 'I've got him now,' I thought exultantly, and went after him at a dead run. But he had remembered what I'd forgotten – the fire escape.

He might have got away then but once again I tackled him rugby-fashion so that I floored him just short of the fire escape. The fall knocked the breath out of me and he improved the shining hour by kicking me in the face. Then, as I was shaking my head in dizziness, he tossed Mark's case into the darkness.

By the time I regained my feet I was between him and the metal staircase and he was facing me with his right hand, now unencumbered, darting to his pocket. I saw the gun as he drew it and knew the meaning of real fear. I jumped for him and he side-stepped frantically trying to clear the gun from his pocket – but the foresight must have caught on the lining.

Then I hit him hard on the jaw and he teetered on the top step of the fire escape. I hit him again and slammed him against the railing and, to my horror, he jackknifed over. He didn't make a sound as he fell the three floors into the alley and it seemed a long time before I heard the dull thump as he hit the ground.

I looked down into the darkness and saw nothing. I was conscious of the trembling of my hands as they gripped the steel rail. There was a scurry of footsteps and I turned to see Geordie darting down the stairs. 'Leave them,' I shouted. 'They're armed!'

But he didn't stop and all I heard was the thud of his feet as he raced down the staircase.

The tall thin man who lived in the next flat came out in a dressing gown. 'Now, what's all this?' he asked querulously. 'A chap can't listen to the radio with all this racket going on.'

I said, 'Phone the police. There's been an attempted murder.'

His face went white and he looked at my arm. I looked down and saw blood staining the edges of a slit in the sleeve of my jacket. I couldn't remember being knifed and I felt nothing.

I looked back up at him. 'Well, hurry,' I yelled at him.

A gunshot echoed up the stairwell and we both started. 'Christ!'

I clattered down the stairs at top speed, all three flights, and came across Geordie in the foyer. He was sitting on the floor staring at his fingers in amazement – they were red with welling blood.

'The bastard shot me!' he said incredulously.

'Where are you hit, for God's sake?'

'In the hand, I think. I don't feel anything anywhere else, and he only fired one shot.'

I looked at his hand. Blood was spurting from the end of his little finger. I began to laugh, an hysterical sound not far from crying, and went on until Geordie slapped my face with his unwounded hand. 'Pull yourself together, Mike,' he said firmly. I became aware of doors slamming and voices upstairs but as yet nobody had ventured down into the foyer itself, and I sobered suddenly.

'I think I killed one of them,' I said emptily.

'Don't be daft. How could you kill a man with your fist?'

'I knocked him off the fire escape. He fell from the third floor.'

Geordie looked at me closely. 'We'd better go and have a look at that.'

'Are you all right?' We were both bleeding freely now.

He was wrapping his finger in a handkerchief which promptly turned bright red. 'I'm okay. You can't call this a mortal wound,' he said dryly. We went out into the street and walked quickly round to the alley into which the fire escape led. As we turned the corner there was a sudden glare of light and the roar of an engine, together with the slamming of a car door.

'Look out!' yelled Geordie and flung himself sideways.

I saw the two great eyes of headlamps rushing at me from the darkness of the alley and I frantically flattened myself against the wall. The car roared past and I felt the wind of it brush my trousers, and then with a squeal of hard-used tyres it turned the corner and was gone.

I listened to the noise of the engine die away and eased myself from the wall, taking a deep shaky breath. In the light of the street lamp on the corner I saw Geordie pick himself up. 'Christ!' I said. 'You don't know what's going to happen next.'

'This lot aren't ordinary burglars,' said Geordie, brushing himself down. 'They're too bloody persistent. Where's this fire escape?'

'A bit further along,' I said.

We walked slowly up the alley and Geordie fell over the man I had knocked over the edge. We bent down to examine him and, in the faint light, we could see his head. It was twisted at an impossible angle and there was a deep bloody depression in the skull.

Geordie said, 'No need to look any further. He's dead.'

IV

'And you say they were speaking Spanish,' said the Inspector.

I nodded wearily. 'As soon as we went into the flat some-one shouted, "Look out!" and then I was in the middle of a fight. A bit later on another man shouted, "Get out of here; don't shoot – use your knives." I think it was the man I knocked off the fire escape.'

The Inspector looked at me thoughtfully. 'But you say he was going to shoot you.'

'He'd lost his knife by then, and I was going for him.'

'How good is your Spanish, Mr Trevelyan?'

'Pretty good,' I said. 'I did a lot of work off south-west Europe about four years ago and I was based in Spain. I took the trouble to learn the language – I have a flair for them.'

The doctor tied a neat knot in the bandage round my arm and said, 'That'll hold it, but try not to use the arm for a while.' He packed his bag and went out.

I sat up and looked about the flat – it was like a field dressing station in a blitzed area. I was stripped to the waist with a bandaged arm and Geordie sported a natty bandage on his little finger. He was drinking tea and he held out his finger like a charlady at a garden party.

The flat was a wreck. What hadn't been broken by the burglars had been smashed during the fight. A chair with no legs lay in the corner and broken glass from the front of my bookcase littered the carpet. A couple of uniformed consta-bles stood stolidly in the corners and a plain clothes man was blowing powder about the place with an insufflator.

The Inspector said, 'Once again – how many of them were there?

Geordie said, 'I had two on my hands at one time.'

'I had a go at two,' I said. 'But I think that one of them had a bash at Geordie first. It's difficult to say – it happened so fast.'

'This man you heard – did he say "knife" or "knives"?'

I thought about that. 'He said "knives".'

The Inspector said, 'Then there were more than two of them.'

Geordie said unexpectedly, 'There were four.'

The Inspector looked at him with raised eyebrows.

'I saw three men in the car that passed us. One driving and two getting in in a hurry. With one dead in the alley – that makes four.'

'Ah yes,' said the Inspector. 'They would have one man in the car. Tell me, how did you come to get shot?'

A smile touched Geordie's lips. 'How does anyone get shot? With a gun.' The Inspector recognized a touch of over-excitement and said dryly, 'I mean, what were the circumstances?'

'Well, I chased the little bastard down the stairs and damn nearly caught him in the foyer. He saw he was going to be copped so he turned and let me have it. I hadn't reached him yet. I was so surprised I sat down – then I saw all the blood.'

'You say he was little?'

'That he was. A little squirt of not more than five foot four.'

'So two men went down the stairs, there was one in the car – and one went over the fire escape,' the Inspector summarized. He had a blunt, square face with watchful grey eyes which he suddenly turned on me like gimlets. 'You say this man threw a suitcase into the alley.'

'That's right.'

'We haven't found it, Mr Trevelyan.'

I said, 'The others must have picked it up. That's when they nearly ran us down.'

He said softly, 'How did they know it was there?'

'I don't know. They may have seen it coming over. I guess the car was parked in the alley waiting for the others to come down that way.'

He nodded. 'What was in the suitcase – do you know?'

I glanced across at Geordie who looked back at me ex-pressionlessly. I said, 'Some stuff belonging to my brother.'

'What kind of – er – stuff?'

'Clothing, books – geological samples.'

The Inspector sighed. 'Anything important or valuable?'

I shook my head. 'I doubt it.'

'What about the samples?'

I said, 'I only saw the specimens briefly. They appeared to be manganese nodules of the type which is often to be found on the ocean bed. They're very common, you know.'

'And valuable?' he persisted.

'I don't think that anyone with knowledge of them would regard them as valuable,' I said. 'I suppose they might be if they were generally accessible, but it's too hard to get at them through two or three miles of water.'

The Inspector seemed at a loss. 'How do you think your brother will regard the loss of those specimens, and his other things?'

'He's dead,' I said.

The Inspector sharpened his attention. 'Oh? When did he die?'

'About four months ago – in the Pacific.'

He looked at me closely and I went on, 'My brother, Mark, was an oceanographer like myself. He died of appendicitis a few months ago and I've just received his effects today. As for the specimens I would say they were souvenirs of the IGY survey in which he was engaged. As a scientist he would naturally be interested in them.'

'Um,' said the Inspector. 'Is there anything else missing, Mr Trevelyan?'

'Not that I know of.'

Geordie clattered his cup. 'I think we were too quick for them,' he said. 'They thought they were on to a good thing, but we didn't give them enough time. So one of them grabbed the first thing he saw and tried to make a getaway.'

I carefully didn't mention that the case had been hidden under my bed.

The Inspector looked at Geordie with something approaching contempt. 'This isn't an ordinary burglary,' he said. 'Your explanation doesn't account for the fact that they went to a lot of trouble to retrieve the suitcase, or why they used so many weapons.' He turned to me. 'Have you any enemies in Spain?'

I shrugged. 'I shouldn't think so.'

He pursed his lips. 'All right, Mr Trevelyan, let's go back to the beginning again. Let's start when you say you first saw the light on in your flat . . .'

It was after three a.m. before we got rid of the police, and they were back again next morning, to recheck the premises and to hear the whole tale yet again. The Inspector wasn't satisfied but neither he nor any of his colleagues could pin down what was wrong. Come to that – neither could I! It was a great way to start my leave. His last word to me that morning was, 'There's been a fatality here, Mr Trevelyan, and that's a very serious matter. I shall expect both of you to hold yourselves in readiness for the inquest. You are not under arrest,' he added in such a way as to make me feel that I was. He strode out of the flat with his myrmidons trailing behind.

'In other words – don't leave town,' I said. 'There goes a very unhappy policeman.'

Geordie said, 'He'll be burning up the wires looking for an expert on manganese nodules. He thinks there's something fishy there.'

'By God, so do I! But he won't find much. He'll phone the Institute of course, and speak to Jarvis or some other big noise and get exactly the same story I told him.'

I got up, went into the kitchen and got a couple of bottles of beer from the refrigerator and took them back into the living room. Geordie eyed them and said, 'You have some good ideas, sometimes. Tell me, these nodules – are they really valueless?'

'I told the coppers the plain truth,' I said. 'But Mark seemed to have some curious ideas about nodule formation – still, the notebooks are gone and I can't check up on his theories without them.'

Then suddenly I remembered something. 'Wait a minute,' I said and went into the bedroom. Sure enough, there it was – the little leather-bound diary, still lying on my dressing-table. The police would have had no reason to think it wasn't mine, and hadn't touched it.

I went back and tossed it to Geordie. 'They didn't get that. I meant to tell you – I found it in a pocket of one of Mark's suits. What do you make of it?'

He opened the book with interest but I watched the enthusiasm seep out of him as he scanned the pages. 'What the hell!'

'That's Mark's patent Pitman variation,' I said. 'I doubt if old Isaac himself could make anything of it.'

'What are all the drawings?'

'Mark was an inveterate doodler,' I said. 'You'd have to apply psychological theory to make anything of those.'

I sat mulling over the events of the previous day, trying to piece them together.

'Geordie, listen to this,' I said. 'Mark dies, and Norgaard, his colleague, disappears. Jarvis keeps his ear close to the ground and knows all the gossip of the profession, and if he says he hasn't heard anything of Norgaard then it's unlikely that anyone else has either.' I held up a finger. 'That's one thing.'

'Do you know anything about Norgaard?'

'Only that he's one of us oceanographers. He's a Swede, but he was on an American survey ship during the IGY. I lost sight of him after that; a lot of comradeship went for a bust when the operation closed down.'

'What's his speciality?'

'Ocean currents. He's one of those geniuses who can dredge up a bit of water and tell you which way it was flowing a million years ago last Wednesday. I don't think there's a name for his line yet, so I'll call it paleoaquaology – there's a mouthful for you.'

Geordie raised his eyebrows. 'Can they really do that kind of thing?'

I grinned. 'They'd like you to believe so, and I've no reason to doubt it. But to my mind there's a hell of a lot of theory balancing uneasily on too few facts. My line is different – I analyse what I'm given and if anyone wants to build any whacky theories on what I tell 'em, that's their affair.'

'And Mark was like yourself – an analytical chemist. Why would he team up with Norgaard? They don't seem to have anything in common.'

I said slowly, 'I don't know; I really don't know.' I was thinking of the highly unlikely theory indicated in Mark's missing notebooks.

'All right,' Geordie said. 'Norgaard's disappeared – you think. What else have you got?'

'The next thing is Kane. The whole thing is too damn pat. Kane turns up and we have a burglary. He knew the stuff was coming – I told him.'

Geordie chuckled. 'And how do you tie in the four Spanish burglars with Kane? Speaking as a non-theoreticist, that is?'

'I'm damned if I know. There's something odd about that too. I couldn't place the accent; it was one I've never heard before.'

'You don't know them all,' said Geordie. 'You'd have to be born Spanish to be that good.'

'True.' There was a long silence while I marshalled my thoughts. 'I wish I could get hold of Kane.'

'You think there's something odd about him, don't you?'

'I do. But I don't know what it is. I've been trying to bring it to the surface ever since I saw him.'

'Mike, I think this is all a lot of nonsense,' Geordie said decisively. 'I think your imagination is working overtime. You've had a shock about Mark's death and another over the burglary – so have I, come to that. But I don't think Norgaard has mysteriously disappeared; I think he's probably sitting somewhere writing a thesis on prehistoric water. As for Kane, you've got nothing but a blind hunch. But I'll tell you what I'll do. If Kane is a seaman he'll probably be down somewhere in dockland, and if you want him that bad I'll put my boys on to nosing around a bit. It's a pretty hopeless chance but it's all I can do.'

'Thanks, Geordie,' I said. 'Meantime, I'd better ring Helen and tell her I've been burgled. She's not going to like hearing that Mark's stuff is gone but there's no hope for it. I can only play it down, tell her it was all worthless anyway.'

'Are you going to pass on the notebook to her?'

I shook my head thoughtfully. 'What notebook? As far as she's concerned, it was all stolen. She could never make anything of that stuff of Mark's – but maybe I can.'

V

I had nightmares that night.

I dreamed of a lovely Pacific island with white beaches and waving palm fronds where I wandered quite happily until I became aware that the sky was darkening and a cold, icy wind had arisen. I started to run but my feet slipped in the soft sand and I made no progress. And I knew what I was running from.

He caught me at last with my back to a palm trunk, and came nearer and nearer, brandishing a rusty kitchen knife. I knew it was the Dutch doctor, although he was screaming in Spanish, *'Emplead cuchillo – cuchillo – cuchillo!'*

He was drunk and sweaty-faced and as he came nearer I felt powerless to move and I knew he was going to stick me with the knife. At last his face was close to mine and I could see the individual beads of sweat on his shiny forehead and his lean dark face. It was the face of Kane. He drew back his arm and struck with the knife right into my guts.

I woke with a yell.

I was breathing deeply, taking in great gulps of air, and I could feel a slick film of sweat all over my body. The knife-scratch in my arm was aching. And I knew at last what was wrong with Kane's story.

The bedroom door opened and Geordie said in a low voice, 'What the devil's going on?'

I said, 'Come in, Geordie; I'm all right – just a nightmare.'

I switched on the bedside light and Geordie said, 'You gave me a hell of a fright, Mike.'

'I gave myself a hell of a fright,' I said and lit a cigarette. 'But I discovered something – or remembered something.'

'What?'

I tapped Geordie emphatically on the chest with my forefinger. 'Mark had his appendix out years ago.'

Geordie looked startled. 'But the death certificate . . .'

'I don't know anything about the death certificate. I haven't seen it yet, so I don't know if it's a fake. But I know that Mr Bloody Kane is a fake.'

'Are you sure about this?'

'I still know the doctor who operated on Mark. I'll give him a ring and check on it – but I'm sure.'

'Perhaps this Dutch doctor made a mistake,' offered Geordie.

'He'd be a damned good doctor who could take out an appendix that wasn't there,' I said acidly. 'Doctors can't make mistakes like that.'

'Not unless he was covering up. Lots of doctors bury their mistakes.'

'You mean he was incompetent?' I thought about that, then shook my head decisively. 'No, Geordie, that won't wash. He'd see the old operation scar the moment he made his examination, and he'd know the appendix had already been removed. He wouldn't stick his neck out by signing a certificate that could be so easily disproved – no one is as incompetent as that.'

'Aye. If he wanted to cover up he'd put down the cause of death as fever or something like that – something you couldn't prove one way or another. But we don't know what he put on the certificate.'

'We'll soon find out. They sent it to Helen. And I want to find Kane more than ever – I want to nail that lying bastard.'

'We'll do our best,' said Geordie. He didn't sound too hopeful.

TWO

I had no more dreams that night, but slept heavily and late. It was Geordie who woke me by shaking my shoulder – and incidentally hurting my arm once again. I groaned and turned away, but he persisted until I opened my eyes. 'You're wanted on the phone,' he said. 'It's the Institute.'

I put on my dressing gown and was still thick-headed with sleep when I lifted the receiver. It was young Simms. 'Dr Trevelyan, I've taken over your old office while you're away and you've left something behind. I don't know if it's valuable or if you want it at all . . .'

I mumbled, 'What is it?'

'A manganese nodule.'

I was jolted wide awake. 'Where did you find it?'

'I didn't. One of the cleaners found it under your desk and gave it to me. What should I do with it?'

'Stick tight to it. I'll pick it up this morning. It's got some – relation to work I'm engaged on. Thanks for calling.'

I turned to Geordie. 'All is not lost,' I said, 'we've got a nodule. You dropped some on the floor of my office, remember, and you left one under the desk.'

'I don't see what all the fuss is about. All along you've been insisting that the damn things are worthless. What's so exciting about this one?'

I said, 'There are too many mysteries connected with this particular lot to suit me. I'm going to take a closer look at this one.'

As I breakfasted on a cigarette and a cup of strong coffee I rang Helen and asked her to read out Mark's death certificate. It was in French, of course, and she had some difficulties over the hand-written parts but we got it sorted out. I put down the phone and said to Geordie, 'Now I want to talk to that doctor as well as Kane.' I felt full of anger and frustration.

'What was the cause of death?'

'Peritonitis following an appendectomy. And that's impossible. The doctor's name is Hans Schouten. It was signed in Tanakabu, in the Tuamotus.'

'He's a hell of a long way from here.'

'But Kane isn't. Do your damndest to find him, Geordie.'

Geordie sighed. 'I'll do my best, but this is a bloody big city, and no one but you and Helen can identify him for sure.'

I dressed and drove down to the Institute, retrieved the nodule from Simms and then went down to the laboratories – I was going to analyse this lump of rock down to the last trace elements. First I photographed it in colour from several angles and took a casting of it in latex – that took care of the external record. Then I cut it in half with a diamond saw. Not entirely unexpectedly, in the centre was the white bone of a shark's tooth, also neatly cut in two.

One of the pieces I put in the rock mill and, while it was being ground to the consistency of fine flour, I polished and etched the flat surface of the other piece. Then the real work began. By early afternoon everything was well under way and luckily I had had the place almost to myself the whole time, but then Jarvis walked in. He was surprised to see me.

'You're supposed to be on leave, Mike. What's all this?'

He looked at the set-up on the bench. I had no worries about that – I could have been analysing anything, and the identifiable half-rock was out of sight. I said lightly, 'Oh, just some homework I promised I'd do when I had the chance.'

He looked at me out of the corner of his eye. 'What have you been up to, young feller? Saw something about you in yesterday's press, didn't I? And I had a chap in from Scotland Yard asking questions about you – and about manganese nodules. And he said you'd *killed* someone?'

'I had a burglary two nights ago and knocked a chap off the fire escape,' I said. I hadn't seen the papers myself and it hadn't occurred to me that the story would be public. From Simms' lack of reaction, however, it seemed not to be exactly front-page news.

'Um', said Jarvis. 'Very unfortunate. Place is getting like Chicago. Nasty for you. But what's it got to do with nodules?'

'A couple were nicked from my place, with other stuff. I told him they weren't of much value.'

'I made that plain to the Inspector,' growled Jarvis. 'And I take it he's now convinced that your burglars were surprised and took the first things that came to hand. I gave you a reasonable character, by the way.'

I had my doubts about the Yard's acceptance of the front story. The Inspector had struck me as being full of deep suspicions.

'Well, my boy, I'll leave you to it. Anything interesting?' He cast an inquisitive glance at the bench.

I smiled. 'I don't know yet.'

He nodded. 'That's the way it is,' he said rather vaguely and wandered out. I looked at the bench and wondered if I was wasting my time. My own knowledge, backed by that of an expert like Jarvis, told me that this was just an ordinary Pacific nodule and nothing out of the ordinary. Still, I had gone so far, I might as well carry on. I left the glassware to bubble on its own for a while and went to take photomicrographs of the etched surface of the half-nodule.

I was busy for another couple of hours and having to use my bad arm didn't help. Normally I would have used the services of a laboratory technician but this was one job I wanted to do myself. And it was fortunate that I had taken that precaution because what I finally found astounded me. I looked incredulously at the table of figures that was emerging, breathing heavily with excitement and with my mind full of conflicting conjectures.

Then I became even busier, carefully dismantling the glassware and meticulously washing every piece. I wanted no evidence left of what I'd been up to. That done, I phoned the flat.

Geordie answered. 'Where the devil have you been?' he demanded. 'We've had the cops, the press, the insurance people – the lot.'

'Those are the last people I want to be bothered with right now. Is everything clear now?'

'Aye.'

'Good. I don't suppose you found Kane.'

'You suppose rightly. If you're so suspicious of him why don't you take what you've got to the police? They can do a better job of finding him than I can.'

'I don't want to do that right now. I'm coming home, Geordie. I've got something to tell you.'

'Have you eaten, boy?'

I suddenly realized that I hadn't eaten a mouthful all day. I felt very hungry. 'I've been too busy,' I said hopefully.

'I thought so. I'll tell you what; I'll cook up something in this kitchen of yours – one of my slumgullions. Then we won't have to go out and maybe get tagged by one of the newspaper blokes.'

'Thanks. That'll be fine.'

On the way home I bought some newspapers and found that the story had already sunk with no trace. A local shop produced me a copy of the previous day's press and the story was a short one, buried in the body of the paper, lacking in detail and with no mention of what had been stolen, which suited me very well. I didn't want to be questioned on anything concerning manganese nodules. I'm not naturally a good liar.

When I entered the flat I found Geordie busy in the kitchen surrounded by a mouth-watering aroma, and a remarkably well cleaned up living room. I made a mental note never to have glass-fronted bookshelves again – I didn't much like them anyway. Geordie called out, 'It'll be ready in about an hour, so you can get your news off your chest before we eat. I'll be out in two ticks.'

I went to the cabinet for the whisky bottle and two glasses, then picked my old school atlas off the bookshelf. Inkblotted and politically out-of-date as it was, it would still suit my purpose. I put it on the table and turned to the pages which showed the Pacific.

Geordie came out of the kitchen and I said, 'Sit here. I want to tell you something important.'

He saw the glint of excitement in my eye, smiled and sat down obediently. I poured out two whiskies and said, 'I'm going to give you a little lecture on basic oceanography. I hope you won't be bored.'

'Go ahead, Mike.'

'At the bottom of the oceans – particularly the Pacific – there is a fortune in metallic ores in the form of small lumps lying on the seabed.' I took the half-nodule from my pocket and put it on the table. 'Like this lump here. There's no secret about this. Every oceanographer knows about them.'

Geordie picked it up and examined it. 'What's this white bit in the middle?'

'A shark's tooth.'

'How the hell did that get in the middle of a piece of rock?'

'That comes later,' I said impatiently, 'in the second lesson. Now, these lumps are composed mainly of manganese dioxide, iron oxide and traces of nickel, cobalt and copper, but to save time they're usually referred to as manganese nodules. I won't tell you how they got onto the seabed – that comes later too – but the sheer quantity is incredible.'

I turned to the atlas and moved my forefinger from south to north off the shoreline of the Americas, starting at Chile and moving towards Alaska. 'Proved deposits here, at the average of one pound a square foot, cover an area of two million square miles and involve twenty-six *billion* tons of nodules.'

I swept my finger out to Hawaii. 'This is the mid-Pacific Rise. Four million square miles – fifty-seven billion tons of nodules.'

'Hell's teeth,' said Geordie. 'You were right about incredible figures.'

I ignored this and moved my finger south again, to Tahiti. 'Fourteen million square miles in central and south-eastern Pacific. Two hundred billion tons of nodules. Like grains of dust in the desert.'

'Why haven't I heard about this before? It sounds like front page news.'

'There's no reason why you shouldn't have, but you won't find it in the newspapers. It's not very interesting. You'd have to read the right technical journals. There's been no secret made of it; they were first discovered as far back as 1870 during the *Challenger* expedition.'

'There must be a snag. Otherwise somebody would have done something about it before this.'

I smiled. 'Oh yes, there are snags – as always. One of them is the depth of the water – the average depth at which these things lie is over fourteen thousand feet. That's a good deal of water to go through to scoop up nodules, and the pressure on the bottom is terrific. But it could be done. An American engineer called John Mero did a post-graduate thesis on it. He proposed dropping a thing like a giant vacuum-cleaner and sucking the nodules to the surface. The capitalization on a scheme like that would run into millions and the profit would be marginal at one pound a square foot of ocean bed. It's what we'd call a pretty lean ore if we found it on land.'

Geordie said, 'But you have a card up your sleeve.'

'Let me put it this way. The information I've given you is based on the IGY surveys, and the one pound a square foot is a crude approximation.'

I stabbed my finger at the eastern Pacific. 'Zenkevitch, of the Soviet Institute of Oceanology – the Russians are very interested, by the way – found 3.7 pounds a square foot right there. You see, the stuff lies in varying concentrations. Here they found five pounds a square foot, here they found eight, and here, seven.'

Geordie had been listening with keen interest. 'That sounds as though it brings it back in line as an economic proposition.'

I shook my head tiredly. 'No, it doesn't. Manganese isn't in short supply, and neither is iron. If you started picking up large quantities of nodules all that would happen is that you'd saturate the market, the price would slip accordingly, and you'd be back where you started – with a marginal profit. In fact, it would be worse than that. The big metals firms and mining houses – the only people with the massed capital to do anything about it – aren't interested. They already run manganese mines on land, and if they started anything like this they'd end up by wrecking their own land-based investments.'

'It seems that you're running in circles,' said Geordie acidly. 'Where is all this getting us?'

'Have patience. I'm making a point. Now, I said there are traces of other metals in these nodules – copper, nickel and cobalt. You can forget the copper. But here, in the south-east Pacific, the nodules run to about 1.6 per cent nickel and about .3 per cent cobalt. The Mid-Pacific Rise gives as much as 2 per cent cobalt. Keep that in mind, because I'm going to switch to something else.'

'For God's sake, Mike, don't spin it out too long.'

I was and I knew it, and enjoyed teasing him. 'I'm coming to it,' I said. 'All the figures I've given you are based on the IGY surveys.' I leaned forward. 'Guess how many sites they surveyed.'

'I couldn't begin to make a guess.'

I took a sip of whisky. 'They dredged and photographed sixty sites. A lousy sixty sites in sixty-four million square miles of Pacific.'

Geordie stared at me. 'Is that all? I wouldn't hang a dog on evidence like that.'

'The orthodox oceanographer says, "The ocean bed is pretty much of a piece – it doesn't vary greatly from place to place – so what you find at site X, which you've checked, you're pretty certain to find at site Y, which you haven't checked." '

I tapped the atlas. 'I've always been suspicious of that kind of reasoning. Admittedly, the ocean bed is pretty much of a piece, but I don't think we should rely on it sight unseen. And neither did Mark.'

'Did Mark work together with you on this?'

'We never worked together,' I said shortly. 'To continue. In 1955 the Scripps expedition fished up a nodule from about – here.' I pointed to the spot. 'It was two feet long, twenty inches thick and weighed a hundred and twenty-five pounds. In the same year a British cable ship was grappling for a broken cable here, in the Philippines Trench. They got the cable up, all right, from 17,000 feet, and in a loop of cable they found a nodule 4 feet long and 3 feet in diameter. That one weighed 1700 pounds.'

'I begin to see what you're getting at.'

'I'm trying to put it plainly. The orthodox boys have sampled sixty spots in sixty-four million square miles and have the nerve to think they know all about it. I'm banking that there are places where nodules lie fifty pounds to the square foot – and Mark knew of such places, if I read enough of his notes correctly.'

'I think you had a point to make about cobalt, Mike. Come across with it.'

I let my excitement show. 'This is the clincher. The highest assay for cobalt in any nodule has been just over 2 per cent.' I pushed the half-nodule on the table with my finger. 'I assayed this one today. It checked out at *ten* per cent cobalt – and cobalt, Geordie, is worth more than all the rest put together and the rocket metallurgists can't get enough of it!'

II

We ate Geordie's stew and very good it was, and by midnight we had just about talked the subject to death. At one stage I said, returning to a sore point, 'I wish I still had those notebooks. They were only rough working notes and Mark seemed to have gone up a lot of false trails – some of the assumptions seemed completely cockeyed – but I wish they hadn't been pinched.'

Geordie sucked on his pipe, which gurgled. 'I could do with knowing why they were pinched – and who pinched them.'

'Then you agree that it has something to do with Mark's death?'

'It must do, boy. He got hold of something valuable . . .'

'And was murdered for it,' I finished. 'But who killed him? Kane? That's unlikely – it's an odd murderer who travels halfway round the world to inform the family.'

That was a good conversation-stopper. We were quiet for some time, then I said tentatively, 'If only we could get hold of Schouten.'

'He's on the other side of the world.'

I said softly, 'I think Mark came across a hell of a big deposit of high-cobalt nodules. He wasn't a bad scientist but, being Mark, he was probably more interested in the worth of his discovery – to himself. His theories were a bit startling though, and they intrigue me.'

'So?'

'So I'd like to do something about it.'

'You mean – organize an expedition?'

'That's right.' Saying it aloud began to jell all the ideas that had been bubbling up in me since the assay.

Geordie knocked the dottle out of his pipe. 'Tell me, Mike, what's your interest in this – scientific or personal? You weren't particularly friendly towards Mark. Is it that you feel that Trevelyans should be free to go about their business without being murdered, or is it something else?'

'It's that and a lot more. For one thing, someone is pushing me around and I don't like it. I don't like having my home burgled, being knifed, or having my friends shot at. And I don't appreciate having my brother murdered, if that's really what happened, no matter what I thought of him as a person. Then, of course, there's the scientific interest – I'm fascinated. A find like this would hit oceanography like evolution hit biology. And then there's the money.'

'Yes,' said Geordie. 'I suppose there would be money in it.'

'You suppose damn right. And if you're thinking in millions, stop it, because you're thinking small – it could be billions.'

He wasn't ready to be enthusiastic. 'So you think it's as good as that?'

'As good as that,' I said firmly. 'There's enough at stake for quite a few murders.'

'How much would such an expedition cost?'

I had already been thinking about that. 'A ship – plus about fifty thousand for special equipment – plus stores and running expenses.'

'Running expenses for how long?'

I smiled wryly. 'That's one of the jokers – who knows in a thing like this?'

'It's a lot of money. And there's over sixty million square miles of Pacific, you said.'

'I know my job,' I said. 'I wouldn't be going entirely blindfold. I know a hell of a lot of places where there aren't any high-cobalt nodules. And there's what I can recall of Mark's theories – perhaps they're not so fantastic after all. Plus there's this – I'm sure we can make something of it.' I held up Mark's little diary, which I was keeping on my person.

Geordie slapped his hands together suddenly. 'All right, boy. If you can find the capital and the running expenses – and God knows where you'll find money like that – I can provide the ship. Would old *Esmerelda* do?'

'My God, she'd be perfect for running on a small budget.' I looked at him closely, trying not to show my excitement too much. 'But why should you come into this? It's a chancy business, you know.'

He laughed. 'Well, you did mention a few billions of money. Besides, some little bastard shot off the top of my little finger. I'm not particularly interested in him, but I would like to get my hands round the neck of the man who paid him. And chartering tourists isn't very much fun after a bit. I suppose you have some ideas about finance? I mean, without a tame banker it's a non-starter.'

I had been thinking about it, for the last hour or two in between our bouts of conversation. The pieces seemed to be dropping into place nicely, so far.

I said musingly, 'I saw Clare Campbell the other day – she's in town with her father, attending some conference or other. He's my goal.'

'Who is Campbell?'

'Jonathan Campbell – never known as J.C. A Scottish-Canadian mining man. Mark worked for him for a while after the IGY – something to do with a mining venture in South America . . .' I trailed off and Geordie cocked his head enquiringly. Something about that statement teased at me but I couldn't identify it and let it go with a shake of my head.

'So he's got money.'

'He's loaded with it,' I said, back on the track. 'He's got the reputation of being a bit of a plunger, and this thing might appeal to him. He lost a packet in the South American business not long ago – something to do with mines being nationalized – but I think he's got enough left to take a gamble on something new.'

'How do you know all this about Campbell, Mike? I didn't know you studied the financial pages.'

'I was thinking of getting out of pure research after the IGY. The pay's small compared with industry, so I thought I'd look about for a job compatible with my expensive tastes.' I waved a hand around my modest flat. 'Lots of other chaps did it – Mark was one – so I did a bit of investigating and Campbell cropped up.'

'But you didn't take the job.'

I shook my head. 'He'd already signed Mark on, you see, and I didn't fancy having Mark as a colleague. Anyway, I was asked to go to the Institute about that time – less pay, but a more interesting job. Mark left the IGY programme early and got out of pure research. I never actually met

Campbell but I did once meet his daughter – in Vancouver. Mark had her in tow. They seemed to be pretty close – they would, she being the boss's daughter.'

Geordie's voice had become as cold as mine. 'Poor stupid cow.'

I thought that she didn't look like his description at all, and wondered how long it had taken for her to read Mark's character. She hadn't struck me then as the sort of girl to be taken in for long. But I hoped that nothing much had happened between them, lest it colour Campbell's attitude towards me when I came to approach him.

'How long did Mark work for Campbell?'

'Not very long – about a year and a half. Then he pushed off into the South Pacific and teamed up with Norgaard, last I heard of it. I don't know exactly what they were doing – they had neither a decent boat nor the right equipment for proper research, as far as I could tell.'

'But if Campbell's a mining man, what makes you think he'll finance a deep sea adventure?'

'I think he might,' I said. 'Metals are his business. Never gold or silver, nor the other end of the scale, the base metals. He's dabbled in tin and copper and had a go at platinum once. Now it seems he's concentrating on alloy metals – titanium, cobalt, vanadium and stuff like that. Now that rocketry is big business there's a boom in these metals.'

Geordie asked curiously, 'How does he go about it – his investing, I mean?'

'He takes advantage of us scientific types. He employs a few good men – people like Mark, for instance – and the number varies from time to time. Most of them are geologists, of course. He organizes field expeditions into remote parts, spots a body of ore, puts a million or so into proving and development, then pulls out and sells to the real big boys at a profit. I heard that in one of his recent ventures he put in two million dollars and a year of his time, then sold out at a net profit of a million and a quarter. Not bad for a year's work, eh, Geordie?'

'Not bad at all. But I'd say it needs experience and a hell of a lot of cold nerve.'

'Oh, he's a canny Scot, all right. I hope he's still in town – I'll find out tomorrow.'

'What about Kane – why not put the coppers on to him?'

I shook my head vigorously. 'Not now. All they'd do would be to pass on a query to Tahiti and I've no positive faith in the activities of the French Colonial Police, especially when there's a convenient legal death certificate handy. The delays would be awful, for one thing. No, I'll see for myself – if I can get Campbell interested. I would dearly like to talk to Dr Schouten.'

Geordie rubbed his chin meditatively. 'I'm thinking of making one or two changes in the crew if we go on this caper. I'd like a couple of blokes I know from the old days. I wonder what Ian Lewis is doing now? When I met him a few months ago he said he found life a little tedious.'

I vaguely remembered a tall, gangling Highlander. 'What was he doing?'

'Oh, he had a place in the Scottish wilderness that he said he'd be glad to leave. You know, I reckon I could get you half a dozen good chaps, all trained fighters and some of them seamen. I've got a couple anyway that I'd keep on for this trip.'

I had a dawning suspicion of what was in Geordie's mind. 'Hold on – what's the idea?'

He said, 'I'd like to see the bunch of thugs who'd stand up against some of your dad's old mob. They may be getting older, but they're not that old and they're all trained commandoes. They're not all settled down and married, you know.'

'What do you think you're doing – setting up a private army?'

'Might not be a bad idea,' he said. 'If the other night is a sample of what to expect we might need a bloody army.'

I sighed. 'All right, Sergeant Wilkins. But no one who's married or has other responsibilities, and you'd better hold your hand until we get Campbell tied up. We can't do anything without money.'

'Ah yes, the money,' said Geordie, and looked very sad.

III

The following morning, quite early, I had a visit from the Inspector and one of his men. Geordie was already out and I was impatient to begin my search for Kane, but tried not to show it. The Inspector was cagey and suspicious, but very casual. I think his trouble was that he didn't really know what to be suspicious of.

He asked, 'Know anyone in South America?'

'Not off hand. No, I don't,' I said.

'Um. The man you killed may have been a South American. His clothes were labelled from Lima, Rio and Montevideo. He could be from almost anywhere except Brazil.'

'I think that answers one question. I couldn't place the accent. What was his name?'

The Inspector shook his head. 'That we don't know, Mr Trevelyan. Or anything else about him, yet. Are you quite sure you don't know any South Americans?'

'Positive.'

He changed tack. 'Wonderful thing, this science; I've found out everything there is to know about manganese nodules.'

I said dryly, 'Then you know more than I do – they're not really my line. Did you find it interesting?'

He smiled sourly. 'Not very – they're about as valuable as road gravel. Are you sure there wasn't anything else in that suitcase that might have been of value?'

'Inspector, it was just junk. The kind of stuff that anyone might carry in a case, apart from the nodules, that is.'

'Looks as though Mr Wilkins might have been right, after all. You surprised the burglars before they could pinch anything else.'

I didn't fall for that one – the Inspector didn't for one moment believe it was an ordinary break-in. I said noncommittally, 'I think you're right.'

'The inquest will be next Wednesday,' he said. 'You'll get an official notification, both of you.'

'I'll be there.'

Then they were gone and I thought about South America. That was nearer the Pacific than Spain, but apart from that it made no particular sense to me. And then, belatedly, I thought of Mark's connection with Jonathan Campbell, and Campbell's reputed connection with some South American mining venture, and I had something else to chew on. But it still made no sense, and for the time being I gave up.

Finding a rich Canadian in London's millions was a damn sight easier than finding a poor Australian. The rich are circumscribed in their travelling. The Institute gave me the address of the conference centre, and they gave me the address of the hotel Campbell was staying at, and I had him at the third phone call. Campbell was blunt and curt to the point of rudeness. Yes, he could give me half an hour of his time at eleven that morning – it was already nine-thirty. His tone indicated that if he thought I was wasting his time I'd be kicked out in the first two minutes. The telephone conversation lasted only that long.

At eleven I was at the Dorchester and was shown up to Campbell's suite. He opened the door himself. 'Trevelyan?'

'Yes, sir.'

'Come in.'

He led the way into a room once a luxury living-room but now fitted out as a temporary office, complete with desk, files and secretary; he sent her out and seated himself behind the desk, gesturing me to sit opposite. He was a broad, stocky man of about sixty with a square, tanned face lined with experience. Somebody once said that after forty a man is responsible for his own face; if that's so then Campbell had had a lot of responsibility in his time. His eyes were a frosty blue and his hair iron grey and grizzled. His clothes were expensive and only the slightest accent indicated his transatlantic origin.

I decided that attack was the best policy. I produced the half-nodule and put it on his blotting pad. 'That assays at ten per cent cobalt,' I said without preamble.

He picked it up and looked at it carefully, masking any curiosity. 'Where did it come from?'

'The bottom of the Pacific.'

He looked up and stared at me, then said, 'Are you any relation of the Mark Trevelyan who worked for me a while back?'

'He was my brother.'

'Was?'

'He's dead.'

Campbell frowned. 'When and where did he die?'

'About four months ago – in the Pacific.'

'Sorry to hear it,' he said but perfunctorily. 'A good scientist.'

I detected the careful note in his voice, and thought that here was someone else who had seen through Mark, or had had some example of how my brother went about his affairs. I wondered if it was a business problem, or if it had had anything to do with his daughter's relationship with Mark. I couldn't assess whether it was going to make things harder or easier for me.

He carried on looking at me rather than at the specimen. 'Trevelyan – I've heard the name more recently. Oh yes!' He turned and produced a tabloid newspaper from a shelf and shook it out. 'Are you the Trevelyan mentioned here? The one who killed a man defending his home? An Englishman's castle and all that stuff?'

I caught a glimpse of the headline: SCIENTIST KILLS BURGLAR. Quite mild, considering the paper. I nodded. 'That's right.'

He pursed his lips and put aside the paper, and then came back to business. 'This is a manganese nodule. There are billions of them lying on the bottom of the Pacific. There are quite a few in the Atlantic too.'

'Not many there,' I said. 'And the quality's poor. Too much sedimentation.'

'True.' He tossed the stone and caught it. 'The highest cobalt assay so far is a fraction over 2 per cent. That one came from the central Pacific. Where did this one come from?'

I looked at him blankly and shook my head. He smiled suddenly and it transformed his face – he had a very charming smile. 'All right, I tried,' he said. 'You'd be surprised how often it works. Do you know why I am able to reel off facts about manganese nodules?'

'I was wondering.'

'Your brother told me,' he said. 'He wanted me to fit an expedition a couple of years back. I must say I was tempted.'

'Why didn't you?'

He hesitated, then said, 'I lost a packet in South America. It caught me off balance and until I reorganized I didn't have any fluid capital. About that time your brother left my company, and he hadn't left me enough to go on by myself.'

'I hope you're better placed now,' I said dryly. 'Because that's why I've come to you – now it's my turn to ask you to fund an expedition.'

'So I gathered,' he said, equally dryly. He touched the nodule. 'I must say you brought more than your brother did. He talked a good story but he never showed any concrete evidence. You say this assayed at ten per cent cobalt?'

'I assayed it myself yesterday afternoon – the other half, that is.'

'Mind if I have this assayed – independently?'

'Not at all,' I said equably.

He laughed, showing his charm again. 'All right, Trevelyan, I won't need to. I'm convinced of this anyway.'

'I'd prefer it if you did,' I said. 'I could do with corroboration. But I must tell you that what you've got in your hand is *all* the evidence I have to show.'

His hand clenched around the nodule. 'Now you do begin to interest me. I think you have a story, Mr Trevelyan. Why don't you tell it and quit beating around the bush?'

I had already decided that if we were to work together at all I must hold nothing back. It was only moderately risky. So I told him everything, and when I'd finished we were well past my original half hour. He listened in absolute silence until I was done and then said, 'Now let's see if I've got all this straight. One, your brother died out in the Pacific; two, a man called Nelson whom you have never heard of sent you a case which contained notebooks and nodule samples; three, Kane shows up and pitches what you think is a cock-and-bull yarn; four, the suitcase is stolen by presumed South Americans with additional violence including one killing; five, you retain *one* nodule, analyse it and find a fantastic percentage of cobalt; and six, you also retain a diary of your brother's which you can't even read.'

He looked at me for a long time and then said gently, 'And on the basis of this you want me to invest maybe a million dollars.'

I got out of my chair.

'Sorry to have wasted your time, Mr Campbell.'

'Sit down, you damned fool. Don't give up without a fight. I haven't said I won't invest, have I?' He saw the look on my face and added, 'And I haven't yet said I will, either. Have you got that diary here?'

Wordlessly I took it from my breast pocket and handed it over the desk. He flicked it open and turned rapidly from page to page. 'Who taught your brother to write short-hand?' he asked disgustedly. 'St Vitus?'

'Basically it's Pitman's,' I said. 'But Mark adapted it.' I could have gone on to say that Mark had always been secretive, never liking anyone to know what he was doing. But I kept my mouth shut.

Campbell tossed the diary aside. 'Maybe we can get something out of it somehow – maybe a cipher expert can sort it out.' He turned in his swivel chair and looked out of the window towards Hyde Park, and there was a long silence until he spoke again.

'You know what really interested me in this improbable story of yours?'

'No, I don't.'

'Those South Americans,' he said unexpectedly. 'South America has been unlucky for me, you know. I lost nearly ten million down there. That's when Mark's expedition went down the drain, along with a lot of other things. And now Mark has come back – in a sense – and more South Americans are involved. What do you make of that?'

'Not a thing,' I said.

'I don't believe in coincidence. Not when it happens like this. What I do have to consider lies outside your domain, perhaps – the complications of international law regarding mining, especially offshore, undersea stuff. International relations – so I have to know more about the areas you want to research. Financing. Distribution. Markets.'

I was a little taken aback. Perhaps I was too much of the research scientist – the hard facts of commercial dealing had hardly occurred to me. But on reflection I could hear no note of doubt or dismay in Campbell's voice, only the sound of a man mulling over the forthcoming ramifications of the deal he was being offered – and liking it. There was undoubtedly the faint note of challenge in his attitude, and this encouraged me. I guessed that he, like Geordie's old pal Ian Lewis, may be finding life a little boring at present and was attracted by the novelty of my proposition.

He poked the nodule with his finger. 'There are two things necessary for industrial civilization – cheap power and cheap steel. What's the iron oxide content of this?'

'Thirty-two per cent by weight.'

'That does it. The cobalt will make it economically feasible and the result is a cheap high-grade iron ore, a hell of a lot of manganese, plus some copper, vanadium and anything else we can pick up. Cheap metals, billions of dollars' worth and cheaper than anyone else can produce. It can be tied into one neat, strong package – but it needs careful handling. And above all it needs secrecy.'

'I know. I've already been stalling off a police inspector who thinks there's more to the burglary than meets the eye.'

Campbell appeared satisfied. 'Good. You've got the point.'

'Then you're willing to finance an expedition?' I asked. It was almost too easy, I thought, and I was right.

'I don't know yet. I want to make some investigations of my own, enquiries which I can make and you can't. And maybe I can find Kane for you. Besides, you may not be in a position to undertake anything for some time – you killed a man, remember.' His smile this time was more grim than charming. 'Not that I blame you for it – I've killed men myself – but let's wait for your inquest before deciding anything.'

IV

It was six days to the inquest, the longest six days I've spent in my life. To fill in the time I got down to writing the paper that I was supposed to turn out. It wasn't a very good paper as it happened; I had too much else on my mind to concentrate really well.

By the end of the week Geordie still hadn't found Kane, though he'd got a lot of other things moving. 'It's hopeless,' he said to me. 'A needle in a haystack would be easier – this is like trying to find one particular wisp of hay.'

'He may not be in London at all.'

A truism which didn't help. But on the morning of the inquest Kane was found – or rather, he found me.

He called at the flat just as I was leaving for the court – Geordie as usual was out ahead of me and would meet me there. Kane was looking a little the worse for wear with bloodshot eyes and a greying stubble on his cheeks. He coughed raspingly and said, 'Sorry to trouble you, Mr Trevelyan, but you did say I was to keep in touch.'

I looked at him in astonishment and choked back the questions that were on the tip of my tongue. I invited him inside and did a bit of fast thinking as I poured him a cup of coffee. Geordie and Campbell had as much at stake in this as I had, and besides I wanted witnesses when I questioned Kane. I decided to play it softly, though I could hardly bear to speak to him without losing my control.

I made myself smile pleasantly at him. 'Had enough of England, Mr Kane?'

'It 'ud be a nice country if it wasn't for your bleeding weather. We could do with some of this rain back in Queensland, my word.'

'But you've enjoyed your stay?'

'I've had a bonzer time,' he said. 'But my stay's over, Mr Trevelyan. I got to gambling again. I'll never learn.'

'I'm sorry to hear that,' I said.

He looked at me hopefully. 'Mr Trevelyan, you said you might be able to arrange a passage for me. I wondered . . .'

'Do you have to get back to the Pacific immediately?'

For some reason that didn't please him. 'Not specially, no. But I've got no boodle. If I had some cash or a job I'd like to stay around a bit. I thought maybe you could . . .'

I said, 'I have a friend who has a yacht which he's fitting out. He and I hope to get in some sailing together, and I think he needs crew. How would that suit you?'

He took the bait eagerly. 'That 'ud be just fine, Mr Trevelyan!'

I put an opened writing pad in front of him, trying to hold back my own eagerness. 'Write down the name of wherever you're staying so that I can get the owner to contact you,' I said. 'He'll want to interview you but I'll make it all right with him. And I'll let you have something ahead of your pay, to cover your rooming costs. How's that?'

He wrote an address down. 'I'll do that. Thanks a whole lot, Mr Trevelyan.'

'That's all right,' I said generously. 'You've earned it.'

I gave him a head start and then left for the court hearing. The encounter had been good for me, giving me something else to think about and making a vital connection in my story for Campbell. I had no time to tell Geordie about it, however, but savoured telling him afterwards.

The inquest was simple and straightforward. A doctor gave evidence of death, then I went on the stand, followed immediately by Geordie. We stuck to straight facts and didn't elaborate but I noticed that Geordie kept his bandaged finger prominently in view of the coroner. My neighbour spoke and then the police had their turn.

As Geordie was giving evidence I glanced round the courtroom and saw Campbell sitting at the back. He nodded to me, then turned his attention to the proceedings.

The Inspector made an appearance and confirmed that he had found a gun, a Beretta automatic pistol, hanging from the right-hand coat pocket of the deceased. The fore-sight was caught in the torn lining. I felt a lot better after this because it had been one of the points I had made myself. I looked the coroner straight in the eye and he didn't avoid my glance – a good sign. The lack of identity of the dead man was briefly discussed.

There was a surprise witness, at least to me – old Jarvis appeared to give expert testimony. He told the coroner what manganese nodules were and even produced one to show what the things looked like. The coroner prodded him a bit about their value and Jarvis responded in his downright, damn-your-eyes way. But that was just for the record.

Then suddenly it was over. The coroner took little time to decide that death was due to justifiable manslaughter. He wound everything up with a pontifical speech to the effect that while an Englishman's home may be his castle, no man had the right to take the law into his own hands and that if a little more care had been taken, in his opinion, a death could have been averted. However what was done was done, and Mr Michael Trevelyan was free to leave the court without a stain on his character.

We all stood up when he swept out and there was a general drift to the doors. An official elbowed his way up to me and gave me a note. It was brief and to the point. *'See you at the Dorchester. Campbell.'*

I passed it to Geordie as he reached me to slap me heavily on the back. 'I hope this means what I think it means,' I said. 'I've got a lot to tell you.'

We drifted out with the crowd and were eventually deposited on the pavement. A lot of people I didn't know congratulated me on killing a man and getting away with it, some reporters had a lot of questions to ask, and at last I caught sight of the man I was looking for. I ran to catch up with him, Geordie behind me. It was Professor Jarvis.

He saw me coming, waved his stick and waited for me to join him.

'Well, that went off all right, my boy,' he said.

'You did your bit – thank you.'

'Damned fools,' he grumbled. '*Everyone* knows that those nodules are basically worthless – not an economic proposition at all.'

'I wondered if you had a moment to talk to me – here, rather than at the Institute,' I asked him. There seemed to be no difficulty and we sat down on the low stone wall outside the courthouse, enjoying the thin watery sunshine.

'I have nothing to tell you, young man,' the Professor said. 'I made a few enquiries about that chap, Norgaard, but there's nothing doing. The feller seems to have disappeared off the face of the earth.'

'When was the last you heard of him?'

'About six, seven months ago – when he was with your brother. They were fossicking about in the islands round Tahiti.'

'When did Norgaard start working with Mark?' I asked.

'Now let me see. It must have been nearly two years ago, after Mark left that Canadian firm he was working for. Yes, that was it – after he had to leave the IGY project he went to Canada and was with that chap Campbell for over two years, then he left to join up with Norgaard. What they were doing I don't know; they didn't publish anything.'

His grasp of events was remarkable, I thought, and then seized on something he had said. 'What do you mean – *had* to leave the IGY?'

Jarvis actually looked embarrassed. 'Oh, I shouldn't have said that,' he mumbled.

'I'd like to know. It can't hurt Mark now.'

'It's bad form. *De mortuis* – and all that, don't you know.'

'Out with it,' I said. 'After all, it's all in the family.'

Jarvis regarded the tip of his highly polished shoe. 'Well, I never did get to the bottom of it – it was hushed up, you know – but apparently Mark fudged some of his results.'

'Faked his figures?'

'That's right. It was found out by sheer chance. Of course he had to leave. But we – the IGY agreed not to make any more of it, so he was able to get the job in Canada, after he resigned.'

'So that's why he left before it was over. I wondered about that. What was he working on at the time?'

Jarvis shrugged. 'I don't recall, but it certainly had to do with the underwater surveys. Manganese nodules, perhaps?' Not too shrewd a guess, all things considered; but I didn't like it. He went on, 'I never did like your brother. I never trusted him and the fact that he cooked his books didn't surprise me a bit.'

I said, 'That's all right – lots of people didn't like Mark. I wasn't too keen on him myself. And it wasn't the first time he rigged his results. He did the same at school.' And at university. Not to mention his personal life.

Jarvis nodded. 'I'm not surprised at that either. Still, my boy, I don't mistrust the whole Trevelyan family. You're worth ten of your brother, Mike.'

'Thanks, Prof.,' I said warmly.

'Forget all this and enjoy your leave now. The South Atlantic is waiting for you when you return.'

He turned and strode away, jauntily waving his stick. I looked after him with affection; I thought he would be genuinely sorry to lose me if the deal with Campbell came off and I went to the South Pacific instead of the South Atlantic. He would once more angrily bewail the economic facts of life which drew researchers into industry and he would write a few acid letters to the journals.

I turned to Geordie. 'What do you make of that?'

'Norgaard vanished just about the same time that Mark kicked the bucket. I wonder if . . .'

'I know what you're thinking, Geordie. Is Norgaard still alive? I do hope to God Campbell comes through – I want to do some field work in the islands.'

'You had something to tell me,' he reminded me. But I had decided to save it up.

'I'll tell you and Campbell together. Come with me to see him.'

V

Campbell was less crusty than at our first meeting. 'Well,' he said, as we entered his suite, 'I see you're not entirely a hardened criminal, Trevelyan.'

'Not a stain on my character. The coroner said so.' I introduced Geordie and the two big men sized one another up with interest. 'Mr Wilkins is willing to contribute a ship – and skipper her, too.'

Campbell said, 'I see someone has faith in your crazy story. I suppose that getting hurt added to your conviction.'

'What about you?' I asked.

He ignored this and asked what we would drink. 'We must celebrate a successful evasion of the penalty of the law,' he said, almost jovially. He ordered and we got down to business. I decided to keep the Kane episode to be revealed at the proper moment and first hear what Campbell had to say.

'I knew my hunch about your South Americans would work out,' he said. 'I've got a pretty good intelligence system – you have to in my line of work – and I find that Suarez-Navarro are fitting out a research ship in Darwin right at this moment. It's new business and new territory for them, so my guess is that they are heading your way.'

I looked at him blankly. That didn't mean a thing to me.

I think he enjoyed my lack of comprehension because he left me dangling for a while before elucidating. 'Suarez-Navarro is a South American mining house, active in several countries,' he said. 'I've tangled with them before – they're a crowd of unscrupulous bastards. Now, why would a mining house be fitting out an oceanographical research ship?'

'Nodules,' said Geordie succinctly.

'How unscrupulous are they?' I asked. 'Would they stoop to burglary?' I didn't mention murder.

Campbell folded his hands together. 'I'll tell you the story and let you judge for yourself. Once I had a pretty good set-up in South America, never mind just where. The mines were producing well and I ploughed a lot back in the interests of good labour relations. I had a couple of schools, a hospital and all the civilized trimmings. Those Indian miners never had it so good, and they responded well.

'Suarez-Navarro cast an eye on the operation and liked the look of it. They went about things in their own smelly way, though. They had a trouble-shooter, a guy called Ernesto Ramirez, whom they used for that type of operation. He pitched up, got at the government, greased a few palms, supported the Army, and then suddenly there was a new government – which promptly expropriated the mines in the interests of the national economy – or that's what they said. Anyway, I never got a cent out of it. They just took the lot and Ramirez vanished back into the hole they dug him out of.

'The next thing that happened was that the government wanted somebody to run the mines, so Suarez-Navarro offered to take on the job out of the kindness of their hearts and a hefty percentage of the profits. I had been paying 38 per cent tax but Suarez-Navarro got away tax free since they claimed it was really government property anyway. They had a sweet set-up.

'They closed the schools and the hospital – those things don't produce, you see. Pretty soon they had a strike on their hands. If you treat a man like a man he kind of resents going back to being treated like a pig – so there was a strike. That brought Ramirez out of his hole fast. He called in the Army, there was quite a bit of shooting, and then there was suddenly no strike – just fifty dead Indians and quite a few widows.'

He smiled grimly. 'Does that answer your question about the scruples of Suarez-Navarro?'

I nodded. It was a nasty story.

Campbell seemed to go off at a tangent. 'I'm attending a conference here in London, a conference on mineral resources.'

'That's how I found you,' I murmured, but he took no notice.

'It's a Commonwealth deal really but various other interested parties have been invited to send observers. Suarez-Navarro have two – you can't keep them out of anything – but another one arrived last week. His name is Ernesto Ramirez.' Campbell's voice was hard. 'Ramirez isn't a conference man, he's not a negotiator. He's Suarez-Navarro's muscle man. Do I make my point?'

We both nodded, intently.

'Well, I'm going to hammer it home really hard. I've found Kane for you.'

'Well, I'll be damned!' I said.

'You were going about it the hard way. I put someone on to watch Ramirez and was told that a man called Kane had a two-hour talk with him yesterday. We had Kane followed to where he's in digs and I have the address.'

I reeled it off.

It was effective. Campbell said, 'What?' disbelievingly, and Geordie gaped at me. I enjoyed my moment.

'Kane came to visit me this morning,' I said, and told them both what had happened. 'I suggest you get him down to the docks and have a serious talk with him,' I said to Geordie.

Campbell frowned and then his great smile broke on his face. 'No, you don't,' he said. 'Don't ask him a damn thing. Don't you see what's happening?'

Geordie and I shrugged helplessly. We weren't quick enough for Campbell in matters like this.

'Ever heard of industrial espionage? Of course you have. Every big outfit runs a spy system. I do it myself – don't much like it, but I've got to keep up with the hard-nosed bastards in the business.' He actually looked as if he enjoyed it very much. 'Now let's reconstruct what's been happening. You got hold of something you shouldn't have – from the point of view of Suarez-Navarro. Ramirez hotfoots it to England – he arrived the day before Kane came to see you, so it's a cinch they came together. Kane comes to you to find out if Mark's stuff has arrived yet, and he knows it has because you tell him so yourself. He spins you a yarn as cover – it doesn't really matter what it is. Then Ramirez tells his boys to snatch the stuff but you surprise them in the middle.' He lifted his eyebrows. 'Does that make sense so far?'

Geordie said, 'It makes sense to me.'

I said nothing. I was a little more doubtful, but if this served to keep up Campbell's interest I was all for it.

He continued, 'But something goes wrong – they leave the diary and one nodule. Ramirez doesn't know this, but he does know you've contacted me and that all sorts of enquiries are out – including questions in court about nodules. Oh yes, I bet he was there – or someone for him. He must have had a shock when you came to see me. You see, he'd keep a tail on you as a matter of routine just to see if you did anything out of the ordinary – and you did. So what does Ramirez do now?'

'I'll buy it,' I said. 'What does he do?'

'He lays Kane alongside you again,' said Campbell. 'You gave him the perfect opportunity – you practically invited Kane to come back. It's Kane's job to find out what, if anything, is in the wind. But what Ramirez doesn't know is that you were suspicious of Kane right from the start, and this gives *us* a perfect opportunity. We string Kane along – employ him, feed him any information we want him to know and keep from him anything we don't want him to know. We also keep him underfoot and don't lose him again. That's why you mustn't ask him any awkward questions – not right now, anyway.'

I thought about it for a long time. 'Does this mean you're coming in with us? Putting up the finance?'

'You're damn right it does,' snapped Campbell. 'If Suarez-Navarro are going to all this trouble they must be on to something big, and I'd like to stab them in the back just for old times' sake. I'll put up half a million dollars – or whatever it takes – and I ask only one thing. That we get there, and do it, before they can.'

Geordie said gently, 'It *was* a good idea of mine, wasn't it?'

'What's that?' asked Campbell.

'Geordie's recruiting a private army,' I explained. 'As he gets older he gets more bloodthirsty.'

A look passed between them for the second time that made me feel like the outsider. Without saying a word they were in full accord on many levels, and for a moment I felt very inexperienced indeed.

Campbell said, 'There's another thing. My doctor is troubled about my health, the goddam quack. He's been pestering me to take a sea voyage, and I'm suddenly minded to accept his advice. I'm coming along for the ride.'

'You're the boss,' I said. I wasn't surprised.

He turned to Geordie. 'Now, what kind of a ship have you, Captain?'

'A brigantine,' said Geordie. 'About two hundred tons.'

Campbell's jaw dropped. 'But that's a little sailing ship! This is supposed to be a serious project.'

'Take it easy,' I said, grinning at Geordie who was already bristling at any slight to *Esmerelda*. 'A lot of research vessels are sailing ships; there happen to be a number of sound reasons.'

'All right. Let's hear them.'

'Some of the reasons are purely technical,' I said. 'For instance, it's easier to make a sailing ship non-magnetic than a powered ship. Magnetism plays hell with all sorts of important readings. But the reasons you'll appreciate are purely economic.'

'If you're talking economics you're talking my language,' he growled.

'A research ship never knows exactly where it's going. We might find ourselves dredging a thousand miles away from the nearest land. Station keeping and dredging take power and fuel, and an engine powered ship would need a hell of a lot of fuel to make the round trip.

'But a sailing ship can make the journey and arrive on station with close on full tanks, given careful management. She can keep on station longer and no one need worry about whether there'll be enough fuel to get back. You *could* use a powered ship to do the job but it would cost you – oh, a million pounds plus. Geordie's boat will be fine.'

'The day's not been wasted,' Campbell said. 'I've learned something new. I reckon you know your job, Trevelyan. What will you need in the way of equipment?'

So we got down to it. The biggest item was the winch, which was to be installed amidships, and storage space for 30,000 feet of cable below it. There was also to be a laboratory for on-the-spot analysis and all the necessary equipment would take a lot of money, and a lot of refitting.

'We'll need a bloody big generator for this lot,' said Geordie. 'It looks as though it'll take a diesel bigger than the main engine. Lucky, isn't it, that charter tourists take up so much space with luxuries.'

Presently Campbell suggested lunch, so we went down to the dining room to do some more planning over grilled steaks. It was arranged that I should concentrate on collecting equipment while Geordie prepared *Esmerelda* and got his crew together. Very little was said concerning the location, or the availability, of the strange treasure we were after, and I knew that I alone could come up with anything of use there. I had some heavy studying ahead of me as well as all the rest.

'If you take on Kane it'll mean we've got him in our sights,' said Campbell, harping back to his favourite subject. 'Not that it makes any difference. Ramirez is sure to have other scouts out. I'll be watching him too.'

I'd been thinking about Kane.

'Your review of the situation was very well in its way, but it was wrong on one point.'

'What's that?' said Campbell.

'You said that Kane spun me a yarn as cover, and that it didn't matter what it was. That's not entirely so, you know – we have independent evidence. The death certificate states the cause of death as appendicitis. Kane and Schouten both told the same lie and I'd like to know why.'

'By God, you're right,' said Campbell. 'We'll get it out of Kane as soon as he's served his purpose.'

Geordie grunted. 'We're going into the Pacific,' he said. 'Maybe we'll get it out of Schouten. At all events, we'll be at the root of it.'

THREE

It was nearly three months before we got away. You can't begin a scientific expedition as though you were going on a picnic. There were a million things to do and we were kept busy on a sixteen hour day, seven days a week. The first thing I did was to hand in my resignation from the Institute. Old Jarvis didn't take it too well, but there wasn't anything he could do about it so he accepted the situation with reluctance. I wished I could have told him what I was doing but that was impossible.

Geordie assiduously recruited his crew and soon they began to turn up. He had kept on four of his own lads and had of course taken on Kane in place of one of the men he let go. Of the other six that he added, all were faces that I hadn't seen since I had been a boy during the war, tagging around after my dad's gang.

Ian Lewis detached himself from his croft with alacrity and Geordie made him first mate; he'd had years under sail and was almost as good as a professional. Ex-corporal Taffy Morgan came along; one night during the war he had killed six Germans with a commando knife in utter silence, earning himself the M.M. Danny Williams had also won the M.M., although I never found out what for since he was reticent about it. There was the burly bulk of Nick Dugan, an Irishman from the Free State. Bill Hunter turned up – he had made a name for himself as an underwater demolitions expert and was the only other regular sailing man among the team. And there was Jim Taylor, another explosives wizard – he had been very near my father when he was killed.

They were now all into their forties, like Geordie, but seemed as tough as ever. Not one had lost his fitness and there wasn't a paunch among the lot of them. Geordie said he could have recruited twenty-five but he'd picked the best of them, and I almost believed him. I was confident that if we ran into trouble we could handle it.

Geordie was confident too, of welding them into a good sailing crew. What any of them lacked in knowledge they'd soon pick up and the enthusiasm was certainly there – although for the time being they knew nothing of the complications in which we were entangled. It was a straight research and survey trip to them all, including Kane, and any hints Geordie may have given his special team they kept strictly to themselves. As Campbell had predicted, Kane was sticking as close to us as a leech; Geordie had simply told him that there was a berth for him if he cared to cross the Atlantic with us, and Kane had jumped at the opportunity.

Campbell had gone back to Canada. Before he left he had a long talk with me. 'I told you I had a good intelligence service,' he said. 'Well, so have Suarez-Navarro. You'll be watched and they'll know everything you do as soon as you do it, even apart from Kane's spying. It can't be helped. We're deadlocked and we know it. So do they. It's a case of we know that they know that we know, and so on. It's a bastard of a position to be in.'

'It's like a game with perfect information – chess, for example. It's the man who can manoeuvre best who wins.'

'Not quite. Both sides have imperfect information,' he corrected me patiently. 'We don't know how much they really know. They might have the exact location of the nodules we're after, and only have to drop a dredge to prove their case, but perhaps they're behind us in planning and need to stop us somehow first. On the other hand, they don't know how much *we* know. Which is precious little. Maybe as much as, or no more than them. Tricky, isn't it?'

'It would take a logician to sort it out. Talking of knowing, have you made any progress with the diary?'

Campbell snorted. 'I gave it to a top-flight cipher expert and he's having his troubles. He says it isn't so much the peculiar shorthand as the sloppy way in which it's written. But he says he can crack it, given time. What I wish I knew was how Suarez-Navarro got on to this in the first place?'

My own thoughts were that Mark, cheated out of Campbell's involvement – I guessed that's how he would see Campbell's loss, only in terms of his own disappointment – had approached them himself. But I still didn't know enough about how Campbell viewed Mark to say so. It hung between us, a touchy subject that we both carefully avoided.

So he went off to Canada to further his own progress, we speeded up ours as much as possible, and it was with great relief that I heard Geordie announce one day that we were at last ready for sea. All he needed to know was where to head for.

I said, 'Do you know the Blake Plateau?'

'Never heard of it.'

'It's just off the coast of Carolina. We'll test the winch and the rest of our gear there, and it's a long enough voyage for you to pull your crew together. I don't want to go into the Pacific to find that anything doesn't work for some reason or other. If there's anything wrong we can get it fixed in Panama – they've got good engineering shops there.'

'Okay. But why the Blake Plateau?'

'There are nodules there. I've always wanted a closer look at Atlantic nodules.'

'Is there any place where there aren't any?' he asked.

I nodded. 'They won't form where there's heavy sedimentation, so that cuts out most of the Atlantic – but the Blake Plateau is scoured by the Gulf Stream and nodules do form. But they're poor quality, not like the ones in the Pacific.'

'How deep?'

'Not more than three thousand feet – deep enough to test the winch.'

'Right, boy. Let's go and scoop up some poor quality wealth from the bottom of the sea. We should be away in a few days now.'

'I can't wait,' I said. I was in fact boiling with impatience to be gone.

II

We made a fair and untroubled crossing of the Atlantic. Geordie and Ian, together with the regular crew members, soon got the others into a good working pattern and spirits ran high. Kane, we were pleased to notice, fitted in well and seemed as willing and above-board as the others. Knowing that they were all curious as to our purpose I gave occasional rather deliberately boring lectures on oceanography, touching on a number of possible research subjects so that the matter of manganese nodules got lost in the general subject. Only two people retained an interest in what I had to say, and to them, in semi-private, I spoke at greater length about our quarry. One was Geordie, of course, and the other, not too surprisingly and in fact to my satisfaction, was Bill Hunter. Already our diving expert, his interest and involvement might well be crucial.

One afternoon they both joined me in the laboratory, at my request, to learn a little more. A quiet word from Geordie to Ian made sure that we weren't going to be interrupted.

Geordie picked up a nodule which I'd cut in half – I had brought a few on board to help my explanation along.

He pointed to the white central core.

'I suppose you'll tell me again that it's a shark's tooth in the middle of this rock. You never did get around to explaining that, did you?'

I smiled and held up the stone. 'That's right, it is.'

'You're kidding.'

'No I'm not – it happens often. You see, a shark dies and its body drifts down; the flesh rots or is eaten, the bones dissolve – what bones a shark has, it's cartilage really – and by the time anything reaches the very bottom there's nothing left but the teeth. They are made of sodium triphosphate and insoluble in water. There are probably millions of them on any ocean bottom.'

I opened a small box. 'Look here,' I said and gave him a larger white bone. It was as big as the palm of his hand and curiously convoluted.

'What's this?'

'It's a whale's earbone,' said Bill, looking over his shoulder. 'I've seem 'em before.'

'Right, Bill. Also made of sodium triphosphate. We sometimes find them at the core of larger nodules – but more often it's a shark's tooth and most frequently a bit of clay.'

'So the manganese sticks to the tooth. How long does it take to make a nodule?' Geordie asked.

'Estimates vary from one millimetre each thousand years to one millimetre each million years. One chap estimated that it worked out to one layer of atoms a day – which makes it one of the slowest chemical reactions known. But I have my own ideas about that.'

They both stared at me. 'Do you mean that if you find a nodule with a half-diameter of ten millimetres formed round a tooth that the shark lived ten million years ago? Were there sharks then?' Geordie asked in fascination.

'Oh yes, the shark is one of our oldest inhabitants.'

We talked a little more and then I dropped it. They had a lot to learn yet and it came best in small doses. And there was plenty of time for talk on this voyage. We headed south-south-west to cut through the Bahamas and the approach to the Windward Passage. Once in the Passage we kept as clear as possible of Cuba – once we came across an American destroyer on patrol, which did us the courtesy of dipping her flag, to which we reciprocated. Then there was the long leg across the Caribbean to Colon and the entrance to the Panama Canal.

By then we had done our testing. There were minor problems, no more than teething troubles, and generally I was happy with the way things were going. Stopping to dredge a little, trying out the winch and working out on-station routines, was an interesting change from what we had been doing and everyone enjoyed it, and we remained lucky with the weather. I got some nodules up but there was a lot of other material, enough to cloud the issue for everyone but Geordie. Among the debris of ooze, red clay and deposits we found enough shark's teeth and whale's earbone to give everyone on board a handful of souvenirs.

Both Geordie and Bill were becoming more and more interested in the nodules and wanted to know more about them, so I arranged for another lab. session with them one day. I'd been assaying, partly to keep my hand in and partly to check on the readiness of my equipment for the real thing.

'How did the Atlantic nodules turn out?' Geordie asked. On the whole he did the talking – Bill watched, listened and absorbed.

'Same old low quality stuff that's always pulled out in the Atlantic,' I said. 'Low manganese, low iron and hardly anything else except contaminants, clay and suchlike. That's the trouble in the Atlantic; there's too much sediment even on the Blake Plateau.'

'Why does manganese behave this way – why does it lump together?'

I laughed. 'You want me to give you a course of physical chemistry right now? All right, I'll explain it as simply as I can. Do you know what a colloid is?'

Two headshakes.

'Look. If you put a teaspoon of sugar into water you get a sugar solution – that is, the sugar breaks down right to the molecular level and mixes intimately with the water. In other words, it dissolves. Right?'

'Right.'

'Now what if you have a substance that won't dissolve in water but is divided into very fine particles, much smaller than can be seen in a regular microscope, and each particle is floating in the water? That's a colloid. I could whip you up a colloid which looks like a clear liquid, but it would be full of very small particles.'

'I see the difference,' Geordie said.

'All right. Now, for reasons that I won't go into now, all colloidal particles *must* carry an electric charge. These charges make the colloidal particles of manganese dioxide clump together in larger and larger units. They also tend to be attracted to any electrically conductive surfaces such as a shark's tooth or a bit of clay. Hence the nodules.'

'You mean,' said Bill slowly, 'that having broken down a long time before, the manganese is trying to get together again?'

'Pretty well just that, yes.'

'Where does the manganese come from in the first place – when it starts clumping, that is?'

'From the rivers, from underground volcanic fissures, from the rocks of the sea bottom. Fellows, the sea out there is a big chemical broth. In certain localized conditions the sea becomes alkaline and the manganese in the rocks leaches out and dissolves in the water . . .'

'You said it doesn't dissolve.'

'Pure metallic manganese *will* dissolve as long as the conditions are right, and that's what chemists call a "reducing atmosphere". Just believe me, Geordie. Currents carry the dissolved manganese into "oxidizing atmospheres" where the water is more acid. The manganese combines with oxygen to form manganese dioxide which *is* insoluble and so forms a colloid – and then the process goes on as I've described.'

He thought about that. 'What about the copper and nickel and cobalt and stuff that's in the nodules?'

'How does the milk get into the coconut?'

We all laughed, taking some of the schoolroom air out of the lab. 'Well, all these metals have certain affinities for each other. If you look at the table of elements you'll find they're grouped closely together by weight – from manganese, number twenty-five, to copper, number twenty-nine. What happens is that as the colloidal particles grow bigger they scavenge the other metals – entrap them. Of course, this is happening over a pretty long period of time.'

'Say a hundred million years or so,' said Geordie ironically.

'Ah well, that's the orthodox view.'

'You think it can happen faster than that?'

'I think it could happen fast,' I said slowly. 'Given the right conditions, though just what these conditions would be I'm not sure. Someone else doing research thought so too, though I haven't been able to follow his reasoning. And I have seen peculiarities that indicate rapid growth. Anyway that's one of the objects of this trip – to find out.'

What I didn't say in Bill's hearing was that the 'some-body' was Mark, nor that the peculiarities I had seen were contained in the prize nodule left from his collection. And there was something else I didn't talk about; the peculiari-ties that led to high-cobalt assay. I was beginning to grope towards a theory of nodule formation which, though still vague, might ease the way ahead. I was becoming anxious to know how Campbell's cipher expert had made out in translating Mark's diary.

III

Ten days after leaving the Blake Plateau we warped into the dockside at Panama. At last we were in the Pacific, all my goals a step nearer. Campbell was waiting for us, jumped spryly aboard and shook hands with me and Geordie, waving genially at the rest of the crew.

'You made a good fast trip,' he said.

'Not so bad,' said Geordie complacently.

Campbell looked about the *Esmerelda* and at the crew who were busy stowing sail and clearing the decks. 'So this is your crew of cut-throats and desperadoes,' he said. He was in a jocular mood – a mercurial man. 'I hope we won't need them.' He took my arm and walked me along the dock, amused at my wobbling land-legs.

'I've booked you into my hotel for a night or so; there's no reason why you shouldn't have a last taste of luxury before the big job. Geordie too, if he wants it. I'll expect you both to dinner – you can't miss the hotel, it's the Colombo, right on the main street. You can tell me all about the trip then. Meantime I want to talk to you in private, now.' He steered me into one of the waterfront bars that always seem to be handy, and I sat down thankfully in front of a large glass of cold beer.

Campbell wasted no time. He produced a biggish envelope from his jacket. 'I had photostats made of the diary pages,' he said. 'The original's in a bank vault in Montreal. You don't mind? You'll get it back one day.'

'Not at all,' I said.

He shook out the contents of the envelope. 'I got the translation done. My guy said it was a bastard of a job – he only hopes he's got the scientific bits right.'

'We'll soon find out.' I was stiff with eagerness.

Campbell handed me a neatly bound booklet which I flicked through. 'That's the stat of the original diary. This one's the translation. There are reproductions of all the drawings at the back. The whole thing looks screwy to me – it had better make sense to you or this whole thing is a bust already.' His good humour had already evaporated, but I was getting used to his changes of mood.

I glanced through it all. 'This is going to be a long job,' I said. 'I'm not going to be able to make any snap judgements here and now; I'll look at this lot this afternoon, in the hotel room. Right now I want to go back to *Esmerelda* and sort out procedures with Geordie, pack my gear and go and take a shower and a clean-up.'

If he was disappointed he didn't show it – clearly what I said made sense. And so it was not until I was lying, damp and half-naked in the blessedly cool hotel room a couple of hours later that I finally opened the envelope. The translation of the cipher was pretty well complete except for a few gaps here and there, but it didn't improve matters as much as I'd hoped. The thing was disappointingly written in a kind of telegraph-ese which didn't make for easy reading. It was a true diary and evidently covered the last few months of Mark's life, from about the time he left the IGY, although there were few dates and no place names written in clear at all.

I wondered if he'd always kept such a diary, and decided that he must have done so – diary-keeping is a habit as hard to break as to develop. As to where the earlier volumes had got to, there was no guessing, nor did I think they would have helped me much anyway. This was the vital period.

It was, on the whole, an ordinary enough diary; there were references to shore leave, films seen, people mentioned by initials only in the irritating way that people have when confiding to themselves, and all the other trivia of a man's life, all in brusque lack of detail. Mark had kept a brief record of his amours which wasn't pleasant to read, but otherwise it was fairly uninteresting on the surface.

Then there were the entries made at sea. Here the diary turned professional with notes of observations, odd equations roughly jotted, analyses of bottom material, mostly sea ooze. Occasionally there were analyses of nodules – nothing very startling, just run of the sea stuff.

I waded on feeling that I might be wasting my time, but towards the end I was pulled up with a start. I had run my eye down the typewritten sheet and was aware that I was at last looking at something remarkable. It was an analysis of a nodule, though it didn't specifically say so, and the figures were startling.

Translated from symbols, they read: *'Manganese – 28%; iron – 32%; cobalt – 8%; copper – 4%; nickel – 6%; other 22%. Wow!'*

'Wow,' indeed.

There followed analyses of four more nodules, all equally rich.

I did some calculating and found the average cobalt in the five nodules to be a fraction under nine per cent. The copper and nickel weren't to be laughed away either. I didn't yet know much about the economics of recovery but it was evident that this might be a paying proposition even with relatively primitive methods of dredging, depending on the depth of water. And I had reason to believe that this was not too great to be worked in. With more sophisticated equipment it would be better than owning a gold mine.

But there was always the snag – nowhere in the diary did Mark say where these riches were to be found. In the whole notebook there was not one place name mentioned. So we weren't really any better off than we were before, except that scattered through the typewritten pages was the phrase, *'Picture Here'* , with a number attached, and at the end was a sheaf of reproductions and a brief account by the cipher expert of these doodled drawings.

It is possible and indeed probable that these drawings are of the nature of pictograms or rebuses. A study of the pictograms leads me to believe that they must indicate place names, and of the 32 drawings, I believe I have successfully identified 24.

To illustrate: the rough sketch of the gas mantle with the word GRATIS beneath may well refer to the Australian town of Fremantle; the bearded man with the sword and the baby is probably Solomon, referring to the biblical story, and may indicate the Solomon Islands; the bearded man looking at a monkey may be a reference to Darwin in the Australian territory; the straight line neatly bisected may refer to either the Equator or Midway Island.

The fact that all these names occur in the same quarter of the globe is a further indication that one may be on the right track in such surmising. Other names tentatively identified are also to be found in the same geographical area.

Tracings of the drawings, together with possible identifications are attached. Of the eight drawings unidentified all I can say is that to solve these one would need to have a more precise knowledge of these geographical areas, together with the need to know a great deal more about the 'artist', since it is obvious that an idiosyncratic mode of thought is here employed, involving a person's training, experience and interior feelings; in fact, a total life.

I looked up the analyses of the two non-standard nodules again. Coming immediately after them were two of the drawings, numbers 28 and 29. I checked them against the tracings. One was of a busty wench wearing a Phrygian cap with underneath it the words, 'The Fair Goddess'. The other was a rather bedraggled-looking American eagle with the inscription, 'The Disappearing Trick'. Neither was identified.

I leaned back and thought about it all. I knew that Mark's ship had been based on Australia during the IGY – hence, possibly, the Australian references. Mark had probably been in the Solomons and might well have gone as far as Midway – he would certainly have crossed the Equator anyway. Did he go as far as Easter Island? I checked the tracings and found it – a rabbit apparently trying to hatch an egg, the traditional fertility symbols of Easter. That was one the expert had spotted too.

It was a hell of a big area in which to find The Fair Goddess or The Disappearing Trick.

I thought about Mark and his 'idiosyncratic mode of thought'. The expert had been dead right there; Mark's mode of thought had been so damned idiosyncratic that there had been times when I thought it wasn't human. He had a strangely twisted, involute mind which delighted in complexity and deception, never taking a straight course but always heading ultimately for one goal – the eventual well-being of Mark Trevelyan.

All my life I had watched him cheat and scheme his way towards the things he wanted, never realizing that if he'd gone about his business in a straightforward way it would have been more efficient. He had a first-class brain, but he was lazy and always looking for short cuts – but you don't find many short cuts in science and thus he tended to lag behind in his work.

I think he was envious of me for some odd reason of his own. I was two years older than he and when we were children he nearly beat himself to death trying to keep up, physically and mentally. The psycho boys have a term for it in their tasteless jargon – 'sibling rivalry' – but with Mark it took an unhealthy turn. He seemed to see his whole life in terms of competition with me, even inventing apparent parental favouritism towards me where I could see none. The only reason that I know for his having elected to study oceanography was because I had done so and not, like me, out of any burning interest in the subject. He once said that he would be famous when I had been forgotten.

It was ironic in a way that he should have said that, because he had the makings of a first rate scientist with a theoretical bent and if he'd lived I'm sure he could have surprised us all – provided he wasn't looking for a short cut at the time.

For years I'd avoided him, physically and professionally, but now I had to match my mind against his. I had to ferret out the meanings of his cryptic scrawls and it wasn't going to be easy. Mark had almost certainly been up to something fishy – no high-cobalt results had come out of the IGY investigations, and Mark had such results. I thought about what Jarvis had said about Mark faking figures during that period, and about Mark trying to persuade Campbell into an expedition to look for nodules. It was beginning to add up.

I was interrupted by Geordie, banging at my bedroom door.

'Aren't you ready yet?' he demanded. 'We've got a dinner date with the boss.'

'My God, the time's slipped away.'

'Found anything?'

I looked up wryly. 'Yes, I've found something but I'm damned if I know what it is. It looks as though we still have to play children's games against Mark's tortuous mind. I'll tell you about it when we're all together. Give me ten minutes to get dressed.'

'There's just one thing first,' Geordie said, hovering in the doorway. 'Kane went ashore and sent a cable.'

'Where to?'

'We were lucky. I detailed Danny Williams to trail him – don't worry, he'll keep it dark – and he managed to hear Kane asking about cable rates to Rabaul.'

'Rabaul! But that's in New Britain – in the Bismarck Archipelago. Why in hell would he send a cable clear across the Pacific? Do you know who he sent it to?'

'Danny couldn't find that out. He should have bribed the counter clerk, but he didn't. The boss says come to the lounge first – it's early for a meal. He wants to talk to us there – about that, I guess.' He pointed to the diary pages lying on my bed.

IV

The Colombo was a modern American style hotel. We went to the reception desk where I had signed in earlier and asked for Campbell, and were told that he was in one of the lounges. It was discreetly lighted and in one corner a trio was playing soft music. It was all very civilized and pleasant and a definite change from life on board *Esmerelda*. Over drinks I asked Campbell to bear with me in setting aside for the moment the matter of the diary, and instead listen while I brought him up to date concerning manganese nodules, to which he reluctantly agreed. He was at his most churlish but I knew that mood would wear off as his interest sharpened. He had already done some homework so I was able to cover the matter of nodule formation and distribution fairly quickly, feeling pleased that I had already brought Geordie up to that point as well. I came at last to the matter of nodule dating.

'I've come to the conclusion that our nodule isn't very old,' I said, producing it from my pocket.

'How old?' Campbell demanded.

'He always talks in millions,' said Geordie wisely, but he was wrong.

'Not more than fifty thousand years,' I said flatly. 'It could be between thirty thousand and fifty thousand but not more than that, I'll stake my reputation on it. Somewhere in the Pacific these things are growing at an explosive rate.'

'Explosive,' said Geordie incredulously. 'Do you call fifty thousand years explosive?'

'From a geological standpoint it's very fast. It's damned unusual, though, and it's very important.'

'Why so?' Campbell asked.

'Look, the whole damn Pacific is covered with these things which have been growing slowly over millions of years. Now we have one which has grown in a fraction of that time. There must be a specific reason for it. My guess is that it's the result of a purely local condition, and if it is the chances are that this condition still exists – in other words, these nodules are growing at the same rate even now.'

'I can't see that that helps us much.'

'It helps us this much. It means we can cut out vast areas – millions of square miles – where I *know* that no peculiar conditions exist in the sea. I'll go along with orthodoxy on that one; the seabed is pretty regular, there are few changes of climate for one thing. What we've got to watch for is the oddity.'

'Got any idea what kind of oddity?'

I nodded. 'I have vague ideas that I'm not prepared to put into words just yet,' I said. 'Maybe I'll get something from the diary translation. It may only need one word to make the whole picture clear – like the last piece in a jigsaw puzzle.'

'We'll come back to that later,' Campbell said. 'Meanwhile I've been keeping tabs on Suarez-Navarro. Ramirez left London and joined that ship of theirs.'

'Where are they now?' Geordie asked.

'Still lying in Darwin – doing nothing. I don't quite get it.'

He glanced up as he spoke and then got to his feet. Coming through the lounge towards us was a young woman whom I recognized as his daughter, and Geordie and I both stood up as she joined us. Campbell introduced us. 'Clare, this is Michael Trevelyan and this is our Captain, George Wilkins.'

Geordie shook hands gravely and corrected his name. As I took her hand she looked at me very carefully but did not react to my name at all. I was on the point of reminding her that I had met her once long before, with Mark, but took my cue from her and made my greeting noncommittal. We all sat down once again, and during the few minutes while drinks were being ordered I assessed her, as a man assesses any woman.

When I had seen her in Vancouver I hadn't been particularly interested. I couldn't be bothered with Mark or any of his affairs. But now I saw that she was really beautiful and wondered why I hadn't noticed it before. She was tall, with black hair and straight brows over grey eyes. Her mouth was generous with mobile corners, a mouth made for laughter but presently in tight control, as though she had learned not to laugh. She was dressed with that deceptive simplicity which means money, not surprising considering that she was Campbell's daughter. She wore, I noticed, no jewellery apart from a small ruby brooch.

We all chatted for a short time about this and that, and I saw that there was something wary and watchful about her, and felt that it concerned me. I wondered how Mark had got on with her. When I saw her with him she had seemed to have a lot more sparkle, and this present introversion wasn't Mark's style at all – he always liked his women to have some animation.

Presently Campbell brought us to the matter in the forefront of all our minds. I was not altogether surprised when he said, 'Gentlemen, you had better know that I've told the whole story – so far as I can – to Clare. She's my right hand, you know, doubles as secretary sometimes, and she's always been involved in my affairs. This one is no different.'

I thought that burglary, forgery, espionage and murder would certainly make it different in my eyes, but perhaps she'd seen all that already, on other missions with her father.

'What's more, when I join ship she's coming along as well,' he continued. He was the boss after all, but he seemed just a little truculent as he said it, as if daring our opposition. Geordie looked faintly dismayed and glanced at me for his cue.

'Why not?' I said evenly. 'Lots of room – and we could do with an extra hand in the lab from time to time. And if you can cook, Miss Campbell – '

'Clare, please. Are you Michael or Mike?'

'Mike, always.'

She smiled. 'I can cook, but I wouldn't want to be chief cookie. I'll spell whoever it is, though.'

Geordie was on the edge of his chair, and finally had his say. 'Have you been to sea before, Miss – er, Clare?' he asked sternly. Clare bore it equably.

'Yes, Geordie, I have – for quite long trips too. I've got all my gear and you'll believe me when you see how worn out it all is. In fact I'm much more familiar with what we're going to do than Pop is.'

Geordie was routed.

Campbell broke in impatiently at this point. 'What about the diary, Mike? You've read through it, I suppose.'

'There are interesting possibilities opening up.'

'How come?'

'The diary was written partly while Mark was with the IGY survey. Now, *he* made a record of those high-cobalt nodules, but the fact never came out in the open scientific record. In other words, he suppressed the evidence.'

Campbell seemed perturbed. 'I shouldn't think your brother would do a thing like that,' he said stiffly. And that told me that any reservations he may have about Mark stemmed from Mark's personal affiliation with Clare, and that he had never plumbed the depths of Mark's personality. I would have to be careful, but it was time to bring things out into the open.

I said, 'Can you think of any other explanation?'

He shook his head. 'I'm at a loss what to make of it – I have been giving it some thought already. Are you serious when you said your brother would do a thing like that? He struck me as a very fine scientist.'

'Mark was never too scrupulous,' I said. 'He wanted something from you and he was showing his cleanest face.'

Campbell didn't like that. My open distrust of Mark offended his sense of fitness. Brothers should be brotherly and blood is thicker than water. I suspected he had a strong puritan streak in him, inherited from his no doubt calvinistic ancestors. He said, almost hostilely, 'There's nothing to be gained by running down your brother – especially as he can't answer back.'

I said softly, 'You should study the Bible, Mr Campbell. There are a few stories in the Book that are very illuminating. Read about Cain and Abel, or Esau and Jacob. There's no hard and fast rule that brothers should like one another – and lots of villains have innocent kinfolk.'

He was acid. 'Well, I suppose you knew him best. I never had any reason to doubt him while he was in my employ.' He caught Clare's eye and faltered just a little. 'Must admit that personally . . .'

Clare's face was calm, showing only a polite interest, but her jawline caught my notice.

I said, 'We must discuss this. We're faced with a problem put to us by Mark and we can only solve it by understanding him and the way he worked. Geordie can support some of what I may have to tell you.' I had them all riveted now. 'Let me tell you something that I'll bet you don't know – Mark was kicked out of the IGY for falsifying figures. That was just before he joined your company.'

'I didn't know that and I don't think I believe it.'

'It's true,' I said. 'Professor Jarvis, my old boss at the Institute, told me about it – and Geordie heard him too. I think he got hold of those nodules at the time, found out their value, and decided to keep the knowledge to himself. Then he moved in on you – and he was using you.'

Campbell was affronted. 'Using *me*!'

'You had the money he wanted for an expedition. He couldn't show you the nodules because you'd want to know where he got them. And that was by stealing them from the people who paid his salary.'

Campbell began to look baffled. 'He never showed me anything. He talked a good story though.'

'That's right. He had a lot of theory and you nearly fell for it. If you had, he'd have wasted his time and your money fossicking round the Pacific for six months and then his "theory" would have led him to a spectacular find. You see, he knew where those nodules came from. Anyway you'd be in the chips and he'd be both rich and vindicated – the great scientist.'

Campbell nodded unwillingly.

I said, 'But something went wrong. You had your run-in with Suarez-Navarro and found yourself strapped for ready funds. You couldn't finance his expedition, and so he left you flat because you were of no further use to him. Isn't that so?'

There was silence while Campbell digested all that.

'All right, you've made your point – don't drive it into the ground. Assuming something like that is possible – what do you suggest we do now?'

'First, another point. You wondered how Suarez-Navarro came into the nodule hunt. I think Mark may have tried the same ploy on them. In fact I think he and Norgaard were waiting in Tahiti for the ship that's being fitted out right now, and that ties everything in squarely together.'

'All right, let's assume that too. We're safer the more we can see into the forest, I suppose.' Campbell was still shaken by what I'd said about Mark. 'What do we do next?'

'Well, we could find out where Mark's IGY ship dredged and drop ours in the same places. But I don't think it will be any of the sites they actually surveyed or this would have come out already – Mark wasn't the only one doing assays. No, I think it was a trial site, one they weren't serious about, and probably didn't even make a record of, though we could check it out.'

We all sat in gloom for a while. The faint drift of music changed tempo and a woman began to sing with the trio, and I turned to watch her. Her voice was nice but she was no world-beater. Her body was better than her voice and set off admirably by a revealing gown. For a moment, lost in something not at all of our troubled world, I relaxed and only caught the end of a sentence directed at me by Clare Campbell.

'. . . to ask you a question – if I'm not distracting you, Mike?' Her voice was calm but when I turned back I saw an ironic sparkle in her eyes.

'Sorry, yes?' I said.

'You say that Mark was kicked off the ship for falsifying figures – but which figures? Not the high-cobalt nodule assay because, as you said, that news hasn't broken yet. So he must have falsified *other* figures which caught him out. What were they and why did he cook them – could they matter?'

That was something I hadn't thought of, and it was a stopper. I said, 'Mark was always a fast boy with a red herring. He cheated once in his school exams, and this is how he did it. He was called into the headmaster's office just before an exam and the master happened to be out of the room. On the desk was a pile of question papers. Mark played it cleverly – he didn't take one, he took six. Then he made a copy for himself and passed the six papers to other boys – anonymously.'

Campbell said, 'I don't get it.'

'It's simple. He told me about it afterwards – he always knew *I* wouldn't tell tales. He reckoned that if the thing blew up in his face he'd see to it that the six papers were all found – in the possession of other boys. He'd be in the clear. It wasn't found out and he got away with it. Now what if he's done something like that here?'

Campbell looked frustrated. He was supposed to be a man with acumen, after all. 'I may be dumb, but I still don't get it.'

'Look,' I said patiently. 'Mark has located a deposit of high-cobalt nodules and he's busy suppressing the information. He knows that if he's found out he's not only in disgrace but he's lost a potential fortune. So – knowing Mark – I'd guess that he'd toss out a few red herrings. He'd falsify some more figures to confuse the issue, and he'd probably revise all estimates upwards. It would add slightly to the risk of discovery, but if it was found out, as it evidently was, he'd be only another glory-hunting scientist, rather too optimistic and looking for professional praise. No one would suspect that one set of figures was wrong for another reason. They may not ever have caught it.' I laughed humourlessly. 'I'll bet that *all* Mark's findings were junked, anyway. None of his colleagues would trust his figures after that.'

'Why didn't they tell the world about it – to protect people like Pop?' asked Clare a little bitterly.

'I think they would feel that commercial folk like your dad can take care of themselves,' I said. 'They're mostly too gentlemanly.'

Campbell was looking at me in wonder, Geordie in silent assent of my assessment. 'Did Mark really have a mind like that?' Campbell said.

I saw that he was hurt; his pride in his judgement of men had been badly undermined. But then, he'd been taken in by an expert. 'He had a mind that would make a corkscrew look like a straight edge. You don't have to take my word for it, either. Geordie can tell you some tales.'

Geordie nodded. 'Aye, the boy was a twister. He caused the family a lot of grief.'

'All right. Supposing that Mark was as machiavellian as you make him out to be, it seems we're back where we started – all we have to go on is the diary.'

'And that's going to be a devil of a job, sorting out his scribbles. I can make a fair stab at the science, but the rest is a teaser.'

'We'll discuss it over dinner,' Campbell decided, to my secret relief.

We chewed over the diary and the dinner together. The dinner was digestible which was more than any of us could say for the diary. Clare asked if she could have it for bedside reading. 'I like that sort of thing,' she said. 'Puzzles, jigsaws.' And I also thought that she might have felt that her own knowledge of Mark's odd mind might be useful.

'You're welcome,' I told her. 'I want a break from it.' I was pleased that as the evening wore on she seemed to lose some of her reserve and her mouth began to lose its tight-locked caution. We were at the coffee stage when a waiter came up to the table. 'Are one of you gentlemen Mr Trevelyan?'

'I am.'

'There's a lady in the foyer asking to see you.'

I looked around blankly. 'I don't know anyone in Panama.'

Campbell looked up at the waiter. 'An old lady or a young lady?'

'Oh, a young lady, sir.'

Campbell's eyes twinkled. 'If I were you I'd be in the foyer now. What's stopping you?'

I got up. 'It's probably a mistake,' I said, thinking that it almost certainly wasn't. 'Excuse me.'

There were several people in the foyer including more than one young lady, but no one approached me. I crossed to the desk and said, 'My name's Trevelyan. I understand someone wants me.'

The clerk pointed with his pen, indicating that I should come into the office behind the desk. The young lady was waiting all right, and I did know her, in a way; she was the singer who had been entertaining us in the lounge.

'I'm Trevelyan. You wanted to speak to me?'

She was nervous, I could see that. She was rather slight and looked, at close quarters, a trifle undernourished, with hollows under her dark eyes and a skin more weathered than tanned. There was an appealing quality about her – I think the best word would be winsome. I was intrigued.

'I'm sorry to trouble you – I saw your name in the register – but I wondered if you were any relation of Mark Trevelyan? From Tahiti?'

'He was my brother,' I said. 'I'm Michael. Obviously you – know Mark.' I didn't know if she knew of his death and I felt it would be unkind to throw it at her without warning.

She nodded, gripping her hands together. 'Yes, I knew him, very well. Have you just come from England?'

'Yes.'

'Do you know his – wife?'

'Yes.'

'Did she get the suitcase I sent?'

I stared at her now. 'Well, I'm damned! I thought you were a man. So you are P. Nelson.'

She smiled and some of the tension left her. 'Yes – Paula Nelson. Then the case did arrive all right?'

'It arrived, thank you,' I said. I didn't say that it had been stolen immediately afterwards because I didn't know just where this girl stood in the complexity of Mark's affairs. But I could try to find out.

'Miss Nelson, what about coming into the lounge and having a drink with me and my friends? We're all of us interested in Mark and in what he was doing out here.'

She shook her head. 'Oh, I couldn't do that, Mr Trevelyan. I'm one of the hired help around here – we're not supposed to drink with the customers. The manager says this isn't a clip joint.' Her nervousness now seemed to include a fear of the manager's imminent wrath.

I said gently, 'Perhaps we could go somewhere else, if you've the time. I would like to talk to you.'

She looked at her watch. 'I could spare half an hour. Then I've got another stint in the lounge. If you'll wait while I get my wrap?'

'It'll be a pleasure.'

I thought of sending a message back to the others but decided against it. I didn't have to account to them for all my actions. We went to a small bar a little way down the street, I bought a couple of drinks and we settled down in an alcove. The bar was deserted except for a solitary drinker. I said, 'You're an American, aren't you?'

'Yes. And you're from – Cornwall. You talk the same way Mark did. I used to tease him about that sometimes.'

Which of course put their relationship on a firmer footing. 'Where did you meet him?'

'In Tahiti. I was working a little joint in Papeete. Mark used to come in with his sidekick, and we got pretty – friendly.'

'Who was his sidekick?'

'A Swedish guy, Sven someone. But this was, oh, maybe two years ago when we first met.'

About the time he left Campbell, I calculated. I said, 'I'm interested in how Mark came to die. Can you tell me anything about it – if it doesn't distress you too much.'

'Oh, that's all right,' she said, but it was a tremulous voice, 'I can't tell you a lot. He died of appendicitis out in the Paumotus – didn't you know that?'

'Yes – but how did you know?'

'I didn't believe it at first, but they let me see the death certificate.'

'Who are "they"? Who told you in the first place?'

'A schooner came in with the news. And I went down to the Government bureau to see the proof. You see, I thought he might have – just – gone away.'

'Did the doctor come to Papeete himself, the one who operated on Mark?'

She shook her head. 'Not much point, was there? I mean, it's over two hundred miles and he's the only doctor out there. He wouldn't leave just to bring the news back.'

This clashed with Kane's story; according to him the doctor had dealt with the certificate and the authorities. Or had he? I thought back to what Kane had said – that he and his partner, Hadley, had left it all to the doctor. Perhaps it only meant sending the papers back on the next convenient transport.

I said, 'Did you know the men on the schooner?'

She was silent for a bit and then said, 'Why are you asking me all these questions, Mr Trevelyan?'

'I could say out of natural interest in the death of my only brother, but I won't,' I said deliberately. 'I think there's something very odd about the whole affair.' As I said it I suddenly wondered if she was a plant – one of the spies of Ramirez of whom Campbell so often warned me. If so I'd already dealt a hand I should rather have hidden, and I felt cold at the thought. But it was very hard to imagine this girl as a crook's agent.

'You think he was murdered, don't you?' she asked flatly.

I tightened my lips. Time for a quick decision, and I thought that I may as well continue. It was already too late to do otherwise. 'You think so too, Miss Nelson?'

There was a long pause before she nodded. 'Yes,' she whispered, and started to cry. I felt better, for some reason – she was ruining her makeup, and surely no spy would do that, not just before making a public appearance?

I let her run on for a little while, then took her hand in mine.

'You were living with Mark, weren't you?'

'Yes, I was. Oh God, I *loved* him,' she said. She was so intense, her grip tightening, that I felt I must believe her.

'Were you happy with him?' I asked. 'Was he good to you, Miss Nelson?'

Amazingly, a smile appeared. 'Oh, I was. Please – don't call me Miss Nelson. My name is Paula.'

'And I'm Mike.'

We were silent for a few moments, then I said, 'What really happened, Paula?'

She said, 'I suppose it all started when Sven was killed – '

'Norgaard? Killed!'

'Yes. He was found out on the reef, outside Papeete, with his head bashed in. At first everyone thought it was the sea – it comes in with tremendous force against the reef. They thought he'd been washed off his feet and had his head smashed on the rocks. Then – I don't know exactly how – they decided he'd been murdered. It was something to do with what the police surgeon found.'

I nodded grimly. 'Then what happened?'

'The police were asking questions and they came to Mark. He said he knew nothing about it, but it didn't seem to worry him.'

I took a deep breath. 'Paula, do you think that Mark killed Sven?'

She hesitated, then shook her head violently. 'No, it *couldn't* have been Mark. I know he could get very angry – even violent – but he couldn't have killed Sven. They were partners.'

I had experienced some of Mark's violence, in my younger days.

'Paula, did he ever hit you?'

She looked down at the table, nodding. 'Sometimes – but I'm hell to live with. I'm untidy and sloppy about house-work. I'm – ' She laughed, but the laugh broke off on a sob and tears rolled down her cheeks. I was appalled.

'What happened then?'

'Mark ran away. He ran from the police. I don't mean lit-erally, not the day they spoke to him, but that night he dis-appeared from Tahiti. And then we heard that he was dead – I've already told you exactly how that was.'

'Who brought the news of his death – in that schooner?'

'It was a man called Hadley – he brought the news. He said that he and his partner had found Mark dying out in the islands.' She had the look of nervousness back, and I thought that it may have been caused by her mention of Hadley.

But I had more important things to think about. This was the break – this was the evidence that showed Kane to be a downright liar. There could have been an honest mistake about the death certificate, but not about this. Kane had told me that he and Hadley had left things to the doctor. This was the crack in his story.

I said, 'Hadley's partner – was it a man called Kane?'

'I don't know, I never met him. I knew Hadley, though; he came to visit Mark often.'

'The devil he did!' I ejaculated. This was a new devel-opment.

'Oh sure. Mark and Sven used to hire Hadley's boat and go off for weeks at a time with him.'

'You've no idea where they went, I suppose?' I said casually.

'Mark never talked to me about what he did,' she said.

'There's just one more thing, but it's very important. You said you thought Mark had been murdered. What led you to think that?'

'It was Hadley,' she said. 'He came to my place and said he wanted Mark's things. The way he talked about Mark – he was so triumphant. I didn't see any reason why he should have Mark's stuff so I gave him the air. He was mad about it but he couldn't do anything then because I had friends with me. But he scared me – he's a bad bastard. I looked at Mark's case and there wasn't anything there that would do me any good, so I sent it home to his wife. Mark talked about her to me.' There was pain in her voice. 'He talked about you too – he wasn't very nice about you.'

'I can imagine. Did Hadley try again?'

'Yes. He came and beat the living daylights out of me and searched my place but of course there wasn't anything there.'

'You mean – he beat you up?'

'Oh brother, you ought to have seen the shiner I had.' She looked at me gravely. 'You don't know much about men like Hadley, do you?'

'Not yet,' I said grimly. 'But I soon will. I'm going to catch up with that bastard.'

She laughed scornfully. 'He'd tear you in half, Mike. Be careful of him – don't come at him from the front, club him down from behind. He'd do the same to you. He's an uncivilized savage.'

I looked at this girl who talked of brawls and beatings so matter-of-factly. No wonder she had that permanently shrinking air – or perhaps it was her manner which attracted violence in the first place. 'I'll remember that.'

She sighed. 'Well, then I got real scared because I said too much. You know what I said? I said I had proof that he was lying – that Mark hadn't died the way he said. He looked at me in a real funny way and said he'd be back – with friends. So I packed a few things and got out. I stayed with someone else the rest of the night and next morning there was a trading schooner leaving for Panama at five o'clock and I was aboard by four. I kept below deck until Papeete was out of sight.'

'What was your proof, Paula?'

She said what I guessed she was going to say. 'Mark already had his appendix out. I saw the scar. He couldn't have died that way.'

'I knew about that too. Mark had his appendix out years ago.'

Paula looked at her watch and jumped to her feet. She still looked ravaged but she seemed a little calmer now. 'I have to get back.'

'Thanks, Paula. You've helped me a lot. Do you think that Hadley killed Mark and Sven Norgaard?'

'I do,' she said intensely.

'Have you any idea why he should?'

She shrugged. 'No idea – but I'm sure he did it.'

'Paula, before I leave here – will you write down what you know for me?'

'I – I guess so, Mike. I – have to be careful.'

She wouldn't come into the hotel lounge with me so I went in alone ahead of her and found Geordie sitting talking to Clare. 'Pop's gone to bed,' she said. 'It's late and he gets tired.'

'I hope Geordie's been entertaining you all right.'

'Oh yes, he's been telling me more about Mark – and you.'

I said lightly, 'I thought I felt my ears burning.'

I saw Paula join the trio. In the dim lounge lighting one could not see any trace of disarray and she began to sing in the same pleasant, husky voice. 'Nice voice she's got,' said Clare casually.

I saw they were both looking at her.

'How was your assignation?' asked Geordie.

'Interesting.'

A mischievous smile played briefly on Clare's mouth. 'We saw you escorting her out of the foyer.'

'Her name is P. Nelson,' I said. Geordie choked over his coffee.

I put Clare in the picture regarding the name, then said, 'She's had a lot to tell me, all fascinating. She thinks that Mark was murdered, and his partner Norgaard too – oh yes, he's dead. And she thinks they were both killed by Hadley, this mystery partner of Kane's. But the consensus of opinion in Tahiti seems to be that Mark killed Norgaard – that's the official police view – and that Mark died by accident while on the run. It's a hell of a mess.'

'Good God,' said Geordie. 'What's she doing here?'

'Ran away from Hadley. I'll fill you all in in the morning. I'm tired.'

It seemed an age since we had come sailing into Panama, only that morning.

Clare looked over towards Paula, who was still singing. 'How well did she know Mark?'

'Pretty well,' I said unthinkingly. 'She was another of Mark's popsies.'

And could have bitten my tongue out the moment I spoke.

V

Next morning at breakfast Campbell came down with a cable. He frowned as he read it. 'Suarez-Navarro have started to move,' he said. 'Their ship has left Darwin, bound for New Guinea.'

Geordie said, 'The Bismarck Archipelago is up that way too.'

'What's that got to do with it?'

'We forgot to tell you,' I said. 'Kane sent a cable yesterday, to Rabaul, which is in the Archipelago.'

'Kane – maybe to Ramirez, telling him where you are. Would your nodule deposit be anywhere up near Rabaul?' asked Campbell.

'There's nothing against it and a few things for it,' I said. 'Though personally I think Mark wouldn't have been so far away from where it is. But from what I could gather from the notebooks Mark was linking nodule formation with vulcanism, and there's a hell of a lot of volcanoes in that part of the world.'

'Not here?'

'Oh yes, all over the Pacific. I'm going to explain that to you when my own ideas are clearer.'

'Do you think he was right in that theory?' said Campbell.

'I don't know,' I admitted. 'It's all very theoretical. There's nothing against it in principle.'

Campbell muttered, 'When I get an unqualified answer from a scientist I suppose the world will be coming to an end. Now, what's all this about the girl last night? Clare's told me a little.'

So I filled them all in and we sat back, aghast and disturbed by the implications in Paula's story. We were running into something which got steadily nastier. Campbell approved of my wanting her evidence written down, preferably legally attested, though I wasn't sure if she would commit herself so far.

Clare said, changing the subject, 'Mike, I've been giving the diary some thought and especially the drawings, and I think I've come up with something. Can we all go up to Pop's suite after breakfast?'

Geordie assented reluctantly. He was anxious to get back to his ship, but we persuaded him that all would be well for a couple of hours more. 'They're good lads, plenty to do and they know where you are if they want you,' I said firmly. So after breakfast we found ourselves seated round a coffee table in the suite, already sweating gently in spite of the air conditioning, and with the sunshine of Panama calling to us through the open windows. Clare laid out the diary and tracings in front of us.

'I've been working backwards, from where we know Mark was, to see if we can identify any more of the drawings. The very last one is what looks like a monocle, and I think I know what it is – but only because we *do* know where Mark was. I think it means Tahiti.'

'How the hell can it mean Tahiti?' said Campbell.

'They're also known as the Society Islands. And a monocle is the epitome of the uppercrust, the "society" bloke. It's lean, but could it do?' She looked anxiously for my opinion.

I laughed. 'As well as anything. Crude but effective. Go on.'

'Numbers 31 and 30 I can't see at all – perhaps Geordie might, if he knows the area well. One's a cow and one's a – well, it's this.' She pointed to an object like an irregular, flattened semicircle standing on a flat base. It was connected to the cow with the word '*OR*', and made no sense at all to any of us.

'Then we come to these. *The Fair Goddess* and *The Disappearing Trick*, a woman and an eagle.'

I interrupted her. 'They are the two that come immediately before his high cobalt assay figures. I think they may be crucial.'

'Good,' she said briskly. 'Because there are lots more possibilities. I've been thinking about the woman. I think she could be La France – you know, Uncle Sam for America, John Bull for Britain and this female – Marianne – for France. You see her in newspaper cartoons.'

Campbell looked at the drawing intently. 'You may have something there. This thing on her head is the Cap of Liberty, isn't it? What's the extent of French territory in the Pacific?'

'French Oceania – about a million square miles of it, including Tahiti, Bora-Bora, the Tuamotus, the Marquesas, the Austral Islands. You'd have to get it down much closer than that.'

'The Marianas Islands,' said Geordie and he sounded very glum. 'The Marianas Trench.'

Clare looked thrilled. 'Where are they?'

'A long way off, too far for comfort. Almost alongside the Philippines,' I said. 'It just can't be there, or else why was Mark so far away from it? I don't believe it.'

But Geordie had thought of something else. 'Suarez-Navarro's ship is heading that way.'

We looked at one another in dismay. 'Just doesn't feel right,' I said, only because I didn't want it to be. 'We want something down this way.'

Campbell said, 'What's this about a goddess? Marianne isn't one.'

'Let's go through a list of goddesses,' I suggested. 'There's Venus for a start. Is there a Venus Island?'

Geordie grinned. 'I've heard of the Good Ship Venus, but not an island. Wait a minute, though – there's a Venus Point in Tahiti.'

'That sounds promising,' said Campbell.

'It's too close ashore – and all round there has been dredged.'

'Not so promising,' said Campbell glumly, 'but we'll keep it in mind.'

'Let's carry on with the goddess list,' said Clare. 'What about Aphrodite?'

We all thought about that. 'Nothing doing,' said Geordie finally.

'It could be a French name,' said Campbell.

I was brutal about it. 'Or a Polynesian name. Or a Polynesian goddess.'

'Good grief,' said Campbell, 'we're getting nowhere fast.'

We ran through the pantheon and couldn't even make a start on the Polynesian tribal deities without a single degree in anthropology amongst us. We switched our combined brains to the problem of the eagle, got nowhere, and came back to La France. Clare gazed fiercely at the drawings. 'All right, one last try. Let's go through it all once more.'

We all groaned.

'Venus.'

'Tahiti,' muttered Campbell, whose attention was waning.

'Demeter.'

Still nothing doing.

'Athena.'

Campbell said, 'I think this whole whacky idea is wrong. Let's pack it up.'

Clare gave a shout of laughter. 'I've got it – she's not La France at all, she's Athena, the goddess of justice. Mark used "fair" in the sense of "fair play".'

'Not that he knew much about that,' Geordie said.

'What about the Cap of Liberty?' I asked.

'It's not – it's a Roman helmet. She ought to have a spear too.'

'But Athena wasn't a Roman,' objected Campbell. 'She was a Greek goddess.'

I said, 'The Roman equivalent was Minerva – what about that?'

Geordie thumped the table and burst out laughing. 'My God! I think that's it – I should have seen it before. *Récife de Minerve*, of course!'

Campbell said, 'You mean there is such a place?'

I was struggling with a memory. I'd read about the place and there was something very out of whack about it, but I couldn't recall what it was. Geordie couldn't stop laughing. 'There's been a shipwreck on it. Oh, this is too damn funny.'

Campbell rubbed his hands, his interest rekindled. 'Now we're getting somewhere – where is it? Obviously down this way?'

'Down south of the Tuamotus,' said Geordie.

'Is it worth a trip?' Campbell asked me. 'You're the expert here.'

I thought that it was only a remote possibility that we'd hit on the right spot on our very first guess, and that there'd probably be a lot of false alarms on the way, unless some much more concrete evidence came up; but on the other hand I didn't want the expedition to founder through lack of either activity or enthusiasm – and we had to start somewhere. 'It could have possibilities,' I said, voicing a little of my reservation. 'It partly depends on where it is, which is what Geordie's going to tell us.'

'Are you kidding?' said Geordie, still spluttering over his private joke. 'Nobody – not even the Royal Navy – knows where Minerva is.'

There was a dead silence. Campbell broke it. 'What the hell do you mean by that?'

'I mean this,' said Geordie, suddenly sober. 'The Navy looked for it but couldn't find it. I suppose it's all in the Pacific Islands *Pilot* – I'd have to look – but there's an account of it in a book I've got on board.'

'But what is it?' Clare asked.

'Just what it says. *Récife de Minerve*. Minerva Reef. It's a hidden shoal.'

Geordie left us to go down to *Esmerelda*. Apart from fetching the book he was anxious to know if all was well, and to supervise the beginning of the restocking for sea. He also had to arrange for a cabin for Clare, which I knew would mean a little crowding up for someone else. We agreed that we might as well get on with things, and that all being well we should be able to sail within a day or so; impatience was in the air. I decided to try and have another word with Paula, who had left a note for me, containing her address. I had another idea that I wanted to try out on her.

I used the phone in the foyer and got her at once. 'Paula, it's Mike. I'd like to talk to you again.'

'Sure,' she said sleepily, and I guessed that late nights singing meant late mornings lying in. 'When – now?'

'If I can.'

'Okay. I'll see you in that little bar up the street.'

She was waiting for me, sitting at the same table. 'Hi,' she said. 'What's on your mind?'

I ordered coffee for both of us. She looked fresh and decidedly less tense this morning, and had obviously decided that I was an ally – as I had concluded about her.

'Hadley and people like him are on my mind. You're sure you don't remember a man called Kane?'

She shook her head firmly.

'Or Ramirez – ever hear of him?'

That drew a blank too. I said, 'Look, how well do you know Tahiti – especially Papeete?'

'Pretty well. I was there a long time, Mike.'

I rubbed my chin. 'I don't know it well at all. And I certainly don't know Hadley. I could pass him on the street without a second glance. What I need is a pair of eyes.'

She said in a small voice, 'You want me to go back to Papeete?'

I nodded. 'But not without an escort or a backup. Scared of Hadley?'

'I'll say I am. I don't mind admitting it.'

I said, 'Paula, I'm here on a small ship crewed by the toughest mob outside of the Mafia – but straight. Most of them are ex-Commandoes and anyone of them could take Hadley with one arm tied behind his back. We're leaving tomorrow, most likely, to sail to Tahiti. If you come with us

I'll assign two of them as your permanent bodyguard when we get there. If Hadley tried anything he'll learn something he never knew about dirty fighting, and probably end up with a broken back, or in gaol.'

I thought that having her on board would be tricky with Kane around, but she said they had never met and it was worth the risk. If I left her behind I might never have another chance to use her.

'You'll have company, by the way – female company, if you're thinking about that. The girl we were with last night – she's coming too.'

She bit her lip. 'Oh Mike, I'd be scared. Besides, I'm on contract here, though it's up in a couple of weeks. I don't want to run out on a contract. Things like that get about in my business.'

I said, 'If it's money you're worried about, we'll pay all your expenses and you'll get a bonus too. Hell, we can buy out your contract.'

'I'm not thinking of money. You're really going to find out what happened to Mark, aren't you?'

'I am,' I said definitely.

She thought for a moment, then sat back and looked determined.

'Then I'll come. Mark was the only man I've ever loved – and I think he loved me, a little. If he was killed I'd like to see his killer caught.'

'Good girl! Look, why not come over on a cruise ship – do they go from here to Tahiti? Can you find out?'

'Wait a minute – I'll see if I can find out anything.'

It was five minutes.

'There's a smallish cruise ship, the *Eastern Sun*, coming through here but not for a few weeks. It'll stop at Papeete. I can get a cabin – and I might even get a job for the trip, which would save you cash. But it's a long time off yet.'

That would suit me. I thought we would be a few days before we could really be sure of leaving, and then might be dredging or searching for several weeks around Minerva Reef, wherever that was. I got the date of the *Eastern Sun*'s arrival in Papeete and promised Paula that we would be there before her, so that she would not be alone. 'I don't want to see you out of pocket,' I went on. 'I'll pay your fare and expenses. If you get a paid job you can let me have it back. Do you have a bank?'

She told me and I said, 'I'll transfer enough to your account. I'm grateful, Paula. I'm glad to have you on our team; and you don't have to break your contract.'

'There's more to this than just Mark's death, isn't there?' she said shrewdly.

'A lot more. I'll tell you about it in Papeete, perhaps after we've found out more still.' A girl like Clare Campbell would have demanded a much greater share of knowledge before committing herself, but Paula seemed accustomed to playing subsidiary roles. As we said goodbye I wondered how in hell Mark could have attracted such widely disparate women, though they had one thing more than their sex in common. Both seemed determined and courageous, and they were both worthy of a better man than Mark in their lives.

I went back to the hotel slowly, looking at shops and enjoying the exotic street scenes around me. I lunched alone, not finding any of the others in, but presently I saw Clare and her father arriving, and soon after we were joined by Geordie carrying a book. Over cold drinks we got down to business once more.

The book Geordie had brought from the ship was a copy of Bill Robinson's *To The Great Southern Sea*.

'Here's the bit. I've looked up the *Pilot* too, but I left that on board for later. I've been rereading Robinson, knowing that we'd be sailing down this way. He sailed from the

Galapagos to Mangareva in his schooner, and here is what he has to say about Minerva. This was published in 1957, not long ago, by the way.'

He passed the book to Clare, indicating a paragraph. She started to read silently but her father said, 'For God's sake read it aloud so we'll all know what's going on.'

So Clare read to us:

'Approaching Mangareva we passed close to Minerva, one of those shoals of doubtful position and uncertain existence known as "vigias". Vigias are the bane of navigators, for one is never sure where they are, or if they are there at all. According to the Sailing Directions, which neglect to state how she got her name, there seems to be no doubt about Minerva's authenticity. A ship named the *Sir George Grey* was assumed lost there in 1865, although the British Navy failed to locate a reef there a few years later. In 1890 the German bark *Erato* saw the shoal. It was again seen breaking heavily in 1920 ten miles from the position reported by the *Erato*.

'To my great disappointment, the *maraamu* spoiled our chances of looking for Minerva. For although the wind had gone down to a fresh breeze and we arrived at the vicinity at midday, there was still a big sea running, which broke in an unruly fashion. It was impossible to distinguish breakers caused by a shoal from those left in the wake of the *maraamu*. We steered a course that took us ten miles to the north of the northernmost reported position of the errant shoal, kept a vigilant look-out, but saw nothing.'

Clare stopped reading and Campbell said, 'Well, I'm damned. Do you mean to tell me that while spacemen are whirling round in orbit and we're on the verge of going to other planets that there's a piddling little shoal like this that hasn't been located?'

'That's right,' said Geordie. 'There are lots of them.'

'It's disgusting,' said Campbell, more accustomed to precise locations on land. 'But if Mark found it we can find it.'

'If he did. I doubt it,' I said. 'If an IGY survey ship had found Minerva they'd have reported it, and they didn't. But it doesn't mean they didn't dredge around there,' I added hastily into three disappointed faces. 'You heard what Robinson said about it. You'd probably only be able to see it in a flat calm, with the tides right.'

'Robinson took damn good care to steer well clear of it,' snorted Campbell. 'Ten miles north of its reported position, indeed.'

'He was a wise man and a good seaman,' said Geordie. 'He didn't want to lose his ship. It might be a shifting shoal and if you can't see where it is it's a good idea to keep clear of it. I'll do the same, believe me.'

Once again they all looked at me – the reluctant expert.

'The conditions I'm thinking of are possible,' I said. 'We have to make a start somewhere, and it would be fun to find it, if we can. Why not?'

One more thing happened before we left Panama. Kane came to see me.

We had ostensibly treated him as just one of the crew, and he'd done his work well and was not a bad seaman. But Geordie had only agreed to take him as far as Panama and now we were waiting to see what his next step would be.

He came down to my cabin one morning and said, 'Mr Trevelyan, could I have a word?'

'Come in.' He looked fit again. Without trying to show it, I had kept clear of him on the voyage, finding it intolerably creepy to have the possible murderer of Mark underfoot, but I couldn't avoid some contacts and this was one I had almost been hoping for.

'What is it?'

'You're carrying on this research stuff, aren't you?'

'That's right. As you know, we're leaving in a day's time.'

'There was a message waiting for me here in Panama from my partner, Jim Hadley. Jim's down in New Guinea and he says he can't come up this way for a while. Now, I know you only promised to bring me as far as here, and I'm grateful, my word I am. But I wondered if I could stick with her a bit longer – you'll need a man in my berth, anyway. Maybe you'll be putting in some place that's nearer for Jim – Tahiti, maybe? That 'ud suit us both.'

I said, 'I don't see a problem. You're welcome to stay on as far as I'm concerned, if it's all right with the skipper.'

'Gee, thanks, Mr Trevelyan. I know I keep asking favours and you help out every time.'

'There's no favour. We will need a man – you work well and you earn your keep. But it's up to Mr Wilkins, mind.'

'Too right. I'll check with him. Thanks again.'

I passed the word to Geordie to accept the expected offer, and told Campbell about it. 'Right, we'll keep him under our thumb,' he said. 'Not much chance of him knowing where we're going if *we* don't know, and he can't pass the word on from out there.'

So friend Kane stayed on with us. And the next day we sailed on a voyage of uncertain duration to an unknown destination which might, or might not, exist.

FOUR

According to local knowledge the *Récife de Minerve* was nothing but a legend, and not an uncommon one at that. The *Pilot*'s preface on vigias showed that there were probably masses of them around, but certainly it said that in 1880 HMS *Alert* had searched the area in which it was said to lie, without any success. And she wasn't the only one – several ships had looked for it, some had found it – but it was never quite in the same spot twice.

We left Panama and made good time at first but in a day or so found ourselves becalmed in a sea of glass. We stuck it for twenty-four hours and then went ahead under power. Campbell didn't like clichés about painted ships on painted oceans, especially after I told him another legend concerning the ship that had floated in the Gulf of Panama for forty years until she rotted and fell apart.

Using the engines was a pity because there would be so much less fuel for station-keeping and dredging, but in Campbell's view time was as precious as fuel, and I couldn't disagree with him. I had Paula to think of. Campbell had sent a spate of cables to his ferrets, advising them that they must keep their eyes on the movements of Suarez-Navarro's ship, and once we were at sea he became nervous. I think he was unused to being cut off from the telephone. He haunted the radio, but though he needed news he half didn't want to get it, and he certainly didn't want to answer. We had a powerful radio telephone that he had insisted on installing; it was an electronic shout that could cover the Pacific. But he didn't want us to use it for fear the Suarez-Navarro would monitor the broadcasts.

News did finally come that they had dropped anchor in Port Moresby, in Papua, and, as in Darwin, were sitting tight and doing nothing. Campbell was as worried by their inactivity as he would have been if they had been constantly on the move.

We all felt better when *Esmerelda* surged forward under the impact of her engine. She forged through the placid seas at a steady nine knots to where we would catch the south-east trade wind and find perfect sailing weather. It wasn't long before we picked up a southerly wind and we headed south-west under fore-and-aft sails only, *Esmerelda* heeling until the foaming sea lapped at the lee rail. As the days went by the wind shifted easterly until the day came when we knew we were in the true trade winds. We hoisted the big square sails on the foremast and *Esmerelda* picked up her heels.

These were Kane's home waters and, while we didn't depend on him, he was free with his advice on weather conditions to be expected. 'A bit further on we'll get revolving storms,' he said. 'Not to worry – they're not very big – but my word they're fast. On you like a flash, so you've got to keep your eyes peeled.'

Campbell turned out to be a poor sailor and spent a great deal of time on his bunk regretting that ships were ever invented. It was unusual for him not to be the master of the situation, and he said he felt like a spare wheel on deck, surrounded by men who were doing all sorts of mysterious things fast and well without his guidance. He must have been hell to his mining engineers on land.

Clare, on the other hand, was a good sailor. She worked hard on deck, wearing the battered sailing gear she had promised us and a healthy tan, and was greatly appreciated by all the crew, who had found her an unexpected bonus on this leg of the voyage. She did help cook and kept watch like the rest of us, but she also absorbed the books in our small library like blotting paper, becoming especially interested in Geordie's collection of small boat voyages, many of which dealt with the Pacific.

One evening she and I talked together and I got another look at my brother, through Clare's eyes.

It was one of those incredible nights you find in the tropics. There was a waning moon and the stars sparkled like a handful of diamonds cast across the sky. The wind sang in the rigging and the water talked and chuckled to *Esmerelda*, and a white-foamed wake with patches of phosphorescence stretched astern.

I was standing in the bows when Clare joined me. She looked across the sea-path of the moon and said, 'I wish this voyage would go on forever.'

'It won't. There's a limit even to the size of the Pacific.'

'When will we get to Minerva?'

'Perhaps never – we've got to find it first. But we'll be in the vicinity in a week if the weather keeps up.'

'I hope we were right about that drawing,' she said. 'Sometimes I wish I hadn't tried interpreting them. What if we're wrong?'

'We'll just have to think of something else. Figuring out Mark's mental processes was never an easy job at the best of times.'

She smiled. 'I know.'

'How well did you know Mark?'

'Sometimes I thought I knew him pretty well,' she said. 'In the end I found I didn't know him at all.' She paused. 'Pop doesn't think much of what you've said about Mark – about his honesty, I mean. Pop thought well of him – mostly.'

I said, 'Mark had many faces. He was working for your father and he wanted something out of him so he showed his cleanest, brightest face. Your father never really knew Mark.'

'I know. Speaking figuratively and with due respect to your mother, Mark was a thorough-going bastard.'

I was startled and at the same time unsurprised. 'What happened?'

She said reflectively. 'I was a bit bitchy the other night and then you pulled me up with a jerk when you called that singer "just another of Mark's popsies". You see, I suppose I could be regarded as "just another of Mark's popsies". It was the usual thing. It must happen a thousand times a day somewhere in the world, but when it happens to you it hurts. I went overboard for Mark. I was all wrapped up in rosy dreams – he was so damned attractive.'

'When he wanted to be. He could switch the charm on and off like a light.'

'He let it happen, damn him,' she said. 'He could have stopped it at any time, but the devil let it happen. I was hearing the distant chimes of wedding bells when I discovered he was already married – maybe not happily – but married.'

I said gently, 'He was using you too, to get at your father. It's not surprising behaviour from Mark.'

'I know that now. I wish to God I'd known it then. Mark and I had a lot of fun in those days, and I thought it was going to go on forever. Do you remember –?'

'Meeting you in Vancouver? Oh yes.'

'I wondered then, why you didn't seem to get on. You seemed so cold. I thought you were the rotter, and he said things . . .'

'Never mind all that. What happened?'

She shrugged. 'Nothing – nothing at all. And I found out at about the same time that Pop was having his troubles with Suarez-Navarro, so I didn't tell him, or anyone –

though I think he guessed something. Have you noticed that he only praises Mark as a scientist, not as a person?'

'And then Mark vanished.'

'That's right. He'd gone and I never saw him again.' She looked ahead over the bows. 'And now he's dead – his body lies somewhere out there – but he's still pushing people around. We're all being pushed around by Mark, even now – do you know that? You and me, Pop and the Suarez-Navarro crowd, your friend Geordie and all your commando pals – all being manipulated by a dead man with a long arm.'

'Take it easy,' I said. She sounded terribly bitter. 'Mark's not pushing anyone. We all know what we're doing, and we're doing it because we want to. Mark is dead and that's an end to him.'

It was time to change the subject. I used the standard approach.

'Tell me about yourself, Clare. What do you do? When did your mother die?'

'When I was six.'

'Who brought you up? Your father was away a lot, wasn't he?'

She laughed. 'Oh, I've been everywhere with Pop. He brought me up.'

'That must have been some experience.'

'Oh, it was fun. I had to spend a lot of time at boarding schools, of course, but I always went to Pop during the vacations. We weren't often at home though – we were mostly away. Sometimes on a skiing holiday, sometimes to Europe or Australia or South America during the longer vacations. I was always with Pop.'

'You're well travelled.'

'It was tricky at times though. Pop has his ups and downs – he hasn't always been rich. Sometimes we had money and sometimes we didn't, but Pop always looked after me. I went to good schools, and to college. It was only last year that I found out that once, when Pop was on a crest, he'd put aside a fund for me. Even when he was busted he never touched it, no matter how much he needed money.'

'He sounds a fine man.'

'I love him,' she said simply. 'When the Suarez-Navarro mob put the knife into him it was the first time I was old enough to understand defeat. I got down to studying stenography and so on, and he made me his confidential secretary when he couldn't afford to hire one. It was the least I could do – he'd lost faith in everybody and he had to have someone around he could trust. Although I didn't feel too trusting myself just about that time.'

'He seems to have survived.'

'He's tough,' she said proudly. 'You can't keep Pop down, and you can bet that in the end Suarez-Navarro will be sorry they ever heard of him. It's happened to him before and he's always bounced back. I still work for him. I – '

'Whatever it is, say it.'

'I had you checked out in London, when you were preparing for this trip. I didn't want Pop stung again. Besides . . .'

'My name was Trevelyan?'

'Oh, I'm so sorry,' she said. 'But I had to. You checked out fine, you know.' For the first time since I'd known her she was a little shy. She went on. 'That's enough about the Campbells. What about the Trevelyans – about you?'

'What about me? I'm just a plodding scientist.'

We both laughed. Plodding certainly didn't describe this airy swooping progress, and it eased her tension.

'Most scientists seem to be looking up these days, not down.'

'Ah, space stuff,' I said.

'You don't seem very enthusiastic.'

'I'm not. I think it's a waste of money. The Americans are spending thirty billions of dollars to put man into space; in the end it could cost ten times that much. That works out at about twenty thousand dollars for every square mile of air-less lunar surface. You could get cheaper and better land on earth and if you poured that much money into the sea the returns would be even better. I think the sea is our new frontier, not space.'

She smiled at the missionary note in my voice. 'So that's why you became an oceanographer.'

'I suppose so – I was always in love with the sea.'

'And Mark? What made him one? I don't think I've ever known two brothers more different.'

I said, 'Mark was eaten up with ambition. How he got that way I don't know – I think some of it was jealousy of me, though God knows what he had to be jealous about. When my father died Mark seemed to go wild; mother couldn't control him. Since she died I've had nothing to do with him – he went his way and I mine. It hasn't always been easy having a brother like that in my line of work. People sometimes confuse us – to my detriment.'

'And his advantage.'

'Why, thank you, lady,' I said and bowed; and our relationship suddenly took a step forward.

'Trevelyan; that's Cornish, isn't it? Are you Cornish?'

'Yes. We're descended from the Phoenician and Carthaginian tin traders. Hannibal is still a popular name in Cornwall, though not in our family, thank God.'

'You're kidding.'

'No, I'm not. It's a fact.'

We had a long, relaxed and easy conversation that night, talking about everything under the sun and moon, and by the time she went back to her cabin I had a better idea about both Clare and her father. Campbell was a difficult man to assess, not very forthcoming about himself and sticking to business most of the time. This talk with Clare had given me something of his background and I felt more than ever that he was a man to be trusted.

And then there was Clare herself. I found myself wondering if she could bring herself to trust another Trevelyan, or whether Mark had soured her on Trevelyans for life. I mentally chalked up another stroke against Mark. I spent a long time thinking about Clare before I turned in.

And then I suddenly thought of what she had said about Mark – of his dead hand pushing people around like pawns on a chessboard. It was true; everything we had done or were doing stemmed from Mark and his character. It was as though Mark had been a showman and we were his puppets as his skeletal hands pulled the strings. It was a shuddery thought to go to sleep on.

II

We entered a region of small revolving storms as Kane had predicted. They ranged from mere waterspouts, ten yards across, to monsters fifty feet in diameter. These squalls provided exhilarating sailing as long as care was taken. *Esmerelda* would be foaming along beneath a brilliant blue sky when the horizon would darken and within minutes the water would be dark and wind lashed, and when the storm had gone there would be rainbows plunging into the sea and the faithful trade wind would pick up again, driving us deeper into the heart of the Pacific towards the southeast corner of French Oceania.

Sixteen days after leaving Panama Geordie figured out the midday sights and announced, 'We're nearly there. We'll enter the search area this afternoon.'

We had decided not to tell the crew too much, and so Geordie gathered them and merely said that I wanted to stooge about looking for a particular sort of water condition, but that everyone was to be on the watch for shoals. Everyone knew there wasn't much land out here and his request may have sounded strange, but they willingly organized for extra eyes on each watch, and we had a man up the foremast with binoculars a lot of the time. To my mind that was just a token that a search was in progress as I didn't think they'd spot anything, but for everyone else it perked up interest. We arranged for some dredging, to give the teams practice as we went along.

I was in the chart room early the next morning with Campbell and Geordie, going over the chart and the *Pilot*.

I said, 'The *Erato* spotted Minerva here – that was in 1890. In 1920 another ship placed Minerva here, stretching east-north-east for two miles. As Robinson points out, there's a difference of ten miles.'

Campbell said, 'It's strange that there should only have been two sightings in thirty years.'

'Not so strange,' said Geordie. 'These waters are pretty quiet, and they're quieter now that power has taken over from sail. There's no need for anyone to come here just for commerce.' He put his hand on the chart. 'There are several possibilities. One of these sightings was right and the other wrong – take your pick of which was which. Or they were both wrong. Or they were both right and Minerva is a moving shoal – which happens sometimes.'

'Or they were both wrong – and Minerva is still a moving shoal,' I said dubiously.

'Or there are two shoals,' offered Campbell.

We all laughed. 'You're getting the idea,' said Geordie. He bent to the chart again. 'Now, we'll put each of these sightings into the middle of a rectangle, ten miles by twenty. That'll give us two hundred square miles to search, but it'll be sure. We'll start on the outside and work our way in.'

Campbell said, 'Let's get to the heart of the matter. Let's go right to each of these positions and see what's there.'

But Geordie decided against that. 'It depends on the weather. I'm not going anywhere near those two positions unless the sea is pretty near calm. You read what Robinson said about not being able to distinguish breakers from storm waves. We might find her too quickly and rip the bottom out of *Esmerelda*.'

'We've got the echo sounder,' I said. 'They should tell us where the water's shoaling.'

'Damn it, you're the oceanographer,' said Geordie. 'You should know that these islands are the tops of undersea mountains. There'll probably be deep water within a quarter of a mile of Minerva. And we could be sailing in twenty fathoms and a spire of coral could rip our guts out.'

'You're right, Geordie. Minerva's probably a budding atoll. Give her another million years and she'll be a proper island.'

'We can't wait a million years,' said Campbell acidly. 'All right, you're the skipper. We'll do your square search.'

So we got on with it. Geordie estimated that we'd have to pass within a mile of Minerva in order to see it. That meant we'd have to cover about 100 miles in order to search a 200 square mile area. We used the engine as sparingly as possible, confined our speed to about five knots and less, and that way a daylight search would take about two days.

The first leg of the search gave us nothing and in the evening we hove-to, knowing that it would be the devil of a job to assess our actual position the next morning because of the rate of drift in this area, and an uncertainty factor of at least one knot. Geordie pointed this out to Campbell to make him realize that this wasn't like searching a given area of land which, at least, stays put. Campbell hated it.

That evening, relaxing on deck, I was bombarded with questions by the crew as we ate our evening meal. They were all curious and I thought that this was not a satisfactory way to deal with them – they'd be more use and have more enthusiasm if they were in the know, of one piece of the story at least. And I was also curious myself as to Kane's reaction, and he happened to be among the off-watch members.

'What is all this, Mike?' Ian Lewis asked.

'Yes, what are we poking about here for?'

I glanced at Geordie, caught his eye and nodded very slightly. 'All right, chaps, we're looking for something a bit offbeat here.'

They were intent, and I knew I was right to share this with them.

'Ever hear of Minerva?' I asked.

It brought no reaction but murmurings and headshakes from all but one. Kane raised his head sharply. '*Récife de Minerve*!' he said in a barbarous French accent. Everyone turned to look at him now. 'Are you looking for that? My word, I wish us all luck then.' He chuckled, enjoying his moment of superiority.

'What is it?'

I told them briefly what we were after, and its tantalising history.

'What's the idea anyhow?' Danny Williams wanted to know.

I said, 'Well, this is an oceanological expedition and chaps like me are always interested in mysteries – that's how we make our living. The waters round a newly-forming island are fascinating, you know.'

They accepted this, though I did hear Danny saying softly to his nearest companion, 'I've always thought there was something crazy about these scientific types, and this isn't making me change my mind.'

Presently everyone fell silent, if a little more alert to the night sea around them, and it was then that Kane came over to join me, dropping his voice very slightly to address me alone.

'Er – this got anything to do with your brother, Mr Trevelyan?' he asked as though idly.

I was wary. 'Why do you ask?'

'Well, he was in the same line of business, wasn't he? And he died not very far from here. Wasn't he looking for something with another bloke?'

I looked into the darkness towards the north-east where the Tuamotus lay a hundred miles on the other side of the invisible horizon. 'Yes, he died near here, but I don't think that he had anything to do with this. I'm not the boss, you know. This is Mr Campbell's party.'

Kane chuckled derisively. 'Looking for Minerva! That's like looking for a nigger in a coal-black cellar – the little man who wasn't there.' He stayed on for a bit but, getting nothing more from me, he moved away and I could hear him chuckle again in the darkness. I realized that my fists had been clenched at my sides.

Next day we were up before the sun, waiting to take a sight and hoping there would be no clouds. Taking a dawn sight is tricky and a bit uncertain, but we had to know if possible how far we had drifted during the night, or the search would be futile.

I was with Geordie, holding the stopwatch, as I told him about Kane's query. 'Becoming inquisitive, isn't he?' he commented.

'I don't know, it was a natural question.'

'I'm not sorry you told the lads, by the way. Otherwise they'd be getting edgy. If you were on board a ship that suddenly started to go in circles in the middle of the Pacific you'd like to know why, wouldn't you? But I wonder about Kane – he tied it up with Mark pretty fast.'

'He tied it up in a natural way. Damn him, he makes a good case for himself as an innocent, doesn't he?' I heard the bitterness in my voice and was glad to be distracted. 'Ah, here's the sun.'

Geordie shot the sun and then said, 'Well, let's find out where we are.' We went into the chart room and he worked out our position which he then transferred to the chart. 'We've drifted about seven miles in the night. There's a set of just over half a knot to the south-east. Right, now that we know where we are we can figure out where we're going.'

We started on the search. Geordie had the man up the foremast relieved every hour because the glare from the sea could cause eyestrain. He stationed another man in the bows with strict instructions to keep a watch dead ahead – he didn't want Minerva to find us. That might be catastrophic.

The day was a dead loss. It had its excitements as when Minerva was sighted only to turn out to be dolphins playing over the waves, to the delight of Clare and the other landsmen. Otherwise there was nothing. We hove-to again and waited out another night.

And the next day was largely a repetition. The last leg of the search took us directly over both reported positions, and we were anxious about it because the wind had veered northerly and the waves were confused, showing white caps. In the evening we held a conference in the chart room.

'What do you think?' asked Campbell. He was at his most brusque and edgy.

'We could have missed it in the last three or four hours. Those white horses didn't make things any easier.'

Campbell thumped the table. 'Then we do it again. Not all of it – the last bit.' He was very dogged about it.

Geordie looked at me. 'Tell me something; when you find Minerva what are you going to do with her?'

'Damn it, that's a silly question,' I said, then immediately had second thoughts as I saw what he was getting at.

'We're probably within five miles of Minerva right now. You said that the conditions that created our prize nodules were local, in your estimation. What exactly did you mean by "local"?'

'I won't know until I find it. It could be an area of ten square miles – or it could be fifty thousand.'

'I think you should drop your dredge around here and see what you can find. We could be right on top of your "locality".'

I felt very foolish. In the mixture of anticipation and boredom that had gone into our two-day search so far I had actually forgotten what we were really here for – and I'd made plans for action earlier in the trip. 'You're right, Geordie. We've wasted some time and it's my fault. Of course we can dredge and keep a lookout for Minerva at the same time.'

Campbell and Clare cheered up visibly. The prospect of doing something other than cruise gently back and forwards was enticing, and I wondered how long it would be before their fresh interest waned once again. I didn't have any hopes of a great find.

So I started to get the winch ready for operations. The seas were choppy and flecked with white and *Esmerelda* was lurching a bit as the dredge went over the side. As we'd done the drills before things went fairly smoothly, though I'd had to take the Campbells aside with a strong suggestion that they should not appear too eager – to the others this was to be a standard research procedure. The recording echometer was registering a little under 15,000 feet.

We dredged two sites that day and five the next. On two occasions operations were interrupted when something was sighted that looked very much like a coral reef, lying some twenty feet under the water, but on both occasions this turned out to be masses of a greenish algae floating on the surface, and we had our share of false alarms when fish shoals were seen. I was kept very busy in the lab analysing the stuff we had brought up, which often included volcanic particles amongst the other material – this pleased me as it bore out some of the theories I was turning over in my mind. We recovered many nodules but test results were poor and disappointing to the others, if not to me. I hadn't expected anything.

I showed a sheaf of papers to Campbell at breakfast, away from the crew. 'Just the stuff you might expect from round here. High manganese, low cobalt. In fact the cobalt is lower than usual – only .2 per cent.'

Geordie said, 'We've only been dredging west of where we think Minerva is – how about a stab at the eastern side?'

I agreed and he said, 'Right, we'll go there today.'

There wasn't much point in pulling the winch down and making sail for such a short trip so we motored across the few miles, starting immediately after breakfast. The sea was calm again with just the trade wind swells and no white-caps, which would make the search easier.

It was Ian Lewis's watch and he had given me a spell at the wheel. I wasn't much of a practical seaman and I wanted to learn while I could, during periods of calm weather, under the watchful eyes of Ian or Geordie.

Clare was sitting talking to me. 'Isn't this the life,' she said. 'I had flying fish for breakfast this morning. Taffy saved them for me – I think he's falling for me.'

'Your dad isn't enjoying it,' I observed.

'Poor Pop, he's so disappointed. He's like this on every new project though, Mike. As long as it's going well he's on top of the world, and when it isn't he's down in the dumps. I keep telling him he'll get ulcers.'

'Like gout, it's supposed to be the rich man's ailment. That should cheer him up,' I said. 'It's only – '

Danny Williams's voice soared up from the bows, crack-ing with excitement.

'Go left! Go left! Go to port!'

Someone else started shouting.

I spun the wheel desperately and *Esmerelda* heeled vio-lently as she came round. Hanging on, I had only time to see a jumble of white waters in the sunshine, and then to my intense relief Ian was with me, taking over at the wheel. I fell away from him, cannoning into Clare who was also off balance. Shouts and the thud of bare feet told me that the whole crew was tumbling up on deck to see what was happening. I noticed the echo sounder and in one incredible second I saw the indicator light spin round the dial. It looked as though the bottom was coming up to hit us.

Ian let *Esmerelda* continue to go about until the foaming area in the sea was well behind us, then straightened her out and the indicator light of the echo sounder spun the other way just as fast. He throttled the engine down and I took a deep breath to steady myself. Geordie came running along the deck.

'What the hell was that?' he shouted.

'I think we damn near speared ourselves on a reef – I think we've found her,' I gasped, still winded. Everyone was crowding to look astern at the jumble of white waters, but from where we were it was already impossible to see anything underneath it. 'Unless it's more fish – '

Ian said, 'No, it was a reef. I saw it – about a foot sticking out. And we shoaled bloody fast just then too.'

Campbell came up from below, looking startled and groggy. He may have been asleep. 'What's happened?'

'I think we've found Minerva.'

He looked aft and saw what we were all trying to get a better glimpse of. 'What, that?' he asked incredulously.

'Is that all?' Clare asked. Some of the crew, the non-sailors, looked equally baffled.

'What did you all expect – the Statue of Liberty?' I asked.

'We've got it, boys, wherever it is we're there!' Geordie was exultant and relieved, and more nervous for the safety of his ship than ever.

Danny Williams came aft to a little storm of back-patting. 'Good job you kept your eyes open,' I told him, and he looked very pleased.

'God, I was never so scared in my life,' he said. 'It came out of nowhere – now you see it, now you don't. I thought the bloody boat was going to ride up on it. You were pretty handy with that wheel.'

There was another murmur of assent and it was my turn to look pleased.

Geordie said to Ian, 'I want you to keep her just where she is. I'll bet that if we lay off a couple of miles we'll never find it again. Christ, it's lucky it's almost low water, it wouldn't show at all otherwise. It'll only dry out to about three feet at this rate.'

'There'll be coral clusters all round,' I said, reinforcing Geordie's warning. 'And deep water between them and the actual reef. There'll be a lagoon beyond that. An atoll is forming.'

I saw that they were all taking an interest, apart from Ian and the on-watch lookouts, so I expanded a little. 'This rock spear that was underneath us can't have been there very long, or it would have been higher – you'd have an island here. But this coral has only just started to form.'

Geordie said suspiciously, 'What do you mean by "only just"?'

'Within the last five or ten thousand years – I'll know better when I can take a closer look at it.'

'I thought you'd say that. But you're not going to look at it. Do you think we could get to the middle of that little lot?'

We all looked back towards Minerva, if Minerva it was. 'No,' I said dubiously. 'No, perhaps not.'

Campbell had a question on his lips that he was dying to ask, but not in public. Headshakes and heavy gestures indicated his desire for a private word, so I extricated myself from the still excited crew and followed him below together with Clare.

Campbell said, 'I'm sorry to interrupt the course of pure science, but how does this tie in with the nodules? Do you think we're going to be luckier now?'

I said soberly, 'That's just the trouble; I don't see how we can. Most nodules are very old, but Mark's was comparatively young. He had a theory which I'm beginning to grasp, to do with them forming very fast as a result of volcanic action. Now there's been volcanic action here all right but much too long ago for my taste. There's been time for a long slow coral growth and it doesn't quite tie in.'

'So this is another goddam false alarm,' said Campbell gloomily.

'Maybe not. I could be wrong. We can only find out by dredging.'

III

So we dredged.

As soon as he could Geordie had taken careful sightings of the reef. 'I'm going to nail this thing down once and for all,' he said. 'Then we'll cruise around it carefully and not too closely, keeping an eye on the depth, and take soundings and chart everything we can see. And then we'll decide what to do next.'

After we had satisfied him we got started. Geordie took *Esmerelda* in as close as he dared and the dredge went over the side. I could imagine it going down like a huge steel spider at the end of its line, dropping past the incredible cliffs of Minerva, plunging deeper and deeper into the abyss.

The operation was negative – there were no nodules at all.

I was unperturbed. 'I was expecting that. Let's go round and try the other side again.' So we skirted the shoal and tried again, with the same result – no nodules.

I thought that there probably had been nodules in the area, but the upthrust of our friendly reef had queered the pitch. We were all calling it Minerva by now, although Geordie and I were aware that it might be a different reef altogether – the seas hereabouts were notorious for vigias. I decided to try further out, away from the disturbance.

This time we began to find nodules again, coming in like sacks of potatoes. I was busy in the lab once more but becoming depressed. 'This is standard stuff,' I told my small audience. 'High manganese – low cobalt, just as before. And it's too deep for commercial dredging. But we'll do it thoroughly.' And day after day the dredging and the shifting of position went on, with the results of my assays continuing to be unfruitful.

Then one evening Geordie and I consulted with one another and decided to call it off. We had been out from Panama for over two weeks, nearly three, and I was anxious to carry on to Tahiti to be there before the *Eastern Sun* arrived. Geordie wasn't anxious over stores or even water – thanks to his careful planning we could stay at sea for up to six weeks if we needed to – but he felt that the activity, or lack of it, would begin to irk a crew which was after all partly made up of people to whom he'd virtually promised action and excitement. Campbell was quite ready to chuck the whole thing in – on a land search he would be more tenacious, but then he was seldom out there himself during the early exploratory days, usually only coming in at the kill, so to speak. And so we decided to call a halt to the proceedings and to turn towards Tahiti the next morning. The news was greeted with relief by everyone, the excitement of finding the reef we were searching for having palled. Campbell walked heavily across the deck towards the companionway, his shoulders stooped. I realized for the first time that he wasn't a young man.

'It's hit him hard,' I said.

'Aye,' said Geordie. 'What do we do now – after Papeete?'

'I've been thinking a lot about that. If it hadn't been for that damned diary then Minerva Reef would be the last place I'd go looking for high-cobalt nodules, but Mark's scribbling has hypnotized us.'

'We don't even know if he meant Minerva. Do you think he was on the wrong track?'

'I don't know what track he was on – that's the devil of it. I only leafed through those notebooks of his before they were stolen, and I couldn't absorb anything much in that time. But one thing did keep cropping up, and that was the question of vulcanism.'

'You mentioned that before,' said Geordie. 'Are you going to put me in the picture?'

'I think another little lecture is in order – and I'll deliver it to Campbell and Clare as well. It'll give him something else to think about. Get the three of you together in here after dinner, Geordie, and put a lad on watch, to keep Kane away. They'll be expecting a council of war anyway.'

And so later that same evening I faced my small class, with a physical map of the seabeds of the world unrolled on the chart table.

'You once asked me where manganese came from and I told you from the rivers, the rocks and from volcanic activity. And I've been doing a bit of serious thinking about the latter class. But to start with, the Pacific is full of nodules while the Atlantic hasn't many. Why?'

The professorial method, involving the class in the answers always works. 'You said it had something to do with sedimentation,' Geordie recalled.

'That's the orthodox answer. It's not entirely wrong, because if the sedimentation rate is high then the nodules stop growing – they get covered up and lose contact with the seawater – the colloidal medium. The sedimentation rate in the Atlantic is pretty high due to the Amazon and Mississippi, but I don't think that's the entire explanation. I want to show you something.'

We all bent over the map.

'One fact about the Pacific stands out a mile; it's ringed with fire.' My pencil traced a line, beginning in South

America. 'The Andes are volcanic, and so are the Rockies.'
It hovered over the North American Pacific coast. 'Here's
the San Andreas Fault, the cause of the San Francisco earthquake of 1908.' My hand moved in a great arc across the
North Pacific. 'Active volcanoes are here, in the Aleutians
and all over Japan. New Guinea is very volcanic and so are
all the islands about there; here is Rabaul, a town surrounded
by six cones – all active. There used to be five, but things
stirred up a bit in 1937 and Vulcan Island built itself up into
a major cone in twenty-four hours and with three hundred
people killed.'

I swept my hand further south. 'New Zealand – volcanoes,
geysers, hot springs – all the indications. South again to the
Antarctic and you have Mount Erebus and Mount Terror,
two bloody big volcanoes. And that completes the circle – a
round trip of the Pacific.'

I turned my attention eastward. 'The Atlantic is pretty
quiescent, volcanically speaking, except perhaps for the Ice-
landic area. There was the enormous Mount Pelée eruption
down here in the Caribbean but as you can see that's only
just off the Pacific ring – and Krakatoa is in it, over Java
way. The only place you find nodules in any quantity is on
the Blake Plateau – and the interesting thing about that is
that the Plateau is exactly where the current runs from the
Caribbean, which I've already mentioned as being volcanic.'

Geordie straightened up from the map.

'You've got a hell of a lot of places to choose from.'

'That's the problem. And there are vents in the Pacific
seabed which we don't know about – hell, we're almost on
top of one now. But I know that high-cobalt area exists and
I'll stake my reputation that we find it in a volcanic area.'

Campbell said, 'As I understand you correctly, the nodules in the Pacific, the ordinary ones which occur in the
greatest number of places, have been slowly growing
through millions of years as a result of long-ago volcanic

activity. But you think there are places where certain nodules might grow faster due to specific and recent volcanic
activity.'

'That's it – and they'll be high-cobalt, high-nickel and so
on because of the fast growth. The metals will be entrapped
while they're still around, before they're dispersed into the
general waters of the Pacific.'

'Um. That still doesn't tell us where to look.'

'I want to stick around the Western Pacific,' I said intensely. 'There are plenty of known undersea vents here,
and it's better fossicking round here than wasting our
time.' I had other reasons, of course – I wanted to begin
my investigation into my brother's death, but I was only
too well aware that in Campbell's eyes the commercial
venture was the main, perhaps the only reason for our
carrying on. He had some personal stake but not necessarily enough.

There was a lot to think about, and talk fell away.
Presently Geordie spoke up. 'All right, let's get on to
Papeete and see what we can decide on the way,' he said
with finality.

IV

We sailed for Tahiti, first heading south to skirt the
Tuamotus, and then on a direct course. Geordie didn't want
to sail through the Tuamotus unless he had to; the name, he
told us, meant 'The Dangerous Isles' and they were every
bit as dangerous as the name implied, a vast area of coral
atolls and sharp-toothed reefs, not all of them charted.

I judged we should arrive in Papeete just about the same
time as the *Eastern Sun*, if she kept to her published sched-
ule. I certainly hoped we would arrive first – I didn't relish
leaving Paula there without protection.

Campbell perked up on this leg of the voyage, gradually returning to his old aggressive self, abetted by Clare. We had talked further about the possibilities ahead of us and I had tried to persuade him that I wasn't taking him on any wild-goose chases, but in fact I had nothing much to go on myself, and was feeling very bothered by this. Clare was back to poring over Mark's diary, trying to unravel a few more mysteries. I almost hoped she wouldn't – we'd had enough trouble over the *Récife de Minerve*. She had hidden the transcript and the photostatted drawings, but had first made copies of these into her own notebook, and studied them covertly from time to time.

It was pleasant enough sailing but not as invigorating as the first part of the trip out from Panama. In spite of the decision to make a new beginning we were all a little depressed, and had all been at sea for a long time. We felt the urge to tread firm ground again.

So it was with relief that everyone heard Geordie's announcement that Tahiti was within easy reach and would be sighted at any time. We were having lunch on deck and conversation was relaxed and easy. Clare sat a little way from the rest of us, still studying those damned drawings.

'Land – dead ahead!' Taffy Morgan hailed, and we all scrambled to our feet to get our first sight of Tahiti. There was only a small smudge on the horizon and we had a long while to go before we would see any more detail. We praised Geordie's navigation and then stood lounging at the rails watching the smudge gain sharpness when Kane came over to Clare.

'You left this on deck, Miss Campbell. It could blow over the side.'

And he held out her open notebook, with many of Mark's drawings in full view. We were all very still, looking at it.

Clare said coolly, 'Thank you, Mr Kane.'

'I didn't know you could draw, Miss.'

'I can't, not very well.'

Kane grinned and flicked at the open pages. 'Doesn't look like it,' he agreed. 'That's a pretty cow, mind you, but it's a pretty scraggy-looking falcon.'

Clare managed a smile as she took the book from him. 'Yes, I'll never be an artist,' she said.

Geordie said harshly, 'Kane, have you spliced that new halliard yet?'

'Just going to, skipper, no sweat.' He walked away briskly and I let my breath out. Clare said in a soft voice, 'God, I'm sorry.'

Campbell watched Kane out of sight and made sure we were out of anyone else's hearing. 'Clare, of all the damn silly things to do.'

'I said I was sorry.'

'I don't think it matters,' I said calmly. 'It's not the actual diary – none of Mark's handwriting shows. And for all we know Kane isn't aware that the diary ever existed.'

'Somebody might,' said Clare. 'That man Ramirez, he sent people to steal Mark's things – he may have known about it.'

'If Kane is a low man on the totem pole then he wouldn't know everything. I don't think it makes a bit of difference what Kane saw. Forget it.'

Clare looked at the drawings again, and suddenly a smile displaced her air of tension. 'Now that he's mentioned the cow, I think I may have one of Mark's awful puns figured out. Don't get excited though, Pop – it's only a wild guess.'

She pointed to the cow and its companion, the squashed semi-circle.

'I've been reading things, and I read somewhere that another name for the Tuamotus is the Low Islands. That's what this flattish object is, a low island on the sea. Then he's put *OR* – and drawn the cow. It's two drawings for the same place – the Tuamotus.'

'For God's sake, why?' Campbell demanded.

'Cows go moo – they low.' And she burst out laughing. I had to join her and even her father started to smile as he saw the joke. If true, it was a good one. We put the incident with Kane out of our minds.

As *Esmerelda* drew nearer to Tahiti the sea gave place to mountains, hazy green, and then we began to see the surf breaking on the beaches as we sailed along the coast. We all turned our thoughts to cold beer ashore.

Papeete, the Pearl of the Pacific, is a pleasant town with all the usual offices – banks, a hospital, shops and so forth, but it is also a collection of tin huts set down on a tropical island and therefore a trifle squalid; but the setting is magnificent. Arriving there we tied up almost in the main street and there are not many ports in the world where you can do that. Looking over the harbour you can see the island of Moorea nine miles away, a volcano which exploded in the far past leaving a jumble of spires and peaks leaning at impossible angles, one of the most splendid sights in the world, and one which must go a long way to compensate for any inconveniences occasioned by living in Papeete.

I looked around the harbour for the *Eastern Sun* but there was no sign of her, so I tried to relax as we waited for customs clearance. Campbell was fretful, anxious to go ashore and see if there was anything for him at the post office. He was too much in the dark concerning the Suarez-Navarro expedition. I wasn't any too patient myself. I had questions to ask and I wanted to try and see the Governor. I believe in starting at the top.

At last a customs officer arrived, gave us a leisurely scrutiny and departed, leaving us free to go ashore. I had asked him when the *Eastern Sun* was due, and one of life's rare miracles occurred.

'The cruise boat, m'sieur? She come any time, I 'ave 'eard on ze radio. She is due tomorrow.'

I spoke to Geordie before everyone vanished. 'Who are the two toughest chaps you have?'

'Ian Lewis for one,' he said promptly. 'Then it's a toss-up between Taffy and Jim Taylor.'

'Whoever it is must be good at unarmed combat.'

'Then it's Ian and Jim. Taffy's the knife expert. Who do you want laid out?'

'Paula Nelson will be in tomorrow, on the *Eastern Sun*. And this place is unhealthy for her. When it comes in I want you to go and meet her, because she'll recognize you, and I want you to take the others along, collect her and bring her back here – unhurt. Anyone who tries anything is to be stepped on hard.'

He listened carefully and then nodded. I knew she'd be in good hands.

'Right. I'll leave you to your own filthy devices, Geordie. We'll want to get refitted so that we could leave almost any time, so warn the crew not to stray. Anyone who ends up in gaol stays there. I'm going to try for an interview with the Governor.'

There was a lot of mail for Campbell at the main post office. He was back even before I went ashore, clutching a sheaf of papers and disappearing below with Clare. I hoped he'd let her out some time, and it occurred to me to ask her to dine with me that night. It would be nice not to eat surrounded by the others, but nicer still with Clare along. I collected a file from my cabin and set out for Government House, and discovered it to be a rambling edifice in Late Tropical Victorian set in a large garden.

I had, as I expected to have, a royal tussle with batteries of underlings, secretaries and so forth, but I was persistent and was at long last shown to a room to await a summons for a brief meeting with the Governor. He was a tall, cadaverous man with a thin hairline moustache, sitting behind an imposing desk cluttered with papers. He did not rise but stretched his hand out to me across the table.

'M. Trevelyan, what can I do for you? Please sit down.'

I said, 'Thank you for seeing me, Monsieur – er – '

'My name is MacDonald,' he said surprisingly, and smiled as he saw my expression. 'It is always the same with you English – you cannot understand why I have a Scottish name – but you should know that one of Napoleon's Marshalls was a MacDonald.'

It appeared that this was one of his usual opening gambits with English visitors, so I said politely, 'Are you any relation?'

'My father thought so, but many Scots settled in France after the abortive revolutions in the eighteenth century. I, myself, do not think I am descended from a Marshall of France.' He became more businesslike. 'How can I help you, M. Trevelyan?' His English was fluent, with hardly a trace of accent.

I said, 'About a year ago my brother died in the Tuamotus, on one of the smaller atolls. There appears to be some mystery about his death.'

MacDonald raised his eyebrows. 'Mystery, M. Trevelyan?'

'Do you know anything about it?'

'I am afraid I have no knowledge of the death of your brother. For one thing I am new here, and am merely the Acting Governor; the Governor of French Oceania is away on leave. And also one would not recall the details of every death, every incident in so large a jurisprudence as this one.'

I wouldn't describe my brother's death, possibly his murder, as an incident myself; but no doubt the Governor would see it differently. I managed to express my disappointment without actually dismissing myself from his office, which had clearly been his wish, and he settled back to hear me out.

'We will have something on the files,' he said, and picked up a telephone. While he was speaking I opened my own file and sorted out documents.

He replaced the receiver. 'You spoke of some mystery, M. Trevelyan.'

'Mark – my brother – died on an unnamed atoll. He was treated by a Dr Schouten who lives on an island called Tanakabu.'

MacDonald pulled down his mouth. 'Did you say Dr Schouten?'

'Yes. Here is a copy of the death certificate.' I passed a photostat across the desk and he studied it.

'This seems to be quite in order.'

I said sardonically, 'Yes, it's a well filled-in form. You note that it states that my brother died of peritonitis following an operation to remove a burst appendix.'

MacDonald nodded. I was going to continue but I was interrupted by the appearance of a clerk who put a file on MacDonald's desk. He opened it and scanned the contents, pausing halfway through to raise his head and look at me thoughtfully before bending his head again.

At last he said, 'I see the British Foreign Office asked for details. Here is the letter and my superior's reply.'

'I have copies of those,' I said.

He scanned the papers again. 'All seems in order, M. Trevelyan.'

I pushed another photostat across the desk. 'This is an attested copy of a statement made by an English doctor to the effect that he removed my brother's appendix several years ago.'

It didn't take for a moment and then suddenly it sank in. MacDonald started as though I'd harpooned him and picked up the photostat quickly. He read it several times and then put it down. 'It looks as though Dr Schouten made a mistake then,' he said slowly.

'It seems so,' I agreed. 'What do you know about him?'

MacDonald spread his hands. 'I've never met him – he never comes to Tahiti, you understand. He is a Dutchman and has lived in the Islands for about twenty years, administering to the people of the Tuamotus group.'

But I remembered his wry mouth and sensed that he knew more.

'He has a problem, hasn't he? Is he an alcoholic?'

'He drinks, yes – but everyone does. I drink myself,' said MacDonald in mild rebuke. He was not going to commit himself.

'Is he a good doctor?'

'There have never been any complaints.'

I thought about Schouten, living in a remote group of islands far from the administrative centre of Papeete. Complaints about his professional capacity would have a way of dying on the vine, especially if most of his clientele were local people.

I said, 'Did Dr Schouten come to Papeete to report my brother's death?'

MacDonald consulted his file. 'No, he didn't. He waited until there was a convenient schooner and then sent a letter together with the death certificate. He would not leave his hospital for so long a journey for one death – there are many, you understand.'

'So no one saw my brother except Dr Schouten and the two men who found him – and no one has made any investigation, no one has questioned Kane or Hadley or the doctor?'

'You are wrong, M. Trevelyan. We are not standing in Hyde Park Corner in the midst of a modern civilized metropolis. The Tuamotus are many hundreds of miles away and we have but a small administrative staff – but I assure you that questions were asked. Indeed they were.'

He leaned forward and asked coldly, 'Are you aware, M. Trevelyan, that at the time of your brother's death he was suspected of murder, and a fugitive from the police?'

'I did hear that cock-and-bull story. It must have been convenient for your police department to have such a tidy closing of the case.'

He didn't like that and his eyes flickered. 'Here in French Oceania we have a peculiar problem. The islands have an enviable reputation, that of an earthly paradise. Consequently, men are drawn here from all over the world, hoping to live in ease and comfort. They think they can live by eating the fruit from the trees and by building a little thatched hut. They are wrong. The cost of living here is as high as anywhere else in the world.

'These men who come here are often, not always, the failures of civilization. Most go away when they find that the islands are not the paradise of reputation. Others stay to cause us trouble. Our work here is not to aid the degenerate sweepings, but to maintain the standard for our own people. And when an unknown white who is already in trouble dies we do not make too much fuss.'

He tapped the file. 'Especially when there is a valid death certificate, apparently in order, especially when we think he may be a murderer, and very especially when he evaded the Tahiti police and ran away to die on some atoll two hundred miles from here.'

I kept my self-control with some difficulty. 'Yes, I understand all that, but will you make an investigation now? My brother, as you will see in there, was a scientist, not a beachcomber. And you will admit that there is something wrong with the death certificate.'

MacDonald picked up the doctor's statement. 'True, a man cannot have appendicitis twice. Yes, we will certainly interview the doctor again.' He made a note on his pad. 'I will appoint an officer to interview him personally, rather than send a message to the local authorities. It will be done as soon as he next goes out to the Tuamotus.'

He leaned back and waited for my thanks.

'When will that be?' I asked.

'In about three months' time.'

'Three months!'

'Your brother is already dead, M. Trevelyan. There is nothing I can do to bring him back to life. We also are busy men; I administer an area of over a million square miles. You must realize that the government cannot come to a stop while we – '

'I am not asking you to stop the government. All I'm asking is that you investigate the death of a man!'

'It will be done,' he said levelly. 'And we will find that the doctor has made an honest mistake. Perhaps he confused two patients on the same day. That is nothing new, but it would be a pity to ruin him for one mistake. We need doctors in the islands, M. Trevelyan.'

I looked into MacDonald's eyes and realized I was up against a stone wall. Nothing would be done for three months and then the whole affair would be hushed up, covered in a web of red tape.

I wrote my lawyer's address on a piece of paper. 'I would be obliged if you would let me know the results of your investigation. You can write to that address.'

'I will let you know, M. Trevelyan. I am sure there will be a simple explanation.' He half stood up, clearly dismissing me.

I went immediately to the British Consul and got no joy. He was urbane and civil, pointing out that everything MacDonald had said was true and that the only thing to do was to wait. 'They'll investigate the matter, don't you worry, Mr Trevelyan. If old Schouten has made a mistake they'll find out.'

But he didn't sound convincing even to himself.

I said, 'What kind of man is this Schouten? I gather you know him.'

The consul shrugged. 'An old Islands type – been here for years. He's done some good work in the past.'

'But not lately?'

'Well, he's getting old and – '

'Hitting the bottle,' I said viciously.

The consul looked up sharply. 'Don't blame him too much for that. He lost his entire family when the Japs invaded New Guinea.'

I said bitterly, 'Does that excuse him for killing his patients?'

There was no reasonable answer to that, and I pulled myself together and changed the subject slightly.

'Have you heard of a man called Jim Hadley?'

'A big Australian?'

'That's the man.'

'Of course he's never been in here,' said the consul. 'We've no official connection, but I've seen him around. He's well known here as a rather hard-headed type, not a man to be crossed I'd say. Your brother chartered his schooner for a while.'

'Is he really that tough?'

He frowned. 'Very much so. Not a consular tea party type at all. I wouldn't recommend him.'

'What about a man called Kane?'

'Is that the other Australian? His partner, I think – I've seen him with Hadley. It's the same answer, I'm afraid; I've never spoken to him.'

'Tell me honestly – do you think the administration is dragging its heels in this matter?'

He sighed. 'I'll have to speak bluntly, Mr Trevelyan. When your brother died he was on the run from the police. He was suspected of murder.' As I was going to interrupt he raised his hand. 'Now, don't tell me that's ridiculous. Most murderers have brothers, like yourself, who refuse to believe anything ill of their kin, especially at first hearing.'

That wasn't what I was going to say, but I kept my mouth shut.

'When he died, complete with death certificate signed by a qualified medical man, the police called off the hunt, and quite naturally so in my opinion. At the present time the administration has a hell of a lot on its plate, and they had no reason to suspect anyone else. But they'll get around to investigating the new evidence you've brought them sooner or later.'

'When the trail is totally cold.'

'I do see your point,' he said. 'I don't think I can do anything about it. But I'll try.'

And with that I had to be content.

When I reboarded *Esmerelda* I felt blue. I think I had expected my news to come with a devastating shock, and it had been dismissed as a hiccup. Clare was on deck and she said sunnily, 'Isn't this a beautiful place?'

'It stinks,' I said sourly.

'What are you mad at? You look as though you wouldn't care if the whole island sank into the sea.'

'It's these damn colonial French. Justice – but at a snail's pace. The British here aren't much better either.'

'No dice with the Governor?'

'Oh, they'll make a new investigation in three months – or three years. He doesn't want to lose his precious Dr Schouten. If he looks too closely he might have to arrest the doctor for unprofessional conduct and he doesn't want to do that, so he's going easy on the whole thing – sweeping it under the carpet in the hope that it'll be forgotten. He's got much more important things to do than to find Mark's killer.'

She was sympathetic and I began to loosen up a little. After a while I even felt cheerful enough to ask her to dine with me, and to my delight she agreed at once. I excused myself and went in search of Geordie, whom I found tinkering with the engine in company with two of the crew. Everyone else had vanished ashore. I took Geordie aside and told him what had happened.

He wiped the oil from his hands and said, 'Then you're stymied.'

'Looks like it, as far as authoritative aid goes.'

'Now's the time to put some pressure on Campbell. You won't get anywhere without him if you want to see Schouten. It's a pity you can't interpret one of those drawings to read Tanakabu – or perhaps you can scare up some good scientific reasons for going there.'

'As well there as anywhere,' I said morosely. 'I'll work on it.'

I spent the rest of the day wandering around the town and picked out a restaurant for the evening, and when it came Clare and I took ourselves off for an enjoyable time during which we both avoided any of the subjects concerning the voyage, and got to know each other better. Campbell had booked himself and Clare into a hotel for the time we were to stay in Papeete, but I had declined his suggestion that I too make such an arrangement, so at the end of the evening I escorted Clare to her new temporary home and came back to the ship feeling weary but reasonably happy.

Early the next morning I saw the *Eastern Sun* enter harbour. Geordie disappeared with Ian and Jim, and I wandered on deck to find Danny Williams just reboarding.

'Morning, Mike,' he said. 'Just back from me detective stint.'

'What's all this?'

'The skipper arranged for some of us lads to keep an eye on Kane. Yesterday he was at the post office and suchlike, and then he holed up in a spot called Quin's Bar. I had Nick follow him today, and I've sent Bill down to hang around

Quin's again – we think it's his meeting-place. Yesterday he was asking for someone there.'

'Good enough,' I said. 'Why not yourself, though? Tired of playing copper?'

'I thought I'd better pull out. I followed Kane all over Panama and I thought that if I did the same here he might twig.'

I nodded in satisfaction. Danny was using his brains. After a while Campbell and Clare came on deck, clearly rested and ready for a fresh start, and I decided that this was as good a time as any to work on him. But he anticipated me.

'Clare's been telling me that you want to go and see this Schouten.'

I looked at Clare. I hadn't told her that but she must have been reading my mind, and I was grateful. I said, 'Under the circumstances, I thought it might be a good idea.'

Campbell frowned. 'I don't know about that.' He dug into his pocket and produced a letter. 'Suarez-Navarro are on the move again – heading towards Rabaul. They should be there by now.'

'Do you know if they're doing any dredging?'

He shook his head. 'My man doesn't say, but I don't think he could know without a flyover.'

'Do you want to follow them?'

Campbell shook his head again irritably as though shaking flies away. 'It's not what I want to do. You don't seem to know where to go next, and apparently Ramirez does. Maybe we should follow him.'

I looked up and saw a small party coming on board, Paula Nelson diminutive between Ian and Jim, Geordie shepherding her with her suitcase. 'Miss Nelson's here,' I said. 'Let's see where this leads us. If she can identify Hadley for me here we may not have to go and see Schouten.'

Campbell and Clare had been told that Paula was coming to Papeete and were both full of curiosity about her. I went over to greet Paula, who looked frankly delighted to see me, and introduced her. I cocked an eye at Ian, who grinned easily. 'No trouble,' he said. 'No one tried anything.'

'Thanks, fellows. We're glad to see you, Paula. Did you have a good trip?'

'It was wonderful! I've never been on one of those big cruise ships before. And say – I hope you don't mind but I didn't work my passage. It was kind of fun to be one of the tourists for a change.'

'That's great,' I told her. Before I had a chance to say anything more I saw Nick Dugan coming up and speaking urgently to Geordie, who then levelled a pair of binoculars at the harbour mouth. I left Paula with the Campbells and joined Geordie at the rails.

Nick said, 'There's the man who was talking to Kane in Quin's Bar.' He pointed. 'He's just gone on board a schooner – and they're getting under way.'

I took the glasses and focused them on the schooner. A big bull of a man was standing at the wheel, apparently bellowing orders to his native crew. They were getting under way very smartly and there wasn't much time to lose. I had a sudden intuition and called Paula over sharply, thrusting the glasses into her hands.

'Look at that ship and tell me if you can identify anyone.'

She had a bit of difficulty focusing at first but then she got it and gave a shuddering gasp. 'It's Jim Hadley,' she said. 'And that's his ship, the *Pearl*.'

Campbell snatched the binoculars and had a look himself.

'Where's Kane?' I asked urgently.

'Still at the bar, last time I saw him,' Nick said. 'Bill's on his tail.'

Ian Lewis had joined us and seemed eager and willing to go on an immediate chase. 'How soon can we get under way, skipper?' he asked Geordie.

'Too long, and half the crew isn't here,' said Geordie. 'But there's no need to go chasing after him – I saw that schooner in Panama. He's following us, damn his eyes.'

I said, 'So Kane lied again in Panama. I wonder what he'll say this time?'

'He'll say that his chum Hadley is nowhere around and he'll ask if he can stay with the *Esmerelda* a bit longer,' Geordie guessed.

Ian looked at him and nodded thoughtfully. 'Skipper, I think it's time we all knew what was going on,' he said gently. 'Who is yon lad, anyway?'

Geordie and I exchanged glances. It was indeed high time.

He said, 'Ian, gather the lads together – just our bunch, that is, not my regular crew. We'll put you all in the picture sometime later today – somewhere ashore I think. I'll be happier with you lot in the know, anyway.'

'Come to my hotel,' said Campbell, taking over as he liked to do. 'I'll arrange for a room big enough for all of us, and we'll pool information. You too, Miss Nelson. I want a word with you, Mike.'

He led me aside.

'I feel as though we're losing out on this thing. I thought we could use Kane to feed Ramirez phoney information, but it's not working out that way. Kane is reporting our every movement, and we're learning nothing.'

I laughed. 'I bet his report puzzles Ramirez. He'd have a hell of a job trying to find the last place we dredged.'

Campbell watched the schooner *Pearl* going out through the pass in the reef. 'What do we do now?'

'We can't go after Hadley; we don't know where he's going and he has too big a start for us to follow. Besides these are his home waters; he could easily give us the slip. If we do anything through government channels we get wrapped in red tape. That leaves Schouten . . .'

'I thought you'd say that. But Ramirez is in Rabaul. What's he *doing* there?'

'Waiting to follow us, at a guess; when he thinks we've hit pay dirt. I'm sure Suarez-Navarro don't know any more than we do, or they'd be there. But this all started with Mark's death and Schouten was present. I think we should talk to him, if only to clear up some unanswered questions.'

He nodded. 'Clare had that idea too. She came up with the idea that perhaps all of Mark's gear wasn't returned to England – that Schouten might have some stuff stashed away. How about that?'

'I'd have to ask Paula – she might know something.'

Campbell drummed with his fingers on the mast tabernacle. 'I tell you – I'm split in two on this thing. After all, we did pull a boo-boo at Minerva, and that was a month wasted. We'll spend nearly a fortnight back-tracking to go and see Schouten and that fortnight might be precious. And God knows what Ramirez will be doing.'

He fell silent and I let him ruminate for a few minutes.

'I suppose we may find something that'll short-circuit the whole damned affair. All right, it's worth the risk. We'll go. But if we get no answers there I'm calling the whole thing off.'

I was too delighted with his decision to worry about the threat. I could take care of that later, if necessary. We went over to rejoin the two girls, who had been chatting together with Geordie.

'We're going to Tanakabu,' I told them briefly and Geordie looked very pleased, while Clare cheered softly. Paula, of course, only looked puzzled.

'Paula,' I asked, 'do you know if the stuff of Mark's that you sent home was everything of his – could he have had more elsewhere?'

'I really don't know for sure, Mike. But I don't think so. He never had much stuff while he was with me.'

I had an idea. 'Paula, you're going to join in the brief-ing this afternoon, which I'm sure you've realized is going to be very confidential. After all, you have a lot to con-tribute. But we may be going off soon after that and as I've brought you here I can't just leave you. You're my responsibility now, you know. Would you like to come along with us?'

I watched them all for their reactions. Campbell had already put on an avuncular act towards her and looked smug, as if it was his idea. Geordie merely looked resigned – now he had two women on board, and even less space to spare. Clare was the problem, but I saw that while she was being rather formal with Paula she wasn't showing any overt hostility, and she appeared to take my suggestion calmly enough, even adding a civil rider of her own.

'Why not? It would be nice for me too, I think.'

Paula looked dumbfounded. Her big dark eyes swept all of us and came back to me, and I could see that she was almost unable to conceive of the notion.

'Think about it. Have you sailed before?'

'Yes, a little. Just locally hereabouts. I was on the *Pearl* once, with – with a friend.'

'You can buy what you need here. It's not too rough, we eat well and you won't have to sleep in a hammock,' I said encouragingly. I also felt that she was probably the only one of us who had faith that Mark wasn't an utter bastard. It would be good to have someone along who was completely on his side.

'What do we do about Kane?' Geordie asked.

'Keep him on ice – we take him with us, if he asks to go. Which he will. Then after I've talked to Schouten we ask him some pointed questions. Until then you just watch him, Geordie.'

'That'll be easy,' Geordie said. 'It's not too big a boat, you know.'

FIVE

We sailed the next day for the Tuamotus, after announcing that we were heading for Indonesia in slow stages. This was not only for the benefit of Kane, who had reacted as predicted by asking to come along on our next leg, but lest MacDonald get wind through the harbour officials that I was going to interview his precious Dr Schouten – he might have objected.

We sailed through the pass in the reef and out into the open sea, continuing west until we were out of sight of land. Then Geordie gave the order to change course northwards. Kane happened to be on the wheel and accepted the order without comment, but a couple of hours later when relieved and with the new helmsman setting a course easterly, he said to me, 'We're going the wrong way for New Britain, Mr Trevelyan.'

'Who said we were going to New Britain?' He had slipped up; New Britain specifically had never been mentioned in his hearing, but I knew he was probably thinking of Ramirez.

He covered it up well. 'Oh, I thought you'd drop anchor in Rabaul for refuelling. It's a prime spot for it,' he said easily.

'The boss has some unfinished business here,' I said briefly, and he left it at that, although I could see he was thinking hard.

I couldn't help goading him. 'I thought your pal Hadley was going to be waiting in Papeete.'

'Yair, he's a fine cobber now, isn't he? But he left a message for me – said he couldn't wait. Anyway, I don't mind giving you a hand,' he said with an air of largesse.

Kane certainly had a nerve – now he was helping us!

Geordie was careful in going through the Tuamotus, careful to the point of keeping Kane off the wheel. We still didn't know what his game was, but we didn't feel like being run ashore deliberately. Geordie kept a sharp eye on the charts and picked a way through the thousand and one islands in the archipelago, always heading for Tanakabu, away on the further side.

Clare liked the Tuamotus. 'It's just like a movie,' she said happily as she viewed an atoll on the horizon. 'Couldn't we go in closer, and have a look?'

I took her elbow. 'Come here. I'd like to show you something.' In the chart room I pointed out our position. 'Here's that atoll – you see the marks here, extending out about three miles from the island. Do you know what they are?'

'Oh God, yes of course. Coral reefs round every one,' she said.

'Nasty and sharp,' I agreed. 'I'm as near to that atoll now as I'd like to be. We only touch on the ones with mapped entrances, otherwise it's all local knowledge hereabouts.' And I thought of Hadley, somewhere out there in *Pearl*. Was he following us?

'I hope we're not making a mistake,' Clare said soberly, catching my mood. 'We must find out something useful. Pop was mad enough over the fiasco at Minerva.'

'We may not find out anything concerning manganese nodules, but I hope we'll find out something about Mark. And one thing may lead to another.' I changed the subject. 'How are you getting on with Paula?'

Clare was silent for a moment, then said, 'I thought I wouldn't like her – you know, two of Mark's popsies should be wanting to scratch each other's eyes out.'

'Don't throw that in my teeth again.'

'I find I do like her, though. I've discovered that I never was in love with Mark, it was infatuation, and when I found out what a lousy creep he could be it all died. That isn't love. Paula knew what he was and it made no difference to her – she still loved him in spite of it. That takes real love – I never had it. We're not rivals any more.'

That was a relief. Two women at dagger's point can cause a hell of a lot of trouble, and especially in a small ship.

As for Paula, she was relaxed and enjoying herself thoroughly. Easily at home among the men and for once away from both danger and professional competition, she had become yet another of *Esmerelda*'s growing assets as far as the crew went. Occasionally she sang for us in the evenings and took pleasure in her small touch of limelight. Campbell seemed to have adopted her as an unusual, but welcome, honorary niece.

When we left the main clutter of islands Geordie was able to set a course for Tanakabu without worrying overmuch about grounding. Kane was aware of this manoeuvre and again spoke to me about it. 'Where are we heading for, more research grounds?' he asked me.

I said, 'Maybe the boss wants another look at Minerva.'

He looked up at the sun. 'Making a bit too much northing for that, ain't we?'

'Or maybe he wants to have a look at Tanakabu?' I suggested, twisting the knife. It was dangerous but he'd find out soon enough.

Kane's eyes shifted. 'Has this anything to do with your brother?'

I raised my eyebrows. 'Why should it?'

'Well, old Schouten lives on Tanakabu.'

'Does he?'

'Yair, but I suppose the old bloke's dead by now. He was hitting the bottle pretty hard when I saw him. A proper old rum-dum, he was.'

I said, 'He's still alive, as far as I know.' I was tempted to play him further but fought it down.

Kane didn't say anything more, but withdrew thoughtfully, and a few minutes later I saw him heading below apparently for some more private cogitation in his cabin, which he shared with two others who were both presently on deck.

We made good time although now we were beating close-hauled against the trade wind and on the evening of the third day we were closing Tanakabu. The sun was dipping into the sea as Geordie scanned the reef with binoculars and then referred to the chart. 'We'll go in under power. The pass is a bit too narrow for comfort under sail. Stand by to hand the sails, Ian.'

He was still looking hard at the sea-pounded reef when Shorty Powell, his radio man, came up. 'I picked up a funny transmission, skipper,' he said, then glanced at me. Geordie said, 'It's okay, carry on. What was funny about it?'

'It mentioned us.'

I pricked up my ears and Geordie swung round. 'Mentioned us by name?'

'The name of the ship,' said Shorty. '*Esmerelda.*'

I said, 'What did they say about us?'

Shorty grimaced painfully. 'That's it, I don't know. I was spinning the dial and caught it in passing, and by the time I'd got back to where I thought it was the transmission had stopped. I just caught a few words – " . . . on board *Esmerelda*. She's . . ." I tell you one thing, though. I'd lay ten to one it was an Australian talking.'

Geordie said, 'I think we'd better get Mr Campbell in on this.'

So we called him up and poor Shorty got the grilling of his life. At last Campbell said, 'Well, how far away do you think it was?'

Shorty shrugged. 'You can't tell that, not unless you've got two directional fixes on the station. But when you spend half your life listening out you get a kind of instinct. I'd say it was one of two things – a hell of a high-powered station a long way off – or a low-powered station damn close.'

'Well, man, which was it?' demanded Campbell impatiently.

'I'd say it was a low-power station close by – but don't ask me to prove it.'

'All right, thanks, Shorty. Stay around that frequency. Maybe you can pick up something else,' said Geordie.

As Shorty left and Geordie turned to his navigation again Campbell said to me, 'What do you make of that?'

'I don't make anything of it. There's not enough to go on – just that some Australian mentioned the *Esmerelda*.'

'It must have been Hadley,' said Campbell positively. 'I'd give my back teeth to know who he was talking to – someone on land there.'

We abandoned speculation as by then we were going in through the pass. It was getting dark and Geordie was on edge. The pass was narrow and there was a dog-leg bend in it and the darkness coupled with the four-knot current made the passage very tricky. But we got through into the lagoon and dropped anchor offshore opposite the lights of a large village. A small fleet of canoes came out to meet us and soon a number of Polynesians were climbing on deck.

I had decided not to wait until morning, but to act right away. It was only early evening, perhaps the best time to see a busy doctor, and there was the fear of being followed to spur me to action. I raised my voice. 'Where can I find the doctor – Dr Schouten?' I asked.

There was an increased babble and a stocky thickset man with an engaging grin pushed his way to the front. 'These boys don' spik English,' he said. 'They spik Française. I spik English. I bin to Hawaii.'

I said, 'My name is Mike – what's yours?'

'I are Piro.'

'All right, Piro. Where do I find the doctor?'

'Oh, Schouten?' Piro waved his hand. 'He round the other side water. He in – *hôpital*. Y'un'erstan' *hôpital*?'

'He's at the hospital, over there?'

'That right.'

'How can I get there?'

'You come wit' me – I take you in jeep.'

I looked into the darkness. 'How far is it?'

Piro shrugged. 'Not far. Twenny minute maybe.'

'Will you take me now?'

'Sure. You come now.' He was suddenly cautious. 'You pay me?'

'Yes, I'll pay you.' I turned to Campbell among the jostling crowd on deck and said, 'I may as well see Schouten tonight. Tell Geordie to keep a close eye on Kane – don't let him get away. He might try.'

He said, 'I'll come with you.'

'No, I think not. But I will take an escort – Jim Taylor, I think.' I said this because he was the handiest, and grabbing him by an arm I pulled him towards me and briefly told him our errand. He smiled and nodded, and went off to find Geordie and tell him.

Campbell looked closely at me, then gripped my arm. 'Take it easy, son. Don't go off at half-cock.'

'I won't,' I promised. 'But by God I'll get to the truth.'

We went over the side and dropped into Piro's canoe, a leaky and unstable craft. Once ashore, Piro introduced us to his proudest possession – his jeep. It was a relic of the wave of war which had washed over the Pacific – and it looked it.

Most of the bodywork was stripped and the engine was
naked and unashamed, very like the naked toddlers who
squalled and chattered, their eyes big at the sight of the
strangers revealed in the flare of torches. We climbed in and
I sat on a hard wooden box, innocent of upholstery, as Piro
started the engine. It banged and spluttered, but caught, and
Piro threw in the gears with a jerk and we were off, bouncing along the beach and swerving round a clump of palms
dimly illuminated by the feeble headlight. It was very noisy.
The sudden change from being at sea in *Esmerelda* was
unnerving.

Piro was very proud of his jeep. 'Best car on Tanakabu,'
he announced cheerfully as we winced at the racket.

'Has Dr Schouten got a car?'

'Ho, no! Doctor got not'ing – jus' stomick med'cine.'

We drove past the dark bulk of a copra warehouse and
then we were on a narrow track through a palm plantation
and Piro waved at it. 'These trees mine. All us got trees.'

'Has the doctor got trees?'

'Lil one lot, not'ing much. He too busy wit' med'cine and
knife.'

We swerved inland and I lost sight of the sea, which
seemed impossible on such a small island, but I could still
hear the unceasing roar of the surf on the beaches, in
between the car noises. After a few minutes we came back
onto a beach and Piro pointed ahead. 'There is *hôpital*.'

In the distance was a large cluster of lights – much bigger
than the village we had left. I said, 'That's a big hospital for
a small island, Piro.'

'Ho, plenny boys come from other islands – ver' sick.
Plenny *wahines* too. Many lepers there, an' boys wit' swells.'

A leper colony! I felt a shiver of atavistic horror. I knew
intellectually that leprosy isn't particularly infectious, but of
all diseases it is the most abhorred and I didn't feel like driving into a colony.

Piro didn't seem worried though, and drove blithely off the beach right into the hospital grounds, pulling up in front of a long low-roofed shack. 'Schouten is there,' he said. 'You wan' I should wait?'

'Yes, you can wait,' I answered. 'I won't be long. Jim, don't come in with me, if you don't mind – but be ready if I call you.'

'Sure thing, Mike.' Jim leaned back and offered Piro a cigarette.

I walked up the two steps on to a long verandah and knocked on the door. A voice said, '*Ici! Ici!*' and I walked along the verandah to a room at the far end. It was an office, the door open, and a big man was seated at a desk, writing by the light of a Coleman lamp. There was a half-empty brandy bottle and a full glass at his elbow.

I said, 'Dr Schouten?'

He looked up. '*Oui*?'

'I'm sorry. I have very little French. Do you speak English?'

He smiled and it transformed his ravaged face. '*Ja*, I speak English,' he said and stood up. In his prime, he must have tipped the scales at two hundred and twenty pounds of bone and muscle, but now he was flabby and soft and his paunch had taken over. His face was seamed and lined and he had two deep clefts from the nose to the corners of his mouth, forming soft dewlaps which shook on his cheeks.

He offered me his hand and said. 'It's not often we get strangers on Tanakabu – at least not at this end of the island.' His accent was heavily Dutch but his English was as fluent as the Governor's.

I said, 'We just came in.'

'I know. I saw the lights of your ship as you came through the pass, and then I heard Piro's jeep coming.' He waved towards the window. 'That is why you see no patients about – sometimes they shock casual visitors, so on those occasions I keep them out of sight.'

He opened a cupboard. 'Will you have a drink?'

I said, 'My name is Trevelyan.'

Schouten dropped the glass he had taken from the cupboard and it smashed on the floor. He turned his head sharply and looked at me over his shoulder. I saw that his face had turned a sickly yellow under the tan and his eyes were furtive and haunted.

'Trevelyan?' he mumbled. He seemed to have difficulty speaking.

'Yes.'

He turned round. 'Praise be to God,' he said. 'I thought you were dead.'

I looked at him in surprise. 'Dead! Why should I be dead?'

He sat at the desk, his hands clutching the edge. 'But they said you were dead,' he said softly. His eyes were brooding and seemed to be looking at something else – something terrible.

Then I caught on – he thought I was Mark! I said, 'Who said I was dead?'

'I wrote out the death certificate – here at this desk. Mark Trevelyan was the name. You died of peritonitis.' He looked up at me and there was fear in his eyes.

I said gently, 'I'm Michael Trevelyan – Mark was my brother.'

He gave a long shuddering sigh, then his gaze dropped to the glass on his desk and he picked it up and drained it in one swallow.

I said, 'Perhaps you'd better tell me about it.' He gave no answer, merely hunching his shoulders and avoiding my eyes. 'You've said too much – and too little,' I pursued. 'You must tell me what happened to Mark.'

He was an old man, rotten with loneliness and drink and the sight of people's bodies falling apart and he couldn't withstand a mental hammering. There was a stubbornness in him but also a softness at the core, and I was brutal in my approach.

'My brother didn't have appendicitis – that was an impossibility. But you forged a death certificate. Why?'

He hunched over the desk, his arms before him with the fists clenched and remained silent.

'My God, what kind of a doctor are you?' I said. 'Your medical association isn't going to like this – you're going to be struck off, Schouten. Or maybe you'll be hanged – or guillotined. A man is dead, Schouten, and you're an accessory. The best thing that is going to happen to you is a gaol sentence.'

He shook his head slowly, then closed his eyes as though in pain.

'You're an old man before your time even now, and ten years in gaol won't improve you. They'll take away your brandy and you'll scream for it. Now, what happened to Mark?'

He opened his eyes and looked at me bleakly. 'I can't tell you.'

'Can't – or won't?'

The muscles of his mouth tightened and he remained stubbornly silent.

'All right,' I said. 'You're coming with us – we're going back to Papeete and you'll tell your story to the Governor. I'm putting you under civilian arrest, Schouten. I don't know if that has any validity under French law but I'll chance it. I'll give you ten minutes to collect whatever you want to take with you.'

Something happened inside Schouten and I knew I was getting to him. He jerked up his head and stared at me. 'But I can't leave the hospital,' he said. 'What will happen to the people here?'

I pushed hard. 'What will happen to this hospital when you're in gaol? Or even dead? Come on – get your things together.'

He pushed back his chair abruptly and stood up. 'You don't understand. I *can't* leave these people – some of them would die. I'm the only doctor here.'

I looked at him without pity. I had a cruel advantage and I had to use it – there was nothing else I could do. 'You should have thought of that before you killed my brother,' I said.

His muscles tensed and for a moment I thought he was going to jump me. I said sharply, 'You may be big, Schouten, but you're old and soft! I'm tougher than you and you know it, so stay clear of me or I'll whale the daylights out of you. I'm sorely tempted.'

His mouth twitched and he almost smiled. 'I wasn't going to attack you, Mr Trevelyan. I'm a peaceful man. I don't believe in violence – and I didn't kill your brother.' ·

'Then for Christ's sake, what's the matter with you? Why won't you tell me what happened?'

He sat down again and buried his face in his hands. When he raised his head I saw that his cheeks were streaked with tears. He said with difficulty, 'I cannot leave the hospital, but you must guarantee its safety, Mr Trevelyan. You see, they said – they said they'd burn the hospital.'

'Burn the hospital! Who said that?'

'What could I do? I couldn't let them burn it, could I?' What I saw in his eyes made me begin to pity him.

I said gently, 'No, you couldn't do that.'

'What would happen to my people then? I had fifty patients – what would have happened to them?'

I took the bottle and poured some brandy into a glass. 'Here,' I said, 'drink this.'

He took the glass and looked at it, then set it down on the desk. 'No. It's past time for that.' His voice was stronger. 'I couldn't help it. They made me do it – I had no choice. It was covering up a crime or losing the hospital.' He threw his arms out. 'I thought the people out there were more important than bringing a murderer to justice. Was I right?'

'What happened to Mark?' I said in an even voice.

His eyes went cold. 'You must promise protection for the hospital,' he insisted.

'Nothing will happen to the hospital. What happened to my brother?'

'He was murdered,' said Schouten. 'On a schooner out in the lagoon.'

I let out my breath in a long sigh. Now it was in the open. All the shadowy suspicions had crystallized into this one moment, and all I felt was a great pity for this wreck of a man sitting at the desk.

I said slowly, 'Tell me what happened.'

So Schouten told me. He had more colour in his face now, and his voice was stronger. His account was factual and he made no excuses for himself; he admitted he had done wrong, but all his thoughts were for his patients. It was a sad and cruel story.

'The schooner came through the pass early last year. She was a stranger, like yourselves – the only ships that put in to Tanakabu are the copra boats and it wasn't the right time for them. She entered the lagoon and dropped anchor just opposite the hospital – out there.' He nodded towards the sea.

'Two men came ashore. One was about your size, very thin. The other was a big man – as big as me. They said there had been an accident and a man was dead. They wanted a death certificate. I took my bag from the corner there and said I'd come aboard, but the big man said no, it wasn't necessary, the man was already dead, anyone could see that, and all they wanted was a bit of paper to say so.'

Schouten smiled slightly. 'I laughed at them and said what they wanted was impossible – that the body must be seen by a doctor. Then the big man hit me.' He fingered the side of his cheek and said apologetically, 'I couldn't do anything – I'm not young any more.'

'I understand,' I said. 'Tell me, were their names mentioned?'

'The big man was called Jim, the other man called him that. His name I don't remember. There was another name said, but I forget.'

'All right. What happened then?'

'I was astonished. I couldn't understand why the man had hit me. I got up and he hit me again. Then he pulled me up and sat me in this chair and told me to write a death certificate.'

My lips tightened. It was only too probable that the big man was Hadley and the other was Kane. I'd have a reckoning with Kane when I got back to the *Esmerelda*.

'I wouldn't do it,' said Schouten. 'I asked why I couldn't see the body and the other man laughed and said it was in a mess and it would turn the stomach even of a doctor. Then I knew there was something very bad going on. I think they had killed someone, and it was someone who could not just disappear – there had to be a death certificate.'

I nodded. 'What happened then?'

'The big man hit me again and kept on hitting me until the other made him stop. He said that was not the way to do it. Then he turned on me and wiped the blood from my face very gently, and while the big man sat drinking he talked to me.'

'What did he talk about?'

'The hospital. He said he thought it was a good hospital and that it was doing good work in the islands. He asked how many patients I had, and I told him – about fifty. He asked if I was curing them and I said yes, some of them, but others were incurable. I just looked after them. Then he asked what would happen if there were no hospital on Tanakabu, and I said it would be a very bad thing – many people would die.'

Schouten caught my hand and said appealingly, 'I told him all this – I told him freely. I didn't know what he wanted.'

'Go on,' I said tightly.

'The big man started to laugh and then he hit me once again. He said, "That's so you'll take notice of what I'm saying. You sign that certificate or we'll burn the whole bloody hospital."'

He dropped his head into his hands. 'What could I do?' he said in a muffled voice.

I was angry, more angry than I've ever been in my life before. If Kane and Hadley had been in that room then I'd have killed them without mercy.

Schouten said brokenly, 'He said that he didn't care if he burned the patients either – it was all one to him.' His eyes looked at me in slow horror. 'He kept lighting matches as he talked to me.'

'So you signed the death certificate.'

'*Ja*. I made it out as they wanted, then I signed it. Then the big man hit me again and the other man said, "If you breathe a word about this we'll know it and we'll come back, and you know what will happen to this collection of grass shacks you call a hospital." Then the big man set fire to the thatch over there and while I tried to beat it out they left. They were both laughing.'

I looked over to where there was a patch of new thatching.

'What nationality were these men?'

'I lived in New Guinea once – that is an Australian mandate and I've met many Australians. These men were Australians.'

'Did you see them again?'

Schouten nodded sombrely. 'The big man – yes. He keeps coming back. He says he is keeping an eye on me. He comes and drinks my brandy and lights matches. He has been back – three times.'

'When was the last time?'

'About a month ago.'

That would be Hadley – not a nice character from the sound of him. There were plenty like him as concentration camp guards in Hitler's Germany but the type is to be found among all nationalities. They weren't a very good advertisement for Australia.

Schouten said, 'I didn't dare tell the police. I was frightened for the hospital.'

I ran over his terrible story in my mind. 'You don't remember the other name you heard?'

He shook his head. 'Not yet, but I think it was the third man on the boat – he was not a local crewman.'

'What other man?'

'He didn't come ashore but I saw him on the deck of the schooner – a very tall, thin man with a hooked nose, very dark. I saw him only once, when the boat was coming in.'

I thought about that but it didn't ring any bells. I said, 'I'm sorry it happened, Dr Schouten. But you realize you will have to tell the authorities now.'

He nodded heavily. 'I realize it now. But I was so afraid for my patients. This is an isolated atoll – there are no police here, no one to guard against violent men. I am still afraid.' He looked me in the eye. 'What is to prevent these men, or others like them, from coming back?'

I said harshly, 'I know who these men are. They won't trouble you again.'

He hesitated and then said, 'So. I will write a letter which you can take to Papeete. You understand, I cannot leave the hospital.'

'I understand.' This would make MacDonald sit up and take notice. I would be very pleased to deliver Schouten's letter in person.

'Will you send people to guard us right away? You have promised no harm will come to us here.'

I thought that we could leave some of the lads with him while we went back, or even send a radio message for assistance before we left. Hadley would follow us back to Papeete, if he was indeed on our trail, and a couple of Geordie's stalwarts would be more than a match for him if he landed after we'd left.

Schouten said, 'The letter will not take long, but you must make yourself comfortable while I write. You would not drink with me before – will you drink now?'

I said, 'I'd be honoured, doctor.'

He went to the cupboard and got another glass, stirring the broken pieces on the floor as he did so. 'You gave me a shock,' he said ruefully. 'I thought the dead had come to life.'

He poured a stiff drink and handed it to me. 'I am deeply sorry about your brother, Mr Trevelyan. You must believe that.'

'I believe you, doctor. I'm sorry for the rough time I gave you.'

He grimaced. 'It wasn't as rough as the time the big man gave me.'

No, it wasn't, I thought, but we'd both operated on the same raw nerve – Schouten's fears for his patients and his hospital. I felt ashamed of myself. I finished the drink quickly and watched Schouten scratching with his pen. I could see it was going to take a while, so I said, 'When will you finish?'

'To tell it in detail will take a long time. Also I do not write English so well as I speak it,' said Schouten. 'If you wait, you will have dinner, of course.'

'No. I'll go back to my ship and make arrangements to leave someone here with you, when we go back to Papeete. I'll come back later tonight or early in the morning.'

Schouten inclined his head. 'As you wish. I will be glad of a guard.' He resumed his writing and I got up to go, and then just as I got to the door, he said, 'One moment, Mr Trevelyan. Something has just come back to me.'

I waited by the door and he rose from his desk. 'You were asking about the name – the one they mentioned. The big man spoke it and the other made him be quiet.'

'What was it?'

Schouten escorted me on to the verandah. As Piro saw us he started the engine of his jeep. Schouten said, 'It was a strange name – it sounded Spanish. It was Ramirez.'

II

We had gone a mile when the jeep broke down. The roar of the engine faded and we bumped to a halt. Piro hopped out, bent over the engine and struck a match. 'She dead,' he said in an unworried voice.

I was impatient to get back to *Esmerelda*. I wanted to beat Kane into a pulp. I know that no man stays angry forever – you can't live on that plane – and I was nursing my anger because I wanted to let it rip. I intended to hammer Kane to a jelly. Jim Taylor had sensed my tension and had wisely refrained from asking me any questions.

Piro struck another match and poked experimentally into the entrails of the jeep. Then he looked up and said cheerfully, 'She no go.'

'What's the matter?'

'No *essence*.'

I said, 'Damn it, why didn't you fill it up? Why didn't you look at the gauge – this thing here?'

'She broke.'

'All right, we'll walk – we just have to follow the beach.'

Piro said, 'No walk. Canoe along here. We walk on water.'

We followed him a couple of hundred yards up the beach to where the road turned inland and he strode to the water's edge. 'Here is canoe, sir – I take you back.'

It was only a couple of miles but it seemed longer in the darkness. We very soon saw the riding lights of *Esmerelda* in the clear air but it took an age to get within hailing distance. Some of the other canoes were still alongside and there was an air of festival on deck, with crew and locals apparently sharing their evening meal. Campbell, Clare and Paula were waiting at the rail as I climbed on board and they saw at once that I was in no happy mood. I said to Campbell in a low voice, 'Where's Kane?' I couldn't see him in my first sweeping survey of the deck.

'Geordie's been watching him. He's given him a job below. What happened, man?'

I said, 'That bastard – and Hadley – killed Mark.'

Paula drew in her breath with a hiss. Campbell said, 'Are you sure?'

'It may not hold in a court of law but I'm sure.' I was remembering the tears on Schouten's cheeks. 'I want to have a talk with Kane – now!'

'He doesn't look like a murderer.'

'Which one does?' I said bitterly. 'I've heard a filthy story. Ramirez was involved too.'

Campbell started. 'How do you reckon that?'

'Can you describe him?'

'Sure. He's a tall, thin guy with a beak like an eagle. He's got a hell of a scar on the left side of his face.'

'That does it. He was there when Mark was killed. Schouten saw him and described him, all but the scar, and Hadley mentioned his name. He's tied up in it all right, right up to his goddam neck – which I hope to break. But first I want Kane.'

Campbell turned to Clare and Paula. 'Go to your cabins, girls.'

Paula turned obediently but Clare argued. 'But Pop, I — '

There was a whipcrack in Campbell's voice. 'Go *to your cabin*!'

She went without another murmur and he turned to me.

'Clear this lot off,' I said. 'Tell Ian. Let's find Kane.'

I went down into the forecastle but Kane wasn't there, nor was he on deck. We roped in the crew and they set out to search the ship but there was no sign of him. My jaw was aching from holding it clenched for so long.

'He's skipped,' said Ian.

'Geordie – where's Geordie?' I said.

But Geordie had vanished too.

I ran up on deck to find that several of the locals were still hanging around. I shouted for Piro and he emerged from the pack.

'Can you help us find two men on the island? Can you search?'

'What men?'

'The captain and one of the crew. The captain is the big man you saw when we came. The other one is thin, tall. Stay away from him – he's dangerous.'

Piro rubbed the top of his head. 'Dan-ger-ous?'

'He's bad. He might fight – might kill you.'

Piro shrugged. 'You pay – we find.'

He dropped into his canoe with two or three of our men, and Ian was already directing the clearing of our inboard launch which was being swung over the side. Piro was shouting instructions in his own language to the suddenly galvanized locals. Campbell came up from below. 'Got a gun?' he asked me.

'I won't need a gun. I'll tear that bastard apart.'

'Come here,' he said and took me under a light. He opened his hand and I saw a round of ammunition in his palm. 'I found that on the floor by his bunk – a .38 slug. Kane must have dropped it in his hurry and that means he's armed.'

'Christ, we must stop these natives making a search,' I said. 'We don't want any deaths.'

I turned to race on deck but he held my arm, pushing something heavy into my hand. 'Here's a gun,' he said. 'Can you shoot?'

I hung onto it tightly. 'I'll soon find out, won't I?' I stuffed it into the pocket of the light anorak I was wearing. 'You'd better stay here.'

'Son,' said Campbell, 'I'm not as old as that – not yet.'

I looked into his frosty eyes and said, 'We'd better make it snappy, then.' We ran up on deck and I dropped into the launch and looked ashore. Little spots of light were moving in the darkness, coming and going, sometimes vanishing and reappearing as the torches were occulted by the palm trees. 'Damn, they've started to search.' I turned to Ian. 'Kane's armed.'

'Let's go – I've got six – the rest are ashore already. They know the score.' The engine started first time off, which was a tribute to someone, and as we sped shorewards I said to the men around me, 'Listen, chaps, we're looking for Geordie. If you come up against Kane steer clear of him. Don't push him too hard – he's got a gun. And as you find the natives send them back to their village.'

Taffy Morgan said, 'What's Kane done now?'

'He's killed a man,' said Campbell coldly.

There was no more talk until the boat grounded on the beach. Piro was waiting, his face alive with excitement in the light of a torch. 'Found 'im,' he said laconically.

'Which one?' I asked quickly.

He gestured. 'The big one – up in hut now.'

I sighed with some thankfulness. This must be Geordie. 'Piro, can you call your men off – stop them? They must not find the other man. He has a gun.'

Piro made a quick sign to one of his friends, who lifted a large conch shell to his lips. The mournful sound boomed out, sending its note across the plantations. I saw the lights begin to drift back to the village.

'Let's see him.'

We found Geordie in one of the huts. His face was a dreadful mess, with deep cuts and gashes across his forehead and cheeks. Piro said, 'We found 'im in trees – asleep on groun'.'

I think he had concussion because he rambled a little, but he was able to speak to us. He had seen Kane slipping ashore in one of the many canoes and had followed in another. He hadn't had time to call anyone because he was afraid of losing Kane. He had followed as Kane skirted the village and entered the trees and then he had been ambushed.

'For God's sake, who ambushed you?'

'It – must have been Hadley. A man as big as an elephant,' said Geordie painfully. 'He stepped from behind a tree and pushed a gun into my ribs. I didn't expect that – I thought Kane was on his own – and he took me by surprise. Then he – made me turn round to face him and he started to hit me.' He was trailing off but recovered. 'With the gun. A big revolver. It was the sight that did – this. And the bastard was laughing. Then he hit me a couple of times on the head and I – passed out.'

He grinned weakly. 'Maybe he thought he'd killed me but I have a pretty hard head. I'm sorry I fell down on the job, Mike.'

'It's all right, Geordie. None of us expected anything like this. I'm only sorry you had to get it in the neck.'

His bloody face cracked in a grim smile. 'Add it to the account with my finger,' he said weakly. 'Give him one from me.'

'You'll have to wait your turn. There's a queue lining up for licks at Hadley – and Kane.' I stood up. 'I think we'd better get you back to the ship.'

Two of his shocked team moved in, gentling him up and setting off for the launch. The others began to gather as Piro called them to the hut. I spoke urgently to him. 'Is there another boat here – the *Pearl*?' I asked. If Hadley had returned several times Piro was sure to know his boat. Piro's answer shocked us all, even though we were already primed for it.

'Yes, it came 'ere. It gone by *hôpital* – one, two hour,' he said.

'Well I'm damned,' said Campbell. 'He came through the pass behind us – in the dark and without lights. He's a bloody good seaman.'

'That doesn't make me love him any more,' I said.

A man ran into the hut and spoke to Piro rapidly in his own language, clearly distressed. Piro looked startled and gestured to me to come outside, where he pointed into the darkness. There was a fitful redness in the sky on the horizon. '*Hôpital*, he burn,' he said.

'Christ!'

The others crowded out to exclaim at the sight.

'How can we get there – fast – all of us?' I damned the jeep, stalled on the beach without fuel.

'Big canoe,' said Piro. 'Go fast. Faster than walk.' He ran off.

I said, 'Hadley's fired the hospital!'

Campbell looked at the glow in the sky. 'Is he plain crazy – why did he do that?' he demanded.

'He threatened to do it. No time to tell you now. We're going in canoes. Piro's gone to organize it. Now where's Ian?'

His soft Highland voice sounded at my shoulder. 'I'm here.'

'Take one canoe and go back to the *Esmerelda*. I want her down at the hospital as fast as you can make it. There's light enough – the lagoon must be safe; you just follow the beach. Just get her there.'

He said nothing but ran off towards the beach. Piro touched me on the arm. 'Come to canoes.'

Most of us could crowd into the launch and the big canoe took the rest as well as a lot of their own men – it held twenty of us. It was also leaky but by God it was fast! The rowers put their backs into it and it skimmed across the water at a great speed leaving a wake glinting with phosphorescence, and easily keeping up with the launch.

The three miles or so to the hospital took only twenty minutes, but by that time we could see that the whole place was on fire. We could see black figures running about, outlined against the flames, and I wondered how many survivors there were. I was so intent on the scene on shore that I didn't see the ship. Campbell shook me by the shoulder and pointed.

A schooner was anchored in the lagoon just off the hospital. We wouldn't have seen her in the darkness of that terrible night but for the raging fire which gleamed redly on her white hull. I shouted to Campbell, 'What should we do – go to the schooner or the hospital?'

'The hospital – we must save the patients.'

The canoe drove onto the beach, a little way below the hospital and we all splashed ashore and ran towards the fire. I saw that Campbell had produced an automatic pistol, a strange weapon with an extraordinary long, thin barrel. I took out the revolver he had given me and pounded onward, barely able to keep up with the racing Commandoes. The whole hospital was burning fiercely, the dry thatch going up like tinder and the flames streaming to the sky in the windless night.

I ran for the open space between two burning huts and came in sight of the hospital's own landing place. A boat was just moving out and I heard the sudden sharp revving of an outboard motor over the crackle of flames.

'They're getting away,' I yelled, and took a shot at them. Nothing happened – I had forgotten to release the safety catch. Campbell squatted in a half-crouch and took aim with his curious pistol, then straightened up and shook his head. 'Too far. I wish I had a rifle.'

'But we can't let them get away,' I raged.

Campbell shook me roughly by the arm. 'Come on!'

I took one last look at the boat disappearing into the darkness in the direction of the schooner *Pearl* and then raced up the beach after the others, who had already dispersed to join the rest of our crew from the launch. I heard someone shouting. 'You can't put those fires out – save the people!' and I ran across to Schouten's house.

It was no use. The place was enveloped in fire, a roaring mass of flames shooting up fifty feet into the night sky. I wondered if it was Schouten's funeral pyre, and whether he had been mercifully dead when the fires started.

I ran round the house to see what it was like at the back and stumbled across a woman sitting in the path. I recovered my balance and looked back to see that she was cradling Schouten's head in her lap. Her wails rose above the crackle of the flames. *'Aaaah, le pauvre docteur, le pauvre docteur!'*

I bent down and saw that her dress was scorched and torn. She had probably dragged Schouten's body from the house. When she saw me she gave a cry, scrambled to her feet and ran away screaming into the darkness beyond the hospital. She must have thought I was one of Hadley's bunch.

I dropped to one knee beside Schouten. He wasn't a pretty sight because he had been shot through the head more than once. His jaw was torn away and there was a small blue hole in the left temple. The right temple was gone – there was a ragged gap big enough to hold a fist and his brains were leaking out onto the path.

I rose and stumbled away, catching on to a tree for support. Then I vomited my guts out until I was weak and trembling, pouring sweat.

I had barely recovered when Nick Dugan rushed up to me, his face blackened with smoke, and took my arm to help me to my feet. 'You all right?'

'I'll – do.'

'Look, Mike – there's the *Esmerelda*. They've been quick.'

I looked across the water and saw *Pearl* getting under way and, beyond her, *Esmerelda* coming up at a hell of a lick under power, her bow wave flecked red by the reflections from the burning shore. *Pearl* was still moving slowly and I could see from the changing angle of *Esmerelda*'s bow that Ian meant to try and stop her by coming hard alongside or even ramming.

But the schooner was picking up speed under her engine and slid out from *Esmerelda*'s threatening bows. Ian changed course again to converge but just at the moment of impact *Pearl* seemed to spin smartly sideways and *Esmerelda*'s bowsprit only grazed her side. As the two ships passed one another there was a fusillade of shots from *Pearl* and an answering staccato rattle from our ship. I wondered who had guns and who was using them.

Then *Pearl* was safely out of reach, heading across the lagoon for the pass in the reef, lights springing up on board as she went. *Esmerelda* gave up the chase and turned towards the shore, and I heard her engines stop. Saving the hospital had priority and it was too dangerous to follow the fleeing schooner in the dark.

They'd got clean away.

III

Dawn revealed chaos. Trickles of smoke still spiralled skywards from the gutted buildings and the patients – the survivors – huddled together on the beach with friends and the remaining hospital staff. Piro had done a count, and the death roll numbered fourteen, not counting Schouten himself.

We were all weary, scorched and depressed.

Campbell looked about him at the scene of that damned atrocity and his face was grey. 'The bastards,' he said savagely. 'The murdering sons-of-bitches. I'll see them hanged for this.'

'Not if I get them first,' I said.

We were crouched over a couple of benches with hot coffee in our hands, brought ashore from the brigantine. We didn't have enough on board to provide adequately for everyone but we had distributed what we could, and the villagers had brought food of their own for the shocked survivors. The few men whom Schouten had trained were performing heroic feats of first aid but much more was needed. And we had received a bad shock of our own – the morning light revealed that our ship's radio had been smashed, presumably by Kane before he jumped ship. There was no way to send for help, save by going for it in person. Ian, who had done wonders by bringing *Esmerelda* down the coast at night, was castigating himself for not having the radio guarded, but we persuaded him that it wouldn't have been thought necessary at the time. I hadn't even been on board to see Geordie yet, though I was assured that he was doing all right, if still confined to his bunk.

Campbell said, 'I can't see Suarez-Navarro going in for this. They're a rotten crowd, as I've told you, but this is unbelievable.'

I wasn't impressed. 'Know any English history?'

His head jerked up. 'What's that got to do with it?'

'There was an English king – Henry II, I think it was – who had a bishop as his conscience, Thomas à Becket. The legend is that the king was at dinner one day and said, "Will no one rid me of this turbulent priest?" So four of his knights went off and murdered Becket in Canterbury Cathedral.'

I scraped with my foot in the sand. 'When the king found out he was horrified. He abased himself before the Church and did his penances – but he came out on top, after all – he didn't have Becket on his back any more.'

I pointed to the burnt-out hospital. 'Suarez-Navarro have a board meeting and some plump, stuffy director says, "I wish we could do something about Campbell and this interfering chap Trevelyan." So someone like Ramirez goes out and does something, and if everything gets done – and Campbell and Trevelyan get stopped – he gets a bonus paid with no questions asked. And the dividends of Suarez-Navarro pile up, and that director would faint if he saw a cut finger so he doesn't enquire too closely into how the job was done in case he gets sick to the stomach.'

'But they didn't attack us.'

'Not directly. This has more Hadley's trademark, sadistic revenge in the meanwhile. But don't think we're not in danger now.'

Campbell looked up the beach to the patients sitting in their forlorn group. He said slowly, 'Then this wouldn't have happened if we hadn't come here.'

There was a coppery taste in my mouth. 'No. Schouten was afraid of what would happen, and I told him he'd be all right. I said he'd be protected. What a bloody mess I've made of everything.'

We both fell silent. There was too much that could be said.

Clare came along the beach towards us, carrying a first aid kit. She looked drawn and pensive, but I was more attracted to her than ever. I would have liked to take her in my arms but something prevented me – and she guessed my intention and saw why I couldn't carry it out.

'Mike, your hands are burnt raw. I'll bandage them.'

I looked at my hands. I hadn't really noticed before but now they were beginning to hurt.

She got busy with my hands and spoke with her head down as she worked. 'Pop, I guess this is where you get busy with your cheque book.'

I said harshly, 'A cheque book isn't going to bring fifteen people back to life.'

'You men are damned fools,' she said and her voice was angry. 'What's done is done, and *you* didn't do it, though I guess you're both blaming yourselves. But the hospital is gone, and what's going to happen to the poor people here? Somebody has to do something – we can't just go away and say, Well, we didn't start the fire, even if it's true.'

'I'm sorry, Clare,' I said. 'But what can we do?'

Campbell dug his hands deep into his pockets. 'There'll be another hospital – a good one. And doctors, and good equipment. I'll endow the whole damned thing.' His voice became harder. 'But Suarez-Navarro will pay for it one way or another.'

He walked away down the beach as Clare smeared a cool emulsion on my hands. 'What's that stuff?' I asked. I had to discuss something less painful, though my throbbing hands weren't the best choice of subject in that case.

'Tannic acid jelly. It's good for burns.'

I said, 'No one else has had time to tell us what happened on board. Can you? I didn't know we had guns.'

'Several of the men have them, besides Pop's little armoury. You can be awfully innocent.'

'Who was doing the shooting from *Esmerelda*?'

'A couple of the crew – and me,' she said shortly.

I raised my eyebrows. 'You?'

'I'm a good shot. Pop taught me.' She began to cover my hands. 'I think I shot one – and I think it was Kane.' Suddenly her voice broke. 'Oh, Mike, it was awful. I've never shot at a man, only at targets. It was . . .'

I was entangled in bandages but I somehow managed to get an arm around her shoulders and she buried her head on mine. 'He deserved what was coming to him, Clare. You've only got to look around you to see that. Did you kill him?'

She raised her head and her face was white and tear-streaked. 'I don't think so – the light was bad and everything happened so fast. I think I may have hit him in the shoulder. But – I was *trying* to kill him, Mike.'

'So was I,' I said. 'But my gun didn't go off. I'm not very good with guns, but I tried and I don't regret it.'

She pulled herself together. 'Thanks, Mike. I've been a fool.'

I shook my head. 'No, you're not, Clare. Killing doesn't come easy to people like us. We're not mad dogs like Kane or Hadley, but when we do come up against mad dogs I think it's our duty to try and stop them in any way we can – even if the only way is by killing them.'

I looked down at the top of her head and wished that this whole stinking business was over. It had suddenly come to me that a burnt-out hospital littered with corpses wasn't the best place in the world to tell a girl that you were falling in love with her. I would have to wait for a calm sea and romantic moonlight, with perhaps the strains of a love song echoing from the saloon.

And for the moment I was sickened of the whole chase. How Mark came to die, where his stupid treasure of cobalt lay, none of it mattered. I wanted to be done with the whole affair – bar Clare. And I couldn't get out of any of it that easily. I recognized the symptoms of exhaustion and sat up, bracing myself.

She saw the expression in my eyes and looked away quickly, but I think she read it all there. She said, 'We've got to go through with this now, Mike. We can't let Suarez-Navarro get away with it – if it is them. All this would go for nothing if we did that.'

'I know; but it won't last forever, Clare. There'll be better days coming. I'm all right now. Were any of our chaps hurt besides me?'

'Scorches, a few scrapes. None worse than you,' she told me.

'Good. We have to start getting clear of this lot, then. The local people must carry on until we can get word back.' I left her and went to where Piro was standing and was aware that she was watching me. I would have given anything to be elsewhere with her than on that beach.

I said to Piro, 'What will you do now?'

He turned a sad face to me. 'We build again. All Tanakabu people built more here – many huts. But no doctor . . .'

I said, 'Piro, Mr Campbell there has money, more than he needs. He will send doctors and you will get a proper hospital, like the one in Papeete. But first we must go back there and tell the police what happened here. Can you write a message for me?'

But it turned out that Piro could not write, nor even sign his name, which was a pity – I wanted a witnessed account of the event to take back, but with Schouten dead there was nobody else to turn to for it.

We buried the dead in the hospital cemetery. I asked about a priest but apparently Schouten had stood in himself for such occasions. They produced a Bible and Campbell pronounced a few words, though few of the locals could understand him. He said, 'We commit to the earth the bodies of those who are the innocent victims of a dreadful crime. "Vengeance is mine", saith the Lord, but it may be He will use men like us as His instrument. I hope so.'

Then he turned and walked away down the beach, a sad and lonely figure.

Schouten was given a grave in a place apart from the others. I thought this might be because of differing religions, but it appeared that they wished to make his resting-place special, and it was clear that they mourned him deeply. I thought that he would have a better memorial than he might ever have realized would be his lot, and was glad of it.

The islanders were already clearing away rubble, and most of the patients had vanished into other homes, when we left that afternoon. There was nothing we could find to take with us as proof of the disaster – the hospital records and all Schouten's personal belongings had been destroyed. We took photographs, though, and I included a couple of the natives gathering round Campbell and Ian to shake their hands, as proof of our friendship, and also of the crew at the mass funeral.

As Ian conned *Esmerelda* out through the pass of Tanakabu he asked sadly, 'What kind of men are they to do a thing like that? You told us they were dangerous – they seem demented, Mike.'

'They must be psychopaths,' I said. 'From what I learned from the Dutch doctor Hadley certainly is.'

Shorty Powell came on deck, white-faced, at the same time that Campbell emerged looking thunderous. 'I've got something to show you,' he said, and took me down to Kane's cabin together with Ian. On the bunk lay a brown-painted gadget which Shorty had clearly recognized and shown to Campbell.

'It's a walkie-talkie, surplus American army stock, selling for about fifteen dollars each. The range on land isn't much over five miles but on water you can keep contact for—?'

'Say about ten miles,' Shorty supplied.

'So that's how Hadley's schooner turned up so opportunely. And that's what that damned transmission was that Shorty picked up. You said you thought it was a low-powered job and very near, but who'd have thought it was from right here on *Esmerelda*?'

Campbell nodded. 'We've probably been shadowed all over the Pacific. Any boat could keep hull-down on the horizon and Hadley could have cosy chats with Kane.'

I picked up the radio and looked at it curiously. 'I don't think Kane was clever enough to think of this himself. This bears the hallmark of organization.'

'Ramirez,' said Campbell decisively.

'Very likely,' I said. I was trying to read any further implications into the find when Paula came looking for me and Ian got back up on deck. 'Geordie's asking for you,' she said. She too looked tired, having spent all morning helping Clare on that dreadful beach, and I smiled and gave her a quick hug of friendship and support.

'How is he?'

'He'll be all right, but he's going to need medical care in Papeete, maybe stitches. I'm not a trained nurse, you know.' Considering the dangers we had drawn her into and the shocking things she had seen, I thought she was holding up amazingly well, but then I think toughness was bred into her

'He may be scarred for life,' she added.

'A pistol whipping is a lousy thing. Damn Hadley!' said Campbell.

We found Geordie sitting up in his bunk, his eyes peering brightly at me through a mass of bandages. He'd been told about the fire and the smashed radio, but was avid for more.

'How are you feeling?' I asked him.

'Not so bad, considering. But I haven't heard the whole story yet. What happened last night between you and the doctor?' he demanded, and I realized with a start that so much had happened since that I hadn't had time to pass on Schouten's terrible story. Having made sure that he was well enough to listen, I gathered Paula, Clare and Campbell into the cabin. They heard me out in stunned silence.

'It's a bad thing,' I said heavily at the end.

'It is that,' said Geordie. 'They must be off their heads.'

I said, 'I don't think Kane's the crazy one. It's Hadley who's the lunatic, a psycho for sure. Kane's cleverer than we thought him to be, though.' I told Geordie about the walkie-talkie.

Campbell said, 'We've been played for suckers and I don't like that one little bit. But with this act I think they've outreached themselves – I have a feeling that Hadley ran amok, and even Ramirez isn't going to like it when he finds out.'

'I've been thinking, trying to put the jigsaw together, you might say,' said Geordie. 'But some of the pieces don't seem to fit.'

'Such as?'

'For one thing, you say that according to Schouten, Kane and Hadley murdered Mark, and that Ramirez was in on it. Why do you think they killed Mark?'

I said, 'I've been thinking about that. It was something that poor old Schouten said – that Hadley had laughed when he asked to see the body and said it would turn the stomach even of a doctor. What would that mean to you?'

'Knowing what we do of Hadley, it could mean torture.'

'And why should they torture Mark?' I should have felt ill at the very thought but somehow it had all become rather academic to me.

'Why does anyone torture anyone? They wanted information out of him.'

'And Ramirez was there. I think they wanted to know where the high-cobalt nodules were to be found.'

'Yes,' said Campbell. 'I've already worked that out for myself. Would Mark tell them?'

'I don't know. He'd look out for his own skin, but he was capable of being very scornful of people like them – he may not have realized that they really meant it until they got down to business, and then it might have been too late.'

The girls studied me in silence, appalled at my implication. But Geordie put it into words. 'You mean Hadley ran amok again and went too far – and he died before he could talk?'

'I think so. They clearly don't know the location, or they wouldn't be tailing us this way. So they buried their mistake, terrorized the doctor, and sent Hadley to get Mark's stuff, hoping for leads there. Hadley bungled it and let the gear slip out of his fingers – thanks to you, Paula – and so Ramirez went to England to get it back, using Kane as scout and contact man.'

'It all seems to fit,' Geordie said.

He lay back on his bunk looking suddenly exhausted, so we left him. We didn't talk about it among ourselves. We were all drained and saddened, and the trip back to Papeete was one devoid of much pleasure for any of us.

We made a quick passage and all went well until we were within about two hours of Papeete, and longing to be ashore. I planned to take Ian, Campbell and one or two members of the crew to the police as soon as we landed, leaving the others to guard the ship, especially Geordie and the girls, zealously. We had no idea where the *Pearl* might be but I wanted to run no risks. I was in my cabin when word came down for me to get on deck fast. Ian, who was acting skipper, pointed to a boat on our starboard beam. It was a fast launch and was cruising around us in a wide circle. 'Yon laddie's come up awful fast, Mike,' he said to me. 'He's up to something. He looks official.'

He handed me binoculars and I saw that it was a patrol boat, naval in style, even to a four-pounder quick-firer mounted on the foredeck. It had a number but no name, and as I looked it turned to approach us directly. 'You'd better call Mr Campbell,' I said.

The launch came up alongside and kept pace with idling engines about fifty yards away. An officer by the wheelhouse raised a loudhailer and a spate of French crossed the water.

I raised my arms to shrug violently to indicate that I didn't understand. Another man took the loudhailer and shouted in English, 'Heave to, *Esmerelda*, or we will fire.'

I looked at the gun on the foredeck. Two matelots were manning it – one had just slammed a magazine in and the other was swinging the gun around to train it just about midships.

'What the hell!' I exploded. But one couldn't argue with a four-pounder. I heard Ian giving brisk orders and the sails came tumbling down everywhere as the off-watch crewmen tumbled up on deck, Campbell among them.

'What the hell's going on?' he asked loudly.

'We're being boarded by the navy,' I said, 'in the traditional style. If we don't stop they'll open fire – the man said so.'

Campbell looked at the little gun in fascination. 'Well, I'll be double-damned,' he said. 'Pirates?'

'Not this close in. It's official.'

The sails were all down and *Esmerelda* lost way and started to pitch a little. The patrol boat edged nearer and finally came alongside, lines went across, and an officer jumped on board followed by three sailors. He had a revolver and the sailors were carrying sub-machine guns. Our men backed up, alarmed and disconcerted by all this, and I saw Campbell make a violent if surreptitious gesture to the girls to keep below decks.

'M. Trevelyan?' the officer barked.

I stepped forward. 'I'm Michael Trevelyan.'

A sub-machine gun lifted until the muzzle was pointed at my stomach. 'You are under arrest.'

I looked at him dumbfoundedly. 'What for?'

Campbell stepped forward aggressively. 'Now look here – ' he began. The officer gestured and the other two sailors lifted their weapons and there were ominous snicks as the safety-catches were released. Ian caught at Campbell's shoulder and he subsided.

The officer said, 'You will learn about it in Papeete. You will please come aboard my boat. You – ' He turned to Ian. 'You will accompany us in under engine. These men will stay on board with you. You will attempt nothing foolish, please.'

I looked into his cold grey eyes and realized that he wasn't kidding. I felt a sense of sick reluctance to leave the *Esmerelda* but there really was no choice, and I swung myself across without a word. I was briefly searched, and then led below to a cabin with a minimum of furnishing – a cell afloat – and once inside I heard the door being locked.

I was on my own.

IV

I was pretty miserable – I didn't know what was going on, nor had I any means of finding out, though I certainly had ideas – too many of them. If only I could have talked to someone I would have felt better, but that was impossible. I wondered how they were all making out.

We went the remaining few miles into Papeete at a speed slow enough for *Esmerelda* to keep up, no doubt still under the threat of the gun. There were no portholes in my cabin and I couldn't hear much either, but the arrival at a jetty was unmistakable, and I braced myself for whatever was coming. Sure enough within a few minutes they were at the door, unlocking it, and then I was brought up into the sunshine to see that we were back in Papeete but not in our old position; instead it seemed to be a naval area. I saw *Esmerelda* tied up alongside us but there were only French sailors on deck, none of my friends to be seen. A police car was waiting for me. My legs felt like lead as I went ashore and got into it.

There was a police station, possibly the principal one, and I was taken immediately and without any formalities into another cell and left there. It was devastatingly bleak. A good couple of hours passed and then I was let out once more, this time to be escorted to a large business-like office, and to confront an angry-looking, mottle-faced man behind the inevitable desk. I stood in front of it with my escort, and another man behind us at the door. I had already decided on a plan of action, such as it was – I was going to go immediately onto the offensive. To be meek was intolerable to me and also foolish, for it might imply guilt where I certainly felt none. So as soon as the man in front of me began to speak I overrode him.

'I want to see the British Consul!'

'Sit down.'

'No. I answer no questions without the presence of the Consul.'

He slapped the table with the flat of his hand, and I was jerked back into a chair. I saw a nameplate on his desk which told me that he was one Jacques Chamant, and with a title which I mentally translated as Chief of Police. I was right at the top, it seemed. It had to be pretty bad. And I already had a ghastly suspicion as to what it was.

'I stand on no ceremony with you, Trevelyan.' Another man with more than passable English. 'There has been a massacre at Tanakabu which you started – and we will have your head for it.'

I stared at him, outraged. 'Are you crazy?'

He leaned his elbows on the desk. 'I have a dossier here on you. You came to Papeete last week and made some very serious accusations against Dr Schouten, on Tanakabu, accusations which would ruin his reputation as a medical man. You were told that someone would take steps to verify your vilifications, but that was not good enough for you. You cleared Papeete with the stated intention of sailing westward, but instead you went to Tanakabu.'

I listened in silence, in spite of my resolve.

'You got to Tanakabu and evidently had a quarrel with Schouten – and you murdered him. To cover your tracks you set fire to his house, and the entire hospital caught fire resulting in many deaths. Your crew is implicated in this as well – you are all guilty men.'

I blinked and sank down in the chair, stunned by the rage in his voice and the whole messy situation. We had made a very fast return trip to Papeete and as far as I knew there were no radio-telephones on Tanakabu, so there was only one way the police could know what had happened. I seized on a couple of things he had said and decided to make the best use of them that I could.

'Can it be that you don't know exactly how many were killed? Have you had any direct contact with the island?' I asked rapidly. I didn't know how much time I would have before he had me silenced.

He hesitated and I knew I was on the right track.

'How did you get the information? Was it a man called Hadley – off a ship called the *Pearl*?'

That went straight to the mark – a bullseye. He coughed, oddly hesitant, and said, 'I do not see that it makes any difference, but you are correct. Mr Hadley described the reign of terror on Tanakabu very circumstantially. He stated that he barely escaped with his own life and that you attempted to run his ship down.'

Good! I had him on the defensive already. It was I who should be doing the talking, not he. I sensed already the faintest thread of doubt in his voice and pressed on.

'You say I "evidently" quarrelled with Dr Schouten. What "evidence" is there? I left him after a long talk, none the worse for it. There was a witness to that, an islander called Piro. He drove me from my ship. He will also attest that we came to save the hospital when it was already burning – and so will many others there. You have no right to arrest me. Or any of us!'

He was listening intently and did not interrupt me. Behind me the policemen stood like statues. I didn't understand why things were going my way but I was feeling stronger by the minute.

'Why don't you study that file, M. Chamant? You've got it down in black and white – Hadley was the man who is supposed to have found my brother, but whom *I* say was his murderer – and Schouten told me so. I can't prove that now, but I can prove everything else.'

I remembered another fact and produced it triumphantly.

'I took photographs. Develop my film. It will tell you everything.'

'M. Trevelyan, I am listening carefully. Of course we will check your camera, and we have already sent a police patrol boat to Tanakabu. But you still have a great deal to explain, and you are not yet released from arrest.'

I said, 'I've got plenty to tell you! That damned bastard and his mate Kane – they're the ones you want. They murdered Sven Norgaard, they murdered my brother, they murdered that poor bloody Schouten and they killed fourteen patients in his hospital – burnt them alive, do you hear – they burnt those poor wretches alive!'

Chamant was gesturing to the two policemen who heaved on my shoulders. I had lost all restraint in my anger, and was trying to climb over the table in my frenzy of trying to make Chamant see the truth. I slumped back, shaking a little and fighting for self-control. There was silence for a moment as we all contemplated my words.

'Where is Hadley now?' I asked him, trying to stay on the offensive.

He regarded me closely in silence still, then nodded gravely. He gave instructions to one of the men in rapid French, and the officer left the room smartly. Then he looked at me. 'I am not yet ready to belieye you. But we will speak again with M. Hadley, I assure you. Meantime, I ask you to explain this, if you can.'

He pointed to a small box on a side-table and one of the remaining policemen brought it to his desk. Opened, it revealed four guns and a little pile of boxes of ammunition. I recognized two of the guns immediately.

'Four guns with enough ammunition to start a war, M. Trevelyan. Not a cargo for a peaceful ship, a scientific expedition.'

'Where did you find them?' But I could guess, and I was troubled. This was going to set back the progress I'd made.

'Three in the cabin of your M. Campbell. One in the possession of M. Wilkins, your captain.'

I made a weak gesture. There didn't seem to be much to say.

'You have seen them before?'

I said, 'Yes, two of them. Mr Campbell gave me that one when we discovered that Kane had gone from our ship. I must tell you the whole story, in sequence you understand. This other one he had himself. But – '

'But?'

'Neither of us fired a shot! If you exhume Schouten you'll see he was shot three times, I think.'

'Only the other two were fired.'

'Yes, on our ship – when Hadley was getting away. We did try to ram him, to stop him – to bring him to justice.' That phrase sounded melodramatic enough even for a Frenchman to gag on it, I thought.

'You will tell me the story.'

So I did, leaving out all references to our search for manganese nodules, to Ramirez and Suarez-Navarro. I thought that made it all far too complicated. I said only that Hadley, once chartering a boat for my brother and Norgaard, had quarrelled with them for reasons unknown, had murdered both of them and had implicated the Dutch doctor in his crime. I had come to seek the truth and had run into a hornet's nest. It was circumstantial and very tidy. He made notes from time to time but said little.

When I finished he said, 'You will write all this down and sign it, please. I am going to allow you to return to your ship, but you will see that you and all your crew are confined to quarters on board. There will be a police guard.'

He was interrupted by the return of the officer he had sent out, who came straight to his side and whispered agitatedly to him. They both got up to look out of the window and went on speaking in urgent undertones, in French. And somehow I guessed what they were talking about.

'It's Hadley, isn't it?'

He turned to face me.

'You've let him get away, haven't you? You've let that murderous thug walk out of here!'

He nodded heavily. 'Yes, he has apparently left. You must understand that there was no reason to hold him, after he placed the information and made a deposition. We would not expect him to leave here – it is his home port.'

Something about the way he spoke told me that he was deeply troubled, to the point of forgetting that he was speaking to a man under arrest. I could guess why. Hadley was surely known here as a tough and a trouble-maker. The police may well have had him under surveillance already, for his connections with Mark and Norgaard, and for all I knew for a score of other things. And in letting him get away M. Chamant had blotted his own copybook rather badly. I was furious and exultant at the same time.

He got himself in hand and gave instructions to take me back to *Esmerelda*, and I was only too happy to go. House arrest seemed insignificant compared to being locked up in a cell. I went on board and was not particularly bothered by the sight of armed police dotted about, a couple on deck and more on the quayside, and a little knot of spectators shifting about as if waiting for a show to begin. In fact I managed a grin and a half-wave at them as I was ushered below, to their delight and the guard's disapproval.

There was a babble of voices at my return and the same air of tense expectancy as on the dockside, only here it was tinged with anxiety and bafflement. They all crowded around me and started firing questions.

'Wait up!' I held them off goodnaturedly. 'Plenty of time – too much, if anything. First, I want a wash-up and about a gallon of coffee and some food. Who's cook?'

I headed determinedly for my cabin to get a change of clothes, leaving the others to see to my inner comforts – and was brought up by the sight of Geordie, still in his bunk in the cabin we'd been sharing all along.

'Geordie! What the hell are you doing here? Shouldn't you be in the hospital?' I was already seething at this in-human treatment, but he waved me down casually.

'I'm fine, boy. It's good to see you. What happened to you?'

'Geordie, I'll tell you together with the rest, once I've washed and had some coffee. Are you sure you're all right?'

But in fact he looked a lot better, and I could see that his face had been professionally attended to, with neat stitches and tidier bandaging. As I stripped he said, 'They wanted to cart me off but I sat firm. There's nothing wrong with me that their pretty visiting nurse can't fix. I'd get her to take a look at you too.'

He nodded at my hands, still partly covered with burnt skin, though they had started to heal pretty well on the short trip back. I completed a quick ablution and was finally seated in the saloon over breakfast and surrounded by the whole of the crew of the *Esmerelda* – bar one. It was an immense relief not to see Kane's face among the others.

I told them as much as they needed to know, reserving a few more private comments for Geordie and Campbell later.

'He's a worried man, that Chamant. Was even when he saw me, and he has to be even more so now that Hadley's skipped,' Campbell said.

'He saw you?'

'Oh yes, and the girls too, and Ian – wanted to speak to Geordie but he was unaccountably sicker just then.' Geordie, propped up on a saloon berth, winked at me, and I realized that my news had cheered everyone up amazingly. Although we, and our ship, were all technically still under arrest it was clear that we weren't in any real trouble, thanks to the various bits of evidence I had offered the police chief, and we lacked only physical freedom – not any of the oppression of spirit that imprisonment usually meant.

'Tell me about your interview,' I asked Campbell.

It had apparently been somewhat hilarious. Instead of being chastened at being caught with a small armoury under his bunk Campbell was airy and unconcerned about it, claiming that the guns were properly licensed, that he was a well-known collector and wouldn't dream of travelling without something for target practice, and that in any case only one of his guns had been fired – and that by his daughter, gallantly defending herself from attack by a shipload of murderous pirates. He was scathing about Clare's poor shooting and seemed not at all troubled by her having winged a man, only irked by her not having killed him outright. It appeared that while in Papeete, Kane had had a small bullet taken from his shoulder, ironically by the same doctor who tended to Geordie. He was not, it seemed, badly hurt, which disappointed Campbell considerably.

He was soundly reproved for not having declared the guns on his arrival and was threatened with their confiscation, but he'd wangled his way out of that somehow; and had got away with their being sealed at the mouth for the duration of our stay.

It turned out that the other gun that I had seen belonged to Nick Dugan, and he was similarly ticked off. According to Clare there had been at least two other small handguns in use during *Esmerelda*'s fight with *Pearl*, but none of them surfaced during the search that was made, and I asked no questions. I also learned that Geordie had a shotgun on board which apart from being legally licensed, had even been declared by him to the Papeete customs – and was the only gun on board that had not seen some action.

Campbell had blustered much as I had and had invoked all the powers he could think of to back his credentials, and apparently M. Chamant had done much what he had done with me – had let him speak at will, listened carefully, and had finally released him back to the ship with a fairly mild request that he write down an account of the affair. Everything pointed to our story being accepted, and indeed later that afternoon the guards began to let us all out on deck in twos and threes for some exercise, after they'd moved *Esmerelda* to a mooring buoy well away from the quayside. Things were looking up, and we all turned in that night a great deal happier than we'd been at the start of the day.

V

A senior police official came on board next morning and took formal statements from everyone on board, which took a considerable time, though some of us had written them out in advance and needed only to sign them in the official presence. My camera was removed as well, and I prayed that my photography had been up to scratch. The doctor came to see Geordie again and Campbell cornered him and asked innumerable questions about the hospital on Tanakabu, and about the possibility of getting another doctor to go out there soon.

We were all beginning to feel restless and uneasy. In spite of some relaxation, we were still confined to the ship and as they kept us battened down apart from whoever was being allowed on deck it was stifling and airless on board.

Some time in the afternoon Geordie sent word that he'd like a word with me and so I went to his cabin. He was propped up in bed and surrounded by books. His face was still heavily bandaged but he was obviously much stronger and the effects of the concussion had long worn off.

'Sit down, boy,' he said. 'I think I've found something.'

'To do with what?' I asked, though I could already guess. Several of the books were nautical and the *Pilot* was prominent among them. 'Has it got to do with those damned nodules?'

'Yes, it has. Just listen awhile, will you?'

I felt a small indefinite itch starting in the back of my skull. At the end of the terrible business on Tanakabu I had felt sickened of the whole search and had wanted nothing more to do with it. The nodules could lie on the seabed forever as far as I was concerned, and with the murder of Mark more or less exposed even the urge to lay that ghost had died away to a dull resignation. But now, deprived of ordinary activity, I couldn't help feeling that it would be interesting to have the problem to chew on again, and my professional curiosity was rising to the surface once more. So I settled down to hear Geordie out without protest.

'I was thinking of that lunatic Kane,' he said. 'He slipped up when he mentioned New Britain – the time he shouldn't have known about it. I got to thinking that maybe he'd slipped up again, so I started to think of all the things he ever said that I knew of, and I found this. It's very interesting light reading.'

He handed me Volume Two of the *Pacific Ocean Pilot* opened at a particular page, and I began to read where he pointed. Before I had got to the bottom of the page my eyebrows had lifted in surprise. It was a lengthy passage and took some time to absorb, and when I had finished I said noncommittally, 'Very interesting, Geordie – but why?'

He said carefully, 'I don't want to start any more hares – we blundered badly over Minerva – but I think that's the explanation of the other drawing in the diary. If it seems to fit in with your professional requirements, that is.'

It did.

'Let's get the boss in on this,' I said and he half-lifted himself from his bunk in delight. He'd played his fish and caught it.

I got up and went to round up Campbell, Ian and Clare and brought them back to the cabin. 'Okay, Geordie. Begin at the beginning.' I could see that the others were as pleased as I had been to have something new to think about.

'I was thinking about Kane,' Geordie said. 'I was going over in my mind everything he'd said. Then I remembered that when he'd seen Clare's drawings he'd called one of them a "scraggy falcon". We all saw it as an eagle, didn't we? So I checked on falcons in the *Pilot* and found there really is a Falcon Island. The local name is Fonua Fo'ou but it's sometimes called Falcon because it was discovered by HMS *Falcon* in 1865.'

Clare said, 'But where's the "disappearing trick"?'

'That's the joker,' I said. 'Falcon Island disappears.'

'Now wait a minute,' said Campbell, a little alarmed. 'We've had enough of this nonsense with Minerva.'

'It's not quite the same thing,' said Geordie. '*Récife de Minerve* was a shoal – exact position unknown. Falcon, or Fonua Fo'ou, has had its position measured to a hair – but it isn't always there.'

'What the hell do you mean by that?' Campbell exploded.

Geordie grinned and said to me, 'You'd better tell them – you're the expert.'

'Falcon Island is apparently the top of a submarine volcano of the cinder type,' I said soberly. 'Every so often it erupts and pumps out a few billion tons of ash and cinders, enough to form a sizeable island.' I referred to the *Pilot*. 'In 1889 it was over a mile square and about a hundred and fifty feet high; in April 1894 there wasn't anything except a shoal, but by December of the same year it was three miles long, one and a half miles wide, and fifty feet high.'

I pointed to the pages. 'There's a long record of its coming and goings, but to bring it up to date – in 1930, Falcon was one and a quarter miles long and four hundred and seventy feet high. In 1949 it had vanished and there were nine fathoms of water in the same position.'

I passed the book over to Campbell. 'What seems to happen is that the island gets washed away. The material coming out of the volcano would be pretty friable and a lot of it would be soluble in water.'

He said, 'Does this tie in with your theory of nodule formation?'

'It ties in perfectly. If these eruptions have been happening once every, say, twenty years, for the last hundred thousand years, that's a hell of a lot of material being pumped into the sea. The percentage of metals would be minute, but that doesn't matter. The process of nodule formation takes care of that – what metals there are would be scavenged and concentrated, ready to be picked up.'

Campbell looked baffled. 'You come up with the damnedest things,' he complained. 'First a reef that might or might not be there, and now a goddam disappearing island. What's the present state of this freak?'

I looked at Geordie.

'I don't know. I'll check up in the *Pilot* supplements – but they're often printed a little behind the times anyway. The locals may know.'

'Where is Falcon or Fonua-whatsit – when it's available?'

'In the Friendly Islands,' I said. Clare smiled at that. 'The Tongan group. It's about forty miles north of Tongatapu, the main island.'

He frowned. 'That's a long way from Rabaul, and that's where the Suarez-Navarro crowd is. And it's a long way from here, where Mark was.'

I said mildly, 'It's halfway between.'

He nodded thoughtfully and we all chewed on it for a few minutes. After a while I spoke up. 'In the light of this information, I think it would be worth concentrating on Falcon – if you're carrying on, that is?' I looked enquiringly at Campbell.

'Yes, of course I am,' he said energetically. His optimistic side was gaining steadily. 'You really think this will be worth trying?'

Clare supported me. 'I was sure those drawings meant something.'

'Minerva meant two months of wasted time,' Campbell said. 'What do you think, Geordie?'

Geordie looked at me but with conviction. 'He's the expert.'

Ian Lewis waited with courteous patience. He was prepared to go anywhere, and do anything that was wanted of him. In spite of the horror of Tanakabu he was having a wonderful time, away from the dullness of home life.

The issue was settled for us while Campbell ruminated. A vagrant breeze from the open port flipped back a page or so of the *Pilot* and I happened to glance down. I looked at the page incredulously and began to laugh uncontrollably.

Campbell said, 'For God's sake, what's so funny?'

I dumped the book into Geordie's hands and he too began laughing. I said, 'It seems we looked at the wrong

Minerva. Look – Minerva Reefs, two hundred and sixty miles south-west of Tongatapu – that puts them only about three hundred miles from Falcon Island.'

'You mean there's *another* Minerva?'

'That's exactly what I mean.'

Geordie handed him the book. 'They're fully mapped. They're on a plateau twenty-eight miles long. It's hard ground – shell, coral and volcanic cinders, at a depth of eighteen hundred to thirty-six hundred feet.'

'Just like Falcon Island but much, much older and well established,' I put in.

'There's no mention of nodules,' Campbell said.

'These are naval records and the navy wouldn't dredge for them. They'd just take soundings using a waxed weight to sample the bottom material. A nodule – even a small one – would be too heavy to stick to the wax.'

There was a rising air of jubilation in the small cabin.

Campbell said, 'Well, that does it, I suppose. We go to Tonga.' He looked at us all fiercely. 'But this time there'd better be no mistakes.'

So it was settled what we'd do after we left Papeete – if we left Papeete.

VI

It seemed a long time.

Apparently a patrol boat had gone to Tanakabu and returned three days later, during which time things had got a little easier for us, but not much. All the crew members had been allowed to go ashore in batches, but Ian, the Campbells and I were still confined, as was Geordie for slightly different reasons. Paula managed to be allowed ashore mainly because she seemed to know everyone, including the policemen, but she only went under Jim or Taffy's escort and didn't stay ashore for long, having little faith in Hadley's having truly disappeared.

On the fourth day we were taken ashore, Campbell and I, and driven to the police station where we were ushered into the same office as before. M. Chamant was awaiting us.

He was quite pleasant. 'Our findings on Tanakabu are consistent with your statements. I note that M. Trevelyan called off the search as soon as he found that the man Kane was armed, which is a point in your favour. I also found that you saved many lives at the hospital, and it is known that you were all aboard your ship when the doctor was shot and the fires started. Also your photographs were helpful.'

It was good news, and as near to an apology as we'd ever get.

'When can we leave?' asked Campbell.

Chamant shrugged. 'We cannot hold you. If we had Kane and Hadley here you would be expected to stay and give evidence at their hearing, but . . .'

'But you haven't found them,' I said bitterly.

'If they are in French Oceania we will find them. But the Pacific is large.'

At least they seemed convinced of Hadley and Kane's guilt, which would have come out sooner or later anyway. Hadley had been seen ashore and recognized by several of the people on Tanakabu, and it made me wonder all the more why they had stopped in Papeete to put the police on a false trail, instead of picking up their heels. But I thought that perhaps Hadley, whose mental processes were not as evident as his brutality, really thought that we would be found guilty of his crime, and so out of his way forever. It was impossible to try and read his mind. Now, if they were being hunted by the law themselves they would have less time to go after us, and we had already agreed to act as if they didn't exist, otherwise we'd get nowhere.

'You can go whenever you want, M. Campbell.'

'We're going west as we originally said,' Campbell told him. 'We're heading towards Tonga. If we see them out there we'll let the authorities know.' We were being cooperative now, wanting no further opposition to our going about our own business.

Chamant said, 'Very well, gentlemen. You may go. I will send instructions for the police guard to be withdrawn. But you will take care to be on your best behaviour for the remainder of your stay here, and I also strongly suggest that you leave these waters soon. Your family – ' He pointed to me. 'Your family seems to cause trouble here, whether or not you intend to. And we do not want trouble on our hands.'

Campbell closed a hand firmly over my wrist. 'Thank you, M. Chamant. We appreciate all you have said. And now can you arrange transport back to our ship, please?'

He was reluctant on general principles but finally we got a ride back to the docks and a short run out to *Esmerelda*, to carry back the welcome news of our release. Everyone deserved a couple of days off, and neither Campbell nor I begrudged them the time. The radio had been repaired and we had a lot of planning to do before we could set sail for the Friendly Islands, one of which might be there, or might not.

SIX

It was good to be at sea again, pounding along under the unfailing impulse of the trade wind. It would take about six days to sail to Tonga and we soon settled into shipboard routine.

Geordie was up and about. Although his face looked like the map of a battlefield he was fit enough otherwise, and took over the command from a reluctant Ian, who had gloried in his brief spell as skipper. The fresh wind blew away the last taint of Tanakabu and everyone benefited, and Kane's disappearance had lifted the last reserve of secretiveness. They were all in the know now, including Geordie's own crewmen, as we felt that it was only fair to warn them all of possible danger ahead, though none had taken advantage of Geordie's offer to pay their fares home if they wished to leave us.

And Paula was still with us. Somehow that had been taken for granted and she had fitted in so well to shipboard life that there was no sense of surprise in her having agreed to come along. She and Clare set one another off nicely.

I immersed myself in text books and charts. I wanted to study currents, so I asked Geordie for pilot charts of the area. 'Not that they'll be any great help,' I said. 'The currents might have changed considerably in the last fifty thousand years. That's why Mark worked with Norgaard – he was an expert at that sort of thing.'

'The pilot charts only have the surface currents,' said Geordie. 'Who knows what goes on under the surface?'

'There are gadgets that can tell that sort of thing, though I haven't one with me. And they can't tell us what went on fifty thousand years ago, more's the pity,' I expounded. 'Here is Fonua Fo'ou. There's a warm offshoot of the South Equatorial Current sweeping south-west past the island. That should mean that any nodule deposits will also be laid down south-west of the island. But it's a surface current – there may be other currents lower down, going in different directions. That we'll have to check, if we can.'

I frowned at my own words. 'The thing is, have those currents changed direction in those last fifty thousand years? I don't know, but I shouldn't think so. It's not very long.'

Geordie snorted.

I put my finger on the chart. 'What I'm really worried about is this spot here. That's the Tonga Trench – our dredge will only go to 30,000 feet, and Horizon Depth in the Trench is nearly 35,000.'

'Quite a bit of water,' said Geordie dryly. 'That's over six and a half miles – a man could drown in that depth of water.'

'If the high-cobalt nodules have formed at the bottom of the Trench we're wasting time,' I said, ignoring his baiting. 'You could dredge them up, but it wouldn't be an economic proposition – it would just amount to pouring money into the sea. By the way, I haven't mentioned this to the boss. It would only cause alarm and despondency, and it might never happen.'

'I won't tell him,' he promised.

But I did seek out Campbell for another reason, and found him on deck in his favourite spot reading a book. We chatted for a few minutes about the ship and the weather, and then I said, 'Is it true what Clare said – that you're a crack shot?'

'I'm not too bad,' he said modestly if a little complacently.

'I'd like to learn how to shoot. I didn't get off a shot back there at Tanakabu, and those bastards were popping off all over the show.'

He grinned.'What happened?'

'I think I forgot to release the safety catch.'

'I thought that might be it,' he said. 'It's obvious you don't know much about the game.'

'I don't know anything,' I said positively.

'Good. Then you won't have any bad habits to get rid of. Stick around. I'll get the pistols.'

He came back with four guns and laid them on deck. Three I'd seen and one which was new to me, but a twin of the one I'd handled. I didn't ask him where it had been hidden. He said, 'I didn't know what kind of trouble we'd be running into, so I took out insurance and brought along these two .38s for you and Geordie.'

'What about yours?'

'Oh, I like this, the .22. They're for me and Clare – she's a pretty good shot, if in need of practice.'

'I've always thought that a .22 was useless against a man,' I said.

'You're like the cops. They always think you can't use anything but a .38 or bigger,' said Campbell contemptuously. 'Look at it this way – who are the men who habitually use handguns?'

I thought about it. 'The police, the army, criminals and hobbyists – like yourself.'

'Right. Now, an army officer doesn't get much time for practice, nor the wartime officer – so they give him the biggest gun he can hold, one that packs a hell of a wallop – a .45. With that gun he doesn't have to be a dead shot. If he only wings his man, that man is knocked flat on his back.'

Campbell picked up a .38. 'Now the police get more practice and they're usually issued with, or equip themselves with, these. A nice handy gun that will fit inconspicuously into a holster out of sight, but because of that the barrel's too short, resulting in some loss of accuracy. You've got to have a lot of practice to be good with one of these.'

He exchanged it for a .22. 'With this you have definitely got to be a good shot; the bullet is small and hasn't any inherent stopping power, so you have to be able to put it in the right place. But the gun is deadly accurate – this one is, at any rate. If you meet up with a man who habitually packs a .22 steer clear of him, especially if he's filed away the front sight, because that means he's a snapshooter – a natural shot.'

I said, 'What's the range of these guns?'

'Oh, they've all got a hell of a range, but that's not the point. What counts is the accurate range, and with any hand gun it's not very much. A guy who is an average shot will stop a man at ten yards with the .38. A crack shot will stop his man at twenty yards. And I'm not talking about target practice on the range – I'm talking about action where the other guy is shooting back.'

He waved the long-barrelled .22. 'With this gun I'll kill a man at thirty yards – maybe a bit further.'

I asked curiously, 'You once said you had killed. Was it with this?'

'Yes, in South America once. The jungle Indians don't like trespassers.'

He said no more about it, and I let it lie.

So he began to teach me how to shoot. He started with the basic principles, stripping the guns and explaining the action. Then he showed me how to stand, and eventually how to hold a gun.

'I'm not going to waste time with you on the classic stance,' he said. 'That's for the police and championship target boys. If you tried you'd be filled full of holes before you sighted on your man. I want you to start with snapshooting.

It's something you have or you haven't – let's see if you've got it. Point your finger at the mast.'

I did so and he followed the line of direction. 'Not bad. If your finger had been a gun barrel – a steady one – you'd have made a hole in the mast just a little off centre. Do it again.'

So I did it again – and again – and again. Then he gave me a .38. 'Now do it.'

I pointed the gun at the mast and he shook his head. 'You'd miss by a foot. Put your forefinger alongside the barrel and do it again.'

I pointed the gun again with better results. 'You won't have your finger there when you shoot,' he said. 'It might be cut off by the action. But I want you to be able to point that barrel just like you point your finger.'

He drilled me for four hours every day on the voyage to Tonga. The rest of the crew crowded around at first, all asking for lessons, but Campbell declined, saying that one pupil at a time was his limit and that in any case there were no spare guns. Geordie endorsed this. Those of the crew who did have guns did a little target practice but no one had much ammunition to spare and soon they left us to get on with it.

I had to learn how to point the gun when standing, sitting, lying down and lastly, after a sudden turn. Then he concentrated on the trigger finger, making me squeeze the trigger gently without a jerk. He filed the sear of the trigger until it clicked at a very slight pressure and then made me practice a draw, snapping off the safety catch, pointing the gun and squeezing the trigger all in one flowing motion.

On the third day I fired my first shot.

Campbell set up a rough target in the bows and when I stood near the foremast and squeezed that trigger I was certain that I had missed. But he led me to the target and pointed to a hole only two inches off centre. 'You'd make a pretty fair ten yard man,' he said. 'Give me another year or two and I'll make a good shot out of you.'

He took his .22 and, standing at the same distance, loosed off six shots in as many seconds. 'Now look at the target,' he said.

He had put a neat circle of small holes round the larger one made by my bullet. 'Give me time and you'll be able to do that,' he said in reply to my honest praise.

'I doubt if we'll have time. Not if I run up against Kane and company in the near future.'

'You think we will? The Suarez-Navarro ship is still up in Rabaul as far as I know.'

'I don't think it will stay there,' I said. 'They'll be on our trail.'

Campbell suddenly seemed depressed. 'How do we know it's the right trail? We're only going on a wild hunch – a hunch that a couple of doodled drawings do mean something.'

He turned and went below, the pistols dangling heavily in his hands.

II

We raised the island of Tongatapu on the morning of the sixth day out of Papeete. Nuku'alofa, the southern port of entry for the Tongan group, is on the north side of the island, so Geordie changed the heading of *Esmerelda*.

He said to me, 'There's a paragraph in the *Pilot* that says you have to keep a sharp lookout for undersea volcanic activity and new shoals in these waters.'

I smiled. 'Sounds good from my point of view.'

'Not so good from mine. I have to skipper this ship.'

But we entered the anchorage without sighting any-thing unusual, tied up and settled down to wait for the port officials. Nuku'alofa was a typical Pacific island town; the wooden houses with their galvanized iron roofs forever frozen in a late-Victorian matrix. At one time it had looked as though Nuku'alofa was going to be the chief trading port and coaling station of the Western Pacific; but Suva, in the Fiji Islands, eventually came out on top, possibly for no more profound reason than that it was an easier name to pronounce. At any rate, Nuku'alofa lost its chance and relapsed into a timeless trance.

Once free to go ashore Campbell headed for the post office as usual. I went off with the two girls who were going to book in at an hotel. Clare announced that she was tired of salt water showers. 'My hair's in a mess and I can't get the salt out. It needs cutting,' she said. 'I want fresh water and luxury for a while.'

I said thoughtfully, 'It looks as though we may be based on Nuku'alofa for some time. Maybe I'd better do the same – get a room for me and see if Geordie wants one. A ship's all right if you can get off it once in a while.'

Paula felt happier here too, with Hadley a remote risk and nobody else around whom she knew either. It was a lot more relaxing for all of us than our second visit to Papeete. We arrived at the hotel and Clare said, 'My God, look at all that gingerbread!' It was a museum piece sprouting galvanized iron turrets and cupolas in the most unlikely places; inside it was pleasantly cool and dark with big electric fans lazily circulating the air.

At the reception desk we ran into trouble when we asked for five rooms – they had only three, one single and two doubles. I said to Clare, 'That's all right if you don't mind doubling up with Paula again. Geordie and I will share and your father can have the single.'

The receptionist was most apologetic. There had been an unprecedented rush on accommodation just recently. I left the desk feeling that perhaps Nuku'alofa was going to give Suva a run for its money after all.

I arranged with the girls to meet them in the lounge in an hour or so and went upstairs to soak in a hot bath, and to lay schemes for getting Clare away by myself somewhere that evening – the first chance I would have had since Papeete. When I came downstairs I found them already in the lounge with tall glasses of beer in front of them, frosted on the sides. 'That's a good idea,' I said and looked at the label on the bottle. It was Australian beer – Swan. For a moment I was back in London on a wet dull day a million years ago. 'That's Kane's favourite tipple. Maybe he'll be around for a drink.'

Clare looked past me. 'Here comes Pop.'

Campbell came over to the table with a sheaf of correspondence in his hand and the inevitable worried look on his face. Clare said, 'Have a cold beer, Pop. It's just the thing for this weather.'

He dropped heavily into a cane chair which creaked protestingly. 'I think we've come to the wrong place,' he said abruptly.

I signalled to a hovering waiter and ordered a couple of beers. 'What's the trouble?'

He unfolded a cable. 'The Suarez-Navarro crowd have moved again to Nouméa in New Caledonia.'

I raised my eyebrows, 'Interesting, but not very informative. I wonder what they're doing there?'

'I don't know but it doesn't look too good to me. According to what we've figured they don't know where the stuff is, so what the hell are they drifting round the Pacific for? It looks as though they're as lost as we are.'

Clare said thoughtfully, 'Maybe Mark gave them a bum steer before he died.'

I shook my head. 'No, if he'd done that they would have been out testing for it, and we know they haven't. But we're not lost – at least we don't think so. We're here for a purpose.'

I glanced through the door of the lounge and saw the receptionist working at his accounts. I said, 'Excuse me for a minute,' and went into the foyer where I had an interesting little five-minute chat with him, which included the passing of a discreet backhander across the counter. I went back into the lounge, sat down and took a long, lingering draught of cold beer. Then I said, 'We're in the right place.'

They all stared at me. 'How do you know? How can anyone know?'

I said, 'One Ernesto Ramirez has booked half a dozen rooms in this hotel. He hasn't turned up yet.'

Campbell looked startled and Clare let out a yelp of pure joy. Paula, on the other hand, visibly shrank back in her chair, and I made a quick mental note of that. I said, 'I thought it a bit odd that the hotel should be so full right now, so I checked up on it. Ramirez booked the rooms and paid handsomely for them in advance; he wrote that he didn't know exactly when he was coming, but that the rooms must be kept free.'

'I'll be damned,' said Campbell. 'But what's he been doing in Nouméa?'

'I think he's been stooging around in this area all the time, getting slowly closer to wherever we were, and waiting to see where we'd go without being too close, so that he could follow easily from a distance.'

'But now he is coming here, and we've not been in a day,' said Clare. 'How could he know? And why come so close now?'

'We saw several ships as we came across, and we made no secret of our destination. My guess is that he's been fed the information somehow. As to why he's closing with us, that I can't guess. But what he doesn't know is that *we* know he's coming, and we have a head start on him – we're here.'

'He must know we've arrived,' said Campbell soberly. 'He's sure to have left a man here. I'll bet they're in touch right now.'

'We're not going to be in for long,' I said. 'We'll be off dredging soon. But we could put it about that we are leaving for somewhere else – that might help draw him into the net. At close quarters we can at least do something.' It was all very dubious though, and we weren't at all sure what was happening around us.

'What kind of a ship have they?' I asked.

'Pretty much the same as ours – a bit bigger. Her name is *Sirena*.'

'Then if he leaves now it'll be over a week before he gets here.'

Campbell put down his empty glass with a click. 'Then we've got to get going as soon as we can,' he said.

I saw Geordie coming into the foyer and waved to him, and he came to the table. He was dirty and looked tired, and the half-healed scars on his face didn't make him look any better. He put a little glass pot on the table with a hand stained black with grease, and said, 'We've got trouble.'

I said, 'Sit down and have a beer.'

'What's the trouble?' Campbell asked.

Geordie sat down and sighed. 'I *would* like a beer,' he admitted. He unscrewed the top of the jar and showed that it was full of grease. He pushed it over to me and said, 'Rub some of that between your fingers and tell me what it feels like.'

I dipped up some of the grease on my forefinger and rubbed it with my thumb. It wasn't slick and smooth as grease should be but seemed gritty. Campbell reached over and tested it for himself.

'Where did you get this?' he demanded.

'It came from the main bearings of the winch motor,' said Geordie. 'And the grease in the bearing of the winch drum is the same – all doctored with carborundum.'

'Christ!' I said. 'If we'd have used the winch the whole damn thing would have seized up. What put you on to it?'

'Partly routine maintenance. But I also thought about what I'd do if I were Kane and I wanted to put a stop to Mr Campbell here. I wasn't looking for anything definite, mind you, but I thought I'd have a look at the winch. I never thought I'd find grinding powder mixed with the bearing grease.'

Campbell swore violently, then looked at Paula. 'Sorry,' he mumbled.

'That's all right. I know those words.'

I said, 'How long will it take to fix?'

'A week,' said Geordie definitely. 'We'll have to strip the winch right down, and that's a big job. But it's not what I'm worried about.'

'Isn't it enough?' grumbled Campbell. 'What else is on your, mind?'

'I'm thinking of things Kane might have done that we haven't found yet. I don't think he got at the engine – but what else has he done?'

I said, 'He can't have done much. He was under observation all the time.'

'He got at the winch,' said Geordie obstinately.

'Geordie's right,' said Campbell. 'We can't take anything on trust. The whole ship must be checked out.'

The girls sat silent through this but I could sense their frustration matched ours. If the intention had been to foul up our operations it might have succeeded. But if it was also intended to dishearten us then Kane had read his man wrongly – Campbell of all of us was the most determined to put things right and carry on.

I drained my glass. 'Let's get to it. I kept the laboratory locked but I suppose I'd better give that a going over too.'

We went back to *Esmerelda,* rounding up crewmen along the way, and I went immediately below to the laboratory. A couple of hours' work showed nothing wrong – the spectro-scope was in order, and the contents of all the bottles seemed to agree with their labels. It was a waste of time from one point of view, and then again it wasn't. At least I knew my lab wasn't gimmicked.

Ian came down with fuel oil samples from the main tanks. 'Skipper wants these tested,' he said.

'Tested for what?'

He grinned. 'Anything that shouldn't be in fuel oil.'

I poured the samples into Petri dishes and burned them. The sample from the starboard tank left little deposit, but that from the port tank left a gummy mess on the bottom of the dish.

I went on deck to see Geordie. 'The port fuel tank's been got at,' I told him. 'I think it's been doctored with sugar.'

Geordie swore a blue streak. 'I thought we were using a hell of a lot of sugar. So that's where it went. How's the star-board tank?'

'It seems all right.'

'Kane couldn't get at the starboard tank without being seen – it's right by the wheel. The port tank is different. I remember he used to sit just about there quite often, when he was off watch.'

'It wouldn't be difficult – a pound of sugar at a time.'

'We've been sailing a lot, too. If we hadn't we'd have found out sooner – the hard way. But all the fuel we've used has come from the ready use tank in the engine room, and we just kept topping that up in port.'

Campbell came up. 'What are the long faces for?'

I told him and he cursed violently.

'We dump it,' I said. 'We can't dump it in harbour – they'd scream blue murder – so we go to sea and dump it.'

'All right,' said Geordie. 'I'll fill the header tank from the starboard main tank. We'll need some power to be going on with.'

'Nothing doing,' said Campbell. 'Kane might have been clever enough to put something else in there. Fill the header tank with new fuel from the Shell agent here.' He paused. 'It's going to be difficult. There's probably a lot of undissolved sugar lying on the bottom of the tank. When you put in new fuel you may be just as badly off.'

I said, 'I can test for sugar in water. We'll keep washing out until we're clean. How are their water supplies here, Geordie? I'd rather use fresh than salt.'

'We're lucky. In the dry season they can run short, but I think right now is okay. We'll have to pay through the nose, though.'

He thought about the job. 'We'll have to wait until the tanks dry out. Maybe I can rig up a contraption that'll pump hot air into the tanks – that should speed the dry-out.'

'Do that,' said Campbell. 'How long do you think it'll take us to get ready for sea again?'

We did some figuring and the answer was again not less than a week. Campbell shrugged. 'That's it, then. But we've lost our lead. We'll be lucky to get out of here before Ramirez pitches up.'

'He may wait until we go,' I said.

But guessing was futile, and we left it at that.

III

Next day we went to sea and pumped out both main tanks and refilled them with water from the fresh water tanks. I checked for sugar and found an appreciable quantity in the water of the port tank, so we pumped out again and went back to Nuku'alofa. We filled up with fresh water again, both in the water and the fuel tanks, much to the surprise of the suppliers, and then put to sea again.

I still found a little undissolved sugar in the port tank, so we did it all again. By this time I reckoned we were clean so we put back to port and Geordie rigged up his hot air contraption to dry out the tanks before we put in new fuel oil. A couple of days was spent on this and we used partial crews each time, spelling the others to have time ashore. God knows what stories were put about in the port, but our lads had orders to remain quiet and ignorant.

While Geordie and one team were checking the winch and its auxiliary equipment, aided by Campbell, Ian set another group to stripping *Esmerelda*. They took down all the rigging, both running and standing, and inspected everything. They found nothing wrong and we were sure we were fit for sea when they had finished. But it took time.

No more of Kane's sabotage came to light. He had carefully selected the two things which could do us the most damage – doctored grease and sugar in the fuel. If he hadn't been watched he might have got away with a lot more, and as it was he'd done more than enough.

Campbell was Napoleonic about the food stores. 'Dump the lot,' he said.

'We've no need to dump the canned stuff,' objected Ian, his thrifty Scot's soul aghast.

But Campbell insisted. 'Dump the lot. That son of a bitch was too clever for my liking. I've no hankering for cyanide in my stew.'

So on our last run out to sea for testing we dumped the food supplies, and also recalibrated the echometers against proven and charted soundings. They were all right but it was as well to make sure. The local tradesmen were delighted at our liberal purchase of fresh food stocks, and no doubt it all added to the gossip concerning the *Esmerelda*. Seven days after we had discovered Kane's sabotage Geordie said, 'That just about does it. We're ready for sea.'

'Let's hope Kane hasn't left any surprises we haven't found,' I said. 'I'd hate to start dredging and then find the bottom falling out of the ship. How's the engine, Geordie?'

He grimaced. 'Nothing wrong there. But we had to pull everything down to make sure.'

'That's the hellish thing about sabotage. Not being sure.'

When we assembled in the hotel lounge that evening Campbell asked me about the next move. 'How do we go about it?'

'I'm working on the assumption that there may be something between Falcon and Minerva. That's a distance of three hundred miles. We go to Falcon and take a bottom sample every ten miles on a direct course to Minerva. If we don't find anything, then we sample on parallel courses east and west.'

'So our first step is to find Falcon Island.'

I became thoughtful, shook my head and presently said, 'No, I've changed my mind. I think we'll start at Minerva – do it the other way around.'

They were interested. 'Why would you do that – why should it matter?' Campbell asked.

'Mark was an oceanographer and he was presumably working on the same lines as we are – volcanic theories much like the ones I've postulated. If the high-cobalt nodules are anywhere near Falcon, why should he mention Minerva at all? I think the nodules are quite a distance from Falcon, quite close to Minerva perhaps. And when Mark indicated them in his diary he thought of the source – which is Falcon – and the vicinity, Minerva.'

'That sounds logical,' said Campbell. 'But it might mean that the nodules aren't placed on a direct course between Falcon and Minerva. Hell, they could be on the other side of those reefs.'

'Or scattered all the way along,' suggested Clare. Which was also feasible.

I said, 'This is what we do. We leave here and sail due west until we hit the track between Falcon and Minerva. We turn towards Minerva and take samples every ten miles. If we don't find anything then, we come back to Falcon and on a parallel course, sampling all the way, go round Falcon and move back again further out. How's that?'

We talked it over for a while and then went in for dinner. I was glad we were going to sea again; every time we put into port something seemed to go wrong, whether it was arson, wrongful arrest, sabotage or just plain bad news.

During the meal Clare nudged me and murmured, 'Look over there.'

I looked around but couldn't see anything out of order. 'What's the matter?'

She said quietly, 'The waiters have just put two tables together over there, and laid them for dinner. There are places for eight.'

I took another look and she was right. 'Ramirez!' I exclaimed and she nodded. 'Could well be.'

We glanced towards the doorway, but saw nobody there.

'Don't tell Pop,' she whispered to me. 'He'll get mad if he sees Ramirez. I don't want us to have a scene – I want us to get him away quietly.'

'You'd better get him up to bed then – if you can. Geordie and I will check out now and go back to *Esmerelda* to push things on – we'll try and leave early tomorrow morning. You be there.'

'I can manage it,' she said.

They didn't come into the dining room while we were there, and Clare and Paula got the old man upstairs without him being aware that he was being moved like a chess piece – they seemed to be good at it, and I was hopeful that they'd handle him as well the next day. As soon as they'd gone I said to Geordie, 'We think Ramirez has arrived. We'd better pack up here.'

'How do you know?'

'Clare's been Sherlocking, and I think she's right.' I indicated the waiting table.

We went straight to the desk and settled up, taking advantage of an empty foyer, and then went up to our room to pack our gear. I took one of the two .38 revolvers which Campbell had entrusted to me and tossed it to Geordie. 'The boss says this is for you. Can you use it?'

He held it in his hand. 'Just let me get Kane or Hadley at the other end of it and I'll show you. Got any ammo?'

We split the ammunition, loaded the guns and went downstairs with our duffle bags. I was conscious of the weight of the gun in my jacket pocket and felt a bit ridiculous, as though I were impersonating a fifth-rate movie gangster. But there was nothing funny about it really – I might have to use that gun.

Halfway down the winding stairs I checked and put out my hand to stop Geordie. The foyer seemed full of people and I heard a drift of conversation. It was in Spanish.

We waited until the crowd had moved into the dining room, led by a tall, thin, hawklike man who must have been Ramirez. He tallied with Campbell's description, though I couldn't see the scar, and I felt a wave of angry nausea in my throat at the sight of him. When the foyer was empty we carried on.

We found Ian on the deck of *Esmerelda*. Geordie asked abruptly, 'Any new ships come in during the last hour or so?'

'Aye,' said Ian. 'That one.' He pointed across the water and I saw the dark loom of a boat anchored a little way out. It was difficult to tell her size, but from her riding light I judged her to be about the same size as *Esmerelda*, maybe a bit bigger but not much.

'That is Suarez-Navarro,' said Geordie and Ian stared at him aghast.

'I want the crew rousted out. I want a watch – two men on each side and a look-out up the foremast. And I don't want any extra lights – I don't want to show that anything out of the ordinary is happening. I want her ready to be moved at a moment's notice. How many are on board?'

'Most of the lads, and I can round up the others easily enough.'

'Do that, right away.'

'Aye aye, sir,' said Ian smartly and went below at a dead run.

Geordie looked across at her. 'I wonder if Hadley's over there – or Kane?' he said softly.

I said, 'They weren't in Ramirez's party in the hotel. Perhaps they're too scared to come ashore – there must be warrants out for them in every port in the Pacific by now. On the other hand, there's no reason for them to be on board her at all. Hadley's still got the *Pearl*, remember, and we've got no proof that they came here, or joined up with Ramirez after leaving Papeete.'

'True,' said Geordie glumly.

'I've got things to do in the lab,' I said. 'I have to make ready for sea. I'll see you later.'

I had been working for an hour when Geordie and Ian came in to see me. 'We've got an idea,' Geordie said. They both looked alive with something that I felt could be called mischief.

'What is it?'

'The boys think that Kane and Hadley may be across there, on Ramirez's ship. They want to go and get them.'

'Christ, they can't do that!'

'Why not?'

'You know damn well they're most unlikely to be there. This is just an excuse for any nonsense they're cooking up.'

'But suppose they are? It would solve a hell of a lot of problems. We hand them over to the police and that scuppers

Ramirez. He'll be too busy explaining why he's harbouring a couple of wanted murderers to be able to follow us.'

I thought about it and shook my head. 'No, it's too risky, too damn close to piracy. Campbell wouldn't like it at all.'

'Look,' said Geordie, 'the boys are all steamed up. They didn't like your stories, they didn't like what those two did on Tanakabu, and they sure as hell didn't like the week's work they've had to put in here because of Kane. They're tired of being pushed around – some of them were shot at in Tanakabu lagoon and they didn't like that either. I don't know if I can stop them.'

I looked at the glint in Geordie's eye. 'I don't suppose you've tried too hard, have you, Geordie?'

He bristled. 'Why the hell should I? I've got scores to settle with Hadley too, remember. He gave me a pistol whipping, don't forget that. And it's *my* ship that Kane's been sabotaging, not Campbell's!'

'Suppose they aren't there after all?'

'We'll be bound to learn something to our advantage.' I noticed he was now including himself in the venture and had given up any pretence of being against it.

Ian said, 'Ach, Mike, it's all laid on. It'll be as easy as lifting a trout from the stream when the keeper's having a dram in the pub.'

'Oh, it's all laid on, is it? Would you mind telling me what the pair of you have been up to?'

Ian looked at Geordie, who said, 'Well, it's like this, Mike. I thought a guard was all very well in its way, but a bit negative, if you know what I mean. So I sent a couple of boys ashore to scout around. They found a lot of the crew of that hooker in a pub, drinking themselves silly. A tough-looking mob, true, but they're almost out of it already. All dagoes.'

'And no Kane or Hadley?'

'No one spotted them. Anyway with your lot at the hotel, there are precious few bodies left on Ramirez's ship.'

I said, 'They'll be keeping a watch too. Ramirez isn't a damn fool, and he knows we're here.'

'Right enough,' agreed Geordie. 'But I've gone into that too. I sent Taffy and Bill Hunter out in a boat to have a look. Bill's the best swimmer we've got, and he had a good look at that ship.' He chuckled suddenly. 'Do you know what he did? He swam right round her first, then he hauled himself aboard on the port side, had a good look round the deck, then let himself into the water on the starboard side and came back to report. That's the sort of watch they're keeping over there.'

'It would have to be done very quietly,' I mused.

'Ach, that's no trouble,' said Ian. 'We're a quiet lot.'

'Just about as quiet as a bunch of sharks. They don't make much noise either.'

'Well, what about it?' said Geordie imploringly.

'There would have to be no guns. No killing. Just bare fists.'

'Or maybe the odd belaying pin,' offered Ian gently.

'You're a bloodthirsty lot. It's a damn silly idea, but I'll agree to it – conditionally.'

Geordie grinned delightedly. 'I knew you had something of your father in you, Mike!'

I said, 'Dad would have had you court-martialled for disobedience and insubordination, and you damn well know it. All right, here are the conditions. One – if you find Kane or Hadley we hand them over to the police intact to the last hair of their heads. We don't want to ruin our own case. Two – if we don't find them you get back here fast. We'll have to get the hell out of Nuku'alofa anyway – Ramirez will be looking for us and maybe the cops too. That means, three – that Campbell and the girls will have to be got aboard.'

Geordie's face fell. 'That means the whole thing's off. He'll never stand for it, not with the girls along.'

'He doesn't have to know about it too soon – if we time it right. You send someone up to the hotel and get him aboard at just the right time.'

'The right time being when it's too late to stop us,' said Geordie. 'Mike, laddie, you're going to have a hell of a time explaining to the old man what we're doing.'

'I'll leave the explanations until afterwards,' I said. 'I've got another condition, number four – I'm coming with you. I've got scores to settle myself.'

IV

The timing was a bit tricky. We didn't know how long Ramirez and company were going to stay in the hotel, nor even if they intended returning to their ship that night. We didn't want to bump into them because then there certainly would be noise.

Again, Campbell and the girls had to be got out of the hotel under the nose of Ramirez, another tricky bit. So we made a plan.

Geordie had picked Nick Dugan to bring Campbell from the hotel. 'He's probably the best scrapper of the lot of us,' he said. 'But he's never quiet in his fighting. It's best we keep him out of the main operation, and he'll not take it well.'

I had a word with Nick and sent him off immediately. 'You've got two jobs,' I told him. 'The first is to keep an eye on Ramirez. If any of them make a move to go back to their ship, you nip down to the waterfront and flash a signal to us. Then the operation is definitely off. Got that?'

'Right.' As it turned out he was surprisingly meek.

'We'll be starting off at eleven-thirty. At exactly that time you get into Mr Campbell's room and give him a note which I'll write. No sooner and no later than eleven-thirty – that's important.'

'I understand,' said Nick.

'Have you got a watch?'

He showed me his wrist watch and, as we synchronized, I wondered how many times my father had done the same before an operation.

'I settled their bills along with mine – they don't need to stop at the desk. No porters. Get them back here as fast as you can, and as quietly – and don't let Ramirez or any of his crowd see you.'

I also had a word with Bill Hunter. 'What sort of watch are they keeping over there, Bill?'

He smiled. 'I suppose they think they're keeping a good one – by their standards. It's nothing to worry about, though. It'll be a piece of cake.'

'Geordie tells me you're the best swimmer, so you'll go first. But you must be quiet about it or the balloon will go up. Your job will be to find the quietest spot on board to get the rest of us up.'

'Not to worry,' he said easily. 'It'll be like the old times.'

As I turned away he said, 'Er – Mike . . .'

'Yes, Bill?'

'It's good to work with a Trevelyan again.'

I was touched. 'Thanks, Bill. You don't know how I appreciate that.'

At last we were ready. Six of us were going – Geordie, Ian, Taffy, Jim, Bill Hunter and myself. Danny Williams was left in command of the ship and the rest of Geordie's non-commando crew, and I said to him, 'Danny, if anything goes wrong, get the hell out of here as fast as you can, once Mr Campbell and the girls and Nick are back on board, even if it means leaving us behind. Mr Campbell mustn't be involved in this, you understand?'

'I gotcha,' he said. 'But you'll be all right.'

Geordie was fussing. 'Jim, got all your bits and pieces?'

'I'm okay,' said Jim. 'Stop binding, skipper.'

I stepped over to Geordie. 'What are these bits and pieces?'

'Nothing much,' he said airily. 'A few tools. Belaying pins and stuff like that. What time is it?'

I looked at the luminous hands of my watch. 'Eleven-twenty-eight.' It had been a rush to get ready but the last few minutes crawled.

'Let's go,' he said. 'It'll be a doddle.'

We dropped into the larger of our two dinghies, Ian and Taffy took the oars and pulled quietly, and the boat moved out. We rounded the stern of *Esmerelda* and Ian steered us across the harbour.

I was thinking of all the things that could go wrong and what Campbell would say when we got back, and damning myself for an idiot. I leaned over to Geordie and whispered, 'If Taffy's got that damned knife of his, tell him to leave it in the bottom of the boat. We don't want even the possibility of him using it.'

'It's all right,' he said in a low voice. 'He left it aboard – I told him to.'

It wasn't long before Ian and Taffy stopped pulling and the boat glided to a stop, rocking gently. Bill was dressed in dark clothing and all I saw of him was the flash of his teeth in the moonlight as he slipped over the side.

'Are you sure the torch is waterproof?' Geordie murmured.

'It's okay,' Bill replied. 'I'll give you a flash as soon as I'm ready.' He moved away without a single splash and we sat quietly waiting for his signal. It seemed a long time coming and as I sat there I wondered what I was doing in this Pacific harbour, contemplating an act of piracy. It seemed a long way from my office at the Institute.

I said to Geordie, 'He's a long time, isn't he?'

'Stop worrying,' said Geordie. 'We're professionals.'

I let out my breath and tried to relax on the hard thwart, never taking my eyes off Ramirez's ship. Suddenly there was a flicker of light, so faint and so quickly doused that I wondered if I'd really seen it or whether my eyes were playing tricks.

'That's it,' said Geordie softly. 'Pull together. Gently now.'

We moved on under the measured slow strokes of the oars until the side of the ship loomed above us. Something hit my face and I started violently. Geordie said in my ear, 'Be still, for God's sake.'

I felt him moving about and he said, always in that low murmur that was so much more effective than a whisper, 'Bill's been a good boy. He's dropped us a line. Make fast there.'

Jim, in the bows, made fast and Geordie said, 'I'll go first.' He swarmed up somehow like a monkey and disappeared over the bulwarks. Ian followed and then I came up, finding that they were using a rope ladder that hung just above our dinghy. My eyes had got used to the darkness and with the help of the waning moon and the dim glow of the riding lights I found I could see fairly well. There was no one about on deck, but a low murmur of voices came from aft.

Someone moved to join us and Bill's voice said, soft and unexpectedly close, 'I've copped one of 'em.'

'What have you done with him?' Geordie asked.

'Nothing much.' There was joy in Bill's voice. 'He won't wake up for a longish time.'

The others had arrived on deck and Geordie said, 'Split into pairs – I'll take Mike. We'll do the old backward-forward trick.'

'What's that?' I asked, trying to pitch my voice low as he had done.

'Quiet! Someone's coming. Jim and Taffy – you take him.'

I watched the two figures snake across the deck and vanish into the shadows. Then I heard what Geordie's quicker ear had caught much earlier – the measured pace of footsteps coming along the deck from aft. The man came in sight round the corner of the deck-house; he was carrying a mug in his hand, being careful not to spill it – probably coffee for someone up in the bows.

Suddenly, to my surprise, a black shape arose quite openly in front of him and Taffy's voice said gently, 'Well now, that's a nice thought – bringing me coffee.'

The man stopped and backed up in amazement. He was about to speak when something flickered in front of his face and he raised his hands to claw at his neck. Taffy expertly caught the falling mug.

The man seemed to be fighting nothing. He staggered two paces along the deck and then collapsed. I saw Jim crouch over him and then they both dragged him over to us, Taffy using only one hand.

'Anyone want some hot coffee?' he said. 'Not a drop spilled.'

'Stop playing the fool,' Geordie growled.

'What happened?' I asked.

'It'll keep. That's two – how many more do you reckon, Bill?'

'There were five on deck when I was here before. But I dunno about below.'

Jim and Taffy were gagging and trussing up their victim. Geordie said, 'We'll finish that. You lot go aft and clear up the deck.'

They drifted away like wreathes of smoke and I helped Geordie finish the job. The man was flaccid and quite unconscious and I whispered, 'What the hell did Jim do to him?'

'A silk cloth with a weight in one corner. We learned that one from an Indian instructor, old thuggee trick. But at least Jim hasn't strangled this one – he'll recover okay.'

There was a muffled thump from aft and he clicked his tongue. 'Someone's being careless. Come on, I want to see if Bill's done his job properly.'

He rose and walked unconcernedly forward, not trou-
bling to hide. He stopped at the forehatch and tested it with
his hand. 'Bill's a good workman. No one can come from
below this way.'

He then searched about until he found what he was
looking for – the prone and unconscious body of the after
watch. He rolled the limp body over and began to tie the
hands. 'Not that I don't trust Bill's judgement,' he said. 'But
it's nice to be safe and tidy. You take his feet – use his
shoelaces.'

It was all a little bit dreamlike. Geordie was expertly
tying the crewman's hands and conversing matter-of-factly
as any good craftsman might as he worked on his bench.
'Sorry to keep you out of the fun, Mike. But you're dead
inexperienced. You've only got to do the wrong thing once
on a lark like this and the cat's out of the bag.'

I looked at Geordie's bulk in the semi-darkness and realized something I'd never thought of consciously before. He
had been trained as a professional killer, and my father had
had a hand in his training. He had been taught perhaps a
couple of dozen ways of putting a man out of action, tempor-
arily or permanently, and he had the professional's amused
contempt for the dilettante. I thought for the first time that
something of Mark's ruthless streak, albeit turned in a strange
and distasteful manner, had been inherited from my father.

I said, 'That's all right, Geordie. You're doing fine. I'm
content to look and learn.'

From the stern came the lowest, breathiest of whistles
and Geordie cocked his head. 'They're finished. Let's go and
see what the bag's like.'

We went forward, walking as though the ship belonged
to us. As we went, Geordie said softly, 'Never dodge about
when there's no need. Nothing looks more suspicious. I
mean, suppose someone's watching the deck right now –
we could be any pair of the crew.'

He slowed as he came to the deckhouse where a stream of light splashed on the deck from the door. He peered cautiously round the edge of the door, then snorted. 'I might have known,' he said resignedly. 'It's Taffy the gutser. What do you think you're doing, Taff?'

He stepped into the deckhouse and I followed to find that it led straight into the galley. Taffy was sawing at a loaf of bread. 'Making myself a sandwich, skipper,' he said.

'You bloody cormorant. How many did you get?'

'Three.'

'Kane? Hadley?'

'Not a sign. If they're aboard, they're below. But they'll be safe – we battened down the hatches.'

'Well, we'll unbatten them and clean up below,' said Geordie. 'It only needs one of 'em to decide he'd like a nice breath of sea air and find he can't get on deck. When you've finished your supper, Mr Morgan, we'd all be grateful if you got back on the job. And before you leave the galley clean up – and then find the flour bin and tip the salt into it.'

'Yes, sergeant,' said Taffy.

We went to the wheelhouse and found the others. Ian was unscrewing the central holding bolt of the wheel-bearing with an adjustable spanner. He looked up at Geordie and said solemnly, 'Might as well cause a bit of inconvenience while we're here.' He withdrew the bolt and casually tossed it overboard, then spun the wheel. 'They'll have a wee bit of trouble in their steering, I'm thinking.'

'Very nice, but a little premature,' said Geordie. 'Let's get the job finished first. Mike and I will take the forehatch and clean out the fo'c's'le. Ian and Bill, take this hatch here. Jim, you'll find Taffy stuffing his guts in the galley – you take amidships. Got your stuff?'

'I've got it, skipper.'

'Right. We'll all go down simultaneously. I'll give the signal – and try not to make too much noise. Come on, Mike.'

When we got to the forehatch Geordie paused. 'We'll give them a minute to get ready.' He shook his head sadly. 'That bloody Welshman.'

I looked aft along the deck. It was very quiet and there was nothing to be seen, and I thought how easy it had all been – so far. These ex-commandoes seemed to take it all as a joke, as I suppose it was to men who had tackled alert Germans. But I wasn't deceived; it was their very competence that made it seem easy.

Geordie startled me by uttering that same hollow whistle I'd heard before. 'Come on,' he said softly. 'Me first.'

He lifted up the hatch gently and went down the companionway. The forecastle was dimly lit by a single lamp and appeared full of shadowy shapes. When I got to the bottom of the steps I found Geordie fastening the door which led to the midships accommodation by means of a small wooden wedge which he took from his pocket. The door fastened, he turned to look round the forecastle. Tiers of bunks, three high, lined the triangular space formed by the bows of the ship. They pack the bastards in like sardines, I thought. There was a snoring noise and Geordie looked round quickly, put his fingers to his lips for my benefit and crept forward very gently, and then waved me forward. He was looking at a middle berth upon which was sleeping a villainously unshaven seaman. He put his lips close to my ear and said, 'Check the other bunks.'

I tiptoed round the forecastle, looking into every bunk, but found no one else. I got back to Geordie and shook my head.

He said loudly, 'All right, let's wake up the sleeping beauty.'

The man snored again, drawing back his upper lip.

Geordie shook him by the shoulder. 'Come on, chum. Prepare to meet thy doom.' The man opened his eyes and looked up uncomprehendingly and then Geordie hit him on the chin with a fist like a hammer.

He rubbed his knuckles and said, a little apologetically, 'I never like to hit a sleeping man. It seems a bit unfair somehow.'

I looked at the seaman. He was out cold.

Geordie looked round the forecastle again. 'Nine a side. They pack eighteen in here. The Board of Trade would never allow this back home. Right, let's see what else there is. The next one might be the lucky draw, Mike.'

He took the wedge out of the door and opened it carefully. We checked all the compartments we came across, even the toilets. 'Nothing like catching a man with his pants down,' Geordie chuckled.

We found nothing.

The ship rocked a little more heavily and we both stiffened but there was no hue and cry and we carried on slowly until suddenly there was a shadow at the end of the passage and Taffy came into sight. He was eating an apple.

Geordie sniffed. 'Look at that. You'd think he'd get fatter, wouldn't you? He was just the same in the army – holding the war up while he rammed himself full.' There were two cabins remaining between ourselves and Taffy and we each investigated one, with negative results.

'What did you get?' demanded Geordie.

Taffy crunched on his apple. 'Ian put one laddie to sleep – he wasn't Kane and not big enough by all accounts to be Hadley.'

'Damn! The bastards aren't here, then. We got another – that's seven.'

'One in the bows and we got two more, skipper,' Taffy said. 'That's seven on board.'

Geordie began to calculate. 'There's no less than fifteen getting boozed up ashore – that makes twenty-two. And there's eight at the hotel – that's thirty.'

'The ship's over-crewed,' said Taffy with the air of one making a profound statement.

'So is a battleship,' snapped Geordie. 'And that's what this is. They wouldn't need all this crowd just to handle the ship. Where's Jim?'

'In the engine room.'

'Good. You nip up on deck and keep watch. I don't think any of the officers will be coming back now, but the crew will, and Ramirez might come back for a check-up.'

We went aft and found Ian breaking open a desk in one of the bigger cabins. I was about to protest when I realized that it hardly mattered what we did now, short of murder. 'Ramirez lives here,' he told us.

The desk gave us nothing of interest or use and we glanced through his clothing quickly. It was elegant and extensive for shipboard life. 'Have you found our birds?' Ian asked as we worked.

'Neither of them,' I said. 'We've slipped up on this one. Campbell is going to be mad.'

Ian was disconsolate. 'My mannie wasn't Hadley. He had a black beard,' he said.

Geordie pricked up his ears. 'Are you sure it wasn't him, or Kane, in a disguise?'

'Na, na,' said Ian. 'It was too long. Kane couldn't have grown it in the time, and Hadley was clean-shaven. And it was real – I pulled it.'

I was looking down and saw Geordie peeling back the carpet, revealing a recessed ring-bolt. 'What's down there?' I asked.

'We can soon find out.' He grasped the ring-bolt and pulled, opening a trap-door. He pulled a torch from his pocket and flashed it down the hole.

'Christ!' he said, and pulled out a sub-machine gun.

We looked at it in silence, and then Geordie said, 'I told you this was a flaming battleship.'

'Let's see what else there is,' I said.

Five minutes later we were surrounded by enough weapons to start a small war. There were four sub-machine guns, fifteen rifles of assorted pattern, half a dozen pistols and a dozen hand grenades.

I summoned up a laugh. 'I wonder what Chamant would have thought of this little lot? He nearly had heart failure at the sight of our four pistols.' But I was feeling a little sick, looking at our haul and my hands, which had been fine up to that moment, were sweating slightly.

Geordie said thoughtfully, 'You were a pretty good armourer in your time, Ian. How would you put this lot out of action?'

'With the bolt-action rifles you just throw the bolts away. With the others, we smash the firing pins.'

'Why not throw the lot overboard?' I asked.

Geordie cocked his head at me. 'We'll do that too. But this mob will then do some skin-diving and I want it to be a wasted effort. Get cracking, Ian, as fast as you can. We've spent enough time here.'

We were ready for leaving fifteen minutes later after carefully dropping the useless guns over the side, with a minimum of splashing. Ian was rolling the last of the bolts he'd taken from the rifles into torn strips of cloth and stuffing them into his pockets. We were about to leave when Taffy suddenly held up a hand. 'Quiet,' he said softly.

We were very still and though I listened hard I couldn't hear anything. Taffy said, 'There's a boat coming.'

Then I heard the faint creak of rowlocks and the splash of oars. I looked anxiously towards Geordie.

'We take them,' he decided. 'We can't have the game given away too soon.' He issued quick instructions and the men spread themselves into the deck shadows. There was a soft bump as the boat reached the boarding ladder, on the other side from our own exit, and a few moments later I saw the outline of a man against the night sky. There was only one man and as he came aboard I drew in my breath sharply.

It was Kane.

'He's my meat,' I murmured to Geordie, who gave me the thumbs up. I moved forward in a crouch. Kane walked forward along the deck and just as he passed me I straightened up and gave him a tap on the shoulder. He turned and I let him have it, as hard as I could to the jaw. Ian tapped him on the head with something as he started to collapse and all in one movement, as it seemed, rolled him into a piece of canvas. Geordie looked over the railings and saw that Kane had been alone in the dinghy. 'That'll get us off the hook with Campbell,' he said with satisfaction.

'I'm not so sure of that,' I said, rubbing my sore knuckles. 'We can't take Kane to the police now. They wouldn't look at all kindly on our methods, and if they find out what we've done to this ship we're for it, right on our side or not.'

'You've said better than you know, Mike,' Geordie concurred. 'We'll leave here right away – and we'll take Mr Kane with us.'

We piled into our boat and pulled for *Esmerelda*, and as we passed under the stern of Ramirez's ship I looked up and saw her name painted there – *Sirena*. Halfway across the harbour I had a sudden thought. 'Geordie, what was Jim doing in the engine room?'

'Nothing much,' he said. Jim grinned briefly in the half-light and I was about to speak to him direct when Geordie interrupted me. 'Heave, you bloody pirates – we haven't much time.' He seemed in a devil of a hurry.

As we climbed the bulwarks of *Esmerelda* I suddenly remembered that Jim Taylor had made a name for himself as a demolitions expert during the war. I hadn't time to develop this thought because Campbell was on to me in a rage.

'What in hell is going on?'

I found I'd stopped sweating and felt very calm. No doubt the reaction would set in later. 'A little bit of direct action,' I said coolly.

Geordie was already giving orders in a quiet bellow. 'Get that bloody engine started up. Slip all lines bar the bow-line. Get that dinghy up smartly now.' The deck was astir with movement.

'You damned fools! You'll get us all gaoled,' Campbell was raging.

'Better gaoled than dead,' I said. 'You don't know what we found on that damned ship.'

'Stand by the warps,' I heard Geordie say. I heard a throb as the engines started.

'I don't care what you found,' fumed Campbell. 'Do you realize you've committed an act of piracy?'

It was lucky that the engine note drowned his voice. In the same moment Ian came running along the deck. 'Mr Campbell, sir. Yon man on the jetty – he wants a wee crack wi' you.'

We both looked ashore in alarm and saw a solitary figure standing just where our gangplank lay. It was about to be pulled inboard, but he arrested it with a gesture. It was Ernesto Ramirez.

'By God, I'll crack him!' I burst out.

Campbell recognized him at once, and I heard a buzz behind me as Nick Dugan breathed the name for the benefit of the crew. I gave Nick a sharp glance and he shook his head slightly, spreading his hands to indicate that there had been no contact before.

Campbell took my arm. 'Easy, Mike, don't go off at half-cock. Let's not compound whatever mischief you've been up to. Hold Geordie, will you?' Amazingly, as my wrath had risen so his had subsided and he seemed in complete control of himself.

He walked away to the gangplank and I shouted, 'Hold it, Geordie! There's a snag – the boss has a visitor.' I followed Campbell.

Ramirez was alone, leaning negligently on a bollard. Obviously he hadn't yet been on *Sirena* – there hadn't been time for that, and he was too composed. Campbell looked down at him. 'Well?' he asked coldly.

Ramirez smiled up at him. 'I just came to wish you farewell. I thought you would be leaving about now.' I realized that, Nick Dugan or not, he'd seen us at the hotel or he'd seen the Campbells and Paula leaving.

He walked straight up the gangplank and stepped onto the deck, elegant in his white tropical suit.

Campbell's voice was icy. 'You don't have to come on board to tell us that.'

'Maybe not, but I am here.'

To give the devil his due, he had no nerves at all. After doing what he'd done I wouldn't have had the guts to come within a hundred miles of *Esmerelda*, let alone without an escort. But he was a subtle and clever man, relying on Campbell's known sense of justice, and maybe he knew that our scruples would hold us back. Still, he had guts.

He said, 'I thought I should warn you. I have plans and I do not wish you to interfere with them. Why don't you give up and go away?'

'I'm not concerned with your plans,' said Campbell stolidly.

'You know what I mean, Mr Campbell. We met in battle before and you came off worst. And so you shall again if you do not get out of my way.' He had the Spanish trick of making gutturals out of his aitches, but otherwise his English was good. I didn't think my Spanish would be as fluent.

My mouth was dry. I said, 'Ramirez, you're a bloody murderer and I'm going to see you pay for it.'

His eyebrows quirked. 'Murder?' he queried mockingly. 'That is a libel, Mr Trevelyan. Whom am I supposed to have murdered?'

'My brother, for one,' I said hotly.

Ramirez threw back his head and laughed. 'My dear sir, I'm willing to go into any court in the world on a charge like that.' His teeth flashed. 'You have no proof, have you – no proof at all.' And he laughed again.

That was only too true. The only man who had seen him at Tanakabu was Dr Schouten – and he too was dead.

Campbell said, 'I fail to see the point of this conversation, Ramirez.'

Geordie tugged at my sleeve agitatedly. 'We've got to get away – now. Before that thing goes bang.'

'What thing, for God's sake?'

He drew me aside and said in a low hurried voice, 'Jim had a small charge of plastic explosive – he slapped it against the crank case of their engine. He wanted to blow a hole in the bottom of their boat but I wouldn't let him – I wish I had, now.'

'When's it due to go off?'

'That's it – Jim doesn't know. He rigged up a time switch from an ordinary alarm clock, and you can't get those right to within five minutes or so. I thought we'd be away by now.'

'It'll rouse the whole harbour!'

'But we'd have been gone – nothing to do with us.' The urgency in his voice was an imperative. I looked across at Ramirez and said, 'I think you ought to have the privilege of cleaning your own deck.'

Geordie caught on and went immediately up to the gangplank where Campbell and Ramirez were locked in a low-voiced, furious argument. I noticed Geordie dab his hand on the winch drum and then signal surreptitiously to Ian and Taffy. Of the rest of the crew all were spellbound except Jim, who was watching anxiously across the water. There was no sign of the girls.

Geordie placed himself squarely in front of Ramirez and was blunt in his speech. 'I'm the master of this ship – and the owner – and I'm particular about filth on my decks. I'd be pleased if you'd leave.'

Ramirez went bleak, looking carefully at his scarred face. 'Ah, the brave and foolish Mr Wilkins,' he said insultingly.

'That's me,' said Geordie. He put out his hand and smeared it down the front of Ramirez's gleaming white jacket, leaving a dirty trail of black oil. 'You're dirty, Mr Ramirez.'

Ramirez was so shocked at the action and at the contempt which lay behind it that he just stood there, making no move – but the fury grew in his eyes.

Geordie said again, 'You're filthily dirty, Mr Ramirez. I think you need a wash – don't you, lads?'

They got the idea fast – faster than Ramirez. With a growl they were on to him, four of them. I saw Ramirez's hand go to his pocket as quick as lightning, but Danny was faster and his hand came down in a mighty chop. A pistol clattered on deck.

Then Ramirez was lifted helplessly off his feet and carried to the side. They swung him twice and then over he went, making a great splash. Geordie wasted no time in useless triumph. He turned, picked up Ramirez's pistol and began chopping out orders again. 'Gangplank in. Don't stand there gawking! Ian, get the wheel, and don't run him down. Cast off forrard. Engine slow ahead.'

Esmerelda got under way even while Campbell was still staring over the side. 'Well, I'm damned,' he said to no one in particular, while staring at Geordie. Geordie was oblivious, watching carefully out into the darkness and giving orders in a low, carrying voice. He conned us out past the sleeping vessels and the marker buoys and Ramirez's splashing progress fell astern.

As we drew level with *Sirena*, anchored in the harbour, there was a dull *thump*, not very loud, which carried over the water. At the same time there was a flicker of lights from a dinghy arriving alongside. The crew returning no doubt, to find a shambles. That would do her engine a bit of no good. Silence held us until we were well past all the shipping and abreast of one of the openings in the fringing reef, and then a babble of noise got up as everyone's tongue was loosened. Ian had to shout to make himself heard, giving orders to get some sail on her. The excitement on board was electric.

Geordie turned and grinned, his battered face alight with triumph. Raucously he began to sing at the top of his voice. *'Oh, we're off to see the Ozzard – the wonderful Ozzard of Whiz!'*

He looked very piratical because of the captured pistol dangling negligently in his hand.

SEVEN

'You pack of damned fools,' said Campbell. 'Whatever possessed you to do a crazy thing like that?'

Ian shuffled his feet, Geordie was clearly unrepentant and I suspected we were in for a tongue-lashing, and didn't relish the thought. The lights of Nuku'alofa were falling astern as *Esmerelda* ran at full speed. Danny Williams was at the wheel and Campbell had gathered the three of us together to take us to task.

'Well,' Geordie began. 'We thought it would be a good idea to go and get hold of either Kane or Hadley and – '

'Kane! Hadley! You won't find them with Ramirez. Ramirez may be a son of a bitch but he has brains – he won't chance himself being linked with those two, not now he won't.'

I grinned at Geordie. 'Where did you put Kane, by the way?' I asked casually.

'We haven't a brig on the ship, but we're making one now. In the meantime he's under guard in my cabin.'

Campbell's jaw dropped. 'You mean you've *got* Kane?'

'Of course,' I said. I didn't say that it had been a near thing, or how close we came to not achieving our objective. 'We thought we'd hand him over to the Tongan police but circumstances – ah – preceded that.'

'What circumstances?'

precluded

'Ramirez's ship got a bit bent,' I said. 'I couldn't control the lads.' I gave Geordie a sly look – I was taking his argument and using it against Campbell.

'How bent?'

'One of us had an accident with some explosive,' I said.

'That thump we heard? As we left harbour? You blew up their ship?' He was incredulous.

'Oh no, nothing like that,' said Geordie placatingly. 'There's a bit of a hole in their engine crankcase, that's all. They won't be following us in a hurry.'

'They won't have to,' said Campbell. 'What do you suppose Ramirez is doing now? He'll have got back to his ship – seething mad thanks to you fools – found it wrecked, and by now he'll be presenting himself at the nearest police station, still in his wet clothes, claiming assault and piracy. I should say that within an hour there'll be a fast patrol boat leaving Nuku'alofa and coming right after us. And we won't get out of it as we did in Tahiti – this time we *are* in the wrong.'

We looked at each other in silence.

'Or maybe he won't,' said Campbell slowly. 'Not after what I told him back there.' He jerked his head astern.

'What was that?' I said. I saw that Campbell's eyes suddenly held the same glint that I'd seen in Geordie's earlier that night.

'I said the Tahitian police were very unhappy. I said they knew about Hadley and Kane and that they had witnesses who'd seen Ramirez with them at Tanakabu, the first time they went there.'

'What witnesses?'

He grinned at us. 'That's what Ramirez wanted to know. I said three of the hospital patients and a couple of staff had seen him. He laughed at me, but it hit home.'

'I don't know anything about any witnesses,' I said.

'Mike, sometimes you're pretty slow on the uptake – there were no goddam witnesses, as far as I know. But someone had to think fast to get us out of this jam. I told Ramirez that the police were looking for more evidence, but that they already had him fairly linked with the events on Tanakabu, and that if he went to the cops in Tonga with any kind of story about us pirating his ship, and if we were picked up, then we'd make enough of a stink to get the Tahitian police down here fast.'

Geordie said, 'Now, that's interesting. We know he was at Tanakabu – Schouten saw him.'

'Exactly,' said Campbell. 'And how does he know that someone else didn't see him too? He can't take the chance – he'll have to lie low. As long as the suspicions of the Tahiti police remain just that – suspicions – he'll be happy. But he won't stir up anything that will give the cops a line on him. At least, I hope not. So I hope he'll dummy up about your stupid raid.'

I said, 'He won't go to the police while we have Kane. Kane is our trump card. Ramirez wouldn't dare let Kane get into the hands of the police.'

'Mike, he's a clever man. Clever and subtle when he has to be. I wouldn't put it past him to wriggle out of that one.'

'And something else,' I said. 'Maybe the raid wasn't as stupid as you think – a bit hare-brained, I'll grant you, but worth while. What we found on that ship was as subtle as a crack on the head with a hammer.' I gestured to Ian. 'Trot out your collection of ironmongery.'

Ian delved in various pockets and brought out the bolts he had taken from the rifles. Campbell's eyes widened as he saw the mounting pile they made on the deck.

'He had *ten* rifles?'

'Fifteen,' I corrected. 'The others were automatic action. We've smashed them and dropped them over the side. Plus four sub-machine guns and a lot of pistols.'

Geordie dug into his pocket and produced a hand grenade which he tossed casually. 'There were a few of these too. I hung on to a couple.'

'Not much subtlety about that, is there?' I asked.

'And he's got twice as many men as he needs,' said Geordie. 'He isn't paying that big crew to stand half-watches either.' Geordie, too, wasn't losing any opportunity to rub Campbell's nose in it.

Campbell's eyes flickered as he watched the grenade bounce in Geordie's hand. 'For God's sake stop that. You'll blow us all up. Let's go down to the saloon and have a drink – it's pretty damn late.'

It was in fact getting into the small hours of the morning but I felt wide awake, and everyone else seemed to share that feeling, even Campbell. Only Clare and Paula, after a brief appearance on deck, had vanished below again.

'No,' I said to Campbell's offer. 'I want to talk to Kane – now. And I want to be dead sober when I do it. Is he conscious, Geordie?'

'Nothing that a bucket of sea water won't cure.'

The three of us went down to the cabin, leaving Ian on deck, to find Jim and Nick Dugan stolidly on guard. Kane was conscious – and scared. He flinched when we went into the cabin and huddled at the end of Geordie's bunk as though by making himself smaller he wouldn't be noticed. Four of us made a crowd in the small cabin, and Kane was, and felt, thoroughly hemmed in.

He looked as haggard as when I'd first seen him in London, unshaven and ill, and carried his right arm awkwardly – I remembered that Clare had shot him. His eyes slid away when I looked at him.

'Look at me, Kane.'

Slowly his eyes moved until they met mine. His throat worked and his eyes blinked and watered.

'You're going to talk to us, Kane, and you're going to tell us the truth. You might think you're not, but you are. Because if you don't we'll work on you until you do. I was at Tanakabu, Kane, and you must know that anyone who was there won't be squeamish in their methods. I'm a civilized man and it may be that I'll be sickened – but don't count on that, Kane, because there are more than a dozen men on this ship who aren't nearly as squeamish as I am. Do you understand me, Kane? Have I made myself perfectly clear?'

But there was never going to be any resistance out of him. His tongue flickered out and he licked his lips and croaked incoherently. He was still reacting to the blow over the head, a physical problem to add to his mental ones.

'Answer me.'

His head bobbed. 'I'll talk to you,' he whispered.

'Give him a whisky, Geordie,' I said. He drank some of it and a little colour came into his face, and he sat up straighter, but with no less fear in his face.

'All right,' I said deliberately. 'We'll start right at the beginning. You went to London to find Helen Trevelyan and then me. Why?'

'Jim boobed,' he said. 'He let that suitcase get away. There were the books and the stones in it. We had to get them back.'

'You and Ramirez and some of his cut-throats, right?'

'Yair, that's right.'

'But you didn't get them all back, did you? Did Ramirez know that?'

'He said – you must have something else. Didn't know what.'

'So he laid you alongside me to try and find out what I had?'

'Yair. And to pass word where you went, anytime I could.' Now he was volunteering information, and it was getting easier. Campbell and Geordie were silent and watchful, leaving the going to me. I was eager to find out about Mark but decided to lead up to that by taking other directions first, which would also serve to confuse Kane.

'You smashed our radio, didn't you?'

'Yair. I was told to.'

'And led Hadley in the *Pearl* around on our track?' We already knew this but I let him confirm it.

'Why did you tell the Papeete police that we'd burnt the hospital? Surely even you could see that we could disprove that pretty easily.'

He looked, for a moment, almost exasperated. 'That was Jim. Bloody hell, I told him it wouldn't wash. You can't tell him anything.'

I nodded and veered off on another tack. 'That time you saw Miss Campbell's drawings on deck, did they mean anything to you?'

'Eh?' He was taken aback and had to readjust his thinking. 'No, why should they?'

'You identified one as a "scraggy falcon". Why did you say that?'

He stared blearily at us. 'I dunno – did it have something to do with Falcon Island, maybe?'

We exchanged glances, and I carried on evenly.

'Go on. Why should it have?'

'I – I suppose it just slipped out. It looked like a falcon, and maybe it was on my mind, see.'

'What about Falcon Island?'

Kane hesitated and I snapped, 'Come on – out with it!'

'I dunno much about it. Ramirez, he talked a bit about Falcon Island, somewhere in Tonga it is. He said once that's where we were going after we'd got rid of you lot.'

'"Got rid of"? How was he going to do that? And why?'

'I dunno that either, Mr Trevelyan. Something about those stones you've been pulling out of the sea – those nodules, you call 'em. He had to ditch you before he could go to Falcon Island, 'cos that's where they were. My word, Mr Trevelyan, I don't know what it's all about!'

Behind me I heard Campbell let out his breath. 'Do you know exactly where they are?'

'No, they'd never let me in on anything like that, none of us except – except the top brass.'

I could believe that. Kane was much too far down the line to have access to such information, but it was a pity. I changed my tack again and suddenly shot the question. 'Who killed my brother?'

Kane's mouth twitched. 'Oh God. It was Jim – and – and Ramirez. They killed him.' He looked mortally sick.

'And you helped them.'

He shook his head violently. 'No – I had nothing to do with it!'

'But you were there.'

'I don't know nothing about it.'

'Look, Kane, stop lying to us. You were with Hadley when he went to see Schouten to get the death certificate, weren't you?'

He nodded unwillingly.

'Then you were in on Mark's death, damn you!'

'I didn't kill him. It was Jim – Ramirez fixed it all up.'

'Who killed Schouten?'

The answer came promptly. 'It was Jim – Jim Hadley.'

'And again you were there?'

'Yes.'

'But you didn't kill Schouten, I suppose?'

'No!'

'And of course you didn't set fire to the hospital and burn fourteen people to death?'

'I didn't,' said Kane. 'It was Jim – he's a devil. He's crazy mad.'

'But you were there.'

'I told you I was.'

'And you'll be sentenced as an accessory.'

Kane was sweating and his whole face quivered. I said, 'Who killed Sven Norgaard?'

Kane didn't answer for a moment, and then under the threat of our gaze he said, 'It was Jim.'

'You're not too sure about that, are you? Now, tell me again.'

'I dunno for sure – I wasn't there. It was Jim or – or your brother.'

'My *brother?*'

I could sense Geordie behind me, a restraining presence.

'The cops were looking for him, weren't they?' cried Kane defensively. 'How was anyone to know he didn't do it? He might have for all I know – I wasn't there, I tell you.'

I said, 'Tell me more about my brother. Why was he killed?'

'Ramirez didn't – didn't tell me,' he muttered.

'Don't be smart. Answer the question.'

'Well, they didn't ever tell me everything. I think he was – holding out on something. Something Ramirez wanted. I think it had something to do with those stones. I never – never killed him or nobody!'

I straightened up and said wearily, 'Well, my lilywhite friend, so you didn't kill anyone, you were never anywhere, and you're as pure as driven snow. I think you're a damned liar, but it doesn't matter. You'll be an accessory all the same. I believe they still use the guillotine out here.'

As Kane flinched I said, 'Anyone got any more questions?'

Campbell said harshly, 'You seem to have covered it. I can't think of anything right now. Later maybe.'

'Geordie?'

He shook his head.

'We'll be back, Kane. As soon as we think up some new questions. I think you've been lying like Ananias, and I warned you what would happen if you lied. You'd better think about that.'

Kane looked at the bulkhead moodily. 'I've told no lies.'

Campbell said, 'I wouldn't make any attempt to break out, Kane, or you'll wind up deader than a frozen mackerel. You'll be safer in a cabin than outside – the crew here don't like you and they may shoot to kill if they see you, so stay put. It's better for your health.'

Outside the cabin we looked at one another bleakly. 'I could do with that drink now,' I said heavily. 'I'm sick to my stomach.'

We sat in the saloon for a while, letting tiredness wash over us and feeling the overwrought emotions of the last few hours seep away. There was too much to think about, and we all needed sleep badly. Geordie had Kane removed to a small cabin that he'd had prepared, which had been stripped of everything bar a bunk, with a padlock to the door, so that we were free to turn in in our own bunks.

Campbell said, 'I want to hear the whole story of this cutting-out expedition of yours, but we'll save it for tomorrow. And I want some ideas about Kane.'

And on that note we turned in, with the dawn already showing at the end of what had to be the most energetic day of my life.

II

The next day started late for everyone except the hands on watch, and it was a quiet and thoughtful start to the voyage. There was an air of reserved jubilation on board which was not entirely shared by Campbell or me. Over a late breakfast I spoke to Clare and Paula about the events of the previous night. 'You got back to the ship smartly,' I said. 'Well done.'

'Nick was great. But maybe not so well done – Ramirez must have seen us leaving,' said Clare.

'Not necessarily. He'll have spotted *Esmerelda* right away and knew we were here. I'm still not sure why he finally joined us. He surely didn't think we'd give up and go away, or hand over our knowledge, simply for his asking,' I mused.

Clare said, 'From what I know about him, he would prefer to bring things to a confrontation after a while. Just to see how we might react to his baiting. I don't think he's as subtle as all that.'

'Where were you during the big excitement?'

'Pop was as mad as a bull when we came on board and he found out what was going on. He was sure it would end up in trouble, maybe a riot, so he made us both go below and promise to stay there.' She giggled. 'We saw Ramirez go overboard, though – it was fantastic.'

'You cheated,' I said.

Paula said sedately, 'And we knew that Mr Campbell would give you a bawling out as soon as we left harbour. We didn't think you'd like an audience so we stayed below.'

'I think we've been forgiven,' I said.

'You've got Kane aboard, we know that,' Clare said and became graver. 'It must have been rotten having to interrogate him. Have you learned much?'

'It was rotten, and we've learned practically nothing. He is wholly despicable.'

Clare caught my hand across the table.

'Horrible for you, poor Mike,' she said and I wanted again desperately to be alone with her somewhere. At that moment, as if by pre-arrangement, Campbell appeared and our hands slid apart. Clare got up to prepare his meal.

Over breakfast, joined by Geordie, I filled Campbell in on the events of the night. When we'd finished the narrative he actually chuckled. 'My God, I wish I'd been there.'

'Pop, you know you didn't approve,' said Clare.

He sighed. 'I know, I know. But there comes a time when you have to hit out regardless of consequence. Maybe I'm getting too old and safety conscious.' He turned to Geordie. 'How long do you give Ramirez to repair the damage?'

'A hell of a long time if he has to depend on facilities in Nuku'alofa. That engine should never run again, if Jim placed his charge correctly.'

'He'll pour out money like water,' predicted Campbell. 'He'll have a new engine flown in with a crew to install it – that's what I'd do. I give him three weeks – not more than four – to be at sea again, and on our tail.'

I said, 'The sea is big. He may never find us.'

'He knows something about Falcon Island, and he can guess we do too. But let's hope you're right,' said Campbell and raised his glass of orange juice. 'Here's to you, Captain Flint. I never thought I'd ship with a pirate crew, and I'm still not sure I approve. But you did a good job.'

He drank, then added, 'I sure hope Ramirez didn't run to the cops.'

'We'll soon find out. I've posted a lookout at the mast-head with orders to watch astern,' Geordie said.

Campbell folded his hands on the table. 'Now let's talk about Kane.'

He was unhappy at the thought of keeping the man on board, for a number of sound reasons. He needed constant guarding, would require food, exercise and a check on his apparently wavering health, and was rather like a stone in one's shoe – a continuing nagging irritation that would work on everyone's nerves. 'As long as we have him with us he's a liability,' he said. 'He's told us nothing of value – I don't think he knows anything much – and he's a danger to us all every moment he's on board. So what the hell can we do about it?'

'You don't think he'd be useful as a hostage?' I asked.

They both looked at me sadly. 'Mike, he's even more worthless to Ramirez than he is to us,' Campbell said. 'They'd knock him off like a shot if they had to, without a moment's hesitation. His only value, perhaps, is in being an eventual witness should there be any police proceedings, and that could work both ways.'

Geordie said, 'It looks as though Ramirez did keep mum. A patrol boat would have caught up with us by now.'

'Maybe,' said Campbell. 'But I want to cover our butts. I want to get him to write a statement that someone on board can witness, someone not directly involved with him. One of your old crewmen would do for that, Geordie. And then I want to put him off somewhere.'

'Maroon him?' I asked. 'More pirate tricks?'

Geordie said, 'I agree with you, Mr Campbell. Let's have a look at the charts.'

He found what he was after almost immediately. Among the northern islands of the Tongan group, and not at all out of our way, lay the small islet of Mo'unga 'one. It had, according to the *Pilot*, one village and a beach where landing in good weather was possible. We tested the idea and could find nothing wrong with it, and so Geordie set about changing our course slightly while Campbell went down to talk to Kane. I didn't want to face him again that morning.

He came back presently and sat down.

'It's fixed,' he said. 'He'll write anything we want, he says, but I've told him to stick to the facts as he knows them – or says he does. He wants to save his own skin but doesn't in the least mind incriminating his great friend Jim Hadley. Lovely man. He's not well. I think a touch of fever from that shot wound, nothing that a few days' rest-cure on a tropical island won't fix. The local people will look after him for a backhander of some kind, till we can pick him up or send the cops for him. It's the only way, Mike.'

And to be truthful I would be as glad to see him off the ship as anyone. The knowledge of him being so close and yet so untouchable was something I found hard to live with.

We lay off Mo'unga 'one for a morning while Geordie and three of the crew took Kane ashore. He was willing, even eager to go, and didn't seem at all concerned as to how long he'd have to stay there. Geordie came back with news of his stolid acceptance by the local inhabitants, who were friendly and incurious. They'd seen many western landing parties in their time apparently. Geordie had asked, with many gestures and a great deal of linguistic difficulty, if they knew anything of Falcon Island, and had got on best after flinging his arms wide and imitating the action of a volcano blowing up. This got grins and giggles, together with agreement that there was indeed just such a phenomena somewhere to the northwards, but Geordie was unable to get any closer details.

So we'd rid the boat of Kane for the second time and again there was a definite feeling of relief in the air. That man may or may not have been a murderer, I thought, but he was certainly bad news.

We got under way again and Geordie said at one stage, 'We're almost on the track between Fonua Fo'ou and Minerva now. All being well, we should be able to start dredging tomorrow – if you intend to stop for that.'

'We'll make use of every moment Jim Taylor gave us,' said Campbell. 'We might as well start. That's what we're here for. Come and have some coffee, Mike; I want to talk to you.'

As I poured the coffee he said, 'You gave me two shocks in Nuku'alofa that night. The first, when I found what you were up to, and the second, when you told me what you'd found. Do you think Ramirez was planning to jump us – real pirate style?'

'From what you've told me about the strikes on your mines I think he's capable of direct action when it suits him. Piracy in these waters wouldn't be difficult either; it hasn't died out. It's supposed to have happened to the *Joyita* not long ago, but they never really got to the bottom of that one.'

'Yes, I read about that.'

'There's plenty of piracy going on even yet, not far from here – in Indonesian waters, down in the Bahamas – all over. I think Ramirez would jump us if it suited him. He'd obviously like us to lead him to the nodule deposits and then scupper us completely. Who would ever know?'

'I think he'd like to scupper us even if he did know where it was,' said Campbell.

'Just to get you off his tail? Yes, you could be right. But he has another problem to solve before he can do it.'

'What's that?'

'Finding us,' I said briefly.

Campbell gave that some thought. 'I can understand that. As you said that night, the sea is a big place. We should be all right as long as we stay out at sea. It's when we put into any port that he'll discover us again.' He drummed his fingers. 'But he might get lucky and find us out here anyway – and that's what I want to talk to you about.'

I lifted my eyebrows.

'Your crew's a tough mob, and I know they can fight if they have to – but will they? You say Ramirez has a crew of about thirty.'

I said, 'It depends on the kind of fighting. We might have cleaned Ramirez out of weapons, and we might not. If he comes up against us with any kind of armament we've had our chips. If it's a matter of hand-to-hand fighting, no matter how dirty, we've got a good chance.'

'At two to one odds?'

'I've seen them in action. Admittedly it was a surprise attack but it went off with about as much excitement as a tea party at the vicarage. Our lot are trained fighting men, most of them. Ramirez has waterfront scum.'

'I hope you're right. But I'd like to talk to our boys anyway. A man should know what he's fighting for.'

'They know what they're fighting for,' I said softly. 'They saw the hospital at Tanakabu.'

'True. But the labourer is worthy of his hire. They don't know the extent of what we're searching for and I'm going to tell them. There's no harm in mentioning a fat bonus at the end of all this – whether we dredge lucky or not.'

I said, 'They'll all be about when we put the dredge over the side. You could talk to them then.'

We had the winch made ready for dredging early the next day, and at ten o'clock Campbell had the whole crew gathered before him on deck. He stepped up onto the winch and sat easily on the control seat, looking down on the men.

'You know some of what this is all about,' he said to them. 'But not everything. So I'm going to tell you – officially. You know we've been dredging in a few places here and there, and I'm going to make it clear what we're looking for.'

He held up a nodule.

'This is a manganese nodule and the sea bed is covered with them. This particular nodule is worthless, but the ones we're looking for are worth a hell of a lot of money.' He casually tossed the nodule over the side.

'Now, a gentleman called Ramirez is trying to stop us. I suppose you all know that – hence the funny things that have happened in the last few weeks. Now, I want you to get this straight. Ramirez is going after those nodules for the money – and so am I, make no mistake about that. The difference is that I think there's enough for all and I'm not greedy. I won't bother Ramirez if he bothers me none, but he's got a big tough crew and he seems to be spoiling for a fight.'

I had my own ideas about that statement. I was quite certain that Campbell didn't want Suarez-Navarro to have any part of the find, but perhaps on moral rather than on economic grounds.

'Now, I want you boys to know where you stand. Before you make any decisions I want you to know that whether we strike lucky or not, there's going to be a sizeable bonus at the end of this trip – you can call it danger money. If we do strike it rich, I'll be organizing a corporation to exploit the find, and I'll put five per cent of the stock aside to be divided among this crew. That may not seem much, but let me tell you it won't be peanuts. You may all end up millionaires.'

There was a babble of talk and a spate of handclapping. Geordie said, 'I think I can speak for all of us, Mr Campbell; that's a generous gesture that wasn't really necessary. We're with you all the way.'

There was a chorus of approval and Geordie held up his hand. 'There's just one more thing,' he said. 'I think Taffy Morgan there will give up his bonus if he can go on double rations for the rest of the voyage.'

A ripple of laughter swept the deck.

Taffy called out, 'I don't want even that, skipper. Just give me the bastard who fired that hospital!'

The laughter turned to an ugly growl, and I pitied Hadley if any of these men came across him.

Campbell held up his hand again for silence. 'That's settled then. If any of you want to know more about these nodules you'd better ask Mike; he's our expert. And now I think we'd better get on with the job before *Sirena* shows up.'

He stepped down from the winch and the work began.

On the first drop the dredge touched bottom at 13,000 feet and when we hauled it up there were plenty of nodules in it. The crew had all seen plenty of them before but this time they were more curious. Danny picked one up and said, 'These could be valuable?'

'They could, and I hope they are. You'll be the first to know,' I said.

I took the first few samples down to the lab and began working. On deck I heard the crew securing the dredge and the bellowed orders of Geordie as *Esmerelda* got under way again. I hadn't been working long when Paula and Clare came in.

'We came to see if we could help,' said Clare. 'You'll have a lot of work on your hands.'

I rubbed my chin. Neither would be able to use the spectroscope without training, but for the rest they could be very useful. 'I hope you're good dishwashers,' I said, and waved at the glassware. 'This lot needs taking down and cleaning after every run.'

'I'll do that,' said Paula. She looked at my set-up. 'It looks like something out of one of those horror movies.'

'I'm not the mad scientist yet, although I might be if this whole thing turns out to be a bust. Clare, there's a hell of a lot of record keeping. You help your father with that kind of thing. Can you cope with this?'

'Sure. Just tell me what you want.'

I got cracking on the analysis. Working in a sailing ship heeled over under canvas wasn't anything I'd been trained for but it was surprising how much I'd learned, and I had rigged up some interesting systems to cope with the movement. We couldn't afford to stay hove-to while I assayed each time, and in fact we'd tried it and that motion was worse. I was checking some rough results when I felt her slacken off and presently the winch engine started again. I knew Geordie had taken up station for another dip over the side.

I said, 'Paula, can you start dismantling this set-up ready for cleaning, please? There'll be another load of nodules here soon.'

She got to work and I turned to help Clare with the records.

'There's the winch report which gives position and depth. There's the spectrograph report, together with the photographic negative list. That's the quantitative analysis, and there's a numbered half-nodule. All that lot must be filed together. This time I've written it out myself, but next time I'll call out the figures.'

I was pleased. This help on routine work made a lot of difference and I reckoned the work would be speeded up considerably. There was a long grind ahead – I didn't expect to hit the jackpot at the first dip, and I hadn't. The result of the first dredge was about average, just what the orthodox oceanographer would expect to find in a normal Pacific nodule.

Clare and I went on deck to get a breath of fresh air and were just in time to see the dredge go over the side. I watched the bubbles rising to the surface and then we strolled away and sat down on the foredeck and I offered her a cigarette. As we went past heads turned and Ian called from the winch, 'Any luck?'

I smiled and shook my head. 'Not yet, Ian, but it's early days.'

Clare said, 'Pop told me about the questions you asked Kane. Do you think he was telling any of the truth?'

'Not a chance. He was lying in his teeth.'

She said, 'You didn't expect him to admit to killing anyone, did you? Of course he would lie.'

'That isn't what I meant, Clare. Curiously enough, I don't think he did kill anyone – not directly. I believed him when he said it was Hadley all the time. I don't think Kane has enough guts to kill anyone, but I could believe anything of Hadley. I think he's a psychopath, Kane implied that even Ramirez can't control him. It won't make any difference in the long run, of course – if we get them all Kane will be as guilty as any of them, and be punished accordingly.'

'Then you think he was lying about something else.'

'That's right – but I'm damned if I know what it is. It was just something about his manner when I questioned him about Mark. There was a look of fear about him, something in his eyes I couldn't place. I think something much more terrible happened. But the outline of the story is clear enough.'

Clare shivered. 'I didn't have much sympathy for Mark – not after what he did to me – but I can't help feeling sorry for him. What a pitiful end for any man.'

I nodded. 'I wouldn't think about it too much, Clare. He's dead and beyond feeling anything any more. The world is for the living.'

And you are one of the living, I thought, looking at her. There was no romantic moon shining across the water; instead we were in the hard white glare of the tropic sun. There was no love song echoing from the saloon, just the rhythmic clanking of the winch and the throb of a diesel. I said, 'Clare, if we come out of this successfully I'd like to get to know you better – much better.'

She slanted her eyes at me. 'And if we don't come through successfully – will you just walk away and never want to see me again?'

'That's not a nice way to put it.'

'That's the way I have to put it.'

I said nothing, fumbling for the right words.

'This is rather a new experience for me,' said Clare with a warmth of humour in her voice. 'I've never had to work at it myself. Most times I've had to fend off the advances – '

'I'm not making . . .'

' – because I wasn't sure if I liked the man, or because I sometimes thought they were after me as Pop's daughter – the ones who never found his money a hindrance. I don't think that's your problem though. Or do you think that rich people should only marry rich people?'

I was about to reply angrily until I suddenly realized that she was teasing me. Her eyes were alight with mischief – and, I thought in astonishment, with fondness. I said lamely, 'Clare, there are all sorts of . . .'

She waited but I was still fumbling.

'Complications? But we could weather them all. Oh Mike, you're an awful fool – but I love you all the more for it.'

I said after a pause, 'Damn it, Clare, it isn't the way I intended this.'

'Am I driving you to the wall, Mike? Why don't you just say what's on your mind?'

So I did. I said, 'Will you marry me, Clare?'

She hung her head for a moment and then looked at me. 'Of course I will,' she said. 'We'll get married by the first priest we come across. I thought you'd *never* get to the point. Girls are only supposed to propose in Leap Year, but I nearly had to break that rule.'

I felt exhilarated and weak simultaneously. 'Well, I'll be damned,' I said, and we both burst out laughing out of sheer joy. I wanted to do the obvious thing and take her in my arms, but there was too little privacy even up here, so we simply clutched each other's hands.

Clare said, 'Mike, let's not tell anyone just yet. Pop has enough else on his mind right now. I think he'll be fine about it but I want to be sure when we tell him, and nobody else should know first.'

I agreed with her. I'd have agreed with anything she said just then.

We talked a lot of nonsense until the dredge came up. I can't remember us walking down to the laboratory – I think we floated.

III

We dredged and dredged, stopping every ten miles on the way to Minerva Reefs. We dredged during every scrap of daylight hours and I worked a sixteen-hour day, taking my meals in the laboratory. The girls were of great service but there was still a lot of work, and I began to fear that my supplies of chemicals would soon run out.

One thing bothered me. We were being continually pestered by members of the crew calling in at the lab to see what we were doing. Not only were they anxious to see good results but I found that Taffy Morgan had organized a sweepstake on the cobalt result of every dredge. I went to see Geordie.

'Look, this is wasting a lot of my time,' I told him. 'Tell them to put a sock in it.'

He smiled slowly. 'Don't want to dampen their enthusiasm, do you? Tell you what; give me the results of the dredge each day and I'll post a bulletin.'

'That'll do it. Get the results from Clare.'

He stuffed tobacco into the bowl of his pipe. 'Campbell started something with his big talk of making us all millionaires. Do you think there's anything in it?'

'I should say he's a man of his word.'

'I'm not doubting his word,' said Geordie. 'I'm doubting whether he can live up to it. If ten to fifteen million pounds is only five per cent of what he expects to make, then I think he's expecting to make a devil of a lot.'

'He is, Geordie,' I said soberly. 'And so am I. I'm hoping that if we hit it all, it'll be big. When I've the time we'll get Campbell to talk in figures. That's going to open your eyes.'

'He's already done that.'

'He's hardly started.'

'We'll see,' said Geordie, unimpressed.

We dredged – and dredged – and dredged. Then we hit shoal ground at nearly 4000 feet. Geordie said laconically, 'Minerva Bank.'

'All right,' I said. 'Nice navigating. We carry out our plan – we dredge all round it. But first I'd like a sample from the middle of the shoal, as far into the shallows as it's safe to go.'

Campbell said, 'Isn't that wasting time?'

'We don't know – not until we've done it. And I'd like to know for the record – and for my own theories.'

We *were* wasting our time. We dredged at 2000 feet and came up with a bucketful of volcanic cinders, dead coral and shell. No nodules at all. The crew looked suddenly worried at the haul but I reassured them. 'I hardly expected any here, so don't worry. Plenty outside still. Now we can cross this area off the list, but I had to be sure.'

We retraced our track to the edge of Minerva Bank and started to circle it at a distance of about ten miles, dredging in deep water. Geordie worked it out on the chart. 'That's about sixteen times we drop – say four days.'

It took us a bit longer than that, but five days later we had made the full circle and still hadn't found anything. Campbell, first up and first down, was getting depressed again and his fretting was agitating the crew, who'd been working manfully. 'Are you *sure* we're in the right place?' he asked me, not for the first time.

'No, I'm not,' I said sharply. I was a bit on edge too; I was tired and not in a mood to be asked stupid questions. 'I'm not sure of a damned thing. I've got theories to offer, but no certainties.'

Geordie was more placid. 'Don't forget that our arrival in Tonga brought Ramirez there hotfoot. I think we're in the right place.'

I wished to God I knew where they were. They'd had time, I reckoned, to repair their engine, and I would have dearly loved to know if they were out at sea searching for us at this moment. If only we had some inkling as to how much Ramirez really knew, we could be better placed to cope with him.

Campbell echoed my thoughts. 'Where the hell is Suarez-Navarro? And where are these goddam nodules? What do we do next, Mike?'

'We carry on as planned. We go back towards Falcon on a parallel track.'

'East or west?' enquired Geordie.

I shrugged and felt in my trouser pocket. 'Anyone got a coin? This is a thing that can be tossed for.'

Campbell snorted in disgust.

Geordie said, more practically, 'Why don't we do both? We use the course we came on as a centre line and zig-zag back. First sample one side, then the other.'

'That's a reasonable idea,' I said. 'Let's do that.'

So we went back, and the same old boring routine went on. The winch motor whined, the bucket went over the side with a bubbling splash and a couple of hours later came up with its load which I then proceeded to prove worthless. There were plenty of nodules but not the gold-plated ones. The crew was kept busy at keeping the decks reasonably clean and at maintenance, and we devised all sorts of games and exercises to use up spare time.

But Geordie was worrying about the maintenance of the winch gear. 'We're overworking it,' he said to me. 'We don't have time for standard maintenance. There's the cable – the lot wants a thorough cleaning and oiling. I'm scared it might break on one of these hauls if we don't check on it.'

Campbell heard him out, tight-lipped, and said, 'No. We must carry on as long as we have the headway. You'll have to do the best you can, Geordie.'

I knew what was on his mind. We had been at sea now for over two weeks and Ramirez would soon be ready to sail. While we were at sea there was a fair chance he wouldn't find us – but to put into any port would be dangerous.

So we carried on, zig-zagging back towards Falcon, fruitlessly dredging the seemingly profitless Pacific.

And then we hit it!

My voice shook as I called the vital figures out to Clare. 'C-Cobalt – 4.32 per cent.'

She looked up, startled. 'I didn't catch that one, Mike – at least I think I didn't.'

I said shakily, 'This is it – 4.32 per cent cobalt!'

We looked at each other wordlessly. At last I said carefully, 'We'll assay again from that last load. More than once. Paula! I want everything washed down again – cleaner than ever.' And the three of us threw ourselves into a routine that was suddenly anything but boring.

The results were dotted around my first one like Campbell's bullet-holes around mine on the target. 4.38 – 4.29 – four times I tested, and every test checked out.

I croaked, 'Hell, I've got to tell Geordie. He's got to change course.'

I dashed up on deck leaving the girls thumping each other's shoulders. Ian was at the wheel. 'Whoa up!' I shouted. 'We're going back to the last site.'

His eyes widened. 'You've never found something?'

'That I have! Where's Geordie?'

'He's off watch – I think in his cabin.'

I left him to supervise the change of direction and pounded below. But Geordie wasn't impressed. 'Four per cent is a long way from ten,' he said.

'You damn fool, Geordie. It's twice the percentage that's been found in any nodule before, apart from the one we had in London. We must have struck the edge of the concentration.'

'Well – what now?'

'We go back and cruise that area, keeping an eye on the echo sounder. That'll probably tell us something.'

He swung out of his bunk and put his trousers on. 'It might tell you something; it won't mean a thing to me. Thank God we've been keeping careful records of our position.'

'Come on – let's tell the boss.'

Campbell had already been told. We found him in the lab with the girls, looking at the figures. He turned as we came in, his eyes bright with expectation. 'Have we found it, Mike?'

I was suddenly cautious. I said carefully, 'We've found something. Whether it's what we hope is another thing.'

'You goddam scientists,' he grumbled. 'Why can't you ever tell a straight story?'

I pulled out the chart I had been making from the recording echometer. 'There's a ridge running along here, roughly north and south,' I said. 'The top is within nine thousand feet of the surface. We picked up our prize nodule here, on the east side of the ridge at eleven thousand feet. I'd like to sail at right angles to the ridge, striking east – this way. I'd like to see how the depth of water goes.'

'You think the depth might have something to do with this?'

'It might. It would be the natural accumulation area for the greatest volume of nodules hereabouts, rather than in the very shallowest areas – even though there's never more than one layer of thickness of nodules anywhere.'

'I thought they'd be there in great piles, humped up together.'

'Sorry, no,' I said. 'That's never been found. The best evidence from some deep-sea photographs is that there are parts of the sea-bed which are lumpy underneath the sediment layer, indicating that many more nodules might be buried there, but in that case they'd have stopped growing anyway, being cut off from their life-line – the sea water itself.'

But for the only time they were not interested in my impromptu lecture. I hastened to correct myself.

'Don't worry, the billions of tons I promised you will be there, even if it does lie only one layer thick. There are lots of things we have to find out still.'

We arrived in the vicinity of the last site with members of the crew, rather ludicrously, peering at the surface of the ocean as if it could show them anything. Geordie said, 'Right – now which way?'

I drew a pencil line on his chart. 'Follow that course, please.'

As we sailed I watched the trace of the echometer with intense concentration. The line showed a gradual deepening of the water – not a sudden drop, but a falling away as though from mountains into the plains. After we had gone about ten miles the bottom began to come up again from 13,000 feet. I made sure it wasn't just a local condition and then said, 'I want to go back about two miles.'

'Okay,' Geordie said, and gave brisk orders. We were doing most of this work under engine as it was tricky for sail, and I was grateful for the continuing calm weather which gave us the minimum of wind and ocean drift to contend with. I thought for just one envious moment of how easy it would all be on land.

Campbell looked at my tracing. 'What do you think?'

'There's some sort of valley down there,' I said. 'We've come from a ridge, crossed the valley and begun to climb up towards the opposite ridge. I want to go back and dredge where it's deepest – it's about 13,000 feet.'

Campbell rubbed his cheek. 'Bit deep for commercial dredging with a drag line. You waste too much time just going down and coming up again.'

'If the stuff's rich enough it should pay.'

He grunted. 'That's what we're here to find out.'

By now everyone knew what was in the wind and there was a lot of tension as the dredge went down. Ian was at the winch and Geordie himself at the wheel, keeping *Esmerelda* on station. It seemed a particularly long time before Ian, watching the cable tension meter, slipped the winch out of gear and said, 'She's bottomed.'

Geordie's hand went to the engine controls. Campbell swung round, fussing like an old hen. 'Careful, Geordie, we don't want any mistakes now.'

Esmerelda crept forward, taking the strain on the cable. I could visualize the dredge at the bottom of the abyss, scraping forward in utter darkness, gathering the nodules and debris into its maw like a vast-jawed prehistoric creature.

Then the job was done and Ian had the winch in gear again. The drum started to turn and the crew began to stow the wet and slimy cable into the hold as it came off the drum. Again it seemed to take ages and the tension increased until our nerves fairly twanged. Taffy said hoarsely, 'For God's sake, Ian, pull your finger out!'

Geordie said calmly, 'None of that, now. Take it easy, Ian – you're doing just fine.'

Thirteen thousand feet is nearly two and a half miles. It takes a long time to haul a full dredge up from that depth, especially when you're not too sure of your cable and taking it slowly. Normally nobody took any notice until the bucket came inboard, but this time everyone's attention was riveted, and when at last the dredge broke surface there were many willing hands to swing the boarding derrick out and bring the haul in.

Geordie had handed over the wheel to Danny and he ran forward to help release the load. A cascade of nodules swept onto the deck, together with the usual lot of slimy mud. Taffy stooped and picked up a nodule. 'This doesn't look any different to me,' he said, clowning disappointment.

Ian said, 'Ye daft loon. Leave it to Mike, would you? He knows what he's doing.'

I hoped he was right.

Campbell said, 'How long, Mike?'

'The usual three hours. I can't do it any faster.'

Nor did I – in fact it took longer. The lab wasn't very big and we had enough trouble with three of us working there. Now Campbell insisted on coming in and watching, and wherever he stood or sat he was in the way. In the end I bundled him out despite his protests, but I could hear him pacing up and down in the passage-way.

At the end of three and three-quarter hours I opened the door and said, 'Congratulations, Mr Campbell. You've just become the father of a 9.7 per cent cobalt nodule.'

His eyes lit up. 'We've hit it! By God, we've hit it!'

'Bang on the nose,' I agreed happily.

He leaned against the bulkhead and sighed deeply. 'I never thought we'd make it.' After a few moments his brain started to function again and he said, 'What's the density?'

'Ten pounds to the square foot. That'll keep you busy for the next few years.'

His smile grew jubilant.

'Come up to the saloon, all of you. Let's have a drink on it. Get Geordie down here.'

In the saloon he opened the liquor cabinet and produced bottles of whisky and gin, and set about pouring drinks with great energy. Clare and I managed to linger in the passage just long enough for a quick hug and kiss before joining him with Paula, and Geordie arrived a moment later, beaming.

'To you, Mike. You've done a great job,' Campbell said expansively.

I included them all in the toast, and we drank it with great cheer. 'It isn't finished yet, though,' I warned them. 'We've got to find the extent of the deposit. There's a lot of proving to be done.'

'I know, I know,' Campbell said. 'But that's detail work. Do you realize we've done it, Geordie?'

'I'm very pleased for you,' Geordie said formally.

'The hell with that. I'm pleased for all of us. How about splicing the mainbrace, Geordie – with my compliments?' He waved to the well-stocked cabinet.

'Well, I don't know,' said Geordie judiciously. 'I've still got a ship to run. The lads off watch can have a dram, but those on duty will have to wait a while yet. There's enough buzz going on up there as it is.' He smiled and added, 'I'm off watch myself.'

Campbell laughed. 'Okay, join us.'

Geordie cocked his head at me. 'We're still hove-to, you know. Where do we go from here?'

I said, 'Ninety degrees from your last course – to the south. Tell the watch to keep an eye on the echometer and to keep to the deepest water they can. We'll go for about twenty-five miles. If the water shallows appreciably or we diverge too much off course I'd like to know at once. And I think Clare had better give you the latest bulletin, don't you?'

Clare produced a sheet of paper with the magic figures, and Geordie took it up with him. Campbell turned to me. 'You trotted all that out glibly enough. I suppose you've got an idea.'

'I've got an idea of sorts. We came from a ridge and dredged in the deepest part of a valley. Now I want to run along the valley to see how far it stretches each way. The echometer record will give us a lot of useful information, and we'll dredge at intervals along the course.'

From the deck we heard the sound of cheering. Campbell stopped in the act of pouring himself another drink. 'Everybody's happy.'

'Everyone except Ramirez,' I commented.

'I wish he'd sink,' said Paula, unexpectedly viciously.

Campbell frowned, then pushed the unwelcome thought from his mind; this was no time for thinking of a chancy future. Geordie came back into the saloon and Campbell pointed to the cabinet. 'Pour your own. I'm no man's servant,' he said. Geordie grinned and picked up the bottle.

I rolled a nodule onto the table. 'Geordie's a bit doubtful as to the value of this. I promised I'd get you to talk figures.'

Campbell poked at it with one finger. 'It sure doesn't look like much, does it, Geordie?'

'Just like any other bit of rock we've been dredging up the last couple of weeks,' Geordie said offhandedly.

'It contains nearly ten per cent cobalt. We don't know much about anything else that's in it because Mike's only checked for cobalt, but we know there should be a fair amount of copper and vanadium and a lot of iron – and manganese too of course. Now, I'm telling you and I speak from experience, that the gross recoverable value will run to about four hundred dollars a ton.'

Geordie was still not convinced. 'That doesn't seem too valuable to me. I thought it was really valuable – like gold or platinum.'

Campbell grinned delightedly and took a little slide rule from his pocket. 'You'd say the density would be pretty consistent over a wide area, wouldn't you, Mike?'

'Oh yes. In the centre of the concentration you can fairly well rely on that.'

'And what would you call a wide area?'

I shrugged. 'Oh, several square miles.'

Campbell looked at Geordie under his brows, then bent over the slide rule. 'Now, let's see. At ten pounds a square foot – that makes it – run to about, say, fifty-six million dollars a square mile.'

Geordie, who was in the act of swallowing whisky, suddenly coughed and spluttered.

We all shouted with surprised laughter. I said, 'There are a lot of square feet in a square mile, Geordie!'

He recovered his breath. 'Man, that's money! How many square miles of this stuff will there be?'

'That's what we find out next,' I said. I saw the two girls looking at Campbell with astonishment and something occurred to me. I said to Paula, 'You're in on this too, you know.'

She gaped at me. 'But I've – I'm not – '

Campbell said. 'Why, yes, Paula. You're one of the crew. Everybody on this ship gets in on the deal.'

Her astonishment must have been too great for her to contain, for she burst suddenly into tears and ran blindly from the saloon. Clare cast us a quick happy smile and went after her.

I could see that Geordie was trying to work out the fifteenth part of five percent of 56 million dollars – and failing in the attempt. I said, 'That four hundred dollars a ton is a gross value. We have to deduct the costs of dredging and processing, distribution and all sorts of extras. Got any ideas on that?'

'I have,' Campbell said. 'When Mark first came to me with this idea I went into it pretty deeply. The main problem is the dredging – a drag line dredge like the one we're using, but bigger, isn't much use at this depth. You waste too much time pulling it up. So I put some of my bright boys on to the problem and they decided it would be best to use a hydraulic dredge. They did a preliminary study and reckoned they could suck nodules to the surface from 14,000 feet for ten dollars a ton or less. Then you have to add all sorts of factors – processing, marketing, transport and other technical overheads – the cost of hiring ships and crews and maintaining them. We'd want to develop and build our own dredges, we'd need survey ships, and we'd have to build a processing plant. That would happen on one of the islands and we'd get a lot of help there, as it'll mean a huge income in many ways for them, but all in all I would have to float a company capable of digging into its pocket to the tune of some forty million dollars.'

He said this in a serious and businesslike tone. Clare was apparently used to these flights of executive rhetoric but Geordie and I gaped at him. It was Geordie's first excursion into high finance, as it was mine, but I was slightly better prepared for it. 'Good God! Have you got that much – I mean can you lay your hands on it?'

'Not before this. But I can get it with what we have to show here. We'd clear a net profit of forty million in the first couple of years of operation – the rest should be pure cream. There's going to be a lot of guys on Wall Street eager to jump into a thing like this – or even take it over.'

He mused a bit, then added, 'But they're not going to. When Suarez-Navarro jumped my mines I swore I'd never hang on to another solid proposition ever again – not if they were as easy to steal as that. So I went back to being a wild-catter; in and out to take a fast profit. But this – somehow this is different. I'm sticking here. I know a couple of good joes back home, men I can trust. Between them and me, and perhaps persuading a couple of governments to take an interest, I want to tie this thing up so tight that neither Suarez-Navarro nor anyone else of their type can horn in and spoil it.'

He got up and went to a port to look out over the sea. 'Tonga's back there. They'll probably come in on the act. They'll benefit by being the ones most likely to get the pro-cessing plant built in their territory – it will be highly auto-mated so it won't mean much steady labour, once it's built, but they'll get the taxes and the spin-off, so I should think they will be happy to cooperate. There's another thing on my mind too; nodules are still forming out there, and from what Mike says they'll go on doing so – at what he always calls an explosively fast rate. Maybe for once we'll be able to do a mining operation without raping the goddam planet.' He came back to the table and picked up his glass. 'And that's an achievement that any bunch of guys can be proud of. Let's drink to it.'

So we drank, very solemnly. I for one was full of awe at what we were doing, and I thought the others felt the same. Campbell had come up with a couple of shattering thoughts.

IV

We stayed in the area for another week, quartering the submarine valley and dredging at selected spots. The material poured in and I was kept busy. A much more detailed survey would be done later – all I was aiming at was to put limits on the area and to find out roughly how rich, and how consistent it was.

Esmerelda was a happy ship in those days. Not that she hadn't been before, but the depression caused by a fruitless search had lifted and everyone was keen and cheerful. There was a lot of skylarking among the crew, although it always stopped when there was serious work to be done.

Once, when I was having a breather on deck, Paula joined me.

'I don't know what came over me the other day, Mike – you know, when Mr Campbell said I had a share in all this.'

'It is a bit of a shock when you find yourself suddenly on the verge of riches. I went through it too.'

'I never thought of being rich,' she said. 'I never had the time, I guess. I've always been on the move – the States, Mexico, Australia, Tahiti, Hawaii, Panama. Guess I was a bit of a hobo.' She looked up. 'That's what you British call a tramp, isn't it?'

'That's right.'

'I guess I was that too – in the American sense, I mean,' she said sombrely.

'You're all right, Paula,' I said warmly. 'Don't worry about it. Enjoy the idea instead. What will you do with all your new-gotten wealth?'

'Gee, I don't know, Mike. I'm not like Clare – she's used to money, but I'm not. And the way her pop talks sometimes makes my head spin, the way he juggles his millions.'

'Maybe you can go on a cruise ship to sunny Tahiti,' I said jokingly.

But she shook her head violently. 'No. I'll never go there again – I never want to see Papeete again.' She was silent for a while and we stood together companionably, and then she said, 'I think I'll go home first. Yes, I think I'll go home.'

'Where's home?'

'In Oregon. Just a small town – there aren't many big ones in Oregon. It's called Medford. I haven't been there for years – and I should never have left it.'

'Why did you leave, Paula?'

She laughed. 'Oh, it's a bromide – a cliché, you'd say. My whole life's been a cliché. I got movie-crazy when I was a kid, and when I was sixteen I won a local beauty competition. That gave me a swelled head and a big mouth – you should have heard me talk about what I was going to do in Hollywood. I was going to knock 'em cold. So I went to Hollywood and it knocked *me* cold! There are too many girls like me in Hollywood. I told you the story was a cliché.'

'What happened after Hollywood?'

'The cliché continued. I drifted around, singing in cheap night spots – you know the rest, or you can guess it.' I was saddened by the bitter resignation in her voice. 'That place where you found me in Panama – that was the best paid job I ever had in my whole life.'

'And you left it – just like that? Just because I asked you to?'

'Why not? It – it was Mark, you see. Oh, I know how you feel about Mark, I've heard you talk. All right, supposing he was a lousy no-good? I guess I always knew that, but – I loved him, Mike. And I suppose I was stupidly hoping to find out if he'd ever loved me. I always wanted to do whatever I could for him.'

I remained quiet. There was nothing I could say to that.

'Yes,' she went on quietly. 'I do think I'll go home. I always boasted that I wouldn't go back until I was a success. I guess they'd call me a success now, Mike?' There were tears in her eyes.

'You've always been a success,' I said gently, and held her shoulders.

She sniffed a bit and then said, shaking her head briskly, 'This isn't getting the glassware washed. I'd better go back to work. But thanks.'

I watched her walk along the deck and for the thousandth time I damned Mark's soul to hell. At a touch on my elbow I turned to find Geordie. 'I didn't want to bust up the *tête-à-tête*,' he said, 'so I waited a bit.' He nodded along the deck. 'Falling for her, Mike?'

'Nothing like that,' I said amusedly, thinking how very off target Geordie's guesses were. 'But there are times when I wish Mark had never been born.'

'Gave her a bad time, did he?'

'Curiously enough, he made her very happy. But he broke her heart by getting himself killed. Not that that matters – he'd have found some way of doing it, sooner or later. What's on your mind, Geordie?'

'I want to talk to you about our next move,' he said. 'We can't stay out here much longer, Mike. The winch and its components really desperately need attention. We're a little low on water – we hadn't had time to top up completely in Nuku'alofa – and that goes for fuel too. And we've been using an awful lot of that for station-keeping. We'll have to put into port somewhere pretty soon.'

'Yes, my lab stocks are running low too. Look, Geordie, we're really finished here – I've got loads of data to work on already. Let's put it to the boss again.'

Campbell said, 'How soon can you finish here, then?'

'I am finished, virtually. This last dredge today could be it – otherwise I could go on tinkering forever.'

'That's it then. But we don't go back to Nuku'alofa, in case Ramirez is still there, or hunting for us in that area. We'll go to Fiji – to Suva.'

I hesitated. 'That's fine, but I'd like to have a look at Falcon.'

'What for?'

I said, 'Well, it's responsible for all this.'

'A scientist to the last, eh? You're not content with finding anything – you want to know when and how and why.'

I was desperately keen to visit the island – or the site of it. I added, to give force to my argument, 'It could well give us a lead to other high-cobalt areas hereabouts. Maybe concentrations of other metals – once we find out something about the mechanism of this thing.'

He laughed. 'Okay, Mike, I guess you've earned it. If Geordie gives the go-ahead we'll go to Suva by way of Falcon.'

Geordie wasn't too certain. He pulled out his charts, measured distances, and grumbled. 'How long are you staying there?'

'Only a day or so, if that.'

'Will you be dredging?'

'There'll be no need to dredge. It's very shallow over the site. A good swimmer like Bill Hunter could go down and collect the samples I want by hand – it won't be more than a few fathoms. And he's dying to show off his talent. We could be away again in just a few hours.'

'It's cutting it a bit fine,' he complained. 'We'll be damned low on water by the time we get to Suva – and it's a good job you don't want to dredge because I really think this one was our last. We have to keep enough fuel oil for manoeuvring and for emergencies – I can't spare any more for the winch motor.'

'Away with you, Geordie. You know you hate sailing under power.'

But I got him to agree in the end. We finished with the dredge and stowed the cable for the last time. The dredge bucket was secured on deck and Geordie set a course northward for Fonua Fo'ou.

That evening in the saloon I said, 'I'd like to summarize what I've found. Can you stand another short lecture?'

We were moving briskly along with a helpful wind, the treasure had been found and any danger seemed infinitely remote and unlikely. My seminar settled down to hear me out in a state of contentment.

Campbell said, 'I'm getting used to being lectured to by scientists; it's sometimes boring and usually profitable.'

I laughed. 'This time it's very profitable.' I produced my charts and notebook. 'The high-cobalt nodules seem to be concentrated in a valley or depression, twenty miles wide and a hundred miles long. The nodules lie in varying degrees of richness and density.'

Clare, whom I had discovered to my pleasure to be a quick natural mathematician, said in astonishment, 'But that's two thousand square miles.'

'Quite an area,' I agreed. 'The richness varies roughly with the depth of the water, from about two per cent at the top of the ridges to a peak of ten per cent in the valley bottom – an inverse curve, if you like. On the other hand, the density varies in a different way. At the extreme north of the valley the density is only half a pound per square foot. At the other end it peaks out at fifty pounds per square foot.'

Campbell said, 'Still at ten per cent cobalt?'

'On the valley bottom, yes.'

'Hot diggety!' he exclaimed. 'A quarter of a billion bucks a square mile!' He and Clare were smiling in delight. Geordie looked dazed – the figures were so fantastic that he couldn't absorb them. Paula looked petrified.

I consulted my notebook again. 'I've worked out some rough figures. I reckon the overall average density over the entire area of two thousand square miles is about eight pounds to the square foot. The overall richness is about six per cent. Considering some of the higher figures, though, you're in for a very fine haul wherever you begin, so systematic mining will pay off.'

Campbell said, 'Those average figures of yours don't mean a damn thing, Mike. What do I care if the average density is eight pounds when I know of a place where it's actually fifty? *That's* where we start – we take the rich stuff out first.' He shook his head in wonder. 'This is fantastic – this is the damnedest thing. We can prove every pound of our resources before we even start. We'll need a detailed survey, though – with you to head it up.'

'I'd be proud to,' I said. I thought of the advanced equipment and systems I could use and rejoiced inwardly.

'I'll give you the finest survey vessel ever built – with no disrespect to *Esmerelda*, Geordie. But then – you may not want to do this. You'll be a rich man.' He got up to pour us all drinks as he spoke.

'I won't be until that survey has been made and the operation started,' I pointed out. 'But you couldn't stop me even then.'

Campbell said, 'I've been thinking this thing out. I'm starting a corporation and I'm reserving five per cent of the stock for the crew. Three per cent goes to you, Mike, and two to Geordie. I'll sell twenty per cent to those two guys I know that I mentioned, for twenty million dollars and let the Goverment – any or all of 'em – have fifty per cent for another twenty million. That starts to take care of the working capital.'

Clare exclaimed, 'Pop, I'm disgusted at you. Don't think I can't add up percentages! You come out with twenty per cent for yourself and you've discovered nothing. All you've done is put up a measly million dollars or so for this expedition.'

'Not quite, Clare,' he said mildly. 'There's your cut – another five, I think. And I have ideas concerning the remaining fifteen. For centuries people like me have been taking metals out of the earth and putting nothing back. We've been greedy – the whole of mankind has been greedy. As I said the other day, we've been raping this planet.' His voice grew in intensity. 'Now we've got hold of something different and we mustn't spoil it, like we've spoiled everything else that we've laid our greedy hands on. I'm keeping five per cent for myself, sure – but the other ten will go into an independent, non-profit making organization which will push my ideas a little further. We have to find a way to take that stuff out of the sea without disturbing the environment more than we can help, and to put something back – somewhere – by way of recompense.'

'There's one way that I can think of immediately,' I said. 'There are phosphorite nodules as well. You can make good fertilizer out of them, but so far no one has thought of a way of dredging them commercially. We could get them up with the rest, and you could be doing agriculture a bit of good.'

'That's what I mean,' Campbell exclaimed. 'You've gone to the heart of it – research is what's needed.' His eyes crinkled. 'How would you like to head up a new foundation?'

'Good grief! I wouldn't know where to start. I'm a field man, not an administrator. You want someone like old Jarvis.'

'You wouldn't be an administrator – I wouldn't waste your time on that. I can hire managers, but you'd be in charge of research.'

'Then nothing would stop me taking it on,' I said, dazzled.

'That's my boy.' He lifted the bottle and inspected it critically. 'Nearly the last of the scotch. Never mind, we can get some more in Suva.'

V

I was below when I heard the engine start, so I strolled on deck to find Geordie at the wheel. It was a calm evening without a breath of wind, and there was no sound except the throb of the engine which drove *Esmerelda* over the placid sea. 'It's lucky you kept some fuel back,' I commented, looking at a steadying sail hanging limply.

'Got a few gallons up my sleeve. I always save a little more than I let anyone know. Mike, what's the depth of water at Fonua Fo'ou?'

'I don't know, Geordie. It varies from year to year. The *Pilot* gives the latest depth in 1949 as about fifty-four feet, with no sign of the island at all, but it was there in 1941 – though there seemed to have been less of it than there was reported in 1939. A shoal at the northern end had vanished in those couple of years.'

He wasn't happy with this. 'We'll have to go very canny then.'

'We've been around shoals before, Geordie. And we know exactly where this one ought to be – so what's the problem?'

'I don't like this.'

'You don't like what?'

'This weather.'

I looked across at the setting sun and then to the east. The sky was cloudless and everything was peaceful. 'What's wrong with it?'

'I dunno,' he said. 'I've just got a feeling. I don't like that yellow tinge on the horizon northwards. Maybe there's a storm coming up.'

'How's the barometer?' I asked.

'Still normal – nothing wrong there. Maybe I'm being a bit old-womanish.'

He called Taffy to him and handed over the wheel. 'Keep a bloody close watch on that echo sounder, Taff,' he said.

'By my reckoning, we should be nearly there – we've been running long enough. Ian, set a watch out. If there's nothing before dark we'll circle back and come up again in the morning.'

He was more twitchy than I'd ever known him, and I couldn't quite tell why. Certainly it didn't appear to have anything to do with a possible chase by *Sirena* – we'd seen nothing and had no reason to suppose that she would find us. She'd scarcely be waiting at Falcon Island as if it were a handy street corner, I thought. And while my weather sense was not nearly as acute as Geordie's I had had my share of storms, and could see nothing in the sky or on the sea's surface to excite alarm. I didn't push him, and finally turned in to leave him pacing uneasily in the darkness, turning *Esmerelda* back on her track for a loop during the night hours.

The morning brought more of the same weather – or lack of it. It was calm, quiet and peaceful as we gathered on deck to watch for any telltale breakers while Geordie brought the ship gently back to her last night's position, and then motored slowly ahead. Presently he throttled the engine back to less than three knots. The echo sounder showed a hundred fathoms. Campbell and the girls joined us on deck and their voices were unnaturally loud in the hush of morning.

Geordie said quietly, 'The bottom's coming up. Only fifty fathoms.' He throttled back the engine still further.

Clare said, 'Is this Falcon Island?'

'Dead ahead. But you won't see anything though,' I told her. 'Just another bit of sea.'

'Twenty fathoms,' called Jim at the echo sounder. Geordie had taken the wheel again and repeated the call, then cursed suddenly. 'What the hell's going on?'

'What's the matter?'

'I can't keep the old girl on course.'

I looked across the sea path to the rising sun. The sea had a black, oily look and seemed as calm as ever, but then I noticed small eddies and ripples here and there – in an otherwise motionless seascape it was a strange and disturbing sight. They weren't large but I saw several of them. I felt *Esmerelda* moving under me, and she seemed to be travelling sideways instead of forwards. Something else nagged at my senses but I couldn't quite identify it.

Geordie had got control again, apparently. As Jim called out, 'Ten fathoms' he put the engine out of gear and as we glided to a rocking stop his hand was on the reverse gear, ready to send it home. Jim was calling steadily, 'Nine fathoms . . . eight . . . seven . . .' At six and a half Geordie touched the engine into reverse and the sounder came back up to hover at seven fathoms. Geordie said, 'This is it. As far as I'll go.' He looked and sounded bothered.

'Is Bill ready?'

Diving in six fathoms – thirty-six feet – was going to be no problem to Bill, who was already kitted up in a wet suit and aqualung, and was dipping his mask into a bucket of sea water someone had hauled up on deck. He already had his orders and they were of the simplest. He was to take down a couple of sample bags and bring me back a little of anything he could see – I didn't expect nodules, but the cinder and shell-laden bottom material would be fascinating to me. I had expected him to take someone else down with him in the accepted buddy system, but he was scathing about it and said he preferred to dive alone.

'When you want a buddy most is on the surface,' he told me, overturning most of my accepted belief at a stroke. 'You get disorientated pretty fast down there, even in clear water like this, and half the time you're not in sight of one another.'

So we'd put the smaller dinghy into the water and it was from there that Bill would launch himself into the sea. 'It won't take long,' he'd promised Geordie, and I felt sure that we could be away in an hour or so.

As he prepared to climb down into the dinghy he paused, sniffing the air, and commented, 'Someone hasn't washed their socks lately.'

That was the thing that was niggling at my mind, and recognition brought a stronger sense of unease. There was a heavy, sulphurous smell in the air. Geordie and I looked at each other and he said, 'Sulphur, Mike?'

'Well, this is a known volcanic region,' I said. 'I suppose it's always a bit niffy here.'

Ian spoke, pointing out to the horizon. 'You can almost see it in the air, skipper.' The sky low down was brightening into the dawn but there was a strange yellow tinge to it.

Bill was in the dinghy now, with Jim and Rex Larkin to row it a few yards off from *Esmerelda*. He sat on the thwart, gave the traditional thumbs-up sign as he made a final adjustment to his mask, and toppled backwards into the sea. For a few moments we could see his body sinking away from the dinghy. He had just disappeared when Geordie said hoarsely, 'Bill – stop him! Don't let him dive!'

It was too late. Several heads turned to stare at Geordie, who had suddenly gone ashen and was wrestling with the wheel, and at the same moment there was a babble of talk from the men at the bows and railings.

'For God's sake, we're spinning!' Geordie said, and I saw then what he meant.

Esmerelda was boxing the compass! Her bows swept slowly over the horizon as she twirled in a complete circle, not very fast, but with a suggestion of power in the colossal eddy that had her in its grip. And at the same time I saw a rising column of mist, darkening even as it rose, that appeared as if by magic out of the sea half a mile or so away from us. There were shouts of alarm from people, and I clung to a staunchion to steady myself as we spun about.

Almost as soon as it happened it had ceased, and *Esmerelda* was rocking tipsily, but steadying up again with the billowing steamy cloud ahead to starboard. I saw other little eddies appear and vanish on the sea's disturbed surface, and the smell of sulphur was suddenly pungent. I heard Geordie shouting but for the moment a ringing in my ears made it sound very faint and distant, and I shook my head to clear it.

'Ian! This is bloody dicey, but we've got to get an anchor down! We'll lose the dinghy and Bill both if we start shifting.'

I heard the anchor cable rattle out of the hawse pipe almost as he spoke, tethering *Esmerelda* to the shallow bottom. I could guess how reluctant Geordie would be to sacrifice his precious mobility at that moment, but it was of course essential to keep station. The dinghy rocked heavily and I saw a line being thrown to her, presumably to keep her in contact with us.

Campbell's body lurched into mine as we swung round the anchor cable, and Geordie called, 'Not enough – she'll swing into the dinghy! We'll have to get Bill up fast!' But he had gone down free-style, without a line, and there didn't seem to be any way to do it. I saw that some of the crew were swinging out the motor launch, and guessed that Geordie would use it to take up the dinghy crew into a more seaworthy craft, leaving the smaller boat in tow.

'How long will he stay down?' I asked, staring over the side. The whole surface of the water was rippling and beginning to chop.

'Not long at all,' Geordie said tensely. 'The moment he breaks surface we'll have him up out of there. With any luck there'll be enough disturbance down below to get him up quickly. Thank God it's shallow – at least he won't have a decompression problem.'

'What's happening?' Campbell's voice sounded as if he'd asked that question several times already.

I said, 'Wait a moment – I'll explain later.' I was staring at the column rising from the sea as if mesmerized. There was hardly any noise but the column blackened steadily, with a white nimbus around it, almost like the smoke of an oily fire, and I knew without a doubt that if there was no underwater disturbance to bring Bill to the surface, there was another phenomenon that would work as well – the sea would be rising in temperature, not to boiling point, at least not here, but several degrees above its normal state. I knew that I was looking at the beginning of an underwater volcanic eruption, and my heart was thudding as if my chest would burst open.

Geordie guessed it too, and a ripple of awareness ran through the crew. Campbell's mouth hung open and his hand fell away from my arm. Eyes were scanning the water near us, looking anxiously for our diver's reappearance, and glances over our shoulders kept us in touch with the increasing activity away on the horizon. *Esmerelda* was still rocking a little roughly but there was no feeling of instability about her. Something broke surface not far from the dinghy.

'There he is!' called Danny, pointing.

We saw the two men still in the dinghy pulling Bill in over the thwarts, the motor launch waiting off to take her in tow back to the ship, when there was a totally unexpected interruption.

Taffy Morgan shouted, 'Ship on the starboard beam!'

I spun round incredulously and pounded across the deck, colliding with someone on the way. Out of the smoke and steam that drifted across the sea ahead of us, half shielding her until the last possible moment, the bulk of *Sirena* came bearing down upon us.

Her yards were bare and she was pounding towards us full tilt under power. I could see figures on deck, many of them, and the lift of her bow wave as she approached.

'Goddam it! We're trussed up here for the slaughter,' Campbell said in vicious unbelief.

Geordie ran up the deck. 'Slip that flaming cable!' he bawled.

But there wasn't enough time. *Sirena* was on us, slewing and with her speed falling off at the last possible moment to lay alongside us with a minimum of seamanship, relying totally on surprise to aid her terrible attack. She didn't quite make the turn and her bowsprit stabbed at us like a monstrous rapier. There was an almighty crash and *Esmerelda* shuddered violently and moved bodily sideways in the water.

I was thrown against Geordie and we both went down in a tangle of arms and legs. I scrambled to my feet, all the breath knocked out of my body, and saw hazily that *Esmerelda*'s yardarm was locked in *Sirena*'s shrouds.

Ramirez had rammed us. The chaos was indescribable.

There was a roar of angry voices and a flood of men poured across the deck from *Sirena*, and I saw the flash of knives in the enveloping glow of that fantastic yellow light.

EIGHT

It was a short fight and a bitter one.

In the fraction of a second before they were on to us I saw Campbell's incredulous face, his mouth open in surprise. Then Geordie roared, 'Stand together, lads!' and I was grappling with a hefty brute who wielded a long and wickedly gleaming knife.

If he had come at me from underneath I might have been disembowelled, but he used the basically unsound overarm stab. I saw the knife coming down, grasped his wrist and pulled. This unexpected assistance sent him off balance. I did a neat sidestep, more suited to the dancefloor than the battlefield, twisted his arm and pushed. He reeled into the scuppers and his knife clattered on the deck.

I looked around and all was confusion. I scarcely had time to distinguish friend from enemy before I was attacked again. I felt a cold burn sear along my ribs as the knife struck, and in desperation I hit out slantwise with the edge of my hand at the blurred figure before me. There was a choked gurgle and the blur vanished – I hoped I'd smashed his larynx.

I staggered up, clutching at a stay for support, and as I wavered about the deck I saw Campbell go down under a vicious smashing blow from a belaying pin – and then I saw the unmistakable bulk of Jim Hadley.

He had got hold of Clare and was twisting her arm behind her back and she was screaming in pain. I couldn't hear her because of the tumult around me but I saw her wide-open mouth and the glaze of terror in her eyes.

I was about to plunge across the deck when there was a staccato rattle of shots and everything seemed to pause momentarily. I took the opportunity to yell, 'Stop fighting! For God's sake, stop fighting!'

The roar began again only to be halted by another fusillade of shots. A voice called, 'Very wise, Mr Trevelyan.' Then came a rapid spate of Spanish, which I was too dazed to follow.

I called out, 'Hold it, lads! They have Clare!'

We had been defeated in less than three minutes.

Everything stopped as suddenly as it had begun. I felt the burning ache along my rib-cage as only the most minor of distractions as I looked hastily around the deck. There seemed to be Spaniards everywhere, far more of them than of us, and three men lay on the deck without moving.

Ramirez stepped delicately across the deck with two armed men at his back. I had time to wonder where he'd got a fresh load of weapons from, and then he faced me. 'We meet under different circumstances, Mr Trevelyan,' he observed with a mocking smile.

I ignored him. 'Everyone all right?'

There was a low murmur and then Taffy looked up from one of the prone figures, white-faced under his tan. 'They've killed Danny,' he said in a level tone.

Over a rising growl I yelled, 'Cut it out – look at Hadley!'

There was a dead silence. Hadley had forced Clare to her knees; he had her right arm up behind her back and in his other hand he held a heavy pistol trained on the nape of her neck. Ramirez stood in front of me, nodding appreciatively.

'You have sense, Mr Trevelyan. You've lost and you know it.'

'Tell him to let her go.'

'In a moment.' He passed along the deck and came to Geordie, who stared at him impassively. 'Ah, the brave Mr Wilkins. I told you that you would regret what you did, one day.' He lifted his hand and struck Geordie across the face with a back-handed blow. A ring cut deep and blood started to drip from Geordie's mouth. He spat on the deck in silence.

Campbell moaned and tried to lift himself from the deck, and Ramirez strolled over to look down at him with an odd expression on his face. It was almost as if he contemplated the defeat of an old adversary with less than satisfaction. 'Come on, old one. Get up,' he said brusquely.

Campbell got halfway up, then collapsed again.

Ramirez made an impatient noise. He pointed to Taffy, still crouched over Danny's body. 'You – carry the old man into the saloon.'

Taffy and Ian between them got Campbell up. There seemed to be something wrong with his side, as if his leg was paralysed. As he lifted his head I saw an ugly blotch of blood on his left temple, and rage rose bitter in my throat at the sight.

Ramirez gestured to Geordie with his pistol. 'You too – into the saloon. And Mr Trevelyan, you too, please. We mustn't forget you.'

A rifle muzzle poked me in the back and I walked help-lessly towards the companionway. I turned my head and saw Hadley dragging Clare to her feet and pushing her for-ward. I wondered where Paula was.

Before we were thrust into the saloon we were brusquely searched. The man wasn't too gentle and I gasped with pain as the heel of his hand slammed against the wound in my side. He just grinned, but it was a mindless rather than a sadistic expression, I thought in that moment that there seemed to be a minimum of brain-power around – these men were mostly obedient puppets, no more than that. It might be useful, I thought, and wondered at myself.

In the saloon I helped Taffy to lay Campbell on a settee and said in a low voice, 'You're sure Danny was killed?'

'I'm sure,' Taffy said tightly. 'He was stabbed in the chest. God, the blood!'

I looked at Campbell. His eyes were open but unfocussed. I said, forcing my voice to a normal conversational pitch, 'The old boy's had a nasty knock. You'll find some water in the liquor cabinet, Ian.'

I looked around for Clare and found her coming to my side. Hadley had let her go and she was very pale but fully composed. Our hands found each other's for an instance and then she was looking at the blood on her fingertips. 'Mike, you're hurt!'

'That can wait. It's nothing. You'd better see to your father first.'

She went to him and began to sponge his head with a cloth dipped in the jug of water Ian held for her, her face clouded with fear and worry.

Paula was thrust into the saloon. She stumbled and nearly fell as her guard gave her a brutal shove before he took up a position near the door, his rifle pointing at us. I took her arm to steady her. 'Paula – are you all right?'

'I guess so,' she gasped. 'I've still got a whole skin.' She looked round and then said to me in a lower voice, 'I saw them putting two of our men in the cable hold, Mike – and they've hauled in the motor launch too.'

'Christ!' said Geordie. He wiped the back of his hand across his mouth and looked without surprise at the blood. He did a quick calculation on his fingers and then said, 'The two on board must have been Shorty and Davie Blake – the rest of us are here or – '

Paula took him up. 'Nick Dugan and young Martin were in the launch. I saw them both. I don't know about the other.'

They were the only two who had been in the launch, and it wasn't surprising that Ramirez had spotted them and fetched them back. But there were still Jim and Rex Larkin in the dinghy, and Bill Hunter. I had a faint surge of hope – had Ramirez missed them? And if so, could they stay hidden in that misty, turbulent sea? Geordie and I exchanged a glance and then looked quickly away.

I crossed over to Taffy, who was helping Clare, and made to assist him. 'Looks as though this is an officer's party, Taffy. You'd better stay pretty quiet unless you want to join the rest of the boys – they're in the cable hold.'

He nodded. 'I'll be all right,' he said, and rubbed the back of his neck in a curious gesture as if he had been hurt there.

One of the men with rifles said in Spanish, 'No speaking! Be silent, all of you.' I pretended not to understand and started to speak, but this time the gesture that went with the repeated instruction was clear, and I subsided. I had time to assess the situation now.

Neither Ramirez nor Hadley had actually entered the saloon with us – there were only the two armed guards. We were seven, and in the cable hold there were possibly four men. Danny lay dead on the deck – I could barely make myself think about that – and three were, with any luck, still at large.

I decided to try a gamble.

'It will be all right to let us speak,' I said in the best Spanish I could muster. 'Mr Ramirez will permit it.'

They glanced at one another, and one of them shrugged. I had guessed correctly – they were so accustomed to being given orders that they would accept this one even from me, spoken as it had been with an air of authority. I turned to Geordie and told him what I had said in Spanish, with a wary eye to the rifles, but to my relief the guards gave no further sign of stopping us.

Geordie said, 'What happens now?'

'That's not up to us. Ramirez has the next move, and I don't like to think what that will be. We can't do much while they're around.' I jerked my head very slightly in the direction of the guards.

'Seven here, four below,' Geordie murmured. He had done the same arithmetic that I had. 'And three – somewhere.'

I looked at Campbell who seemed to be recovering. 'They're a murderous lot of bastards, aren't they?'

'I wish I'd given Jim his head when he wanted to blow a hole in *Sirena*,' said Geordie viciously.

'Wishful thinking won't help us now. What bothers me most is that I think that's what they may be going to do to us.'

He shook his head irritably and we all lapsed into silence. Clare came over to me, unbuttoned my shirt, and proceeded to patch up what luckily proved to be no more than a skin graze, though it hurt me more than the slight wound warranted. I thanked God that we kept small first aid kits all over the ship. As she worked I felt her hands shaking just a little, and I grasped them to try and reassure her, but it was a wretched attempt.

There was a lot of movement on deck and a great deal of shouting. Ian looked up at the deckhead speculatively. 'I'm thinking they're having trouble, skipper. There's a hell of a tangle at the masthead.'

That was all to the good. The longer they took to separate the two ships the more time we would have to think of a way out of this mess. I looked at the guards and felt very depressed. They looked as though they'd murder their grandmothers for two pesetas, and they'd certainly have no qualms about shooting us if we tried anything.

It was nearly an hour before anything happened. We used the time to some little advantage; all of us achieved better control over ourselves and Clare brought her father to a degree of coherence. He had a pretty bad concussion – his speech was affected, although his thinking seemed clear enough.

'Goddam sonsa-bitches,' he said indistinctly. 'Why d'you quit, Mike?'

'Hadley had Clare,' I said briefly.

'Haaaah,' he sighed, and sagged back on the settee. 'I shoulda lef' her behind,' he muttered. 'Never lissen to a woman, Mike.' He closed his eyes and turned his head away, and Clare and I exchanged worried looks across his head.

'It's my fault,' Geordie burst out. 'I should have kept the lads up to scratch. We should have kept watch. We shouldn't have been surprised like that.'

'Shut up, Geordie,' I said. 'That won't get us anywhere. There's no blame – not on us. *We* weren't looking for trouble.'

'Aye,' said Ian softly. 'Yon Ramirez has a lot to answer for.'

Presently there was a rattle at the door and one of the guards opened it. Out of the corner of my eye I saw Taffy slide into a corner, half-hidden behind the settee, and then Ramirez came in, as elegant as ever. 'I trust you are comfortable,' he said solicitously.

'Let's not have any blarney,' I said bluntly. 'What's the next move, Ramirez?'

He smiled, and seemed to be enjoying a huge joke.

'Why, I have to introduce you to someone,' he said.

He leaned out of the door and beckoned to someone in the passage. He turned back to me and said, 'I told you once that you shouldn't make libellous statements that you couldn't substantiate.'

The man who came into the saloon was about my size, dark and heavily bearded. He carried my laboratory note-book in one hand.

Ramirez said, 'An old friend for you. I think you all know Mr Mark Trevelyan.'

II

As I looked into Mark's eyes I think my heart seemed to miss three full beats and I felt the hairs bristle on the nape of my neck. It isn't often that one is confronted by a dead man – especially a dead brother.

There was a sound as of a long-pent breath being released throughout the saloon and then the silence was total. Ian was the first to stir. 'That's the mannie I found . . .'

His voice tailed off as Mark switched his eyes to him. 'Ah, Ian Lewis. So it was you who clobbered me, was it?' he said pleasantly, and then his voice hardened. 'You'd have done better to stay in your Highland hovel, you Scots peasant.'

The whole pattern of events of the last few months had suddenly been shuffled like the pieces in a kaleidoscope, to present an entirely new picture. It was no wonder that Ian hadn't recognized the bearded man he found on our raid on *Sirena*; he had last seen Mark as a boy. I might have recognized him, but I hadn't taken the trouble to look. We weren't looking for a dead man that night in Nuku'alofa.

I looked round at the others. Their expressions were a mixture of amazement and slowly dawning comprehension. Clare gave Mark one long, measured look, then made a small contemptuous sound and turned back to her father. Campbell took her by the wrist protectively, never taking his eyes off Mark. He said nothing.

Ian was furious and showed it, while Geordie merely stared speculatively at Mark under lowered brows. Paula had made a sudden move as if to go to him, but she shrank back and hid in the shadows at Geordie's back. Taffy didn't show himself at all.

Of them all, Mark was watching me. 'Hello, Mike,' he said soberly.

I said, 'Mark, for God's sake – I – '

He was urbane where I was dumbfounded. He lifted the notebook and some papers in his hand. 'I've been rooting about in your laboratory. So kind of you to have done the preliminary survey for me. I couldn't have done it better myself.'

He dropped the papers on the table.

Ian looked at him with black anger in his eyes. 'I wish that I'd hit you a bit harder,' he said harshly.

Mark smiled at him but said nothing. He picked up my notebook again and flicked the pages with one hand. 'We seem to have struck it rich, Mike. There may be billions in all this, don't you agree? A pity you wasted your time but never mind, you saved me a bit of work.'

I spoke through a dry throat. 'You're a bastard, Mark.'

'Oh, come on, Mike. Aren't you maligning mother?'

He looked around. 'And who else have we? Yes, Wilkins, isn't it? What's it like on Tyneside these days, Geordie?'

Geordie showed his disgust. 'A bit cleaner than this saloon.'

'We will have our little jokes,' said Mark lightly. 'And my dear old boss, Mr Campbell, the fallen warrior – and Clare. I'm sorry you had to be here, Clare.'

She refused to look at him and said nothing. It irked Mark and he shrugged petulantly, turned away and peered behind Geordie. 'And who's the young lady sitting in the shadow?' he asked. 'I didn't know you were such a one for the ladies, Mike.'

He moved round the table and stopped suddenly. His face went very pale. 'Paula!' he whispered. He turned his head quickly to Ramirez. 'You didn't tell me she was aboard.'

Ramirez shrugged. 'Just another woman,' he said casually. For an instant they glared at one another and I had an insight into their relationship.

Paula stood up. 'Mark – oh Mark! I thought you were dead. Why didn't you come to me, Mark? Why didn't you trust me?'

Ramirez laughed softly.

Mark actually looked troubled. 'I'm truly sorry,' he said. 'Sorry you had to be on this ship.' He made a curious gesture as though wiping her away, and a prickle ran up my spine. In that one sudden movement he had rejected us all – wiped us out of his world.

Paula took a step forward. 'But Mark, I . . .'

Ramirez snapped out a curt phrase in Spanish and one of the guards lifted his rifle. The meaning was unmistakable.

Paula stopped dead and looked at Mark with the comprehension of horror. His eyes flickered and he looked away from her and she slowly fell back into a chair and buried her face in her hands. I heard the racking sobs that shook her, and saw Clare move to put her arms round her shoulders.

I had to force myself to speak calmly. 'We all thought you were dead. Why did you do it?'

'I had to die,' he said. He perked up – the change of subject took his mind off Paula. 'The police were after me and getting a little too close, so I conveniently killed myself.'

I suddenly knew another black truth. 'You did kill Sven Norgaard, didn't you.'

He turned on me. 'What else could I do?' he said defensively. 'The bloody fool wanted to *publish*. Him and his bloody scientific integrity – he wanted to give it all away, billions of dollars that belonged to me – to *me*, do you hear that? I made the discovery, didn't I?' His voice tailed off, and then he added softly, 'I *had* to kill him.'

The silence was murderous and we all stared at the egomaniacal horror that was my brother. He straightened up and said, 'And then I killed myself. The police would never look for a dead murderer. Wasn't that pretty clever of me, Mike?'

'It was stupid,' I said flatly. 'But then you always were a stupid man.'

His hand crashed on the table and we all jerked at the sudden violence. Only Ramirez watched him unmoved and dispassionate. 'It wasn't stupid!' he yelled. 'It was a damn good idea! But I'm surrounded by bungling idiots.'

'Like Kane and Hadley,' I said.

'That's right, them,' he agreed, suddenly calm again. 'Those damn fools gave me appendicitis, of all things. I could have killed that madman, Hadley – there was no need to invent extra details.'

'I'm sure you could,' I said. 'But it was you who bungled it. You should have told them precisely what to say.'

He betrayed for the first time his lack of authority. 'It had nothing to do with me,' he said sullenly. 'Ernesto fixed it.'

I shot a sidelong glance at Ramirez. 'So he's a bungler too?'

Ramirez smiled sardonically and Mark said nothing. I went on, 'You bungled again when Hadley let your papers and the nodules go. You should have taken them with you – that was bad planning.'

'They got them back though.'

'Not quite, Mark. I had a nodule still – and I had your diary.'

He reacted to that with white-faced fury, then subsided and nodded thoughtfully. 'You were lucky. You read it?'

'Oh yes,' I said casually. 'A simple code, really.' And watched him swallow his ire yet again as item by item I did my best to undermine his self-confidence. Then he suddenly laughed.

'That lunatic, Hadley. But you all thought I was dead anyway. And poor old Ernesto here was getting all the blame. That was really funny.'

Ramirez, who had been leaning negligently against the bulkhead, suddenly straightened, his face cold. 'This is a pointless conversation,' he said shortly.

Mark said, 'Let me have my fun, old boy. It isn't often a corpse can hold an inquest on himself. I'm getting a kick out of it.'

Ramirez looked at him contemptuously. 'All right. It won't make any difference,' he said dismissively. I knew that he was only waiting for word that his crew had separated the two ships before he did what he was going to do – and I had a good idea what that was.

I rubbed my ear – there seemed to be something getting in the way of my hearing, and Ramirez's voice had seemed to vibrate in a curious way. The ship creaked and rocked uneasily, and I wondered what was really happening outside. But it was also important to me to hear what my brother had to say, and I pushed the thoughts that were bothering me to the background.

'My inquest,' Mark said again. 'Let's develop this interesting theme.'

'Yes, let's do that,' said Campbell suddenly.

I turned to find him sitting up on the settee, waving away Clare and Ian. 'Let's do that,' he repeated, and I noticed that his voice was stronger and his speech clearer. 'Let's consider the burning of a hospital and the murder of a doctor and fourteen of his patients.'

Mark flinched. 'I didn't do that. It was Hadley again.'

'Hadley again,' I said caustically. 'You sound as pure as Hadley's pal Kane.'

'You condoned it,' said Campbell relentlessly.

'It was *nothing* to do with me. I didn't even know about it until afterwards. That man's beyond controlling.'

Ramirez had picked up my injudicious reference to Kane and was looking at me enquiringly. He was very acute.

'You have spoken to Kane again, Mr Trevelyan? He was supposed to come to me in Nuku'alofa, but I didn't see him there.'

I tried to make the best of my slip. 'Yes, we've spoken to him. He's told us a great deal too – enough to condemn the lot of you, so think carefully about what you're planning, Ramirez.'

'Might one ask where he is?'

'Where you won't find him, and all ready to sing like a bird.'

He looked thoughtful and did not speak again for a moment, and Campbell, sensing a faint opening, was quick to take advantage.

'What were you planning to do with us? It won't work now, you know.'

'You speak stupidly,' Ramirez said. Mark watched us fascinated, all his boasting silenced. He'd shocked us but he'd failed to impress us, and now things were taking a turn that he didn't like. It was slowly becoming obvious to me that in spite of Mark's almost insane posturing, it was Ramirez who was the more powerful of the two, and possibly the more dangerous.

Campbell said, 'You've decided that you can't leave us alive, haven't you? That would be too much to expect. You've already killed some seventeen people – another dozen or so won't make any difference. But you won't get away with it. We have covered our tracks, Ramirez, and for another thing your own crew will talk about all this, sooner or later.'

It was a bold try and I had never admired Campbell more.

Ramirez threw back his head and laughed. 'My crew – those morons?' He gestured to the stolid guards. 'Those oafs? They do what I tell them and nothing else. They have no mind of their own – I am the only brain they have. And who would believe them if they talked? They have never understood what it is all about, not one of them. Besides, that can be taken care of too.'

'A series of unfortunate accidents?' asked Campbell sardonically.

'Regrettable, isn't it?'

I listened to this ghastly conversation with a feeling of unreality. Ramirez was prepared to kill us without compunction. What was more, he was equally prepared to kill his own crew as well. I could just imagine how it would be arranged. The men would be well paid, split up and dispersed and then there would be, as Campbell foresaw, a series of accidents. A man found dead in a harbour here, a fatal car smash there, until the whole crew was disposed of.

'All right,' Campbell was saying. 'You still won't get away with it. Quite apart from Kane's evidence, you don't suppose I haven't made my own arrangements, do you? My agents have sealed letters which will be handed to the police if I don't turn up somewhere soon. There's going to be one hell of an investigation if I go missing.'

'You're an old fool,' said Ramirez brutally, the gloves off at last. 'The barometer has dropped three points in the last hour, there's a storm coming up and that thing out there is going crazy. You're going to be lost at sea – the lot of you. We will not be anywhere near here. There will be no proof – no proof of anything.'

Campbell shuddered and Clare pulled a little closer to him. Watching Ramirez, I was fascinated by a movement outside the port light behind his head. Nobody else had seemed to see it, too appalled and horror-stricken by the finality in Ramirez's voice. I saw Taffy, crouched at the end of the settee, fumble again with that curious gesture at the back of his neck, but his eyes never left Ramirez.

Campbell said slowly, 'Ramirez, you're a bloody-minded butcher.'

Ramirez spread his hands. 'I don't like killing for killing's sake. I'm no Jim Hadley – he was stupid back on Tanakabu and I abhore that, putting pleasure before business. I kill only from necessity. But when I do, whether it's seventeen or seventy lives doesn't make much difference. Lives are cheap, my friend, when there are large stakes. I consider my measures necessary.' He was as cold as a snake.

I switched my gaze back to the port and caught my breath. There was a face out there. An eye winked.

Bill Hunter was back on board.

He was a hidden ace that Ramirez must not become aware of. I cautiously lifted my hand to my mouth, coughed, and then made a slow downward movement, being careful not to jerk. I didn't want to catch anyone's attention. The eye winked again and the face disappeared.

Campbell was still speaking, desperately searching for arguments to persuade Ramirez not to go ahead with whatever plans he had for us. Again there was that vibrancy in my ears, a curious beat in Campbell's voice as though there were some sort of aural interference, some note so low as to be inaudible. Not far away there was a sound as though an engine were letting off steam. *Esmerelda* shuddered and the noises on deck increased suddenly.

Ramirez interrupted Campbell, turned and to my horror strode over to look out of a porthole. I tensed but then he turned back and spoke again, and I realized he'd not seen anything untoward.

'Whatever is going on out there will serve its purpose,' he said coolly. 'As soon as these idiots of mine have parted the two ships we go our separate ways. You won't have far to go – a mile or so straight down. We will tow you into deep water – or point your nose into that thing out there.' He turned on Geordie. 'We have borrowed an idea from you, Captain. We will set an explosive charge against your hull, and that storm out there will do the rest.'

Geordie ground his teeth together but said nothing.

Somebody ran across the deck over our heads and a voice called out. Ramirez cocked his head and glanced upwards. 'It sounds as though they are about ready.'

I heard a clatter of heavy boots on the companion steps and there was a thump on the door. At a gesture from Ramirez one of the guards opened it and Hadley came in. He looked at us with an oafish grin that didn't reach his pale, cold eyes and bent to whisper to Ramirez, who immediately turned to look out of the porthole again. I thanked God that Bill had kept out of sight. Or had he?

Ramirez turned back. 'Which would you choose? Deep water or Falcon Island? There seems to be increased activity over there.' He smiled and said to Mark, 'This is lucky, you know. Where else should a survey ship be wrecked but in investigating Falcon Island a little too closely at the wrong time? Keep our friends happy for a little while.'

He turned on his heel and left the saloon, followed by Hadley.

Geordie watched them go and then transferred his attention to Mark. 'You're a poor specimen of a man,' he said with contempt. 'What makes you think I'm going to sit back and let you wreck my ship and murder my crew? If I'm going to be killed I might as well take you with me.' He began to rise from his chair. With Ramirez's departure a curious change had come into the atmosphere. It was as if we could all recognize that where Ramirez had real authority and total amorality, Mark had only his ego and his self-seeking veneer of toughness over a very insecure personality.

As Geordie started to rise Mark snapped out a command in Spanish and the guards' rifles lifted to the ready. 'Be careful,' Mark said. 'They are trained killers.'

'So am I,' said Geordie with menace. He continued to rise slowly and Ian started to get up as well.

Mark spoke again in Spanish and one of the guards casually fired his rifle, apparently without aim. The noise was appalling and we flinched back as splinters flew from the bullet as it struck the cabin sole just by Geordie's foot. He hesitated and I spoke sharply. 'Cut it, Geordie – you haven't a chance. You can't move faster than a bullet.'

Geordie glared at me under his lowered brows but I made a quick slashing gesture with my hand and, taking a chance, winked at him. His brow smoothed and he sat down again, as did Ian. Both were watchful, and I knew that I had succeeded in alerting them.

There was a sustained racket from overhead. Geordie said, 'They're making a muck-up of it out there, aren't they?'

'Mind if I smoke, Clare?'

I put my hand into a pocket and stopped as a rifle barrel turned and the muzzle pointed unwaveringly at me. 'For God's sake, Mark, can't I even have a cigarette?'

He looked amused. 'Smoking's bad for you, Mike. Go ahead – but you'd better have nothing but cigarettes in your hand when you pull it out.'

Slowly I withdrew my hand as he spoke to the guards again. The rifle barrel drooped a little and I opened the packet and put a cigarette in my mouth. And at that moment I saw Bill's face at the port once more. The sound of the rifle had brought him back, as I'd hoped it would.

The saloon door opened and there was a brief exchange between one of our guards and a man outside, and then it closed again. Clearly Ramirez too had sent to ask about the shooting. I put my hand to my pocket again and said to the man with the rifle, '*Fósforos*?' He made no sign and I managed to get the matches out without being threatened.

I lit the cigarette and said, 'Look, Mark. You know everybody cooped up in this saloon. Some have been your friends – others have been more than friends – a lot more. In God's name, what kind of a man are you?' I found it hard to speak to him without my voice betraying me.

'What can I do?' he asked petulantly. 'Do you think I *want* to see you all killed? It's out of my hands – Ramirez is in control here.'

Clare's voice was cutting. 'He washes his hands – the new Pontius Pilate.'

'Damn it, Clare, you don't think I want to see you at the bottom of the sea? I can't do anything, I tell you.'

Campbell said, 'It's no use, Mike. He wouldn't do anything to save us even if he could. His neck's at stake, you know.'

This was my chance. To speak to Campbell I had to half-turn away from Mark and the guards in a natural fashion. 'He'll join us anyway,' I said. 'Ramirez has got what he wants now. He doesn't need Mark any more – he only needs to take my notes with him – and I'm damn sure he'll want to rub out *any* witness to all this – including Mark.'

I was printing on the back of the cigarette packet with the stub of pencil I had taken from my pocket with the matches. The words, as large as I could make them, were 'CABLE HOLD'. I drooped my eyelid at Campbell and he caught on fast. He shook his fist at Mark to divert attention and started acting up a little. 'You damned murderer!' he shouted.

'Shut up,' said Mark venomously. 'Just shut up, damn you.'

I held up the cigarette packet towards Campbell and said, 'Take it easy. Have one?'

'No, no,' he brushed my offer aside, but the job was done, and Bill had had a clear vision of my message over Campbell's shoulder. I hoped to God that he had good eyesight. Clare saw the message too and her eyes widened. She bent her head over the still prostrate Paula to hide her expression. I saw her whisper in the other girl's ear, apparently still soothing her.

I said to Mark, still playing for time, 'Why the hell should he shut up? We've got nothing to lose by telling you what we think of you. I'm sickened at the thought of you being any kin to me.'

Mark's jaw tightened and he said nothing. I had to goad him into speaking. I risked a glance at the port, and saw that the face had gone, to be replaced with a hand. The middle finger and thumb were joined in a circle. Bill had got my message.

Whatever happened now I had to give him time to act on it. Now he knew where the rest of us were and might be able to do something about it. I wondered if he was alone or if Jim and Rex were still with him. It was a slim chance but it was all we had. I reckoned that the only thing we could do to help was to get at Mark in some way – and in his highly nervous state that might prove deadly dangerous.

I said, 'What put you on to us? The sea's a big place, Mark. But of course you always knew where that high-cobalt nodule formation was, didn't you?'

'I only knew approximately. I wasn't the only one doing assays on that damned IGY ship, and I couldn't get at all the information I wanted.' His sullen tone implied that such information should have been his by rights, which was typical of him, but I was on the right track in getting him to talk about his own cleverness. Few genuine egotists can resist such an appeal.

'Who had the bright idea that found us here, then? We could have been anywhere. We could have been a hundred miles from here. You couldn't know where we were.'

He laughed. 'Couldn't I? Couldn't we? I know you like a book, Mike. I knew that you'd find that deposit given time to survey properly – so I gave you that time. And I knew that once you'd found it you couldn't resist investigating the source. I knew you'd *have* to come to Fonua Fo'ou, to Falcon. Ramirez couldn't see it, of course. He can be a stupid man at times. But I convinced him that I knew my own brother. We've been hanging round here for two bloody weeks waiting for you to turn up.'

I said, 'How did you get tangled with Ramirez?' We already knew the answer to that one but it kept him talking.

'Campbell there couldn't finance me and Suarez-Navarro could. It was as simple as that. Who else should I go to but them? They'd just shown that they weren't too scrupulous by what they'd done to his mines, so they were just what I wanted.'

'And then they led you into murder. You had to kill Norgaard.'

'That was an accident,' said Mark irritably. 'All Sven was doing was tying up loose ends. We were waiting for the hue and cry to die down, and then Suarez-Navarro were going to provide us with a proper survey ship to find this stuff.' He thumped the papers and notebook. 'Meantime that damned fool decided that he wanted to publish. You see, he didn't know much about Suarez-Navarro and that's the way I wanted it. We had an argument – he was a pretty excitable chap – at first in words, and then it came to blows. The next thing I knew was that he'd cracked his head open on the coral. But I didn't mean to kill him, Mike. I swear it. All I ever wanted to do was to shut him up.'

'All you ever want to do is to shut people up,' I said flatly. 'How do you go about shutting up a good scientist, Mark? It seems to me that the *only* way is to kill him.'

I was cold inside, chilled by his amoral egocentricity. Everything he had done was justified in his own eyes, and everything that had gone wrong was the fault of other people.

Mark waved me aside. 'Hadley knew, of course. He was my liaison with Ramirez. They helped me to cover it up, but somehow the police got onto it.'

'My God, you think *I'm* naive,' I said. 'Look, Mark, I wouldn't be surprised if Ramirez didn't tip off the police himself. It wouldn't matter to him – he was in the clear. He arranged for your "death" and that was that. But he had you neatly wrapped in a package from then on, and you couldn't do a thing without his say so.'

'It wasn't like that,' Mark muttered.

'Wasn't it? Even when the first plan went wrong and Hadley was implicated in your so-called murder Ramirez wasn't worried. That's why he laughed his damn head off when I accused him. He knew that all he ever had to do to clear himself and Hadley was to produce you, and you can be sure he'd do it in such a way that would earn him the congratulations of the law.'

'What do you mean by that?'

'He'd produce you dead – or dying, Mark – just so you couldn't talk. And the police would pat him on the back for capturing Mark Trevelyan, the murderer of Sven Norgaard, and maybe the mastermind behind the killing of Schouten. By God, I was right when I called you stupid. You'd really got in over your head, hadn't you?'

He was angry and baffled, and I could see that my attack had hit home; doubt was in his every action.

Campbell said, 'It doesn't make any difference now. Mark, you're for the deep six along with the rest of us. Ramirez will see to that.'

Geordie laughed without humour. 'Do you think you can trust Ramirez?'

Mark thought deeply and then shook his head. 'Maybe you're right,' he admitted, and I don't think he had often used those words in his lifetime. 'But it still makes no difference. You want me to help you, but I can't. You'll never beat him – and if you did I'd still be wanted for murder. I'd rather stick to Ramirez and take my chances. He still needs me.'

I wanted to try and tell him how wrong he was, but something else had finally penetrated to my consciousness. There was a whistling sound in the distance – high pressure steam was escaping somewhere. Mark looked out of the porthole and what he saw over the water made him acutely unhappy. 'Damn them, what are they doing on deck?' he muttered. 'This is no time to be hanging around here.'

His nervousness increased and he conferred with one of the guards in a low voice. An argument seemed to develop as the guard answered back, but Mark overbore him. With a black glance and a reluctant shrug the guard opened the saloon door and went out.

I looked at Geordie with hopeful eyes and he nodded grimly. The odds were improving, but anything we tried would have to be done before the guard returned. Geordie's hand crept towards the heavy glass ash tray on the table and then relaxed near it. He couldn't throw it faster than the guard could shoot – but he was ready if a chance came up. We were all sitting tensely.

There was a reddish reflection in Mark's face as he went again to look out of the porthole. Evidently things were stirring on Falcon. I said, 'What's going on out there, Mark?'

His voice was strained. 'It looks as though Falcon is going to bust loose.'

I felt suddenly colder. Mark and I were possibly the only two people on either ship qualified to have any understanding of what that might mean. I said, 'How close are we?'

'Maybe a quarter of a mile.' He straightened his back and added, 'It's happened a couple of times this week already. It's never amounted to much. A great sight, but that's all.' But he was not convincing.

We were much too close to Fonua Fo'ou. To Ramirez and Hadley it might seem a good safe distance, especially if they had been watching pre-eruption patterns all week, but Mark and I knew better. We knew what volcanic eruptions could do.

No wonder Mark was scared. So was I.

He looked at the remaining guard, hesitated, and then spoke to him. The guard shook his head vigorously, and as Mark started to leave he stepped in front of the door and raised his rifle.

Campbell said ironically, 'What's the matter, Mark? Doesn't he trust you?'

The whistling and belching suddenly increased and *Esmerelda* lurched, her joints squealing a protest. We swung round, still locked with *Sirena*. There was a sudden blast of an acrid sulphurous smell in the air. Mark's eyes darted from the guard to me and our glances locked as tightly as the ships.

Mark said sharply, 'He doesn't want to be left here alone with you lot. I must wait for the other guard.' He crossed to the porthole and looked out again and I felt bile rise in my throat.

Geordie said, 'What the hell's the matter. . .?'

He didn't have time to finish. *Esmerelda* gave another great lurch and went over almost on her beam ends. I slithered helplessly towards the side of the saloon and jarred my head against the table as I fell. There were sounds of bedlam above decks.

The ship righted herself and we fell back in a jumble of bodies. I heard Campbell groan; it must have been hell for him in his condition. Geordie was up first. He grasped the ashtray and hurled it at the guard, and then leapt the length of the saloon. The guard tried frantically to retrieve his rifle from the deck where it had fallen. He had his fingers on the butt when Geordie kicked him with precision in the jaw and his face disappeared into a bloody ruin.

Ian had gone for Mark and any trace of his normal Highland gentleness had vanished. His face was a mask of rage. Geordie had grabbed the rifle and turned it on Mark. They converged on him, but Mark managed to evade them both and scrambled towards the saloon door.

There was a curious flicker in the air and he slumped, his hand clapped to his right hip, and I saw blood welling between his fingers.

I had raised myself to go after Geordie and a shouted word of protest was already on my lips, but as Mark fell both Ian and Geordie came to an abrupt stop, the momentary blood-lust dying from their faces. All eyes were on the gleaming, bloodied blade on the floor beside Mark.

'Who threw the knife?' I demanded.

Taffy came from the far end of the saloon. 'I did.' He saw the look that sparked in my eyes and added hastily, 'I wouldn't have killed him, Mike – even though he deserves it. I know where to put a knife.'

'Well, you'd better come and get it,' I said.

He came forward to take it from the deck and carefully wiped it on his trouser leg. Clare was looking at him ashen-faced, but Paula had already pushed forward to Mark's side.

I said, 'I saw you searched like the rest of us, Taffy. How did you hide the knife?'

'I had it dangling down the small of my back on a piece of string. It's an old trick but they fell for it.'

For the moment the crisis was passed. I looked anxiously out to sea. There was a haze of steam in the near distance and beyond it the swell of sullen black clouds still rolled sky-wards. The sea was choppy, with little eddies swirling here and there, and around the fringe of the steam there was a white roil of froth. The smell was fitful and nasty. Closer in, I saw our motor launch swinging astern with nobody on board her. There was no sign of Bill, nor of anyone else on deck.

In the saloon Ian was helping Campbell back onto the settee with Clare to lend him a hand. Paula was bandaging Mark and Geordie was searching the prostrate guard.

Taffy was missing.

'Geordie, where's Taffy?'

'Danny Williams was a special mate of his, you know.'

'Damn it, we need team work, not singleminded heroics.'

'Easy now,' Geordie said. 'Taffy never was a good team man, but he's deadly on his own. He'll do a hell of a lot of damage.'

'All right for him, but we need a plan of action urgently. Taffy's loose and Bill is somewhere on deck, and with luck Rex and Jim are with him. Maybe they've been able to do something. And there's us – three men and a rifle.'

'Four men,' snapped Campbell, getting to his feet. 'And if those sons of bitches haven't searched our cabins there'll be guns in them.'

He met my eyes with a cold blue glare. He was right; he'd be no good in a brawl but give him one of his target pistols and he could be deadly. Clare looked from her father to me and there was something of the same hard wildness in her face.

'I'm coming with you,' she said.

'Clare, you can't . . .'

She cut in decisively. 'I'm a pretty good shot too, remember? Better than you, Mike. You're going to need all the help you can get.' She was determined to stay close to me and her father, and she was right. We would need her. And if it came to the worst, for her as for the rest of us, death by a bullet was preferable to drowning, clawing for air in a scuttled ship. My throat closed up with fear for her but I couldn't argue with her decision.

She moved to the liquor cabinet. Several bottles had broken in the roll, and she picked one up and stared at the jagged edges. She said slowly, 'I've seen them do this in movies.'

I thought that she could probably never use it, but it gave her some confidence. Geordie actually chuckled from the doorway. 'That's the stuff,' he said. 'Come on. We haven't much time. Me first, then Ian. Mike, you bring up the rear.'

Paula was bending over Mark. She met my eye and shook her head slightly. Mark lay back with his eyes closed, though whether he was unconscious or shamming it was impossible to guess. 'Okay, Paula, you stay here with him,' I said.

Geordie opened the door and slipped out.

One by one we followed him cautiously into the passageway. He hadn't gone more than a few feet when he stopped, stepped over something and then moved on. It was the body of our second guard. He must have been on his way back to the saloon when he met up with Taffy. His throat was cut in a gaping gash and the front of his shirt was sodden and dyed scarlet with blood. Clare swayed a little as she looked down and I took her firmly by the arm and pushed her past.

We moved ahead to Campbell's cabin and went inside to find that it hadn't been searched. Campbell took his valise from the bottom of the wardrobe and unrolled it, looking satisfied and stronger with every movement. There were three guns in it, his own and Clare's, and the one Geordie had taken from Ramirez back in Nuku'alofa. Father and daughter quickly loaded their weapons and Clare discarded the jagged bottle with obvious relief.

In our cabin Geordie and I found our two pistols untouched, and as we loaded them Campbell nodded with approval. 'Now we've a fighting chance,' he said.

We crept on without interruption to the aft companionway. Geordie climbed up cautiously, then ducked back. There was a man standing above on the deck silhouetted against that yellow-glowing sky. He was holding a rifle. Geordie laid his own weapon aside and moved slowly up the steps. Then he motioned me to follow – Ian was the professional but, being much slighter than the Scot, I had a better chance of reaching the deck simultaneously with Geordie.

Geordie leapt swiftly up and took the guard from behind, one arm swinging round his neck and the other grabbing the rifle. I scrambled after him and clubbed the man with the butt of my gun. He collapsed in a heap.

We dropped him down the companionway like a sack of potatoes. With a grim smile Geordie said to me, 'You're learning, laddie.' We followed the body down again.

We now had three rifles and a small assortment of handguns. The odds were getting better all the time. Geordie, making his disposition of his troops, said, 'Mike, I want us to take a look at Falcon. You come with me. Ian, cover our rear. Mr Campbell, you and Clare keep watch down here, and shoot anybody who tries to come down that passageway – as long as they aren't ours.'

We slipped quietly on deck and I got my first full look at Falcon. The yellow glow seemed to be diminishing but there was a lot more steam, and sheets of a rain-like substance were falling to one side of the troubled area. In the middle of it all the dense black smoke billowed upwards with fleeting streaks of red intermingled in it. The sea there was heaving and broken, but the ships were still in an area of almost untroubled ocean, save for the hurrying turbulence on the surface. The whistle of high-pressure steam was deafening, a bad sign, and the smell was gut-wrenching. I stared in utter fascination.

But once on deck Geordie was more concerned with his ship. He looked up at the foremast. 'Christ, what a mess! They haven't cleared her yet.'

In the dazzle of sunlight looking upwards I could see that the two masts were almost separated; they now seemed to be locked only somewhere high up. The taller *Sirena* leaned over *Esmerelda* at an angle and there was a hellish tangle of lines, broken spars and general debris scattered everywhere. The motor launch still hung astern but from where we stood there was no sign of our dinghy.

'They're still busy,' Geordie murmured. 'We'll make for the winch. We can hide there while we try to open the cable hold.'

There was nobody at the wheel but ahead I could see knots of men at the foot of each mast. Some were up the masts working to free the wreckage, and I hoped to God they were too occupied to look down and spot us.

'We'll have to chance it,' Geordie said, and gestured to Ian to follow us. We ran forward in a crouch, keeping to the shadow of the deck house. At the end of it Geordie paused, caught my arm and pointed. There was a slight movement in the shadow of the winch drum, and to get there we would have no further cover.

'Bill – or Taffy,' he breathed.

A hand came out into the light and fumbled with the fastenings of the hatch cover. Ahead the men on board *Sirena* seemed to be watching the attempt to clear the mast or looking back towards Falcon, and there was a good chance that they wouldn't see a man if he moved stealthily across the deck. A wild dash would be suicide.

The disembodied hand was still working on the hatch cover. 'I'm going to undo the other side,' I said quietly to Geordie. 'Cover me.'

A rumble came clearly across the water from Falcon cutting through all other noises, and the red flashes of light in the black cloud suddenly flared higher. Voices were raised in alarm and there was a stampede of running footsteps. The diversion was well timed and I slid along the deck, clutching for the edge of the hatch, and pulled myself to lie close alongside. Groping for the catches, I saw that my companion was Bill Hunter. I had released one catch and was attacking the other when there was the sharp crackle of gunfire and a thunder of feet. Ian and Geordie were on their knees, firing at *Sirena*'s men who were pounding aft towards us.

A contorted face loomed over me, the butt of a rifle poised over my skull. I jerked to one side and it slammed into the deck. Then I heard the distinctive 'spaat' of Campbell's target pistol and my assailant grew a third eye in the middle of his forehead and crashed on top of me.

I shoved his body aside and grabbed for the hatch. The second catch came free and Bill and I heaved the cover up and flung it open. Four men came boiling out of it, ready for blood.

Geordie screamed, 'Aft! Get aft!'

We all tumbled down behind the deckhouse. More shots rang out and Ian scored a hit. The rest of *Sirena*'s crew retreated back to the mast as covering fire came from on board their ship. It seemed to come from their deckhouse, but it was hard to tell in the confusion. Geordie looked us over, counting heads and to my intense pleasure the face of Jim Taylor was amongst them. At least one of the dinghy crew was safe, which gave me hope for Rex Larkin. Bill gave me a quick thumbs-up sign.

Sporadic fire came from *Sirena*. There was at least one sharpshooter up the mainmast, and Geordie ducked as a bullet sent splinters flying just above his head.

'This is no good,' he said. 'There's not enough cover, and we're running out of ammo.'

Then came the methodically spaced shots from Campbell's pistol. There was a scream from the yardarm and a dark figure fell, all spinning arms and legs, to *Sirena*'s deck.

Geordie got us moving aft, leaving Nick and Ian to cover our retreat. In the companionway Campbell was reloading the pistol as we swarmed below. His lips were curled back in a fierce grin. He motioned us aside curtly and aimed at the yardarm, crouching to steady himself in the hatchway. Another body plummeted down, this time into the sea.

'That's the lot,' Campbell said. He looked drawn and white and near the end of his endurance. In the passageway Clare was standing with her pistol held in a steady hand. The alarm in her face subsided when she saw us. I caught and held her briefly.

The men gathered below and there was a swift redistribution of weapons. Nick lifted a brawny fist. 'I won't need a gun,' he said. He was holding a huge Stillson wrench.

A few more shots came from above but they died away, and a short time later Nick and Taffy reported that *Esmerelda* was clear of enemies below decks at least. With the exception of my brother.

Jim and Geordie went to reconnoitre the forward companionway, after a brief word with Campbell. Somehow he persuaded the Canadian to stay back in the saloon with Mark, Paula and Clare, and I forebore to ask him whether he'd done it by tact or threat. I was deeply relieved, either way.

'They've retreated – they're all aboard *Sirena*.' Geordie was back with a report. 'I didn't see any sign of Ramirez, but Hadley's all over the place, bellowing orders. He's making a right foul-up of the job too. We're still locked on, damn them.'

'What about Falcon?' I asked.

'The same as before – it's pretty fierce out there. But we've checked the engines and there's no sabotage there, thank the lord. We're going to have to get clear of *Sirena* and away bloody fast as soon as we can. But how?'

We all looked at one another, desperately searching for ideas.

Geordie swung round to Hunter. 'Bill, how did you get back on board? And where's Rex. Is he okay?' Bill didn't know about Danny yet, but I'd seen his eyes scanning our bunch and he looked grim. It took him a moment to reply.

'I'm sorry, skipper – we lost him. We saw some of *Sirena*'s lot take over the launch. They held guns on our lads and threw them a line to haul them in. They hadn't seen us, so I got Rex and Jim here to slip over the dinghy side and we swamped her. Jim and I got back on board okay, up our ladder, but we had Rex between us and when *Esmerelda* lurched over he – let go. God, Geordie, I – '

'You did your best. It's another one to chalk up to Ramirez,' said Geordie curtly. I left them together and went up to take another look at Falcon, feeling sick and depressed. The launch still bobbed at the end of its line, but somewhere under that twitching sea lay our dinghy and one of our crewmen.

The distance to the belching gout of smoke seemed less. Either we were dragging our anchor, which was very likely with the disturbance under her hull and the extra weight of *Sirena* alongside, or the area of eruption was enlarging – an even more alarming prospect. There was even more steam than before and I longed to know what was going on behind that red-lit misty curtain. I would have very much liked to ask Mark's opinion.

I went back down to Geordie. 'We've got to get out of here before Falcon really starts acting up.'

He looked across the sea. 'It's weird, I'll grant you, but is it that serious? Lots of observers have seen eruptions at sea before now. And Mark said it's been going on for days already.'

'This is just an overture,' I said. No time now to begin a lecture on undersea vulcanology. 'I don't think we should be around when the finale's being played.'

'Oh, I want out too, make no mistake. But we've got a closer problem than Falcon right now – our friends out there. I wish to God I knew where Ramirez was, and what he's planning. Bill, could you see any sign of tampering with our hull? They've threatened us with explosives.'

Bill shook his head. 'No, skipper. At least not that I've seen.'

My warning about Falcon seemed to have passed Geordie by – it was something quite out of his experience. He was still wholly concerned with unshackling *Esmerelda*, and certainly for the moment he was right.

I asked, 'What the hell can we do?'

'Well, whoever's in command over there – Ramirez or Hadley – will want to get free as much as we do. They're in danger just as we are. And I don't think they'll find it so easy to retake us now, or blow us up as they threatened. Knowing Ramirez he may be prepared to cut his losses.'

'And try another time?'

'Another time isn't our problem right now. Let's solve this one first.'

He was right, and we waited in silence, aware that a plan was forming in his mind. At last he said, 'I reckon we should call a truce. If we send a man up the mast they won't fire at him if they know why he's going up there.'

'What's the good of sending one man up? They've had a dozen men up there for an age and they haven't been able to achieve much.'

'I've got an idea about that,' Geordie said, and passed the word for Jim to join us. 'Got any more of that plastic explosive, Jim?' he asked.

Jim shook his head. 'No, I only had the bit I used on their engine.'

Geordie pointed to the masts. 'See that yardarm – where it's tangled with rigging? Could you blow it off if you fastened a hand grenade on each side of the spar?'

I stared at him, but Jim was already immersed in technicalities. 'It would be a bit tricky, skipper. Grenades aren't exactly meant for that sort of thing.' He peered at the spars doubtfully. 'It's steel tubing.'

'Of course,' said Geordie. 'If it was wood they'd have chopped it through by now. Steel halliards too.'

'I dunno,' said Jim honestly.

'It would weaken the spar though, wouldn't it?' Geordie persisted.

'It wouldn't do it any good, if that's what you want.'

'Hell, come down to brass tacks. Suppose I have the engine going and put a strain on the yardarm after the grenades are blown, do you think that would do the trick?'

'I reckon it might,' said Jim slowly. 'It would be a nice job to place the grenades right.'

Geordie had trapped him neatly.

'You'll have a go then? You're our expert.'

Jim grinned. 'I'll give it a bash – if they don't shoot me.'

'Good,' said Geordie briskly. 'We'll take care of that part of it. You gather together what you need and I'll get those grenades. I knew we'd find a use for them. Mike, you'll be the best man to negotiate. Try to settle terms for an armistice with that bunch of pirates.'

I wondered if Ramirez would realize that if he let us go he might never catch up with us again. We would forever be a threat to his freedom, and he might never agree to such terms. There seemed to be too many imponderables. And there was Falcon . . . We were very vulnerable – underarmed, undermanned, and in no position to dictate terms. And then I thought of Clare, and how precious she had become to me. Whatever else, I was determined that she should survive, and to hell with the rest.

I crawled into the wheelhouse, keeping below window level, and raised the loudhailer.

'Ahoy, *Sirena*!' I shouted. 'Ahoy, Ramirez – can you hear me?'

A shot was fired at the wheelhouse. I heard the smash of broken glass and a small shower of it fell near me. There was shouting and then silence. The only sound came from the ships as they creaked and groaned together and from the hissing of the volcano behind us.

'*Sirena*! Ramirez! I want to talk to you.'

My knuckles were white round the loudhailer. The silence was finally broken by a harsh voice. 'Well?'

'Is that you, Ramirez?'

'Yes. What do you want?'

'That volcano – it's going to erupt at any moment. Hell, it's *started*.'

'I know.' He sounded frustrated and I almost smiled with relief. He'd cooperate.

'We have an idea.'

'What can you do?'

'We want to send a man up the foremast. We can clear that rigging.'

His voice was full of suspicion. 'How can you do that?'

I did not intend to tell him our plan. I called, 'We have an expert here. We want you to guarantee that he won't be shot at.'

There was an even longer silence this time. Someone tapped me on my shoulder and pushed a note into my hands. It was from Geordie and read, 'Got to slip the anchor. Quiet as possible. Good luck.'

The silence was broken by Ramirez. 'All right, *Esmerelda*. We don't shoot.'

I called, 'Ramirez, if our man is shot at you'll be dead within the hour. Every man here will make you his personal target.'

'You terrify me.' Was he laughing? 'You can send your man up the mast in five minutes. I will arrange things at this end.'

I crawled out of the wheelhouse and joined Geordie, who had Campbell beside him. Geordie said, 'We heard that. What do you think?'

'I think he'll hold off,' I said. 'He's in as big a jam as we are and he knows it. And he must accept that we do have more expertise aboard here than he has.'

'It's not your neck,' said Campbell sharply. He was right back on form. 'Jim will be an Aunt Sally if he goes up there.'

'It will be his decision,' Geordie said. 'I've got some lads up in the bows to slip the anchor. They've timed it in with that, to cover any noise.' He nodded towards Falcon.

I said, '*That* makes this really urgent – it scares me to death.'

Jim had joined us and was listening gravely as Geordie explained. Then he said, 'All right, I know the odds. I'll have a go.'

I said, 'We've got three minutes left. At one minute I'll call Ramirez again.'

We waited, huddled in the corner of the wheelhouse. The minutes ticked by as we listened to the ominous rumbling and hissing from the sea. I turned to Geordie. 'We're only forty odd miles from Nuku'alofa – a fast boat could reach us in a couple of hours. Surely that would be some protection for us. What's the chance of getting off a radio message?'

Geordie's voice was bitter. 'The radio was the first thing they smashed. It's fated. Shorty's trying to whip up a spark transmitter out of the wreckage, but he says it'll take time.'

There was one other faint hope, the possibility of the pall of black smoke being seen and investigated. But we knew only too well how few ships there were in this locality. None of them would be very fast – and as soon as any sensible skipper came near enough to see what was happening the chances were that he would keep well clear. Every track of thought seemed to lead to a dead end.

I crawled into the wheelhouse again and took up the loudhailer.

'Ramirez!'

'I hear you.'

'Our man's going forward now. In the open. He has a bag of tools with him. No shooting!'

'No shooting,' he agreed. 'I have told my men.'

I watched through the window as Jim walked to the foremast, a satchel slung round his shoulder. He climbed the mast steadily. Almost all our crew were watching from various hidden vantage points, several with rifles or pistols handy. Jim reached the yardarm, paused, then swung the satchel in front of him and put his hand inside. He'd have to clip his way through some of the tangle first. On board *Sirena* there was no one in sight; like us, they were staying in cover.

There was a sudden lurch of the two ships as an eddy caught us. I was braced and swaying with the movement, hoping to God that Jim had a firm handhold and that he wouldn't drop a grenade. Suddenly from *Sirena*'s wheel-house came a babel of voices, and a second later Hadley came running on deck, into full view. He was laughing, and he carried a sub-machine-gun. Swiftly he raised it and fired a burst at the foremast.

Jim toppled from the yardarm, falling with limbs awry to slam with a dull thud across the starboard bulkhead. If the bullets hadn't killed him, then that fail would surely have done so.

There was an angry roar from *Esmerelda* and guns began firing. Hadley stepped back into the shadow, still laughing, and sprayed the rest of the magazine across our decks. Splinters flew on deck at the madman's feet but he seemed to dance away from the bullets and vanished into cover.

Hadley's blast had shattered the rest of the wheelhouse windows. I catapulted myself out of there towards Geordie and Campbell. Geordie was speechless with rage and grief. Campbell was snarling. 'The goddam maniac!'

'I'll have his guts,' Geordie said stiffly.

The firing from our crew died away and I saw faces staring, stunned by the horror of what they'd seen. Two men broke cover to go and collect Jim's body. No one shot at them. Slowly I followed the others below for a council, and found Clare waiting for us in the passageway, white-faced and rigid. She came and clung to me and I held her tightly, and for a moment the only reality seemed to be my love for her.

'Dear God, Mike – Pop – what happened up there?'

'Jim's been killed,' Campbell said shortly.

'They've got a raving maniac over there,' I told her. 'Hadley – he's lost all control.'

'I'll kill him,' said Geordie.

'Geordie, wait! This isn't a war and you're not some bloodyminded general who doesn't care how many men he loses to the cause. We've lost Danny and Jim – and Rex – and other men are wounded. We haven't a hope of getting aboard *Sirena* – we'd be massacred.'

'Hell, what other way is there?' he asked, still spoiling for a fight. There was a growl of approval from most of our crew. I felt as they did, but I had to stop them.

'Look, Hadley's run mad and there's no knowing what he'll do next. But I'll bet those Spaniards over there are even more scared of him than we are. I think Ramirez will have him dealt with, for their own safety.'

Geordie's face was still shuttered and frozen. He wasn't going to listen. Then Campbell said, 'Don't forget we're drifting now. You slipped the anchor.'

And that brought Geordie fully to his senses. He frowned, and it was an expression of worry that was far healthier for all of us than his glare of bitter hatred. 'Christ, yes! We could drift right into that thing. We've got to get the foremast right out of its housing, clear the shrouds, the lot. Dump it all overboard. It'll hamper *Sirena* if she tries to give chase. Taffy – Nick – ' His voice rose in command.

The men gathered round, grasping their weapons and waiting for him to order them into battle. Instead he began to give firm orders for freeing *Esmerelda*, and they recognized the urgency and sense in his voice. The fighting craze began to leave them all.

I turned to Clare. 'Are you all right?' I asked quietly.

'Better now, darling.'

But even now there wasn't time for more than that one quick moment of comfort. 'Where are Paula and Mark?' I asked her.

She nodded towards the saloon. 'They're still in there. He's not too seriously hurt. He was sitting in a chair the last time I looked in. But he won't give us any trouble, Mike. I've never seen him so subdued.'

'There are all the signs that Falcon will get rougher soon. I want you to get both of them up on deck – it'll be safer than staying below. And stay with your father, Clare. Keep them all together.' I kissed her and then she went into the saloon without a word.

Geordie and the men had gone up on deck and I followed. On board *Sirena* there was frantic activity as men wrenched and struggled with equipment at the base of the foremast. A similar scene was being enacted on our ship. There was no shooting, and of Hadley there was no sign. With any luck they had killed him themselves. I had a brief glimpse of our motor launch, still attached and dancing wildly astern, of the litter strewn on deck, of Jim's body being passed below. I started to go forward and make myself useful.

And then Falcon blew.

There was a mighty roar as thousands of tons of water exploded into superheated steam. A bright flickering glare shone on us and the sunlight was dimmed as a pillar of steam ascended into the sky.

The first wave reached us in less than fifteen seconds. As I staggered, grabbing for support, I saw it racing down towards *Esmerelda*, silhouetted against the raging furnace. It was a monstrous wave, rearing mast high, creamed with dirty grey spume and coming with the speed of an express train.

I crouched on the open deck, trying to flatten myself into the planking.

The wave broke against *Esmerelda*. She heaved convulsively and ground against *Sirena*. There was a rending crash and I thought that both ships must have been stove in. A flood of near scalding water washed over the deck, and I writhed as I felt it in the stab wound in my side.

Then the wave was past us and the ships dipped in the afterwash, creaking and groaning in every timber. There were four more huge waves, but none as high as the first. I staggered to my feet, feeling the ships' curious writhing motion on the water.

The waves had done what we had failed to do. *Sirena* was dipping and bobbing in the water about fifty yards away from us. *Esmerelda* was free, and she had no foremast at all. It had been plucked out by the roots.

But every time *Sirena* rolled there was a crash which sent a shudder through her. I stumbled to the side and looked down into the water. Our foremast hung there, still tethered to *Sirena*'s mast by a cat's cradle of lines and spars. As I watched a surge of water sent it slamming against her hull like a battering ram and she shivered from stem to stern. She wouldn't stand much more of that treatment.

I fell over a body lying in the scuppers. Nick lay there with blood oozing from a wound in his forehead, but as I turned him over he groaned and stirred and opened his eyes. He must have had a constitution like an ox because, in spite of the massive contusion, he began to struggle to his feet at once.

I shouted, 'Let's look for the others!' and he nodded. We turned and then stood frozen in amazement as we caught a glimpse of Falcon.

There was *land* back there. Land that glowed a dull red shot with fiery gold streaks and which surrounded the pit of Hell itself – a vast incandescent crater which spewed forth red hot cinders and streams of lava. Falcon was building an island once more.

The sea fought the new land but the land was winning. Nothing could stop the outpouring of that huge gaping red mouth, but the sea did its best, pitting water against fire, and the result was an inferno of noise. There was a great ear-splitting hiss as though all the engines of the world were letting off steam together, and under that a rumbling bass from the depths of the chasm.

Great gouts of fire leapt up from the crater, half hidden behind the red mist, and the water boiled as it encountered the blazing heat of the new Fonua Fo'ou. There was the sound of surf pounding along a reef, but such surf as none of us had ever seen before. Mighty columns of tephra, all the pent-up material that Falcon could fling into the air from its huge maw, seethed and erupted in spasms, hurling ash, magma and boulders high into the sky. A hazy brown cloud of fragmentary pumice hung over all, obscuring the sun.

Esmerelda was pitching as helplessly as *Sirena*. Black figures moved on both decks, outlined against the red glow of Falcon, and I felt a great leap of relief. For a moment it had seemed that Nick and I were the only two creatures alive. I hoped to God that Clare was safe.

Nick's eyes were glazed, not in fear but in awe. He was tougher and far better trained for danger than I, but I had one great advantage. I knew what was happening across the water, and my knowledge helped steady me. I shook him roughly and consciousness crept back into his face. He breathed deeply and then led the way across the littered deck.

On *Sirena* a ship's boat dangled from one davit. Clearly some of the crew had tried to get away, but those terrible waves would have made nothing of their chances. One of the falls had parted and the men must all have been tipped into the sea.

As we made our way forward, incongruously, it began to snow. The flakes came drifting from the sky, featherlike, to settle everywhere. I brushed one from my shoulder; it was a flake of ash. The air was becoming poisonous with fumes, the increased stink of sulphur and the worse stench of sulphuretted hydrogen. I looked at the sea. It was bubbling like a mud pool. Great fat bubbles were coming up from the seabed and breaking on the surface, adding a dangerous smoke to the haze of steam. I realized with sick horror that we were not drifting closer to the source of the eruption – it was expanding under the sea, coming to meet us.

III

There was a shattering roar from Falcon as a second vent opened, only a few hundred yards away from the two ships. The waves this time weren't as massive as before; this was a smaller vent. We clung to handholds during the first swamping rush of hot steamy water and then emerged gasping into the foetid air. Nick was nursing one arm and my rib-cage was alive with pain, but we'd survived. Figures struggled to their feet on our foredeck, and I recognized Ian's bulk among them, and then Geordie.

Sirena lurched and wallowed in the turmoil of the sea. Then she began to spin as *Esmerelda* had done when we first reached Falcon. The eddy that caught her moved on and after a few turns she steadied up again, still dragging the wreckage of our mast.

A plume of water suddenly shot up from the sea not ten feet to starboard and drops of warm gritty water fell on my head. Another waterspout shot up a little further out, and then another. It was for all the world as if we were under shellfire.

The whole angry sea was pock-marked as though by a mighty rain. It was a welter of spouting water as rocks from Falcon's second vent, hurled high in the air, fell vertically and straddled the two ships. Smoke wreathed about us and steam coiled everywhere.

The falling tephra didn't straddle for long. There was a crash from midships. Splinters of wood leapt into the air to mix with the hail of ash and burning magma. As we stumbled forward we found a ragged hole on the galley roof and a huge glowing ember beginning to eat its way through the deck planking inside. Already small flames were starting to flicker and gnaw at the woodwork.

'Fire, by God!' Nick said. 'How the hell do we cope with this?'

The answer was dramatic and swift. With a booming roar another vast wave engulfed us. We emerged miraculously still intact to find the embryo fire completely doused at the cost of a drenched and sodden galley.

At last we managed to join some of the others. By clinging to anything stable enough we were able to steady ourselves. Of cuts and bruises there were plenty, but everyone was on their feet again. Except Geordie who'd vanished. I caught someone's arm.

'Geordie – he was here. What's happened to him?'

'Gone to try and start the engine,' Taffy bellowed in my ear.

A moment later there was a steady rhythmic throb underfoot as our engine started, and the sound gave me a wild surge of hope.

A warm rain, condensing steam mixed with the slippery and treacherous ash, was falling all around us. The acrid stench was still heavy in my nostrils and the banshee sounds of the ships' timbers mingled with the high-pitched whistlings and rumbling from Falcon's new orifice, threatening to pierce our eardrums. A fresh rain of tephra assailed us. Three or four larger flaming rocks crashed down on Sirena's deck, a couple on ours. Sirena was almost level with us and her rails were lined with men. Several of them jumped, some into the sea itself, some trying to reach our decks.

'Bring lines!' Ian yelled, and I pounded after him to the ship's side as he and Nick began throwing them over the rails. One man battling in the water seized a trailing end and Ian and Shorty dragged him on board. Nick threw another line out. Esmerelda was buffeted by a sudden wave and his feet slid across the ash-strewn deck. He cannoned into me and we both crashed down against the railing.

All the breath was knocked out of my body and for a moment I blacked out. Then I started to struggle to my feet, in time to see Nick about to topple clean over the ship's side into that raging sea. I got him in a tackle around his knees and wrestled to keep him on deck, but the slippery footing and his own weight were proving too much for me. He seemed to be unconscious.

Then another wave poured down across both of us, tipping *Esmerelda* the other way and doing what I couldn't manage, forcing Nick's body back inboard. We slid away from the railings together, half submerged in the gritty water that cascaded down over the deck.

I landed spitting and spewing up sickly-warm sea water. Hands helped me to stand up, and one of them was Clare's.

'Mike – are you all right?'

She was trembling and so was I.

'I'm okay. How's Nick?' I was still panting and spluttering. But I was comfortably aware that our engine was still running, and Geordie was backing us steadily away from *Sirena*.

Clare gave me a fierce hug and I winced.

'Mike – you're hurt?'

'Don't worry, it's really nothing. But go carefully with those hugs for now.'

Campbell limped up to us, his face blackened with smoke, his clothes scorched and sodden. He and I exchanged a look over Clare's head and he smiled briefly.

'How's Paula?' I asked him. 'And Mark?'

'Both all right. We haven't lost anyone else,' he said grimly. 'The boys pulled two Spaniards aboard and two others jumped across.'

Taffy was helping Nick to his feet. Apart from his arm which was obviously crippled and the abrasion on his face there seemed to be little wrong with him. Again I marvelled at his strength. Taffy said, 'We've sent all the Spaniards below and Ian's got 'em locked in our homemade brig.'

I said, 'Surely they aren't a danger to us now?'

'Well, there could be trouble,' said Taffy. 'We've got – '

A stunning crash interrupted him. The hail of ash and magma had died down briefly, but now it started up again as a fresh pillar of smoke and steam boiled skywards from almost dead ahead of us. Our ship rocked wildly as another barrage of waves hit us. *Sirena* reemerged from this last assault on fire in several places. We heard men's voices faintly through the uproar.

I'll lay odds that Geordie Wilkins must be the best seaman ever to put his hands on a wheel. With consummate skill and an astonishing use of gear and throttle he edged *Esmerelda* nearer and nearer to the doomed *Sirena*, to aid the stricken men. As we closed in we saw that one of Falcon's barrages must have sheared through the rigging and brought down the main gaff. Struggling men lay pinned to the deck. Others were trying frantically to release them, but the fires were closing in, eating their way along the deck timbers.

Clare screamed, 'Look – Ramirez!'

A man was staggering across the deck of *Sirena*. Oblivious to the cries and struggles of his crew he never took his eyes from *Esmerelda*. Through the smoke as it was lit by an occasional red glare I saw that he was carrying a rifle. His torn clothing appeared scorched and blood-stained, and his face was a mask of smoke, blood and fury. He had crawled like a deadly spider from its crevice to use its poison for the last time.

I don't know if he had given up all hope of surviving and was bent only on revenge, or if his mind had given way. I didn't believe that cold intellect, so unlike Hadley's unreasoning savagery, would break as easily as that. But there was an implacable singleminded purpose about him that was terrifying.

He aimed the rifle across the water.

I flung myself down shielding Clare – I had no idea who he would choose for a target – and I heard the gun fire, sharp and crisp against the background bedlam. It was followed almost instantly by a terrible grinding roar, louder than anything we had heard before. We staggered to our feet in time to see Falcon play its most horrible trick.

It was Geordie, intent on his delicate steering, who first saw the danger. I don't know if he'd even been aware of Ramirez. *Esmerelda* sheered off violently as he spun the wheel so that we turned in a half-arc as fast as the one in which the eddy tide had taken us. Then he pushed the throttle in until the engine was pounding at maximum speed, to carry us away from the arena.

Behind us I saw *Sirena* jar to a sudden halt and Ramirez flung across the deck. The ship rose grotesquely in the air and tipped over on her side, looking like a small sailing boat stranded by the tide. But this was no sandbank. It was a bed of writhing red-hot lava. The sea recoiled from it in a tempest of steam.

In that last fraction of a second Ramirez rolled back down the deck, his clothes a mass of flame. He was flung straight overboard into the raging lava bed and vanished instantly. *Sirena* went up like a funeral pyre, before banks of smoke and steam rolled across to blot her out of our sight.

IV

The rain of fire from Falcon continued. In all we were hit by four of those fiery bombs. An exhausted and shell-shocked crew was kept busy dousing fires, using the hoses for the biggest, buckets for the rest, and praying that we would not run out of fuel. The hoses worked only as long as the engine continued to run. And we knew that there wasn't the slightest possibility of rigging sail.

Even with the engine at full speed there were times when *Esmerelda* began to drift back towards Falcon, caught in the grip of a cold water current as it rushed in to replenish the vaporized water. An occasional eddy swung her round by the bows and Geordie had to take her out in reverse.

It was three hours before we were well clear of Falcon, a mad jumble of fire, steam, smoke and lava falling mercifully astern of us. Geordie had been spelled at the wheel by Ian and Taffy; the rest of us had managed to extinguish the fires, hurl the worst of the debris overboard, and bring some faint semblance of order to the ship. We took turns to collapse with exhaustion. Clare worked steadily taking care of burns and wounds.

Some parts of *Esmerelda* were in better shape than others. By a strange miracle the launch still clung to our coat-tails, though we had no time to stop and haul her up on davits. I found to my great relief that my notes and the bulk of the lab files were in order, though most of the apparatus was wrecked. It was better to work on things like that than to dwell on the last appalling few hours. But there were a couple of matters that had to be taken care of, that could not, for all my wishing, be put off much longer.

Mark was still on board and had to be dealt with.

And so was Hadley.

Taffy had started to tell me, just before Falcon blew its top. Hadley had been one of the two men who had leapt to our deck, and was being held in the brig with the other men from *Sirena*. It was dismaying to know that he was with us, but for me the most serious problem was Mark.

He and Paula had stayed together in the saloon during the whole of the encounter with Falcon. Now I had to face him. I pulled myself to my feet and went wearily below. Paula looked up as I entered and her face, like everyone else's, was drawn and shadowed.

'Are we safe yet, Mike?' she asked.

'Pretty well. You should both come up on deck and get some air. It's remarkably peaceful up there now. Paula, thank you for standing by.'

She smiled a brief acknowledgement and she and Mark got up together. He was very pale under the heavy beard, and limped a little, but he seemed fairly strong. He had said nothing as yet. I led the way on deck and they followed in silence, numbed by the sight of so much damage. Nobody spoke to Mark, but more than one of the crew reached to pat Paula's arm or give her a quick smile as she went by.

We stopped outside the deckhouse, a shattered and burnt-out shell. They stood together looking astern at the now distant ascending cloud of smoke.

'I wish I'd seen it,' Mark said. He sounded wistful.

'It was fantastic, but too close for comfort,' I said. 'I'm going to tape my impressions as soon as I can. There's a lot to be learned from such close-up observation. Do you know what happened to *Sirena*?'

'Clare told us,' Paula said, and shuddered. Mark seemed unmoved. He was not going to be overtaken by conscience as easily as that. I didn't mention Hadley or the other prisoners.

'Mark,' I said abruptly, 'I have to talk to you.'

'I'll go,' Paula offered.

Mark took her arm and held it. 'Stay with me,' he said. She was the only one he could be sure was on his side, and he needed a friend at court. He turned to me and a hint of the old arrogance was back in his voice. 'What's it going to be? One of your little lectures on decency?'

I felt grim and tired. This wasn't going to work.

'For God's sake, Mark, ease off. I'm not going to lecture you – it was always too late to get you to listen to reason. But we have to work something out before we land, or before someone sights us.'

I wanted above all things to lie down, right there on the deck, and sleep for a week. I was physically beat up and exhausted, but the onus of Mark was a heavier burden. I wished I could have had Clare to stand by me, as he had Paula, but I wasn't going to bring her into it.

We stared at one another in stalemate.

My jumbled thoughts were interrupted by a bubbling scream. The sound came from below. Taffy and a couple of the others dived down the companionway, and Ian came past us at a run. I made a move to follow but then held back, leaving it to the professionals.

I said, 'I think it's one of the Spaniards. He must be hurt, poor devil.'

'What Spaniard?' Mark asked.

For answer there was a crash from below, and Hadley burst into view through the burnt-out galley and onto the deck where we were standing. He had a kitchen knife in his hand. I backed away from his red-rimmed crazy eyes as he came at me like a bull.

I booted him on the shin but it was like trying to stop a truck. He leapt on me in a bear hug that jarred excruciatingly on the knife-graze in my side. His knife hovered near my throat. Desperately I clawed at his face as we fell. Hadley landed on me with all his weight but thank God his knife-arm was pinned beneath us. I chopped viciously at his throat and he choked. His grip loosened. I jerked a knee up into his crotch and broke free.

But Hadley recovered fast and rolled over onto his feet. Agile for his bulk he leapt on me as I gasped for air. He pinned my arms and I felt the breath being squeezed from my lungs and a rib cracked agonizingly. Blackness surged in front of my eyes.

Suddenly he lost his balance and we both crashed to the deck. Nick, crawling up from behind, had seized Hadley's ankle and had yanked his foot out from under him. I rolled free and Hadley got the full force of a bullet from Ian's gun in his belly.

Astonishingly he regained his feet and swooped for the knife which lay on the deck. For a near-fatal instant we all stood paralysed. With an unearthly bubbling scream of rage and agony he plunged towards Mark and the knife flashed viciously in the sunlight.

Mark flung Paula aside and met the attack full on. The knife sank into his side and he collapsed without a sound.

The weapon fell to the deck. Hadley took two staggering paces backwards, clutching his stomach, and then in a full back arch he went over the railings into the sea.

Silence hung in the air after his fall.

I stood shakily clutching my ribs and breathing in short painful gasps. Clare and Bill Hunter were first at my side. When Campbell went to help Paula, she brushed him aside and ran to Mark, who was still lying on the deck. But he was conscious and trying to sit up.

Geordie arrived at a run and a babble of voices told him what had happened. Taffy said harshly, 'My fault, skipper. I let the bastard out. We heard a man screaming and I thought someone was in pain in the brig. I went in with Bill but Hadley went through us like an express train.'

Bill said, 'No wonder that poor devil was screaming. Hadley had near taken the arm out of his socket; to get us to open up.'

'He was quite mad,' said Ian soberly.

To dispel the air of gloom Geordie said briskly, 'Well, he tried and he failed. And that's the last of them. The others won't make any trouble. Now, lads, back to work. We're not home and dry yet.'

They dispersed slowly. Geordie turned to me and said softly, 'The last of them – bar Mark. What are you going to do about your brother, Mike?'

I looked at him bleakly.

'I don't know. First I must see how badly he's hurt. But I can't just hand him over to the police.'

'I don't think you've any choice, laddie.'

'I guess not. But it's a hell of a thing to have to do.'

Clare, her arm comfortingly firm around my rib-cage, waited in silence for me to come to a decision. I said, 'Geordie, I have to talk to him alone. Take Paula with you, Clare. Look after her. God knows she's had enough to cope with. Keep everyone away from us for a while, would you?'

'I'll do that,' Geordie said.

Clare gave me a smile of compassion and warmth and then walked back to the deckhouse. Mark was sitting propped up against the railing with Paula as always by his side. I waited until Clare took her gently by the arm and the two girls went below to join Campbell. I wanted to speak to Mark, perhaps for the last time, with no one to act as a shield between us.

He looked stonily at me as I squatted beside him.

'How is it?' I asked.

He shrugged his shoulders. 'Not good,' he said breathlessly. He was sheet-white and his eyes were cloudy.

I said, 'Mark, thank you for saving Paula.'

'Don't thank me. That was my business.' He did not want to hear praise from me. 'I told you that man was off his rocker.'

'Well, he's out of it now. Ramirez too. Which leaves only you, Mark. And puts me in a devil of a fix.'

I expected his usual sneering retort, but instead he surprised me. He said, 'I know that, Mike. I've caused you a lot of grief, and I'm sorry. I'm likely to cause you a lot more as long as I live.'

'No, I – '

'Which won't be long. I'm no doctor, but I know that much.'

'Mark, we'll be back in port pretty soon and you'll be in medical hands. We may even be sharing a ward,' I said, trying to speak lightly. Mark was sombre and less arrogant than I had ever known him, and I was dismayed.

'Don't be a fool, Mike,' he said with a touch of his old acerbity. 'You're going to have a million questions to answer as it is. It's not going to make things easier for you if you suddenly turn up with your long-lost, murdered, murderer brother, is it?'

I knew that he was right. I foresaw nothing but trouble for both of us. I shrank from the thought of turning him over to justice, but I could see no other way. Mark let me think about it for a while.

'Mike, I have one chance, just one, to make things easy for you. I've never done anything for you before. You have to give me this one chance.'

I said slowly, 'Dear God, what can I do?'

He pulled himself more upright and swayed a little. Then he said, 'Mike, I'm going to die.'

'Mark, you don't know – '

'Hear me out.' His voice shook. 'Remember, Mike, I'm already a dead man. Without me you have every chance of coming clean out of this. There will be nobody to contradict your story. You were sailing to meet up with Ramirez on a survey expedition, and got caught up in the shambles of Falcon. By now the world will know it's blown. There'll be scientists overflying, ships coming to look, the lot. You know that. Your stalwart fellows can wipe out all traces of a gunfight. And you can persuade those Spaniards you've got on board to shut up.'

He drew in a harsh breath. He was drenching in his own sweat.

'Christ, do I have to spell it out for you? I'm not going to recover. I can do one thing for you, if you'll help me now.'

I asked, knowing the answer, 'Help you to do what?'

'Help me to die.'

I had known. 'Mark, I can't kill you.'

'You won't need to.'

Something glittered in front of my eyes. It was the kitchen knife Hadley had used on Mark, bloody at the tip but winking in the sunlight. I swallowed, a hard lump in my throat.

'What – do you want me to do?'

'Get me over the side, into the sea. It'll be as quick for me as it was for Hadley.'

Silently I got up and began to pace the deck. He watched me carefully, saying nothing, giving me time. This was the only completely unselfish thing he would ever have done in his life. But he gave me a dreadful choice.

At last I came back to him.

'All right, Mark. God forgive me, I'll help you.'

'Good.' He became brisk. 'Don't let anyone see us. The story will be that I climbed over on my own, after you'd gone. I would do that, but I need your help.'

There was nobody in sight. Geordie had done his work well.

I could find nothing else to say. Mark gave a short hard cough and his head drooped, and for an instant I thought that he had already died, sitting there. And then he raised his head and looked me in the eye. For the only time in my adult life our gazes locked without antagonism.

It took only a couple of moments. I got him over to the railing and we both looked down into the sea where the bow-wave ran along *Esmerelda*'s side. I remember thinking how quiet it was.

He hooked one leg over the rail and I helped steady him as he lifted the other across. For an instant I held him.

'Goodbye, Mike,' he said clearly.

I let go. He fell backwards and disappeared into the spray. I turned blindly away and with my head in my hands huddled down by the side of the deckhouse.

After a while I stood up shakily. It was done. And I must go and talk to some of the crew. Not to Paula, not yet. But I must give Mark's plan a chance to work. I turned to leave.

The knife had gone from the deck.

I stood for a moment riveted, a flood of thoughts pouring into my mind. Then I swung round to look at the deck where Mark had been lying. There was still no knife, and now that I came to think of it, very little blood.

In two strides I was at the rail, looking aft, my thoughts erupting as the volcano had done. The motor launch which had been running in tow was gone, and the painter dangled loosely over the stern. Across the water I thought I could see a tiny dancing speck, but I couldn't be sure of that, or of anything.

Slowly I walked aft and hauled in the painter. The end of it had been cut across, newly-severed and just beginning to fray.

There was fuel in the launch and iron rations, for it had always had the function of a lifeboat. There were fishing lines, blankets, flares, a first aid kit. There was everything needed for survival.

I stood at the railing, alone as I'd asked to be, and bade my brother a final, ironic farewell. And yes, I wished him luck.

INTERVIEW WITH DESMOND BAGLEY

On Friday 29 September 1978, the London
Evening Standard published this rare inter-
view with Desmond Bagley, in which
Maureen Cleave explored the background to
his novels, including his approach to writing
The Snow Tiger.

BAGLEY'S EQUATION
AND HOW IT SOLD TEN MILLION BOOKS

Thriller writers give away *what* they mean to *when* they mean to, no more and no sooner. Mr Desmond Bagley has perfected this skill in his appearance – in it he gives away nothing at all.

A small neat man, his clothing is subfusc; tie grey, suit dark grey; shoes black; socks black; while most of his features are obscured by a beard (grey) and spectacles (black) – all, that is, but a prominent square brow rather like Lenin's, the sort that mothers fondly suppose to be bursting with brains.

Hampered by a stammer, Mr Bagley is also sparing with words; he says only what he means to say. If indeed his mother did think he was clever, few others did. Late developer, dark horse, call him what you will, it wasn't until 1963, when he was 40, that he began his career as an author. His 12 novels have sold 10 million copies.

He comes from Kendal in Westmorland. He took some Kendal Mint Cake with him to the South Pole but, he says, his companions found it chilly fare. His father was a miner, but when the family moved to Blackpool they ran a theatrical boarding house.

'Frank Benson,' Mr Bagley said, 'the Laurence Olivier of his day, broke his leg falling down our front steps.'

During the War he made bits of Spitfires and after it determined to leave as soon as possible. He crossed Africa by land, working as a clerk in gold mines and asbestos mines, until he finally fetched up in South Africa as a nightclub photographer. He had to learn to distinguish on sight who was with his wife and would like to be photographed, and who wasn't and would not.

All this experience was grist to be milled later. The Sahara in 1947 was stored away to emerge as the background for his novel, *Flyaway*. 'I always try,' he said, 'to use the background as another character which plays its part.' Because of this strong sense of place, when filming his books, there's no question of mocking up the Cotswolds in Spain. *Running Blind*, which is soon to be seen on television, is set in Iceland, and in Iceland it had to be shot.

As *late* developers do, when he moved he moved fast. He met his wife Joan at a fencing club and decided within two days to marry her. As for many childless couples in middle age, theirs seems to be a true union of souls. She ran a bookshop and from her he learned that thrillers sold best, and that Collins published the best thrillers.

He wrote *The Golden Keel*, which Collins accepted, wrote a second novel and decided to leave for England.

'I was aware that all publishers had a letter permanently set up that said: "We regret that Mr So-and-So's second novel does not measure up to his first . . ."' When he arrived at Collins, one look at his editor's face confirmed that such a letter was being circulated about himself.

'What was the point of this then?' he said, and passed across the desk the third novel he had managed to dash off before his departure.

His work is famous for its highly technical content. He has had to learn geology, ship-building and Mayan history; he knows about hurricanes and avalanches, genetic engineering and computers. He reads a book every day of his life.

DISASTERS

Here are explicit instructions based on his book *The Snow Tiger*, on how to write a thriller. In 1963 he wrote a letter to his editor to say he would be writing a book about an avalanche.

'Thriller writers,' he said, 'are always in search of good disasters but there are almost insuperable problems writing about avalanches; they are *highly* technical.' Years passed. Mr Bagley continued. 'Then in 1968 I had the great good fortune to go to Antarctica with the US Navy where I would talk to the physicists who specialised in snow and ice.

'They gave me lots of specialised stuff, six mathematical equations to the page. Oh of course I understood them, though I had to simplify them for the reader.'

Mrs Bagley here interrupted to say that her husband had a retentive memory and, even when absorbing the most specialised information, rarely wrote anything down. 'Experts find it very disconcerting,' she said.

Mr Bagley resumed: 'There's no point in setting your avalanche in Antarctica; there are thousands of avalanches but nobody underneath. On the way back we landed in New Zealand on the ice fields by Cook Mountain. I asked a few questions and discovered that the ski industry was booming. So I invented a little community called Hukahoronui. . .'

Years passed. It is 1974 before Mr Bagley approaches the typewriter.

'Now,' he said encouragingly. 'You've done your research, you have your setting, what you need is a *theme*. My theme here was a natural hazard being compounded by the stupidity of people. The theme of *Othello* is the corroding influence of jealousy. Having got your theme, you need a plot to illustrate it. Shakespeare used what is known in the trade as an *idiot* plot.

'If Desdemona had said to Othello: "Oh dear me, I lost my hankie in the laundry," the play would have come to a shuddering halt.'

'Thrillers with idiot plots,' Mrs Bagley said, in one of her many helpful comments, 'are those where the heroine hears a funny noise in the night and comes down in her nightie – whereas you or I would stay in bed and phone the police.'

Mr Bagley's habit is to start with hardly any plot at all, idiot or otherwise.

'You have a strong opening situation and then it grows like a tree organically for the next 300 pages. I read each day's output to Joan and at the end I say: "Any idea what's going to happen?" If Joan can predict what's in my mind then it means – another technical expression – I am telegraphing my intentions.'

He alters his intentions at once. In his books, the virtuous are rewarded and the bad are punished. He has even killed off his hero for behaving badly towards his father-in-law. There are no sex objects and not much sex. 'Sex,' he says, 'gets in the way of the plot.'

Joan is his helpmeet. It is Joan who nurses him through that appalling affliction, writer's block. 'You don't know when it will all end,' she said, 'if it will end. It can last for years. He mopes around, not eating, not sleeping. . .'

Success came to Mr Bagley as a wholly delightful surprise. They live in Guernsey in comfortable rather than grand style. His one little extravagance is computers. 'I don't know if you keep up with the micro-computer world?' he inquired politely. That very day £18,000's worth of computer had been ordered to replace his old one. It would arrive on January 9. Mrs Bagley came to the rescue once again. 'He's a self-trained computer programmer,' she said, 'and a very good one. Before the computer arrived, we had these hand-written figures on scraps of paper all over the house and shelves and shelves of books – all equations, statistics, symbolic logic.

'You see,' she said almost apologetically, almost as though it were a secret vice, 'Desmond's a recreational mathematician. It's his idea of fun.'

Maureen Cleave
Evening Standard

DESMOND BAGLEY

'The best adventure stories I have read for years.'

Daily Mirror

THE GOLDEN KEEL

When the Allies invaded southern Italy in 1943, Mussolini's personal treasure was moved north to safety under heavily armed guard. It was never seen again. Now, an expedition plans to unearth the treasure and smuggle it out of Italy. But their reckless mission is being followed – by enemies who are as powerful and ruthless as they are deadly . . .

THE VIVERO LETTER

Jeremy Wheale's well-ordered life is blasted apart when his brother is murdered. The killer was after a family heirloom – an antique gold tray – which sets Wheale on a trail from Devon to the tropical rainforest of Yucatan. There he joins the hunt for a lost Mayan city. But in the dense cover of the jungle a band of vicious convict mercenaries are waiting to strike . . .

'Bagley has no equal at this sort of thing.'

Sunday Mirror

978-0-00-730477-6

DESMOND BAGLEY

'Bagley is one of the best.' *The Times*

HIGH CITADEL

When Tim O'Hara's plane is hijacked and forced to crash land in the middle of the Andes, his troubles are only beginning. A heavily armed group of communist soldiers intent on killing one of his passengers – an influential political figure – have orders to leave no survivors. Isolated in the biting cold of the Andes, O'Hara's party must fight for their lives with only the most primitive weapons . . .

LANDSLIDE

Bob Boyd is a geologist, as resilient as the British Columbia timber country where he works for the powerful Matterson Corporation. But his real name and his past are mysteries – wiped out by the accident that nearly killed him. Then Boyd reads a name that opens a door in his memory: Trinavant – and discovers that Bull Matterson and his son will do almost anything to keep the Trinavant family forgotten forever . . .

'Very much of the moment. The characters are sympathetic and believable' *Sunday Times*

978-0-00-730479-0

DESMOND BAGLEY

'Stories charged with suspense.' *Financial Times*

WYATT'S HURRICANE

Ferocious Hurricane Mabel is predicted to pass harmlessly amongst the islands of the Caribbean. But David Wyatt has developed a sixth sense about hurricanes. He is convinced that Mabel will change course to strike the island of San Fernandez and its capital, St Pierre. But nobody believes him, and the hurricane is only one of the problems that threaten San Fernandez . . .

BAHAMA CRISIS

Tom Mangan was a sharply successful entrepreneur who lured the super-rich to his luxury hotels in the sun-soaked Bahamas. Then violent tragedy struck: his own family disappeared, and a series of misfortunes, accidents and mysterious epidemics began to drive the tourists away and wreck Mangan's livelihood. Fatally, he becomes determined to confront his enemy – and the hunt is on . . .

'Tautly written adventure, packed with exhaustive detail. You will be out of breath when you finish.'

Books And Bookmen

978-0-00-730478-3

DESMOND BAGLEY

'Bagley in top form.'   *Evening Standard*

THE SPOILERS

When film tycoon Robert Hellier loses his daughter to heroin, he declares war on the drug pedlars, the faceless overlords whose greed supplies the world with its deadly pleasures. London drug specialist Nicholas Warren is called upon to organise an expedition to the Middle East to track down and destroy them – but with a hundred million dollars' worth of heroin at stake, Warren knows he will have to use methods as deadly as his prey . . .

JUGGERNAUT

It is no ordinary juggernaut. Longer than a football pitch, weighing 550 tons, and moving at just five miles per hour, its job – and that of troubleshooter Neil Mannix – is to move a giant transformer across an oil-rich African state. But when Nyala erupts in civil war, Mannix's juggernaut is at the centre of the conflict – a target of ambush and threat, with no way to run and nowhere to hide . . .

'Bagley is a master story-teller.'   *Daily Mirror*

978-0-00-730480-6

DESMOND BAGLEY

'Compulsively readable.'   *Guardian*

FLYAWAY

Why is Max Stafford, security consultant, beaten up in his
own office? What is the secret of the famous 1930s aircraft,
the Lockheed Lodestar? And why has accountant Paul
Bilson disappeared in North Africa? The journey to the
Sahara desert becomes a race to save Paul Bilson, a race to
find the buried aircraft, and – above all – a race to return
alive . . .

WINDFALL

When a legacy of £40 million is left to a small college in
Kenya, investigations begin about the true identities of
the heirs – the South African, Dirk Hendriks, and his
namesake, Henry Hendrix from California. Suspicion
that Hendrix is an impostor leads Max Stafford to the Rift
Valley, where a violent reaction to his arrival points to a
sinister and far-reaching conspiracy far beyond mere
greed . . .

'From word one, you're off. Bagley's one of the best.'
                                                       The Times

978-0-00-730476-9